DEFY THE SUN

'This is an outrage.' Julie glared at the high-handed officer. 'It is most urgent I get to Paris immediately, and you are forcing me to remain here.'

Although the main expression on his face was one of polite sorrow, Nicolas's light eyes were insolent as they traveled over her, finally lingering boldly on her mouth. 'My regrets. You are quite right, it is an outrage. But His Majesty's business must take precedence over his subjects' private affairs.'

'I cannot believe the king would countenance your impertinent midnight marauding of a lady's conveyance just to bring some poor criminal faster to his dungeon,' Julie snapped. 'I shall surely report this to the authorities.'

'In this case, dear lady, I *am* the authority.'

And before she could move, with one arm he swept her tight against the gold buttons on his coat and clamped his lips down on hers. In her astonishment her mouth remained soft, helplessly accepting of his hard, insistent kiss.

She staggered a step back. 'Oh! You——!'

He bowed in the face of her speechless indignation and took his leave. 'Your humble servant, madame,' he murmured with an infuriating, completely unabashed grin. 'It is my fondest hope that we shall meet again in less trying circumstances. . .'

Mallory Dorn Hart is a former public relations executive who lives in New York.

Also available by this author in *Worldwide*

JASMINE ON THE WIND

DEFY THE SUN

Mallory Dorn Hart

WORLDWIDE BOOKS
LONDON · SYDNEY · TORONTO

All the characters in this book have no existence outside the imagination of the Author, and have no relation whatsoever to anyone bearing the same name or names. They are not even distantly inspired by any individual known or unknown to the Author, and all the incidents are pure invention.

All rights reserved. The text of this publication or any part thereof may not be reproduced or transmitted in any form or by any means, electronic or mechanical, including photocopying, recording, storage in an information retrieval system, or otherwise, without the written permission of the publisher.

First published in Great Britain in 1990 by Worldwide Books, Eton House, 18–24 Paradise Road, Richmond, Surrey TW9 1SR

This edition published by arrangement with Pocket Books

© *Mallory Dorn Hart 1988*

ISBN 0 373 58479 2
10/9006
Printed and bound in Great Britain by William Clowes Limited, Beccles and London

To my handsome husband, George,
bagagiste, conducteur, compagne, enthousiaste par excellence.
Among other swell things. . .

CHAPTER
~ 1 ~

Stumbling over a rain-glistened paving block, the wan young woman recovered her balance but didn't bother to look behind her to see if the tattered wharf rats carrying her belongings were following her up the quay. She had no wish to put her eyes ever again on the wallowing masts of the broad-beamed Channel ship that had brought her home to France. 'I shall never put another morsel of food in my mouth,' Julie mumbled to herself. She was certain that anyone chancing to peer under the damp hood of her cloak would bolt in fright at the haggard visage created by days of violent seasickness.

Doggedly, she climbed up the long ramp toward Saint-Malo's welcoming gates, the *skreek* of gulls wheeling overhead causing her to picture the precipitous plunge of the ship's bow in the three-day gale they'd weathered. The very images stirred up her lingering nausea. Hurrying along through the round-towered stone gates, she knew she would feel better as soon as the city's broad ramparts blocked the sight and sound of the sea.

By dint of arriving at the nearest inn before the other travelers, who were straggling along behind her, Julie secured the best chamber the *patron* had to offer, plus the services of his slovenly daughter to help her undress and bathe. The *patron* showed her to her upstairs chamber and then hastened along the two porters, who tottered up with her trunks. Rubbing his hands together briskly, the innkeep asked, 'Will you breakfast, madame? Something to warm you—a boiled sausage, perhaps, or fresh fried tripe with mushrooms or hot bread, very tasty——?'

Over her rising gorge, Julie protested weakly. 'Not now, landlord, not now. Some weak broth, if you have it. What is more important is that I should like to hire a coach to take me to a place called Saint-Léonard-sur-

Loire, to the west of Bourges, and thence to Paris. Would you be good enough to arrange this for me? I would like to leave tomorrow.' With a tired hand, she undid the button of her cloak and dropped the sodden garment to the floor.

The innkeep beamed. Here was a nice commission to be picked off that rascal Poilettier, for the blackguard would charge plenty for the long trip. The lady was traveling alone, without even a serving maid, and had unremarkable traveling clothes. But she was unmistakably quality, and quality was prone to travel incognito to guard their fat purses.

'*D'accord*, madame. I will see to securing you a conveyance immediately,' he assured her. He went off, and Julie heard him yelling for his daughter, Agathe.

She stepped over to a small mirror hanging on the wall and stared into it as she dragged off the limp scarf covering her hair. '*Peste!*' But the curse was more like a moan. Two great haunted eyes stared out at her from a paper-white face stiff with salt. Her black hair hung lank and lusterless, and as she lifted a strand of it, her mouth twisted in disgust. Was this the French beauty who even at fifteen had intrigued the gentlemen of the court of Charles II? In a week of voyaging, having no one to do for her and being too deathly sick most of the time to care, her toilette had been of the skimpiest—with the disastrous results she now saw in the mirror.

A loud crash and rumble outside, and another storm flung itself from the low-hanging clouds in a torrent. Thick sheets of rain lashed heavily at the inn's stucco walls. Stepping to the mullioned window, Julie could see nothing in the narrow street but a river of rain flowing down the gutter in the middle. She turned about and surveyed the room, which, other than the warming glow from a charcoal grate, had little to recommend it. If this was the innkeep's best, she would hate to see the worst. There was a low bed with a lumpy-looking mattress, a scarred table, an earthen chamber pot under the bed, a cane-back chair, and a bare plank floor that creaked. But it was solid and stationary and dry and in France— and that alone started her heart rising and lifted the corners of her weary mouth in a smile.

Agathe arrived, hauling behind her on a sledge a wooden tub in which rode three buckets of hot water. The girl was sullen and had an offensive body odor, but she was competent and helped Julie out of her clothes with a minimum of clumsiness. Agathe's vigorous scrubbing with a rag washed the salt and the belowdecks grime and smell from Julie's body, and the coarse soap at least got Julie's hair clean. Grateful that the stinging soap had not landed in her eyes more than a few times, Julie allowed herself to be dried and wrapped in a grayish flannel. She then directed the raw-boned wench to open one of her trunks and withdraw fresh linen and garments and her curling irons.

She sat backed up against the brazier so that her hair would partially dry. It was an uncomfortable procedure that roasted her rear, but it made sure that her toilette would be completed before she lost Agathe's services. Julie sipped the last of the watery broth the host had sent, then put down the mug. Carefully, she showed the girl how to use the curling rods, twisting a long lock of hair around and down to the handle of the solid rod, then slipping the hollow brazier-heated second rod in a snug fit over the first and holding it there for a moment.

Agathe nodded and picked up a heavy lock of hair, prepared to do her duty as a hairdresser. But Julie, catching a glimpse of the girl's stupid expression, suddenly imagined the smell of burnt hair and the look of singed curls, and she pulled back in haste.

'Never mind, Agathe,' she gasped. 'I've no patience to sit still now. When my hair dries fully, you can brush it well and dress it back in a plain Psyche knot. That will have to do.'

In half an hour, the rain stopped as precipitously as it had begun. The wind shredded the clouds and blew them away, and suddenly the autumn sun blazed out on the resumed bustle of the port. And with the sun arrived the coachman for hire recommended by the *patron*. He was a hulking, stoop-shouldered man with a sly, weathered face who announced his name as Jules Poilettier and told her his price as he stood before her, hat in hand.

'Five hundred francs!' Julie cried, astounded.

Poilettier shrugged heavy shoulders. '*Eh bien*, madame, it is a long journey from here to Paris, especially going south and out of our way to the Loire Valley as you demand. There is feed and stablin' for the horses and an allowance for meself for so many days on the road there and back, and a tiny pinch o' profit for me trouble. Add it all up, madame, and you'll see I am practically driving for nothing. It is me best price, assuredly. I cannot do't for one sol less, or me five little ones will have no bread in their mouths.'

'I had not thought the cost would be so steep.' Julie frowned.

'Y'er just arrived on the Channel ship from Bournemouth? Ah, then madame does not imagine how hard are the times in France. Prices are high, taxes terrible, food scarce.' He spread his callused hands in a take-it-or-leave-it gesture. 'I hire out me coach for short trips in the area; it brings enough to keep the horses and a bit left o'er. But in the time it would take to drive you to Paris and return, I could earn as much with me fishing nets and not leave me poor wife alone. It may sound a mighty sum, madame, but these days it buys little enough.'

'Two hundred,' Julie offered.

'Five hundred is me price, and there ain't no other vehicle about you can hire for Paris.'

'Three hundred, then.'

The coachman appeared to struggle with his better sense. 'Four hundred fifty,' he conceded.

'Three seventy-five. You'll get three hundred and seventy-five francs and not a penny more,' Julie concluded in a determined voice. 'If you won't agree, then I can get on a northbound vessel to Le Havre and reach Paris from there for half of what you ask.' She could think of nothing more horrible than reboarding a pitching, rolling ship, but she was not going to let him know it.

Poilettier, though complaining mournfully that he would have nothing to show for his trouble, finally accepted her offer of three hundred seventy-five francs—half now and the rest when they reached Paris.

She thought the coachman, fearing to lose his passenger and his 'tiny pinch o' profit,' had been taken in by her attitude, her indifferent shrug. But her triumph in driving a good bargain was soon deflated—she did not miss the smirk of derision on Agathe's homely face as the tavern wench ushered out the departing coachman.

As it was, a serious recounting of the gold coins in her purse dashed her, for there would not be much left after the hundred eighty-seven francs she had agreed to give Poilettier the next morning. There was some money waiting for her in Paris, but she had been loath to send for any of it and had merely exchanged for francs and traveled with the thirty pounds left after the London creditors had finished with her. She had never expected the coach part of her journey to cost so much. Ah well, the carrot was cut; one could not stick it back together again. Her funds would last until Paris if she managed frugally and traveled fast.

Natural exuberance took over once more, and she laughed and did a few hopping dance steps around the room, toes pointed, skirt lifted. She was home, she was back in France, and in Paris she would find all the entertainment and freedom and living that had been denied her in the country manse where she had wearied away five years of her life. Julia Mountmerry, Countess of Lowry, she had signed the channel ship's register, and for the last time in that particular way. She had never been Julia Mountmerry, no matter what the marriage papers said. Julia maybe, for the pitiful little time that Richard had fondly called her that. Handsome Richard, admirable Richard—her lip curled. But Mountmerry, never. Charming Richard had ruined that.

She was Julie de Lisle Croixverte. So she had left France, and so she returned. And if the Mountmerry must be legally added, then so be it and damned to it. She was no longer the wide-eyed girl of fifteen, the silly romantic awed by the adventure of accompanying her father, Henri, Vicomte de Morlé, to Whitehall. She was a grown woman who had weathered the loss of her father, the bitterness of her marriage, the death of her husband, the trial of squeezing a legacy from the wrecked estates of both parents and mate, all in so short a time. Yet she was sure she was returning to France much better off than when she had left it.

Her duty had been first to her father and then to her husband, but now the slate was clean: she was a widow of almost twenty-two, very pretty, so some had said, and free to do exactly as she wished with her life.

But in spite of herself, a wave of anxiety washed over her, taking some of the sparkle from her eyes. The frightening fact was that she was alone in the world. And it would not be easy to maintain independence on the paltry sum of money her father had left her. She would want to purchase an appointment at court; her wardrobe was a shambles; she had little jewellery or frippery to adorn her. To live meant to enjoy the dazzling swirl of the court of Louis XIV. And that took money.

Sudden anger gripped Julie at the irony of it all. Would anyone believe it? The daughter of the respected Henri de Morlé, late French ambassador to England, and the widow of the wealthy, infamous Richard Mountmerry, Earl of Lowry, wondering how to stretch her little remaining gold to cover the requirements of her position?

Thank God there was at least La Vallette, the estate left by her mother and the reason for her long trip to Saint-Léonard-sur-Loire. She had never been to La Vallette, but her mother had often spoken of its beauty. And since she was being forced to sell it for lack of cash, Julie thought it would be wise to see it first, so that a prospective buyer would not be able to take her in by offering less than it was worth.

Suddenly Julie felt hungry, for the first time in many days. Ravenous, in fact. She slipped on a simple gown of wool with lawn sleeves and realized that it hung on her. The tiny-waisted, rounded figure that had drawn admiring glances in London was on the edge of being skinny. Bones will never do for Paris, she scolded herself. You must eat, my girl. She decided to start with the landlord's fried tripe and sausage, just the thing to build her strength for the long journey that would begin in the morning—pray God the sun would hold and dry up the mud quagmires sometimes called roads.

The next day, refreshed by another good breakfast and a good night's sleep, even though the bed had seemed to roll and pitch underneath her, Julie drew in deep breaths of the fresh sea air and then stepped jauntily into the coach Jules Poilettier pulled up before the inn with a loud flourish of 'whup-whups' to his two rump-sprung horses. And in a moment, Julie and her baggage were jolted away from Saint-Malo. Settling herself with her feet up on the opposite seat, which also held a pannier of provisions for a midday meal, she happily watched the fruitful farms of Brittany jounce by.

They kept up a tolerable pace in spite of the mucky roads, but after many days of racketing and bouncing and as many uncomfortable nights in hostels, much of Julie's effervescence had been sapped. Then, finally, they were past Le Mans and into the valley of the Loire, heading toward Blois.

Julie daydreamed along the way, viewed the passing countryside, and spent a good bit of the time dozing in spite of the coach's careening. But sometimes, despite the several years that had elapsed and her determination to stay with the present, the last dreadful scene with Richard at Cuckfield, the last time she had seen him alive, passed again before her eyes.

He was standing in the center of the mansion's reception hall, slim, decadent, his face a pale marvel of that cool, chiseled beauty so seductive to women. She was dark-haired and of medium height, her eyes, so deep blue as to seem purple, now rimmed with red. He was very drunk and dangerous, a man in love with self-destruction. She was trembling violently, assailed by shock and heartbreak. Thinking no more could be said between them, she whirled to leave the room, her breath coming in dry sobs, wanting only to run out of the house and into the fields, run and run a thousand leagues to where she could no longer hear his voice tearing her apart.

But she was too slow.

The Earl of Lowry flung a small chair out of his way so fiercely that it cracked apart as it hit the floor. Ignoring the crash, he made one swift, unsteady lunge, grabbed his frightened wife by the arm, and jerked her around to face his drunken spite. Physical violence excited him. She knew he was hoping she would bite and scratch and curse him, but only a muffled wail escaped her, and so he despised her all the more.

'You will stay here in the room, madam, I've not finished with you yet,' he ground out.

'Oh, let me go.'

'Not until you've gained some idea of how stupid you are. And truly!'

'Could there be more, Richard? What have you left to destroy me with? You do not want me. I disgust you. You shudder at my name.' Tears began welling in Julie's eyes again.

'Aha, so it has finally sunk into your brain, has it? It has taken two hours and a whole carafe of my best brandy to get you to comprehend that much. Then let us go on to other things.' The finely molded face, so reminiscent of an ancient Greek athlete's, was disfigured by an ugly leer. Malice burned in his gray eyes. Lowry was wallowing in the joy of eradicating a lesser opponent, a weak life that was fun to crush because it went *pop*! He enjoyed tears and pleading and anguish.

'Please let me go,' Julie begged, distraught. 'Do whatever you wish. Whatever you wish, do you hear? I no longer know who you are or what you are. Let me go to my father——'

'Ah, your father. Now, there's a man, b'God's grace.' He hooted, and with fearful heart, she knew she had played right into his hands.

Roughly, he shoved her into the tapestried armchair behind her. He planted his booted foot on the edge of the chair so that she could not escape and leaned over her in mock coziness. 'Your father, my blind, stupid woman? Your own father detests you, too, didn't you know? And so many tuppence for parental devotion!'

'That is a falsehood. My father loves me. He has always——'

'Pah! What do you know, with your feelings and mewlings and dainty reservations, sniveling over poetry?

Your father forfeited you to me as if you were a slave or a piece of furniture, like the puling simpleton you are. You meant nothing more to him than the luck of a card.'

'You are mad,' she gasped. 'I wanted to marry you. I loved you. I begged him to arrange the marriage. And you courted me. You loved me, too.'

Sculpted lips twisting contemptuously, he removed his foot from the chair and lurched to the heavy oak table, where the almost empty decanter sat. His mouth hung slack as he filled a crystal goblet. He turned to her once more and, with heavy irony, raised his glass, the strongly spiritous wine sloshing unnoticed onto his velvet coat and lace cuffs.

'Yes, indeed, I loved you, madam. I loved you the amount of your dowry—ten thousand pounds' worth and not a tittle more. And that only half paid off the sum your sanctimonious sire owed me. I plan to squeeze him for the remainder presently. Or, if necessary, squeeze you like a pressed grape until he honors his gambling debts like a gentleman. Bloody frog!'

'God help you, Richard. You did care for me those months in London, and if I was fooled, how could my father know better? You sat at my feet and kissed my fingers. When we married, we were happy; you told me you adored me——' She pressed a sodden lace handkerchief against her eyes for a moment, overwhelmed by disbelief. 'You sent me away from London last year to keep me safe from the plague, because you loved me——'

'To get you out of my way, you imbecile. Oh, I'll give you the few months you beguiled me with your blushes and dimples and fine, firm rump. You see, wife mine, once in a while a man needs a change, a little time to catch his wind, and that is what you offered. A little time for playacting: Lord Lowry, the simple, romantic clod living blissfully with his young wife to the slow-measured tempo of a *courante*. But virginity and domesticity, once tasted, lose all savor. And then I was bored. The devil's arse, how I was bored!' Exasperated, he turned his back on her in disgust but then whirled and pointed his finger. 'And you—always spying on me, questioning me, your fingers clinging like burrs to my arms. I had acquired a new mistress when I sent you out of London to grace these Sussex dells. She's an Englishwoman, worth ten of you. She doesn't ask me to play gallant lover. She's happy enough for any sticking I give her, and she asks me for it ten times a day.'

Swaying, grinning, Lowry drained his glass with one hand and made a lewd gesture with the other. But his speech came out unslurred, a torrent of venom savagely disgorged.

Julie jumped up and stumbled away toward the door. She was a wounded animal fleeing in dumb terror from a tormentor.

'Eh, where are you going, madam? You'll stay here until I am finished with you,' Lowry screeched, falling again into a fury, elegant nose pinched white. He hurled his empty glass at her back, missing widely, then darted across the sparsely furnished, echoing room to bar the doorway.

'In fact, you'll stay here forever, for the rest of your life, you wailing baggage. I'll not have you spoiling my amusements at court. You're nothing but a vouchsafement, a piece of collateral, and you don't even know it. You make me sick!'

Julie remained where his dash for the door had stopped her. Some of the shock had worn off. Turning to him across the pain of her ripped heart, she stared stricken at the man who fourteen months before had sighed blissfully when she lay beside him. It was obvious he meant just what he said. Now, for once, he meant every word he crushed her with.

Warily, she backed up, rigid with fear as he came toward her, weaving, white-lipped, clench-fisted, visibly obsessed with the urge to hurt.

'For the rest of your life, I order you to remain here in Cuckfield, madam. How long is a life, madam, eh? Answer me that, you shivering rabbit.'

A table hit the back of Julie's legs, and her hand groped behind her for the heavy pewter candlestick she knew stood there. Her husband was wrong. There were fires in her he had never seen or known, because she was not certain herself how to either enjoy or control them. Now control made no matter. What mattered was the leap of hate in her breast, her urge to strike out at him. Grasping the candlestick firmly behind her back, she lifted her chin and glared warning, sparks leaping out from her tear-swollen eyes. Her shallow breath came in audible pants. Her heart pounded with terror. 'If you come one step closer, Lowry, you will regret it.'

He was too drunk and too near passing out to listen. With a snarl of rage, he lunged, catching her by the long black ringlets clustered over her ear, yanking her head back. She yelled in pain and fear. His distorted face loomed over her, the reek of wine filled her nostrils, and then he was falling, crushing her up against the table, sliding bonelessly down her body.

For a moment, she stood rooted, looking down at her supine husband in horror. Then she swiveled to set the candlestick carefully back on the table. She twitched the hem of her gown out from under the sprawled drunk. As life began flooding back into her veins again, she clapped a hand over her mouth, sickened to realize that she might have killed him if she had hit him. With a dry sob, she whirled and ran and fled from the dour manor house to take refuge with the sympathetic old gentleman on the neighboring estate.

When she returned in the morning with an empty pistolet hidden in the fold of her gown—for she was determined to defend herself against Lowry's insane rage—he was gone. She never saw him again, her handsome, engaging Richard, not in the four more years she was forced to weary away at Cuckfield, unaided by her father, who dropped his eyes in shame the one time he came to visit her.

Julie squeezed her eyes shut and shook her head, forcing into oblivion the destructive past, the remaining shreds of anger against her father. Today was another day; she was another person. She opened her eyes and, looking from the coach windows, rejoiced in the sun sparkling amid the currents of the wide river purling its way just below the road. At a crosspath where Poilettier was forced to pull up to let a long straggle of goats and their herder pass, she stuck her head out of the window. 'Ho, Poilettier, is this the river Loire?'

'*Oui*, madame, just so. Finally. Once we pass Sancerre, the very next village is Saint-Léonard. So they told me at last night's halt.' He hawked and spit onto the rocky road and grumbled, 'At least most of the way is behind us on this endless journey.'

Julie smiled and settled back on her seat. The coachman would not be happier than she to have done with this duty.

They reached the village of Saint-Léonard-sur-Loire at about four in the afternoon, and Julie decided to make arrangements for the night before she drove out to see La Vallette. The small gaggle of thatched-roof cottages and tiny church offered no public inn, so she directed Poilettier to drive up before the only residence she could see that boasted a tile roof and more than two rooms, and she told him what to say. Poilettier swung down from his seat and prepared an officious knock for the plank door, when it suddenly squeaked open in his face and a woman in a white peaked cap poked out her head, grimacing, 'Eh?'

'Is this the house of the mayor? Yes? Well then, tell him to come out here.'

The beady old eyes looked past him at the dilapidated coach, which certainly didn't belong to the tax collector, the *abbé*, or any of the minor gentry in the area. 'And who wants to see him?'

'Madame the daughter of the Vicomte de Morlé.'

'Eh?'

'The mistress of La Vallette, that's who.'

'The mis—oh, oh! *Ma foi*——!' The white cap disappeared.

The rotund mayor, who was also the village barber and blacksmith, appeared quickly and all in a dither handed Julie ceremoniously out of the coach and conducted her into his house, which consisted of a large kitchen and two small bedchambers. He offered her a chair with a rush seat and fluttered over her while his old mother bobbed curtsies in the background and grinned toothlessly.

'Oh, but if only Mademoiselle de Croixverte had notified us of her arrival,' he apologized, wringing hamlike hands in nervous excitement, 'we could have prepared to greet her more appropriately.'

'Do not be troubled, good mayor. I am bound for Paris in all haste and will only stay with you the night. Can you accommodate me?'

'Beyond doubt, mademoiselle, what my humble dwelling has to offer is at your disposal.'

Julie smiled pleasantly. 'Not mademoiselle,' she corrected him. 'I am now the Comtesse de Lowry.'

'Ah, a thousand pardons for my ignorance, Madame la Comtesse. It has been years since La Vallette has been graced by the presence of its owners. . .'

The old crone surreptitiously wiped the dust from a treasured silver cup with the corner of her apron and set it before their guest. 'A sip of nice wine to refresh yourself, madame?' she quavered. To be gracious, Julie accepted the wine from the work-gnarled hands and nodded her thanks.

'I've come to inspect my property and the chateau,' she informed the flushed mayor. 'This afternoon, so that I may be on my way by tomorrow early. Is the road to the chateau marked, or will a guide be advisable to show my driver the way? I imagine the place is in quite rundown condition after all this time of neglect.'

The mayor's smile became a puzzled stare. 'Rundown, madame? Are you making a joke? Can it be that you do not know?'

'Know, Maître le Maire? Know what?'

The mayor smote his forehead with an anguished hand and cried, 'Ah, of course not, how could you know? Oh, madame, I kneel at your feet in regret, I beg your forgiveness—I had meant to communicate the disaster to Monsieur le Vicomte so soon as it happened, but with my cows giving sour milk and the river overflowing not a week later and all the village in danger of being washed away, and then both brothers Legrand dying of the pox. . .I thought I had sent a message, but now that I consider it, alas, I did not. It was terrible, terrible. It happened just after the rent collector came in the spring.

For three days I smelled trouble—no wind, too hot, too still. And then such a violent storm as madame could hardly conceive, great claps of thunder and lightning that lit the whole sky for many hours, and then the rain—for days without mercy. Alas, madame, but the chateau is no more, demolished by fearful lightning bolts, three of them, some say, and ravaged by rampant fire. We could do nothing to save it——'

'Oh no,' Julie breathed.

Oh no, she thought in horror. It can't be burned and ruined and worthless. I need it, I haven't enough money, I was going to sell it, La Vallette was all I had left. . .

'——but I am sure Monsieur le Vicomte will be happy that the fire did not spread to the stables, at least,' the mayor finished lamely, his smile anxious.

'My father is deceased. La Vallette is—was mine.'

The man's porcine face wrapped itself in condolences. 'So! What a loss. A man in his prime, God rest his soul, full of vigor and grace, so kind, so considerate, so——'

'I will go out to the chateau now.' Julie cut him off, rising. 'Kindly show my coachman the way.'

'But, madame, there are only ruins!'

Without answering, Julie swept out of the house. Shrugging his shoulders, the mayor followed her to the coach, helped her in, and, with a good enough grace, heaved himself up beside Poilettier. Julie did not doubt that the man told the truth, but she wanted to know firsthand the extent of the damage. If the blow of tragedy was to fall again, it should do so quickly.

The chateau was not far from the village, built on level ground surrounded on three sides by a long, gentle curve of the river. It was reached by a private avenue lined with unkempt trees whose branches clawed at the coach and hid the gardens and mansion from sight until the last minute. The depressing vista that greeted Julie's stare as the trees fell away was shocking to someone who had known La Vallette only through her mother's glowing descriptions—a fairy-tale castle where good little girls who minded their nurse might go and slide down the wondrous marble chute that sloped from the terrace into the river. The chute had been designed by Julie's grandfather as a novelty for his children. When wetted, it made a swift slide that dumped the children laughing and delighted into the placid current.

When Julie was a child, her father had had other estates, more convenient to reach and closer to the king's residences, and Julie was never taken to La Vallette. After her mother's death, her infrequent leaves from the convent school were spent with her father in Paris or at Clamienterre, an estate now sold. But her mother had always had a wistful love for La Vallette, the reason, perhaps, for which the Vicomte had left this remnant of his daughter's inheritance untouched.

Now there was no slide, no terrace or spired turrets, no berries big as your thumb growing along the flower-dotted banks of the river. Only one gaunt wing of the mansion remained standing, a scorched shell with a caved-in roof, stark as a skeleton. The rest—the towers, the tapestried rooms with fireplaces higher than the height of two men together, the fanciful mosaic pavement in the great hall—all vanished, buried in a rubble of stone, as if some giant had ground down a malicious thumb upon the site. The wide marble steps that had led to the main portal were intact and somehow free of debris, but they were steps into nowhere.

La Vallette's gardens, Julie's mother had recounted, had had square beds of hollyhocks, yellow lilies, and blue lupins edged with ground ivy, in the Italian manner, and Italianate fountains and statues adorning the grottoes. One might have expected them to be overgrown now, but what Julie found was desolation, erosion, and dead hedges, where not even the outlines of the former flower beds or the gravel paths were visible anymore. Coarse grass and weeds had taken hold.

'What happened to the park?' Julie whispered to the mayor, aghast, for so gloomy was the aspect of the place, so melancholic in the slanting rays of the sun, that a normal tone would have jarred.

'The floods, madame; the river overran its banks and did not fully recede for two weeks, a catastrophe not in the memory of our oldest inhabitants. The current was so powerful it washed away topsoil, plants, roots, everything. The village is on higher ground, the merciful Seigneur be thanked, but you can see from this costly destruction'—the wave of his hand took in hectares of despoiled gardens—'what muddy misery the flood made of our fields.'

All Julie could think of at that moment was her long-departed mother, who had cherished La Vallette. Oh, Maman, I am sorry, she thought sadly. And then her own situation confronted her as she noticed that even the stone stables standing forlorn behind the chateau's wreckage were roofless. It was a small estate to begin with, and the tiny dependency of the village of Saint-Léonard returned tiny rents. With residence and park destroyed, what buyer would purchase an isolated woodland preserve that offered no shelter of convenience and only squirrels and hare for hunting? If she could sell it, it would be for 'pence, not pounds,' as they said in Sussex, and that was poor comfort to a woman who had hoped to direct her life with an unfettered hand.

With a final, defeated survey of La Vallette's ruins, Julie drew her head back into the coach and slumped against the seat while Poilettier guided his horses back to the village in the gathering twilight.

A restless night in the mayor's lumpy bed—the only real bed in the hamlet, he had told her proudly—didn't help Julie swallow the awful reversal. She got up in the morning, wrathful at the peabrain who called himself a mayor for not having tried to notify her of the debacle that had occurred to La Vallette; the message would have gotten to her through her father's notary and at least saved her this expensive and useless journey. She gave the bumbling fellow a very cold goodbye as he stood, hat in hand, with the other gawping inhabitants of Saint-Léonard-sur-Loire behind him. Poilettier cracked his whip, and away they bucketed—north, at last, toward Paris.

As the leagues passed, Julie's brooding lifted. There was, after all, her uncle de Montespan. He surely would not desert her, although she hardly knew him. But she *did* know his wife, Athénais, her dearest friend at the convent school, who had married him. Julie so clearly remembered how, during the last of their convent days, Athénais had blushingly confided that Julie's own uncle, the Marquis de Montespan, was suing for her hand, and how she prayed her father would consent to give her to the middle-aged but dapper and distinguished soldier who was her idol. And how they had giggled to think that in such a case Athénais would suddenly be Julie's aunt; and how Julie would twit her friend and give the other young ladies something to gabble about by addressing her as *'ma chère tante'* every so often.

The happy marriage had come about just before Julie's father had taken his fifteen-year-old daughter to London. And it was Athénais, as soon as she received Julie's letter telling of Richard's death, who insisted that Julie return to Paris and remain as her guest as long as she wished. Julie responded to her just before she left London, so Athénais and her uncle would know the approximate date of her departure, the fifteenth of October 1669, and the date was significant—it was the date of her final deliverance from the web of sorrow and lawyers and creditors England had spun for her. Oh, she was anxious to see Athénais again, her bosom friend from the convent, her dear correspondent whose infrequent but welcome letters brought the bubbling diversions of the Sun King's court to the forsaken young wife in the drafty manor house in Sussex.

Giving herself up to lively daydreams as the tall wheels rumbled, Julie imagined the court's constant round of balls and picnics and masquerades. She imagined herself the laughing center of an avid group of admirers, acting as nonchalant and gay as if she had enjoyed seven years of such tribute at Charles II's English court—oh, *fi donc,* Monsieur le Duc, you are too flattering; dear Monsieur le Comte, do bring me an ice; would Your Highness *truly* care to hear my opinion of the English Protestants, well. . .Against the stretches of stately poplars lining the road, she conjured up images of herself taking the air along the Cours de Reine in a dashing coach-and-six, splendid in satin and jewels and drawing from the impressed onlookers an intrigued 'Who is that lady?' Not even the bone-rattling discomfort and mildewed seats of Poilettier's coach prevailed against her runaway projections, even though they were so at variance with the state of her pocketbook.

Later, another recounting of her remaining cash reminded her of Richard's taunt that she had no head for finances. *Sale cochon!* What business had he ever let her transact? He gave even her household accounts over to Cuckfield's ferret-eyed chatelaine, Mistress Battersby. Niggardly to his wife, disdainful of his mounting debts, the Earl of Lowry could lose thousands of pounds in one day's gaming without turning a hair. Was that what he called a head for finance? At any rate, she saw she would barely have enough to cover the remainder of the journey—if she reduced herself to less expensive accommodations and a subsistence diet, that is.

One day, having been thrown sliding across the width of the seat, she recovered herself to realize that the coach had just taken a curve on two wheels. Enough was enough. Holding on tightly to the window ledge, she leaned across the facing seat and banged on the coachman's trap. It took a few minutes before the noise she was making was noticed above the racket of pounding hooves and groaning axles. Finally, the little door opened to a view of the coachman's stubbled jaw as he leaned down to hear her.

'Yes, madame?' he yelled.

'Poilettier, you are shaking me to pieces. Why must you find every hole and rut in France?' she shouted. 'Why are we going so fast?'

'Getting dark. Innkeep back there warned there were dangerous highwaymen on this stretch, said it was infested with 'em, murder 'un for a sol. I ain't fancying to travel in the dark. We have to make Lagle. Brace yourself against t'other seat, and it won't take you so bad.'

And the trap clapped shut.

Muttering, Julie fell back and tried to wedge herself more firmly into a corner. She was annoyed. Provincials sometimes magnified one varlet with a club into a whole army of bandits. But just then, they sped by the charred remains of a coach that had been run into a ditch and burned, and a bit further on, Julie spotted a rotting saddlebag that had been slashed and rifled. It came to her that *she* might know she had nothing worthwhile for anyone to rob, but a gang of marauders would not—not until they had killed her and Poilettier and then searched their bodies and luggage. Imagination gripped her with visions of her ravished body left broken and bleeding by the wayside. She shrank fearfully into her corner and held on.

They were just outside Lagle when she thought she heard the sound of galloping horses behind them. Poilettier lashed up his team in one last spurt, and they rattled into the village and up to an inn in a billowing cloud of dust. The bone-jarring arrival, in addition to her accumulated travel-weariness, really raveled Julie's composure. And Poilettier's growled warning served further to set her nerves on edge.

'See to't your door's well barred tonight,' he cautioned. 'If there's thieves about, there's no telling but the innkeep's in with 'em and they'll steal your money whilst you sleep. Happened once outside of Saint-Malo, and a man and his wife murdered, cut up to ribbons in their bed——'

The *patron*'s wife was ill, and he had no other female help that night, so Julie struggled with her own buttons and lacings and wearily combed out her hair. She ate her frugal supper in the surprisingly decent chamber rented her, washed the dust from her face, and slipped on her white linen nightdress, grateful that the weather was holding a pleasant temperature. But before she got into bed, she rummaged in her smallest trunk and pulled out the heavy, ball-handled dueling pistol she had found among Richard's effects, along with the little paper cylinders containing shot and powder.

With the pistol tucked under her pillow, she felt calm enough to draw her hand mirror from her trunk and, for the hundredth time, take stock of her assets in the game of living, for her destination was no more than a few days away. The face she saw was quite agreeable, take away the fatigue lines caused by travel: large, lustrous violet eyes that deepened into purple when she was angry, fringed by short, thick black lashes and emphasized by winged brows, a milky, satiny complexion marred only by a few faint freckles, and a mass of wavy hair so ebon it sparked blue in the sunlight. Her hair color was natural, and she would leave it that way, no matter that so many ladies in the courts of Europe bleached their tresses to the highly fashionable golden blond; it was different and would stand her out from the horde of flaxen-haired females surrounding the glittering Sun King.

Her mouth was nicely curved and showed a sprightly humor, she thought. Her teeth were even, her chin delicate but pleasingly round. Compared with the tininess of her waist and her slim hips, her breasts were large, firm and full. Sir Hubert, her kind neighbor in Sussex, had screwed up his wrinkled eyes and deemed her a perfect Diana, but she would be nothing but candid with herself and, turning her face from side to side in the mirror for a better look, decided again that her nose was a trifle too tilted to win her the accolade of classic Greek beauty.

As for character, she thought she knew her faults: mainly impetuousness, a tendency toward sudden shifts of mood, and a slight stutter when she was upset—balanced, she hoped, by a generous nature.

So then, she was pretty and amiable, and she had manners, a measure of wit, and a fine name. And she could play the clavier well. These were the things she could offer a prospective husband, one who might value them above a good dowry. Not that she wanted to marry right away. She wanted to be gay and young again for a while, but she had to face the facts—when her little bit of money ran out, and if a suitable gentleman was available, she would have to relinquish her liberty.

She knew exactly the sort of man she wanted if she could have her choice: he would definitely not be the handsome, selfish, overbearing sort of rake who had just put her through almost six miserable and lonely years. He must be an older man—of proper rank, of course—a stable, solid, virtuous gentleman of good means who would treat her kindly and cherish her. His looks and grace would not matter. If he could give her respect and comfort, she would bear his children and be loyal to him and look forward to their years together with contentment. After being singed in the evil pyre of Richard Mountmerry, she was now going to be smart enough to put her life into the proper hands.

'So much for the nightly reminder of my path to happiness,' Julie yawned and climbed into bed, hoping to fall asleep right away. But the difficult trip was telling on her nerves. She lay wide awake in the dim room, and the shadows made by the candle reminded her that there were blackguards who could be creeping up. She jumped at each scrape of a leaf along the roof, each creak of a shutter below, each scrabble of a mouse in the walls, until she swore at herself for a timid idiot and hauled over on her side, eyes determinedly shut.

She must have finally dropped into an exhausted sleep, for the next she knew, her chamber was filled with the violent racket of an assault upon her door, and from below her night-darkened window she heard the loud snorting and blowing of hard-run horses and the clink of spurs. She flew bolt upright, struggling to awaken, then clasped her hands in dread. Even by the small light of the night candle—*mon Dieu!*—she could see clearly that in her preoccupation with the pistol, she had stupidly forgotten to bolt her door, which now shuddered under the insistent pounding of a heavy fist.

The pistol! Gasping with fright to hear the noisy cutthroats outside boldly shouting commands at the poor innkeep, Julie fumbled the pistol out from under her pillow, tore at the paper cylinder with her teeth, and poured the ball and powder down the bore. She pulled back the ornate cock with shaking hands and slid out of the bed to where she could have an unobstructed aim at the blackguard who was battering on the door. 'Poilettier! Thieves! Poilettier, help me!' she cried out as the pounding broke off and the latch jiggled.

Desperately, she steadied the pistol in two hands and, as the door flew open, closed her eyes and squeezed convulsively on the trigger.

At once there was a thunderous report, a splintering

of wood, and an astounded curse. As she staggered back under the pistol's recoil, she opened her eyes to see a man, dressed in the dusty but unmistakable gold-buttoned blue and red coat, gold sash, and high boots of a king's officer, pressed against the wall by the doorway. She heard him call out to a companion that he was all right, madame had merely mistaken him for a target. The innkeep's voice now rose from the courtyard outside, and even in Julie's extremity, she recognized the apologetic anxiety that hostel keepers reserved for paying guests, not highwaymen.

The heavy pistol dropped from her trembling hands and thudded to the floor. Oh, *Sainte Vierge*. In her blind panic, she had almost murdered someone! A buzzing blur arose behind her eyes; she swayed, buckling at the knees, and was just saved from crumpling to the floor in a semifaint by her visitor, who quickly leaped forward from the doorway to catch her in strong arms and hold her upright.

Helplessly, she leaned against him until her head cleared. In a moment, she was enough recovered to push away from his support and snatch up her cloak from a stool, not missing, in spite of her confusion, the brash intruder's grin of regret for her recovered physical fortitude—her nightdress was opaque, but the linen was thin and soft. Obviously, it had been pleasant to hold her. She drew herself up, hiding her state of *déshabille* behind her cloak and her outraged dignity.

'How dare you batter down my door like a thief in the night, monsieur! Is it so that the gentlemen of France treat unprotected ladies? For you are a gentleman, I presume from your dress, and not the common cutthroat you act!'

He answered her anger by plucking his plumed hat from his long locks and sweeping her a low, exaggerated bow. He was broad-shouldered, cinnamon-bearded, merry-eyed, and a man obviously unrattled by women swooning at his feet.

'Nicolas de Courcillon, Captain of His Majesty's Garde-du-Corps, at your service, madame. And I did not batter down your door. I scratched politely, and then

I knocked and called, and then I pounded, but it seems you rest most soundly or you are a trifle deaf, and I thought I had better go shout in your ear. I did not imagine you would shoot me down first and ask questions later.'

'Since you seem to believe that a lady would take kindly to a strange man entering her room and shouting in her ear, you will one day meet a better shot than I and pay dearly for your insouciance!'

The intruder laughed and responded insinuatingly. 'Ah, but had I known what an exquisite ear rested behind this portal, I would have used a more soothing manner of awakening you than shouting and bruising my fists on the door. I cannot express how deeply sorry I am, both for my intrusion and for my ignorance that it was a *young* lady I had to arouse——'

'Rather than impudent apologies, monsieur, I would like an explanation. What do you want of me?' Julie broke in, ice in her voice.

'Since we are just new acquaintances—alas—at this point, only your coach, madame.' He smiled boldly, showing white teeth. Clapping his wide-brimmed hat back on his head, he strode to the window to check on the bustle in the courtyard. 'Good. My men are hitching it up now. We are transporting a most important prisoner to the fortress at Pignerol and have had the bad luck to break an axle on our vehicle. We woke the local smith, who says it will need at least a day or two to repair the damage, and this miserable village hasn't another closed conveyance in it except yours. Since we are in the utmost of haste to deliver our prisoner, I took the liberty of waking you to request the exchange of your coach.'

'To *commandeer* my coach, is the phrase, monsieur, since you are already hitching your horses to it without my consent. I am going to Paris, and I am also in the utmost haste, and you will call down to your men to undo their work. You may not have my coach.'

'In that case, and a thousand pardons for the inconvenience to you, we shall just have to take it. My orders are to brook no delay in getting this prisoner to his destination, and a broken axle means enormous delay.'

'By what authority do you seize a private vehicle in this high-handed manner?'

His answer was pleasant but firm. 'By the authority of Louis of France, in whose name I must require you to exchange your coach for ours.'

It wasn't the loss of Poilettier's uncomfortable, ungainly coach that provoked Julie into such a strong objection, but the embarrassing fact that the other vehicle might not be ready for another two days and she simply did not have enough money to cover the extra nights on the road unless she borrowed some from Poilettier. It was a mortifying situation that she might have to ask a mere coachman for a few francs, but she was certainly too proud to explain her problem to this irritating swaggerer.

'This is an outrage,' she said, glaring at the high-handed officer. 'It is most urgent that I get to Paris immediately, and you are forcing me to remain here. May I remind you that *I* am not your prisoner to order about, monsieur, and that you are taking great advantage of a helpless woman.'

Although the expression on his face was one of polite sorrow, his light eyes were insolent as they traveled over her, finally lingering boldly on her mouth. 'My regrets. You are quite right—it is an outrage. But His Majesty's business must take precedence over his subjects' private affairs. If madame will tell me her name, I will see that His Majesty has full knowledge of her cooperation with his projects, and I am sure he will want to thank her for her graciousness.'

'I cannot believe the king would countenance your impertinent midnight marauding of a lady's conveyance just to bring some poor criminal faster to his dungeon,' Julie snapped.

His easy baritone laugh curled around her. 'Ah now, madame, would he not?'

'Oh, you are inconsiderate and most intolerable!'

He stepped closer to her to peer into her eyes, and it raced through Julie's mind that such rugged looks and bumptious confidence might be attractive to some women.

'And you, madame, are uncooperative and cranky. But had I the fortune that you *were* my prisoner, there would at least be time for me to smooth your ruffled feathers in a gentler manner.' The generous, strong mouth under the trim, light moustache quirked up at the corners. 'Too bad that we only cross paths. A man could happily lose himself in your beautiful eyes, *ma belle voyageuse.*'

'Your unwanted flattery will avail you nothing. I shall surely report this to the authorities.' She was too angry to yield and step back from him.

'In this case, dear lady, I *am* the authority.'

And before she could move, with one arm he swept her tightly against the gold buttons on his coat and clamped his lips down on hers. In her astonishment, her mouth remained soft, helplessly accepting of the hard, male-tasting, and, a few seconds later, upsettingly interesting kiss. Then she felt his other hand caress her buttock and give it an appreciative squeeze. With an outraged squeal, she bucked, and he released her, laughing, shrugging ruefully at his lack of time to pursue the subject further.

Julie staggered a step back. 'Oh! You——!'

He bowed in the face of her speechless indignation and took his leave. 'Your humble servant, madame,' he murmured with an infuriating, completely unabashed grin.

The intruder strode to the door, then turned and said, 'Oh, and I must insist upon settling with the innkeep for the extra time our emergency may force you to stay with him. Please allow me at least this gesture, I beg you, for it is my fondest hope, dear madame, that we shall meet again in less trying circumstances.'

Julie watched the door close on his lithe but heavy-shouldered frame with a mixture of shock, ire, and relief. She immediately ran over and slammed the bolt home, then ran to the window to watch wide-eyed as, on the far side of Poilettier's coach, two of the king's men urged a hooded figure forward. The prisoner jerked to a stop just before mounting the vehicle and tilted his head back as if to take one more look at the spangled black sky. The hood slipped back a bit.

Julie gasped softly. The man's face, just above his mouth and unkempt beard, was concealed by an appalling, polished, hard black leather mask with small eye slits and a grim, molded nose. Had she not been looking at him from above, she would not have seen the weird disguise the slipping hood revealed.

Impatiently shoved from behind, the grotesquely shrouded prisoner dropped his head in resignation and mounted into the coach, which creaked as the guards climbed in after him. Their own driver was already seated on the box, and six armed soldiers waited on horseback, ready to be off.

The captain emerged from the inn and stopped to speak to Poilettier, who pulled off his cap and nodded his head eagerly. In the yellow nimbus of the lantern held up by the *patron*, the arrogant captain's shadow loomed along the ground like an ebon giant, and the intricate basket hilt of the sword at his side gleamed golden. The officer finally swung onto his horse and signaled. The coach driver cracked his whip and bawled out, 'Ho, ho, hyup! Gar!' and the equipage clattered off into the night, preceded by two torch-bearing soldiers and followed by the rest of the watchful escort.

Julie's eyebrows pleated together as she contemplated the poor wretch she had seen, not only manacled but masked. And how could one single person be such a danger to the state that it required devoted haste and night travel to get him locked up? she wondered. But she was bone-weary and too wrought up to puzzle any longer about what didn't concern her. People were arrested every day, and terrible things happened to some of them. She padded over to test the door bolt, then threw off her cloak and slipped back into bed.

He hopes we shall meet again, does he, the presumptuous oaf? Pulling her blanket up, she thought of the cavalier peevishly and tried to calm herself. Well, he was a perfect example of the soulless Richard type, whose thin veneer of courtesy is a screen for brutality; attractive maybe, and dashing enough to steal a kiss, but entirely repugnant to her. In her mind's eye, she saw him again and thought of the conceit of the short, close-trimmed beard, which just outlined his jaw and chin. Fashionable men went cleanshaven or sported the veriest wisp of a divided moustache, in imitation of the king. Only the doddering grew regular moustaches and beards today—and that was hardly a description of the strapping officer she had just encountered.

What color were his eyes? Gray? Pale blue? He had perhaps a head more than she in height and heavy, broad shoulders tapering to a narrow waist. The charm of his easy smile didn't fool her; in her opinion, his firm mouth showed the obstinacy hidden under that insouciant expression. She turned on one side and then the other, then tossed over onto her back. *Ciel!* How had she noticed so much about him in so short a time?

Her fingers crept up to touch her lips, where she could still feel the pressure of his kiss. The problem was, she decided, that it had been so terribly long since a man had kissed her—or done anything else with her—that any embrace was pleasant. In London, she had been too beset with problems to welcome any attentions from the several gentlemen who tried to gain her interest, and five years before, she'd been too inexperienced. There had only been Richard; but, oh, she had learned some things about her body in the short time he'd favored her.

The familiar aching, like the yearning of an empty vessel to be filled, radiated from her loins and crept out along her limbs so that she curled up and hugged herself tight to stop the lonely demanding. No wonder she had paid attention to—de Courcillon? Was that his name? She was just hungry for the company of men, the flattery, the admiring looks, the excitement of charming them, their wonderful weaknesses and strengths. De Courcillon was just the first, she hoped, of a long line of gentlemen whose amusing presence would dispel the last vestige of her bitterness.

She had to admit to herself that it had been good to feel his arms about her waist, easily supporting her, and now she allowed herself a tiny smile at the memory of his strength and his astounded oath when she'd shot at him. Still, she wished she hadn't been so silly and come so close to fainting when she thought she'd committed murder. That sort of cowardly reaction to surprise and fright had happened twice before, and it embarrassed her; she preferred to see herself as braver.

Julie forced herself to think of the good times ahead in Paris. Mollified as well by the fact that her extra board bill was paid, she finally slept.

The incident actually brought more ease to the rest of her trip, for the coach she had received in exchange was sturdier than Poilettier's old heap, and the seats were well padded to absorb the jouncing. Poilettier, of course, was delighted with the best end of the bargain and beamed at Julie, the lucky talisman that had brought him such a windfall. He sang out in a booming bass easily heard over the rumbling wheels.

The first day in the new coach, as Julie leaned to open the basket of cold provisions she had bought to serve them both as midday dinner, her eye was caught by fresh white scratches in the varnished wood along the side of the seat. She bent closer and saw that the scratches, laboriously made, as if by the edge of a manacle, spelled out a name—'Ed. Courbier'—with the last letter trailing off jaggedly. Using an idle finger, she traced the letters and then shrugged. The name, maybe that of the mysterious prisoner being hastened to his captivity, was unfamiliar to her. Forgetting it, she found a roast pigeon in the basket and tore off a joint to nibble at while she watched the countryside roll by, flat and uninteresting but bringing her ever closer to her goal.

They jolted through the town of Ivry and then into Paris, more than two weeks after she had reached the coast of Brittany exulting that she was home at last and free. But in spite of the wearisome trip, the tragedy of La Vallette, and the midnight skirmish with the brash officer, Julie peered out of the coach window as the city engulfed them and twisted about on her seat with more excitement than a child at his first Twelfth Night feast.

CHAPTER
~ 2 ~

For eyes dulled by the forced contemplation of Sussex farmland, Paris put on a heady show. Even London, still showing the violent black gouge of the Great Fire from London Bridge to Holborn, could not compare with the bright, vigorous bustle of Paris.

True, the streets were very narrow and slanted toward the malodorous, slop-laden gutters in their middle. Refinements such as raised sidewalks hardly existed amid scores of cramped, unnumbered buildings, which reared steeply pitched roofs five and six stories high, cutting off light and air from the common Parisians who swarmed in the complex of alleys. Julie stared at the widespread poverty and misery—hordes of maimed beggars, dirty children, and threadbare students from the Left Bank colleges lugging satchels of books—but this was a condition of every city.

Paris, to make up for it, offered sections on both sides of the river more prosperous than anywhere in the world. *Le Roi-Soleil*, the glittering, imperious Louis XIV, ruled over a city of seven hundred thousand people that under his centralizing hand flourished and grew and now had become a magnet for all of Europe.

The river Seine was the true center of the city, where all Paris gathered for commerce, fêtes, or revolts. It was edged on both sides with crowded quays supporting every type of stall and market, offering all sorts of merchandise from fresh mackerel to rare books. Flowing past on the river was a jostling traffic of barges laden with freight, rafts, water coaches like floating houses, delicate shallops, and gilded pleasure galleys with pennants fluttering in the wind. The riverman's shout of ''Way there—'way!' as the beating oars of another vessel threatened to cut across his bow was a continuous, cursing cry across the bosom of the gray and rippling high road.

The Vicomte de Morlé had once remarked to Julie that anything one's imagination could conjure up was available in Paris if one had the money—not only European goods and luxuries but also the exotic crafts of Africa, Arabia, and the Orient and the furs and spices of Canada and the American Indies. One could rent anything from a potent's rabbit's foot for luck to a curled and waved perruque. And on the rue Saint-Denis, lined with inns and restaurants and pastry cooks, one could hire for a banquet an elegant chandeliered room complete with silver and crystal goblets for as many guests as one's pocketbook could stand.

As Julie mused on these marvels, the coach emerged from the confusion of Left Bank streets and rattled along the cobbles of the Quai des Augustines. Poilettier pulled up to ask a passing artisan for directions to the Ile-Saint-Louis, but Julie just looked out and drank in the bustle around her with the greedy joy of the returned exile. They'd stopped in a bread market where round white and dark loaves were displayed on boards resting on overturned baskets. There were also live chickens in crates and some geese that had gotten loose, which scuttled, honking, from the paths of the strong-porters. Merchants and mounted men passed along the quay, as well as peddlers with handcarts or baskets on their heads or hanging from their tattered backs, all of them calling out their wares: 'Soap, soap to sell and fine brushes'; *'Voilà les petits pâtés, tous chauds, voila!'*; 'Death to rats and mice, ho ho!'; 'Cakes called *oubliés*! Very good'; *'La Gazette Nouvelle, La Gazette!'*

Poilettier clucked to his horses, and they crossed the river by the Pont Neuf, which gave access to the islands sitting in the middle of the Seine like beans obstructing a gullet. The semicircular bays of the bridge were occupied by various mountebanks and sideshows, and Julie remembered her father's annoyance at the riffraff always clogging the busy roadway across the river—jugglers, conjurors, idlers, and grotesque beggars who pulled out teeth or glass eyes to amuse people for a few sols. Then Julie's eye was taken by the gray bulk of the palace of the

Louvre, stretching along the river bank and connected by a long gallery to the Tuileries palace. She wondered if the king was now in residence there with his Spanish queen and his court. Or, if not in the Louvre, then perhaps at the Palais Royal, just across the road, the palace that Cardinal Richelieu had willed to the crown.

They passed the famed cathedral of Notre Dame, and Julie blinked to make sure it was real. And finally, they jogged onto the bridge connecting with the Ile-Saint-Louis, which, in concert with the exclusive quarters of the Left and Right banks, was an enclave of townhouses; the gilded and classic *hôtels* of the wealthy, with their high corniced windows, paved inner courts, and walled, geometric gardens.

A shiny calèche trundled past, its elegant female occupant leaning on the head of a slim walking stick. Making a disgusted moue with her mouth, Julie compared her own simple cloak and gown to the expensive chic that had just passed, and sighed. How could she come on the scene dressed like some country mouse and expect to make a favorable impression?

After one more stop to ask the way, Poilettier finally pulled up with a flourish before the tall iron portals of the Hôtel de Montespan and shouted. The gates opened, and they drove into the paved court and stopped before a short double stair. A footman in crimson and gold emerged from the house and ran down to hand Julie out from the coach. Impassive, he conducted her into a marble foyer with a checkerboard floor, where she gave the liveried butler her name and said she was expected.

'Ah yes, Madame la Comtesse, we have been apprised of your coming. Madame la Marquise will receive you in her chamber.'

But Athénais had peeked out from a window at the sound of the coach, and now she flew down the curving staircase and ran to Julie with her arms stretched in welcome, a fair, round-cheeked, full-bosomed beauty with a glorious halo of golden-blond curls framing her face and pearly white teeth sparkling her smile.

'Ton-ton, dear!'
'Coco!'

Crying the pet names of their girlhood, they hugged each other in a transport of reunion and then kissed each other on both cheeks. They were of the same height, though of strikingly different coloring, and where Julie's tone was normally soft, Athénais's voice trilled out like a flute.

'But where have you been, my dear? I have expected you every day for weeks!' the Marquise gurgled, holding Julie out from her, the better to see her.

'In the Loire Valley,' Julie said, smiling, 'and the story is too long to tell now. But it was a wasted trip and cost every sol and franc I had with me.'

'By the Loire? But what were you doing down there? You poor creature, you must be exhausted from such a trip. Come with me right this instant!' Her hostess grabbed Julie's hand and pulled her to the staircase. 'Guillaume, see that madame's trunks are immediately unloaded and transported to her chamber, and tell the kitchen to prepare a *gouter* to be taken in my apartment.'

Another butler quickly divested Julie of her dusty cloak. In her luxurious chamber, Athénais pressed her guest into a high-backed armchair to rest and then drew up a cushioned folding chair for herself so that their knees almost touched. Flushed with excitement, Julie laughed, still breathless that she had finally arrived. 'Oh, Coco *chérie*, I am so happy to be here, I can't tell you. How very much the same you are. I was afraid we would be strangers after so long a separation.'

Athénais was several years older than Julie, yet the two of them had been drawn together in a companionship that had weathered many girlish spats. Few of the budding demoiselles at the convent school had liked Athénais de Rochechouart-Mortemart, for she was vain of her appearance and of her ancient family, aggressive and clever, and she often displayed a sharp wit that entertained while stabbing its squirming victim through like a rapier. But Julie had admired Athénais's fearless spirit and was not at all bothered by her high-flown pretensions. And after a few heated quarrels, when Athénais learned that Julie would not be bullied or treated disloyally, they had grown as close as adolescent friendship could bring them.

'But Athénais, you look absolutely *ravissante*, more beautiful than I remembered.'

The spectacular blonde grasped Julie's hand and said, 'If I should not have improved my looks in seven years, Julie, I would run this moment and break all my mirrors. But it is you, *ma chère*, we must talk about. You have lived through such a purgatory. You are charming to look at, as you always were, but your unhappy years show in your eyes, in your wistful smile. What has happened to the breathless romantic I knew at Sainte-Clothilde?'

'That one? She died of disillusionment in her English cage. For five years, I had nothing to look at but a big, empty house, the mill, the stables, the dairy and laundry, and had no one to talk to but myself and a sullen housekeeper and the maids. Once in a while, I'd purchase some little nonsenses in the village just to have something to do, but mostly I would put on a boy's shirt and breeches and ride, ride far and fast, and hope I would break my miserable neck.'

'*Ma pauvre!* But why didn't you flee? You could have always come here.'

Julie looked down at her hands. 'I was ashamed to tell you in my letters. Richard held over my father's head heavy gaming wagers he was owed, and he threatened to ruin him if I behaved badly. He would have broken my father and besmirched his name with the king, and all the two of us had left at the time was the pride of the Croixverte name. The fact is, after my father died, I simply had no money.'

Athénais's eyes flashed blue fire. 'Oh, what a devilish tormentor, your English earl. *Sale cochon!* Well, take heart, I'm sure the gentlemen of France make better husbands—for the most part. Now tell me, we never have kept secrets from each other—did you have him killed?'

Instead of gasping at such a terrible idea, Julie only laughed; she knew better than to take her friend's deliberately shocking question to heart.

'No, dear savage. I am desolate to disappoint you, but my late, unlamented husband was mortally slashed during another of his drunken duels, this time by a man who accused him of cheating at cards.' She added hastily, 'And I swear I didn't hire the man or even know him.'

'Don't mock, Julie. I was perfectly serious. One must have a lion's share of courage to advance in this world. I know. I have had much experience.' A sparkle of triumph appeared in her blue eyes.

Athénais's excitement relaxed as a servant entered with the *gouter* and set the table between them with rolls and biscuits, fruit, little dishes of jelly, and decanters of barley water and muscat wine. Then she continued, 'But you must forget England now and recover your spirits, Julie. You are here and in the best position in the world—a widow, free to do as you like. In fact, I have some excellent news for you. There is a court post coming vacant immediately, a high one that could put you in a most important and lucrative position.'

'Yes? Which one?'

Smirking, Athénais popped a bit of biscuit in her mouth and licked a jelly drip from a plump, white finger. 'Wait. First I have to relate to you the latest scandal, a story that is true but almost too ridiculous to believe. Julie, listen, this is quite priceless.' She set her goblet down and leaned forward avidly toward her guest, who was happily devouring a juicy, greenhouse-grown pear such as she had not enjoyed in years. 'There is a personage at court, one of the very highest quality, who has fallen madly in love with a man vastly below her in rank. And so incensed with passion has this person become that she flings herself headlong and openly into her embarrassed lover's path at every opportunity. The whole court is snickering at her unblushing pursuit of this fellow. Oh, it is an incredible spectacle!' Athénais threw back her head in a melodramatic laugh. 'Well, I give you that such aggressive women are not so unusual, but it is the identity of the lady involved that is just astounding. Come, guess who it is, I dare you. You won't choose the right one in a thousand years, it's too unthinkable.

But guess, guess——!'

Discarding the fruit stem, Julie wrinkled her brow in puzzlement. 'But really, Athénais, I know very little of the court intrigues at the moment. I couldn't imagine—Madame de Guise, perhaps, or the Comtesse de Soissons?'

'Oh no, no, I knew you wouldn't pick the most impossible name you could think of. Do you give up? *Bien*, listen to me. It is—oh, shall I tell you? You won't believe it, it is too droll. It is Mademoiselle!'

'Mademoiselle who?'

'*The* Mademoiselle, silly goose, Mademoiselle de France, Mademoiselle d'Orléans, Mademoiselle de Bourbon, Mademoiselle la Duchesse de Montpensier—forty-three years old and at last captured by that tender passion she disapproved of so loudly all through her youth! And who, might you ask, is the object of this late-blooming infatuation?' Athénais was thoroughly enjoying herself. 'The Comte de Lauzun is his name, a self-seeking, posturing little climber for whom the king has curiously shown much partiality and who now has the gall to think he can presume to a lady of the royal family. There! Now, didn't I say you would be thunderstruck?'

It was like old times at Sainte-Clothilde, the breathless tidbits of rumor and gossip to be whispered, gasped at, and giggled over. Only this time, Athénais was right, the news was really bizarre. Julie pressed a hand to her chest. 'Saints! I can't believe it. Mademoiselle in love? The Amazon warrior of the Fronde showing the weakness of a mere woman? Oh, Athénais, you're making fables——'

The heavy-lidded blue eyes were alight with catty enjoyment. 'No I'm not, and perhaps you'll soon see for yourself. Mademoiselle's lady-of-honor, Madame de St Gênet, has lately entrapped a foreign noble and is leaving to be married in Milan. She will sell her post for fifty thousand livres to whomever of the applicants Mademoiselle approves of. So, there you are. Mademoiselle has not yet chosen, and although she has no great love for me, her good *amie* Montglat, the reclusive one she calls Delphinia, tells me she had always had a kind of respect for your father. I have already apprised her of your imminent arrival. If you please her—and you should be good contrast to the solemn de St Gênet—you will have a position of honor almost as fine as mine.'

Athénais was lady-in-waiting to Queen Marie-Thérèse, Louis's dull, neglected Spanish consort.

But Julie frowned and bit her lip. 'Fifty thousand livres! Oh, but that is just wonderful. I have not even got fifteen.'

'Are you joking?'

'You know how little my father left, and I was lucky I did not have to part with even that to free me of Richard's numerous obligations. That's the reason I went to Saint-Léonard-sur-Loire; I have remaining one small estate of my mother's, and I went there to see how much it might bring me—except that I found it in ruins and worthless.'

'*Ciel*, I did not realize you were in such financial straits. But that is terrible, *ma chère*. One cannot move without money.'

'I was hoping I could borrow enough from my uncle to buy myself a court post and then repay him slowly from my yearly allowance and prerogatives. Only I didn't realize what it would cost. Oh dear, Athénais, what shall I do? Do I dare ask the Marquis, your husband, to loan such a sum?'

The heavy lids dropped as Athénais studied her ring-bedecked fingers. 'I expect not,' came from the rosy-red lips. 'You cannot ask my husband. He doesn't have it to lend, and he is not here. He is in exile at his chateau in the Pyrenees, and for all I care, he may rot there.'

Julie's mouth opened in astonishment. 'Athénais! My uncle, banished to Bellegarde? B-but why? He was always so high in the king's favor. What did he do?' There had been no mention at all of trouble in Athénais's few letters. She searched the lovely round face for any hint of a joke, but there was only a flare of the dainty nostrils to label Athénais's last remark as pure understatement.

'What has he done?' Her snort was without humor.

'Why, nothing less than dare to oppose His Majesty's wishes. One doesn't do that, of course, even if one's wife has chosen to become the king's mistress.'

'The king's. . .'

'Oh, calm yourself, Julie, you look like a startled goldfish. What is so surprising about that, when you, above all, know the ambitious paths my mind could conjure? Be proud of me, dear friend. I have attained the most dizzying pinnacle of success a woman could dream of—the heart of a king! Louis is my slave, he adores me, and I shall do anything necessary to ensure he never stops. I have a fortune in gold, in jewels and gifts, I have the whole of the court at my feet, begging favors. I am the true queen of France, and this is yet only the beginning. The king of France shall never fall out of my hands.' Again the blue eyes sparkled with triumph.

'But—but Louise de La Vallière?' Julie stammered out the name of the infamous woman who had in the past nine years been the Sun King's undisputed favorite.

'That swan-necked country bumpkin? That guilt-ridden, mealy-mouthed nun? The king was almost pathetically glad to be rid of her martyred tears and whines. But he pitied her and fancied himself loyal to his first grand passion. I had to step very cleverly to detach him from his withered romance. You know how little patience I have; it was torture to play the game slowly. But ah, the reward was worth the effort.'

She became aware of Julie's disturbed reaction. '*Écoutes*, dearest Julie, do you think I am debauched, a married woman whose husband is still alive and well, openly acknowledged as the king's mistress and living at his palace in suites connected with his own for convenience? Well, it was Montespan himself—your uncle, my own dear husband—who cruelly urged me to sleep with Louis to further his own fortunes and then was infuriated when the situation finally began to appeal to me.'

'Oh, Athénais, but you both seemed so happy when you married, even though he was so much older. . .'

Athénais pushed back her seat abruptly, jumped up, and moved away a few paces, her small fan moving rapidly. 'Henri was so blind, he thought I could be another La Motte-Houdancourt or Comtesse de Roure or any other light o' love the king had for a night or two and then discarded. You know I have never been content with a lesser prize when a greater one is possible.' Her smile appeared for a moment, brilliant and hard. 'But it's too long a story, the struggle I had to dethrone La Vallière. Anyhow, at last I gained what I wanted; Louis fell so deeply in love with me, there was no question of it being a casual dalliance. Because of my married position, we had to be very discreet. My chamber adjoins La Vallière's, and, at first, when everyone took for granted that the king was with her, he was actually with me.

'The arrangement worked for a while, although La Vallière, having been set aside, begged to be allowed to join a convent. But he would not allow it, my royal lover, for she was too convenient a masquerade.'

There was a nearby *jardinière*. Athénais picked off a dead leaf from its bouquet of flowers. 'I would still like the arrangement. Louis's daily routine is so fixed and public that any least page in the household could tell you the exact minute of the day the king makes love. I enjoyed letting La Vallière carry the embarrassment of that schedule.' She dropped her tone an octave; Athénais had always mimicked voices easily. ' "I shall have to speak with His Majesty," says the courtier. "Well, not now," says his friend, squinting at his timepiece. "His Majesty is just at this moment about to caress his mistress's thigh." And meanwhile, Louis and I took our pleasure privately, like normal lovers. However, the court was not long hoodwinked, even though no one dared admit it. And at last even my husband's eyes opened, the fool!'

She shrugged in the face of Julie's wide-eyed attention. 'He was like a madman, *ma chère*. He threw a tantrum and beat me, and when I ran to the king for protection, he raised a miserable scandal, dressing in deep mourning, insanely comparing His Majesty to King David in the Bible. Once he even tried to assault the king, like a man bereft of his wits. Exile to Bellegarde was lenient for a man who dared dispute with his ruler a gift he had presented so calmly and casually in the beginning.'

The bitterness underlying the last sentence even yet mirrored the hurt a young wife must have sustained. Julie was overwhelmed, unable to say anything more than 'Oh, *mon Dieu!*'

Athénais let her fan dangle on its wrist strap and calmly arranged the single long, blond lovelock that fell on her dimpled shoulder. 'Actually, what is most important, *mon amie*, is that I have a little daughter and, recently, the sweetest infant son by His Majesty. I am sure Louis will soon acknowledge them, and all the children I may have, since he did so for La Vallière's brood. So I have a royal lover, and my children will be legitimized with the purple blood of *Roi-Soleil* in their veins. Be happy for me, Julie. Without doubt, I have climbed as high as a woman can go who is not born a queen.'

She stood there jubilant and proud in a shaft of sunlight, and she looked every inch a queen. Her heavy, lustrous gold damask gown was flounced and parted to reveal a pleated white satin underskirt and jewel-buckled shoes. The gown had white voile sleeves gathered into puffs in several places by gold rosettes and ending at the elbow in a shower of exquisite lace that met long white kid gloves. Her waist was drawn very tiny. Her pointed bodice, embroidered with seed pearls and thread-of-gold and cut square and very low, revealed a seductive expanse of smooth white bosom adorned only by a simple pearl choker—simple, that is, if one did not know the value of the large, perfect pearls in that single strand. A white ostrich plume was fastened among the clusters of bright golden curls by a diamond brooch and curled charmingly to her rounded chin. From a ribbon about her waist hung a small purse of embroidered cloth-of-gold, and her painted fan showed carved ivory vanes.

The sunlight streaming from the tall windows at her back formed a luminous aureole about her blond beauty; she was radiant, proud, assured, and vain. Julie was only human. She suffered a twinge of jealousy, even though the mercurial love of a king held no interest for her. But

Athénais was her friend, and there was no real begrudging in her heart. 'If you are happy, then I am happy, too, Coco. And I would so much like to see your little royal son.'

'And so you shall, one day soon. Oh, he is beautiful, a fine, big boy with his sire's strong nose.' She swept over to sit down again beside Julie and impulsively grabbed her hand. 'Ah, but Julie, no more of me, we must talk about you now. As for buying your appointment, don't worry your head, I have coffers full of money and can lend you the entire sum. You'll pay me back as you can. More important is that you must present an elegant front and not let anyone suspect that you have been left without a sol from your wealthy English marriage—one is never pleased to have to pity a woman. Mademoiselle especially likes fashionable ladies about her, a compulsion left over, I suppose, from her embarrassment years ago with the antique little court her father kept at Blois. How is your wardrobe?' Athénais inquired bluntly.

'Frightful, now that I see the current fashion here,' Julie mourned. 'My necklines are too high, my bodices not long or pointed enough at the waist, and my sleeves come almost to the wrist. Worse, I haven't many gowns. Richard would not pay for his wife's clothes when he could spend his funds so much more agreeably on his mistresses and his gambling.'

Athénais studied the lavender tie about Julie's waist with a calculating eye. 'Hmmm. Well, you certainly must leave off that widow's sash. The gowns you already have must be altered immediately, and meanwhile we'll order some new ones sewn. Now, let's see. I will send a page to notify my tailor, the draper, and the milliner to attend you first thing tomorrow morning, and one of the maidservants I keep here is experienced at hairdressing. We must waste no time introducing you to Mademoiselle. What pure fortune that I came back here today to confer with the upholsterer on new furniture for the reception rooms.' The Marquise de Montespan's blue eyes smiled. 'Heavens, how selfish I've been, keeping you chattering when you must be fainting from fatigue.'

'Oh no, I'm not really tired.'

'Nonsense, you are practically drooping. Your complexion will suffer if you don't rest.' She drew Julie to her feet. 'Let me show you your chamber now. I've sent my lady-in-waiting on an errand, and as soon as she comes back, I must return to the Louvre. Oh, Julie,' she cried, hugging her. 'I am so delighted that you are here.'

In the chamber assigned her, a servant had already unpacked Julie's chests and put her things neatly away in the tall carved armoire, and an enameled tub of hot water already sat steaming on the marble hearth. The maid helped Julie disrobe while Athénais gaily entertained her with more of the latest court gossip, her tone alternately acid or approving, depending on the situation. Informed that her lady-in-waiting had returned, she jumped up from the bench she'd been perched on, bent over the tub to kiss Julie on both cheeks, and promised to be in touch with her shortly. In a cloud of rose perfume, she made her departure.

Left alone, Julie could not contain herself; as soon as she was dried off and in a dressing robe, she hugged her arms about her in excitement and did a lively, mock *bourrée* all around the tub, singing her own accompaniment and laughing, to the silent amusement of the maid. She had experienced more adventure, heard more stupefying news, seen more sights in the past two weeks than in all the miserable years in England put together. If Athénais felt somewhat sorry for her now, provincial and uninformed as she was, the king's beloved would soon change her mind; given a little time to gain familiarity with the complicated world of the court—and assuming her lack of funds did not impair her confidence—Julie intended to shine as brightly as any other female in the firmament around the Sun King.

The hot, fragrant bathwater had soaked divinely into her bones. It had relaxed her body but not her mind, for while she washed she'd made a mental list of the gowns she owned, trying to decide which of them a good seamstress could salvage, and she would certainly have to dip into her slender capital for some new accessories—there was no help for that. Better to die of hunger than look like a ragpicker.

The rest of the day, she went through her trunks, wrote a note for delivery to her notary, ate a good supper, and finally climbed into the great curtained bed to sleep away her travel-weariness.

She woke the next morning fresh and bright-eyed, ready for the adventure to begin, and was enjoying a cup of bouillon when a footman escorted the hulking Poilettier into her chamber. There was more than a hint of awe in the shrewd eyes that darted about the finely appointed room where Julie sat in her dressing robe. He pulled off his felt hat from his greasy locks and greeted her with a broad, respectful smile.

But Julie felt consternation; she had forgotten the other half of the fare she owed him. 'Oh, Poilettier. Ah yes, your money, *mais oui*. But I don't have it at the moment.' She saw the smile fade. She added hastily, 'I will have it tomorrow, though, for I intend to visit my notary and will be able to pay you in the evening. Staying one more night in Paris should not be so onerous for you. Go across the bridge to the quartier Saint-Michel and see the sights.'

'I have to return to me wife and four children,' he muttered, not too pleased.

'Four? I thought you said five.'

Poilettier cleared his throat. 'Ah, did I? Well, one is grown and gone from the home.'

'You and your horses will be well accommodated here for another night. It is the best I can do.'

The coachman acquiesced, shrugging. '*Très bien*, madame, I will wait, then. And I shall go about Paris as you suggest. I had in mind to do as much. Never been here before.' He bobbed his head, his grin reasserting itself, and withdrew.

Now Julie's attention was claimed by the costume merchants who arrived, laden with boxes and bolts and panniers, and danced about in transport over the excellence of their goods. They cunningly spread out before her desirous eyes an array of wares designed to tempt the devil himself, and to convince this newly arrived noblewoman of the absolute necessity of doing regular business with them.

The draper unrolled, with flourishes, bolts of gorgeous fabrics, shimmering satins, heavy silk brocades, velvets, and velours, ranging in shades from purest white to scarlet to an ebony touched with the sheen of moonbeams. Julie stroked the naps and fingered the weaves, exclaiming over each bolt. For her new gowns, she finally chose—with Athénais's tailor at her side to determine the yardages required—a lavender brocade, a deep red velvet, and a pale cream satin. Not nearly enough, but a start.

The basics accounted for, she gave her attention to the vital accessories—gloves, handkerchiefs, stockings, muffs, fans, masks, ruffles, ribbons, and bow knots. She bought Brussels and Venetian lace, had her feet measured for two pairs of high-heeled satin-and-kid slippers, and had the merchants count out a number of lengths of silk ribbons. She selected fine lawn for some new underclothing and two silver-clasped purses, and she added to these from the perfumer a pot of rouge, a charcoal stick, and pulverized mother-of-pearl face powder, along with a new flask of her favorite scent—which she had just about used the last of—oil of white hyacinth.

She chose plumes and feathers from the milliner and topped it all off by yielding to a set of garnet-studded buckles for her shoes and a frivolous but adorable patch box with an enameled and gilded lid.

Compelled like a starving wretch invited to a feast, she went far over what she had intended to spend, but she rationalized away her extravagance by considering that she might not get the appointment to Mademoiselle's train if she appeared less than well dressed, and without an appointment she could not stay at court. She would be reduced to begging her uncle to let her join him in his exile—horrible thought. One must spend to gain, she stoutly encouraged herself as she purchased from the tailor a curving, pointed corset of whalebone and linen that laced tightly in front and pushed her full bosom high. Her good straight-sided, sober English back-lacer she consigned to limbo.

The tailor pleaded that he couldn't possibly produce

her new gowns in less than a month, so she promised the seamstress an extra bonus if she would work speedily to redo the old gowns.

That evening, supping alone in her chamber, she began to have qualms about the expensive garnet buckles and patch box. After all, she could live without them, and she had very few livres left to sustain her. She would have to decide about returning them in the morning. She said a brief prayer and climbed into bed, but she lay awake plotting what she might say to impress the august Grande Mademoiselle.

A message came in the morning from Athénais, saying that the Duchesse de Montpensier would receive them both the next day, and Julie spent the next twenty-four hours fretting that the gown she had decided to wear would not be ready in time. But the seamstress was diligent, and when Athénais's impressive coach pulled up before the Hôtel de Montespan, Julie was as prepared as she would ever be for her interview.

Athénais seemed preoccupied as the coach-and-four trotted them off the Ile-Saint-Louis and rumbled along the Left Bank toward the Palais du Luxembourg. To start a conversation, Julie said brightly, 'I chanced to meet the Comte de Vosges at my notary's yesterday. Do you know him?'

'*Chérie*, the Lémoustons have collected rents on half of Picardy for centuries. The Comte de Vosges is terribly rich. But some say he is suspected of having Huguenot leanings.'

'He seems a very pleasant man.'

'But dull, and he doesn't cut much of a figure,' Athénais sniffed.

There was some truth to this. Poilettier had driven Julie to the rue de la Truanderie to see her father's notary Giles Le Crandeau, a well-to-do bourgeois of a respected family, a calmly precise man in a stiff brown perruque and white neckband. Seated at his writing table, which was neatly arranged with seals, papers, pen, and ink, Le Crandeau had expressed due regrets over the destruction of La Vallette and dryly doubted that Julie could realize much money on the sale of such indifferent property. At her request, he had handed over to her gold equal to half of her ten thousand livres and, with a slight rise of his scanty eyebrows, expressed his hope that she would guard her money more wisely than her parent had. He conducted her to his door to bid her a polite good morning.

As Julie hesitated on the threshold with half a mind to return to safekeeping part of the money he'd given her so she would be forced to economize, the heavy purse she carried under her cloak slipped from her grasp and crashed to the ground.

A coach drew up before the house as gold and silver coins escaped the loosened drawstring and rolled crazily about her feet. Maître Le Crandeau bent his creaky bones to collect some of the fallen coins for her, and his servant came from behind the door to chase those that were rolling away. A gentleman who had alighted from the coach limped over to join the scramble, gallantly gathering up the louis and écus Le Crandeau had missed.

The gentleman spilled them into her purse and blushed when she thanked him effusively. The spare notary, straightening his back, had quickly made the introductions since he was not so old that he did not see his good client's shy appreciation of Madame de Lowry's beauty.

'De Vosges is ridiculously bashful of women,' Athénais continued, warming to her subject. 'Which, I suppose, is why he doesn't marry. He is a frequenter of Madame de Sévignée's salon and discourses quite impressively on the literature of ancient Greece, but there are certain delights of society that seem to have escaped his notice. Oh, I don't mean he lacks masculinity, like Louis's brother Philippe, but he lives such a spartan, solitary life. I imagine you might call him a dedicated scholar.'

For some reason, Julie had immediately liked the slim, stoop-shouldered man who had a twisted foot and who had kissed her hand so gently when they were introduced. His dark eyes glistened sadly. His divided black moustache served only to accentuate the paleness of his face. But his shy smile was pleasant and without guile. In fact, he seemed to her like a forlorn puppy suddenly discovering a friendly face. His subdued costume, of fine fabric and cut, displayed little ornament.

The coach rode over a hole and jounced the two women into each other, and they laughed. 'However,' Athénais continued, readjusting the chiffon scarf over her deep décolletage and enjoying her role as instructor, 'it wouldn't hurt for you to coquette with him if he seems interested. It is always soothing to be courted by a wealthy man, especially if he cares to shower you with gifts. Even a boring cripple like Mercure de Vosges can come in handy when one needs a favor or a faithful rival to keep a lover on his mettle.'

'I rather like him,' Julie said mildly.

A rowdy wedding party blocking the narrow street slowed them down, and Athénais knocked up to the coachman in irritation. The *canaille* gave way as the coach lurched forward, but the painted device on its doors gave rise to murmurs of 'Montespan' and 'la Reine-Marquise' while the numerous wedding guests crowded as close to the slow-moving vehicle as the footmen allowed them, to ogle the king's gorgeous mistress.

'Wish me luck, Madame Marquise!' the unblushing bride shouted out from the head of the party. 'I am on my way to church to cheat the devil of a much less splendid sinner than you!' A coarse burst of laughter applauded the girl's bold insult.

Finally, the coach picked up speed, and Athénais's face relaxed from the haughty, unseeing stare that had not deigned to notice the outspoken rabble of Paris. 'I am damned for a double sin,' she muttered to Julie. 'A married woman openly consorting with a married man. Had I requested a guard this morning, they'd remember fast enough that the "man" in this case is their ruler; a few pikemen, and they'd quiver in their boots lest an impertinent thought cross their minds. The vulgarity!'

'What think the members of the court?'

'I could not care less. The women are sick with jealousy, and the rest have enough regard for their own skins to keep their opinions to themselves. No one dares treat me without deference, and most find it advantageous to ingratiate themselves with all speed.'

Athénais, her inborn disdain now increased to arrogance, probably had not one true friend at court, Julie thought. She wondered why she had always felt a touch of pity for this quite capable beauty. Maybe because she knew how hard it was for Athénais to trust anyone. Even surrounded by adoring husband and lovers and fawning companions, Athénais would always suffer loneliness.

Athénais grumbled something else about 'cursed insolence,' and suddenly a cinnamon-bearded face came into Julie's mind. It was not the first time she had entertained the image of the brazen de Courcillon, but it was the first time she did not erase it immediately, with annoyance. Giving in to her curiosity, she asked in a casual tone, 'By the way, do you also perchance know of a Nicolas de Courcillon, a captain in His Majesty's Garde-du-Corps?'

'*Ciel!* Nicolas d'Aubièrre, the dashing Marquis de Courcillon?' In amusement, Athénais raised a golden eyebrow cosmetically darkened to fawn brown. 'But who doesn't know him? That cavalier has broken more hearts and won more duels than any gentleman in France, and he has paid not a sol of punishment for such illegal combat because the king enjoys his temerity. And I suppose, because he is a valuable and experienced officer. But has his reputation crossed the Channel to England, then?'

Julie wanted to tell Athénais of her midnight encounter with de Courcillon, but they were already approaching the palace, and there was no time. 'I learned his name here in this country, and I'll tell you about it when we've a better chance to chat.'

'Yes, and remind me sometime to tell you about Madame d'Aubièrre. There's a story to make you wonder,' her companion said casually, already distracted with last-minute primping.

Julie bit the inside of her lip, vexed at the tiny disappointment that had struck her heart. How ridiculous of her to care a whit whether the Marquis de Courcillon was married or in Paris or sported two heads.

All along she had had the measure of the man—oh, she knew his sort well. The devil take him, she thought, for I certainly would not.

She drew a small hand mirror from her purse. 'How do I appear?' she inquired, and received a reassuring pat on the hand from Athénais. She wished she could have worn a new gown, but she had on the best of her old ones, a pale green velvet with silver bow knots drawing up the sleeves into puffs above a cascade of delicate lace falling to the elbow. The bodice, scrolled like brocade, was altered now into a smooth, long line to emphasize her small waist and ended in the billows of her skirt. The neckline had been lowered off the shoulders and was edged with a looped-up rope of green beads. She wore long white gloves and pendant pearl earrings, and her shining black hair was formally dressed, wound into a Grecian knot behind and caught over the ears in romantic clusters of long curls, with ringlet wisps blowing on her forehead. A white ostrich tip nodded above her head, not so grand as Athénais's large purple plumes festooned with pearls and diamonds, but stylish indeed, and anchored with a pouf of green silk ribbon.

Her new embroidered purse hung from a narrow sash about her waist, and a little satin-lined velvet cape with a high collar protected her bare shoulders from the chill air. She had applied a touch of pink rouge to her cheeks and lips and pasted a tiny felt patch in the shape of a heart, called an *assassin*, high on her left cheekbone to point up her violet eyes.

Julie came nowhere near the magnificence of Louis's pampered mistress, who wore three patches and carried a gold-and-ivory walking stick, but she was a far cry from the somberly dressed and miserably seasick provincial who had stepped from the ship at Saint-Malo.

Their vehicle proceeded at a good pace down the hotel-lined rue Tournois; the coachman blew a flourish on his horn, and then the Italianate bulk of the Luxembourg was before them. Numerous fine coaches were already standing in the paved enclosure before the ornately sculpted entry. Mademoiselle's *lever* was well attended this morning.

CHAPTER
~ 3 ~

It was customary to use honorary titles to designate certain members of the royal family. Thus, the king's oldest son and heir to the throne could be referred to merely as Monseigneur, if not as the dauphin. The king's oldest brother, in this case Philippe, Duc d'Orleans, was designated by one word, Monsieur, and his wife the Duchesse Henrietta, sister of Charles II of England, was Madame. The princess who was senior daughter of Monsieur was always known as Mademoiselle until she married.

The Duchesse de Montpensier, spinster granddaughter of Henri IV and daughter of Monsieur, Louis's late uncle, Gaston d'Orleans, was Mademoiselle. But when her cousin Philippe, the present Monsieur, was blessed with a daughter, the Duchesse was given the distinguishing title of La Grande Mademoiselle—some say because this royal princess was of Junoesque build, and some say because she was that much older than Philippe's little girl. But La Grande Mademoiselle had a further dimension than just her royal blood to recommend her. Indeed.

Her mother, Marie de Bourbon-Montpensier, had died giving birth to her but in recompense had left her an income of seven hundred thousand livres a year and various immense properties all over France. Anne-Marie-Louise d'Orleans was the wealthiest woman in all of Europe.

When the court was in Paris, Mademoiselle resided at the palace of the Luxembourg, which she owned and which had been built by her grandmother, Marie de Medici.

Mademoiselle usually took her weekly bath in the morning during her *lever*. This was an eccentricity according to many among the noblesse, who preferred their all-over irregular washes in the afternoon or at night, when hearth fires burning all day had taken the chill off the room. They reserved the morning for a quick dip of hands and face and a brisk rubbing of the limbs with a damp flannel cloth. Mademoiselle's painted bathtub was placed inside the *ruelle*, a private section of the bedchamber containing her curtained bed and nightstand and separated from the rest of the room only by a low balustrade. This day, she was attended there by her maid, her ladies-in-waiting, and the visiting Marquise de Charost, whose prerogative it was to hand her the washcloth.

On the other side of the *ruelle*, the large bedchamber, bright with morning light from its tall brocade-draped windows, was occupied by casual knots of chatting courtiers interspersed with Mademoiselle's doctor, tailor, liveried footmen, and pages.

For modesty's sake, a bucket of milk had been added to Mademoiselle's bathwater to make it opaque and shield her nudity from the eyes of the male visitors. There was little privacy for anyone in palaces, where corridors were few and one room opened onto another so that even bedchambers were thoroughfares—a good reason for curtained beds and painted screens. But for members of the royal family, whose every waking (the *lever*) and retiring (the *coucher*) and childbirth was attended by protocol and jealously guarded ceremony, even bathing in privacy was an unknown luxury.

The king had his *lever* and *coucher* and the queen had hers; and so did the rest of the royal family and the loftiest of the nobility, the number of visitors to each according to the host's importance. Even the highest types were forced to rise very early and retire very late in order to have their own ceremonies and yet be on hand to protect their prerogatives in the dressing and undressing rites of the monarchs. Below the rank of prince and duke, titles were sold with the land and so carried little precedence. Accordingly, a viscount of wealth and ancient bloodlines could hold more importance than a marquis without such. And prerogatives of honor, often handed down along with the title, added much luster to one's rank.

The *lever*, especially, was the time for petitions, interviews, gossip, and back-biting. Attendance was not compulsory except for the official ladies or gentlemen-in-waiting, but it would be a black mark against manners to be too long absent from any of the royal *levers*, and manners were much stressed by Louis XIV. Anyway, one wanted to be present at the royal awakenings and retirings because it was there that one heard all the news worth hearing and encountered the newcomers to court.

Mademoiselle's bedchamber had walls of extravagant white brocade divided into panels by gilded and scrolled molding, an elaborate ceiling brilliant with paintings of Apollo and his golden chariot ushering in the day, and heavy chandeliers of crystal and gilt bronze, which were reflected in big mirrors at either end of the room. Square-backed chairs and settees were upholstered in red brocade to match the rich velvet of the looped-up bed drapes. But even the wide and blazing fireplaces at either end did not erase the early-morning chill from a room so high-ceilinged and large.

The Duchesse, hair wrapped in a gauze turban, splashed irritably in the cloudy, shoulder-high water in her metal tub. 'God's mercy, de St Gênet, can't you move that screen to get the draft off my back? You've twiddled with it for twenty minutes. I shall probably suffer my death at your hands.'

'I've placed it everywhere I could think of, Your Highness,' her maid-of-honour whined, picking up the small tapestry screen and depositing it farther to the left of the tub. 'It's just that the whole room is cold. The drafts are coming from everywhere.'

'Well, move the brazier close to me, then. Use your head for a change,' her mistress chaffed, raising one dripping arm to rub a sponge over it. She then turned her attention to the Marquise de Charost. 'Well, continue, madame. What did the Duchesse de la Vallière say on her return to the Louvre? Your habit of lingering in anterooms should net you more than a mere outline of fact.'

The portly Marquise twisted her fan in an eagerness to impart all the scandal she knew. 'Highness, when a woman flees embarrassment by escaping to a convent forever and yet is forced by royal authority to return and assume her empty position, what can she say? His Majesty, on his way to the queen's apartments, barely greeted La Vallière. In fact, he looked at her with such coldness that I myself shivered where I stood for the timid creature. "I have need of you by my side, madame, and I bid you remember your prayers can be heard from here as well as your refuge in the convent. Do not again require me to have you dragged from the selfish solitude you seem to crave." So he said very icily, and she, pale as death and with tears on her cheeks, knowing full well her presence is required solely for a certain party's benefit, whimpered, "My lord, have mercy on me and release me to seek my peace," to which he merely replied, "Your peace is in obedience to me, madame," and he passed on his way.'

Mademoiselle shrugged and leaned forward to allow her personal maid, Dant, to scrub her back with a stiff brush. '*Tiens*, the same story year after year. She must do as he wishes, of course, but she could have various consolations if she would only ask for them. One must hope the little martyr will one day be permitted to enter her nunnery so we can be quit of the monotonous accounts of her uninspired behavior.'

Behind her, she heard one of her ladies-in-waiting, petite Mademoiselle de Greu, whose blond curls were wired to stand out from her head, whisper to Madame de St Gênet, 'Do you think His Majesty will take Madame de La Vallière along when the court goes to Flanders?'

'Why not?' de St Gênet whispered back. 'He certainly will not leave a certain lady behind, and he is evidently not ready to drop the pretense that it is La Vallière he visits.'

'Still, one cannot help feeling sorry for her,' the Marquise de Charost concluded, shaking her head.

But Mademoiselle had no use for weaklings. She sniffed imperiously. 'The poor creature is a fool. When one consorts with a sovereign, one must be ready to swallow disappointment bravely and without falling to pieces.' She signaled that she was finished with her bath, and her maid held up a voluminous towel. Madame de St Gênet rapped sharply on the balustrade, and the footmen ushered all the males from the chamber for the moment.

Anne-Marie-Louise d'Orleans was no stranger to disappointment herself, but in her case the blood told, for she had borne her embarrassments with the true *sang-froid* of a daughter of France. She had been comely in her youth, and her rank and vast possessions certainly portended a splendid marriage with a crowned head of Europe, if not, as many had expected, a match with her younger cousin Louis. Such great expectations—and such painful disillusionments. Mademoiselle shrugged to herself as she stepped from her bath on this fall morning. No one could discern from her ordinary goose-pimpled female form the tumultuous political past of a woman who during her younger years had been unsuccessfully proposed for wife to, or had rejected, an emperor, three reigning monarchs, Louis's brother Philippe of France, and six sovereign princes.

Mademoiselle de Greu handed her mistress's silk chemise to the lady-of-honor, de St Gênet, who handed it on to the Maréchale de Grammont, whose privilege it was to give it to Mademoiselle, who sat partially naked and shivering in the chilly air but was conditioned to wait while the ceremony was enacted. Mademoiselle passed the chemise finally to Dant, who with the Maréchale's aid, dropped the low-necked undershirt over her mistress's head. Next came her silken underdrawers—for she was not among those scandalous coquettes who, *à L'Anglaise*, did not wear them—and then flounced petticoats of winter thickness and the stiff, pointed corset that, with much tugging, laced her middle into a fashionable small waist. At this point, she was considered covered, and the footmen summoned back the plume-haired and ribbon-bedizened male visitors into the room.

A shield cape was thrown over Mademoiselle's shoulders, and she advanced to her silver dressing table, where she sat to have her hair combed and coiffed. Her favorite poet, Segrais, came to bow before her, holding half-unrolled a parchment written on in elaborate script. One of her ladies signaled the three musicians who always began the Duchesse's day with the serenity of airs for viol and lute, and Mademoiselle nodded to Segrais to begin proclaiming his muse. She knew what it was, anyway, a long panegyric of praise dedicated to Madame de Motteville, which she had commissioned in honor of that lady's birthday, and she listened with only half an ear.

In the mornings, she allowed herself a critical appraisal in her gilt-framed mirror, a brave gesture after the passing of what prettiness she'd had in the first flush of youth. The middle-aged face staring back at her could be called interesting and definitely aristocratic, but in no way either lovely or sweet.

Her face was too long. She thought people's eyes went immediately to her long, overpowering jaw, heavier now with the telltale folds of skin under her chin. Her lips were overfull, her nose, following the shape of her face, was long and high-bridged and sharp, and the lines running from nose to mouth had deepened into grooves. Her complexion was coarsening, the pores large and visible, and, worse, her skin mottled into too high a raspberry color on her cheeks at the coming of cold weather.

But three assets softened the mirror's assessment and drew her eye to pleasanter contemplation. Her hair, darkened through the years from blond to brown and now colored by special preparations of root juices to blend the proliferating gray strands into the rest, was very thick and wavy and fell in luxurious masses of curls, which were the envy of younger women who needed false hairpieces to fill out their coiffures.

Her figure, tall and big-boned, was still good, too, curved in the right places, the inevitable thickening in the waist and the drooping of the bust well hidden by her corset. Her shoulders and arms were yet smooth and firm, and the inevitable extra poundage brought on by rich diet and middle age was, fortunately, camouflaged by her height.

But she felt it was her eyes that lifted her appearance into the appealing. They were a lively, glowing blue, and their almond shape, under heavy brows, served to remove attention from the crease between them. They had often been praised as fascinating, so she emphasized their appeal with blue tint on the lids and kohl under the lashes and lately conceived the habit of thrusting her face close to Monsieur de Lauzun when they sat and spoke, so that his gaze would stay on her eyes and not stray to her wrinkles.

She was aware that her stare was often considered sharp, and she regretted that the disappointments of the years had so embittered her regard, but now, since the thrilling advent of de Lauzun, she thought the expression reflected in her morning mirror was much gentled, even full of goodwill.

She gave her wrist to the doctor to take her pulse, as he did every morning, and with the other hand she picked up the cup of sage tea that always preceded her breakfast. Segrais finished his declaiming and stepped back, his gaunt face flushed with pleasure as she offered her congratulations. The visitors scattered about the room continued to chat and laugh softly about this and that, but they always had an ear cocked to the business of the petitioners who, one by one, came up and bowed before her.

Madame de La Roche, daughter of an old friend now dead, asked for sponsorship as governess to Monsieur's children, a post the woman was little qualified to fill, and Mademoiselle put her off with the truth, that Madame would hardly favor any recommendations from her. The Marquis de Pomperant, troubled of face and creaky of knees, begged her to intercede with the king to allow the return of his only son, who had been exiled along with Monsieur's unsavory bosom friend, the Chevalier de Lorraine. This request started a round of whispered gossip that Philippe had so bedeviled his wife for her part in the exile of the chevalier that now poor Henrietta preferred Lorraine's return to the disgraceful homosexual liaison with her husband rather than the shattering quarrels his absence brought on.

Mademoiselle Le Fontagères-Villy shyly brought remembrance from her parents, whose estate was neighbor to Mademoiselle's chateau at Thiers, and a request to be attached to Mademoiselle's household—already too large, with eight ladies-in-waiting, a lady-of-honor, equerries, stewards, guards, footmen, pages, a doctor and a legal adviser, a treasurer, and about a hundred other attendants.

The Duchesse de Navailles, who arrived late, asked for a subscription for her pet charity, a Dominican orphans' home; the jeweler Reynaud unveiled a pair of diamond-and-pear drop earrings in an unusual design he was sure Her Highness could not live without; a lieutenant of the king's Garde-du-Corps arrived with His Majesty's invitation to an intimate supper and entertainment the next evening (intimate meaning no more than sixty persons). Several other courtiers engaged her attention briefly.

By now, with the help of her ladies, Mademoiselle sat fully dressed in a brocade gown and train of pale blue velvet with seed pearls and silver scrolls and a white wool scarf looped about her bare shoulders for warmth.

A rustle among the assembled company brought her attention up from the mirror in time to catch, in dramatic pause upon the threshold, the striking and haughty Marquise de Montespan, accompanied by an unknown young woman. Mademoiselle deliberately kept her eyes from narrowing as Montespan approached, preparing instead a cool smile. Once she had rather liked the clever marquise, but that was before her Jupiter-cousin had put the corrupting wand of power in Montespan's greedy hands.

The king's mistress swept up before her chair in a cloud of rose scent and bowed just long and deep enough to satisfy minimum protocol to the royal family.

'Your Highness,' she murmured. 'I hope you will forgive me for not paying my respects earlier, but certain matters conspired to detain me. I do trust Your Highness is in very good health this morning?'

'That is what my doctor informs me, the *bon Seigneur*

be praised. But tell me, madame, do you bring any news of the proposed tour to Flanders? I hope His Majesty will not require us to prepare to leave overnight?'

'Oh, so do I,' chimed in the Duchesse de Navailles. 'And I do hope the journey won't be before full spring! I can just feel the cold of that low, damp land freezing my bones already. My astrologer says this is going to be a hard winter in Paris, much less what it will be farther north.'

Mademoiselle thrust her hands into a little muff. 'Tut, Navailles, you are not made of rose petals. A little snow won't harm you.'

The black-clad, lace-cravated Abbé de Prestembois, standing nearby, an obsequious man quite popular with the older matrons, found a ready flattery for the fluttering, obese Navailles. 'Madame surely need not fear a winter journey,' he demurred. 'Snow would not dare to fall on her for fear of comparing badly with her pure complexion.'

'My doctor says snowflakes are beneficial to health, Duchesse,' Athénais de Montespan remarked, her pleasant expression barely covering the contemptuous glitter in her eyes. 'Droplets of water in such pure, cold form give vigor to the blood, and, of course, the broader the area they fall on, the greater their salubrious effect. Broader, as he must have meant it,' she innocently added to the fat Navailles, 'in a sense of exposed, don't you think?' Julie, behind her, swallowed a laugh. Athénais was in fine form today.

Mademoiselle raised an eyebrow. 'How interesting. I wasn't aware, Marquise, that you are so admirably informed on the newest medical discoveries. But we have passed from the subject of Flanders. Can you tell us nothing concrete about the journey?'

'Why, it seems that the date of departure depends on General Turenne's assessment of the state of the lower provinces,' Athénais drawled, always enjoying the position that put her privy to the king's projects even before some of the court's more important figures. 'The time, therefore, is still in question. Of course, those in His Majesty's confidence may have more information than merely this morning's rumors,' she added, in lip service to the shredded secrecy, which fooled no one.

'Of course,' echoed the Maréchale de Grammont inanely.

The conversation was becoming tiresome, Mademoiselle decided. In order to change the subject, she asked, 'And who is your companion, Marquise?'

Athénais now drew Julie forward. 'With your permission, Your Highness, may I present to you a niece of Monsieur de Montespan, just newly arrived from a sojourn at the English court. Madame Julie de Lisle Croixverte-Mountmerry, Comtesse de Lowry.'

Croixverte? Surprise darted through Mademoiselle's mind. *Ma foi*, did stern de Morlé really produce this striking and lissome brunette? How droll.

Julie curtsied deeply. When she looked up, the piercing blue eyes were regarding her with curiosity. 'Your Royal Highness,' Julie acknowledged the introduction with her most charming smile, although her heart was beating rapidly.

The thick lips stretched in an answering smile, a cool, polite one. 'So, the daughter of my ancient friend, the late Vicomte de Morlé. I believe it was mentioned to me by Madame de Montespan that you had lately lost your husband as well and you were returning to France. My sympathy in both your bereavements, madame.'

'Your Highness is kind to share my grief.'

Never caring to dwell on death, Mademoiselle went on, 'And how did you find your adopted home across the Channel? I hear the English are more amusing on their own soil.'

The question followed the convention of petty conversation and required a casual answer of 'Quite charming' or 'An admirable country, once one gets used to it,' but Julie lacked practice in polite patter, and besides, intuition or something about the impatient boredom she sensed beneath the imposing façade of the royal lady led her to assert her personality.

'I found England distressing, Your Highness—chill, vulgar, unfriendly, and uncomfortable. I know I would never care to return there of my own accord, not even if

I were offered all the jewels in the Tower of London as inducement.'

A light of amusement crept into Mademoiselle's eyes. 'I trust, madame, that you did not speak so disparagingly of England before my cousin Charles Stuart? He is rather touchy about Frenchwomen who disdain his country.' A titter ran around the room. In her youth, Anne-Marie-Louise d'Orleans had turned up her nose at marriage with the exiled Charles, whose father had been so ignominiously beheaded, for she believed the penniless young man would never regain his throne—a mistake for which Charles had never forgiven her. Nor had she forgiven herself, in spite of her joking attitude.

'I met the king only a few times just after my father and I arrived at the English court, and at that time I was more impressed by England. But for the remainder of my stay I lived in Sussex, and, unfortunately, His Majesty never passed that way.'

'In Sussex? Then you do not care for court life?'

'Oh, indeed, I much prefer it, Your Highness, but circumstance forced me to reside in the provinces.'

'Circumstance. Ah yes.' Julie did not wonder at the hint of sympathy in her tone. Mademoiselle at one time had been exiled to the country. But Mademoiselle's eyebrows rose in a question. 'And do you intend to remain with the court here?'

'I greatly desire to—if I am able to obtain an appointment.' The unwavering and forthright scrutiny to which she was being subjected made Julie drop her eyes in discomfort.

'I suppose Madame la Marquise told you that my lady-of-honor, the Comtesse de St Gênet, is leaving my service?'

'Yes, Your Highness.' Julie looked straight at her again, bringing back her shoulders. 'And it is my hope that you will approve my bid to purchase her place.' She met the intent gaze upon her with a genuinely hopeful expression, for there was prestige attached to this woman, and a certain uniqueness. The association probably would not be easy, but it promised not to be dull.

The king's first cousin relaxed against the high back of her chair. 'If the king makes a triumphal tour of Flanders this spring, I have every intention of going with him. That might mean snow, cold, bad accommodations, worse food, and lost baggage. Would such an excess of discomfort bother you, Comtesse, or are you of a more rugged breed than Navailles here?'

The purse-lipped smile was meant to make the question seem no more than a little dig at the abashed Navailles, but Julie had a feeling she was being plumbed for more than just a coy protest.

'Your Highness, I am certainly no hardier than Madame la Duchesse; such a journey would plague me into grumbling. I would complain, probably, but only to myself. In fact, I have had enough of sedentary life, and would much rather endure all the hardships of a foray into Flanders than stay home and miss the excitement.'

Mademoiselle's tone was dry, but a little gleam appeared in her eyes. 'You can be sure you would complain only to yourself, madame. I could not tolerate any whining women around me.' A tiny pause, and Mademoiselle cocked her head. 'Tell me, do you leave your hair so dark by choice? Is it not unfashionable that way?'

'The color is my own and suits my personality, Your Highness,' Julie blurted out, startled by the tactless question.

'One hopes that is a misleading answer. Would you have me believe your black hair matches a black heart?' Mademoiselle chuckled, amused to tease this newcomer.

Julie recovered herself, her own eyes bright with humor. 'No, Your Highness, a mourning heart, if the analogy must be made. But the truth remains that it is because I stubbornly prefer my natural shade.'

'Well. You have the courage to be individual. I like that. I liked your father, too; I was well acquainted with him. Next to the gaming tables, he preferred to attend my salon and argue interminably the merits of Boileau's satires with the Duc de Nemours. He was a very astute and loyal friend, de Morlé, in his humorless way. Are you as well read as your parent, madame, or where do your talents lie?'

It surprised Julie how pleased she was to hear the praise of her father. 'My father did send me numerous volumes to keep me entertained while I lived in Sussex, but alas, I would not be able to discuss them with as much erudition as he. However, I do play the clavier, Your Highness.'

'With skill? Don't be modest.'

'With great skill, Your Highness.' Julie grinned.

Mademoiselle looked pleased, but at that moment the Marquise de Charost murmured about the fleeting of the morning. Mademoiselle nodded and rose, a signal to all that the *lever* was over. De St Gênet settled a velvet cape edged with ermine on her mistress's shoulders, and, with a rustle of wide skirts and ribbons, bobbing plumes and lace-bedecked cloaks, her visitors opened a path for her and prepared to follow her to attend the king at chapel.

Julie had not realized how unusually tall the woman was. But Mademoiselle's almond-shaped blue eyes looking down at her held a glint of approval. The Duchesse now had the last word in their conversation. 'Madame de Lowry, it is not just erudition that counts in a discussion but imagination, and that is my favorite point of contention. We must take up this particular subject at another time.' She turned her attention to Athénais, who was standing back with a smile bland as cream. '*Je vous remercie*, madame, for bringing the Comtesse de Lowry to my *lever*. I am sure His Majesty will find her a most attractive addition to his court.' The smile she returned to her cousin's mistress was an insinuating one.

Unstung by the sniping, Athénais bowed as Mademoiselle swept past her. But she straightened almost immediately and put out a beringed hand to halt de St Gênet, who was following in the Duchesse's wake. 'Attend us a moment, madame, if you please.' It was said mildly, but it was an order.

De St Gênet's face took on a noncommittal expression as she halted before them and allowed herself to be drawn aside. Her little eyes shifted from one to the other, then rested on Julie.

Julie said, 'As you have been informed, madame, I wish to purchase your position of honor to Mademoiselle.'

'Ah, yes. Madame la Marquise indicated as much to me. Well, it does appear that Her Highness has no outward objections to you, madame. But then, she also approves of Mademoiselle de Charmions, who has already offered me sixty thousand livres. Mademoiselle de Charmions is my dear departed mother's cousin and is most anxious for the post, *vous savez*. She might even be prepared to go a thousand livres higher. . .' The nasal voice trailed off suggestively.

Julie hesitated, shocked at such numbers, but from behind de St Gênet, Athénais nodded her head encouragingly and opened her eyes wide.

Taking the cue, Julie countered, 'Then will you take sixty-three thousand livres for your appointment? For I fear that if that doesn't suit you, I will be forced to look elsewhere.'

De St Gênet's nose twitched greedily. 'Sixty-three thousand livres? *Tiens*, it suits me very well, madame. I don't believe Mademoiselle de Charmions could match that. So then we have an agreement. Since I am departing at week's end, I shall send my lawyer around to you with a receipt by Friday. I presume he can find you at the Hôtel de Montespan?' She swiveled to look at Athénais for confirmation. 'Well, I do wish you all good fortune at court, Comtesse, and I hope you have a good, round hand for copying. Mademoiselle is writing her memoirs, but one cannot read her scratching and so it all must be recopied.' She wiggled her right hand as if it ached. 'There were nights I could not get my fingers to loosen their grip upon the quill.'

All three made brief curtsies, and de St Gênet hurried off to secure a place in one of the crowded coaches headed across the river.

Athénais chuckled as they walked slowly among the stragglers. 'So, there you are. For a few thousand livres extra, de St Gênet slits the throat of her dear departed mother's cousin, who never offered her more than fifty thousand anyway, I'll wager. Well, you have a better name than de Charmions, and you are younger. La Grande Mademoiselle sets much store by youth these days—as if some of it might rub off on her. I'm sure you made a good impression.'

'Perhaps I shouldn't have spoken so vehemently about England,' Julie fretted, remembering the blue gaze fixed intently upon her. 'But when she asked me how I cared for the country, the truth just tumbled out.'

'All the better, since she was expecting the usual polite and insipid answer. You startled her by being direct, which is exactly what she admires.'

'She seems rather crusty——'

'One moment pompous, the next moment fluttery—one can never describe her without using extremes. You really interested her with your unself-conscious honesty. I think you can consider the post yours.'

'Dear Coco, I am so very grateful to you. Sixty-three thousand livres is a fortune to lend. Believe me, I shall do my best to pay some of it back to you the very moment I sell my land.'

'Oh, take your time, Julie. You'll need to spend what you have on clothes at first anyway. However——' she seemed to have another thought '——there is a little thing you might do for me in the future, very confidentially, *mon amie*. You see, His Majesty is often hard to amuse, as that dull little La Vallière discovered. He really has very little sense of humor, and he has much less culture and education than he would like anyone to know. Even for me, it is sometimes difficult to keep him entertained, keep the conversation going. But he does enjoy the petty gossip of the court, and I tell him whatever interesting tidbits I hear.

'He is particularly amused by his middle-aged cousin's love affair—happy, in fact, that she has found a man to melt her unemotional heart. You will be with Mademoiselle constantly. Should any funny or quaint or special incident occur between her and de Lauzun, I would appreciate your relating it to me. It would truly help me keep the king from becoming restless of afternoons, and both the principals are so oblivious to court chatter, it wouldn't matter to them in any way.'

Julie shrugged. Graciousness required that she acquiesce to the request, and it didn't seem much to ask. At her murmur that she would keep it in mind, Athénais's pearly smile shone out, and the Marquise patted her arm.

A faint tintinnabulation of church bells from Saint-Sulpice came through the windows. Athénais's smile disappeared, and a frown marred her marble-smooth countenance. '*Merde!* Nine o'clock already. I have an appointment for which I am terribly late, and here there's but one carriage between us and no time for me to return you to the Ile-Saint-Louis. *Sainte Vierge*, why can't I ever apportion my time correctly?'

'Could I deliver you to your destination, then go home and send the carriage back for you?'

'Yes, I suppose that would be a solution.' But Athénais's obvious hesitation and the way she bit at her lip hinted at a highly private destination.

A little embarrassed, Julie offered, 'Well, perhaps one of the company going to the king's chapel will later pass your hôtel and let me off there. If we go quickly, we can catch those who haven't gone off yet.'

Athénais's relief was visible. 'Of course, the very answer. I am truly sorry, Ton-Ton. . .'

There was a gentle cough, and an apologetic male voice sounded from behind them.

'Ah. . .your pardon, mesdames. I, ah, was just passing by, and, ah—I would be honored to convey Madame de Lowry to the Ile-Saint-Louis. It would be my pleasure indeed. . .'

'Why, Monsieur de Vosges!' Julie cried, surprised to see the crippled gentleman she had encountered at her notary's. 'How nice to meet my gallant knight of the rolling coins once more. I did not know you were present here.'

De Vosges blushed hotly. 'I. . .was in the window alcove conversing with the scrivener Monsieur Herriot all this time. But it would be my great pleasure to be of service to you. If you will allow——?' He bowed to the two of them.

Julie dimpled and accepted. 'If you are sure it will be

no trouble, I do need a ride to the Hôtel de Montespan. I seem to have to lean on your gallantry every time we meet.' The light of esteem in de Vosges's dark eyes was doing Julie's vanity no harm. She took his proffered arm, and Athénais, forced to be courteous and take the other, swallowed her impatience as they moved off slowly to accommodate his hobble. Finally reaching the courtyard, they parted.

Julie and de Vosges watched Athénais's coach rumble off, and then a footman handed Julie into de Vosges's own dark maroon and silver equipage. Well, she reflected, sinking into the plush upholstery, he *is* rich. And gentle and fine, in spite of his twisted foot. It would be clever of me 'to have several strings to my bow,' to quote Athénais, and this shy man seems to find me interesting.

But Mercure de Vosges sat across from her nervously fiddling with the fur cuffs on his gloves, at a loss for how to begin a conversation. He seemed to have had more assurance in the presence of Le Crandeau and Athénais, as if company supplied some of the courage he needed to deal with women. Julie wondered if he was sorry now that he had locked himself up with a terrifying member of the female sex. But she remained silent for the moment, with just a quiet smile to reassure him. She considered how solid and sober he appeared in his plain brown silk brocade coat, which showed a glimpse of the puffed tan breeches that met the white hose covering his calves. But in fact, this morning he also sported a butterfly bow of white lace at his neck and large green ribbon knots on the instep of his square-toed shoes. His straight dark hair fell to his shoulders and emphasized the translucence of his complexion. The impression she had of this retiring man was not of bloodlessness but rather of subdued emotions twisted into subjugation, just as his foot was twisted.

When he finally brought himself to look at her without glancing away, she liked his eyes. They were so black, with delicate, feathery black lashes, that she could hardly discern a pupil; but they were neither fathomless nor sinister and, in fact, displayed a soft, gentle luster which spoke of sensitivity.

Julie turned up the warmth of her smile, and de Vosges smiled back uncertainly. He cleared his throat and smoothed his minute moustache, but still he said nothing. She wondered where he had found the courage to offer her a ride. And so, to relieve his discomfort, she pointed out the window and inquired about the various houses and imposing new structures they passed. Eased by being able to direct his attention outside the coach, he told her about Mansard's ambitious Hôtel des Invalides, whose immense dome was rising in the distance. Architecture seemed of great interest to him; he became so warmed to the subject of Paris's bustling construction projects that he forgot to blush every time he looked at her. What he said grew so technical that she lost some interest, but she managed to ask intelligent questions, and he seemed to take this as an indication that she, too, was fascinated by the structural details of the new buildings. Shy pleasure was written all over his face.

It was difficult for him to alight from the coach, but she tactfully did not dissuade him from helping her out when they reached their destination. She thanked him again for the lift, and he kissed her gloved hand and stammered that it was a rare treat for him to drive with such a gracious and learned lady. And to Julie's surprise, he added that he hoped to have the pleasure of her company again, perhaps a drive next Tuesday on the Cours de Reine along the Seine? When she willingly consented, he blushed and backed away. He did not make his ungainly climb back into his coach until Athénais's butler had opened the tall, carved portal for her.

Julie ran up the stairs to her chamber after requesting that the butler have some hippocras punch brought to her. Breathlessly, she flung her little cape and her fan on a chair and skipped over to throw the tall window wide so she might draw in the wonderful, adventurous air of Paris.

A servant brought her a goblet of spiced wine, and she stood for a while in a buoyed-up state, dreaming out at the walled garden and statues of fauns and satyrs below.

Presently, Athénais's request came into her mind—that she keep her ears open for any sort of juicy gossip, and so she would. But she did feel sorry for Mademoiselle, whose ungainly romance served to keep the king and his callous courtiers in conversation. The Duchesse certainly did not appear the type to let herself in for such ridicule, and so the Comte de Lauzun must be a truly extraordinary man. It seemed that love—or perhaps the idea of it, as Julie had unfortunately discovered—made women accept humiliations they would otherwise refuse to tolerate.

There was still a chance, of course, that Julie's bad fortune was not yet played out. Mademoiselle might find something about her to object to, and in that case Madame de St Gênet was out her extra three thousand livres, and Julie was out a most prestigious position.

She swallowed the last of her spicy hippocras, feeling luxuriously wicked for such an indulgence in the morning, and then crossed her fingers behind her back for good luck in her plans. She even said a little prayer for divine help, although being a product of her age, her prayer was not very impassioned. Religion was more a matter of routine and obligation than actual faith. One worshiped in a cathedral presided over by an unordained, politically appointed bishop; one knelt praying among rouged nuns, unconfessed involvements of the church; one began to doubt the necessity and spiritual truth of religion.

But Julie prayed anyhow. Deep down, she believed in God.

On Wednesday, a page decked in de Montespan's red and gold livery brought a heavy casket of money and a few scribbled words of assurance from Athénais.

And on Friday, Madame de St Gênet's lawyer called on Julie, carrying word that her transaction with his client had been approved and writing her a receipt for sixty-three thousand livres, in purchase of the post of lady-of-honor to Her Highness Mademoiselle la Duchesse de Montpensier.

CHAPTER
~ 4 ~

'*Ciel,* can you not hurry, madame? Your fumbling will make me late to receive the king, saints forbid! What are you doing?'

'In a moment, Your Highness,' Julie replied calmly as she worked with the clasp of the emerald necklace around Mademoiselle's neck. 'The catch refuses to close properly. Ah! There, it's done.'

'Well, and where is my fan, the lace and gold one I chose?'

Madame de Plessis-Rabat quickly put it in her hand. 'Right here, Your Highness. I've been holding it ready.'

'I've changed my mind. Bring me the ivory one with the painted silk and silver tassels. It's more colorful with this gown. *Vite, vite.*'

De Plessis-Rabat ran to the chest where the fans were kept as Mademoiselle de Greu bustled into the chamber.

'The actors have arrived!' she panted.

'And high time! Remind Maître Gaspar that they are to be ready for an eleven o'clock performance, and see they are given some wine and cakes to sustain them. Come, ladies, I am ready.'

Mademoiselle paused before the decorative mirror and preened, opening her fan and waving it before her face for effect, majestic from the top of her pearl-wound coiffure to the end of her eight-foot satin and fringe train, held up by two pages.

'Your Highness looks especially lovely tonight,' Julie murmured.

Mademoiselle cocked her head to further consider her image. 'I believe you, madame,' she said.

Great crystal chandeliers blazing with hundreds of tapers were suspended like sparkling stalactites from the painted ceiling of the Luxembourg's grand reception hall and the ballroom and the salons adjoining. Huge swags of glittering silver tinsel and artificial flowers decorated the brocaded walls and hung from the marble pilasters and the paneled mirrors. Motionless lackeys in the Duchesse's silver and green livery supported flaring candelabra every few feet, or gilt poles with balls of fragmented colored glass which, as they were twirled, captured the brilliant light and swirled it about in gay rainbow patterns. The huge rooms were awash with peacock nobility, the gentlemen in gold gallooned coats and ribbons, wide, plumed velvet hats, and red-heeled shoes; the ladies bare-shouldered and splendid with jewels. Their tinkling laughter rose above the music of the violins and *hautbois* from the ballroom and the stentorian voice of the herald announcing the arriving guests from the head of the foyer staircase.

Eau-de-vie, fine wines and punch, and tremendous *épergnes* of fruit weighted the buffet tables, along with pyramids of cakes and ices in cunning shapes, *bons-bons*, almond pastes, candied melons, and preserves, just a little *collation* to stem the appetite until supper was served after midnight.

In the salons, card tables for *reversi* and *ombre* and boards for *trou-madame* were set up, and there were billiard tables, too, as well as little conversation groups of pillowed folding chairs for the weary. One could dance or nibble or gamble or flirt or chat, or draw one's lady into the seclusion of a shadowed corner for a kiss.

Mademoiselle had invited six hundred of the *haut monde* to her ball and entertainment, and since the pursuit of pleasure and royal invitations was of foremost importance to the courtiers, everyone came.

Accompanying La Grande Mademoiselle down the marble hallway, Julie glanced over the balustrade into the foyer below, where the guests were still arriving. Tonight, only a few days after joining Mademoiselle's train, would be her first meeting with many of the luminaries of the court and, most especially, with the king. She was endeavoring to hide her excitement and fight off timidity by breathing deeply, concentrating on her carriage, gliding smoothly along with head high as the nuns had taught her. She thought she appeared calm.

But a fan tapped her lightly on the elbow, and she turned to look into Mademoiselle's shrewd but sympathetic smile. 'Are you nervous, Comtesse? Well, you needn't be. They will be as curious about you as you are about them.' With a confident nod, she motioned Julie to go on.

They entered into the swirl of the brilliant ballroom. The Duchesse moved with stately graciousness among her guests, the ladies curtsying as she stopped to greet them, the gentlemen kissing her gloved hand and going into fulsome poetic compliments about her appearance. Julie was confronted with a kaleidoscope of names, faces and first impressions to remember: the Duchesse de Valentinois; the Maréchal de Villeroy, former tutor to the king; the Marquis de Mascarille; the Comtesse de Bussy-Rabutin; the Bishop of Condom; Monsieur de Bossuet; the Duchesse de Montausier, daughter of the famous Rambouillet salon; and Monsieur de Crequé, governor of Paris, among others.

In a stir of ceremony, Monsieur and Madame arrived, Philippe round-bellied, powdered, and pouting; Henrietta small, chestnut-haired, very vivacious, with that English coloring that recalled an exquisite porcelain doll. After a perfunctory greeting to his hostess, Philippe hastened to the gambling tables, leaving Henrietta to the host of admirers who immediately swarmed around her. Henrietta openly enjoyed the plethora of gallants who freely admitted they would slay dragons for one meaningful glance from her dark eyes. Indeed, before La Vallière, the youthful King Louis and the lovelorn English Duke of Buckingham had both been rumored to covet her affections; but she was so pitied for the unnaturalness of Philippe's sexual diversions that few blamed her for casting eyes. What made even more interesting gossip was that although Louis's passion for her was long over, he had discovered that she was politically astute, and it was said that he planned to send her as emissary to her brother Charles to smooth the way for a French-British commercial alliance.

One of Henrietta's ladies suddenly broke away from the circle about her mistress and launched herself at

Julie. '*Ma foi*, is it Julie de Croixverte? I thought you were in England, my dear.'

'Eloise L'Amiels! How wonderful to see you again.'

Eloise, a former schoolmate at Sainte-Clôthilde, had always been a prattler; she soon put Julie straight on which of their companions was now Comtesse this and Duchesse that and Prioress of so-and-so, and of course there was always Athénais de Rochechouart-Mortemart—would you believe it? Eloise herself had married a newly elevated vicomte, which didn't much further her rank, 'but he's a very wealthy man, *bien sûr*!' she confided.

Two gentlemen in elegant perruques and gold-hilted swords thrust into wide baldrics diagonally draped from shoulder to waist broke in to beg the Vicomtesse to present them to her enchanting companion, and they were soon eagerly joined by a third. Delighting in their gay badinage, Julie nevertheless took note of the page darting among the guests in haste to get to the leader of the orchestra. She quickly excused herself and made her way over to the group surrounding Mademoiselle.

The music stopped abruptly, a customary signal for all attention to be centred on the main doorway, and in a moment the herald's voice rang out: 'Clear the way! Clear the way for His Most High and Christian Majesty, His Royal Highness, Louis of France!'

Two long-haired royal pages proceeded solemnly through the wide portico. They were followed by the king's officers currently on duty, de Lauzun, captain of the Garde-du-Corps, and de Passy, captain of the Cent Suisse, stiffly elegant and wearing their shoulder ribbons of commission. And then, accompanied by the flourish of a drum roll, the threshold was invested with the imperious majesty of France's absolute monarch, Louis de Bourbon, *Le Roi-Soleil*, straight and imposing and giving the impression of height in spite of his medium stature; the personification of royal purple and rule by divine right, the most autocratic and powerful of French sovereigns because he had so willed it, Louis XIV, called the Sun King, called the Jupiter King, called the God-given, *Le Dieu donné*.

Broad-shouldered and strong-nosed, in his thirty-first year and with his own dark and luxuriant hair falling on his shoulders, Louis dazzled the eye. He was garbed in shimmering cloth-of-gold frothed with lace and rows of diamond buttons. There were jeweled buckles on his red-heeled shoes and a gem-banded, wide-brimmed beaver hat with a double row of white plumes on his head.

And on his arm, like the triumphant clash of cymbals, floated the breathtaking blond-and-white beauty of the Marquise de Montespan, set off by a pearl-festooned scarlet gown, her six-foot-long train carried by royal pages.

With one motion, the entire company swept a low bow, moving back to open a path to the gilded armchair under a red canopy prepared for the king—a single royal chair, since the queen often avoided unnecessary meetings with the Marquise by becoming indisposed.

Her long train still not detached for dancing, Mademoiselle sailed up the living aisle and folded her big-boned body into a curtsy before the smiling monarch. 'Your Majesty, I had scarcely dared hope you would honor the Luxembourg with your presence this evening. I bid you welcome. And you, Madame la Marquise,' she carefully added.

One of Louis's most amiable habits was his unfailing courtesy to women: a king need not remove his hat to anyone, but Louis was known to occasionally give even a maidservant that respect. Now he doffed his elaborate hat and projected his full warmth upon his hostess.

'Nonsense, dear cousin. You know I would never allow a mere touch of indigestion to keep me from one of your delightful *soirées*. Come, but where is the music? I am always annoyed that my entrance means a hiatus in the festivities. Tell the musicians to strike up and give my good *mesdames et messieurs* their pleasure.' His cordial smile was emphasized by his tiny, divided black moustache.

'The pleasure of your subjects is always dependent upon Your Majesty's presence. Now that you have graced us, we can truly commence this evening.'

'You are not only silver-tongued this evening, Mademoiselle, but more ravishing than I have ever seen you,' he responded. He then conspiratorially lowered his head and his tone. 'You give yourself away, dear cuz. Only the intrigue of romance could bring such sparkle to a woman's eyes. It is not *my* arrival but Lauzun's that animates you thus.' Affability kindling his shrewd dark eyes, he twitted her, vastly amused by the maiden's blush on the cheeks of a forty-three-year-old spinster. 'But be good enough to spare some little time from your gallant later; I've found no one to step the *gaillard* as lively as you.'

'A generous flattery, Your Majesty,' Mademoiselle returned, ever up to the formulas of *politesse*, 'but my success in the figures is really just the skill of my royal partner.'

Beaming, she took the free arm he offered, and all three proceeded down the bowing ranks, Louis stopping here and there to greet one of his nobles or gracefully compliment a lady. When he reached his chair, he did not sit but accepted a goblet of wine from Mademoiselle's maître d'hôtel and stood conversing amiably with his nobles and his sister-in-law Henrietta. Madame de Montespan's attention was engaged by the saturnine Marquis de Louvois, Louis's Minister of War.

Julie found herself within the shifting group about the king, whose back was toward her. The music recommenced, and from the corner of her eye she saw one of the gentlemen she had recently met, the moist-browed Chevalier de Rohan, coming toward her purposefully. She picked up her short train and glided closer to Mademoiselle. She didn't want to dance now; she wanted to be presented to the king.

Mademoiselle, breaking off her animated prattle with the Comte de Lauzun and the Venetian ambassador, di Granciano, to place her empty goblet on a lackey's tray, realized that her lady-of-honor stood beside her. Amiably, she drew Julie forward and presented her to the gentlemen with a confident pride of patronage. The rouged di Granciano kissed Julie's gloved hand with the appreciative warmth of an aging *roué*, holding her fingers in his insistent grip a little too long.

But the Comte de Lauzun completely surprised her. Somehow she had expected La Grande Mademoiselle's passion to match the royal lady, to be a most imposing man. Instead, although well formed, the captain of the royal Garde-du-Corps was unusually short, and the tart expression on his face was hardly softened by his pursed smile. Still, his words, however abrupt, were the pleasantries of the court, and he deferred to Mademoiselle with much pomp and formal respect. He bore himself with stiff pride, vain of his military reputation and the favor of the king, and in spite of his grotesque lack of height in comparison to Mademoiselle, Julie thought she discerned the masterful appeal that had captured her mistress.

'Did you perhaps know my cousin by marriage, the Marquess of Baimbridge?' de Lauzun questioned Julie. 'I hear he had been appointed first gentleman of the bedchamber to King Charles.'

'No, monsieur, I was not acquainted with the gentleman.'

'Ah, so much his lordship's loss,' di Granciano wheezed, 'to have missed the pleasure of conversing with so fair a French lady. I cannot understand how he failed to seek an introduction.'

'Madame de Lowry found no liking at all for the English court, signore, and resided in the country, where the Marquess could scarcely find her,' Mademoiselle explained.

Julie demurred, 'Your Highness puts it a bit strongly. I did not dislike the English court. I merely found their proceedings different from ours, and I suppose I am shy of customs I do not understand.' She had decided that to casual acquaintances ignorance caused by bashfulness was less mortifying than admitting her late husband's dismissal of her.

'Very interesting. I am intrigued,' de Lauzun responded. 'And what did you find wrong with the Stuart court to prompt you to absent yourself, may I inquire?'

At this moment, Louis, with Madame de Montespan,

turned to their group, and the ruler's deep but modulated voice broke into de Lauzun's question. 'Who is it, monsieur, who has found my cousin Charles's country disagreeable? I usually hear quite the reverse.'

Julie made an elaborate curtsy, butterflies suddenly fluttering in her stomach. 'It was I, Your Majesty. I found the English lacking in subtlety. They lack the cultivation of the finer arts and are entirely unaware of the more gracious manners and deportment for which Your Majesty's own court is envied. A young girl brought up with the last degree of French refinement finds it hard to exist among ruder tastes. . .' She faltered to a stop as she realized he was smiling at her self-conscious pomposity, and, blushing furiously, she lowered her eyes. 'And besides, I was just childishly homesick,' she finished, then looked up at him again, irrepressible laughter in her glance.

'Madame is refreshingly candid.' Louis chuckled appreciatively as he smoothly shifted his experienced gaze to take in her entire form. 'Charming——'

Mademoiselle quickly made the introduction. 'Sire, allow me to present my newest lady, the daughter of the late Vicomte de Morlé, Madame la Comtesse de Lowry.'

A momentary surprised flicker of the eyelids, and then Louis recovered himself. 'Ah, I had wondered even from a distance who was the lovely unknown with the raven hair and pink plume. And by that name I now have the explanation of madame's intimate knowledge of English habits. I had heard mention of the Earl of Lowry's untimely demise, but we could not think we would be so fortunate as to lure his widow and my late ambassador's daughter away from her adopted home and possessions. Doubly fortunate, I will say, now that I have personally encountered her.'

'Your Majesty is so kind,' Julie murmured, smiling, color rising in her face.

Athénais de Montespan snapped open her fan to bring attention back to herself. 'The Comtesse and I are ancient friends, sire, since we both suffered the rigors of the convent school together.' Then she added, sweetly but very clearly, 'And we are even related in a way, for madame is Monsieur de Montespan's niece and godchild.'

Louis, who would not again repeat the terrible uproar of wresting a relation from the intrepid Montespan, understood very well the jealous warning in the last remark. 'You are, my dear Marquise, a veritable well of information,' he told her dryly, and then, held by the magnetic appeal of his mistress's blue gaze, he succumbed and smiled fondly at her. 'But you are absolutely unique,' he assured her. His large, expressive eyes, inherited from his Spanish mother—eyes that could freeze with disdain, blaze up with rage, or, as at the death of his mother, Anne of Austria, swim with crocodile tears—now returned mildly to Julie.

'Since your father's tragic accident, I have missed the name of Croixverte about me. I shall hope, madame, that circumstance or your heart will not again deliver you to a foreign lord and remove your beauty from my court.'

Signore di Granciano crinkled his rouged cheeks. 'Your Majesty is hardly generous to us foreigners who have an adoring appreciation for French ladies. You leave us quite desolate, sire.'

'Come, signore,' Louis drawled, 'the gentlemen of Venice already have a sizable collection of my female subjects to their credit. But how say you, Madame de Lowry?'

'It would be rude of me to express any preference, sire, in the contest of your kind words and Signore di Granciano's,' Julie answered, flattered by his interest. 'But if I were absolutely forced to leave France again, I hear that Venice is truly an enchanting city.'

'The Comtesse so plainly inherits from her father,' Louis declared. 'A true diplomat. I compliment her, and you, dear cousin, on your astuteness in choosing your ladies.'

The orchestra struck up the first chords of a stately air.

'Ah, Your Majesty's favorite?' Athénais murmured.

'So it is. Well then, with your permission, mesdames, messieurs. . .' His genial nod took them all in, but the glance that rested a moment on Julie held beneath its approval a look curiously like speculation. He gave his arm to his mistress and led her out onto the floor.

Mademoiselle's cheeks were mottled, and her pitch of gaiety high as she turned to de Lauzun. 'Oh, the *Grand Pas Son Majesté*. How I love its measures, don't you, messieurs?' she purred, fanning rapidly.

'Will Your Highness honor me?' De Lauzun took her cue with a solemn bow, and, tucking his lace handkerchief into a shallow pocket in the skirt of his coat, he escorted her off, for all the world like an elegant bantam rooster shepherding an ostrich.

There remained Julie and di Granciano. But before the eager Venetian could open his mouth, they were smoothly joined by another gentleman in a dark coat whose features were underscored by a grim sword scar along his jaw. The man's lanky frame folded in a bow.

'Madame de Lowry, permit me the liberty of presenting myself, for my manners are strained before the enchantment of your beauty. I am François Michel Le Tellier, Marquis de Louvois, and I plead the honor of this dance, if the signore will graciously excuse us?'

Julie, still tingling with the attention the king had bent upon her, felt herself a butterfly emerging from the cocoon. She looked up into de Louvois's smiling but shadowed, deep-set eyes and smiled back brilliantly. 'I should be pleased, monsieur.'

And old di Granciano, whose sixteen-year-old wife was at home in her last days of pregnancy, could do nothing but shrug sourly and mutter, 'Of course, Monsieur le Ministre, your servant.'

On the shining parquet floor of the long, brightly lit ballroom, the Comte de Lauzun led the Duchesse de Montpensier in a short promenade step before the next figure.

'I was expecting you to appear earlier this evening, monsieur,' Mademoiselle coquetted, her long train now detached, the smaller one which had been underneath gathered in loops over her arm.

'Your Highness did not realize that today began my three-month tour of duty with His Majesty.'

'Ah, how disappointing. That means you will have few moments to spare for me this winter.'

'Unfortunately so, Your Highness,' the little beau answered stiffly. But the glance he darted at her spoke eloquently of constrained sighs.

'Oh, monsieur, it is too cruel to expect me to put aside our little conversations for so long a time. Your arguments are so instructive and diverting. I look forward to our meetings,' she encouraged him, simpering. 'Truly I do——'

'I am told we shall have a performance of a new play by Molière before supper,' the suave Minister of War remarked, taking Julie's hand in his thin, strong one and walking her slowly about in a cadenced circle.

Julie nodded. She glanced provocatively at him from the corner of her eye. 'I don't believe we have met before, Monsieur de Louvois, and yet you knew my name. How is that?'

'There is little that passes in Paris that I don't know, madame, if you will forgive my immodesty. And the arrival of a most lovely, violet-eyed temptress in all her unique beauty was a signal event to my agents, certainly. They made full report on your arrival.'

'Oh, you are mocking me. You must have heard me presented to the king.'

'But will you allow me to view tonight's drama at your side, madame? For otherwise I shall not enjoy it.' Louvois smiled, persisting.

'Does His Majesty's minister give such personal attention to every newcomer his agents mention, or shall I consider myself a special case?' she flirted.

They separated, changed places in a precise, three-measure maneuver and faced each other again. The look he bent upon her was too penetrating, a habitual expression, she decided, for a man who supervised France's army as well as her intelligence network and prisons. But Julie felt the true impression she was making on him throbbed in the lean male hand that pressed her fingers.

'You *are* a very special case, Comtesse, but to

François Le Tellier, not the Minister of War,' he breathed in her ear, glancing down at her décolletage as she wafted past him.

'Then I shall grant your request with pleasure, monsieur, if you can make your way through the crowd of agents you say is spying on me.'

His narrow smile warmed up a bit as he chuckled. Even the scar along his jaw seemed less sinister. He has a certain sensuous appeal, she thought, as long as one is not intimidated by the tremendous power he wields. Which she was not.

Julie laughed and mentally thumbed her nose at the memory of the forlorn little wife of Cuckfield Manor.

Passing the beautiful Madame de Montespan before him in an elegant turn, the monarch of France muttered, 'Why did you not tell me de Morlé's daughter was in France?'

'Why? I did not have any idea it would interest you.'

'It does, in a fashion. How well do you know her?'

'We are very *intime*.'

'Good. You are in a position to influence her. She will have many swains. If she marries again, it must be to one of my courtiers and not a provincial or one of the foreign nobles that swarm about us. Now that she has returned to France, I want her under my eye.'

Athénais looked up sharply from beneath her lashes at the king, whose impressive height came from his high-heeled shoes and not from nature. 'Does Your Majesty seek to have me play La Vallière to her de Montespan?' The red mouth carried a small smile, but wrath was poised to leap from the blue eyes.

'Peace, madame. Would I be fool enough to mention it to you if I did? It is purely a political question that you seem qualified to help with.'

'My friend is very pretty,' Athénais sulked.

'And very insignificant in your wake, my dear Circe. Do as I ask, and lay your claws to rest. My purpose has nothing to do with her charms. I charge you to see that she stays at court.'

'I will do what I can if she shows any disposition to

leave,' his mistress consented grudgingly, then dropped the subject. She had other, less quarrelsome means of finding out what political question he meant.

The last figure was finished. With a slithering rustle of silks and velvets and patterned brocades, the dancers parted and bowed solemnly to each other. Rising from her deep curtsy to the king, Athénais cast a swift sidelong glance at her old friend Julie and the absorbed Marquis de Louvois, who stood a bit down the line.

Yes, she would surely be able to find out what was up.

CHAPTER
~ 5 ~

Julie's chamber in the Luxembourg was furnished with a good bed, several tall, armless chairs, a writing table to which she had added her own silver ink pots, and a chest. It was small but comfortable and had a pleasant view of the palace's fountains and precisely laid-out gardens. Julie had not had to supply anything for her living quarters besides linen and quilts, which was a kindness to her pocketbook and a fairly new innovation. In her childhood, all residents of a house were expected to supply their own personal furniture and accessories, guests included. Even the king, when he traveled, had to take with him his bed, chairs, rugs, dishes, pots and pans, and any household necessity he might need, since his hosts and even his own chateaux did not supply them. But Louis had lately begun the custom of keeping his various palaces fully furnished, and the nobles who could afford it immediately followed suit, at least in their Paris hôtels and main properties.

When she first came to the Luxembourg, the chamber had been strange to her, a part of the whole novel enchantment of being at court, but now that the winter was almost over, the dream had passed into normal routine, and the cozy chamber was hers, familiar, as were the animated gatherings and suppers and salons and promenades that adorned her days and evenings. Julie stared out at the frost-sparkled yew hedges and the washed tranquility of the gravel garden paths under the clear, faintly purple winter sky. Heedless of the chill, she threw the windows wide so that she could draw a deep breath. It lacked another six weeks till spring, but this time she did not have to dread the arrival of the season of renewal with its proddings of her passion to live. This year, Richard of Lowry and Cuckfield and England were just witches' fables she had invented somewhere between her promising girlhood and this expectant moment.

'No, no, I've changed my mind. I will not step one foot from this chamber today for anyone else's *lever*. I am still sick, sick, do you hear?' The stentorian tone, flung after a retreating courtier, rang through the room. Two huge sneezes punctuated Mademoiselle's complaining, and she pressed her handkerchief urgently against her reddened nose to abort another sneeze. As Julie solicitously bustled up to her chair with a fresh lace-edged square of silk to catch the royal coughs, the Duchesse said hoarsely, 'Just get them all to leave, madame, I haven't recovered enough to bow and scrape today. But I'm not too sick to work. I want my peace. Send them out,' she ordered.

Hiding a smile, Julie turned to catch Mademoiselle de Greu's comprehending eye. That the Duchesse still suffered the remains of a bad congestion of the head was obvious, but Julie understood a stronger reason for missing the social scene four days in a row. Mademoiselle had been gripped by her erratic muse and was in a lather to continue pouring out the novel that had displaced her memoirs for the moment.

'Mesdames, messieurs, Her Highness is again much indisposed this morning and elects to remain in her chamber to rest,' de Greu called out to the chattering courtiers in her high, sweet voice. 'Pray continue your round of morning honors at this time. Her Highness requests solitude to care for her catarrh.' She nodded to the head footman, who then signaled his fellows, and they began shepherding the visitors out.

'Good.' Mademoiselle snuffled into her handkerchief as the last visitor bowed a perfunctory goodbye. A gray-haired gentleman approached her with a vial in his hand, along with a page carrying a spoon and saucer on a tray. 'Oh, *Dieu me sauve*, Doctor Benoit. Do you really expect me to swallow that nauseating concoction again?' she cried, eyeing the viscous brown liquid the physician was carefully pouring into the spoon. 'It's disgusting.'

'Please take it immediately, Your Highness,' her

doctor ordered in a firm tone born of long acquaintance and his popular no-nonsense approach. 'And *le bon Dieu* will have an easier time in attending to your appeal.'

Julie moved to take the spoon and saucer from him, but Mademoiselle, with an annoyed glance that said she was capable of taking her own medicine, grabbed both, made a face, and swallowed down the potion. 'Gahh——'

'That is to soothe your cough, a special blending of senna and syrup of roses, along with licorice root. Now, if you would only allow me to bleed you, as by the example of the king who every last quarter of the moon rids his body of the toxic humors that accumulate in the center of the system, the catarrh would be gone by tomorrow and. . .'

'Monsieur Benoit, you will not belabor me with bleeding. The answer is no. Pure and simple. The king my cousin is surely wiser than this poor woman, but it is not my will to be bled just as a matter of course. Leave your noxious medicine with me if you must, and I will take it.'

'Every three hours? And you will rest and drink my herbal infusions as hot as you can stand it?'

'Yes, yes, now do leave me. Madame de Lowry, accompany the good doctor to the foyer and then immediately attend me in my boudoir. We must be at our work.' Mademoiselle nodded impatiently to dismiss her private physician, although she knew he would be returning in several hours to take her pulse and badger her with another vile medicine. Putting down her gilt mirror on her dressing table, she rose, turning her head on a neck beginning to go crepy. 'Where is Madame de Plessis-Rabat? Or Dant? Ah, there you are, Dant.' She spied her personal maid. 'Bring me as many handkerchiefs as are laundered, and if there aren't enough, ask one of my ladies to go purchase some more. My nose is running like the Seine in full flood.' She allowed the bowing doctor to kiss her hand, sparing him a suffering smile, and then swept away in her velvet morning gown toward a door that was cleverly concealed in the moldings of the wall behind her bed and which led to the small, sunny white-and-gold boudoir where she enjoyed writing.

Mademoiselle closed the door behind herself with a satisfied sigh, her double chin quivering with anticipation. *Bon!* She would have a whole morning to work before joining the king on his promenade prior to one o'clock dinner (unless one was dying, one did not stay out of *Le Roi-Soleil*'s sight too long). Arranging herself on a small stiff-backed settee placed against the tall window, she took up a writing board on her lap and bent her head to her labor.

In a moment there was a scratching, and the door opened to admit a swish of skirts and a soft step on the polished parquet. Mademoiselle knew it was only Julie de Lowry, but she looked up anyway, just to enjoy the sight of her smiling and lissome lady-of-honor garbed in a yellow silk gown, which seemed to embody the cheerfulness of the unusually golden-bright winter morning. There was a yellow knot of ribbons and silk flowers caught in de Lowry's dark, shining curls and a rakish *assassin* patch applied to one side of her piquant mouth. It was no wonder she had blossomed into this radiance in so few months, this English comtesse of French birth, with so many gentlemen swooning over her raven hair and incredible violet eyes.

What *was* the wonder was Mademoiselle's own pleasure in the woman, for the Duchesse was well aware that beautiful women usually caused her goodwill to frost over. Well, perhaps it was because of her own lightness of heart lately, a certain expansion of her soul, that her lady-of-honor's comeliness did not annoy her.

But what was more, de Lowry had an interesting personality of varying hues and shades that engaged the interest. For some reason, she had fallen very quickly into a certain rapport with old de Morlé's daughter. Unless she was becoming a silly old fool, she sensed from the first a sort of empathy between them, although she wished she could fully trust that intuition. Still, even without any personal connection, de Lowry was certainly intelligent, she was talented at the clavier, and she had an infectious smile. Thus, she was amusing.

Julie dropped a casual curtsy, unaware of being the object of Mademoiselle's musings, and glided over to seat herself at the turned-leg table that served as a desk and where she was recopying in a clear hand all her royal mistress's scribbled pages so that the printer could read them.

Without ado, she took up her goose quill and turned over another page from Mademoiselle's untidy stack, but at that moment Mademoiselle was seized by a violent coughing fit. Jumping up, Julie hurried to pour some water into a goblet from a silver ewer on a nearby table. She put it in the reddening lady's hand and then watched helplessly as the Duchesse tried to quell the insistent tickle of the cough with sips of water. She wondered what she could do to cheer up the sufferer. She truly liked the Duchesse de Montpensier, and having tried to put her finger on the why of it, she had decided that, in part, it was because Mademoiselle was honest: she said just what she meant, and there was no need to look over or under or around her words to discover any secondary sense. Yet, for all her position, it seemed to Julie that the high-born lady was much more vulnerable than she realized.

Julie hadn't quite been born when La Grande Mademoiselle had her days of glory—or infamy, as many said—as a female general during the War of the Fronde, the bloody revolt of the nobility against Cardinal Mazarin during Louis's minority. But who in France did not know the history of this unique royal spinster, so often rejected in royal marriage arrangements, so often rejecting of proposed suitors, so openly disdainful of human passions? Although Julie saw Mademoiselle through eyes admiring of her legend, she also perceived her now as a lonely middle-aged woman fully controlled by her awesome Jupiter-cousin and her own egocentricity, a pawn of the throne who possessed every prize but a woman's most natural need, a husband and children.

Julie saw nothing ridiculous in Mademoiselle's passion for the Comte de Lauzun, for she had learned how hollow it was to choose by rank and airs and handsomeness rather than virtue. As she had observed him through the winter, de Lauzun had struck her as a worthy man who pleased the king with superior capabilities and thereby earned the jealous detractions of the court. She thought de Lauzun's assured and proud demeanour the perfect complement for Mademoiselle's sometimes visible, if incongruous, longing to be helpless and protected.

Wanting to be kind to the sniffling Duchesse, Julie came up with another of her little untruths to ease the strain of the lopsided courtship which, because de Lauzun was so careful of the bounds of rank, placed Mademoiselle in the unfeminine position of prime initiator.

'I was at the gallery of shops in the Place Royale last evening, Your Highness, and happened to meet Monsieur de Lauzun at the lace merchant's.'

Mademoiselle did not look up from the mostly blank page she had gone back to contemplating. 'Well, I suppose he must purchase lace at one time or other like anyone else.'

'He was in a great hurry, having taken a few moments from his Garde-du-Corps duties while His Majesty was in his cabinet, but he stopped to inquire very seriously of Your Highness's health and asked me to convey his sincerest respects to you.'

Now the Duchesse looked up with unconcealed hopefulness. 'And did he ask if I was going to attend Madame's ballet tomorrow evening?'

'N-no,' Julie fumbled, unwilling to overembroider her lie, for Monsieur de Lauzun had not really asked after Mademoiselle. 'He was in such a rush, we only said a few words. But he peered anxiously into my eyes as if to make sure I was not deceiving him when I reported you were recovering from your congestion.'

Mademoiselle licked her dry lips and returned to her concentration, but her long face was suffused with a glow. 'Monsieur de Lauzun is a very considerate man,' she murmured to her writing board.

Julie did not feel one bit guilty to have offered some little prop to Mademoiselle's courage.

In the companionable silence and warmth of the

boudoir, the two quill pens scratched out pages and pages of the romance of Arabaze and Iphidamente. Plunging into a long, boring description of the paradisiacal glade of Cantamont, Julie's thought divided into two levels as she worked, one directing her pen on the paper, the other bringing up and toying with the memory of Monsieur de Louvois's flirting words to her at the supper given at the Tuileries the night before, after the opera. 'You are dangerous, madame, dangerous to me. . .' he had murmured, leaning over her. And as her eyes widened, questioning, he had gone on. 'Because you are causing sweet bonds of affection to wind about my heart, and yet I know you are only trifling with me.' To that, she'd come back with some coquettish answer simply because it was difficult for her to believe the mighty, cold-eyed Minister of War felt any more for her than simple male desire.

And yet his attentions were much upon her, and open—thus, the envy of numerous ladies and a feather in her cap. It was flattering. And yet intimidating, because she sensed he was not a man who waited too long when he wanted something. Some women were able to control suitors, playing them on lines as suited their fancy for countless months, but Julie was not adept at this. She would soon need to decide whether to keep de Louvois's friendship or not.

Nevertheless, a smile trembled on her lips even as her eyes carefully followed the course of the scribbled line she was copying. How lifting to the heart it was to have admirers. There were others besides de Louvois. The Chevalier de Rohan, who was a prince, for one, young and insincere, but whose boyish enthusiasm made his company most charming. And Mercure de Vosges, whom she often encountered at Mademoiselle's Thursday salons or those of Madame de Sévigné or the Comtesse de Soissons rather than at evening affairs, for he was self-conscious with his inability to dance or promenade through the galleries. But when she was free, he took her for drives in the Bois de Boulogne and had almost lost his shyness with her, discontinuing his nervous habit of pressing down his moustache once he saw she would not giggle at his serious and elevated concerns or display the female archness that always unnerved him. They shared stories of their previous years, and she heard about his surprisingly happy youth, raised by his mother, a bachelor brother, and a tutor he revered.

Julie smiled to herself. Mercure was so sweet, so reliable; so gentle was the regard in his liquid, dark eyes. She knew he had swayed toward her several times because he wanted very much to kiss her, but then quickly drew back, afraid of rebuff. She resolved that the next time she was going to help him.

And then there was the attractive Seigneur de Creque, an eligible and sought-after gallant whose eyes ate her up and who needed no prompting to steal a quick kiss or squeeze whenever she neglected to watch him. And one or two others. She did not lack for cavaliers.

Then, as usual, her mind jumped to Nicolas de Courcillon, and as usual it annoyed her. One solitary meeting, and she kept remembering that bearded, insouciant face looking down at her, white teeth gleaming. He had not put in an appearance at court all winter, and she sometimes wondered why—although it was no concern of hers, of course. Again, she forced her mind away from de Courcillon. Athénais's assessment of him months ago had been more than enough to warn her off.

She finished copying a long sentence and then with a sigh laid down her pen. She stood up to stretch, wriggling her shoulders to release them.

From where she was frowning at her page and biting on her quill, Mademoiselle looked up.

'May I be excused for a few moments, Your Highness?'

The sharp blue eyes smiled. 'Certainly. When nature calls, one answers. My father, Gaston, passed down to me the only good trait he possessed, a large inner reservoir. Go, and on the way, order the herb tisane Doctor Benoit was mewling about. And I need more handkerchiefs.'

'Yes, Your Highness.' Julie nodded, and in a swirl of yellow skirts, she slipped through a door hidden in the paneling which led to a dark interior stair and the little hall connected to her chamber.

Nicolas wasn't sure what was buoying him up most—riding once more through the hurly-burly of midday Paris with sight piled upon view and scent upon odor, experiencing again the powerful feel of the city and its grand buildings and vital life all about him; or the fact that the earnest young Breton accounts keeper he'd left in charge of his warehouse had done a surprisingly fine job of matching records and receipts with inventory, vindicating his employer's selection of him by intuition several years ago. The bright day was cold, his horse's breath tracing fine plumes on the air—all the more perfect weather for his business, which was the wholesaling of furs to vendors to resell to the rich. And in which his personal involvement was the scandal of the court.

His mounted companion followed along behind him. Nicolas grinned with pleasure as he guided his horse through the confusion of Parisiens and conveyances coming and going off the Pont Neuf and headed the animal toward the rue Tournois. Business was excellent. His partner in Canada would rejoice. But he was personally looking forward to shaking the oppressive solitude of Pignerol from his spirit with a merry dive into the entertainments and the women of the court. Home only two days, he had first slept, bathed, sent for the tailor and the barber, kicked the lazy asses of some of his servants, reported on his mission to de Louvois, sent messages to his friends and greeted his brother, and investigated his business affairs. And he was now headed toward the Luxembourg to pay his respects to the one other person besides his brother he deemed close family.

The night before, Apollon de Vivonne, a good friend from his days with the regiment in New France, had helped him put away three bottles of wine, a huge sausage, fried chicken, and a chestnut pudding, meanwhile filling him in on the political and social news of the past three and a half months. Alternately interested, bored, and finally drunk, there was only one item that gave him real concern: the hardening rumors and speculations about the liaison between the Duchesse de Montpensier and that scorpion de Lauzun. He would have to see about that.

The gold-buttoned, white-stockinged butler who met him and his manservant at the foot of the palace's grand staircase knew him. 'But Monsieur le Marquis, Her Highness is somewhat indisposed. She is involved with her works in her boudoir and wishes to remain undisturbed.'

'Don't be foolish, man. Her Highness will be delighted to see me. I am one of her works, too.'

'But monsieur. . .'

Nicolas shoved by him and the two footmen and bounded up the stairs, his passage unopposed not so much because of his relationship with the Duchesse but rather because of the menacing glare of the huge, bronze-skinned savage who followed in his wake, incongruous in coat and breeches and with a feathered felt hat jammed over long, straight black hair that was interspersed with thin braids.

Making his way across Mademoiselle's ornate bedroom, Nicolas overtook a servant just arriving at the study with a steaming pot and cup on a tray and appropriated the burden before the startled man could protest. 'Wait out here,' he ordered Skandahet-se, his large companion, as well as the hand-wringing butler. He knocked at the door with a cheerful tattoo instead of scratching and, with the tray balanced on one arm, entered.

'Her Highness's tisane has arrived!' Nicolas announced, setting the tray clinking on the desk.

Mademoiselle's startlement turned to instant joy. She quickly put aside her writing board and held out her big but shapely hand in welcome. 'Nicolas! How wonderful! They have finally released you from that miserable service.'

Sweeping off his plumed hat, he went to one knee before her, bending his head to kiss her hand warmly.

Mademoiselle smiled down at the thick cinnamon locks that fell forward across his face and the slight tickle of his soft beard on her hand. 'Oh, I am so glad you've returned to court. I've missed you, miserable rogue.'

Nicolas raised his head, his light blue eyes teasing and merry. 'And I you, Your Highness. Never was there anyone in all those dreary months to disapprove of my behavior or tell me I was disgracing the very essence of my station. I felt abandoned, bereft. . .'

'Oh, *tais-toi*,' Mademoiselle clucked. 'How happy I am you are here. Come, get up, sit by me.' Ignoring the protocol she often observed to its very letter, she patted the pillow next to her on the settee. 'The winter has been much too peaceful'—she sneezed into the handkerchief—'except for this damnable congestion.'

Holding up a finger for patience, Nicolas first strode to the tray, poured out a porcelain mug of the steaming brew it held, and strode back to place the cup in Mademoiselle's grateful hands, which she protected from the heat with her heavy satin handkerchief. 'So!' she gasped between sips. 'But tell me about that dreadful Pignerol.'

He slipped his sword forward so he could perch on the damask-covered seat with her. 'There is little to tell.' He shrugged his big shoulders. 'It is a moot question in those godforsaken mountains who in the fortress is the most punished—the prisoner in his dungeon or the jailer in his tower. It was a bit of bad luck the governor, St Mars, became so ill just as I arrived with my charge. But fortunately, he finally recovered, or I would still be discharging his duties for him and pacing and cursing those hoary battlements.'

'You saw, of course, Le Tellier?' Mademoiselle asked, referring to the king's deposed and disgraced former minister of war.

'Yes, we had many a game of chess together. He fares as well as any man can in a dismal, lonely cell, in spite of the comforts provided him. His hair has turned more white than dark, and his shoulders stoop. . .'

The corners of Mademoiselle's ample mouth began to droop. 'Ah, yes, we all grow older. . .'

'But not you, dear godmother.' With practiced grace, Nicolas hastened to drive away the less pleasant mood he saw coming. 'Your Highness is looking most wonderfully well, in spite of your indisposition. As radiant as a fifteen-year-old.'

She flushed with pleasure but attempted to be sober. 'Come now, don't cozzen me with that glib tongue, de Courcillon. I have a few bones to pick with you, monsieur.'

'Lectures already? And I am but a day in Paris. I came to see you directly I made myself presentable, because in all of France there is no one else whose presence I missed so much.'

She knew he was fond of her, and she returned the affection, and so her eyes were soft. 'Oh, very well, knave,' she chuckled. 'Later, then. In fact, I———'

There came a muffled shriek from outside the door, a grunt, and small shuffling. Without even a scratch to beg entry, the door flew open to admit two women. The second one, a servitor, ruffled up with indignation, carried a tray with a tiny cup of medicine and some handkerchiefs on it.

But it was the first one, sweeping in with a rustle of silk skirts, who made Nicolas start and then catch his breath. There, astonishingly, was that beautiful face, those lash-fringed, wide violet eyes that had come to his mind so often in Pignerol. Before him was the unknown woman in the nightdress whose carriage he had commandeered outside of Lagle! That time, in those few moments, the ebon hair faintly scented with hyacinth had spilled freely onto her shoulders in silky waves, mysterious as midnight against the pale luminosity of her face. Now it bobbed fashionably dressed in clusters of curls adorned with bright ribbon knots, and there was a piquant tiny black patch at the corner of her coral mouth. But the wide, lovely eyes were just as startled now as when he'd first seen her, missing only the veil of fear.

He jumped to his feet. The young woman, her startled smile tentative and her glance traveling between him and Mademoiselle, glided toward them like an advancing ray of sunshine in her yellow dress. His unprepared heart leaped of its own accord and turned over, causing as much surprise to be mirrored in his eyes as in hers, but for different reasons.

'What in the world was that commotion out there?' Mademoiselle demanded.

'It was nothing, Your Highness. . .' Julie started to reassure her.

'Nothing, was it, *mon Dieu!*' The Duchesse's personal servant, Maîtresse Dant, outspoken with the confidence of long service, bristled under her starched linen headdress, her thin mouth pulled even thinner. 'A monstrous savage without, Your Highness, copper-skinned and beady-eyed and big as a house, and he tweaked my—uh—arm as I went by so that I near to fainted.' Dant's indignant eyebrows rose to touch the iron-gray hair peeking out from under her stiff coif.

Nicolas had to compress his lips to hide a grin. 'But you know Skandahet-se, Dant. He's irrepressibly child-like. Allow me to apologize for him. I've had little success in teaching him manners. He's just frisky to see me back.'

Dant curtsied but was little mollified. She quickly set down her tray, offered the cup to Mademoiselle, who drank it down with a face, and after another sketchy curtsy, she hastened out the opposite door, muttering.

Mademoiselle wiped at her runny nose with a clean handkerchief. 'Really, monsieur, must you keep that wild man who afrights half of Paris and scarcely understands a word of French? Even the king tired of the redmen sent to him from Montreal and sent them home, and they were at least ordinary size. Aren't there enough servants in France from which to choose?'

Then her glance took in Nicolas and Julie staring at each other, and her heavy lids half-drooped over her blue eyes. 'Ah, but presentations are in order. This is my new lady-of-honor, the Comtesse de Lowry, who acts also as my secretary. Allow me to introduce to you, madame, the Marquis de Courcillon, my godson.'

The light, merry blue eyes leveled on her gleamed in recognition, Julie saw, although the Marquis kept a gentleman's formal manner. He swept off his soft-brimmed, plumed hat and bowed deeply. 'Madame,

I am truly enchanted.'

'Monsieur,' she acknowledged, but her curtsy was as stiff as her smile, for she had not forgotten his high-handedness at invading her chamber and purloining her coach. Of course, at present his form was more elegantly clothed than when he had hammered at her door at midnight. His knee-length, silver-scrolled coat of blue brocade had wide velvet cuffs turned back to show the lace-trimmed sleeve of his shirt. It was topped with a brief blue cape showing a crimson lining. A silver and crimson baldric running from one shoulder to just below the opposite hip sported a slender sword. The bagged breeches that showed briefly below his form-fitting coat, as well as the silk stockings that outlined his muscular calves, were white. His square-toed shoes showed heels less fashionably high than most. And like the king at times, he wore no perruque; his own light reddish hair, parted in the middle, waved to below the crisp white lace of his neckband.

Julie admitted to herself that de Courcillon cut a fine, if somewhat restrained, figure in a court where the gentlemen strolled about in ribbons and gee-gaws and heavy cascades of lace at neck and wrist. And his bearded face was ruggedly attractive. But Julie did not care for his egotistic, cocky sort at all. So why was her mouth so dry?

'Lowry must be an English county. Have you then recently arrived in France, madame?' de Courcillon inquired, acting the innocent.

'Almost four months ago, monsieur.'

'I trust you had a pleasant journey, with no mishap on the way?'

'Yes, quite pleasant.'

'I ask that because I seem to remember a report at that time of an Englishwoman traveling alone to Paris and being very rudely relieved of her coach by certain ruffians who broke into her bedchamber at an inn.'

'But I am French, not English, in spite of my title, monsieur. So you see, I am not that lady you speak of.' Her tone was short, and she was aware that he was carrying off their little charade much more smoothly than she.

'For that I am thankful, Comtesse. It would incense me to think it was you who suffered such villainy. No man in his right mind would distress such an exquisite pair of eyes. . .'

'You are very kind, monsieur,' Julie interrupted through her brittle smile, and she turned to Mademoiselle. 'Does Your Highness wish me to retire now?'

Mademoiselle's alert gaze had been jumping from Julie to de Courcillon all during the curious conversation, one eyebrow slightly lifted. '*Mais non*, Comtesse, stay. Monsieur has spent the winter at Pignerol substituting for the governor, who was ill, and his adventures as he recounts them are usually fascinating, if not shocking.'

Nicolas pushed up his hat ruefully. 'Not this time, I'm bound. Pignerol, Madame de Lowry, is in the southern mountains, just on the border of Italy. It is a solitary fortress-prison more gloomy and dark than the Bastille, inhabited by brutes of guards and forgotten wretches the king has deemed too dangerous to incarcerate elsewhere. For four months I did nothing more exciting than fill out supply requisitions and plead with the doctor to deliver St Mars from his coma with all speed, curse my luck. And here you ladies were, dancing and holding gay court to all of Paris, and you, Mademoiselle, growing younger every day without one thought for the poor cavalier chaffing away the winter in isolation.'

'You're wrong, dear Nicolas. I thought of you often,' Mademoiselle protested dryly. 'In fact, I was quite cheered when His Majesty informed me that he had ordered you to substitute for St Mars. Separation from the court is good for cogitating on one's follies, as I can well attest, and after that insupportable brawl with Monsieur d'Enghien, you were in need of some meditation to alter your ways. Don't look to me for sympathy.'

Nicolas's white teeth flashed through the short beard. 'Your Highness, the Duc d'Enghien is an idiot and his vain Duchesse a liar with a vengeful imagination. She is not a woman to appeal to me. The notion that I divested him of his sword and knocked him unconscious into a watering trough in the presence of some sadly drunken witnesses is merely all rumor. As ridiculous, in fact'—he strolled nonchalantly to lean back against the writing table—'as the rumors I heard last night concerning you.'

Mademoiselle's head came up, her red nose shiny in the light reflected from the window. 'And Monsieur de Lauzun, you mean, of course.' Her voice was hoarse. 'What morsel did they feel you should know?'

'That you might be entertaining some idea of marrying him. I informed them, of course, that the notion was ridiculously absurd.'

He fell quiet as Mademoiselle rose up angrily, snapped open her fan, and turned her back on them to walk to the window. 'Yes, of course, you would say that. All my heirs take the same bleak view of the subject.'

Nicolas had plucked from a table a bunch of African grapes to munch on. Now he put them down on the desk slowly, and Julie was surprised to see anger darken his eyes, too. 'Why not, Your Highness?' he growled. 'Why should your half-sisters and illegitimate brother and all the rest take kindly to a parvenu like Monsieur le Comte decimating their inheritance? And I, naturally, am one with them. Your kindnesses to me do not mean that I am solely concerned with your personal happiness, and the devil take your fortune!'

His impertinence made Julie gasp and then purse her lips in disapproval. How did the man dare speak so openly to Mademoiselle about his selfish designs? He was either a fool or insane.

But Mademoiselle swung around to face him with a contrite expression. '*Mon Dieu*, that was monstrous for me to say, and I didn't mean it. Forgive me, Nicolas. But Monsieur de Lauzun has become a touchy subject, and I suppose I am oversensitive. The truth is, I am very pleased with the gentleman's company, but as for the gossip you hear, it is based upon little. I have not decided on my course, nor has Monsieur de Lauzun declared himself in any way.'

'Surprisingly reticent for a man of his nature,' Nicolas muttered.

'He has a great measure of modesty to commend

him—a quality other people I know could sorely use,' Mademoiselle said pointedly. 'I do not understand your antipathy toward him.'

Nicolas tried greater tact. 'Ah...I don't dislike him, Your Highness. As you say, he has certain points to recommend him. But I am wary of Monsieur le Comte. He reminds me of those ice mountains afloat on the northern seas—interesting and harmless on the surface but hiding dangerous potential underneath.'

'That is because you do not know him at all well, and I do. What I see of the inner man is good. Admirable, in fact.'

'Women in love are easily fooled,' he responded. Now he turned his clear, mocking gaze upon Julie. 'Don't you agree, Madame?'

Julie did indeed, but she did not care to take his side. 'That depends on the woman, monsieur,' she answered coolly. 'Those of intelligence have no trouble in discerning the worth of a man in addition to his obvious characteristics.'

'And *you* will concede I have some intelligence, Nicolas,' Mademoiselle added. 'You needn't worry that I will do anything foolish. Now tell me,' she asked, firmly changing the subject, 'have you had any news of Madame d'Aubièrre?'

He made a careless gesture with one hand. 'I hear she is as usual.'

There was a small scratching at the door, and Madame de Plessis-Rabat stuck her head in. 'Your Highness, Maître Lebrun has been waiting in your anteroom for several hours. Do you wish to see him today?'

'Certainly I do, and in my bedchamber. I have no intention of living through tomorrow without my horoscope cast to guide me.' Mademoiselle strode to de Courcillon, as tall as he, and kissed him on both cheeks. 'I am really happy you've returned, monsieur, in spite of your impertinence and the outmoded hair you wear on your face.' She chuckled affectionately and turned to Julie. 'Monsieur le Marquis spent a number of his youthful years in the frigid climate of New France, far across the Atlantic, and needed to wear a muff on his face to keep it warm. Now, in the center of civilization, he insists on retaining both it and that strange Indian servant.'

'To say nothing of my disgraceful penchant for engaging in business,' Nicolas added drolly.

'Business?' echoed Julie.

'Furs. The finest beaver, otter, and fox pelts to be had, madame, waiting patiently in my warehouse to grace, with their soft and downy warmth, the enchanting shoulders of beautiful women.' He grinned, appreciating his own eloquence.

'Oh, de Courcillon, you are indeed strange.' Mademoiselle clucked indulgently, shaking her head. 'Then see your merchant brings me a shoulder cape of that purest white fox you've been promising, and bid him not charge me as if it were sapphires. At any rate, I shall expect a good amount of your attention at the ballet tomorrow night, if the other ladies will release you.' She offered her hand imperiously, and her favored godson kissed it.

'Without a doubt, Your Highness. The honor will be mine.'

Mademoiselle picked up her train and draped it over her left arm. 'Madame de Lowry, do accompany the marquis to the main foyer and see if that flibbertigibbet de Greu has returned yet from the queen's *lever* with an answer to my note to Madame de Sévigné. We shall speak more tomorrow night, Nicolas.' She swept past Julie's curtsy and through the door to her bedchamber, where her astrologer awaited with his charts and papers in a corner.

De Courcillon grabbed up the twig of grapes and with a bow invited Julie to precede him from the room. Her head held high, she walked quickly through the large bedchamber with only an askance glance for the somber savage who fell in behind them as Nicolas strode along beside her.

'I can see you haven't forgiven me for borrowing your vehicle,' he remarked mournfully, and he offered her a grape, which she ignored.

'You were doing your duty, monsieur. There is

nothing to forgive.'

'There was one activity I enjoyed this winter that I neglected to mention before the Duchesse. I thought of you. Often. I thought of your great violet eyes and coral lips, of your raven hair and pliant grace, which could not be missed even hidden in that voluminous nightdress——'

Julie felt her cheeks color up and halted to face him with embarrassment.

'——of a pistol ball whizzing by my head,' he finished, unperturbed, looking down at her with a pleasant smile. 'You are one of the reasons I did not go mad from boredom at Pignerol. You kept me quite busy wondering who you were and where I might find you again.'

'I hope your curiosity is now satisfied, monsieur,' she said ungraciously, and she turned on her heel and walked on. He came after her, undaunted.

'But my imagination is faulty. You are much more beautiful and temperamental than I remembered.'

'I am not temperamental,' she huffed.

'Could you not at least tell me your full name so I may be formally aware who it is who cannot forgive a small kiss between a man and a maid?'

Julie raised her chin and glanced at him sideways. 'Kiss? What kiss?' Why give him the satisfaction of knowing she'd thought about it, too? Then it occurred to her that she really was being much too hard on him. And he was, after all, very much favored by her royal employer. She stopped again to face him, dropped a stiff curtsy, and with a wary smile responded, 'My name, monsieur, is Julie de Lisle Croixverte-Mountmerry.'

His smile faltered, and she saw surprise spring into his eyes. Staring, he automatically took the hand she offered him. 'Did you say Croixverte?'

'Why, yes. My father, *le bon Seigneur lui donne la paix*, was the Vicomte de Morlé. He died in a ship lost at sea several years ago.' She was puzzled by his reaction. His eyes traveled over her face in serious regard. She tried to withdraw her hand, which he was squeezing too hard. 'Monsieur. . .?'

'I. . .uh. . .I'm sorry, madame. It's just that I. . .at

one time knew your father.'

Nicolas reluctantly let go of the Comtesse de Lowry's soft hand, regretting the flickering out of existence of the single charming dimple that had flashed for a second beside her little black patch.

De Morlé had said his daughter was in England and comfortably settled in the country. Nicolas's mind darted back some years, and for a moment, superimposed upon her face, yellow candlelight kept the night at bay in a rude house of logs, and the lined and bitter man who was sitting there by the plank table said, à propos of nothing, as he stroked the silky fur of a pelt, 'She is a beauty, my daughter—dark-haired, pale-skinned. The Englishman who took her to wife got a good bargain, more than he deserved. Although, in spite of that, he'd dearly love to lay hands on me.' Briefly, the old man shook lank gray locks, sighed, and then continued with the subject they'd been discussing, how to coax the Algonquins into letting trappers pass through their territory. . .

Nicolas's vision cleared, and he saw de Morlé's daughter, head tilted quizzically, staring back at him. 'How did you know my father, monsieur?'

'Uh. . .well, in my youth I was attached to a regiment sent by the king to Quebec to help quell the Indians. The vicomte traveled on the same ship with us, and later, when he acted for a time as intendant at Trois Rivières, I was assigned to him as special aide.' Which was the truth.

That makes him about thirty or so, flitted through Julie's mind under her train of thought. 'Yes, that was before we went to England, where he was the king's ambassador.'

'Did you not care to stay in England then, madame?' Nicolas inquired carefully.

'I am a widow, monsieur. My husband recently died, and I felt a stranger in that country and so I came home.'

'From England to Paris by way of Lagle?' Scratching his earlobe, he confronted her with so puzzled an expression that she had to laugh.

'Well, I first made a journey from Saint-Malo to Saint-Léonard-sur-Loire, where my mother had left me a small property. But unfortunately, the chateau had burned and the park had flooded, and the whole thing was worth little. In fact, it was probably that long and useless trip that made me possibly short-tempered when we first met each other,' she found herself admitting.

He had recovered his aplomb. 'Ah, but you were magnificent. The worst shot I have ever encountered, fortunately.' The smile that quirked up one corner of his mouth gave her absolution, but Nicolas wanted to know more about her. 'And when you reached Paris you took service with La Grande Mademoiselle?'

'She knew my father, too, it turned out, although my introduction to her was through my dear friend the Marquise de Montespan.'

'Ah,' Nicolas uttered thoughtfully. 'The magnificent Athénais.'

How ridiculous to feel jealous because he said Athénais's name so reverently, Julie chided herself as she turned and continued walking toward the entry. Besides, Mademoiselle had just inquired about a Madame d'Aubièrre, and that was probably his wife. At court, it was good form for a married man to openly admire other women, single or married, as long as his respects were paid in a light manner and in the company of others, and Julie had her amusing share of these attached gallants who held out no future. She did not need another, despite the fact that the man matching his stride to hers had a resolute yet sensitively shaped, sensual mouth and exuded an aura of physical power that drew her like a magnet.

They had come to the head of the stairs. She gave him her hand, and this time he kissed it, lingeringly, so that she felt his breath on her skin. She withdrew her hand, somewhat flustered, and bid him a civil *au revoir*.

'Until tomorrow night, then, Comtesse. I shall sleep well tonight with the thought that you might allow me a few moments' conversation at the ballet performance. Perhaps you might tell me more about England. It is a country I have never visited.' Smoothly, with a gleam in his light blue eyes, he saluted her and departed, the silent-treading Huron hard on his boot heels.

Julie watched him take the marble steps at a nimble clip, dodging several more sedate visitors on their way up. He is of the nobility and yet a seller of furs? Julie wondered. Well, that in itself was curious enough, she decided, for her to ask a few delicate questions about him of Mademoiselle and yet not be considered too interested.

Nicolas lounged, musing, on the outside stair waiting for Skandahet-se to bring their horses from the stables. Imagine. The Vicomte's daughter, not a married matron safely ensconced in England but widowed and by herself in the midst of the court of France. And not too affluent, either, he reflected, for he had noted a small faded patch on the shoulder of her gloriously becoming yellow gown. In his experience, well-born women didn't appear in old gowns unless they were forced to do so. There was more to her story, and he wished to know it, but not from her; pride would make her gloss things over. He would have to lay aside his antipathy for Athénais de Montespan long enough to ask her some questions about her good friend, questions any eager beau might pose.

Which, he reflected wryly, recalling again the Comtesse de Lowry's sweet mouth, always slightly parted because of an alluring, short upper lip, might not be stretching the truth too far.

CHAPTER
~ 6 ~

Mademoiselle had deliberately not sat in the high and specially erected royal box to view the dancing along with the queen and other members of the royal family. Claiming that her lingering cough might spoil the performance and that she preferred sitting near one of the gallery's portals for a quick escape, she was now ensconced in a high-backed armchair and surrounded by several orderly rows of higher nobility, seated on their traditional upholstered tabourets. Lesser lights were on folding chairs or stools or stood along the wall—a performance being the only time anyone besides the royal family and very highest nobility got to sit down.

Mademoiselle was hoping very much that the Comte de Lauzun might find the boldness to join her, and she had prepared for such a happy occurrence by asking Julie de Lowry, in that case, to give up her foldstool so that the Comte could watch the performance seated beside her.

Six liveried heralds came forward on the performance floor, their trumpets ready to signal the start of the ballet. The orchestra members, sitting on a platform, raised their instruments, and the audience stopped rustling and grew expectant. Mademoiselle sighed in disappointment but kept her face forward so as not to have to exchange remarks with the Duc de La Rochefoucauld, sitting on her left. She gave her attention over to the section of the parquet floor that would be the stage. The heralds blasted out their news, but just as the music began, she heard a whisper and some scraping and movement to her right. She turned her head, and there, poised elegantly on the foldstool beside her and nodding most formally, except for the warmer greeting speaking from his eyes, was that most superior and dashing of men beside the king—her Lauzun.

A happy shiver ran down her spine to be near him; excitement caused the short hairs on her arms to stand. Uncaringly bold, she unfolded her fan against her mouth, leaned toward him, and whispered under the cover of the musical introduction, 'You came neither to my *salon* nor to my *lever, méchant monsieur,* and I almost expiring of the croup. Must I surmise you care not a fig whether I live or die?'

Most of the candle sconces had been snuffed, so the only lighting was the chandelier above the stage area. Under cover of the darkness, and with crowding as an excuse, she could feel his leg boldly pressing against hers.

Fervently he whispered, 'Might you surmise, Your Highness, that I could not bear to see you suffer, even with a minor complaint? My sensibilities allow me to kill an enemy in the field with impunity, but to see the least pain in someone I. . .ah, revere, turns my heart to jelly.'

His knee and leg pressed more intimately against her satin skirts, taking away her breath with the idea that crowding had nothing to do with this mute declaration. But since they were drawing discreet but fascinated stares, they could say no more and turned toward the stage. Mademoiselle's full lips were smiling when she refolded her fan. She remembered to hold her head up high to minimize her double chin, and she was blithe-hearted with the Comte's confident and open settling beside her in full view of the court.

From nearby, Nicolas had noticed the Comtesse de Lowry rise and slip away toward the doors as de Lauzun, strutting like a bantam cock, made his pompous approach toward Mademoiselle. Unwinding the petulant-mouthed Madame de Conti's arm from his with a whispered apology, he ignored the princess's seductive pout and made a quiet exit from the room.

Julie emerged into the Salle du Garde, a large, arched room where a few courtiers lingered in conversation or in coquetting in the deep window alcoves. She intended to find an alcove, too, and pass a short while looking out at the Tuileries gardens, then finally slip back into the gallery to view the rest of the ballet, which she loved, from the back row.

It had thrilled her romantic heart almost as much as Mademoiselle's to see the Comte de Lauzun in his wide baldric and elegant gold-picked coat of rose satin approach to join the lofty lady with whom he had only lately allowed himself more open friendship. As she stood quietly before the chill glass panes watching the winter moon spread opaline light over the precisely rectangular bushes and shrubs in the park, she allowed herself to recollect wistfully the short months she, too, had known what it felt like, being in love, and how happy she had been, and she hugged her arms about her to hold on to the pitifully short memory of the sweetness of loving and being loved in return.

She was aware of him then as a faint aura of turbulence and male heat behind her before she felt the light touch on her arm.

'I prefer the moon myself to all that silly posturing in there,' came the bluff baritone voice. Her heart skipped a beat, and she turned about.

'Oh, Monsieur le Marquis.' This time her smile was warmer, for she had discovered that the Madame d'Aubièrre both Mademoiselle and Athénais had referred to was de Courcillon's widowed sister-in-law, a sick woman, and that, to Mademoiselle's disapproval, there was not yet a Marquise de Courcillon—although the only interest this held for Julie was that the Marquis was at least not a philanderer. She teased him, 'But *fie donc*, monsieur, the king adores the ballet and adores to dance the leading roles himself, and anyone who can at all keep a graceful balance prays to be asked to take part. It is your *duty* to admire the ballet.'

'If the king ordered me to admire a six-legged horse, I would. But since he has totally neglected to speak to me of the dance, I would prefer to admire you.'

He took up her hand and kissed it, and the touch of his lips and soft beard shot a tingle up her arm. She felt the color rise in her cheeks. She retrieved her hand and turned partially away from him to view the shadowed gardens made ethereal by the muted strains of Lully's ballet music floating from the gallery. 'Does the moon shine as brightly as this in New France, monsieur? Or is there any moon at all in that faraway place?' she ventured.

'Alas, *chère* madame, it has been some years since I left New France, and for all I know there may not be. But I used to watch it rise over the vast, dark forests that surrounded each of our little towns—a huge and swollen orb, as silent and lonely and mysterious as the land below it. Somehow this friendly companion that floats above Paris seems much more civilized, pouring its pale benediction upon the midnight activities of our beggars and bourgeois alike.' He paused, watching with enchantment the dimple that appeared above one corner of her smiling mouth.

'How poetic you make it. But did you care for the life of the Canadian frontier? Or were you happy to come home?'

His admiring eyes looked into hers for a moment, and then his gaze strayed over her shoulder to study the vista outside. His tone took on a moody introspection. 'In fact, I loved that huge land—and I hated it. The best of it was the challenge to survive, for sometimes our farther forts were surrounded by hostile Iroquois and Senecas, whose bloody ambushes make our European battle-grounds seem dainty and whose sieges often cut off our food supplies. I arrived as a young officer with the Marquis de Tracy's Carignan-Salière Regiment, twelve hundred men strong. The first besieged winter my company spent at Fort Tasdousac, twenty men died of starvation before a relief column arrived from Quebec City. The country is swarming with Indians—Algonquins, Montagnais, Etchamins, Micmacs—and yet the vast land rolls on and on in an endless ocean of wilderness, dwarfing any human settlements into insignificance.'

His earnestness caused his brows to draw together. Julie could see he had wrestled with his ambivalent feelings for the struggling French colonies before. 'There is such a sense of loneliness pervading the whole panorama that it often sapped at my mood and reassurance, I must admit. I don't suffer fools gladly, but I am by nature gregarious, and when my brother Eugene and his infant son died and the title passed to me—no, madame, I was not unhappy to return to France.'

'In fact, I understand you very well,' Julie sympathized. 'I once had cause to contemplate nothing but fields for years on end and was often demoralized by it, too.' She felt a certain awe, though, for him. New France was so terribly far away and so savage. He not only had endured it successfully, but he had come away, so she'd learned, with a good investment in raw furs as well.

Now a look of humor lit his eyes as he looked down at her. 'Ah, but there were marvelous things, too. Some of the tribes were quite friendly, Skandahet-se's Hurons, for instance. When I left the king's service to wander a short time in the wilderness and meditate on my existence, they adopted me and taught me how to live the life of a brave—and of a trapper. Understanding what the New World is about is like turning an uncut crystal in one's hand; it shows different aspects from every side. And when one lives like the natives, their land does not seem so intimidating.'

De Courcillon did not impress Julie as a man who could be easily intimidated, yet there was a refinement to his observations. Yes, ran the cynical whisper through her head, just as the poems Richard scribbled out impressed you, too.

But she queried, 'But how do the townspeople live? Surely not in hide shelters, as I have heard?'

He gave an amused bark of laughter. 'Not anymore. Except for the governor, who dwells in a small chateau, the several thousand Europeans living in Quebec City have quite respectable roofs over their heads, laid out in streets and squares—and in Beaupré and Montreal, too. Although why anyone would want to live in Montreal, with the Jesuits strangling whatever gaiety can be mustered, is beyond me.' He paused, and his strong, mobile mouth quirked up under the cinnamon moustache. 'But I followed you out here to talk about you, Madame de Lowry. And to give myself the pleasure of looking into your remarkable eyes again.'

For a moment, Julie had been comfortable with him,

but his return to honeyed banter disconcerted her. To cover this, she gave him a weak smile and turned her head toward the moon once more. She was acutely aware that he stood close behind her, close enough so that the light essence of hyacinth she'd dabbed on her curls was surely confronting his nostrils. And driving him mad, she hoped, with female perverseness and an imaginary toss of her head.

That de Courcillon was strongly drawn to her she could feel down to her toes, for his intensity was not just that of the experienced courtier making polite compliments. That she felt the same helpless, strong attraction toward him she could not deny, either. So these things went, she supposed—without rhyme or reason and contrary to will. But her self-confidence had increased in the past months. So she could argue with herself that she could enjoy such an infatuation because she could control it and never entangle her emotions too deeply with the audacious de Courcillon, captain of the king's bodyguard.

'Why do I sense that you shy away from me, madame? I am not going to bite you—although propriety does not allow me to admit that I would like to,' he whispered huskily in her ear. He was gazing down at her profile, making her self-conscious about her less-than-perfect nose.

'I am merely timid, monsieur. You don't understand that I passed a number of years very quietly in the English countryside. The court ways are new to me.' She shrugged with feigned helplessness. She was much pleased with herself that his forwardness had not rattled her.

But Nicolas, inspecting her beguiling face, knew more about Julie than she was aware of. It was information he had squeezed from de Montespan, who found his breezy flirting pleasing to her fantasies, and whose love of unique furs knew no bounds. He was more involved with Julie de Lowry than she could imagine or would learn from him.

What he didn't understand was why this one female, no more lovely than any of the court's other ravishing temptresses who had not tempted him any further than their warm beds, gave him a weak feeling somewhere below his breastbone and an uncomfortable sense of losing his grip on the respectful but eminently realistic attitude he held toward women. Maybe it was the unforgettable way they'd first met, when he'd seen a terrified young woman swaying and holding a smoking pistol trained on his chest. Or those damnably beautiful eyes—like flowers, whose clear depths held both innocence and wariness in appealing war. Or the somewhat breathless way she had of speaking, as if she were afraid the other person would not stay to hear her out.

Nicolas moved some inches closer to her; she gracefully moved some inches away—of necessity, further into the window alcove. 'Don't you believe it was fate that brought us on the same road at the same time?' he drawled, following her, his breath so close it stirred the white satin plume descending from satin ribbon knots to curl at the side of her face.

His fingers ached to feel the smoothness of her white shoulders and the swelling bosom which rose above the low neckline of rosette-caught chiffon. Her graceful neck, encircled by a simple strand of small pearls, seemed carved alabaster against the dark cloud of her curls. Her unmarked brow was brushed by tender wisps of ringlets, which would be nice to stir with a lover's gentle breath, he thought.

She turned to fully face him again, and the elusive dimple made her smile roguish. 'Fate, perhaps, but for what? To teach you to knock less heavily upon a lady's door?' she teased.

It was absolutely the wrong move to make with this woman, but Nicolas was gripped by an urge he did not fight. His arms were around her before she could stir. He pulled her tightly against him and took her mouth hungrily, like a tomcat at the cream, tasting her lips, pressing her body against his, and drinking in the sublime feel and breath and yieldingness of her, so carried away by his heart-pounding reaction to the essence, the presence of this one woman in his arms that it took moments before he realized that she wasn't fighting him, that she had willingly raised her face to his, that her pliant lips were clinging to his, responsive, moving. For a few seconds, they stood there, enmeshed. Through the thin gathered chiffon at the top of her bodice, through his brocade coat, he could feel her leaping heartbeat, and he gathered her more passionately against him.

Suddenly, she gave a muffled cry and pulled her head sideways, tearing her mouth from his with a sharp intake of breath and tearing a rip in his being at the same time.

He had only meant to quickly kiss that seductive, parted mouth and then release her, but all thought of release had fled at the taste of her warm, velvety lips. Now he let her go.

For a second, she stared at him, huge-eyed, her breath shallow, her expression astonished. He stared back, sober and silent, and there was no way he was going to apologize for this second embrace he'd had of her, not when it was obvious that she had enjoyed it as much as he. She blinked, and a flush of rose flooded her face, as if sanity had returned.

Consternation shook her. Not looking at him, she swept up her small train and stuttered, 'You ought not to have d-done that, monsieur; y-you are indeed t-too forward. I must return t-to the performance.' Head high, she shoved him aside with a stern hand and pushed past to sail away toward the gilded portals of the Grand Gallery.

He did not follow her but stood watching as her skirts billowed out and her curls bobbed with the haste of her progress away from the commencement of an affair she could not escape. Nor could he. Not that he wanted to. It had been a very long time since any woman had set up the clamor inside of him produced by that hot, brief, but intoxicating surrender. He rubbed a thoughtful thumb across his lips. One played it carefully with a skittish woman like that, he presumed.

The footman pulled the door ajar slightly, and Julie slipped inside, enveloped by the elegant music and the welcome shadows, unnoticed by an audience engrossed with the quite expert, lithe, and sensuous movements of *Le Roi-Soleil* as he partnered Madame de Vigny in the intricate *Branle*. Julie slid along the wall and then leaned her head back, trying to quiet her hammering heart. *Morbleu*, what a fuss her heart was kicking up over an embrace, stolen as it was. She was grateful that he hadn't followed her. She needed some time to get over her brazen reaction to his arms going about her, his ardent kiss. . . The minute he had touched her, just the act of raising her face to his to order him to desist and she'd been lost—drawn by his magnetism. And then there was his heated, insistent mouth upon hers, the hard muscles of his upper arms under her protesting hands, the smell of him, the way her body fitted into his. She had been drawn willy-nilly into an abandoned response to him with her lips, the pressure of her body. . .

Mon dieu, she was acting like a silly virgin. Her hand crept to where the pulse beat in the hollow of her throat. She knew what this was, this breathless feeling of falling into the vortex, this leaping excitement. Once she might have called it love, but now she knew it wasn't. It was lust. And she wasn't happy about it.

CHAPTER
~ 7 ~

Julie desired to be practical and clever like Athénais, but she suspected she was much more a dreamer, seeing the world not always as it was but as she would prefer it to be.

Yet even her lively imagination had not dared to dream such a reality as Le Crandeau's surprise visit to the Luxembourg one evening, drawing her from a game of *trou-madame* with his urgent request for her attention. She conducted the notary to her small chamber and, seating herself on an armless chair and smoothing down her wide skirt, waved him to another.

He began without preamble. 'Madame, it is my pleasure to tell you I have sold your property, La Vallette, and I am here to render you account.'

'Why, Maître Le Crandeau, I am delighted. And for how much?'

The notary's face took on the aspect of a mourner at a grave. 'I beg you believe it. For two hundred thousand livres, madame—nine thousand gold louis!'

Julie felt her breath leave her body. 'W-what?'

'No, madame, I am not bereft of my senses. I was offered, without introduction, this great sum for your land, asking no conditions and especially without care for the valueless chateau and outbuildings. And although I had, in all honor, to point these out, the offer remained firm and insistent.'

'Nine thousand gold louis? A fortune!' Julie gasped in awe. 'But why? I do not understand. For so small an estate?'

'It would please me to tell you I astutely sought out so liberal a buyer, but that would not be true; not even my excellent contacts had turned up much interest except at shocking discount.' His lips twisted in disapproval. 'No, madame, this offer came from a stranger, a legitimate petit-bourgeois named Jean Beraite, who sought my office two days ago and said he was an agent for a party greatly desiring to own La Vallette and then forthwith made this offer with no bit of hesitation or dickering involved. It was take it or leave it, and so, after making sure the man understood exactly what he was buying, as your agent I felt constrained to accept forthwith the note he tendered for the deed.'

'Constrained? But, *mon Dieu,* Maître Le Crandeau, the man must be crazy. Was the note good?'

'Yes, perfectly, but drawn on the banker Flederman, a man not given to revealing his clients.'

'B-but whom might the agent be representing who so deeply wished to own La Vallette? Would he not say?'

'He was adamant about secrecy, madame. Something to do with a family feud. All he would impart was that La Vallette some centuries ago had belonged to this family, which had then fallen on hard times and sold it, and that a more wealthy descendant was now endeavoring to reclaim his ancestral lands.' The notary shook his head and steepled his fingers before his chest for emphasis. 'I have little respect for eccentrics, madame, who doggedly purchase their will with no care for any opposition or any value received. However, by this quirk you have received a most comfortable fortune, and I a commission, and so the more we must value such peculiarities.'

'Indeed,' Julie agreed, still shocked.

Le Crandeau unbound the buckles of a stiff leather pouch and withdrew a flat, sturdy wooden box. He flicked open a hooked latch and lifted the cover to reveal the gleam of tidy stacks of gold louis and ducats. 'I've taken the liberty of bringing you here an immediate sum for whatever use you may have for it. The major part of the money, minus my commission, remains safely with the banker, to swell your yearly allowance appreciably. I trust, madame, I have acted appropriately?'

'Without question, maître, *je suis ravie de votre service,*' Julie murmured, staring at the windfall of money and experiencing an almost painful twinge of joy. '*Dites-moi,* he couldn't take it back, could he? Change his mind, I mean?'

The notary allowed himself a smug smile. When his own surprise and brief pangs of guilt had abated he had written up a tight agreement that not even the king's lawyers could abrogate, he felt. He now drew some parchments from his case. 'These documents of transfer, already signed by the agent, await your hand. Once on file with the Provost of Deeds, which I shall implement first thing in the morning, the matter is legally sealed as it stands. We need only a witness.'

Julie jumped to her feet, motioning for his patience, and ran out to make a sweep of the adjoining salons, where she netted Mademoiselle de Greu flirting cozily on a high-backed settee with a swain. Murmuring apologies, Julie propelled the young woman back to the chamber. Parchments duly signed, the nettled but curious de Greu and the stiff Le Crandeau, who had made a pretty penny on the transaction, both departed with her thanks in their ears. Julie was left alone to savor the giddiness of being financially solvent.

The exorbitant sum paid for La Vallette would handily remove some of the constraints upon her, an extra thousand livres a year of income easily paying for new apparel, a more impressive necklace of pearls, even a personal serving wench—for by the time she had accompanied Mademoiselle through the woman's active day and presided over the Duchesse's late *coucher*, she sometimes flung herself down on her own bed without thought to her rumpled gown on the floor or the strength to find a servant to clean the mud from the soles of her fragile shoes.

But her greatest pleasure would be at the retiring of her debt to Athénais de Montespan. It was not that the generous Athénais had made any mention at all of repayment. It was that her friend often plumbed her about Mademoiselle and the progress of that lady's awkward romance, and Julie had felt constrained by her indebtedness to relate various details even though, as time went on and her regard for the Duchesse grew, she found it distasteful to be adding tales to the already heavy yammer of court gossip. Such as, for instance, the conversation she had chanced to overhear as Mademoiselle took de Lauzun aside one afternoon in the anteroom of the queen's private oratory.

Looking at him with a coy tilt of her head, Mademoiselle laid her hand lightly on the little beau's arm and murmured, 'You have been my good friend and an honored one for a long time, Monsieur le Comte. May I now presume upon that to beg your advice?' She was simpering, not even realizing she had her shoulders slumped to reduce the difference in height between her and the haughty little man. 'I hear the king may seek to marry me to the Prince de Lorraine. But I wish to remain in France, where I am convinced my true happiness lies, since I can only love what I esteem. I am really fearful he might insist on Lorraine. What do you think of such a situation?' And she tucked in her chin and gave him her best provocative glance.

'Why, I would be grieved, of course, to see you leave the court, Your Highness, most personally grieved. But do you never entertain the thought of marriage, then?'

'Yes, of course, passionately. And especially every time I overhear my heirs guessing amongst themselves who will inherit this of my lands and that of my castles. It so vexes me. They talk as if I were an old woman with one foot in the grave. You do not deem me old, do you, monsieur?' Her smile was arch, but she was quite serious as she continued. 'People of my quality, of my station, are always young, you see. One dresses young, one continues to dance, one keeps a blithe and romantic outlook on life. . . *n'est-ce pas?*'

But Antonin Nompar de Caumont, Comte de Lauzun, was regarding her with dispassion.

The eavesdropper, discreetly glancing over, was reminded that de Lauzun had been heard to remark that all women, including royalty, deserved to be treated brutally in order to make them submissive, and then, were a soothing balm applied afterward, it would make them grateful. Even so, it was appalling to hear how sternly he replied. 'Your Highness, you are right to wish to marry. There are times, such as the present, when even a dear friend is forced to wound you by reminding you that you cannot forever play the gay sprite. An unmarried woman of forty-three should not be wrapped up in the pleasures of the world like a girl of fifteen. At that age, a woman should take the veil or at least live a quiet and devoted life and remain at home in modest dress. For a lady of your high rank, perhaps one or two acts of the opera might be permitted at long intervals, but as a spinster it is more your duty to attend vespers, listen to sermons, support charities and hospitals. Gaiety is not for you.'

The astounded Julie, hazarding a full look at them, thought Mademoiselle would surely rear back from this unheard-of rudeness and slap the impertinent man, but, amazingly, the woman regarded that ferretlike face with unalloyed adoration. Masterful, Julie thought. That was what Mademoiselle said she liked about him, that he was so masterful.

'Oh, you are too cruel, monsieur,' Mademoiselle responded softly, stricken. There was gentle reproach in her eyes; her cheeks were vividly colored.

De Lauzun nodded, unrepentant, pleased with himself. But his tone turned more soothing. 'Therefore, dear Highness, the alternative is to marry. For, once married, a woman can go anywhere at any age. She dresses fashionably to please her husband, of course, and goes to every and all amusements because it advances him. Anyone not blind can see the folly in a woman not marrying.'

Mademoiselle turned from him slightly, her lips pouting, her bosom rising and falling, her painted fan moving quickly. 'So is it your advice, then, for me to accept Lorraine if he is offered?' She was trying to seem nonchalant, but the eyes that slid toward him held painful rejection.

A spasm took de Lauzun's facial muscles, as if he were losing control of his strict façade. He raised a protesting hand. 'Ah, most royal of ladies, not one moment would I ask such sacrifice from you, so sensitive a person, for I have been at other courts and I have observed the burden of playing at royal consort not worth the honor of it. A foreign queen, an empress, can become quickly bored, for few courts are as scintillating as our own, and she is heavily bound by the strictures of her position and her lord's humors.'

He stepped about so that she faced him fully again, and with intense solemnity, he took her large hand in both of his. 'My advice to you, Your Highness, is certainly to marry, but here, in the highest flowering of civilization. Do you forget you have such wealth that it is in your power to raise up any estimable man to equal most rulers in grandeur?'

'Yes, yes, that is true,' Mademoiselle whispered eagerly, trembling that he held her hand without regard to the glances all about them.

De Lauzun's thin hair was blond mixed with gray. It was hidden by a wig whose curls he now nervously plucked with one hand while he looked at her with eyes red-rimmed from too much poring over plans and logistics of the coming Flanders journey. 'Above all, would not such a man be deeply grateful for the pleasure you would take in bringing him to prominence, and for it return to you sheer adoration? In that way the formula for true happiness is complete. Don't you agree?' The grooves between his nose and chin softened as he stared meaningfully into her eyes. Then he started, as if remembering his place, and with a twisted smile he bent to kiss Mademoiselle's hand.

Her restrained passions were evident in the trembling of her thick underlip. 'Ah, alas, but where is such a man?' she said breathlessly. 'Where might I find him?'

If de Lauzun had noticed the tremor in her hand, he gave no indication of it. He straightened up and became the cool, aloof soldier again, reserve once more settled on his face. 'If you will give me time to think on it, I might recommend several for your consideration, particularly from the younger group.'

Some of the light died in Mademoiselle's expectant eyes. *'Vraiment?* Such as who?'

He shrugged noncommittally. 'Perhaps the young Monsieur de St. Paul, for example, heir to the Duc de Longueville.'

Julie would not have wondered if acid had dripped from Mademoiselle's voice at this point, but the

Duchesse merely persisted encouragingly. 'But there are others, monsieur, whom I would be more inclined to take for a husband. A man, for instance, whose interests and age and sophistication were more coincidental with mine. Don't you agree?' Dismissing the fact that he was seven years her junior and that the literature and music that were so important to her were of little moment to the uneducated de Lauzun, Mademoiselle still stared at him hopefully. Then she realized from the little step back with which he formally distanced himself from her that the wily Comte had once again withdrawn from the running. It was because he was modest, was her reasoning, unable to find the courage to give her the avowal, the declaration she longed for, and such unique reticence fanned even brighter the flames of love in her thirsty soul.

'There are others, Your Highness knows as well as I. Perhaps when the court returns from Flanders, some other candidates can be distinguished. . .'

The oratory doors were flung wide by two footmen, and the queen, short, stubby, with an overshot lower jaw, emerged, blinking in the brighter light of the anteroom. The chatter and laughter of a room full of people released momentarily from the round of court duty faded as the gathered nobility awaiting her bowed, then fell into the wake of the wan, blond royal consort to take the fresh air on the Louvre promenade along the Seine, a twice-weekly event.

Mademoiselle and de Lauzun parted, she with melancholy eyes, he with a suspicion of yearning in his last glance, which somewhat consoled her. And thus Julie had been able to describe to Athénais how the peculiar Comte de Lauzun had so harshly denounced a royal princess for her unwillingness to face up to her age and how humbly his scolding had been received.

Five minutes afterward, she hated herself for her disloyalty.

But that was finished now. Heaving a great sigh, Julie slid the heavy box of money under her bed and prepared to return to the mirrored salon designed for Marie de Medici, where Mademoiselle and her guests were playing cards to the tune of mild swearing and substantial sums.

Tomorrow she would count out sixty-three thousand livres and then have delivered to Athénais at the Louvre a note stating that she desired to repay her loan, if Athénais would indicate where the money should be sent.

Having suffered the meticulous morning ministrations of his valet, Nicolas, followed by the silent Skandahet-se, descended his stairway to attend the king's *lever* and from there to a meeting of high-level officers. But in the marble foyer of the Hôtel de Courcillon, he encountered his brother, just stumbling through the portal, muzzy-eyed and with a two-day stubble of black beard.

A grunt of impatience escaped him. It did no good to disapprove of Jean-Pierre Anselm d'Aubièrre, Monsieur l'Abbé of a small congregation of Petits-Augustins, for he would only listen guiltily, swear to improve, and continue on with his debauched ways. In any case, he was twenty-two, a grown man, and it was Nicolas, in fact, who supplied him with the heavy purses that supplemented his increment as leader—usually in absentia—over the monks in residence at the abbey house near Dijon. Nicolas was inclined to indulge his younger brother, who had suffered much from the early loss of their parents.

'Was she so good that you could not come up for air all this time?'

'Good enough,' Jean-Pierre mumbled, straight dark hair hanging in his eyes. He gave Nicolas a lopsided grin and tried to slide past him, but Nicolas stood firmly on the bottom step. Jean-Pierre shrugged. 'But her husband came home.'

Nicolas bumped him with his chest to keep him off the stair. 'From the look of you, you barely had the fortune to get out intact. Are there not enough unguarded young maidens yearning for you that you have to risk having your testicles fed to you by an angry husband? Some men do not care for the fashion of loaning their women.'

Undaunted, Jean-Pierre made a coarse gesture with his third finger. 'That for de Mauriante. He could not stick an ox in the side with two men holding it down.' He swayed from his night's endeavors, the pallor of fatigue showing under his olive complexion. Even as a child, his dark coloring and delicate frame had made such a contrast with his fair and heartier-built two older brothers that Nicolas as a boy had been upset to overhear scurrilous asides about a *mésalliance* on his mother's part. Jean-Pierre's face looked squashed together, with small features between a high brow and a boxy jaw, but his ready grin provided the charm that opened many a bedchamber door and also kept his bishop blind in one eye.

Nicolas nodded. 'You're right about de Mauriante, but others are not so clumsy, and you are not that polished in defending yourself, Abbé. I ask you to have a care for yourself. We are all that remains of this branch of the d'Aubièrres.' That his reproof was mild was not so much from affection—for Jean-Pierre seemed to him a half-formed person, as if the skin of a man had been pulled tight over an empty space—as from a certain guilt for having spent so much time away from Jean-Pierre in his youth. Eugene, too, the oldest and original inheritor of the title, had given the littlest brother scant thought.

Jean-Pierre squinted amiably at him. 'No, I beg to differ. We're not all that remains. Have you forgotten my little Randolphe? Illegitimate, I grant you, but a d'Aubièrre just the same. And what of your get in Canada, eh? My heart is too soft to forget all these little bastards as you do.'

Determined to ignore a sore subject he should never have confessed, Nicolas eyed the wine stains on the Abbé's neckcloth and misbuttoned coat. He said abruptly, 'Go find your chamber, and have a change of clothes while you are at it,' and grudgingly stepped aside.

'Oui, ma mère.' Jean-Pierre saluted. 'And *pax vobiscum.* There is no doubt in all good Christian minds that you love me.' He shuffled up the elegant switchback stair and airily waved away the servant who had descended to

help him. 'But right now I need neither clothes nor bath nor sex nor cautions,' he called back to Nicolas. 'I need a bed.' Whistling off-key, he continued on his way up.

Nicolas had learned that there was no way to deal with the willful Jean-Pierre other than to immediately dismiss him out of mind, and so, with an effort, he did. He swung up into his saddle, neck-reined his horse away from the groom, who had steadied the animal, and trotted out into the bustling Marais. Once a swamp, it was now an enclave of the rich and titled, where Nicolas's grandfather had built his fine townhouse. He was concerned with the coming meeting, where it would be decided how many regiments would be marching under the Comte de Lauzun's command during the procession to Flanders. In view of the object of the exercise, which was Louis's egoistic desire to impress the cities newly wrested from Spain with France's military might and glorious court, he did not deem it wise to take too many troops away from the Holland border. Nicolas recognized de Lauzun's self-seeking need to build up his command, but he would not hesitate to speak his mind to Louis and General Turenne. And it was sincere opinion that motivated him, not competition. The king's favorite, unlikely as the insolent, posturing de Lauzun seemed for the signal honor, was a military hero and would probably get his way. But that didn't bolster Nicolas's confidence in the man's decisions.

What was bothering him, what kept chasing from his mind the arguments he might marshall to impress the king and have him revise de Lauzun's requests, was the fact that he was going to have a confrontation with Julie de Croixverte-Mountmerry, the beauteous Comtesse de Lowry, and it wasn't going to be pleasant.

They had not avoided each other these past weeks so much as they sought no occasion to be with each other privately. Neither of them mistook the tension of attraction between them. It was almost a palpable thing, and they played with it deliberately, like tossing a ball back and forth, and even stoked it whenever they met, with flirting eyes and provocative glances, but always safe in the bosom of a crowd. He assumed that his own uncharacteristic lack of aggressiveness was merely to build up the anticipation of the eventual encounter, although he could not deny that there was a certain instinctive apprehension in him that once the thing was started, there would be no turning back.

But today he was riding a thin edge of dislike for the woman. She had seemed different, de Morlé's appealing daughter, excited with the headiness of court life and easily becoming a part of it, yet with a reserve. He sensed that a bit of her stood aside, sensitized to the more obvious posturing and silly excess of the fashionable life, just as his own years on the frontier had made his perspective different from that of many around him.

Now, disappointment pinched him and made him even angrier over what he had learned, thanks to the Maréchale de Grammont's throwing her daughter Elize under his feet at every moment. Sometimes, to be nice to the mother, he danced with the girl, silly and fluttery as a plump partridge. And it was Elize who giggled out the latest gossip to him, that Mademoiselle had allowed the Comte de Lauzun to call her an old maid and insult her and advise her to become a nun. And the Duchesse did not even give the little man the slightest reproof and thus was even now secretly packing her trunks to take the veil and ease her broken heart. Oh, it was all over the court, Elize had trilled, and she had tapped him coquettishly on the shoulder with her single-plumed fan. Oh, of course it was true. The Marquise de Charost had it from the king himself, who had it from Madame de Montespan, who always had the latest succulent morsel directly from Mademoiselle's own lady-of-honor.

Mademoiselle's lady. But hardly of honor, Nicolas boiled.

He came up right behind her as she worked her way through an intricate chaconne on the Duchesse's elaborately painted clavier. Again, she sensed his presence before he spoke, even though there were numerous people around her, sitting or walking about as they awaited the appearance of the infamous writer Bussy-

Rabutin, who was late to Mademoiselle's Wednesday salon.

'I would like to speak with you, madame. Privately. Now.'

Her hands did not miss one resonant note on the keyboard, although his peremptory command sent mild apprehension coursing through her. '*Ciel*, monsieur, you sound as if the sky has fallen down,' she responded lightly.

'Perhaps it has, in fact,' he growled. 'Will you indulge me? Please?'

In fact, you sound more like my old nurse when I was naughty and headed for a slapping, Julie huffed to herself. But curiosity and the fact that his presence sent a tingle up her spine overcame her inclination to bristle at his attitude. She shrugged and bent her head, returning her attention to the music spilling from her arched and flying fingers, and in a few minutes she offered up a faultless coda to those who were listening closely. Her hands remained poised over the keyboard for a second at the finish. Then she relaxed, pushed back the seat, and looked up to repay with a dazzling smile the approving finger snapping and *bravas* of the company and Mademoiselle's proud nods.

Nicolas took her firmly by the arm and steered her past the knot of male admirers waiting to congratulate her. She laughingly wafted apologies behind her to cover his rudeness, even though she was shocked by the grip that propelled her and hoped it was not obvious to everyone.

When they emerged into the anteroom, she jerked her arm away from him angrily and turned to scold him, but before she could open her mouth, he gave her a thin smile and strongly indicated that she pass into the small, more private chamber whose access was through a flush, seamless door.

Ruffled, she complied, her curiosity still in charge. After the passionate embrace at the ballet weeks ago, he'd been very pleasant and very polite whenever they'd met, but he gave no indication of wishing to continue a closer friendship, even though she often accidentally caught his eyes on her and their gazes held. His reticence puzzled her, hurt her, if she had to admit it. Obviously, she did not compare with the flashy, fawning females who hung on his arm.

The small room offered a cold fireplace, an Oriental carpet on the shiny parquet, and an inlaid table. Julie pulled her velvet and fox capelet closer about her bare shoulders and flounced her dark curls in a gesture of disdain as she whirled about toward him. 'How dare you handle me like that, monsieur? I demand an explanation and an apology.'

But he clasped his hands behind his back and began to pace, not looking at her. 'I believe you are aware, madame, that I am extremely fond of my godmother, who, although not old enough to be my mother, surely acted as a loving relation during my lonely childhood.'

Julie stared at him in confusion.

From under drawn-together brows, he met her glance for a moment, then looked away again.

'Therefore, I am not inclined to stand aside while slander and lies and ridicule are passed daily about the court in a vicious attempt by a newcomer to ingratiate herself with various powerful personages by degrading a royal lady. What have you to say for yourself?' Now he stared at her. The bold eyes that were usually so cheerful had frosted over into pale blue ice. A muscle twitched under his cheekbone as he waited for her answer.

Taken completely aback, Julie could only defend herself indignantly. 'I don't know what you are talking about, monsieur. But I strongly protest the insulting tenor of it.'

'Then I will explain it to you, madame. More clearly.' He stopped pacing and leaned on the small table. He fixed her with a baleful stare and proceeded to report in an accusing tone some of the tales Elize had repeated to him, emphasizing who the girl had quoted.

'I will not allow you to continue spreading such falsehoods about Mademoiselle la Duchesse, if I have to go to her myself and demand your removal from her household.' His face had grown as ruddy as his close-clipped beard.

Julie's panicked eyes opened wide. 'But they are not falsehoods,' she protested under his attack. 'That is. . .I mean. . .I didn't m-make any of that up.'

'Ah, then you admit you talk about her cruelly behind her back.'

'No. . .'

'Betraying the unusual confidence she has shown in you. . .'

'No. . .I m-mean. . .n-not really. . .'

In two determined strides, he reached her, then roughly grasped her wrist. 'What does that mean, not really? Do you deny you have been a conduit to the malicious little ears of the Marquise de Montespan, who has been neatly skewering Mademoiselle for the delight of the court ever since the gnome de Lauzun appeared in her life? Do you deny that?' He scowled blackly, shaking her by the wrist.

Julie stared at him, dismayed by his anger. Suddenly, as if illuminated in a shaft of white light, the depth of her careless stupidity was apparent to her, and it pierced cruelly through to her pride. A burn of tears started in her eyes, and desperately she blinked them back. She quivered and whispered, 'No, I do not deny it. But I swear I did not mean her any harm.'

Evidently, he had marked as genuine the shock that had jumped into her violet eyes, for he shook her again, but less roughly this time. 'And what did you think such a violation of a woman's privacy would do besides make her a laughingstock?'

'I didn't think. It never occurred to me. It was Athénais. . .'

No, it was not Athénais who had played her for a fool; it was her own unsophisticated gullibility, coupled with a selfish desire to repay a debt she feared she could never retire otherwise. Julie twisted her wrist from Nicolas's grasp and walked to the fireplace, where she leaned her burning brow on the coolness of the marble. Behind her, Nicolas was silent, waiting.

He had a right to consider her poisonous, although her heart and her pride ached that he did. She cast about frantically for something to excuse herself with, even to herself, but, horribly, there was nothing but her blind and self-centered credulousness. Yet she was desperate that he not betray her disloyalty to Mademoiselle, for more than losing her position, she feared the loss of the lady's trust and goodwill. She truly liked Anne-Marie-Louise d'Orleans, in spite of the woman's haughty faults and pettiness. She admired her courage and intelligence; she wanted her approval. She would be heartbroken to be summarily dismissed, and in disgrace.

Julie turned around to him, her head drooping. 'When I first came here, monsieur...' Her voice broke. But she cleared her throat and straightened her shoulders, willing her gaze to lift to his and her quivering voice to come stronger. 'When I arrived here from England, I had very little money. My uncle, the Marquis de Montespan, was unavailable. Therefore, it was Athénais who advanced me the sixty-three thousand livres necessary to purchase the appointment to Her Highness's household, and she did so with little hope of repayment. In exchange, she merely asked for some bits of harmless gossip to amuse a restless king—and for him alone, I thought at the time. If that appears gross stupidity, then so it was, the ignorant trust of a woman unused to court intrigue. I felt beholden to the Marquise de Montespan. I had no idea the confidences would go any farther than the king's ear. Mademoiselle, after all, is the king's first cousin!'

'Louis has no real love for her,' Nicolas said with a stony stare. 'Not since she accidentally directed the cannon on the Bastille walls to fire at him during the War of the Fronde. He has played harshly with her life ever since.'

Drowning in dismay, Julie blurted out, 'But it will not happen again, I promise you that. Not only because my wits have finally returned to me, but also because I have lately repaid my debt and now owe the marquise nothing.'

He cocked his head. 'I thought you had no funds. How did you manage to find sixty-three thousand livres?'

Too chastened to tell him it was none of his affair, she dutifully replied, 'Do you remember I once mentioned a small, ruined estate I possessed on the Loire? Well, it was purchased by someone, and my representative was clever enough to squeeze out a very good price.' She shrugged. *'Voilà.'*

Nicolas continued to contemplate her. His fingers, rubbing his beard, were also covering his mouth, still pinched in contempt, she thought. Then he put his hands behind his back again and resumed pacing. And now she waited. Finally, he threw her a look over his shoulder and burst out in exasperation, 'I do not see, woman, how you can excuse such rank calumny, such ignorant cruelty. . .'

But she was tired of being tongue-lashed. She drew herself up and blinked back her tears. 'I cannot excuse it, monsieur. I was in error. I can only make a deep and heartfelt apology and give you my sincere promise to make amends by offering Her Highness my most devoted service.' Her voice trembled. 'Y-you may not believe it, but I c-care m-much for her, too.'

He did not miss either the honest regret or the silent petition behind her words. He walked up to stand close to her and looked down to search her eyes. 'You do not wish me to tell her, do you?' It was a statement.

'N-no.'

'Very well, then I will not. In my life I have made foolish mistakes, too. I accept your explanation, that you were unthinking rather than mean and were taken in by a guileful friend. And that it will not happen again. The situation is over. Gone from my mind, Madame la Comtesse, never again to be thought of. I give you my word on it.'

Julie blinked at his generosity. 'B-because you believe me?' she asked.

'Because I believe you,' he murmured. There was a softer look in his eyes and, for once, no hint of flippancy.

She dragged her gaze away from his and curtsied. 'Thank you, monsieur.' There was relief in her voice. 'I must return to the guests now, if you will excuse me,' she mumbled. Turning her back, she marched away from him, anxious to be gone with her embarrassment. But he called after her.

'Julie!'

The familiar use of her name stopped her short, and she swung around to watch him approach.

'Julie, my inimitable godmother has snubbed or rubbed the wrong way most of the court at one time or another. She has few deep and true friends—Madame de Sévigné, the Princesse Palatine, the Duc de la Rochefoucauld, one or two others, and myself. And now you. Perhaps we could act in concert to protect her from her myriad detractors, you and I.'

But mortification was making Julie smart, and, childishly, she could not help venting her anger. 'You should have thought of that before you so quickly ascribed to me such churlish motivations.'

He laid a cautioning finger on her lips and withdrew it. 'Ah-ah! We have consigned all that to the rubbish heap, gone and forgotten, madame. From now on, we go forward. As friends.'

But Julie was still suffering acute humiliation. One minute he was reviling her, and the next he wanted to make an ally of her? She lifted up her chin to ignore his peace overture, aware as well, deep inside her, that some of her ire was because he had made no move toward her these past weeks. With stiff dignity, she informed him, 'I am in your debt, Marquis. Now I must return to help Mademoiselle greet her guests. I bid you good day, monsieur.'

'Nicolas,' he said, the smile that had come into his eyes finally touching his lips.

'I fear we do not know each other well enough for that,' she responded.

His scrutiny of her did not waver. 'We will,' he promised softly.

Her answer was to flee the room, as if from the devil himself.

CHAPTER
~ 8 ~

Athénais studied in turn each person's face in the rocking coach, relaxed as they were by the motion of the wheels and ingestion of a too-heavy dinner—although it was the best meal she'd been served in the weeks they'd been traveling. Even the dauntless Louis had removed his hat to lay back his head on upholstery and close his eyes for a few minutes. She sat opposite him alongside a window, and their knees pressed together in a contact all the more intimate and fun for seeming the innocent effect of crowding.

This day, Louis had invited his consort, Marie-Thérèse, to ride with him, for the road was smooth along this stretch between Combles and Cambrai, with no water to ford, and so he was assured not to have to endure too many of the queen's complaints about the horrors of the trip. Athénais, however, had a feeling the journey was going to get worse today before it got better. She hardly enjoyed the discomforts of the road either, but her lover was an intrepid traveler; he hated timid women, anyone who needed to pee more than twice a day, and grumblers. Not having quite the privileges of a queen-in-name, Athénais—and the other ladies, too—had to continue to smile and suffer in silence the hard assaults of rain and dust and cold, not to mention the punishing lurching of the ungainly coaches.

Next to the dozing, pasty-faced queen, who was wrapped head to toe in a traveling cloak, sat the Marquis de Louvois, back erect, spikes of dark lashes lowered on his high cheekbones, although Athénais doubted he slept; she wondered if de Louvois ever slept. He had been her lover once, briefly, before the king had succumbed to her spell and installed her as recognized mistress; for even before her success, she had thought it might be wise to bind so powerful an official to her with a stronger tie than just poignant glances. He had not relished giving her up to the king, and even now there was a strong message in his cold black eyes when they rested upon her, although he dared not do more. But it was comforting to know that she and the Marquis de Louvois were often allies, a case of one hand washing the other.

At the window and next to de Louvois nodded Madame, the Princesse Henrietta. Athénais sniffed, piqued that the cold only tinted the English beauty's cheeks all the pinker, while for her it did nothing but redden the tip of her nose. She buried her hands more deeply in her ermine muff.

The broad shoulder bumping hers belonged to that blasé military tactician the Prince de Condé, in late middle age now but still a warrior to be reckoned with. The handsome jowled face, relaxed in a quick nap, was suffering the puffiness of drink and excess, a legacy of his years in disgrace for commanding the civil war of the nobility called the Fronde. The dwarfish Princesse de Condé, whose uncle had been Cardinal Richelieu, lolled her head against her husband's arm, and at the far window nodded Louise de La Vallière, twin pinched furrows between her eyes, a tormented woman longing for retreat. As usual, the king was traveling with his 'three queens,' as the *canaille* called them.

Athénais sighed, wondering why she was so wide awake, for the company was hardly scintillating. Actually, she missed Monsieur's presence. Louis's brother ordinarily sickened her with his womanish ways, but he always brought with him when he joined the king some choice bits of gossip to digest, or started up word games to pass the time, or in the evening ordered out the musicians and gave an impromptu dance in any barn that was handy. Philippe was amusing sometimes, even to the fits he took if his rouge and powder case could not be found amongst the huge piles of his baggage.

She brushed a stray blond curl back into her hood and peered out at the freshly turned fields and flat countryside. Peasants, standing transfixed like statues under the still-leafless trees at the roadsides, gawked at the incredible procession jangling and rattling past them. To escape tedium, Athénais did the mental gymnastics of trying to see with their eyes, for to them, it must appear as if the entire city of Paris had pulled itself up to come streaming down their road.

Just the king and the royal family alone, including herself and the pitiful La Vallière, accounted for a great train of more than two thousand people, and this did not include the escorting army regiments. The royals traveled with all their official honor attendants (each of whom had a suite of his or her own), plus doctors and astrologers and musicians and domestics of all kinds—pages, footmen, valets, and valets of valets. And since no one in the court had dared remain behind, every aristocrat of both sexes had also joined them, along with their own households and domestics. A convoy of a thousand private carriages carried the pomp and glory of France north to impress the new territories won in 1668, having assembled and departed from the palace of Saint-Germain the minute the winter was over.

The baggage carted along by this tribe required extended lines of heavy carts and pack mules, for the higher-ranked nobility took complete sets of furniture with them, and those obliged to keep open table had domestics and kitchen equipment enough to staff several inns. The king had brought several sets of bedroom furniture, including an immense bed upholstered in green velvet, which was embroidered with twenty-four-karat gold, although only rare accommodations afforded the space for him to use it. The queen insisted on having her Gobelin tapestries, her silver chandeliers and wall sconces, and certainly her silver plates.

Athénais's lip curled in cynical amusement thinking of the utter confusion in uniting luggage and owners when the slower baggage train finally reached the evening resting places, which often covered an entire group of straining villages whose resources and patience were stretched to the limit. Just the evening before, Marie-Thérèse had been distraught because her cooks had somehow lost the way, and if many of the ladies were frantic not to find their cosmetic cases in the disorder, so were the gentlemen, whose private stocks of this food or that wine were somewhere behind in the long line of drays.

Tiring of the game of trying to see this remarkable congregation with peasant astonishment, Athénais turned her vision inward, and a sigh escaped her. She was pregnant again, although it did not show yet. She truly disliked being pregnant. It was a miserable nuisance, but, facing reality, she realized it would be only through her children that her future could be assured. Louis had finally recognized her little daughter and her infant son, Louis Auguste, the Duc de Maine, just as he had done with La Vallière's sickly brood, only two of whom yet survived. But there was a difference, and she bit her lip in vexation. Louis had settled no income on the head of her little bastard prince. She was not foolish enough to expect a sum near the two hundred thousand livres a year he allowed the nine-year-old dauphin. But here she had provided him with this healthy and charming little son, and all she got back was promises; so far, no fat purse or rich county to make her son wealthy. And if Colbert's dire warnings and lectures about the depleted state of the treasury were to be believed, none might be forthcoming.

Her gaze shifted to de Louvois and remained on his brooding face. Not in any least way was she going to be stymied in providing her firstborn with the means to live as the royal prince he was—in her most secret dreams, perhaps even in line for the throne should all Louis's and Philippe's children die childless. Her frustration had led her to formulate a bold if chancy strategy, one she had already revealed to de Louvois since his devious mind often picked greater possibilities from a skein of deceit that she might see. A further encouragement to her ally was that, should her idea succeed, it would humiliate the half-insane Comte de Lauzun, and de Lauzun's abasement would give the Minister of War great joy. Over and over, de Louvois had tried to thwart the little flea's rapid climb to the heights of military command and, for all his power, was defeated each time by the inexplicable favor in which the king held the man.

In the course of outlining her plan to de Louvois, she had mentioned to him her annoyance that Julie de Lowry, having come into a good sum of money, had paid back her loan and then seemed to close her mouth about the private events at the Luxembourg, drying up a source that had been helping her determine when to pounce. De Louvois commenced immediately to probe sharply about where Julie had gotten the money—one could almost see his ears prick forward on the alert—and this had narrowed her eyes a bit. She did not for one minute believe that de Louvois was dancing about and paying court to her friend because he was smitten with her; Julie de Lowry was too proper for him. Yet all Athénais's not-too-subtle prodding for more information about why this unimportant young woman had taken the interest of both king and minister alike had drawn nothing but a thin smile, a debonair shrug, and a remark about Julie's appealing beauty.

The attention focused on Julie subsiding, they had returned to their main conversation—how to manipulate the situation between La Grande Mademoiselle and de Lauzun. The minister did not seem too concerned. 'Don't worry, *ma chère amie,*' he soothed her, sliding a hand up her bare upper arm with an intimacy she did not like. 'I have various other means of getting you the information necessary to your scheme. We will see to it that the situation plays itself out just as you wish.'

'You are being very good to me, François Michel.'

The dark head inclined in sarcastic agreement. 'I am also being good to myself, as you well know.'

As Athénais sat in the king's coach remembering this exchange, de Louvois's eyes opened, as if he had been watching her all this time through his lashes. As if he had read her mind, she told herself, seeing a sardonic smile twist his mouth. The smile said not to worry, that when and if the Duchesse de Montpensier became serious in this grotesque farce of marriage with de Lauzun, Athénais would be the first to know.

Raining, raining! If it rains anymore, I shall grow green with moss like a river bank, Julie grouched to herself, wincing as a huge drop blown from the coach's overhanging gilt trim hit her on the head. She pulled her head back from the window. 'Your Highness, it seems His Majesty has stopped the procession in order to confer with the commander, Monsieur de Lauzun. Perhaps new orders?'

'What? Is that poor man standing outside again in this torrent?' Mademoiselle cried and pushed her own hooded head out the window into the beating rain to look down the line. 'Ah, *Sainte Vierge!* See how he stands there drenched, with his hat under his arm, while the king speaks out from his carriage. How pitiful!' She drew her head back into the coach again, heedlessly wiping the rain off her own cheeks, which were mottled high with indignation. 'The poor Comte is soaked through. My cousin should think to command him to cover his head, at least; he will be ill.'

Without any apology, Monsieur, the king's brother, casually leaned all the way over Julie to see for himself what transpired, crowding her against the back of the seat with no more attention to the body he was pressing against than any woman might give. 'Heavens, you should see him,' Philippe called back snidely to Mademoiselle's other guests. 'But nothing could get me to show myself in such a condition. His hair is uncurled and dripping; his clothes are plastered about him. I have never *seen* a man look so hideous. *Tellement bas!*' he cackled. With a final, disdainful snort he drew back and allowed Julie her breath once more.

Could looks kill, Monsieur would be breathing his last on the carpet floor of the coach, Julie saw. But Mademoiselle restrained herself, limiting herself to a dignified, 'Monsieur de Lauzun is a man I would never consider ugly in any state, cousin. Never. And the king's great esteem for him is obviously not marred by the Comte's placing his duty above his person.'

Philippe's answer was merely to raise a crayoned eyebrow and smirk behind the three beauty patches plastered about his mouth. He went on lazily peeling the orange whose aroma perfumed the close air of the carriage and chased the acrid smell of their charcoal foot warmers.

'Well, maybe they are deciding whether we shall make the chateau at Landrecies this evening, don't you think?' offered the youthful-looking Cardinal de Montigny, who was the reason for Monsieur's presence in Mademoiselle's coach. The prelate slid suggestive, languid eyes toward Philippe.

'Oh, the Lord knows I hope so. This day has been so especially grueling,' Mademoiselle's good friend the Princess Palatine moaned. 'It frightens me to see so many coaches and carts sunk to the top of their wheels in mud holes, with all their animals dead of exhaustion in their traces and who knows whose baggage overturned in the muck.'

With patronizing calm, Mademoiselle assured her. 'Rest easy, *ma chère amie*. We have a very good coachman who has expertly kept us from becoming bemired so far and will continue to do so. Your man does very well, madame,' she remarked to Julie.

It was Poilettier on the box. It seemed he had not been able to tear himself away from the great city to go back to Saint-Malo. Having sold his good coach and spent all his money, he suddenly turned up a month ago, hat in hand, and asked Julie for employment with Mademoiselle's household. Mademoiselle had casually agreed. One more in so large an establishment of servants made little difference.

The conversation droned on, the Cardinal relating a long tale of a desert storm he was once lost in during a sojourn in Egypt. Julie's thoughts drifted away from them to Nicolas de Courcillon, as usual, whom she had assiduously avoided whenever the preparations for this miserable journey had allowed him to join any social events. Actually, the procession had departed without him, as Mademoiselle had happened to mention, for he was assigned to coordinate the ranks of the regular army and Swiss guards left to patrol the royal palaces in Paris. But he had caught up to them after they had left Lille, galloping up to their coach to greet Mademoiselle merrily through the window and throw Julie a wink and a smile. He had been given the responsibility for the rear of the great straggling train of coaches and wagons and its escort, but he averred that he would spend some time with them whenever he came forward for orders. So far, they had not seen much of him, which was fine with Julie, who feared that the weary weeks of journeying had caused her to look as travel-strained as she felt. Still, even though he was kept occupied an hour's ride behind, the trip suddenly seemed more interesting the moment he joined it.

The damp, unusually cold spring air made its way up through the floor, so she snuggled her feet more comfortably on the small, wooden charcoal-burning foot warmer she was sharing with Mademoiselle. In spite of this and her heavy skirts, a chill wriggled up her spine. She prayed she wasn't becoming ill, although it was possible she'd never feel rested again. The number of nights they were able to lodge in big chateaux or decent village houses was not as many as the halts they were forced to make in primitive accommodations. Two nights before, the small and dilapidated Chateau de Pol in Labroux burst at its seams to host even the most important of such a caravansary, with the result that the nobility who could squeeze in slept anywhere there was a space, even upon straw if a camp bed wouldn't fit. Two of the queen's ladies had to settle themselves in a storage cupboard on some wheat, and Julie had to make do near Mademoiselle's pallet on a mound of charcoal covered with a blanket. Her back still pained her, and the night just past, spent stretched on a hard bench in a commandeered village house, had not helped it.

She wished heartily that Mademoiselle were not such a stoic, for the woman never grimaced at a bad supper or at being forced to sleep on a chair if it meant impressing the king with her fortitude. The Duchesse wouldn't even sleep in the relative comfort of her own carriage, as many people did, changing into dressing robes, donning night bonnets against the drafts, if resting on a too-short cot or a heap of pillows exercised her royal privilege to remain close to the king. But she had one failing to be the sort of good traveler approved by the king, and it was a grave one. She had the same insurmountable terror of water as the queen. If the procession was forced to ford a stream, she screeched and quivered as loudly as Marie-Thérèse, and never mind the king's impatience.

Now the coach lurched up again and, with wheels squelching, bumped slowly along for a half-league or so. Then it came to another halt. Looking wearily at each other, the passengers could hear shouting and horses whinnying, and suddenly an officer wearing the *justaucorps* of the king's elite bodyguard, a blue coat lined with red and scrolled with gold and silver braid, appeared on horseback and bent to the window. Mademoiselle released the cord that lowered the glass.

'We are just before Landrecies, Your Highnesses.'

Philippe smiled with relief and answered for all, 'Very good, monsieur. We are looking forward to dry chambers and a hot dinner.'

'But Landrecies is just on the other side of the Sambre River, which we shall have to ford. It is ordinarily a very placid and shallow little stream, but the rain has swollen it much.'

It was meant to be a caution from Louis to his fearful cousin, but it did no good. 'What, what?' Mademoiselle immediately cried. 'Do you tell me I shall be forced to plunge with my carriage into a mad river in this downpour? Oh, *le bon Seigneur me sauve*, I won't do it. I can't do it. . .' Her eyes bulged with the fright of her phobia, and she seemed to shrink into her fur-lined cloak. Her long, heavy-jawed face had gone ashen, and she grabbed at the Cardinal's arm as if it were a lifeline to stay her from drowning. She rolled frantic eyes at the faces of her embarrassed guests, seeking help, but the coach started up again, and she was reduced to pitiful squealing, her hand fluttering against her heart. 'Oh my! Oh my!'

Julie let down her window and looked out. They had bumped slowly down a small embankment and were now pulled up at a muddy, wheel-rutted landing, where the royal coaches in the lead had stopped just short of the swiftly rushing water. The king had dismounted from his coach and stood in the rain, conferring intently with a number of men. Julie leaned farther out and spied a top-heavy coach stuck out in the middle of the river, the water breaching its doors and several men wrestling in the flood to unharness the wildly plunging horses. But several other test coaches had made the opposite bank, a three-minute crossing when not against the pressure of swirling water. Their drivers stood shouting encouragement to those struggling in the river, and one ran to aid two sopping gentlemen assisting each other to wade from the water.

Mademoiselle took a peek out and, to everyone's consternation, fell back gasping as if she were dying. 'No, no, no, I am afraid we shall perish, drowned and blue. I will not cross over, not in such a rain, never, never,' she screamed out, her whole body stiff with terror, eyes starting, her shrieks loud enough to be heard in Landrecies.

Julie heard the same sort of cries and heavy weeping coming from without, emanating from Marie-Thérèse's coach, where several ladies were bending forward trying to console and calm the distraught queen.

'We shall drown, we shall be swept to our deaths!' the petrified Mademoiselle blubbered, crushing the helpless Cardinal's arm to her convulsively.

'*Oh merde*, cousin, you are acting an utter old fool,' Philippe sniffed at her in disgust. 'Let me get out, and I shall determine what the king wishes to do.'

'Yes, yes, I will descend, too,' Mademoiselle agreed, and she knocked wildly to the coachman to be helped out as Julie tried to catch her fluttering hand to calm her. Poilettier dutifully placed the steps in the mud and opened the door. They all hastened to climb out after the royal princess into what was becoming a mild drizzle.

The king, wearing high leather boots, stalked up, accompanied by de Lauzun, who glared at Mademoiselle, and by several officers of the Musketeers and the Royal Garde-du-Corps. The edge of Louis's cloak was thrown up on one shoulder to keep it from the mud, and the aggressive royal nose jutted from beneath a sodden-plumed velvet hat. There followed what was to Julie's uninitiated eyes an incredible scene. The proud, pompous Duchesse de Montpensier grabbed the king's hand, brought it to her lips, and fell to her knees right there in the mud, weeping wildly not to be forced across the fearful flood; and one could hear the same sobs issuing forth from the queen's vehicle.

Although he was toweringly irritated, nevertheless the purse-lipped ruler cast some measuring glances over Mademoiselle's head toward the several abandoned conveyances that had not made it across the river. Finally, he spoke to de Lauzun from the side of his mouth, and Julie thought she heard the words 'pontoon bridge.'

De Lauzun nodded. 'We would regroup, Your Majesty, go in two sections. The heavier drays could make it across today. . .'

'We shall have to do so, for this flood may get higher. Bring up what squadrons you need. . .' They conferred a few minutes.

Louis rescued his tear-stained hand and pulled the sheet-white Grande Mademoiselle to her feet. Without comment, he passed her shuddering body over to Monsieur de Romecourt, his special adjutant, while de Lauzun stood mud-bespattered and stiff, mouth compressed as if he had tasted something bad. The king craned his head about. *'Voilà!* I spy a habitation of sorts over there, messieurs,' he rumbled. 'To please our affrighted ladies, we will rest under it this night, or each one in his own carriage, and that will have to suffice.'

'A messenger from Monsieur de Courcillon brings word that the commissary wagons have fallen behind, sire, and are floundering in sloughs. They are hitching up extra teams to drag them.'

'Then send a delegation to Landrecies for food, and see they are not niggardly about it. Remount your coaches, mesdames, messieurs. There will be our shelter for the night.' He jerked his head toward the rude little structure sitting alone at the edge of a bare field.

Monsieur squinted at the hovel and made a face. 'Hardly for me such elegant accommodations. Romecourt, see that my own carriage draws up there, just in case.'

'Good, Your Highness.'

* * *

It turned out that the thatched-roof hut had a sod floor and only two rooms. The smaller room Louis designated military headquarters, and a conference of all commanders was immediately scheduled. The larger room, which had neither hearth nor window, the king placed at the disposal of the royal family and their intimates. Various coaches and wagons pulled out of line to circle the little building, and servants began to slog back and forth from the baggage carts and mules farther up the road.

Since nightclothes were always carried in private coaches for just such emergencies, nightfall saw the coach curtains pulled and people getting undressed, preparing for rest. Or they wolfed down whatever they had saved in their hampers from the last meal they'd had—that morning, in fact. The males having departed Mademoiselle's coach, Julie, Mademoiselle, and La Palatine struggled together to help each other remove heavy skirts and corsets, their stomachs grumbling, since they had nothing to nibble but a few biscuits the Princesse Palatine had saved in her pocket. Poilettier knocked on the door. 'Your maids are without, Your Highness.'

Astonished, Mademoiselle pushed open the curtains, and there in a small cart, damp but unbowed, were Dant and three other serving women. 'We were allowed to come forward by special order of Monsieur le Comte de Lauzun, Mademoiselle,' Dant proclaimed proudly. 'In fact, he insisted.'

The warmth of the thrilled smile that slowly curved Mademoiselle's lips was like the sun coming out. All remnants of her panic left her. 'Monsieur de Lauzun is surely one of the most gallant men in France,' she exclaimed proudly as Dant climbed into the carriage to lend her expert hand to the undressing routine. When that was over, Mademoiselle laid back her head and tried to doze, worn out from her bout with gut-wrenching fear. All three women, in fact, tried to rest.

In a while, Mademoiselle's head footman, who shared a canvas shelter with Poilettier on the coach roof, squished up and knocked on the window to announce that hot cooked food had finally been delivered from

Landrecies and would be served in the hut. His famished mistress's eyes lit up for the second time that day. Fortunately, the liveried footman was a big man. Julie, in all her extremity of hunger and fatigue, had to smother a wild giggle in her cloak to see the august Mademoiselle mounted on the fellow piggyback, her ruined soft kid shoes jutting to either side as he jogged her solemnly across the trampled sea of muck between her coach and the hut.

The footman returned to do the same for the Princesse Palatine, but when he returned for Julie, he was waved away, for the Comte de Vosges in a mist-glistened cloak had already ridden up and hoisted her onto his saddle for the short trip. She was wrapped in her cloak, uncomfortable with chill, and her hair was knotted and tucked into a white lace night bonnet tied under her chin. She had been pleased to grasp de Vosges's gloved hand and then lean back against him as the horse picked its way through the milling servants and arriving officers. She was so disgusted with the sufferings of this miserable trip that she wanted to cry, only peripherally noticing the slight tremor in the arm about her waist and the quick, wistful touch of his pale, cold cheek to hers.

She thanked de Vosges sincerely as a royal page helped her down from the saddle at the hut's threshold and answered his usual blush with so grateful a smile that his tiny pencil moustache turned up and his dark eyes glowed. 'Will you sup with me when we reach Landrecies, dear madame?' he ventured.

'I would be very pleased to, monsieur,' she promised, and if it was only the thought of a town and a dry, warm house and a decent dinner that put such fervor into her tone, he did not know it.

De Vosges, flushed with pleasure, saluted and turned his horse. Julie entered the hut to find a new royal crisis brewing in the field of thin mattresses being laid out all over the floor of the dormitory room. Marie-Thérèse, her pasty, flat-planed face skewed in distress under her Spanish lace head shawl, was refusing the arrangements. 'How can you ask this of me?' she wailed. 'The whole family sleep together all in one room?' But that is execrable. It is indecent. It is a sin before God.'

'Don't be ridiculous, madame,' Louis snapped at his wife as he stood hands on hips in the middle of the room. 'You are fully dressed, as is everyone else. There can be no harm or embarrassment in merely sleeping. I find none at all. Do you, dear cousin?' He turned for arbitration to Mademoiselle, who, no longer threatened by rushing water, was her stately self again.

She gave him a flattered nod and pulled in her chin smugly, content that they were committing no impropriety. 'Not at all, Your Majesty. In such emergency as this, it is obvious decorum is served by the very size of the company alone.' Her voice carried farther than necessary, probably to reach the ears of the Comte de Lauzun, who was threading through the maze of mattresses to get to the other room, where the king's officers were already supping on the thin bouillon and hard roast chickens sent over in a heavy dray by the city of Landrecies.

Appeased for the moment by the promise of the only bed which had been brought down the line and from which, with curtains open, she would be able to observe everyone, the queen flopped down upon a mattress like everyone else and drank her soup and struggled to pull apart the tough chicken, muttering over and over that she could not imagine what was the pleasure in such journeys. Julie noticed that Athénais, who had answered her wan smile and small wave with a conspiratorial grimace and roll of her eyes, had spread a scarf on the ground so she could subside gracefully right at the king's feet, her uncomplaining endurance in direct contrast to the queen's lamenting.

After the unsatisfactory supper, the king and Monsieur betook themselves to join their commanders in the candlelit room, where maps detailing the remainder of the trip were laid out in military style, for Louis enjoyed giving the ladies an idea of the hard work a real battle campaign would require. The rest of the august ladies and gentlemen, more than twenty of them, including the queen, Madame, the king's two mistresses, Athénais's sister Madame de Thianges, Mademoiselle and her half-sister the Duchesse de Guise, and several ladies- and gentlemen-of-honor, stretched out as best they could in the airless room and, covered with blankets, tried to sleep.

But there were not enough mattresses or even floor space, forcing Julie and Madame Bethune, the queen's lady-of-honor, each to choose a corner, wrap up in a blanket, and try to rest sitting up. Officers coming and going on business to the smaller room stumbled repeatedly over supine royal bodies until Louis, hearing the indignant outcries of his relatives, ordered his gentlemen to use a hole in the outer wall of the command room to issue their orders.

Outside, at the end of a path, two narrow canvas tents had been set up to surround the pot chairs serving as royal latrines, with a corps of domestics passing the used containers to be emptied in the river. At one point, Julie came back in and, in the light of the few small lanterns left burning, slipped back to the low stool she had propped into the corner at Mademoiselle's feet and miserably wrapped herself up again. Leaning against the wall, she tried to doze, but a few tears of fatigue welled from the corners of her eyes as she listened to the restless rustlings and turnings and heavy sighs of the highest flower of France, in their fancy dressing robes and nightcaps, struggling to rest on the dirt floor of an abandoned peasant's hut.

She heard a murmur of men's voices behind the plank door of the second room and, from outside, the muffled noises of the regiment of men and beasts laboring by flare and lantern light to construct a temporary bridge over the river. She was aware of the chink and plod of harnessed animals passing close to the hut and the distant shouts of the engineers and the soldiers who were working below the banks.

Semicomatose, she knew the door of the small room opened once in a while to admit someone, showing the brighter glow of the candles from within. And soon there were snores and snufflings from the mattresses about her, even from the queen's bed. Once she hearkened enough to realize that de Lauzun had emerged and was squatting near the half-raised form of Mademoiselle and in a low, harsh whisper was berating the lady for her ridiculous dread of water, which had caused so much trouble. Julie could not hear the Duchesse's answer, only her tone, apologetic, pacifying, but she did hear a muffled giggle from the direction of the young Madame de Guise. De Lauzun stood up abruptly, glared about, and departed.

Sometime later, she knew that the king and Monsieur had emerged and sought their mattresses. She was not really sleeping; she was dozing and drooping. Her shoulder ached, her back was twisted, and one leg was almost numb. She was desperate to stretch out her cramped body, even on the hard floor. The night was cold, but the crowded room was airless and soon warmed by crowded bodies; she twitched the blanket off her shoulders. She felt heavy-hearted every time she flickered back into consciousness and realized where she was.

Suddenly, she was aware that someone was hunkered down before her and shaking her gently by her gloved hand.

'Come on, de Lowry. You will never last another day if you try to sleep sitting up like that. Come along with me.'

At first, she thought she was dreaming that it was Nicolas de Courcillon, but although his face was in darkness, there was no mistaking his silhouette and sonorous baritone. Or his domineering manner.

But she was too wilted to do more than mutter a weak, 'Come where?'

'Out to the coach, where you can at least stretch out.'

'It's cold. . .'

'At least you'll have some air to breathe,' he insisted. He stood up and tugged at her, and she did not resist, for he had said a magic phrase: *stretch out*. Clutching the blanket, she let him lead her through the narrow spaces between the sleepers and then she stood swaying, heavy-eyed, while he opened the door. He scooped her up in his arms and carried her toward Mademoiselle's empty coach. The damp wind, however, revived her will.

'But I don't wish to be out here by myself.'

'You won't be. I haven't the energy left to ride all the way back up the line to my own carriage. And you, *chère* Comtesse, not being royal, have no need to impress the king by ruining your health with no sleep.'

'But it will look very peculiar. I mean, you and I. . .' she fretted as he strode across the soggy ground.

'Look peculiar to whom? Most people are either asleep or looking peculiar themselves. Now, tell the fellows up there who you are, madame.'

Julie answered Poilettier's sleepy grunt from the roof by telling him he wasn't required. Nicolas, managing to get the door open without dropping her, deposited her on the carpeted floor inside and then, when she had raised herself to the seat, climbed in after her.

The charcoal foot warmer was out, and the air was chill, but the vehicle was nevertheless softly upholstered and cozy and silent. Perching warily on the seat opposite where she and her companions had piled all their clothes, she watched de Courcillon reach over to draw the curtains.

'No, don't do that,' she said stiffly, staying his hand.

'I'm merely trying to keep the light of the torch from your eyes.'

'It's very dim. It doesn't bother me.'

He studied her and then shrugged. 'If that suits you. . .'

She gave him a brief, weak smile and tried to arrange herself comfortably but not quite full length on the seat, since to stretch fully out seemed to her improper. And, in fact, with her head propped in a padded corner, she was content with the greater ease to her muscles and joints. But her problem was the cold. All day she'd suffered chills, and now she could not stop shivering, in spite of the cloak and blanket. Hazily, she thought how stupid a custom it was to change into sleeping clothes on the road, wearing only a dressing robe over a flimsy chemise rather than staying dressed in warm petticoats and skirt.

Through her lowered lashes, she saw Nicolas frowning. Having put aside his hat and sword and without a cloak, he was clad in his blue uniform coat, breeches, and tall boots. He had unbuttoned his lace cravat at the neck. One side of his face was in the shadows; the other showed, in the feeble light of the flare, the golden tips of reddish hair and beard. And above them his concerned gaze, riveted on her.

He sat there on the opposite seat watching her. Finally, disconcerted, she opened her eyes fully, wondering what he was about. 'Aren't you going to sleep, monsieur?'

'How can I sleep, madame, when there is a person in this coach whose teeth are so noisily chattering together?'

'My teeth are *not* chattering together.'

'Well, then it must be your knees knocking. But whatever part of you is doing it, I don't like that shivering. Perhaps you've taken cold and have a croup coming on. I shouldn't wonder. Females are not made to endure the miseries of a vast company on a long march.'

'I'll beg you to remember that ladies often slept in the field with their armies during the War of the Fronde, monsieur,' Julie huffed. 'In fact, they led those armies, just as hardy commanders as the men they replaced.' Nevertheless, she was unsuccessful at stopping a convulsive response to a chill climbing her back.

'Ladies like my godmother, you mean, whose army captured Orléans? Yes, I suppose. Women were more iron-natured then, perhaps. But not anymore. Now they are faint and fragile. They quake with cold. Like you.'

At that, he seemed to come to a decision. With a deft movement, he swung across to her bench, insinuated himself between her and the window, and firmly gathered her into his arms, cradling her against his chest like a baby. In her surprise, she let go of the blanket and it slipped down. Ignoring her wiggling and protests, he reached over and drew up her posterior so that the rest of her lay comfortably along the seat. Propping his leg against the opposite bench, and supporting her with one arm, he used the other hand to open his coat, push back her cloak, and huddle her close to him so that she could draw up his warmth, which was considerable. He resettled the blanket around her shoulders and answered her attempts to pull away by whispering in her ear, 'Don't be foolish, Julie. I have enough heat for both of us. Do you want to be ill in such a place? And see, the curtains are open and the driver is up top. Nothing could possibly happen. I give you my word as a gentleman.' His arms gave her what might have been nothing more than a reassuring squeeze.

She had no strength to maintain a demure distance between them, and he was right. The heat of his broad chest radiated right through his soft shirt and warmed her cheek and neck and the rest of her; his parted woolen coat held away the drafts from her face so that her breath warmed the air about her. She knew she would be askance with herself in the morning to have, without a word, allowed such familiarity, but only an iron woman could have rejected his help in such extremity of fatigue and uncontrollable tremors. Wisdom was to accept now and deplore later, she decided. Like a child, she snuggled more comfortably in his arms. Her shivers were already disappearing.

'Thank you,' she murmured, and soon her muscles began to relax.

She was aware that he was looking down at her. His chest rose and fell evenly, but the strong heart under her ear was thumping. As her body warmed, her mind began to function again, to signal her. He was a man, after all, and her dressing gown was made only of thin stuff. Their bodies were pressed together in most intimate contact. He had never been shy before. Wasn't she being naïve to think he would honor her just because he said so, just because he was quietly lending her heat? Nose buried in his shirt, she breathed in the dry, pleasant odor of the soft linen that had been washed in lavender water. And then there was the muskier, sensual smell of his skin beneath it, and a faint whiff of sweat mixed with the pungent hint of leather always present on a rider. In spite of her qualms, his scent excited her, making the pulse beat in her throat. The paradox of it was that she was also soothed being in his arms, comforted by a sensation of rightness and safety that flooded through her. Her breath came out as a quivering sigh because she desperately wished that such were true.

She felt his beard brush her face. Then she realized that it was his lips touching her forehead in a gentle kiss. Startled, she pushed back a bit and looked up at him. He wasn't smiling. She waited for him to say something, waited for herself to pull away, to jump up and run from this trap of intimacy.

'You look like an innocent, small girl in that simple cap,' he finally murmured. His hand came up to play with a lock of silky black hair that was straggling against her neck. 'But, *Dieu me sauve*, you are not a little girl, madame. I think you are a siren. You have crept into my bones, and I cannot sleep for thinking of you'—his quirked smile came out wry—'a condition which has never confronted me before.' His finger strayed beneath the edge of her cap to stroke the lobe and rim of her ear.

Alarm bells must have rung somewhere in her brain, but they were so damped down by the lulling quiet and peace in the carriage that she easily ignored them. She felt heavy, languid, and her protest sounded milder than she intended. 'You must not mistake this, monsieur, the trust of an exhausted woman, for something more than it is.' Halfheartedly, she made a movement to escape him, but he held her more tightly. 'Please——' Now she pushed harder against him, although he scarcely seemed aware of it. At last she heard the alarms.

Instead of letting her go, he arranged a hurt look on his strong features. 'You have my word as a gentleman, Julie, that it is not my intention to molest you. But no one was paying the least attention to your pale face and the tremors you were suffering, certainly the result of fatigue. I noticed your condition when I first arrived at the hut, although you were too busy aiding Mademoiselle to see me pass through. Am I to be blamed for wanting to help you?'

She lay very still against him, wishing she could see his eyes more clearly. 'Why do you want to help me? A few weeks ago, you despised me for being two-faced.' She felt the pounding of her pulse in her temples.

He sighed. 'Ah, madame, how I wish I could despise you. I wish I could do anything but'—he hesitated, and when he spoke there was a thickness to his voice—'desire you as much as I do. Because from the way you have assiduously avoided my company since the day we first met, it is obvious you do not want me.'

But his tone struck her as more theatrical than sincere, and she stiffened. 'I do not believe in desire, monsieur. I believe in marriage.' The moment she uttered the leaden, pompous statement, she wanted to take it back. She felt her cheeks redden.

She could see his slow grin and the gleam of his teeth, even in the darkness. 'But you have already had marriage. Now, why not try the joy of the other?'

'I have had both,' she lied stiffly, immediately annoyed again that pride had made her sound promiscuous.

'I don't think so,' he drawled, maddeningly sure of himself. 'You shy like a colt to the bridle when offered even the hint of an encounter between man and woman. A woman who has been loved would crave it. Would crave me, very frankly.' His appreciative laugh rumbled in his throat.

She decided not to take such monstrous ego one bit seriously. But to let the dangerous conversation go on to an inevitably unpleasant conclusion would surely lose her the warm nest, and his appraisal of her condition as it had been several hours ago had frightened her. She was afraid to fall ill. So she escaped by letting her head roll sideways, away from him. 'Please. I beg you, monsieur. I am *so* tired,' she whispered in a defenseless little voice, and it was no lie.

She heard his even breathing. 'Sleep, then,' came his soft agreement. But she felt him lay his warm hand flat against her neck and cheek in a momentary tender caress of good night, and an astonishing flare of wanting leaped up inside of her, accompanied by a smoldering, interior whisper of his name. 'Oh, Nicolas.' This was followed by an even more incredible jab of rebellious resentment that she was forcing herself to erect walls against this man simply because she distrusted his character. She was a grown woman, wasn't she? Didn't her safety really lie in her complete awareness, this time around, of the fleetingness of such a male's interest? And, armed by this knowledge, couldn't she just enjoy what life was offering and avoid spinning a common liaison into foolish romantic dreams? Her woman's heart and her longing body were so starved.

Deliberately, she turned her face full up to him under his caress. Her invitation was unmistakable and was rewarded with a convulsive tightening of the stomach muscles against which her side was resting. Swiftly recovering his balance, he stared at her. He continued to hold her eyes with his probing gaze while his long, blunt fingers gently pulled open the ribbons of her cap and slipped underneath again to stroke and caress her ear, a simple action that sent a deep thrill of desire to the very pit of her stomach. Her lips, offered to him, parted involuntarily. His head swooped down, and she closed her eyes. She felt his kiss on her neck, burning there against the skin, sending waves of heat through her. He pressed his lips slowly several times along the curve of her throat and then along the line of her jaw, kisses that printed indelible marks on her soul, and when he finally guided her mouth to his with spread fingers against her cheek, she was almost expiring from need of his embrace. She had teased herself with the memory of the stolen kiss at the king's ballet at least once a day for many weeks.

Opening wide the gates, she flung her free arm about his neck and clung to him with her mouth and her body in a burst of pent-up emotion that blotted out everything with its intensity. Her lips moved under his, her mouth opened under the onslaught of his relentless tongue, eager to join her need with his. The taste of him was like cloves; the compelling, musky smell of him sent pangs of yearning lancing through her.

She matched his ardor hungrily and soon cared nothing for her cleverness or awareness or anything else other than that he claimed her mouth again, and once again. And he was greedy in his turn, each kiss passionately bestowed from a slightly different angle. She felt his heart pounding against hers. She knew the closed bud of her sensuality was opening up, poised to burst into exotic bloom.

With a swift, determined movement, his hand dove under the blanket and slipped up between her legs to press there, and she threw back her head and caught her breath convulsively, for in spite of the fragile fabric of her chemise, caught between his hand and her flesh, she pulsed feverishly against his touch. He found her mouth again with his demanding lips. But then a moment passed and he did not move his fingers. A strangled moan escaped him. With an effort, he pulled his lips from hers, grinding out a curse. Then he sighed huskily in her ear. 'No, darling. Not now. Not here. But we will have each other. And it will be right.'

Reluctantly, he removed his hand, and in a reflex action she curled herself up, rolled her face into his chest, and whimpered pitifully, achingly, 'Oh my God.'

But he pressed her back to make her look at his somber face. 'You are weak and tired and entirely defenseless, *minette*,' he muttered. 'How would I like myself if I were brute enough to take you now?' The light blue eyes moved possessively over her face. His voice was ironic. 'But don't mistake me for a martyr, Julie. It is not fine breeding that banks the fire you pour through my veins, preserving your honor and strangling my groin, but amorous imagination. And the infernal damned fact that I gave you my word.'

Her lip quivered. She was suddenly aghast with herself, off balance, vulnerable to him. She would almost have preferred that he had played the beast and taken her on the coach seat rather than crack her defenses with such gallant forbearance. It was not true to the picture she had of him. In emotional disarray, she revealed her deepest heart. 'Oh Nicolas, I am afraid.'

Her little cap had fallen off, and her hair fell like a cascade over the arm that supported her. Brushing away the ringlets on her forehead, he stroked the silky midnight tresses back from her forehead. 'Afraid? Of what, *douce coeur*? Your own womanly sensuality? But your beauty would be empty and meaningless without the warmth of your soul behind it.' He looked away from her then, blinking sandy lashes, staring out the night-darkened window into a distance only he could see. 'I knew a woman once who gave up her life for lack of beauty—because she did not understand that the singular spirit she so wrongly dispensed with *was* her beauty.' He allowed himself a moment more of introspection, shaking his head. And then he was gazing down at her again, a softness in his shadowed eyes.

Suddenly, his expression changed to a grimace. 'If you absolutely need to be afraid,' he muttered, 'be afraid that my leg has become so numb that it is going to fall off in a second and you, dear Circe, will land on your lovely arse on the floor.'

It was so incongruously earthbound a remark that she laughed in spite of herself. 'How do you know it's lovely?' she couldn't help teasing him.

'I told you. I have a most vivid imagination.' He grunted, shifting her weight so he could turn his hip and take the strain off his leg.

'I don't know what you must think of me. . .'

He grabbed her hand and put the backs of her fingers to his lips. 'I think you are enchanting and lovely,' he said against them gruffly, his pale blue gaze warm under his heavy brows. 'I always have, from the moment you tried to kill me. And charming and desirable, and if I tell you any more, that little cap will no longer fit on your head. And I intend to press my suit with you, madame. No matter how many others you dangle on a string, I shall cut them away one by one. And that is what I think of you, my sweet Comtesse.'

'I told you a lie before,' she whispered, 'about having. . .having had both kinds of love.' She felt her cheeks flare, and she bit on the inside of her lower lip. She expected him to tease her.

But he didn't and instead said softly, 'I know. In spite of the passion of your mouth, there is still a pristine innocence in the depths of those beautiful violet eyes. For all you were married, I think you are scarcely awakened. Which makes you a lady both precious and seductive. You will have a hard time, madame, ridding yourself of me.'

She stared at him wordlessly, and somewhere inside

her a bird began to sing, and streamers of flowers reached to wrap around her heart. She wanted to memorize his face—the solid, bearded jaw, the mobile mouth, the straight, strong nose, and eyes that could merrily twinkle or coldly tyrannize or look at her with gentle pleasure the way they were doing now. As she unfolded her fingers, she thought there must be wonder glowing in her eyes, and tenderness, too.

'Now slip down along the seat,' he ordered, patting her rear and letting her go, and when she obediently did so, he bunched up her cloak and made a pillow of it against his thigh and pressed her head down on it. He tucked the blanket about her. 'Now go to sleep, madame, for I trust you are warmer? You have worn out my nobler impulses for the evening.' From upside down, he traced her lips tenderly with a reassuring finger. Then he slid down a bit on his spine, folded his arms across his chest, and firmly closed his eyes.

Julie stared into the shadows of the coach for a bit, her mind skittering about between elation and fear. Then she snuggled deeper into the blanket, putting off all regrets and all blushing examination of the explosion of her suppressed desire until daylight, content to rest against him and reknit the strands of her strength in his shelter. The man confused her, he intrigued her, his aggressive masculinity seduced her. She wasn't even sure how much she liked him. But she was infinitely glad to be with him.

When Julie woke in the blue light of earliest morning, stiff but warm and more rested, she found he had already quietly gone to his duties. She pulled herself together, dressing in the carriage as best she could. The footman knocked and then poured clean, cold water from a bucket into her cupped hands; she drank and then washed her face, wiping it on the blanket. Then she picked her way across the yard to see what help she could be to Mademoiselle. The company was just beginning to stir as she entered, with valets and maids edging between the pallets and adding to the confusion. They were a pitiful sight to behold, these most glorious of all personages of France, as they staggered up groaning from their crowded and uncomfortable mattresses, locks disheveled and hanging, faces haggard and with wrinkles pressed in, limbs stiff.

Mademoiselle was just opening her eyes and seemed not to have noticed Julie's absence from the dormitory, for which her lady-of-honor was grateful, guilty to have slept in less glory but much more comfort. She found a basin and held it steady while lackeys filled it with water from a large jug and then offered it to Mademoiselle. Dant, who had just hurried in, handed her a cloth. The Duchesse yawned, sat up, and swabbed at her face and hands with the wet cloth, then raised her eyes to sourly survey Julie. 'How can you look so fresh, you and the king, too, so I see, when everyone else seems about to expire? It is a scandal,' she muttered. 'Sleeping sitting up must agree with you, madame. Dant, for heaven's sake, where is my cosmetic case. . .'

But then she spied the Comte de Lauzun entering the communal bedroom to find the king and urgently pulled at the cloak still wrapped around her lady-of-honor. 'Quick, Julie,' she hissed. 'Stand before me. I don't want Monsieur de Lauzun to see me, not like this. Pretend you're concerning yourself with my coiffure and conceal me.'

Julie did as she asked. In fact, she was pleasantly surprised. Mademoiselle had never before addressed her by her first name. She offered to the top of the Duchesse's head, 'Your Highness is being modest. Your color is very good this morning.'

'Too good. Probably red as a beet, it's so hot and close in here. Just stand there until he leaves. This sort of circumstance is not fair to a woman's beauty.' Mademoiselle gripped her dressing robe together and sat squeezed small in Julie's and Dant's shadow as they pretended to fuss with the strings of her nightcap. Later, she would dress as she had undressed—in the coach.

Julie listened to the hoarse chatter going on amid the hawking and coughing all about her. It seemed the bridge was finished and the procession could now go on.

The night she'd spent huddled against Nicolas might

have been a dream, except that she no longer had chills.

In Landrecies, everyone went first to morning mass with the king and then hurried immediately to bed in their comfortable billets to sleep most of the day. Julie took supper, as she had promised, with Mercure de Vosges and the next day was pleased to be invited to ride with de Louvois in his carriage. But to her great disappointment, the duties of shepherding and leading such a host were so enormous that neither she nor Mademoiselle saw much of de Courcillon or de Lauzun.

They made a detour northeast to Roubaix, where, of all of the women who pressed behind the king on the battlements pretending to absorb his explanations of the military tactics used to take the city, only Mademoiselle listened with real understanding—followed up by a modest blush as she saw de Lauzun's sour but approving smile upon her.

Nicola did manage to sup with them several times, bringing Mademoiselle's cooks gifts of fresh eggs and cheese and cider. Perhaps he made roguish, fascinating observations, perhaps he only chatted politely with them about the journey, Julie didn't care. She was afraid everyone could hear her heart hammering just because he was within an arm's length of her.

Their eyes met continuously, loath to part. He caressed her with his eyes when there was no better way, and several times as they stood close together, his hand groped for hers and their fingers clasped firmly behind the folds of her skirt. She could feel the pulsing of the blood in his fingers, she wanted to feel his mouth on hers, and she knew he cursed at the overcrowded accommodations as she did, for circumstances conspired never again on the trip to allow them an empty room or unoccupied coach for some privacy. However, the frustration of such cheek-by-jowl waking and sleeping with her neighbors was at least balanced for Julie by the way it neutralized François Michel de Louvois's mounting ardor.

The procession turned back south again, and the plan was to reach the royal palace of Saint-Germain, outside

Paris, early in June. It wouldn't be a moment too soon for everyone involved, even the tireless king, who at last understood that there was a qualitative difference between taking the field with regiments of hardened, seasoned veterans calloused to riding long hours and accustomed to hardships, and an army of ladies and gentlemen whose greatest effort ordinarily was choosing between one scent and another and keeping a smile during weary hours of standing through court events.

CHAPTER
~ 9 ~

'*Ma foi*, I have no patience for this.'

Mademoiselle jabbed in her needle, shoved aside her tapestry, and popped up from her armchair in a sudden fit of pique. 'Please go, leave me, all of you,' she ordered her ladies, motioning them out of the sitting end of her bedchamber, where they were enjoying the soft breeze from the bank of tall open windows. 'How unseasonably hot it is,' she complained, grabbing up her painted fan and wielding it ferociously.

'Shall I bring Your Highness a draught for her headache?' inquired Madame de Plessis-Rabat, gathering up her sewing. The several older noblewomen attendant upon the irritable Duchesse obediently rose and brushed out their skirts.

'No. If I wanted one, I'd ask for it. Your kindness to me would be to depart instantly so I can lie down to rest.'

Although the gaggle of ladies bobbed respectful curtsies, they glanced cautiously sideways at her as they left. Her Highness had been in very short temper since the court had returned from Flanders several weeks ago. Gliding past Julie, Mademoiselle de Greu rolled up her eyes in a sign of martyred patience.

The Duchesse tapped Julie with her fan. 'Not you, Madame de Lowry. You remain.'

Mademoiselle had seemed distracted all morning. Now Julie stood and watched patiently as the tall lady paced up and down in a swirl of rustling taffeta skirts, pounding a balled fist against her thigh. A green emerald, pendant from her pearl necklace, glittered at the base of her throat. 'Oh, he is driving me to lunacy, that man,' she muttered. 'Lunacy. He is impossible.' Mademoiselle stopped abruptly and eyed Julie, standing quietly awaiting her orders. 'Did you know, Comtesse, that before we reached Paris the king revealed to me some dreadful news?' she demanded, indignant, as if it were Julie's duty to know. 'Well, he did, in fact. He informed me that Charles of England was considering putting aside his barren Portuguese wife and was seriously casting eyes in my direction again. *Mais oui!* Remember that night you saw me weep but you didn't know what for? Remember?'

Julie nodded, wary but curious.

'Ah, but *he* knew very well. He saw me weep, too, and his only reaction was to pretend he thought it was because I did not wish to leave France.'

'He, Your Highness?'

'Don't be stupid. The Comte de Lauzun, of course,' Mademoiselle snapped. She clasped her hands together in passionate remembrance, her high brow crumpled, her lips drooped. 'But he knew—ah, that gentleman did not mistake why I wept, for he was just as pale and distraught at the idea I might be snatched from him. And yet, being of such a modest and correct nature, he did not dare to say how he felt. But *I* should have. Just then and there, I should have said what was in my heart. And then, as always, he slid away from the subject, quite literally that time, for one of his lieutenants interrupted us and called him away. And the occasion to speak the truth, as always, evaporated.'

She sat down with a thump on a settee and moodily gazed over its back out the open window toward the delightful June flowering of the Luxembourg gardens and the great central fountain spouting its geyser of shimmering droplets into the hazy blue Paris sky.

Julie didn't know how to respond. As anxious as she was to like de Lauzun, she had to admit he was somewhat peculiar, a man who pretended to elegance but who enjoyed crude practical jokes and who now and then went out of his way to insult Mademoiselle in public—perhaps in an attempt to squelch the rumors of romance he felt were embarrassing the royal lady. But nothing the man did to her angered the Duchesse. The smitten woman saw nothing but modesty and great respect in his sometimes churlish behavior. And when one considered it, Julie thought, perhaps loving a woman so exalted that she was considered for a consort by kings and princes made one a little crazy.

'And *is* there serious possibility of a suit from the king of England, Highness?' she finally asked.

'No, so it seems now. Or perhaps my cousin *Le Roi-Soleil* was just having some sport with me. Charles has decided not to set aside Catherine of Braganza just because she has not conceived. He has plenty of children by others, and a brother as well. What went unspoken is that I am probably too old to produce a royal heir, and the king of England has never forgiven that years ago I rejected his suit.' The curled and coifed head, usually so erect on its crepey neck, drooped. Dejection was dulling the usual ring of her voice. 'I am so weary of feeling a pawn produced at every death of a queen in any royal house of Europe, of being shoved this way and that by politics. And what has my loyalty to duty got me but loneliness? So now I think if I married, the lottery would be over, finished.' She squeezed shut her unhappy blue eyes for a moment. She pounded her fist slowly on the settee's gilded arm. 'The irony is, there finally *is* someone I would marry, if he would only declare himself!'

Mademoiselle turned her drawn face up to Julie then and threw out her hands in dramatic appeal. '*Dis-moi*, Comtesse. You are young, but you have more experience with these things than I did at your age. What is a woman to do? I am a daughter of France. I hint and I hint, but I cannot throw myself at the Comte's feet. I know he yearns for me, but he conceals his true feelings behind a façade of propriety, which is exactly correct but which will in the end ruin our lives. If only I could find a way to dissolve his reserve. If. . .' Her hands collapsed in her lap.

Julie glided up to her and briefly touched her bare shoulder with a sympathetic hand. 'I am afraid my experience does not justify your confidence, Highness. I am not so worldly with men as I might be. If I only knew how to help you, I would do so gladly.' She meant that. For some reason, Mademoiselle had put great trust in her over the eight months she had been at court and had slowly made of her a confidante. Julie felt both flattered and responsible to uphold that trust, and because so much gladness had come into her own life, her spirit brimmed with an elation she wanted to share with the lovelorn royal lady.

Mademoiselle eyed her with a certain speculation. 'But. . .perhaps you can help, madame. Sit down. Here.' She indicated the upholstered stool beside the long settee. 'I have something to discuss, and I do not wish my voice to carry.' She kept her large but shapely hands clasped tightly in her lap as Julie sat down, and then she leaned forward, peering straight into Julie's eyes. 'Can I trust you? Implicitly? *Comme une vraie amie?*'

'Without doubt, Your Highness. I am truly most loyal to your designs.'

Mademoiselle stared for a moment more and then, with a nod and a sigh, drew back, satisfied at what she read in her lady-of-honor's eyes. 'So. I will come directly to the point. I have lately been entertaining a certain idea which I am forced now to employ.' Her eyelids fluttered. 'There are certain potions, I have heard, which, when they are ingested by a man, will break down the inhibitions that block his more tender emotions. Love potions. They are said to be very successful, and, in fact, my Jupiter-cousin's *amour fou* for Athénais de Montespan is strongly rumored to be caused by powerful love spells casting unbreakable magical chains about the liaison.' To cover some embarrassment, she looked down to fiddle with the fan that lay beside her on the settee, then glanced from the corner of her eye for Julie's reaction. She then sat up straighter. 'Therefore, that is what I desire. A love potion to dispense to the Comte de Lauzun.'

An uneven flush rushed up Mademoiselle's neck and face, in spite of the matter-of-factness she was trying to maintain. 'And you shall obtain it for me.'

'A love p-potion, Your Highness?' Julie stammered, surprised. 'But where?'

'*Zut*, you know where as well as I do,' came the impatient response. Now that the worst was over, the

Duchesse had regained some of her poise. 'From La Voisin, of course. You surely have heard of her.'

Who had not heard behind-the-hand tales of the superior practitioner of fortune-telling called La Voisin and her confreres, dispensers of palm-reading, love spells, *poudres d'amour*, and beauty creams—to say nothing of the darker whispers about sorcery, necromancy, poisons called *poudres de sucession*, and methods to help unwanted babies into, and out of, the world. Even the recent shocking trial of the Marquise de Brinvilliers, a mild noblewoman convicted in absentia of poisoning to death her father and brothers and making attempts on the lives of other relatives, had not arrested the widespread clandestine trafficking in magic practiced by many highborn women in a reaction to their powerlessness in a male world. In fact, the blackest whispers of all hissed about the actuality of the obscene rites of the Black Mass or, worse, the Bloody Mass, at which an infant was strangled. Most people, however, wanted to believe that a little dabbling in harmless philters by silly women had been blown up by rumor-mongers out of all proportion.

'If you truly wish to help me, Julie, you will help me in this manner. No matter how I went masked to buy from the sorceress, I should be instantly recognized; you will not deny that I stand out amongst women in my height. But you can go masked and disguised and with discretion obtain for me just the aid that will change my life.' Her lips trembled as shame made Mademoiselle mottle again. 'Or do I ask too much of you? You must speak up if you have no heart for the task. I will not hold it against you. I realize it is not just a trip to the lace vendor in the Place Royale that I request.'

Glad for a chance to prove her loyalty, Julie responded, 'Ah, no, Your Highness, I am quite willing to obtain this potion for you. Only. . .I don't know how to find La Voisin.'

Mademoiselle retreated to her dignity again. 'And neither do I. In all my life, I have had no dealings with such people except for my astrologer, Monsieur Visconti, who is well above the level of such flotsam. But you might ask the Marquise de Montespan. There is no doubt she could guide you, especially if you make it seem your own quest, as you must do to protect me. She would not deny you such help in the cause of love, would she?'

'I don't think so. I can only ask her.'

Impulsively, Mademoiselle reached out and took Julie's hand, her penetrating gaze softened by her distress. 'See, madame, I can think of no other way by which finally to dissolve Monsieur de Lauzun's reticence and yet preserve a shred of my pride in case my heart leads me wrong—which I do not believe for a minute. The man adores me. He needs only a slight push. Therefore, I rely on you, Comtesse.'

As usual when the Duchesse referred to her bantam love, two hectic spots of red appeared on her cheeks and a light glowed in her eyes.

But Julie had to push away a nervous gripping of doubt. She remembered a conversation she'd had with her father just before they'd left for England and the Vicomte's disgust with the flimflammery he saw mesmerizing the ladies of the court—a reaction, he opined in his analytical way, to the devaluation of their status and freedom after the heady emancipation they had enjoyed during the Fronde, when, after the deaths of their fathers, husbands, and brothers, they had directed their own fortunes, made the military decisions, and taken over the armies.

And even in England, Julie had heard of the trial of the murderous Brinvilliers. The truth was that it went against her grain, even just for a harmless love potion, to mingle with the sinister dregs of Paris who purveyed these goods and services. It somehow seemed debased, unworthy of her birth. But she had offered to help Mademoiselle, and she would keep her word. And so, on the surface, her calm remained in place.

She smiled into Mademoiselle's troubled stare. 'Please do not worry, Your Highness. I will obtain the love powders you need.'

'The most *puissant* of them?' A gleam of anticipation crept into the blue eyes.

'I promise.'

Mademoiselle gave a conspiratorial squeeze to the slim hand in hers and warned, 'But not a mention to anyone, madame, heed me. Not even to my godson, de Courcillon, as he walks you so tenderly about in the garden. Men have absolutely no understanding of affairs of the heart.'

Julie flushed, smiling, modestly lowering her lashes at the allusion to Nicolas's attendance upon her. 'I give you my parole on that, Mademoiselle. Not a word to him, or anyone. No one will be the wiser, and Athénais will believe it is I who seek help.'

'I am grateful. You have given me hope, madame. Now, do it quickly,' Mademoiselle commanded, withdrawing her hand to sit with straight spine and head high. Her expression grew bedazzled as she already contemplated the happy spectacle of Antonin Nompar de Caumont, Comte de Lauzun, on his knees before her.

Accompanied by her personal maid, Julie left Paris that afternoon via the Porte Maillot to reach the nearby chateau of Saint-Germain-en-Laye, where Athénais had remained with the king to rest from the sudden, nameless indisposition she'd suffered in Clermont, on the way home from Flanders. 'Miscarriage,' she'd whispered miserably the next day to Julie, who had come to her and was clasping her hand in concern as she lay pale and weepy. 'Stay with me for a while, Ton-Ton. . .'

Now the June air was delightful in the countryside, even if Poilettier was taking the turns and bends in the road at his usual debonair clip. Her new serving maid, Blanchette, sober, silent, wispy in her simple high-necked dress and white kerchief, suffered from sickness if she sat above with the coachman, and now she was perched opposite Julie, quietly enjoying the breeze from the lowered windows. The soft wind slipped like silk along Julie's bare shoulders and tickled her nose with the scent of wildflowers, primrose, and cowslip blossoms, wafting like little giggles above the hearty shout of new-made hay. The coach rattled along the hard-packed highroad, past stands of silver beeches shaking delicate leaves, and elm and oak trees of every shade of green. In spite of what Julie considered in her heart of hearts the beginning of an unsavory errand, a gay tune floated around in her head, and she hummed snatches of it through her smile.

The smile was because Nicolas was at Saint-Germain, having begun his three-month tour of duty as commander of the royal Garde-du-Corps. Nicolas was the joy and terror of her life, for it shook her that an entire room sprang into brighter color when he strode into it; that what began as an ordinary day could turn festive just by the arrival of his note begging her company for a sail down the Seine on the Duc de Longueville's sumptuous pleasure barge, with a picnic afterward; that the merest touch of his hand on her elbow as they wandered the graveled paths of the Luxembourg or strolled with the couples in Louis's wake during the monarch's daily turn about the Louvre gardens was enough to make her heart jump in her chest.

As circumstances would have it, they hadn't had opportunity to be alone in the two weeks since the return from Flanders, but they stole every fleeting second they could to join their lips in the sweetest of kisses, their bodies in hungry hugs, their eyes in bold, flirting promises. And Julie delighted in his male jealousy. Several times, he had allowed the Marquis de Louvois hardly a minute to talk with her before he sauntered up to join them, jauntily disregarding the ire in the cold, black eyes that bored through him.

Her smile faltered a bit when she thought of de Louvois. She was not sure just how to handle the aggressive Minister of War. At first, months back, she hadn't minded his sometimes impolitic curiosity, such as the way he had admired her new set of pearls, meanwhile insinuating how large a sum the necklace must have cost and how smitten must be the suitor who had presented it to her—neither of which indiscreet questions did she answer. Considering that she merely accepted his flattery politely without otherwise leading him on, his interest in her had developed to the point that each look he gave her, each kiss of the hand, held intense meaning. She had begun to find him too precipitous, too presumptuous even in the voluptuous atmosphere pervading the court of *Le Roi-Soleil*. By dint of deft maneuvering, which surprised even her, she had managed to avoid finding herself alone with him without being obvious about it. On the surface, the intriguing de Louvois was in every way a gentleman, paying court to her in the prescribed elaborate manner and ritual, but she'd begun to dislike the impatience she sensed beneath his suavity. And now that Nicolas had looped tender bonds around her, she cared for de Louvois's insinuating tension even less. She would soon have to risk offending him by making clear that their friendship was merely one of sociability.

But that was soon. Now she was being carried along toward Nicolas. She leaned back, a smile playing on her lips again. The Princesse Margarethe and several other court belles he had abandoned for her stared daggers through her. In fact, Diane de Greu, with whom she'd formed a friendship, told her that the disappointed princess was actually languishing sequestered in her hôtel in pique, and taking little nourishment. 'She could live on her fat for a month,' had been Julie's catty, if inaccurate, response. That there had been an affair between de Courcillon and the willowy Margarethe did not surprise her; Nicolas had a lusty view of life and did not willingly put aside its pleasures. Well, she had decided, neither would she, for as long as it pleased her. Nor would she try to kill herself when it was over.

Julie laughed cynically to herself and primped up the crisp fabric of her pink taffeta skirt, which was drawn up by bows to show a pleated white silk underskirt, one of the elegant costumes her newfound prosperity had brought her. The skirt was topped by a tight, pointed bodice festooned with silver ribbon at the neckline, which pushed up her round bosom in fashionable and tantalizing display, although not cut as low as some worn by the bolder ladies which hardly covered their nipples. She wore her old, smaller strand of pearls, and there were tiny daisies scattered through her dark hair. It was too hot for anything more.

She laughed to herself. Decided not to put aside pleasures, had she? Compelled was more like it, forced to throw any caution to the wind by a need for him that she simply couldn't control. She enjoyed being with him; she enjoyed his conversation, his humor, his intelligence. But more than all of these, she wanted him physically, and so bold an admission had been hard for her to make to herself. But she would be cleverer than Margarethe, understanding from the beginning that nothing was forever, especially passion. And the only watchword in Louis's court was discretion. You might take whatever your amusements were with discretion, and none would fault you for more than providing the gossip on which the aristocracy lived.

None would fault you, except possibly yourself. Julie allowed the thought to invade her mind. Now the pale face of the Comte de Vosges danced with the motes in the beam of sunlight lancing across the opposite seat near Blanchette. He was so sweet, Mercure, so sensitive, so sincere, so unfortunate in the defect that made a mockery of his given name. He did not excite her, but she very much trusted him and admired him. Oh, if only she could dare to trust her dashing, commanding de Courcillon. But that would be stupidity, and stupidity was something she had left behind in Sussex with the ruins of her marriage.

The coach sprinted away from the hamlet of Marly and plunged into the deep green forest of Saint-Germain, traveling the turning, twisting road that climbed toward the vast stone and brick chateau perched on the crags high above the valley of the Seine. Now and then, a party of riders from the castle would rejoin the road behind them from the maze of paths and *allées* tracing through the woods. Looking up, Julie spied the walled terrace built by Henry IV running along the height for more than a league and affording stunning views of the vineyards and orchards of the countryside and of the silvery Seine snaking along the plain below. It was from this long, wide terrace that the radiating avenues of the chateau's park stretched to join the *routes* of the great forest.

Julie had already been at Saint-Germain just before the Flanders journey, for the king usually moved his court at Easter week to Saint-Germain or Fontainebleau. Sniffing the spicy scent of flowering bushes, Julie saw in her mind's eye the lavish park laid out behind the fortresslike bulk of the great chateau where Louis had been born, and allowed herself a daydream of strolling among the formal flower beds arm-in-arm with her bearded cavalier.

They rattled through the main gate of the palace and joined the myriad coaches, calèches, and assorted fine conveyances drawn up before the wide steps. As always, where the king was in residence, so was much of his nobility, either in the chateau or at accommodations in the town. Numerous richly dressed gentlemen and ladies were in evidence, mingled with petty professionals of all kinds, tradesmen and petitioners, all scattered throughout the palace's salons and gardens on that charming afternoon.

Informed that Madame de Montespan was on the terrace, Julie hurried there, trailed by Blanchette. She checked her appearance once more in a mirrored wall panel, settling the beaded bodice more squarely, adjusting her shining black curls and tucking back into her hair an errant daisy. She bit her lips to brighten them, although just for general effect, for she had already learned that the king was on a ride with his gentlemen and Nicolas was surely with him.

A striped awning had been erected beside the stone balustrade of the terrace, and under this lounged the king's favorite love, along with various ladies and gentlemen of her choosing. Julie heard her friend's bold, flutelike laugh even before she stepped out onto the breezy terrace.

Blond curls dancing about her head, Athénais turned her classic profile, her eyes widening as she spied Julie. She jumped up from her armless chair and came forward, holding out her hands affectionately. 'Ton-Ton, what a surprise! I thought Mademoiselle was resting in Paris and that I would not see you until Fontainebleau. But you look lovely, *infiniment belle*,' she cooed, her reception somewhat gushing, thought Julie, surprised.

'And so do you,' she retorted, squeezing the hands that held hers. But it was a bit of a tale, for Athénais had still not fully recovered the luminous glow of her skin or the roses in her cheeks. 'I am here by myself, actually, to have a private word with you if you have a moment. It's very important.'

Athénais's blue eyes peered into hers. *'Mon Dieu,* how solemn. I hope nothing has gone wrong with you, *chère amie.'*

'No, no, it is nothing terrible, Coco, just. . .well, if we could talk for a moment. . .'

'Of course. Come with me.' Leading Julie by the hand, she called back to the group she'd left. 'I will return presently, everyone, and then let's have a game of *il fait comme il faut,* but no cheating!' Smiling at the chuckles all around, she glided away, reentering the palace and guiding her guest to her apartment, which was on the coveted first floor, only one story above the ground, right next to the chamber of Louise de la Vallière and not far in the stately progression of rooms from the queen's. Athénais closed the scrolled door behind her, and they were alone in the sumptuous, quiet chamber, which smelled of her rose perfume and the musky, intimate redolence that attaches a space to one particular female. 'What is it, Julie, that you have come all this way from Paris? You look upset.'

Julie drew a deep breath and composed herself, but her hands felt sweaty even though the breeze was finding its way in through the open window. She hated to lie to her friend, but then Athénais had once not been truthful with her either, and what she was about to say would at least hurt no one. She had forgiven Athénais for trying to use her. Craftiness was simply welded to the woman's nature, and Julie should have remembered so and watched out for it. 'Coco, my astrologer cast the same horoscope for me three days in a row—that a certain gentleman for whom I care greatly would soon leave me. To come up in the stars three times leaves no room for doubt, and I am devastated. The friendship is still a new one—if you take what I mean—and I've no chance, with only ordinary means, to bind this man to me. It will break my heart to lose him.'

Athénais moved around her. 'And may I know the name of this gentleman who has captured your heart?' she asked softly.

Julie hung her head, hoping to soften the lie. 'I'd rather not say.'

'Pah, why bother with girlish blushes with me? It's Nicolas de Courcillon, isn't it? Oh, you needn't deny it. The gossips have already been babbling over his preference for you. And yours for him,' she finished dryly. 'Well, heavens, who can blame you? The man is divine. I have to tell you that did I not adore Louis so much, I would surely give you a battle for him.' She chucked Julie under the chin and then went to pour out a glass of barley water from a splendid gold ewer on her writing table, and another for Julie. Ice tinkled in the pitcher. Athénais tilted her head as something struck her. 'What do you mean, with only "ordinary means"?'

'I. . .uh. . .mean, without a certain sort of help.' Julie gratefully accepted the cool goblet Athénais handed her. Her throat was dry from the dust of the road. But her other hand was behind her back, her fingers crossed to keep her misleading information from coming to the attention of the devil, who might then make the tale true. 'I am told there are certain powders which, when mixed with wine or sprinkled on food, can make the object of one's affection more. . .affectionate. I wish to obtain one of these potions.'

Athénais put her goblet against her cheek to cool her skin. Her expression was of false horror. 'What are you saying, madame? Surely the virile Marquis does not need the help of magic to bring him success in the bed of a beautiful woman?'

'Athénais, don't mock me. You don't understand. I want him to *love* me. To love me so that he would not consider the charms of another woman. I am frantic to hold him. Surely you, of all people, can understand. Oh, you must help me.'

'But what do you think I can do?'

'You must know where I can obtain these powders. I am told half the court uses them and that there are perhaps four hundred spell-makers in the city. There is nothing that happens in Paris that you are not aware of.'

'Oh? What have you heard?' Athénais's voice sharpened.

'Why, nothing. But I just presumed that you know. Or that you can tell me who might know where I can find the best of those sorcerers who vend magic potions.'

'Such as La Voisin?'

Julie put down her cup. She was faintly agog at how easily deception came to her. She clasped her hands passionately in an appeal to her friend. 'Yes, La Voisin. Because I hear she is the most expert in obtaining the required responses.'

'You seem to hear a lot,' Athénais remarked with a sardonic edge to her voice. 'And yet you don't know where to seek out the help you need.'

'The salons are full of idle chatter'—Julie shrugged helplessly—'but no one would ever admit. . .oh, Athénais, I appeal to you.'

Athénais narrowed her eyes at Julie for a moment, her stare taking in the raven ringlets on the white brow; the smooth, tilted nose; the round-busted, tiny-waisted figure in the fine summer gown; the wide, lustrous violet eyes gazing so desperately into her own. There was no doubt in her mind that the Comtesse de Lowry had a dark loveliness that might even match her own golden splendor. The king had noticed her, inquired mildly once in a while about her. Friend or not, Athénais considered every comely woman a potential rival for the exalted place she had worked so cleverly to obtain. If Julie's heart was imprisoned by love for de Courcillon, all the safer—and, as she remembered, Julie had a well-developed sense of honor and probably would not so easily cross her up.

Athénais came to her friend's side and took her hands. 'Can we trust each other?'

Dumbly, Julie nodded.

'I need to trust you, Julie. Yes, I know where La Voisin lives. I was first introduced there by the Comtesse de Soissons, and I have been back several times with other ladies. Actually, the woman is an astonishing clairvoyant. She turns up the tarot cards or inspects your palm and predicts your future within a hair's breadth of the truth. And I have purchased love philters from her as well.' Athénais's red lips curled in self-mockery. 'Don't think it is easy to keep the undying ardor of a man such as Louis, who loves women well and surrounds himself with all the young and gorgeous flowers of his realm.' Her dimpled shoulders lifted above the rose faille, pearl-sewn bodice in an angry shrug. 'Women are the most impotent of creatures. We have no rights, no power, nothing but our own being to bargain with. Who doesn't need help to arrange her life to some advantage?'

Peering into Julie's eyes, she said, 'It has been in my mind to visit La Voisin again, but this time for a stronger spell to be pronounced over me, a special one.'

'But Athénais! The king worships you.'

'No, it is not his love I seek to bind this time. It is actually. . .well, a fertility charm.' Her gaze slid away from Julie, and she stepped to the table to refill her glass from the ewer. 'I abhor pregnancy. I detest my body growing more and more heavy until I'm just a misshapen lump that can't move. I hate the pain, the mess, and the futility of laboring under babies who die. I don't even like children much. I am tormented to look so grotesque while the Jupiter-king, father of my unborn child, flirts about with the beauties Madame seems always to nurture in her suite. She does it on purpose, that Henrietta, and in fact I myself was a lady to her when I met the king. But since she cannot have him, she tries to undo me by placing tempting morsels of female flesh under his nose.'

Julie watched Athénais open a drawer in the table and pull out a stoppered silver flask. She then poured a stiff measure of white liquid into the small amount of water in her goblet and looked inquiringly at Julie, who shook her head. Twice Athénais threw back her head and downed the drink in two gulps. She sighed as if feeling better, sidled another glance at Julie, and poured more of the spirit into her glass. 'To strengthen my blood,' she muttered defiantly, drinking it down straight.

When she centered her attention on Julie once more, there was a more relaxed gleam in her eyes. 'But the king loves and cherishes children, *vois-tu*, especially his own. Yet, except for the dauphin, the queen's issue have all died. She births children made of rotten stuff—the Spanish line is bred out. Not one had the sturdiness of the daughter and son I have given Louis, and for this he dotes on my children. And I will give him more. Many more, in spite of the fact that I hate the process, for by that I will bind him to me, and the royal blood in the veins of my children will provide for me in my old age.'

'Have you had trouble conceiving, then?'

'No, hardly, but I have had two miscarriages in a row, and that worries me. I do not wish to seem weak. His Majesty does not like weak women.'

How well Julie knew that. Even so human a thing as needing to urinate seemed a weakness to the king, for he seldom had to, and on the Flanders journey the women about him, royal or not, had suffered tortures because the king would not allow the coaches to stop so that the ladies could relieve themselves.

'Therefore,' Athénais continued, 'I, too, need the intervention of something to help nature behave. We shall share the visit to La Voisin. In fact, I prefer your company to anyone else's, for I can rely on your discretion. So it works out well, doesn't it? I shall have the comfort of your company, and you shall have your potion to enslave your lover.' Her pearly-white smile lit the room.

Julie blinked, her mission achieved. 'When?' she asked breathlessly. Athénais had so easily wrapped up a neat package.

'Next week. We are returning to the Louvre before embarking on the barges to Fontainebleau. I will arrange everything and give you exact instructions.' She casually stroked the silky blond lovelock that fell to her shoulder. 'But you do understand that we will be without the law in attending upon a witch, white as she may be. I rely on you to be totally silent, say nothing to anyone—or we are lost. Agreed? Your word before God?'

'Agreed.' Julie nodded. 'And thank you. I am much relieved.'

The blue eyes gleamed, and the Marquise de Montespan's tone grew gay. 'Ah, but what are friends for if not to help each other? Come, let us go back to the terrace. I have changed my mind. We won't play *comme il faut* but hide and go seek. To watch the jelly-bellied Duc de Nemours staggering from being whirled around, and groping about in all his fatness, is too hilarious——'

Julie was trying to assimilate two opposing feelings, one of satisfaction at having accomplished part of her task for Mademoiselle, and one of trepidation. For at the point when Athénais had underlined the true nature of La Voisin, that of a witch, she was sure she had seen a quick flinch dart across the soft, round-chinned face.

Amid a clinking of spurs and a rumble of laughter and conversation, the king and a group of his gentlemen, followed by two Swiss guards, entered the marble foyer leading from the Queen's staircase just as Julie and Athénais reached it. Louis, outstanding among them even in the simple brocade riding coat that clothed his well-made frame, strode erect and confident, ebullient, the heat plastering his dark curls to his forehead. His keen, intelligent eyes lit at the sight of his mistress, who gave him a radiant smile and a deep curtsy, as did Julie. Ever courteous to women, Louis doffed his plumed beaver hat and swept it to his chest.

'I am truly enchanted, mesdames. I did not think to have such visual pleasure before submitting myself to my gentlemen for the debooting ceremony, as well as to the ministrations of my valet to make me presentable. Contemplating the bountiful charms before me will give me courage to go forward into their hands.' His intensely pleased gaze, sweeping over the two women before him so contrasting in their lush beauty, gave truth to his compliment.

The gentlemen about him chuckled, smoothing down their long hair, brushing dust from their sleeves, for they had ridden far and fast along the country lanes, an alternate recreation to the king's beloved hunting. Julie caught herself envying them. The one thing she missed about Sussex was the wild rides through the fields and over the hills that had relieved the monotonous years of her incarceration.

'Did Your Majesty enjoy the ride?' Athénais murmured, knowing she would hear about it when he came to her at his usual hour of eleven, after supping with the queen. They would sit and talk, for more often it was at their early-afternoon trysts that she tempted him with a wicked, seductive *déshabille* and they would roll about in the uninhibited, lusty lovemaking they both craved. She looked up at him through her lashes, ever Circe.

Louis teased her. 'Indeed, madame, it was exhilarating. There are few activities I can think of to match the stimulation of a long gallop. And yet there are a few. So I am told.' His full lips smiled beneath the tiny moustache.

Not a bit of pink marred Athénais's smooth cheeks. She merely smiled back and looked straight into his eyes in the bold, direct manner that had first captured him with its challenge.

He flicked his dark-eyed gaze to Julie. 'I am happy to see you, Comtesse, but surprised nonetheless. Will I have the pleasure, then, of greeting my good cousin shortly?'

'Alas, no, sire. With Her Highness's permission, I have come to Saint-Germain on some business of my own and will return to Paris and the Luxembourg tomorrow.'

If Louis was curious about what business she had with Madame de Montespan that could not wait until the court passed through Paris the following week, he did not show it.

'Will Your Majesty give permission for Madame de Lowry and her maid to stay the night under his roof?' Athénais asked formally.

'With pleasure, Marquise. Monsieur L'Evremont, will you ask my steward to find a comfortable accommodation for this lady? We have *appartements* tonight, mesdames. I shall hope to greet you there.' Louis nodded and returned his hat to his head, preparing to walk on. But his glance had not missed Julie's covert search through his gentlemen and quick peek toward another group of courtiers coming up the stairs.

The king of France prided himself on his wide knowledge of all his courtiers, their genealogies, their wealth, their loves, enemies, and past and present follies. As he passed by Julie, he leaned above her low bow and murmured conspiratorially, from the corner of his mouth, 'Monsieur de Courcillon separated from our group as we entered, to confer with his officers in the Salle du Garde. I imagine his pleasure at your presence with us, madame.' And, smiling, he walked on.

With short, polite bows and appreciative smiles to the two beauteous young women, his attendant noblemen strode after him, bootheels striking the polished marble.

For a moment, Julie and Athénais simply stared at the retreating royal back of the Jupiter-king, who, in the midst of directing the affairs of a powerful state, had spared attention to a warm involvement developing between two of his train. They turned to each other, each with a raised eyebrow, and broke into a laugh.

But Julie's heart was filled with joy. In fact, it was knocking rapidly in her chest just to know that Nicolas de Courcillon was somewhere in the near vicinity.

Nicolas gazed through an open window in the vast groin-vaulted and tapestry-hung guard room, occupied now by his own company of fifty gentlemen currently on duty, a company of the cavalry called Mousquetaires, and a unit of the Cent Suisse, all part of the king's personal household troops. His attention had been drawn outside and below by faint laughter and cries coming from a small lawn just before the mossy paths leading into the forest. Casually, he watched the gaily dressed group of men and women, looking like summer flowers against the shady greensward, cavorting in the children's game of *cache-cache*—hide and go seek—until one woman caught his eye. Actually, it was the charming pink color of her gown that reminded him of one Julie had worn to a picnic, with devastating effect on him. Then he took in the dark hair curled about the small head and the particularly lissome grace of arms as the woman whirled, laughing, out of the grasp of the blindfolded searcher. He thought the distant laugh he heard was Julie's, a set of chimes only she could ring. Frowning, he tried to make out the face. He wanted it to be the Comtesse de Lowry.

A last wave to his two lieutenants, who were reading out special assignments to their subordinates, and Nicolas clapped on his hat and strode out of the hall. With a bounce in his step that wasn't there before, he headed out to the lawn beyond the *parterre*, heedless of his dusty riding clothes. 'You, monsieur, are dancing to a fine tune in your dotage,' he growled to himself. 'Pinioned to starry eyes and a single roguish dimple at the side of the mouth and lips luscious enough to bite. It might not even be her, fool——'

But he could feel the pulse at the base of his neck beat stronger, like a drum, when, as he drew closer, he saw that it was.

As he came up to the tittering group of players, the lot had fallen to Julie. She was blindfolded with a white chiffon scarf and was being turned about to get her all muddled by the enthusiastic, lanky young Duc de Tremouille, whose busy hands almost spanned her waist. The others surrounded her in a rough circle, calling out teasing remarks to get her to grope toward them. Nicolas nodded silently to several who spied him—Athénais de Montespan, Mademoiselle de Cluny, and the Comte de Rigaurau of the Condé family—then he watched with interest as the group scattered. Julie tottered forward, giggling, her ungloved arms, dripping silk and lace, outstretched, trying to choose which taunting voice to follow. The flaxen-haired dauphin, whose strict and oppressive tutors had somehow allowed the plump nine-year-old this respite among the adults, had a high, piping voice that stood out, and Julie decided to follow him first.

Restricted to the small lawn and just a short way—until the gravel stopped—along the paths leading into the forest, the group danced around their 'blindman,' who then whirled about to lunge at a passing voice or, calling her own threats, launched a rush at a spot where someone had been. Once on a path, the tormentor who inveigled her forward could not escape to the forest on either side but had to slip past the blindman's flailing arms or else go over the boundary mark and lose.

'Aha, I've got you now, Monseigneur. I know your voice. You will not dodge me again,' Julie called out merrily to the grinning dauphin, who danced back just beyond her wiggling fingers, his feet crunching on the gravel.

''Tis not that person. You have the wrong target, madame,' the boy called back, deepening his voice into a comical false tenor to mislead her.

Walking silently on the sandy ground at the edge of the path, Nicolas came up behind Julie, finger on his lips to warn the dauphin to silence. The boy grinned and put his hand over his mouth to stay quiet at this new deception. Following the rules, Julie could not turn back. She had to go forward until her object was forced over the boundary, was caught or touched by her, or managed to sidle past her—in which case she must turn about and choose another of the teasing group to follow. Athénais darted up, smirking, to pull her curls, and a gentleman tugged at her skirt. She swung around grabbing the air, then immediately turned back to keep the dauphin from sliding past her.

But Nicolas had substituted himself for the dauphin, who was cheerfully cooperating by still calling her forward.

'Oh, you will be past the boundary in a trice, whoever you are,' Julie called, pretending the boy had fooled her with his imitation of an adult voice. 'You shall not escape me!' She crouched and flung her arms as wide as they could go, swinging them around. 'And in a moment you will be *it*!' she crowed.

'Oh!' Expecting to catch in her arms a boy shorter than she, she bumped blindly, chest first, into Nicolas, who was standing solidly in her way. *'Mon Dieu!'*

Since the blindman also had to name who it was he'd tagged, by a good guess or by feeling various features— the part of the game most enjoyed by adult players—

Julie's startled 'Oh!' turned into an embarrassed giggle. 'No matter,' she called out to the others. 'Whoever it is has lost to me, and I'll easily name him, too. My fingers are clever in spying out secrets,' she boasted.

Oh they are, are they? Nicolas chuckled to himself.

Her hands slid up his coat again to the plateau of his shoulders, one momentarily fumbling with the embroidered sword baldric slung over his left shoulder. Moving in, her fingers tangled in the waves of his long hair, which hung forward as he looked down at her in amusement. 'Ah, no wig! That leaves you out, Monsieur de Rigaurau, and you, Monsieur d'Arcy. But not you, Tremouille.' She raised her soft fingers upward and the dimple at the side of her chin flashed into being. 'Then it would have to be. . .*Ciel!* A beard? *Nom de Dieu!*' she sputtered, laughing.

Nicolas grabbed the hand fluttering on his cheek and brought it to his lips. With her free hand, she tore off the scarf. Two shining violet eyes, the short, thick lashes fringing them matted by the blindfold, blinked at him.

'Monsieur de Courcillon! Why, what did you do, grow from the forest floor?' she trilled gaily, but the slim fingers against his mouth tightened about his hand in private welcome. She turned to the grinning group behind her and protested, 'Not fair. Even had I guessed who it was, monsieur was not in the game.'

'Therefore, I relinquish the status of "it,"' Nicolas conceded, 'but not the fair seeker. If you will forgive us, mesdames, messieurs, pray continue in your game. I have several private messages for Madame de Lowry which cannot wait to be delivered.' He made a mock bow to the groaning company and with a quick dip swept Julie up in his arms, her long skirts trailing the ground, and carried her away down the path into the cool, soft twilight already gathering under the verdant trees and rhododendron bushes.

Behind them, the usually complacent dauphin capered up and down, caught like the lot of them in the high spirits caused by the clean air. 'I will be "it," I will be. I forfeit my rights. . .' They heard a gurgle as someone took the child up on it and pulled his hair for a chase.

Around a turn in the path was one of the leafy Grecian grottoes dotted about the woods of Saint-Germain for the pleasure of strollers, lovers, and poets. Nicolas deposited his giggling burden on a curved marble bench, and when she had removed her arms from around his neck, he sat down beside her and solemnly straightened some of the daisies in her hair. 'We cannot have you going about looking molested,' he announced.

'This is scandalous behavior on your part, monsieur. Madame de Rigaurau gasped at you like a fish out of water.'

'She looks like a fish out of water.'

'His Majesty, whom I happened to meet, mentioned you were with your company in the Salle du Garde.'

'I was. And at this moment I should have returned to my duty a pace behind and a step to the left of the king. But I have shirked my responsibility in order to say *bonjour* to you, madame, as I have shirked everything else in the past weeks because all I do is think about you.'

'I am glad. That you came to say hello. And that you think about me.'

Nicolas smiled down into the glowing face lifted to his. Her short upper lip kept her lips slightly parted, a sweet situation that shredded his control more than usual after their separation. And control was what was needed here, for he knew that under her fascination with him there was a lurking wariness, like that of a doe pricking her ears while nibbling the sweet grass leading to the huntsman's lair. 'I thought Mademoiselle had begged leave to spend a few weeks in Paris. Or has Monsieur de Lauzun cured his gout and arrived here at Saint-Germain?'

A small irritation at the way he put this almost—but not quite—made Julie's smile waver. Even though the connection he'd made between Mademoiselle's desire to be in Paris and Monsieur de Lauzun's presence there was true—their coaches always seemed to accidentally meet on the Cours de Reine—she didn't like the flippant cynicism in Nicolas's remark. But because she believed he thought he was merely being droll, she let it pass.

'The Comte de Lauzun is still at his hôtel, I believe, as Her Highness is at the Luxembourg. I just came here on an errand for her and must return in the morning.'

'Peace, peace. You needn't get huffy.' He frowned. 'What sort of errand?'

Julie chuckled. 'Sometimes, Nicolas, you act as if you are your godmother's father. It is merely woman's business. The name of a special perfumer Mademoiselle just had to have from Athénais de Montespan.'

'Couldn't she send a page?'

Julie deflected the question with an arch glance. 'I asked to go. I was longing for a breath of country air. It has been so hot in the city.' She watched as he took one of her hands in both of his and held it against his chest like a precious thing. She saw a tiny quiver in the lower lid of one light blue eye.

'You came to see me.'

'Most certainly I did not.'

'Most certainly you did.'

'You would have preferred a page, you just said. Then perhaps you should find one.'

He shook his head in mock disapproval. Carefully, he removed the white-plumed hat from his head, putting it behind him on the bench. An errant ray of the sun struck through the leaves behind him and touched gold to his coppery locks. 'Women who tease will surely pay a price,' he told her.

'Sometimes they may be prepared to. . .'

He drew her closer to him. She so wanted him to kiss her that it made her toes curl in her satin shoes. Her hand remained imprisoned in his. She stared at the strong cheekbones rising above the beard, which was a bit darker than his hair, and saw his lashes lower and then rise again as he took her all in, in deliberate, careful inspection. She saw the straight eyebrows draw together. 'I have missed you, damn it!' he whispered fiercely, and pulled her against him.

He took her mouth roughly, as if he were angry, but his lips soon told her that he was hungry for her. When he let her go, finally, fervid eyes challenging her from behind half-closed lids, her own ardor drove her to lace her arms around his neck and pull his mouth down to hers again.

Her heart was hammering. She could not think of one thing more delirious, more necessary in this world, than the feel, the texture, the hot pressure of his mouth, the insistence of his tongue probing against her lips, the exciting sensation of yielding, of letting him in, coming to meet him. Had she been standing, her knees would have wobbled dangerously.

He broke the kiss to hug her like a bear. 'Oh, Julie——' His breath came ragged against her ear, as if he had been running. 'It seems to be me who cannot pay the price. I cannot touch you without wanting to ravish you, a most unseemly lack of courtesy for a gentleman. And yet'—he held her out from him so that they were staring at each other—'I would even be happy to just look into those limpid eyes all night. As long as you stand a pace away from me,' he conceded, mouth twisted into a self-mocking grin.

She cracked in half. One part of her, the part that was her heart, her spirit, leaped for joy that he desired her. The other part, struggling with her brain, remembered Richard Mountmerry saying almost the very same words—'I would be happy just to look into your limpid eyes the rest of my life'—a miserable memory. But this wasn't Richard, this was Nicolas, a totally different man. More direct, less precious, less dissolute—and yet the same: beloved of the ladies, convinced of his unassailable rightness. To want the beauty of such a man was to forfeit one's soul to him and then to suffer terribly if he turned away. And she was afraid.

Laughter and talk came through the trees. Several people were slowly approaching on the path. Relief flooded through Julie, along with an aching sense of loss. Gently, she squirmed away from his grip. 'Nicolas, there are people coming,' she pleaded, removing his hands from her waist.

'*Nom d'un chien!*' he muttered. 'Their timing is abominable.'

She rose and stood before him a moment, her knees touching his eloquently, intimately, a silent expression of what she was feeling. Then she straightened her skirts and smoothed down her bodice. Patting her curls back into place, she murmured, 'I don't care about being sociable right now. Let's go farther on and find our way back on another path.'

With a resigned sigh, he stood, resettled his plumed hat, and offered her his arm, a regretful quirk on his mouth. She chuckled softly and took his arm, giving the hard muscles a gentle squeeze, leaning in toward him for the quick peck on the lips she wanted as remembrance. They started off, in a few minutes nodding to a footman coming the other way who was lighting the lanterns that showed evening strollers the paths.

'I'll be in for one of Louis's infamous deadly stares if I don't change my costume and return to his side right now.' Nicolas considered the waning light above them. 'He is dressing now to attend the collation before the *appartements*. Will you meet me there this evening, *petit chou?*'

'I shall be delighted, monsieur.' She looked up into his eyes, her smile dimpled.

Three times a week, the king held social gatherings other than the frequent plays, operas, and ballets he commissioned, and since these evenings of gambling, concerts, and billiards till all hours of the morning were held in the series of state salons, or *appartements*, of whichever palace the king was in, they had taken on the name of their location. Julie wasn't fond of cards; she couldn't give it the concentration necessary to play wisely. But a new fad from Rome, a flat, whirling horizontal wheel with a tongue of leather licking between upright spindles to land on a number, was effortless and exciting, and now that she had some discretionary écus to buy counters with, she enjoyed small wagering.

She was just about to tell him he would find her at *la grande roue*, when he caressed her shoulder with strong fingers. 'What chamber have they assigned you?' he asked. She wondered at the gruffness in his tone.

'I don't know yet, but my maid Blanchette must

already be there. One of the footmen will find out for me.'

Nicolas turned her around to face him, his grip hard on her shoulders, although his voice remained low. 'Will you tell me tonight where I can find it?' he demanded with his usual directness.

Alarm bells went off in her head even as a thrill of excitement climbed her spine. Her imagination spun. In that brief second, she imagined being alone with him in the total privacy of a fragrant bedchamber, their bodies naked together and silken, passion darkening his eyes, the heat of his hand on her back as he gathered her into his hard embrace, the silvery light of the moon from the window striking across the strong, sensuous mouth that she wanted to trace all the curves of her body, to kiss her all over, over and over——

Her eyes went wide. She felt a hot blush climbing her cheeks, spreading across her forehead.

He shook her slightly, waiting for a response.

Flustered, she managed to give him an enigmatic smile. 'Perhaps,' she said, turning her head away as if in sudden coquetry. But the clanging bells of warning kept up a clamor inside of her. She just wasn't ready yet.

They walked onto a cross path ahead. Nicolas's gaze slid to her seductive profile. She confounded him. She had left him no doubt that she was a loving, passionate woman. And she was the survivor of a long marriage, not some shrinking maiden. And yet there was something virginal about her, a decorous reluctance to follow her own inclinations, so opposite to many women at Louis's romance-infatuated court. Already he regretted having frightened her with his aggressive suggestion, for if she demanded patience, she would get it. He was certain that eventually she had to yield to her own lust, which he had tasted on her clinging lips, felt in the pressure of her body against his, seen smoldering in her eyes gone deep purple with desire—and which was driving him mad to satisfy.

Just as he was certain, finally and not without a struggle, that he loved her, Julie de Croixverte-Mountmerry. And that he would never force her will.

She had too much of his heart in her delicate hands. Damn it!

Helplessly, Nicolas yawned behind a polite hand and cast another despairing glance around the salon, searching among the groups engaged in animated, witty repartee, scanning the tables of intent card players for the one face that held any interest for him. She wasn't to be seen. She wasn't at the clacking wheel of chance in the gallery, either, among the press of gamblers whose often ruinous debts were not disagreeable to the king—debts and idleness kept his nobility under his thumb. Nor was she in the small audience in another salon listening to a singer and lute or with the young people dancing to a violin in another. Her charming laugh was not to be heard amid the company's chatter and laughter and the occasional victorious shouts from the winning plungers at Hoya. Julie de Lowry was nowhere about the public gathering rooms of Saint-Germain, and her self-appointed cavalier was fretful and beginning to worry.

'But really, Monsieur le Marquis, you aren't listening. Do I bore you?' The tall, blond Clemence de Nataleys pouted her thin-lipped smile, sleek and bland as a thoroughbred. She tapped him on the arm with her fan. 'As Monsieur de la Rochefoucauld often says, "It takes two to make a bore, *n'est-ce pas*?"' She winked. Her long curls, the color of pale champagne wine, were modishly wired to stand out wide from her head. A lovelock fell past one shoulder to point discreetly to her deep décolletage.

'Your pardon, *chère* madame. It was but a momentary lapse, the result of a long day of riding with the king,' Nicolas apologized. He had always regretted the flirtation he'd carried on with the cool lady a couple of years back, a brief and tiny flame, soon out, but one which she tried to rekindle at every opportunity.

De Nataleys daintily took two candied fruits from a tray carried past by a servant and handed him one. 'It seemed to me you'd care to know the latest scandal from New France, dear Nicolas. The curé in Montreal I was mentioning, who tore out so many pages he considered objectionable from de Coramont's precious copy of Petronius, did not fare too well. You remember de Coramont. He was exiled for dueling. My brother writes that the man swore he would tear just as many tufts out of the priest's beard, and he did do so and very roughly. Antoine writes that the bishop is considering excommunicating de Coramont...can you imagine?' She paused to laugh. Such high-handed behavior from the church was unacceptable in Paris.

Nicolas laughed with her, politely, but he had heard the news before, several times, a silly bit of business. Just then his friend Jean de Fort passed by them unnoticing, his eyes fixed on some goal across the room. With a dart of his hand, Nicolas snagged de Fort's arm and in a trice had slipped the surprised but willing gentleman into their tête-à-tête. '*Tiens, mon ami*, I do not think you have had the fortune to meet the Baronne de Nataleys? Let me hasten to rectify this oversight. Madame, may I present to you my colleague in the Garde-du-Corps, Monsieur de Fort?'

Dazed by the precipitous introduction, de Fort fumbled to kiss the statuesque blonde's hand and stammered his delight to make her acquaintance.

'My friend here once confessed to me that he had gazed admiringly at you, madame, from afar at many gatherings,' Nicolas fabricated, edging away as de Nataleys made a raised-eyebrow survey of the stocky, red-cheeked young guardsman. 'I thought perhaps you might rescue this languishing gallant from his shyness.'

The young woman's cool demeanor didn't extend to being one bit immune to flattery, and de Fort, good-naturedly going along with a situation he promptly understood, was not shy, certainly not in the case of this patrician, jewel-covered lovely. In a moment, the two were caught up in the verbal minuet of sounding each other out, so that after a sketchy bow, Nicolas was able to detach himself and slip quickly away.

The palace steward was not hard to find. He was in his cluttered little office at the rear of the great mansion. It took only a wink and a silver écu to obtain the location of Madame de Lowry's chamber on the second floor.

Making his way by a back staircase, Nicolas soon presented himself at the apartment in question. But as he raised his hand to scratch at the door's dark, waxed wood for admittance, he stayed it a moment. From inside, he heard Julie's voice speaking a calm, short phrase. She seemed to be standing quite close to the door, although he could not get the exact words or her maid's answer. Well, at least she was up and about and not prostrate with some illness. With his square, blunt nails, he politely scratched for entry.

Halted in her restless pacing of the room, Julie stood transfixed between one step and another, the hooped embroidery she had been attempting to fill the hours with forgotten in one hand. She had just informed Blanchette that she would commence to disrobe, now that the hour seemed too advanced for her to attend *appartements*. She felt tired from the strain of her divided desires: to go down to meet Nicolas or not. Yet she was relieved that she had found the fiber to sit out the evening by herself rather than fall prey to the great allure of the man.

Finger on her lips, she made a silent urging motion to the servant, who was hesitating. Blanchette finally approached the door and called out a timid, 'Who is there?'

'It is Nicolas de Courcillon. I wish to see Madame de Lowry,' came the muffled reply.

Blanchette's response was to roll questioning eyes at Julie, who stood rigid as a statue, her lower lip clamped under her teeth. She had never expected that he would make his way to her door. She shook her head emphatically and waved her hand at the nonplussed Blanchette. Then, with more violent motions, she urged the woman to say something, anything, to put a stop to the insistent scratching and get him to go away.

'Ma-madame is not here. She's not here, monsieur. She is at gaming with Ma-madame de Montespan. Below,' Blanchette cried out desperately, improvising as best she could.

There was a momentary pause during which Julie tried to still her heart by hoping Nicolas had believed the maid and gone away. But only the polite scratching had gone away. Now his knuckles rapped loudly.

'Madame *is* in there. I heard her speak just now. Julie! What is wrong? Open up.'

Julie continued to chew on her lip. She nodded frantically again to encourage Blanchette, who was very bad at lying and knew it.

'Uh. . .*oui*, monsieur, she is ill,' Blanchette cried, and Julie smote her forehead. *Peste!* The little idiot! She had meant for her to insist that her mistress was elsewhere, that the gentleman had been mistaken. Now her eyes darted about, as if she had some chance of hiding. She was beginning to feel ridiculous.

'Ill?' came Nicolas's muffled exclamation. 'Of what? Tell madame I am very concerned and I must see for myself how she is,' he demanded. Julie bridled, even in her embarrassment, at such arbitrary assumption of responsibility for her.

'She's very ill, sir, and don't wish to see anybody tonight. Tomorrow she'll be better. So. . .so please go away. Sir,' Blanchette quavered doggedly, 'Madame don't wish to see you.'

The door latch jumped and jiggled, but by luck, Blanchette had turned the key in the lock. Now the puzzled man outside turned irate, using his fist to pound on the door so that Julie ducked her head and held her ears. *Sacre Dieu*, the whole palace will hear him, she thought in a panic, kicking off her mules and tossing the embroidery to a chair. Had he no sense of propriety?

'Listen, woman. First madame is not in her room but with the Marquise de Montespan, and now she is so ill she cannot admit a friend who wishes to help her! What is going on in there? I command you to open this portal immediately, or I will bring some help to break it down,' the king's captain barked, pounding heavily on the thick old door. Julie threw up her hands and fled to her bed. Blanchette, undone by the ruckus, skittered after her.

'I will keep up this racket until everyone in the palace rushes to see what's amiss,' Nicolas thundered. 'Please let me in, Madame de Lowry!'

There was no time to undress. Julie yanked the pins

from her hair with one hand and whipped back the bedclothes with another. She flung herself onto the pillows, pulling the sheets up to her neck to hide her gown. 'Allow him in,' she hissed at Blanchette. 'But do not leave this room, on pain of death. No matter what he says. Act as if I'm sick.'

Blanchette bobbed her head distractedly and then ran to unlock the door, opening it to catch Nicolas's fist in midair. Red in the face, he marched past her and looked about to see Julie in the bed, reclining in an attitude of suffering, a presumably wet handkerchief posed on her forehead. He strode toward her. 'I don't understand, *madame*, why I must use a battering ram against your door to have a simple interview with you.' He stopped and studied her carefully with his direct gaze. 'Although at least this time you didn't welcome my entrance with a lead ball. I suppose I should feel some sort of friendly progress has been made.' He chuckled darkly, his sense of humor returning. 'Do you have a headache, madame?' he added with solicitude.

Julie sighed. 'Oh, Nicolas, how kind of you to come. But even you can't really ease my suffering. My head is like a drum being beaten. Oh, it is painful.' To herself, she wondered uncomfortably, How in the world did I get myself into this? She was not at all enjoying the pretending.

'The fact is that I became alarmed when you did not attend *appartements*, so I came to look for you. What can I do to aid you, *pauvre petite*?'

'Nothing, truly, but I do appreciate your concern.' Julie invented a pained grimace and then a pitiful moan, then glanced up through her lashes covertly to see if he was affected enough by her extreme discomfort to go away. 'Just leave me here to my faithful Blanchette, and I'll be recovered tomorrow.'

'But Julie, *chérie*, tomorrow you will be heading back to Paris.'

'Yes, unfortunately, Mademoiselle expects me. And that truly makes me sad. I shall miss you, Nicolas.'

He stepped closer, tilting his head in contemplation of her. 'Why did Blanchette at first say you weren't here?'

Julie gave him what she hoped was a shame-faced smile. 'Oh, that was rude of me. I beg your pardon. I just didn't want you to see me this way.' She had the grace to blush a little for all her subterfuge.

His tone was sympathy itself. 'Do you get this sort of misery often, poor *minette*?'

She shrugged as well as she was able under the sheet she held taut over her shoulders. 'Once in a while. My poor mother suffered from headache, too, I remember. She always needed rest and solitude to cure it.'

A repressed expression seemed to be tugging at the corner of his mouth. He clasped his hands behind him and rocked on his heels, contemplating her with eyes glinting like chips of aquamarine from under his half-closed lids. 'How very peculiar. You seemed in excellent health this afternoon. And in fine spirits.'

'Yes, didn't I,' she agreed in a weak and martyred voice, nervously swallowing down the feeling that he was playing with her. 'These miserable afflictions do come on so suddenly.' Her arms were getting tired from her convulsive clutching of the sheet.

'*So* suddenly that you neither divested yourself of your earrings, necklace, nor the very ribbons in your hair, madame?' he accused.

Julie gawked at him, her heart dropping into her stomach with a thud. Now she damned the telltale color for coming up in her face.

'In fact, my dear, a blind man could easily see under that sheet the outline of the gown you neglected to take off when this mysterious affliction hit you.' He sounded exasperated. 'You look superbly well to me, the picture of health. I suggest you get out of that bed and make an attempt to explain what this game is.'

She balked at his officious manner. Using indignation to cover her mortification at being discovered in such a silly deception, she huffed, 'How dare you order me about, monsieur. I am not your wife to bully.'

'Nor even my lady,' he muttered, 'and at this peculiar rate might never be.' He moved toward her as if he was going to rudely pull her from her cocoon. Aware that such a peremptory move was not beyond him, she quickly sat up. She swung her legs off the bed and stood erect, suffering Blanchette's rush to smooth down her skirts.

Chin tilted, she still clung forlornly to brazening her way past her embarrassment. 'There! Now are you satisfied? Really, monsieur, your unkindness in the matter of my hasty need to lie down has quite exacerbated my headache.'

But he wouldn't let her off the hook. He studied her down the length of his nose. 'Headache, my arse. You have no headache! But maybe you were awaiting someone? Someone other than the susceptible gallant with whom you had made a prior rendezvous at the giant wheel?'

'Oh, *cochon*, would you perhaps like to look under my bed?' she gritted, happier to be angry than to feel foolish.

He took her by the upper arms, peering with genuine puzzlement into her eyes. 'Julie, I'm sorry, forgive me. That wasn't nice. It was merely the jealousy of a disappointed man. *Doux coeur*, won't you tell me why you did not come to meet me and why this charade when I came to see you? Did something occur to make you angry with me?'

Her mouth opened, but nothing came out, and then her lip trembled. What could she tell him? That he attracted her so much she was frightened of her own responses? She did not care to sound like a child who could not control her own emotions. Actually, it was the pace she found too fast; this was backward of her, perhaps, but the truth. She wasn't ready.

But Nicolas was not naïve in the retreats and advances of women. He saw her blush and hang her head and realized he had made a misjudgment earlier. Her head had not caught up with her heart. He let her go then and said, 'It was my crude suggestion this afternoon, wasn't it? I frightened you. *Comme tu es ingénue, madame*. Did you think I meant to attack you?'

'No, of course not. But I-I suppose I'm yet a country cousin in many ways. It—it didn't seem quite proper for you to attend me all alone in my chamber.'

'But your maid would have been present,' Nicolas reminded her reasonably, glancing at Blanchette, who huddled on a stool in the farthest corner from them. 'Just as she is now. You wound me, Julie. Do you consider me such a beast that you cannot trust yourself in a room with me?'

She felt pained that he might think such an untrue thing. She took a deep breath and looked up into his hurt eyes with sudden courage. The role of shy maiden wasn't really her. 'You've said it correctly, monsieur, but with the wrong emphasis. Trust *myself* is what is wrong.' Abashed, she dropped her eyes involuntarily. 'I am so very drawn to you, Nicolas. That could hardly be a secret to you. I seem to lose my equilibrium when you touch me.'

He pushed up her chin with a finger. 'And what is wrong with that?'

'N-nothing. But I am unused to such a situation.'

'I certainly hope so. But does it displease you?'

She sensed that only the truth counted now. She obeyed her desire and reached up to caress the soft, short beard along his jaw. 'No. It makes me more happy than you can know, to lose myself in someone else. I just need some time to get used to it.'

Suddenly, he grinned. 'A lot of time?'

Listening to the insistent clamor of her heartbeat as the heat of him came through her fingers, she could only utter, 'No, Nicolas, just a little.'

'I will take you at your word, *ma douce*. Be warned.'

Her gratitude for his understanding, her very need of him, beamed out in her smile. 'Oh, Nicolas, I am not always the coward I appear at the moment. You must know that.'

He moved back a bit and shook his head. 'What I know is that sometimes you baffle me, madame. And it is not my habit to feel off balance, either.' He tried another tack to make sense of her. 'You said you will miss me when you leave. Is that true?'

Feeling much more confident of her safety, she stood close to him and put her arms loosely around his neck. 'I swear it. I have missed you terribly all along. You are not so easily done with, Monsieur le Marquis.'

'Very well, then, *cher coeur*. We shall see what the future brings. Will you at least allow me a good-night kiss?' With a finger, he toyed with a shining strand of black hair lying on her shoulder, then gently pushed it away to join the others.

'Of course.' She laughed, relieved beyond measure that his patience with her still held. Hands on his shoulders, she reached up and quickly pressed her lips against his, hard, passionately. Then she danced back before he could enfold her, or her own feelings entice her into more than that. The feel of his lips, the essence and scent of him were reaching out to imprison her.

He let her go and gave her his quirky smile, though his eyes were merry once more. 'That was far from satisfactory, even for a friendly good-night embrace. But since you must leave tomorrow, we will let it do. I will see you at Fontainebleau, madame, if not in the morning at chapel.'

They stared at each other for an instant. Love's silent promises traveled between them.

Then he saluted her and was gone, and with his absence the atmosphere of the room seemed to deflate like a balloon. There was emptiness. Already she missed him. Already she was beginning to regret her simpering. She was completely aware that she could not temporize with Nicolas as she could with Mercure or the others. He was too aggressive. He had magnanimously allowed her some skittish coyness this time. He wouldn't again.

A pestilence on her irresolution. She didn't want him to allow it.

CHAPTER
~ 10 ~

Monsieur La Reynie, Prefect of the Paris police and a top-notch administrator, considered himself a moral man. Placed in a position that allowed him to do good or evil to even the highest among men, and to command the lives of the poor, he had tried hard to maintain scrupulously fair standards set to produce as little harm as possible. He was proud of the headway he'd made in mopping up the cesspools of humanity in Paris, proud of the protection he'd given Huguenot property and churches against Catholic persecution, and aware that he had made certain efforts to ease the lives of the humble, the beggars, the foundlings, and the vagabonds inhabiting the city's underworld.

But he had been too dumbfounded to know how to cope with the horrifying facts that one night came tumbling from the mouth of the anguished black-and-white-robed priest from Notre Dame. The cleric had agonized for months about keeping the secrets of the confessional, but finally God had sent him to La Reynie to whisper in distress the word *poison*. Too many of the good father's parishioners were confessing to him to murdering someone by poison. The horrified priest would name no names except those of two rascals mentioned over and over as practitioners of the unsavory arts.

By nature a cautious man, La Reynie first sent an accomplice to buy from a Madame Bosse and a Madame Vigoreaux a vial of poison for the express purpose of dispatching an inconsiderate husband; and as this purchase was accomplished with no difficulty, the two were arrested and taken to the dungeons of Vincennes. They insisted that they were only fortune-tellers, but under the right persuasion, they were able to name many of those in Paris who were also dealers in vile potions.

One of the names they gave most importance to was a Madame Catherine Monvoisin, commonly called La Voisin, popularly considered merely a superior reader of palms and cards, with a large circle of highly placed clients. So highly placed, in fact, that sweat broke out on La Reynie's high forehead to contemplate going to his director, de Louvois, the Minister of War, with such a volatile story. It was still as unproven as all the other trumped-up tales whispered about Black Masses and human sacrifice and revolting couplings between man and beast. The guilty must be apprehended—that was justice. But it seemed to the Prefect that it would be better to have some proof of evildoing other than confessions under torture before taking the chance of dragging some of France's most illustrious names through a scandalous muck.

Accordingly, he organized a secret raid on the premises of La Voisin with the object of going before Monsieur de Louvois with solid evidence. But—in the interests of tact and an intuitive fear that the sky might fall in—he determined to make sure that any innocent clients caught on the premises would have their identity protected from the public.

Monsieur La Reynie was a responsible official. He would not contemplate shirking the investigation of such whiffs of horrendous behavior, in spite of what he feared he might unearth.

The sky was a dark slate, still heavy with clouds, although the rain had stopped. The cobbles of the sodden, littered streets still glimmered as Poilettier drove Julie in a trim calèche, with a dark cloth pasted over the Duchesse de Montpensier's coat-of-arms, toward a rendezvous with Athénais on the Right Bank of the Seine.

Was it close to five o'clock, Julie wondered? She wished she could see the face of her new timepiece hanging from a fine link chain about her neck, and she hoped she wasn't late. Mademoiselle had been in a nervous tizzy all afternoon, first wishing Julie luck on her quest, then deciding she shouldn't go, then changing her mind in a cycle of fits and starts so that when she finally ordered Julie to go, it became a question of speed to make the appointed rendezvous—hence the swift little calèche.

But Julie fingered the tiny clock, even if its message was unreadable in the uncommon gloom of threatening weather. It was a lovely present from Nicolas in apology for having offended her at Saint-Germain, and it had been delivered with a note warning that if she did not accept his most penitent offer of contrition, he would arrive in person and camp before her door until she did. The knave! But even before the gift arrived, she had already examined her own infantile behavior at Saint-Germain—barring herself in her room that evening with an 'indisposition' and not allowing Blanchette to open it to him when he came to inquire on her health, then departing in haste at dawn the next day. She had cringed at the memory of her stupid panic, insulting him where no insult was meant. And so she gratefully accepted the gift, sending back a note of thanks and her own embarrassed apology. She would not forget the fast drive back to Paris when, in the sunny June morning, she recovered her senses and considered how pleasant a threat, truly, she was fleeing. A few anxious tears had slid down her cheeks then with the thought that he might return his attentions to the less silly Princesse Margarethe.

The small timepiece was lovely, with a black face and a gold hand and a rotund back of gold inlaid with enameled flowers and her initials, 'J. de L.' She loved it. Her fingers stroked it often.

They arrived before the imposing length of the Hôtel de Ville, the City Hall. A coming and going of damp Parisiens squelched across the puddles on its wide plaza, which was called the Place de la Grève, and conveyances to hire were lined up in the center. At one end of the open area, an unmarked carriage waited silently, its leather curtains down, and Poilettier headed directly for it. Julie drew up her black velvet mask; it covered all of her face to her mouth and chin. Masked aristocrats of both sexes caused no comment on Paris streets as they went about their business shielded from prying eyes, or from the sun's tanning rays, or even from impurities in the air that caused skin ulcers.

The leather curtains moved, drawn aside slightly by a gloved hand as Poilettier pulled up and hailed the other coachman garbed as he, without livery. He set the steps, and Julie descended from the calèche. She had on a simple gown of dark blue serge, and a white chiffon scarf covered her hair and shoulders. From the other coach, the footman handed down Athénais, dressed in the same plain manner, her blond hair concealed with a pale blue scarf. But her maroon velvet mask was decorated with embroidered gold bumblebees.

'Wait here, both of you,' Athénais ordered the drivers, 'for however long we shall be, and it may be hours. Talk to no one, tell no one for whom you attend. And don't leave. Come, madame.' She took Julie firmly by the elbow and guided her off. 'You are late,' she hissed. 'I must return and dress before eleven tonight, which is the hour Louis visits my apartment. We must hasten!'

They hurried across the plaza to the public hire station where coaches and sedan chairs waited, and Athénais hailed one, convincing the sullen driver with an offer of thirty écus that he wished to go all the way out to the suburb of Villeneuve-sur-Gravois. It was a sum he could not otherwise hope to make in a week of driving.

Athénais was in a removed mood and said little as they rattled along, but she pulled off her gloves impatiently, and her fingers twined and intertwined. She cracked her knuckles. Her red mouth twisted sometimes with an unexpressed thought, and she bit her lip. Julie had never seen her domineering friend so nervous, but then, neither was she herself so calm.

'They say it may have been La Voisin from whom the Marquis de Brinvilliers obtained the arsenic with which she murdered her family.'

A small shrug. *'O là, on dit?* One can buy arsenic or antimony from any apothecary. You slip it into your loved one's weekly enema, and, *voilà*, you have achieved your purpose.' A typical Athénais answer.

'Madame de La Fayette related to Mademoiselle's salon one day the tale of a man whose clothes had been dusted with arsenic and who developed in his groin every terrible symptom of syphilis.'

'*Tant pis*. The pig should have brushed his clothes out before he wore them.' Athénais turned to stare at Julie. 'Why is your conversation so morbid this evening? You are only coming along for a little *poudre d'amour*. And from the way de Courcillon carried you off from our little game at Saint-Germain, you've scant need of it.'

'Very well, I won't be morbid. But then, why are you so nervous? The woman is just going to say a spell over you, isn't she?'

'Yes, she and some assistants to help her. It's just that I. . .' Athénais looked down at her hands, picked at a nail. 'Well, it's possible, Julie, that the process may take long. Do please wait for me, even if another customer should offer you passage home.'

'*Mon Dieu*, I would never do such an impolite thing as to leave you.'

Athénais's smile was strained. She patted Julie's hand. 'Yes, I know. I just wanted to make sure.' She turned to look out of the window again, subsiding into brooding silence.

Julie's unease deepened. Athénais, usually so sure, so cocky, was sitting taut enough to jump out of her skin. Something was shaking her, and Julie did not believe it was the possibility of being seen trafficking with conjurers of love potions and fertility charms. Perhaps she herself was a fool to carry her devotion to her employer so far as to mix with the sinister riffraff of palm readers, magicians, and gypsies. But the die was cast; she wouldn't turn back now. She remembered Mademoiselle's bright cheeks as the woman related to her exultantly that de Lauzun, his eczema under control, had come to call just the evening Julie had been at Saint-Germain. She had threatened the stiff little Comte that she would breathe upon a mirror and write her true love's name thereon, and he threatened to leave if she would do such a thing and blushed furiously. But yet he held her hand to his lips so desperately and with such poignant looks...The love potion was all the more vital now, while the iron was so hot, Mademoiselle had decided at the last, and sent Julie off.

The hired coach left Paris by the Porte Saint Denis. Not too long after, the horses slowed and under heavy skies plunged off the main road into a rutted path, lined with trees and tangled brush, along which they bumped for at least ten minutes. The end of the road proved to be their destination. Driving through a thick arch in a stone wall, they pulled up at the portal of a very old, large, and gloomy stone manse with round towers at either side of the entry. In the cleared space before the door waited several unmarked conveyances, drivers slumped patiently on their boxes or sitting hunched against a wheel. No light shone from the abode, for all the windows were shuttered, a curious thing for a warm if rainy evening. And even more curious, Julie noticed, black smoke was puffing out against the shifting clouds from a chimney somewhere behind the house. A chorus of whispers filled up her head again, susurrating about furnaces that burned the bones of aborted babies and sacrificed animals, and hundreds of little graves hidden in the woods in unconsecrated burials...

They descended the coach, and a pock-faced servant at the thick iron-bound door inspected them silently. After receiving some coins from Athénais, he grunted and pulled open the portal by its iron ring. Except for the squeak of the door hinges and the constant rustling of the leaves of the trees surrounding the house, there was an uneasy silence pervading the storm-threatened evening, no sound of bird or peep of frog. Not even a human voice from within the manse. The door yawned open, and they entered into gloom. Julie suppressed a little shiver and followed in Athénais's more bold steps. They found themselves in a large flagstoned hall empty save for wavering shadows cast on dirty stucco walls by candles burning in a single standing candelabrum.

Coming across the echoing hall to greet them was a servant, a perfectly ordinary woman in white apron and cap who bobbed a curtsy when she reached them. 'Ah, *c'est* Madame L'Abeille,' she greeted Athénais. 'You are awaited. Come with me, please.'

They followed her through a door into a passageway, lit by a grudging flare here and there, whose low ceiling, after the expanse of the shadowy hall, added a feeling of constriction to Julie's throat. Except for the click of their high-heeled kid mules and the servant's shuffling raffia slippers, the silence continued as they passed a series of closed doors. They went up several steps to another level, then went around corners and down a few steps. The old country house was built like a maze, with numerous nooks and crannies and side passages. With a sinking feeling, Julie realized that one would have a difficult time finding the way out without a guide.

But Athénais stepped along more confidently; she had been this way before. 'We are to see La Voisin herself,' Athénais whispered, squeezing her hand. 'She has a number of associates who help her, because her readings and divinations are as much in demand as Monsieur Visconti's, the queen's horoscopist. But rank has its privileges,' she boasted with smug satisfaction, 'and I deal only with her.'

'Surely she doesn't know who you are,' Julie whispered in return.

'She only knows me as the lady with the bee-embroidered mask. She calls Madame de Soissons, "the green mask," and my sister-in-law, the Duchesse de Vivonne, "the silver bow knot." But subterfuge is useless, as you will see. One can hide little from a woman with such powers of looking into the unknown. But don't be fearful. La Voisin's fortune—and her powerful contacts—are built upon her utter discretion.'

'Where are the owners of the carriages we saw outside?'

'Closeted in this room or that throughout the house conducting what business they came for, with her assistants Le Sage, a master of magic, or Broulet or the tiny La Pertingai—I'm sure you've heard of her. She is the most successful with powders to alleviate male impotence.'

At last, the succession of doors appeared to end. The servant stopped before a dim alcove in which was a wider portal. It was bracketed with heavily carved moldings. Before it, teetering on a stool, was a coarse-looking, burly man in a food-stained cassock. He got up to make an awkward bow, and Julie noticed the tip of a wide sword scabbard protruding beneath the hem of his gray robe, definitely not one of the dressy rapiers worn mostly as an accessory by male fashionables about the court. The maid opened the heavy door, which moved back with hardly a scrape, and nodded them in. The moderate light that greeted them from several burning candelabra seemed like a blaze after the murky passages they'd traversed.

There were no windows. The unoccupied room was enclosed all about with crimson velvet draperies suspended from a ceiling of velvet pleated and draped like a pavilion. The floor was covered with thick Oriental carpets. The air was still, laden with the sweet smell of incense. In the middle of the floor was a round table covered with a crimson cloth, the drop of which displayed a huge, double-headed gold eagle with a writhing lizard in its claws. At the table were three seats: a gilded armchair of regal proportions and two upholstered tabourets.

Athénais guided Julie to a tabouret and took the other for herself. It was hot in the muffled chamber. They both lowered their scarves off their shoulders and drew small, plain parchment fans from their skirt pockets.

Athénais's golden curls gathered a gleam of light from the tapers in the iron chandelier suspended above the table. She perched in silence at the edge of her stool. In a few moments, she gave Julie an encouraging smile, but her fingers drummed nervously on the purse of silvered leather attached to a sash about her waist and resting on her lap. Julie wondered tensely if there was enough air to breathe in the room. And then one of the red draperies was pushed aside, and a small woman stepped in, to move with slow dignity across the carpets.

It was La Voisin herself, Julie had no doubt, for the woman was arrayed in an incredible costume. She wore an exaggerated, widely puffed gown of shimmering green silk heavily sewn with beads and winking colored stones. Over it floated a billowing, spruce-colored mantle showered with double-headed eagles so gleaming bright they must have been embroidered with pure gold thread. And riding high on her head was a fantastic headdress fashioned of felt, gray feathers, ivory, and two polished jewels of flashing brown amber—the staring head of an owl, symbol of wisdom.

The seer glided silently toward them, stopped at the armchair, and, with gloved fingers lightly touching the table, nodded to them in greeting. Since visitors were incognito here, bows and prerogative demanded by rank were ignored. In fact, La Voisin seated herself in the sort of armchair reserved for a queen.

'*Bonjour*, Madame L'Abeille, and you, madame'— she studied Julie for a moment—'Raven Hair. Madame L'Abeille and I had a prior rendezvous for later this night, therefore I understand we sit together for you, Raven Hair. I am at your disposal. State what you wish.' And when Julie hesitated to answer, she continued encouragingly. 'A lotion to clear the face of blemishes? A powder to rejuvenate an aging husband? A foretelling of your future?' The voice flowed softly.

Julie opened her mouth, but nothing came out. In fact, the middle-aged face under the fantastic headdress was hardly sinister. It was the face of an ordinary matron, plump-cheeked, comfortably double-chinned, with a few crooked teeth to be seen as the prim mouth stretched in a smile. A goodwife's face. But it was her eyes that told the story, eyes the color of mud, of silt, of a nameless shade. They impaled Julie from their deep, loose-skinned sockets and pierced shockingly into hers as if drilling a hole through bone and flesh to see every secret written on her heart since she was born. La Voisin's lips twitched as if they and the strange, sharp eyes were laughing at her mental scramble to bury deep her identity and her real purpose for venturing into this den. But the woman's calm expression and soft tone did not change.

'Well, what shall it be, then, madame?'

Sternly, Julie pulled herself together, angry with her timorous response to this challenge. 'I am seeking something to help a certain gentleman find the boldness to approach me with his suit. Something to make him desire me so strongly that all obstacles will be swept from his mind and he will love me forever.'

'Forever?' laughed La Voisin with the chuckle of an older, wiser woman. 'I have no potion for eternal love, my dear, nor has anyone else. But I can help you for the here and now, and into the foreseeable future. The love philter you are after, to make the gentleman you covet fall into your arms, will be mixed to my specifications as long as you have brought with you the required materials.'

'*C'est ça*, madame. A *poudre d'amour*, that is my wish,' Julie agreed, feeling more confident. 'And I have brought what you require.'

Athénais gave La Voisin a tiny nod. The little woman leaned back in her armchair and tented her fingers under her fat chin. 'That is well, madame. But first, I must look into your hand. It is necessary for me to read your history in the past, in the present, and in the future in order to divine which magical substance will draw affection toward you. Ours is an exact science. We would not wish to make an error which could mistakenly divert your lover into other arms——'

Suddenly, Julie heard her father's stern voice command in her inner ear: 'Don't give her your hand. Don't let the seer take such power over you.' But it was her own head that told her it was Mademoiselle's palm that should be scrutinized in this instance, not hers. Unprepared for the demand, Julie looked desperately at Athénais. 'I would rather not have a r-reading today. The date is not propitious for me.'

La Voisin leaned forward again, and it seemed to Julie that the woman searched her face with four eyes, her own deep-set ones and the hard, lustrous depths of the owl's jeweled orbs. The gloved hand reached out. 'Give me your hand, Raven Hair,' she demanded quietly. 'It is necessary. Since you do not wish it, I will not do a full reading, but then I must ask you to remove your mask. The lines of the face tell a quicker story than those of the palm. Passion and anxiety are difficult to conceal in the features.'

Seeing Julie's hesitation, and La Voisin's questioning glance toward her, Athénais murmured, 'Do not be afraid, *ma chère*. All is secure here. Do as she asks you.' The king's mistress shifted on her seat. There still was tension underlying her voice.

'I can do no reading of velvet physiognomies,' La Voisin stated bluntly.

It could not be helped, and so Julie complied, unhooking the wires from her ears and lowering her mask, praying that the fortune-teller's perusal of her would not shift the focus of the love potion to her. She might have even tittered at the thought of sour little de Lauzun chasing her about in a paroxysm of love if the strange eyes now studying her face did not seem to come forward in their sockets, burning with an unnatural light, suggesting powers that belied the prim, starched smile on the matronly face. The diviner gave no indication of any recognition, but Julie had a powerul feeling that this fabled person infallibly knew the name and rank of all her clients. The lashless eyelids closed a moment. For a moment, the plump face seemed vacated.

'You have been on a sea voyage not long ago,' La Voisin intoned. 'It caused you sickness; you were vomiting.'

Julie drew a sharp breath. She'd never mentioned to anyone being seasick.

'And you shall make another voyage by sea—and another as well.' La Voisin opened her eyes. 'But whether along with your love I cannot say, since you will not give me your hand.'

Automatically, Julie's fingers clenched protectively over her palms and whatever might be her private destiny, which had nothing to do with the Duchesse de Montpensier's *poudre d'amour*.

'Still, I can see passion in your face and a great womanly capacity for giving and receiving love, in spite of your deep fear of the vulnerability this produces. The man to whom you address your efforts will finally come to realize his good fortune, madame. So. Have you brought the nail parings and hair?'

Julie nodded, drawing a small packet from her skirt

pocket and handing it over. Mademoiselle's servant Dant had experienced no difficulty in bribing the Comte de Lauzun's barber, a man who, given the superstitious wallowings of the court, made notable clandestine sums from the detritus of his noble clients.

'*Très bien*, madame. I shall have your potion made up for you.' The eyes now sank back, drab-colored again in the round, calm face. 'It will be a colorless and almost tasteless elixir bottled in a small vial and easily concealed. Just a few drops in wine or cider will suffice, but because the potion is benign—a solution of powder of cantharis, heartsease weed, and other herbs dissolved in purest maiden's tears—its strength will build only slowly. Several usages will be needed to bring it to full efficacy. Do you understand, madame?'

At Julie's nod, the seer stood, her headdress of sagacity casting its weird shadow against the red velvet drapes. 'Wait here, then, and it will be brought to you. I hope to greet you again, Raven Hair, and next time perhaps for a full consultation with the tarot oracle. Without a glimpse of the future, one lives uncomfortably and blind, in a directionless present. *Adieu,* madame.' The measured-out smile showed the broken teeth again, and then La Voisin turned to Athénais. 'Come with me, Madame L'Abeille. We must prepare you for your *séance*.'

Athénais stood up calmly, lips smiling below her disguise, but the blue eyes behind the mask's slanted eyeholes shifted about. She leaned over Julie and muttered, 'Be sure to wait for me, Ton-Ton, no matter how long. The spell is difficult. It will take a while.'

'I will come with you.' Julie started to rise.

Athénais's 'No!' was sharp as she pushed her down. 'Please, just wait here.'

The door opened silently, as if by itself, and La Voisin motioned to her client to precede her. Julie caught a glimpse of a masked man and woman flitting past in the passage with the aproned maid leading them in the direction of the entry hall, and then the door closed behind Athénais's stiff back and La Voisin's voluminous cloak and eerie headdress.

So, that was the infamous La Voisin. Hardly prepossessing, in spite of her regalia. Just a short, pudding-faced, soft-voiced little woman who must be coining coffers of money at her business. Except for her eyes. It was the strange eyes, which seemed on the brink of spinning like a dun pinwheel, that suggested one was dealing with more than the ordinary seer who cast fortunes and devised simple charms.

Prepared to wait, Julie slumped on her backless seat, fanning herself with her little parchment maker-of-breezes. The worst part was that the room was so soundless. She minded that more than the stifling warmth. She consulted her little timepiece—it was a quarter before the hour of seven.

Her mind ran again over the just completed brief séance. In spite of the chamber's stuffiness, in spite of the fact that she saw no evidence of sorcery or diabolic practices, or was able to distinguish nefarious witchcraft in La Voisin's businesslike manner, a light chill ran along her spine and raised the hair on her arms.

The Vicomte de Morlé would have disapproved most fiercely of her dealing with 'filthy vendors of superstition,' as he had tagged them in one of the long monologues she was conjoined to hear during the enforced intimacy of their journey to England. Her father deemed himself a man of pure reason, and after having viewed twice in his youth the grisly spectacle of six hundred witches and warlocks all at once piled with faggots and straw to their necks and burned alive, he had made a thorough, scholarly study of the occult arts to discover what was this enduring heresy that the Christian church in sixteen centuries had not been able to stamp out.

Julie could see him yet, sitting with her on a bench below the ship's high prow to take the fresh sea air, his straight gray hair blowing behind him in the wind and baring his narrow forehead, where a blue vein throbbed. 'It is actually a true religion,' he expounded to Julie, 'not an aberration of our own. It descends from the rites of the ancient Gaulish tribes and those early men called Celts who lived throughout Europe and were ancestors to the Gauls. It was not these ancestors but the Christians who named their strange deity Beelzebub and identified him with the Satan of our Bible. These cultists follow a teaching more ancient than our own, although a mistaken one. Therefore, they are not guilty of heresy, to my mind, but of ignorant clinging to ingrained old beliefs.'

'But, Father, what of their malevolence, their death spells, their evil eyes, their blood sacrifices upon black altars?'

'Evil can be found everywhere—even, I fear to tell you, in our own true church of Jesus. It is my opinion that their most vile practices are done more in defiance and hate than in the tenets of their religion. Those who perform such maleficent liturgy that crops fail and sheep sicken deserve execution, to remove their tainted spirits from among us. But many that the righteous put to death are merely crazy old women or simple herbalists. Still, for your soul's sake, I bid you stay away from the casters of horoscopes, card readers, concocters of noxious powders which have no efficacy, charlatans, and cheats with sleight-of-hand as their only power. They prey upon certain ignorance and hysteria, which should be the shame of anyone not of the lowest caste.'

The young Julie had listened wide-eyed, not a little titillated, enjoying thrills of horror as he related in his pedantic way what he'd read and seen of certain scandals—the Abbé Mariette, for instance, an ordained priest hauled before the Chatelet court on sorcery charges, who, under torture, admitted to practicing astrology, alchemy, phrenology, graphology, magic, and the preparation of root of mandrake potions passed 'under the chalice' in a black rite! The Vicomte exposed Julie to the knowledge he liked to roll off his tongue, accounts of wild witches' sabbaths; reported compacts signed by Beelzebub, Lucifer, and Satan; fiendish ingredients used to control people or murder them—and then the stomach-turning punishments meted out to those master warlocks and witches who were caught.

Sitting in the palm-reader's gloomy manse and shifting from buttock to buttock, then walking about as the time wore on, Julie was glad much of the ugliness her father repeated was in the past, for in her own lifetime it seemed that the practice of true black sorcery had been checked and reduced to only occasional accusations and trials here and there in the countryside. The ordinary casters of horoscopes and diviners of futures were considered harmless. Indeed, Primi Visconti counted among the sometimes two hundred coaches lined up in his courtyard names such as Soissons, Poitiers, Louvois—and Bourbon.

She cleared her throat just to hear a sound. And then, behind the table, the curtains that must have concealed another door stirred with a breeze. Quickly, Julie adjusted her mask. There were slow footsteps, and the crimson drapes were parted by a portly man on matchstick legs wearing an askew brown wig. His mouth drooped sadly. 'I am Monsieur Monvoisin,' he announced, as if such a fact pained him. 'And here is your purchase.' He held out to her a little drawstring pouch of yellow silk tied with ribbons. 'That will cost you one gold louis.'

'Yes, of course.' Julie fumbled in her purse, withdrew the shiny coin, and put it in his moist palm.

'Madame Monvoisin has also included a small gift of an unguent made with oil of almonds, crushed violets, and other ingredients, very fine for enlarging the bosom or encouraging longer eyelashes,' he announced in a singsong voice.

'*Merci*, monsieur.' The man turned to go, but Julie reached out to detain him. 'Please, can you tell me how much longer I must wait for Madame de. . .L'Abeille? It is over an hour already.'

'Alas, madame, I am merely a deliverer of packets. I have no other connection with my wife's activities, or my daughter's. Nor would I wish to. Therefore, I can tell you nothing. *Adieu*, madame.' The drapery swished forward and back, and the sad old man was gone.

Julie's back ached from sitting so long on the tabouret. It was easier to stand. Stand and stand, that was what one did all day long at court. But the crimson-cushioned armchair opposite her seat was not especially sinister-looking, and it beckoned her with its wide-seated comfort. She might as well ease her long wait. La Voisin hadn't sounded as if she intended to return, anyhow. She walked around the table with the golden double-headed eagle and seated herself in the armchair, unhooking the uncomfortable mask and leaning back with a sigh.

The silence grated on her nerves. She drummed her fingers on the chair's carved arm. What should she think about to keep her mind occupied? Nicolas? She smiled to think what would be his reaction to her being in this isolated house surrounded by dense forest, suffocating crimson draperies, and creepy silence and intimidated by soothsayers and alchemists. Strong, to say the least.

She leaned forward and laid her head down on her arms on the table for a moment, the better to reflect dreamily on Nicolas de Courcillon, remembering their first midnight meeting on the road to Paris and their wary second at the Luxembourg; dreaming, dreaming that she and—the Comte de Lauzun, was it—were dancing a ballet, and a great stag from the hunt at Fontainebleau nudged her up on his back with his antlers, and she rode away toward Cuckfield, where Mistress Battersby waited in the neglected garden with a large spoon, beating time, beating, beating——

With a start and a small groan, she woke up, the little watch that she held clutched in her hand ticking against her ear. She sat up, disoriented, then realized with dismay that she was still in the seer's sanctum. She rubbed her eyes, stretched, and finally squinted at her timepiece and gasped to see it was almost nine o'clock. Where was Athénais? The king was punctual to the minute. If his mistress was not in her apartment at eleven o'clock, he would know it. He might even send out the guards to look for her.

Julie's back and shoulders ached, her neck and forehead were perspired, her mouth was dry. The situation was precarious. She had to find Athénais and warn her of the time. Creaking to her feet, she smoothed her skirts, adjusted her head scarf and mask, and stepped across the carpets to the portal. Tentatively, she pulled on the ring, and the heavy old door swung toward her. Opening it all the way, grateful for the cooler air that bathed her moist face, she was prepared to demand that the guard direct her to Athénais. The guard was easy to find, for he was wedged between the wall and his low stool, snoring away, his head drooping on his chest. Keeping a wary eye on him, she edged out and tiptoed from the alcove into the passageway. In either direction, the passage turned a corner, but she knew that to her right were all those forbidding closed doors. Never mind. She would just open one at a time and brazenly inquire for Madame L'Abeille. The situation called for a certain bravado, and so did her frayed patience and nerves.

And then, as she quietly distanced herself from the guard's snoring, she heard it—a low, slow, sonorous chant, deep bass voices in a measured litany, the words unintelligible, a vibrating, menacing rumble that seemed to come from unspeakable depths.

Julie froze in midstep, for the monotone chorus filled her with dread. It seemed to seep from the stone walls all around her, filling the air with malignancy. Yet her shrinking heart told her that where she would find the unholy singers she would also find Athénais. She turned about slowly, ears straining, and finally decided the sound was loudest before her. She went forward cautiously in the dim passageway of twists and turns, seeing to her surprise that the shallow-arched chamber doors she now passed stood half open, the inky dark behind them testifying to their emptiness. The chanting here became more intense, until she discovered hidden in the shadows of another alcove a narrow stairwell leading down like some mysterious throat from which the hypnotic singing was issuing. At the base there was wan light on a landing.

Pulled forward as if by a hook, Julie put her hand on the wall to steady herself and tiptoed down the straight flight of stairs. Turning at the base, engulfed by the grumbling, muttering chant, which now sounded vaguely like Latin, she entered a large space that was barely lit by several black candles in iron wall sconces. A thick wall with three low archways faced her, each opening obscured by heavy black draperies. The center one was painted with a shocking, leering face, a bearded and horned red demon, its purple tongue lolling out.

Julie made a convulsive grab at her chest to keep her heart from jumping out. She tried twice to swallow. She was trapped. She was in a devil's nest, but how could she get out? She would surely get lost in the bowels of the sprawling house. And intuition still pressed her that it was here where Athénais must be, behind those arches, whose drapes, undulating, were traced with strange golden writing that surely warned that this was the abode of Lucifer. Nevertheless, she could not, would not, leave without Athénais, even if she might hit-and-miss find the entry. She heard her father's voice trying to convince her, 'It is not actually Satan they call upon but gods of another religion,' and she deliberately slowed down her breathing and pulled her shoulders back to bolster her courage.

She took off her shoes and flitted barefoot across to one of the smaller arches, whose draperies had not been pulled quite closed. Breathing shallowly to mitigate the choking effect of the heavy incense fumes, she wished she could put her fingers in her ears to shut out the fearful bass threnody saturating the air about her. Warily, she applied her eye to the slit between the drape and the time-battered stone of the arch.

It was not hard to see. Placed about the walls, tall tripods supporting great black bowls of fire illuminated the large chamber beyond the drape, their leaping yellow flames matching those from a low iron bowl in the middle of the floor, which stood on a dais before a black-draped table. Over this travesty of an altar was suspended a large black cross with the crucified shape of a fork-tailed devil hanging upside down. Behind stood a rank of black-robed and cowled figures, hands obscured, faces blurred behind deep hoods. If not for several open windows high above, the smoke from the flares and incense would have been suffocating.

To one side of the altar, on planks supported by rough-hewn sections of tree trunk, sat six velvet-masked and cloaked spectators, men and women, whose stiff posture suggested some trepidation. Opposite them, a similar rude bench held fantastic figures in billowing black robes, their heads totally encased in painted masks, which were frightful depictions of horned and fanged demons, a virulent glint of human eyes to be seen behind the black-rimmed eye slits. Julie found herself counting them. There were thirteen. A cabal!

Too stunned to be frightened, she finally admitted what she was secretly witnessing—a Black Mass! Almost as her father had described it. And taking place here, on this day, and barely a league from the streets of Paris. The realization was stupefying.

A stir ran round the room as from behind a black curtain strode three more diabolists in flowing robes, one in the mask of a mad-eyed, green-feathered rooster, another wearing the grinning face of a horned and bearded goat, and the third, of much smaller stature, enveloped in a black velvet cloak embroidered with glinting symbols of witchcraft. Two slim acolytes in black pages' outfits followed them out, supporting between them a blond, cloak-wrapped woman, her face obscured by a vizard picked with yellow bees, her wobbling head encircled with a garland of hellebore and witchweed. She was walking but would certainly have stumbled or sunk to the ground without the aid of the acolytes.

Julie gasped, then moaned, the sound luckily lost under the drawn-out mouthings of the chant. It was Athénais de Mortemart, Marquise de Montespan, beloved of the Jupiter-king of France, who was being laid on that unholy altar. Julie gasped again, and her spine went rigid as the three celebrants' wide sleeves fell back and she could make out the crescent marks of the devil's hooves tracking their arms. A second later, she desperately muffled her betraying mouth with a trembling hand as the shortest of the priests of the black rite grasped the cloak of the woman lying on the altar, triumphantly pulled it off, and held it up.

A great crescendo of bass chanting greeted the sight of Athénais's complete nakedness, her soft, voluptuous, quivering body milk-white against the black altar cloth. Only her white silk stockings, secured about her thighs by red garters, and her shoes were left on.

Drugged. She is drugged, Julie muttered wildly to herself, for even headstrong Athénais would not so shockingly desecrate herself of her own free will.

Abruptly the singing stopped, sending Julie's heart lurching in the dead silence.

All eyes were on the shortest celebrant, who threw back her hood and stood revealed as La Voisin, a black band with glittering blood-red stones wrapped about her forehead. One of the priests threw a handful of powder into the iron bowl before her, and violent purple leaped up, tinting with evil the pudgy, unsmiling face of the sorceress, the grotesque masks of her priests, and the inert body on the altar. Another handful of powder, and the flames writhed angry yellow.

The goat-masked priest intoned, 'Hear, O true chosen ones, followers of the Great Horned God Cernummos, hear all ye demons, incubi and succubi, witches and warlocks, magicians and wizards, hear in the dark of the moon the words of our Lord, the Prince of Devils. Hear and believe.' The voice issuing from the goat's muzzle ended with a hoarse break, and Julie blinked—she had heard that peculiar manner of speech before.

'Hear, followers of the black heart!' the rooster-head boomed out. 'Hear the petition of a most pious, a true worshiper.'

Now La Voisin, high priestess, prophetess, sacrificer to the old gods, raised her hoof-marked arms, flung back her black-wrapped head, and called out, 'Hear, darling minions of Asturoth and Asmodeus, Princes of Darkness, beloveds of Lucifer, Leviathan and Belial, hear the words of the ultimate Power!'

Her eyes burning unnaturally, like glowing coals, La Voisin now made the sign of the cross against her black vestment, but backward and with her left hand. Closing her eyes tight as if to capture their fiery strength against her lids, she began to intone, slowly at first and with deep feeling. Then, her voice becoming lower and lower in pitch, faster and faster she spoke, and finally a weird, deep voice spilled gibberish from the prim lips, to become a roaring bass voice pumping out incomprehensible syllables. The masked spectators on the right bench quaked under the violence of that evil torrent, while the members of the coven fell to their knees and bowed their concealed heads. One of them, whose *papier-mâché* chalk-white caricature mask was of a distorted human face with purple cheeks and black lips, jumped up and commenced to shudder, limbs jerking out in all directions like a puppet worked by a madman, and his kneeling colleagues joined in with wild shouts and moans and growls, hands outspread toward the black cross over the altar.

Then, as precipitously as it had begun, the insane babbling stopped, and it seemed to the stunned Julie that she hadn't breathed for all that time or even blinked her eyes. La Voisin seemed to deflate, to collapse within her robes. Her head dropped, and her fellow priests supported her. But in a moment, her eyes snapped open and she straightened, staring with those terrible dead-leaf orbs, so Julie thought with a pang of terror, directly into the shadowed archway and into her own eyes as she peered through the gap in the curtain. But the priestess's hands swept out, and the fire in the low cauldron leapt up crimson, green, cobalt, orange, magenta, sparks snapping.

'Hear us, Lord of Lords, King of the Netherworld,' La Voisin called, now in her own voice. 'I conjure you to grant the petition of this woman who offers herself on your altar to receive the substance and fluid of your body in union with your Power, to accept the sacrifice of new life which we make to you in return for favors asked: that this petitioner shall have and keep the love of the highest-born prince, which she craves; that the consort of this power-among-men shall become barren so that he leaves her bed to come to this woman, who begs your favor; that he grant this petitioner whatever she asks, include her in his council, and that his love for her shall grow and flourish. Above all, Dark Ruler of Men's Destinies, grant this female the fecundity she desires, give her children in abundance to this prince, children we will acknowledge and cherish, so the more to worship her and, in her, you. We beseech this of you!'

A chorus of amens sounded. The lay spectators—and Julie was sure she recognized behind a lace-trimmed vizard the red hair and sharp-tipped nose of the Comtesse de Soissons—sat silently, some clutching each other's hands. Julie squinted hard at Athénais and saw her head move to follow La Voisin's movements and thought she saw a gleam of blue behind the bee mask's eye slits. Athénais was at least awake, then, and somewhat aware. But her arms hung limp to either side of the altar, and her legs, which hung from the knee down over the edge of the black-draped table, were motionless.

From a platter presented by the acolyte, La Voisin took a slab of black bread and placed it on Athénais's smooth, round belly, which was fluttering with her breath. 'This is the Body of the Loved One baked of blackest bread and Spanish fly to bring passion, to bring living proof of carnal desire,' she crooned, her face shining with sweat and an unholy rejoicing.

She held aloft an onyx chalice, then lowered it to receive the substances she took from the acolyte's tray and named each carefully as she poured or sprinkled them into the balefully reflective cup. 'Powder of mandrake root to thicken the blood; witches' thimble to strengthen the heart; tincture of cantharis to quicken the loin; semen of bull to nourish the seed; powder of cocks' combs and testicles to fortify the womb; urine of blind man, fat of dead baby, water from a drowned mouth. . .'

She fell silent, waiting. Another priest, robed and hooded, came from somewhere beyond Julie's range of sight carrying before him a small cloth bag in which something mewled and moved fitfully. He stood facing his high priestess, his back to Julie, and deposited his burden on a smaller black stone altar. Julie could see nothing beyond his broad back, but something told her to be glad, for the man pulled from his sleeve a wicked knife, flashing in the light, and she heard the bag being ripped open. La Voisin threw back her head, calling, 'Accept. Accept. New life for new life!' The long blade flashed down, there was a ghastly gurgle, and then blood spattered to either side of the stone altar and onto the floor. The priest held up his crimsoned knife.

The chanting erupted, deep and triumphant, rolling over the gasps of the spectators, two of whom had clapped shaking hands over their eyes.

Julie fought nausea, terrified that she would be sick. She moved away from the drapery, clutching her stomach and mouth. Oh, *le bon Seigneur*, at least let it be a tiny lamb whose throat had been cut! Human babies, her father had muttered, the bones of hundreds of them buried in the rich loam always surrounding witches' dwellings. Oh, that wicked Athénais! How could she have given herself to such abomination? Mopping her damp forehead with her sleeve, Julie moved with reluctance and dread back to her peephole.

The priest with the knife, back still toward her, finished pouring a deep red fluid into a black cup, and the cup was taken back to La Voisin, who reverently put it to her lips and drank from it. She then poured the remains into the black chalice and stirred up the mixture with a baton. The chanting from beneath hoods continued but diminished in volume, remaining a sinister muttering in the background as La Voisin touched Athénais's forehead, holding aloft the cup. Dipping her hand into the nauseating mixture, she rubbed the viscous stuff over the supine woman's naked breasts. Athénais flinched, at which Julie thanked God, for Athénais's limpness, her immobility, had been a prime worry. The priestess applied the potion to her subject's belly and thighs, and thickly in the groin, all the while murmuring dark incantations.

The cabal of masked devil worshipers, unlit black candles in their hands, stood up from their bench and filed toward the altar, coming to rest on either side of it. One dipped his candle to the flame of the iron bowl, and the others passed the flame on, each small flicker illuminating from below the grotesque masks and giving them a diabolical semblance of life.

The taller priest stepped forward. He called out, 'Hear, oh darling Beelzebub, maker of wondrous creatures dark of blood, red of skin, black of tooth, of hair, of bone, give to this petitioner the fertility of your body so that she might bear living children of her race. We beseech you.' Julie heard the peculiar break, the hitch in the voice again, and, remembering finally, bit hard on her lip. She'd noted it before and thought it a rather endearing little defect the several times she'd chatted with Nicolas's affable, lively brother, the Abbé d'Aubièrre. It could only be he under the goat mask. She felt sick again.

D'Aubièrre approached Athénais to stand before her knees. Suddenly, the blond head in the bee mask rolled from side to side on the black altar cloth and the body twitched. The two acolytes stepped up to her, and each pinned down an arm. The priest's fingers worked with closures along his garments, and then, as the unholy chant rose in volume again, he flipped back his robe, under which he was entirely naked, a goat-faced, horned satyr with oiled, dark skin and muscles bulging above gold armbands and—Julie's eye's popped—what had to be an artificial male member strapped to his groin, for she could not credit any human to be so hugely endowed. The priest moved closer to Athénais, the phallus stiff before him, his intention unmistakable. The coven members swayed on their feet in ecstasy.

Julie's skin crawled. If he penetrated the prostrate woman with that obscene device, he would surely rip up her tissues. She had to stop it. Athénais had been wickedly arrogant to think she could withstand the ministrations of the devil's brethren, but Julie could not stand by and let her be lacerated in her stupor. Her desperate idea was to burst through the curtain and cry that the king's police were coming, and she opened her mouth to shout, but the next moment it was too late and the shout turned into a gurgle of fright as her arms were caught from behind and she was jerked backward against a pudgy chest. A breath fouled with garlic fell hot on her cheek.

'A little spy, eh, putting yer nose where it doesn't belong? That will cost you dear, bitch.' It was the guard who had been snoring in front of the séance room.

'Let me go!' Julie cried, struggling.

'Sure, why not? Get in there, since yer so anxious to see all,' he snarled, and he shoved her through the curtain, holding one arm painfully twisted up behind her back. 'They'll know how to dispose of you. . .'

At the disturbance, the tableau at the altar had frozen. La Voisin turned her head slowly toward the interruption. Her piercing glare quelled Julie's bucking, riveted her to the floor, and clamped the guard's mouth shut on the announcement of a spy in their midst. The cold fury of the seer's stare and her hollow command—'Hold her silent!'—stopped all motion from the hard-breathing guard and his frightened prisoner. The paralyzing stare withdrew. La Voisin and her confederates turned back to the grim business of the white flesh arched on their black altar.

The goat-headed priest took another few steps toward Athénais, his mask glimmering gold in the flickering flames of all the fire bowls, shadows playing on it so that the ugly, hair-fringed muzzle seemed to gloat. Another step, and the phallus gently touched Athénais between her thighs; the chorus of bass chanters raised an excited, pulsating drone. D'Aubièrre, in his role as chief priest of Satan, put a black-gloved hand on each of Athénais's thighs and pulled back his hips preparatory to making a thrust of the large, obscene device into the willful woman who for magic favors would thus painfully make a union with the devil.

He moved, and Julie's paralyzed stance broke. Horrified, she cried out, 'No, no!' to stop him, and at the very same moment, shockingly, a bone-rattling, shriller, and louder scream came from above amid the fearful flap of great wings. All heads jerked up to see a giant screech owl swooping in through one of the windows. The bird shrieked again, circling and swooping about the ceiling on gray and white pinions, finally coming to perch on the sill, yellow eyes blazing.

It screamed out a third time.

Pandemonium! The spectators jumped up, bumping into each other in panic. The silenced chanters fell back. The fanged and pointed-eared masks of the coven members turned wildly about. Only La Voisin and her priests kept a measure of calm at this sudden appearance of a devil's familiar. Julie saw her motion to one of them and snarl, 'Get her off there and take up that altar cloth.' She flung out at the acolytes, 'Gather up those black candles.' And into the confusion of frightened celebrants, the devil's witch shouted, 'It is the signal from our confederate. Troops approach. Come with me instantly, and none will suffer!'

''Tis La Reynie's riders, I'll wager, the police, scarce minutes away,' the guard gasped in Julie's ear. '*Sauve qui peut*, bitch. I've me own arse to haul out of here.' He shoved her away from him and rushed to help others tear down the demon-painted plaque fixed to the black draperies.

Julie staggered into a stone column from the force of his push, but at least she was free. She made herself small against the column, shifting to keep as far out of sight as possible. The priest whose voice was Jean-Pierre Anselm d'Aubièrre's had whipped his cloak about him again, covering the lewd dildo. He and his confederate lifted the groggy Athénais up and snatched away the telltale altar cloth from under her. Impatient with her limpness, they dumped her on the floor and tossed her cloak onto her smeared body. With determined steps, La Voisin marched to a corner of the stone wall and pushed on a hidden lever, and the entire corner section swung in on well-greased hinges.

'This way, this way,' the priestess of black arts urged, motioning her anxious spectators and followers into the dark recess. 'It leads to the forest. We can stay well hidden until they go.' An acolyte with a flaring torch went first; the others scurried behind him. The tallest of the masked coven, a string-bean figure, had run to a rope that lowered the blasphemous cross to the ground. Another helped him carry the heavy thing to the secret door and maneuver it through. 'Hurry, hurry,' the second acolyte called, fright in the young voice.

The two priests got Athénais up so she leaned woozily against the table, but they could not get her to walk. They looked toward the receding backs of their congregation and then glanced at each other. 'Leave her, leave her,' the fallen Abbé ordered. 'She will only slow us up. You know who she is. No one would dare to accuse her openly of consorting with sorcerers. Leave her——'

The two priests hurried away toward the closing door.

'Wait!' Julie cried out, stepping hastily from behind the column, but they did not hear her. The door swung shut.

The silence, after all the scuffling and running, was sudden. A shiver of panic shook her. In spite of the thick walls, Julie thought she heard the hoofbeats of the wardens of the peace closing on the house. She had to get out, she and Athénais. They would be arrested, accused, burned at the stake, *Dieu sait*. Pulling on her shoes, which somehow had stayed in her hand, she ran up to Athénais, who was shaking her drooping blond head like a wet dog, pitifully trying to clear it of the drug they'd plied her with. Julie wrapped and fastened the cloak around the slumping body. 'Come, Coco, come hurry, lean on me, we must go. Coco dear, come!' She tugged her friend's arm about her shoulder, and, with strength that came from she knew not where, she lifted her up and supported her in a clumsy shuffle to the corner, where the hidden door was located.

Propping Athénais against the wall, she fell on her knees as she had seen La Voisin do and felt with trembling fingers along the dark crack where floor met wall, where there must be a spring catch. Now she did hear something from above, a loud slam and crash as if a door had been burst open, and then the muffled stomp of boots. *Sainte Vierge!* Sweat from heat and fear trickled off her brow and seeped under her mask; her armpits grew sticky, and her back, too. Her fingers scuttled back and forth along the seam La Voisin had touched; she moaned in frustration to find nothing but tiny bits of loosened mortar. Now she heard muffled shouts. In a few moments, they would reach the stair and descend. These two fine ladies would be discovered in this strange house, alone, Madame de Montespan unclothed and besullied, Madame de Lowry with a vial of witch's drops in her pocket——

She found a cleft, pushed her finger in, and wiggled it.

Nothing happened. Desperately, she pulled against one side of the cleft. Nothing. Hopelessly, she pushed on the left side. And she almost fell through as the whole side of the corner before her swung silently open on a pivot. With a gasp, she jumped up, grabbed the blinking Athénais by her arm, and propelled her through the opening with a strength made of terror. Once through, she shoved the heavy section of wall with her shoulder to swing it shut on its pivot. None too soon. Through the tiny slit, before the door stones joined seamlessly, she saw the thrust of a pike violently ripping away the drape covering the central arch.

Athénais whimpered, still struggling to consciousness. Julie hissed a warning and put a hand over her mouth. At least it wasn't pitch dark in the low passage; farther in, black candles had been stuck in a wall sconce and lit. Panting, Julie allowed Athénais to sink to the dirt floor. She could hear muffled men's voices, boots stomping, excited cries when something was found. And then a sound like heavy thumping, coming closer. Holy Mother, they were testing the walls for a hollow sound, looking for an escape door.

She turned back to Athénais. 'Get up, madame, we have to go on. Coco, *chérie*, get up,' she pleaded in a whisper. 'I can't lift you all the way from the ground.' Athénais's face was a white blur against the hood of Julie's dark cloak. The mask had been jostled off and hung from one ear. A glisten of sweat covered the marble forehead. 'H-help me,' Athénais stammered back hoarsely and got up on her knees. Tugging under her friend's arms, Julie staggered under Athénais's weight but somehow quickly got her on her feet. She took a second to refasten the bee mask just in case, and then, supporting the woman about the waist, she hustled Athénais along the oppressive earthen passage. Just barely, she stifled a scream as two red-eyed black rats, tails stiff, scuttled squeaking across their path and disappeared into a fall of brick from one of the buttresses. She heard one more low, distant *clung* against the wall of the chamber they'd just left, and then the passage turned and nothing more reached her.

It seemed like an agonizingly long tunnel, lit here and there by candles to guide the faithful. Finally, they staggered around another corner and there was only darkness before them. Swallowing, Julie squeezed Athénais's waist, held out her free hand, and groped slowly forward into the black, about a dozen steps. Her hand touched rough, splintery boards. She pulled it back with a gasp, then like a blind woman began to feel about on the wooden wall blocking their way. There had to be another door here. Leaving Athénais to sway alone, she ran her hands up and down the edges of the planks where they joined the earthen walls and found nothing. Just then, her hip struck something, and, to her surprise and grateful relief, her fingers found an ordinary latch, one with a toggle, which, when lifted, opened the bolt.

'Athénais, make no sound. We are going out,' she muttered into her friend's ear, and she felt the bedraggled curls brush her cheek as Athénais nodded.

With infinite care, sweat trickling down between her breasts, Julie lifted the latch and pulled. In answer to her prayer, the secret door opened inward smoothly, without even a creak. And a blessing of fresh forest air, along with a faint night glimmer and the rustle of leaves and branches, rushed in to revive them and evaporate the wet film of fright from their bodies. They stumbled up a short flight of dirt steps and out behind a stack of firewood into what appeared to be a three-walled shed.

Pulling Athénais along, Julie approached the open side of the shed and found herself looking into purple-shadowed deep woods. She heard nothing but the wind in the trees and an occasional *skreek* of a night bird. Then she looked up, and there, where no branches intervened, were the blessed stars hard-bright against a velvet sky, thousands of them shedding a pale bluish light along the twig-carpeted forest floor. There was neither sound nor sign of the others who had preceded them in flight down the passage. The traffickers with Beelzebub had melted away like wraiths at cock's crow. And behind them all was quiet, too. But even though they could not hear pursuers from here, the police might just find the passage. At the least, they would surely make some sweep of the woods around the manse.

'We must get far away from here. We can hide safer far out in the forest,' she told her companion, who was standing more steadily now, and Julie was encouraged to see that Athénais's head was clearing and she had more control of her muscles. But she was shivering in the warm night.

They slipped out of the shed and, holding hands so as not to lose each other, started off through the forest, stumbling, treading on sharp stones that hurt them through the flimsy soles of their shoes. Julie wasn't even sure they were heading away from the house, but she prayed they were. On they scurried, as fast as they were able, until their breath came in wheezes.

'Uh, I can't anymore,' Athénais wailed softly. 'I am perishing of thirst. My head is bursting and throbbing. I must rest, Julie. Please.'

Julie's legs felt wobbly, too. She looked around into the shadows about them. She made out a thicket at the base of a large tree that had a brake they could crawl into, and she pulled Athénais toward it. With trepidation, they edged into the bracken, silently dreading snakes and spiders, worse, surely, than foxes or wolves, which had been hunted out in the areas around Paris anyway. Gingerly, they lowered themselves onto the damp leaves to rest.

'Unless they intend to comb the entire forest between here and the main road, I think we're far enough away so that they won't find us.' Julie said this to be cheerful, but Athénais answered by putting her head down on her drawn-up knees and bursting into sobs. Finally, she ran the back of her hand under her dripping nose.

'*Merde!* I stink to heaven,' she choked out, pulling the cloak away from her neck to take a whiff and gagging.

'Yes, you do,' Julie agreed, thinking it served her right. 'They smeared you with filth.'

'That detestable Abbé d'Aubièrre! He left me there helpless, unclothed, muddled in the head. I'll see him arrested and hanged,' Athénais raged, knowing full well that if torture ever loosened the man's tongue, she herself would be compromised beyond redemption.

'Was he the one who introduced you to this?' Julie asked, almost fearful to know. Nicolas had made several dry remarks about his brother's intemperate ways. What would his shock be to know the true degradation of the man?

'*Merde!* My stupid tongue ran away with me.' Fingernails dug into Julie's arm. 'You must pretend you did not hear that name, Julie, please. You cannot understand how much I need this help. I cannot afford to offend any of them. I beg you. . .' Athénais's low voice quivered.

'You needn't. I am as trapped in this as you are,' Julie muttered disgustedly, then froze. 'Shhh—I hear something.' She heard it again. A soft snuffle, the jingle of bit, a low-pitched neigh. 'A horse! I'm sure I hear a horse over there. Do you think it would be from the house, scared off and wandering free? Maybe we could catch it, ride it out of here! I'm going to look.'

'No! You'll get caught. It is probably La Reynie's men just skulking about, hoping to net someone.' Athénais's alarm was evident even in her whisper. 'Don't give them cause to look back here——'

'I won't. I'll be careful. But we must try. What will you say tomorrow if you are not in your chamber awaiting the king tonight?'

She could hear Athénais grinding her teeth. 'Something. I'll think of something.'

But Julie didn't stay to argue. The darkness was sufficient to hide her from eyes not expecting her, and the past fifteen minutes had given her experience in stepping lightly over the sodden twigs. She crawled out of the brake and, in a cautious, stop-and-start lope, made her way toward the horse's soft snorting. Finally, peering through a bush, she saw in the dim starlight a coach and team of four horses standing behind some shrubs just off the road, the driver a silent shadow on the box, waiting. She couldn't tell if there was anyone inside the vehicle. Suddenly, the driver's slouch straightened, as if he was listening to something; then, like a turtle, he pulled his head into his jacket and clucked softly to quiet his horses. The thunder of hooves on hard-packed earth came to Julie's ears, a distant drumming growing louder and louder, and then in a great rush and swoosh of wind, the raiding troop of police wardens galloped past toward Paris, eighteen or twenty of them, the two forward riders with streaming torches. In the rear was a careening cart in which several figures jounced.

The crescendo of noise diminished, and then they were gone, headed for the highroad and the Porte Saint Denis.

'Now then,' she heard the coach driver mutter to his horses in the backwash of silence. 'It's back to the weird house for us. We'll try to collect those ladies if it weren't them they took. Ain't going to come out all this mucking way without our pay, thirty écus it was, and damn well worth it for all this trouble——'

Julie let her breath rush out. She felt indescribable relief, for it was their own hired coach, surely. Afraid to hesitate too long and dilute her courage, she stood up straight and boldly called over, 'Psst. Coachman! Here we are. Over here. Your passengers.'

'Wha——?' The turtle's head stretched out and jerked around.

'Just stay right there, driver. Don't move, *mon bon homme*. I will be right back.' And she scrambled back through the dark brush and trees to fetch Athénais, taking the first real breath into her tense body in several hours, thanking God the tenacious coachman, who had probably been sent away by the police, had refused to leave without the special fare promised him.

'*Comment vas-tu?*' Julie asked Athénais in the coach, patting her knee. They would soon come up to the Louvre and with hardly time to spare for Madame de Montespan to reach her apartment.

'Not terrible.' The tired voice dragged with the residue of the drug and tension. 'It is good Louis always sups with the queen before he sees me. I certainly won't bump into him coming up the servants' stairs.' Athénais had released her mask and was slowly fanning herself with it. 'I feel so pale and pinched, though. And I must have a thorough wash.'

Julie was silent for a moment as a horror flitted across

her mind, the picture of a goat-masked celebrant with the grotesque dildo coming determinedly toward the waiting body of this arrogant supplicant to Satan. 'He almost entered you with that—that filthy caricature. It would have hurt. It would have torn you.'

'I know. Anything efficacious usually does hurt,' Athénais answered sullenly. 'The cursed interruption was most inopportune. The spell was cracked and broken. I shall have to try again.'

'And what would you have told the king to see you so wounded?'

'A fall from a horse——'

'Athénais, you must not subject yourself to such odiousness. You cannot! It is vile and blasphemous. And dangerous. If the police had found you——'

'*Tais-toi,* Julie,' the nerve-shredded Athénais burst out. 'You don't know whereof you speak. I am gambling for the love and respect of a king, the power of being almost as exalted as a queen. Whatever methods I use to win, however much of my soul I must throw into the wager, does not equal the worth of the sun for which I reach. But you needn't worry. I will not trouble you to come along with me again.' Her classic, arrogant nose wrinkled as she caught another whiff of herself again. 'Phew! Pray God that lazy Ninon has my bath ready——'

Indignation rose up in Julie's throat. Well. The same rude person she'd known in school—not a *merci*, not an appreciation that Julie had saved her skin, nothing but an irritated promise not to trouble her again. 'It was not my trouble in helping you I was worrying about,' she retorted stiffly.

The remainder of the trip, until they pulled up at a side door in the Louvre courtyard, was passed in silence, Athénais slumped in a corner chewing the edge of a fingernail, swearing now and then under her breath. A figure detached itself from the dark doorway, then another. 'My maid—and my footman,' the king's mistress muttered. 'I must hurry. I need to wash, to redo my hair.'

'I will send your coach back to you from the Place de La Grève.'

Athénais had donned her mask again. Julie's borrowed chiffon scarf hid her tumbled yellow curls; the wrapped cloak hid her besmirched, nude body. The red lips, still with a beauty patch at one corner, lifted in a cynical curve as the footman opened the door. Athénais reached for Julie's hand. 'I imagine you think I am ungrateful? Ton-ton, listen to me, *chérie*. Of anyone there, it was only you who had the courage to risk your own reputation to help me avoid being found undressed and drugged in a house suspected of sorcery. I am not so selfish that I ignore that. It is only that I am upset. But I will not forget. If a time comes when I can help you, I will not fail you. There is my word. Thank you, *chère amie*.'

She leaned forward and brushed Julie's cheek with her lips. Then, holding the cloak carefully closed, she climbed down from the coach and hastened away through the little-used portal toward her nightly rendezvous with her royal lover.

Julie knocked up with the stick used for this purpose, and the coach turned about and continued on to the open area on the banks of the Seine where her own coach waited. Athénais had always enjoyed living on the edge, she reflected with resignation. Then she started, remembering. But a pat on the pocket of her skirt told her that the silk pouch containing the love potion for Mademoiselle had not been lost. She allowed herself a deep, wavering sigh that the distasteful errand—which had almost turned into tragedy—was done. She had no strength to think about the depraved Abbé d'Aubièrre now, but what was certain was that she was in no position ever to breathe a word about his apostacy to his brother. It would mean having to explain how she knew.

It wasn't until she was in her own snug, overly warm chamber and a yawning Blanchette roused from her cot was undressing her—not so sleepy, however, that she did not murmur her surprise at the mud and bits of leaf and bramble caught in her mistress's clothes—that Julie saw to her horror that the chain of her little clock had broken and her timepiece was missing.

Tears of chagrin welled in her eyes. How would she

explain to Nicolas the loss of her precious bauble?

'The trouble with females without husband or family is that they have no one responsible to supervise them, and so they sometimes fall afoul of the law,' the Marquis de Louvois remarked suddenly, watching Julie from the corner of his eye as his coach drove them leisurely along the pleasant and scenic road north of the Tuileries called the Cours de Reine.

'Oh?' Julie lilted in an ascending tone that was both a question and a disagreement. By this time, she had removed the white vizard she had worn to this unavoidable outing with the Minister of War as a precaution to keep any false gossip from spreading through the court. It now lay in the lap of her white silk and organdy gown, which was scattered with embroidered sprigs of pale primroses and green leaves, some of which, in their fragrant actuality, were also adorning her dark hair. She wished the curtains of the big coach were not so suggestively half closed, but then, it allowed removal of the mask, which had a tendency to make her perspire.

'You, for instance, madame, in the regrettable death of a husband should not have been left as well without a father to guide you,' de Louvois continued. He scratched the end of his nose contemplatively. 'Do you miss the Vicomte, *ma chère* Julie? Perhaps you wish he were still with you?'

She was surprised by two things: the use of her first name—for it was the first time de Louvois had uttered it—and the question attached to it. In fact, Julie was not sure yet why he had insisted on meeting her privately. His whole rather mysterious attitude seemed ominous. She answered him with a shrug. 'Miss my father? Why, sometimes, although we did not spend much time together in his last years. And what's strange, once in a while I think he is still with me. I hear his voice in my ear propounding this and that, giving me lectures and advice——' She paused, deciding she was sounding maudlin.

'So? Almost as if he were alive, eh?' came the soft comment, and de Louvois's dark eyes rested on her with cool concentration.

'Yes. Almost. Although it is more than five years that he is dead.' She smiled tentatively, not understanding where all this might be leading.

For a moment, de Louvois continued to stare at her, his thoughts unreadable. Then he blinked, seemed to switch gears, and his expression clarified into one of grave concern. 'The situation remains, Comtesse, that without the intervention of an older or wiser head that might have controlled your actions, you have put yourself in a compromising position. One that could work to your detriment had you not found in me a devoted friend.'

Julie stared at him silently. She was beginning to guess, and dread, what he was referring to.

His arm shot out. The strong, lean hand opened to display an object on the palm.

'Oh! Why, where did you get that, monsieur?'

'Then it *is* yours, madame? I hadn't supposed there were many J. de L.'s at court.'

Julie's throat almost closed up in her distress. She wanted the little timepiece back desperately, and yet she feared to be branded as one of La Voisin's clients. Now, at least, she knew the motive behind de Louvois's insistence that she meet him where the Cours de Reine commenced and ride with him in his carriage. The wording of his message had made it clear that there was something more important on his mind than a sociable ramble along the Seine. Therefore, with Mademoiselle's permission, she had ordered the calèche, and it was now following their coach-and-four at a discreet distance. She swallowed and stammered, 'Oh, I. . .you see, I did own a timepiece something like it. It was filched from me at the Palais Royal—you know those awful crowds about the merchants' booths? How terribly sad it is to realize what a fine living the thieves make mixing among good people and stealing their belongings. It's a true disgrace. . .'

She glanced up through her lashes to ascertain the effect of her indignant complaint on him. He was sitting much too close to her, having maneuvered her next to him as he drew her into the carriage. But because Nicolas's precious present was in his hand, now was no time to insult him by moving away. He sat regarding her with a little smile, his dark eyes cynical, and she understood that her excuse hadn't deceived him. 'But where did you find it, monsieur?' she asked in as bright a tone as she could muster.

'It was given to me yesterday by my chief of police, Monsieur Le Reynie, who found it during an official sally against certain premises. Pray tell me, madame, what were you doing in the house of a suspected trafficker in black magic and poisons?'

Julie widened her eyes and opened her mouth to protest that she did not know what he was talking about, but looking further into the astute, unwinking stare, she saw that it was no use lying about her presence at La Voisin's. She blushed and looked down an instant at her fingers, encased in white silk gloves, then bent the full force of her violet gaze upon him. 'But you shock me, monsieur. I had no idea of such allegations against Madame Monvoisin. I merely went there two mornings ago for a complexion lotion,' she dissembled. 'I must have lost my little clock then. How fortunate I am that it was found and returned to you.' There was artless relief in her smile.

His long fingers closed on the timepiece again, and he withdrew his hand. Julie's gaze followed it.

'Now listen to me, *chère* Comtesse. You must no longer patronize this woman. She was quick and clever enough this time that we found no evidence, no proof of nefarious workings. But eventually, we will get what we are after, and anyone named as one of her clients will be tarred with dark suspicion. Perhaps worse.'

Julie tried to efface her memory of the dark night of the Black Mass with an appearance of wide-eyed innocence. 'I am astounded at your attitude, Monsieur de Louvois. Do you suspect *me* of buying noxious substances and consorting with sorcerers?'

'No, I believe your business with La Voisin was as innocuous as you say. But that is because I have some knowledge of your character, and I care for you. A special tribunal of judges soon to be appointed to deal with an abomination so fearful as witchcraft may not be as easily convinced. Therefore, I have seen to it that the mention of finding this incriminating bauble has been deleted from the records. Promise me that from now on you will buy your lotions and potions from the public apothecaries on the Rue Vigny only.' De Louvois chucked up her chin so she was forced to look at the intense expression on his hard features. 'Promise me. I must have your word, madame.' The fist that held her timepiece in its grip lay quiet on his knee.

She had no recourse, in spite of the fact that she felt like a scolded child. '*Bien sûr*, you have it, monsieur.' She nodded, and her obviously relieved agreement brought him a small smile; de Louvois never smiled very broadly. But Julie's answering smile was earnest. The import of his statement about being devoted to her had finally struck her. It did certainly pay to have friends in very high places. Athénais would approve.

He reached a finger to touch the dimple that had appeared at the side of her mouth, and the lines about his own mouth softened. 'But there is a forfeit, *ma belle* Julie, eh? Nothing ever is given for nothing in this world, isn't that true?' He leaned toward her, a fervid look in his eyes. 'And so you must pay me with a kiss.'

Nor will it be a token kiss, Julie thought, for de Louvois's gaze was heating further as it wandered her face, dropping to her bare shoulders and bosom rising in creamy smoothness from the draped and bow-knotted neckline of her gown. Still, it was little enough to pay for the return of her cherished little timepiece and for his squelching of any suspicion of her. She looked at his thin but defined lips, eloquent now of controlled desire. His teeth were sound, his breath good. A double-plumed beaver hat rested elegantly on his curled, dark hair; the lace fall at his throat was lavish. The taut-featured, powerful official was an attractive man even if a veiled one. It might not be unpleasant. Resigned to thanking him in the coin he requested, she put up her mouth in assent.

His dry, hard kiss was not unpleasant, she discovered, but it left her unaffected and politely waiting for it to be over. Yet his mouth went on claiming hers, and when she moved to make an end to it, one long arm shot about her waist, and his other hand held the back of her head in an iron grip, making it impossible for her to break off. His tongue fought against her frantically closed lips, his tense body, smelling of spiced perfume, pressed into hers, pushing her along the seat. She wriggled and struggled, finally wrenching her mouth away. 'You presume too much, monsieur,' she gasped. 'I beg you. . .'

'I have been longing for you,' he whispered ardently, as if her protest didn't exist. 'You cannot refuse me at least a caress, a little hug, perhaps a discreet rendezvous soon? There is a small inn outside of Ivry——'

She shoved the heels of her hands against his shoulders. 'How dare you! Let me go, I tell you. Where is your honor, sir?'

'Michel, you must call me Michel,' he murmured with intimate insistence, 'for your message is so well delivered by those incredible amethyst eyes.' He continued pressing her backward. 'You flirt with me, tease me. I do not miss, my dear, the way you invite me with looks that speak of passion, that call to the man of affectionate ardor who resides within me——'

Julie twisted her head from side to side, straining to break from his relentless grip. 'No, not true. I have no interest in you, monsieur, other than amity. I demand you release me immediately!' But his hand caressed her shoulder with firm insistence and began slowly to move down.

'How much patience can a man have, *ma chère* Julie, after so many months of being in your thrall? I burn, I am aflame with my desire to hold your lovely form in my arms, to feel that soft skin under my touch, your ripe lips under mine. . .'

She was astonished at how the normally restrained de Louvois was transformed, undone by infatuation, oblivious in his unwelcome declarations, almost squeezing the breath out of her. 'For shame, monsieur, to mishandle me like this,' she said, fighting him off angrily. 'I can never forgive such boorish behavior.'

'As you surely forgive it in that swaggering fox of a merchant prince de Courcillon?' he cried, having backed her into a corner of the swaying coach. 'Yes, I am engorged with jealousy to see you so often in his company. I am not blind to his appeal for women. He is rich, he is handsome. But I am power, madame, raw command, and that is very attractive to the female gender, both vertically and horizontally. Would you let me demonstrate, I could easily change your mind. Come, don't pull your head aside, *ma petite*, don't play shy. Give me your lovely mouth again——' Eyes glowing like dark embers, he reached out to force her head toward him once more, crushing her against the plush seat. Like a cornered and furious ferret, she sank her teeth into the fleshy part of his hand just below the base of the thumb.

With a howl of rage, he pulled back, clutching his hand, the thin scar along his jaw twisting like a serpent. God help her, Julie prayed. She had just wounded the man whose orders filled the dungeons of Paris. His next expression of love to her could be a *lettre de cachet* that would name her a confederate in any number of witches' plots and guarantee a trialless trip to prison.

'You miserable bitch,' he snarled, glaring at her. He yanked a lace kerchief from the bosom of his coat and wiped away the tiny wellings of blood in the tooth marks on the side of his hand.

Conquering her fright, Julie answered him by straightening her spine, giving him an icy, disdainful stare, and knocking up to the driver. 'Stop this coach immediately,' she called. De Louvois made a small motion toward her, but she held up her hand with a stern confidence she forced herself to feel. 'Unless you intend to throttle me, Monsieur de Louvois, I shall scream to the high heavens if you so much as put one more finger on me, and I am sure we have company all about us on this road. Now, please order your coachman to stop, since he won't obey me.'

De Louvois stared at her for a second, nostrils white, mouth pulled into a straight line. Then his scowl lost its intensity. It broke and dissolved into a sarcastic smile. He returned his handkerchief to its place and indicated his bruised hand. 'I admire your spirit, madame, but not your intelligence.'

'I do not care for your admiration, monsieur, not when you have forgotten the obligations of a gentleman. No lady appreciates being forced into intimacy when she isn't ready.'

De Louvois's fury at being balked seemed to have swiftly dissipated. His thin smile did not waver as he asked her, 'Does that imply that sometime in the future the queen of ice will be ready?'

Here was an opening to smooth the hawk feathers of this dangerous wielder of vast prerogative. Julie took a bit of the starch out of her voice and attempted some diplomacy. 'No, monsieur,' she told him. 'It only implies that I understand impetuosity. It is a failing we all have from time to time, and it must be forgiven. And forgotten.' She tilted her head, favoring him with a milder, more conciliatory expression. 'And friendships can begin anew. So, if you will be good enough, sir, to allow me to descend now——'

She could hardly credit that de Louvois coveted her enough to swallow his pride and grab at this straw, but so he did. With only a tiny twitch of the lips molded into an empty smile, he said, 'Your charity both shames me and gives me hope, *ma belle*. This was, unfortunately, neither the time nor the place for me to forget my manners. I would like to apologize for it, but I do not withdraw anything I said. I can feel you, I can feel the fires within you. But if you must be coy longer, then so be it. I shall press my suit again, though more gently, if you give me leave.'

She was willing to say something ambiguous just to get away from him. 'It would be a most unusual woman who would not enjoy being sought out by you, Monsieur le Marquis,' she murmured with what she hoped was a convincingly provocative glance.

'Graceful, *chère* Julie, graceful.' He chuckled without

mirth. Drawing the driver's attention by knocking with the silver head of his walking stick, he ordered the coach to halt and was immediately obeyed. Julie drew up her small mask to cover her eyes as the footman opened the door and placed the steps.

'*Adieu*, monsieur.'

De Louvois touched her arm as she prepared to alight. 'But you have forgotten something.' He bent and retrieved the little timepiece, which had fallen to the floor in their tussle. He offered it to her.

Julie took it gratefully, offering in return a small smile. A relaxed blandness had descended upon his face, although a remnant of foiled will and anger still lingered in his sharp, deep-set eyes. 'You are very kind, Monsieur de Louvois,' she thanked him.

He kissed the hand she gave him. 'Your devoted servant, Comtesse.'

The calèche pulled up for her. She could feel his gaze burning through her back as she collected her skirts to keep the delicate summer fabric from under her feet and the footman gave her his hand to help her down. It was not until the door of her own conveyance had closed and she found the fan she had abandoned on the seat there and wielded it to dry her damp forehead that she took a deep breath and let it out in a long sigh. It was hard to tell what de Louvois's attitude had been in the end. She prayed she hadn't made an enemy, although the lips that had brushed her hand were cold. Even in her short time at court, she had learned that it was not wise to offend the king's potent minister by refusing his attentions and chomping on his hand as if he were a common thug.

'Well, what could I do?' she argued with herself. 'Let him fondle me, perhaps even force himself upon me, just because he wished to? The line had to be drawn, and I drew it. Let him court me to his heart's content. I do not love Monsieur de Louvois, and I will not accept his advances.'

She put the little timepiece to her lips tenderly. If de Louvois had only known he was returning his rival's gift! And, *merci à Dieu*, she had it back in her possession.

Still—there was a part of her that felt flattered. Nicolas was not the only one who could claim a languishing 'Princesse Margarethe.'

CHAPTER
~ 11 ~

Accompanied by a footman, the three gentlemen ran up the Luxembourg's long flight of marble stairs in a clatter of heavy boots and rattling swords, piquing the curiosity of the courtiers who had attended Mademoiselle's *coucher* and were just straggling down. The lead gentleman, in the fitted red and blue coat of the king's Garde-du-Corps, strode up to Julie in the anteroom and, somewhat out of breath, demanded audience of Her Highness.

Julie had just closed the lady's bedchamber door behind her. 'But Mademoiselle has recently retired for the night,' she objected.

'Then you must wake her, madame. This is the king's business. It is urgent that I deliver a message to her. Immediately.' Authority snapped in the man's voice.

Mademoiselle de Greu and two others of the ladies attendant upon the Duchesse de Montpensier, on their way to their own beds, fluttered back in from the salon beyond the anteroom to see what the disturbance was. Julie turned about on her heel and reentered Mademoiselle's chamber, the courtier close behind her, while his escort of two musketeers, pistols stuck in their belts, remained outside. Dant, who was not yet abed in the cot she occupied at the foot of her mistress's couch, looked up from her task of sorting stockings. Stepping to the ornate bed, Julie parted the flowered summer curtains and gently shook the sleeping woman awake. She murmured to her that the king had sent a messenger bearing urgent news.

Mademoiselle stirred. 'At this hour?' she complained fuzzily. And then, full consciousness returning, she struggled up and clutched the light coverlet to her, her eyes startled, anxious. 'Well, bring the man here,' she instructed Julie hoarsely, and she shivered. 'What bad news could this be in the middle of the night?'

Julie motioned the man forward through the marble *ruelle* that fenced off the bed, and then she discreetly retired at a distance. The curtains unfortunately muffled the short mutter of conversation, but she did hear one harsh gasp from the occupant of the bed. Then the man withdrew to rejoin his companions, and Mademoiselle slipped from the bed.

'Julie, come here and help me make ready to go out. Dant, bring me some clothes. No, there is no time to go to the wardrobe room. I'll wear those and be dammed with it.' Mademoiselle indicated the gown and petticoats she had earlier removed, which still lay draped upon a table waiting removal for cleaning. 'Dant, call my page. He must be outside.'

'Shall I send for your other ladies and your maids, Mademoiselle?' Julie asked as she took the heavy silk skirt from Dant and draped it over her arm. She did not ask directly what had drained the long face of the gaiety it had evinced earlier in the evening after a private visit with Monsieur de Lauzun, now replaced with pallor and nervous frown, nor what emergency had come up to demand a midnight foray.

'No, I shall need only you. Make haste. Help me with the corset, both of you. The lieutenant who was just here, the young Comte d'Ayen, is alerting my hostlers to get ready a coach. We must make for Saint-Cloud as soon as my body is decently covered. Never mind my hair. I'll wear a scarf. Dant, just bring me a handkerchief and a bottle of that heavy heliotrope perfume.' A sigh escaped her.

Curiosity put special strength into Julie's arms. Hauling on the corset strings to draw them tight as Dant held Mademoiselle back from being pulled forward, she finished the task with alacrity and then served for a leaning post as Mademoiselle stepped into her linen petticoats.

'Incredible, incredible,' the Duchesse muttered to herself through stiff lips.

'Mademoiselle?'

'It is Madame,' the royal lady burst out, sweeping

Dant out of her way, too impatient for last-minute adjustments. 'The Duchesse d'Orleans. She is dying! Dying, imagine! The entire royal family has been summoned to attend her last hours. Quickly, Dant, a scarf, a scarf...'

'Oh, *mon Dieu*, dying!' Julie almost dropped the delicate mule she was holding for Mademoiselle to slip her foot into. 'But Your Highness, I only saw her several days ago, before they went to Saint-Cloud——'

'Yes, I, too, of course, at the concert of viols and hautbois at the Tuileries.' Mademoiselle clasped her hands before her chest in disbelief. 'Incredible——'

'She was laughing, full of spirits, joking with General Turenne——' Julie draped the large white scarf over Mademoiselle's head and shoulders.

'But Henrietta's health has always been delicate——'

'Yet she stood up for almost every dance at the *soirée* that followed. She did not seem at all sick——'

Mademoiselle accepted the handkerchief and scent from Dant. She stared reflectively at Julie. 'In fact, she wasn't sick. It happened last night, suddenly. One minute she was perfectly well and ready to retire, having left Monsieur and his unsavory cronies still at cards, and the next minute she was writhing in pain. That is what the officer tells me.'

'But to be taken so badly——'

'Are you ready, madame?' the Duchesse demanded. 'There is no time for you to fetch your shoulder wrap. Dant, give her one of mine.' Mademoiselle's regal figure sailed toward the gilt-scrolled door. Julie waited for a moment for Dant to give her a blue challis scarf run through with gold and silver threads. Then she caught up with her mistress.

At the door to her bedchamber, Mademoiselle turned, eyes still dark with shock, to Julie. 'Poison can take one badly, Comtesse.'

'Poison! Oh, *Sainte Vierge*!'

They stared at each other, each thinking of the innocent-looking vial of colorless and odorless liquid Julie had put into Mademoiselle's eager hand several days ago.

'Never say I said that. Never, you understand? But there are certain men who could carry on their disgusting and unnatural practices more easily without Henrietta's constant interference. It was only a matter of time, once d'Effiat was allowed back into the country, before the gang of them would make a move to pave the way for Lorraine's return. They cannot seem to live without him. . .'

There was a rap on the door. 'Your carriage is waiting, Your Highness,' came a muffled voice.

Mademoiselle swept out, Julie beside her, Dant hurrying along behind through the empty, echoing anterooms. 'When will you return, Highness?' the maid asked.

'I have no idea. But surely not tonight. Follow as soon as the sun comes up, and bring us both a change of attire and cosmetics. And bring Madame de Lowry's maid as well and whatever we may need for a short stay—God grant *la pauvre petite* does not suffer long. I never cared much for her,' she confided to Julie in a hoarse voice. 'She is too thin, too delicate, not like you or me with a womanly bosom and hips. But, *Dieu le sait*, she is too young to die.'

Several footmen preceded the hastening women down the main steps of the palace. Two jumped from the seat behind the heavy coach to assist the passengers to mount, one of them still surreptitiously buttoning his livery coat. Two link boys holding large torches were mounted before, and an escort of guards was ready behind. The driver cracked his whip, and the lumbering coach rolled out of the Luxembourg gates and into the sleeping streets of Paris, meeting on its way the coaches of the Maréchal de Grammont and several ministers of state. They made a small procession hastening out of the city in the night, toward the beautiful country chateau belonging to the king's brother.

Madame, Princesse Henrietta, who was also the Duchesse d'Orleans, had just recently returned from a triumphant visit to her brother, having been sent to England by Louis as an ambassadress to negotiate a treaty of commerce and alliance. Philippe, jealous of her successful mission and still outraged by her maneuvering which had resulted the year before in the exile of his favorite playmates, refused to meet her and her suite at Calais on her return, and gave her an obviously cold welcome when she arrived to report to Louis at Saint-Germain. But when the two of them left for Saint-Cloud, seemingly in a better rapport, Henrietta's pretty and delicate face glowed with her usual gentle humor, though she murmured a bit about being tired.

A number of coaches were already standing in the court when they arrived, although the echoing halls of the huge house through which Mademoiselle and Julie hurried were empty except for footmen and guards standing in attendance. They came to the gold and white anteroom to Madame's bedchamber, with walls lined from ceiling to floor with paintings, and there they found twenty or thirty people conversing. These dropped low bows as the king's cousin entered the room.

'Has His Majesty arrived yet?' The Duchesse singled out the quick-witted lady of letters Madame de La Fayette, an intimate of Henrietta's. The writer's fine gown was of modest neckline, her hair dressed simply in a Grecian knot at the back of her head.

'No, Mademoiselle. But he should be here momentarily.'

Mademoiselle studied La Fayette's slumped shoulders and drawn face, with eyes red-rimmed from no sleep. 'How is she?' she inquired hoarsely, dreading the answer.

'Ah, pitifully sick, Your Highness, and in much, much pain. She turns alternately white, then livid, and writhes on her bed crying out she cannot bear the agony. Monsieur Esprit, the *premier médicin*, the king's own doctor, is with her and is treating her—for colic.'

Drawing the woman aside, Mademoiselle demanded, 'What happened? Monsieur d'Ayen would only give me a bare outline.'

'Two days ago, she bathed in the Seine, although she had complained of a pain in her side. Yesterday, she said she felt peevish, but her bad humor would have been the good humor of any other woman. She attended mass, went to see the English painter Lely, who is doing her portrait, and returned fatigued, so she went to bed. She awoke looking so ill that Monsieur sent for me. She called for a glass of chicory water to be poured out for her and drank it down when Monsieur's valet handed it to her. Then she suddenly clutched her side, screaming out that the pain was intense. The doctor was sent for, he diagnosed her complaint as mere colic, which would subside. But she kept crying. . .' Madame de La Fayette paused to wipe away a tear, then looked dubiously at the lady who was listening so intently to her.

'Yes? What? Go on, madame,' came the impatient order.

'She kept crying that she was poisoned, and to bring her an antidote. She said the chicory water was to be examined. Monsieur, of course, was unperturbed by her notions. He took a goblet and poured some of the water for himself and drank it, just to calm her, and he even ordered some sort of antidote to be made up. It seemed, alas, to make her all the worse. All day she has suffered, *la pauvre petite*. She weeps that the pain is so excruciating that she would kill herself were she not a Christian. Through the hours she becomes more and more sunken, more feeble. Her spirit seems ready to depart her suffering body. Three doctors attend her now—which could be a death sentence in itself,' Madame de La Fayette said sadly. Tears wetted her pale cheeks. *'Ma pauvre belle Madame.'*

Mademoiselle's face was ashen. 'Thank you, Marquise. I will wait for the king before making my farewells,' she muttered, and turned away to take the chair the Maréchale de Tréville had vacated for her. But just then, the sound of many approaching feet announced the arrival of the king, and Louis came through the door with the queen on his arm, followed by mesdames de Montespan and de La Vallière, the Comtesse de Soissons—who was the spoiled niece of the late Cardinal Mazarin—General Turenne, and others.

'Ah, cousin.' The king acknowledged Mademoiselle softly as she came out of her bow. The brow beneath his waved wig was a field of red furrows, and the dark eyes he bent on her reflected both shock and sorrow. 'Come along. There is no moment to lose, I am told. Alas, alas. . .' Louis had never lost his fondness for the kittenish Henrietta, even though the fleeting, high passion of a young man had soon faded. As a lackey opened the bedchamber door, the king removed his hat. Philippe was standing just inside. As Louis stalked in, Julie saw him give his brother a long, hard look.

Julie moistened Mademoiselle's handkerchief with the heavy perfume she had brought, and the Duchesse held it determinedly to her nose, both to ward off infectious vapors given off by the sick and to neutralize the odors of the sickroom. Mademoiselle followed the royal couple into the lavish, gold-draped chamber, where Madame lay suffering upon a great carved bed that seemed to reduce the woman of twenty-six to the size of a child.

Julie followed Mademoiselle as closely as she could, a vial of ammonia salts Dant had pressed into her hand at the ready, for the Duchesse could not abide to witness sickness and death and had been known to turn faint. Julie's own heart was heavy within her. She set her teeth against the terrible cries coming from the bed. The doctors hovering about the invalid parted and stepped away to allow the royal family to surround the bed. Julie caught a glimpse of Henrietta, and tears of pity sprang to her eyes.

It could not be that the disheveled figure lying curled up on the bed was the gay Duchesse d'Orleans. Her linen nightdress lay open at the neck to allow her to breathe, the short, puffed sleeve displaying the thinness of an arm she had flung over her forehead in misery. Her dark hair lay atangle all over the pillow. Her face had lost any semblance of prettiness and was nothing more than a waxy mask of suffering, mouth drawn taut in a grimace, pain etched into every line and plane. Her eyes were closed and sunken. Her labored breathing was interrupted by her shrieks of pain as her body thrashed every few minutes to mitigate the torment.

Julie was not the only one to cry. There was quiet sobbing all around her, a pervasive pity for this young and charming woman being caught in the toils of so frightful a death. Even her embittered husband, whose excesses she had managed to check for a while, had runnels of tears tracked through the heavy powder and rouge on his cheeks.

Louis bent his dark head over Madame to briefly kiss the burning forehead. Julie saw him murmur to the sick woman, saw her open her eyes, and heard her weak voice whimper, 'Ah, see what a state I am in, Majesty.' In a few minutes, the queen took Louis's place, looking distraught, wringing her hands. Then, in quick succession, the Marquise de Montespan, her former lady-in-waiting, and the Duchesse de La Vallière, Henrietta's old rival for the king's affection, made their brief farewells. Mademoiselle, refusing to approach closer than the end of the bed, said a sad goodbye from there. Olympe de Soissons, Henrietta's sometime rival, sometime confederate, knelt weeping at the side of the bed. The king approached once more to take her hand, his face set against the shrill cries and tormented tears issuing relentlessly from the pitiful soul. The doctors, conferring in a corner near a towel-draped table holding basin, wooden syringes, and lancets, were preparing to bleed her again.

Two gentlemen were admitted through the door. One of them Julie recognized as the English ambassador Lord Montague, who strode forward to the bedside of his monarch's sister.

But the self-serving pragmatism of the members of the court was never far from the surface. Now Julie heard a low remark somewhere behind her. 'They will waste no time choosing someone to succeed her as Philippe's wife. Do you wager it is La Grande Mademoiselle?'

'Oh hush. Madame is not yet a corpse. Anyway, it is probably more in the king's interest to seek a foreign alliance.'

And thus, slowly, their grief mitigated by speculation they could no longer contain, the spectators to the dying of Madame began to sigh, talk freely, move about the room; there was even some quiet laughter in the groups that had coalesced to whisper about the succession. Julie caught several times the mention of La Grande Mademoiselle as people passed her.

That august person, aroused from the melancholy contemplation of her dying cousin-in-law, suddenly looked around in surprise and then loudly demanded that Philippe send for a priest, which no one had remembered to do.

Still snuffling into his large lacy handkerchief, Monsieur looked at her with startled eyes. '*Nom de Dieu*, dear cousin, but you are right. We have no priest.' He peered at her earnestly. 'But whom shall I send for? Bossuet? Grandhomme? Whose name do you think will appear more chic in the *Gazette*? My wife must not appear slighted in any manner. Her funeral will be the most impressive ever seen in the country.'

The two then went on to discuss the merits of various clerics of fashionable name, although Mademoiselle—pausing to glance at Henrietta and seeing in the pain-filled eyes the woman's anguished perception that she was already considered dead, that the dried tears and buzz of conversation in the room represented speculation about her successor—had the grace to draw Philippe away from the bed to continue their conversation.

Julie was disgusted by this callousness but not surprised. Only the death of the king, around whom their very lives and privileges revolved, would move these courtiers to more than a few token tears. Death dwelt intimately in every house, taking children and youths, middle-aged and old, with impartial frequency. It was a circumstance of life much decried but in its familiarity not too long lamented, except by those few who were truly bereft.

The windows of the bedchamber were shut tight and the drapes drawn. The air was stagnant, fetid with the breath of illness. Julie backed away and then turned to the portal, seeking a few minutes' relief from the sick woman's suffering. Henrietta was a scant few years older than she, and already the grim reaper had lifted his scythe in the princess's path, her high standing and money erased of meaning and availing her no help. She lay clothed in only her poor and frail human body, unable to stop the fall of the killing blade.

With a wrung heart, with lancets of the fear of death stabbing her as sharply as the knives now opening the veins of the mortally ill Madame, Julie stumbled through the door, pulling the too-warm blue scarf from her shoulders. And then she saw Nicolas in his blue and red coat approaching her through the scattering of people who had hastily assembled in the anteroom. He had evidently come with the king's party from Saint-Germain. He took one look at her tear-stained cheeks and opened his arms, and she gratefully flung herself into his comforting embrace. With his arm about her shoulder, he walked her to a more private corner of the room. Already she felt safer, the specter of harsh fate fading in the presence of this strong, sure man.

'How does she do?' he asked gruffly.

'Badly, very badly. She looks not to last the night. Ah, Nicolas, I can't believe this is happening. The poor woman suffers so.'

He looked down at her. 'Death is never pretty, *ma petite*. And it is, eventually, unavoidable.' He hugged her against him and rubbed his soft beard comfortingly against her temple.

'They are already tossing about the names of women they think will become the second Madame,' Julie told him, indignant in spite of the fact that she knew, as her father had always said, the living must go on living. 'They mention Mademoiselle. Is that possible?'

'More than possible. Probable. Philippe would be delighted to get his hands on her fortune, and Louis has never denied his brother anything, ever.'

'But he is—he is not a fit husband.' She pushed back to look up into his eyes. There was shock in her retort. '*Écoutes*, the poor Duchesse cried out about poison, Madame de La Fayette told us. She kept insisting that she was poisoned and kept demanding an antidote, which didn't work when they administered it to her. Why would she cry such a thing? And who knows if she isn't right?' Her tone took on a dramatic darkness as she concluded, 'It would be perilous for Mademoiselle to marry so desperate a man, who might prefer to quickly inherit all her money rather than share it!'

Nicolas frowned disapproval into the wide violet eyes staring at him and put a finger on her lips to quiet her. '*Doucement, doucement*, Comtesse. Keep those biased and dangerous thoughts to yourself. In my opinion, Philippe is not a murderer, no matter how his wife dismantled his preferred amusements. In fact, Mademoiselle would never ride him so hard to change his habits as did Henrietta, whose youth made her demanding of him and jealous of his lovers. Mademoiselle would get to be Madame, second consort in the land to the queen. Such a position would not distress her.'

'But she has so much already. She is the richest woman in all Europe. A duke carries her train in processions. What little would being Madame avail her if it meant a liaison with that—that preening egoist?' Julie could not bring herself even to whisper the word *pederast*.

Nicolas grinned. 'Why, she would move up to a better place in the king's carriage when he invited her to ride. How many times she has complained to me that she hates to be sometimes relegated to the outside seats when he invites the dauphin to fill in the sixth place in the coach.'

Julie was impatient with how obtuse men could be. 'You are wrong, Nicolas. It would be the death of her if she were ordered to marry Philippe. Her heart is elsewhere. She loves someone else.'

'*Love* is a word not considered for royalty. And to whom do you refer, the Comte de Lauzun? Pah! She is a grown woman, not a silly girl. She could not be serious. All her life, my godmother has taken the demands of her station most literally. When she was young, she had a history of turning away some very exalted suitors.'

'Like the king of Portugal, a madman smotherd in ulcers and partially paralyzed?' Julie huffed.

'Like the young Charles of England, or the Duc de Savoie,' Nicolas finished smoothly. He smiled, refusing to be riled.

Pulling back, Julie was going to disagree, not too pleased with the acceptance of practicalities that seemed to blind Nicolas to Mademoiselle's humanity, her woman's need for love, and the strength of the passion that bound a virgin heart suddenly awakened.

But Nicolas continued on, seeming not to notice her small recoil. 'All her life, my godmother has insisted upon protocol and the fitness of alliances. I just don't believe she would turn ridiculous now, in midcourse.'

'Ridiculous?'

But the man with the merry light blue eyes refused to be drawn into arguments, and, shaking her arm gently by the sleeve to change the subject, he said, 'Would you care to know how I miss you, *mon coeur*? Following the king about is not the most edifying of tasks. My superintendent at the warehouse sends word to me that one of our finest merchant ships is overdue and feared lost, my brother has difficulty staying sober, and yet only you fill my thoughts. It is a situation that can only be alleviated by your presence. . .' he murmured, leaning closer, and Julie found she could not tear her gaze from his strong mouth. '. . .By your warm arms about my neck and your kisses, by your beautiful eyes. When will you leave Paris for Fontainebleau and relieve my languishing?'

His brief mention of his brother had given her a jolt, but Julie quickly pushed away the horrid picture of a green goat's head and looming male organ that invaded her mind. She would deal later with the guilt of keeping silent about something Nicolas should know. Now she just wanted to wallow in his life-affirming pleasure in her. 'Close upon your arrival. In a few days,' she murmured.

'Good. For I warn you now, I am planning to——'

He broke off, turning about at the flurry of activity behind them, to see the king stride forth from the sickroom, followed by his suite, his women, and his brother. As was the custom, Louis was being hastened away by his minions after saying his goodbyes to his sister-in-law, for the monarch of France was not allowed to look upon the crassness of death.

Mademoiselle rustled up to them, and Nicolas swept off his hat and kissed her hand. 'Ah, de Courcillon! I am charmed to see you,' Mademoiselle warbled, having recovered her poise. 'But the king departs for Saint-Germain, and so must you, I suppose. Promise to steal a moment from your duties to His Majesty to attend me at Fontainebleau. I have something most important to discuss with you.' There was a demanding glint in her blue eyes.

'Indeed, *chère* Highness, I vow that hungry lions could not keep me from you,' he teased. He transferred his gaze to Julie, and his eyes were full of promises. 'Nor from you, madame,' he said. He jauntily saluted them both, then wheeled and strode away after the king, his bootheels striking the parquet with firm assurance.

The gaze of the two women followed him. 'The rascal,' Mademoiselle muttered, unsuccessful at holding in a smile. 'He has no solemnity.'

'Nor any propriety,' Julie added, looking yearningly after the retreating broad shoulders and strong back, her cheeks pink with embarrassment over her own private thoughts.

The steward assigned to them a partially furnished chamber commensurate with the Duchesse de Montpensier's rank, a grand, paneled room with a canopied bed for her, and a small chamber attached to it, where a cot was set up for Julie. Two maids were sent to help them undress and bring what nourishment they might need. But having determined to return to Paris as soon as it was light, Mademoiselle instructed them only to remove her gown and loosen her corset. Then, as soon as the maids shut the door behind them, she grabbed up her discarded gown, felt about in the pocket, and withdrew a small vial. Julie, standing in her petticoats, recognized it as the love philter La Voisin had sold to her.

True to her sense of drama, head erect with regal determination, Mademoiselle marched to the cold hearth and unhesitatingly dashed the glass vial against the firewall, where it shattered with a tinkle, the liquid pouring down to make a dark puddle on the charred brick floor. She turned and eyed Julie with defiance. 'You needn't stare so, madame. I have carried that concoction with me ever since you fetched it. But now I think, how do we know what horrid stuff is in it? You could have been recognized and considered an emissary for me and your true mission surmised. Monsieur de Lauzun has many enemies who could have reached that sorceress and easily influenced her to do him harm.'

'Oh, Your Highness, that is difficult to believe. You are just unnerved by this dreadful calamity tonight.'

Mademoiselle reached out one toe to gingerly stir the shard of glass. 'Perhaps so, although, for your information, I believe my dear cousin Philippe is completely incapable of the crime of murder. But not his vile henchmen, who enjoy their control of him. They have long hated her, poor wretched creature.' Shrugging, she turned her back on the shattered fragments, walked tiredly to the bed, and sat down. 'She has truly upset my plans by dying. How unfortunate,' she rasped.

At this moment, with the Duchesse pursing and unpursing her mouth nervously, Julie thought better of remarking that poor Madame was not dead yet.

'Don't you see, Julie? I have no time left to play love games with slow-acting potions meant to urge Monsieur de Lauzun on. I am very aware that I am being matched with Monsieur in my Jupiter-cousin's mind, and should he order me to become Philippe's wife, I would have to obey or risk lifelong exile from court. But he cannot order a woman to marry who is already openly betrothed. Tomorrow I shall confront the Comte de Lauzun with the exact situation—which I am sure he already has been apprised of—and once the veils of his modest reticence have been torn away, he will surely know what we must do.' Her face picked up a glow from the thought of de Lauzun's usual masterful confrontation with most situations. The long, bumpy nose twitched in anticipation.

Julie helped her swing her feet onto the bed, although the Duchesse insisted on sleeping atop the bedclothes, as if the soft linen sheet might in some way hinder their quick departure in the morning. Then, blowing out most of the candles, Julie went to find her own bed in the dressing room next door. And so, partially clothed, each woman lay on her couch to try to find sleep for a few hours before dawn broke.

Julie could hear Mademoiselle tossing and turning, muttering in her sleep as if the woman were calling in her disturbed dreams for her *cher* Antonin, her stern soldier who was capable of fixing all things. Julie couldn't sleep, either. Her mind was too full of whirling images both horrible and wonderful: Henrietta, the frightening Abbé d'Aubièrre, Nicolas, the glamorous prospect of soon being at Fontainebleau and perhaps the half-finished palace of Versailles as well, life, death, the loneliness of each soul imprisoned in its body, no matter how beloved of someone else. . .

She dozed at last, and in a moment it was morning.

CHAPTER
~ 12 ~

'Bring him in.'

At the order from one of the king's private secretaries, Nicolas left his second-in-command outside the room and shoved the plump, pale *valet-de-chambre* forward. It had been easy to arrest the man without Monsieur's being the wiser, for Philippe was away. He would never miss one of the lavish hunting parties that set the tangled woods of Fontainebleau echoing with horns and baying hounds and crashing with men in full chase of giant wild boar. Philippe would be gone for hours, acting the hunt leader in the absence of the king, who supposedly nursed one of the massive headaches which lately assailed him.

Another shove, and the valet stumbled through the open door and into the chamber, although the servant, bald spot shining since he'd been given no time to don his wig, kept a steady demeanor. Nor did his aplomb desert him under the hawk-nosed regard of his king and the gimlet stare of the Marquis de Louvois. Nicolas delivered him a thump on the back. 'Mind your manners, man!' The valet hastily bowed to Louis, murmuring 'Sire' in a high but calm voice.

'His name is Marcel Gomberon, Your Majesty,' Nicolas said.

Still dressed from head to toe in the milky lavender of mourning, Louis sat erect in a massive high-backed armchair, an imposing figure, even seen against the vivid allegorical paintings covering the walls of his private cabinet. The great carved ball-footed table at his side was piled with papers and charts and dispatch cases. Close by, in front of the fireplace, stood his Minister of War, whose agents, since the death of Henrietta, had kept the suspect under close observation in case he'd had any intent of slipping away before reaching Fontainebleau.

'Bring the person forward, Monsieur de Courcillon, and remain with us. Another witness besides Monsieur de Louvois is necessary, and I trust your discretion.'

Nicolas nodded. He urged the servant forward until the man halted just before Louis, and then moved aside, standing easy, although one hand rested lightly on the pommel of his duty saber. He was pleased to have been invited to stay. Once Madame's massive funeral was over in Paris, life around the king—who this year was chafing under the absence of any war frontier—had taken on a hot-weather somnolence. This secret interrogation of Philippe's valet provided a ripple of interest on the great glassy sea of the court's frivolous pursuits. He had to admire Gomberon's coolness, though. He didn't look like the kind who would face being dragged before the king and de Louvois with such outward composure.

Louis's hard eyes looked the man up and down. The king leaned forward, hands white-knuckled on the clubbed arms of his chair. A huge emerald glittered balefully on his forefinger. '*Mon ami*, listen to me. You have a simple choice and no time to consider. If you tell me everything you know and hold nothing back, no matter what part you may have played, I give you my word I will pardon you and you will return to your duties. But if you conceal any fact you know from me, I shall easily divine it, and the captain of my bodyguards, who hastened you here, will help you to leave this room as well, but dead and stuffed in a trunk.' Louis paused, but the valet stood solid, a respectful but unquailing expression on his face. Louis continued, 'So. We understand each other. My sister-in-law was poisoned, is that not the truth?'

'Yes, sire,' the man answered.

There was a moment of silence as the import of that short, blunt answer sank in. Louis's ringed hand trembled on the arm of the chair. He demanded, 'Who poisoned her, and how was it done?'

'It was a special preparation of antimony. The Chevalier de Lorraine had it made up and sent it to Monsieur de Beuvron and the Marquis d'Effiat. But when they first approached me to help them, I refused, as then they made it appear as if they only joked.'

'And did my brother know of this murder plot?'

'No, sire, they said he absolutely did not.' And with the confidence of an intimate who had served Philippe for twenty years, he added, 'In fact, they would have been fools to tell him. He cannot keep a secret. Sooner or later, he would have blurted it all out.'

With an explosive sound, the king let out his breath and leaned back in his chair, unconcerned for the show of relief that was visible in every line of his body. He exchanged a quick glance with de Louvois and then continued. 'Relate to me, then, Gomberon, how the deed was accomplished.'

'I can only speculate, sire, since I believed that without my help they could not effect so dastardly a plot, and I thought no more about it. But on the day Madame fell ill—in fact, just before she returned from her portrait session—I entered her room and discovered Monsieur d'Effiat there, just in the act of rubbing Madame's crystal and gold goblet with a thick piece of paper. I demanded to know what was his business there, and he said Monsieur had sent him to fetch something, he'd gotten thirsty, and since the cup had been used, he was wiping it out. Very calmly, sire, he put down the goblet and went out, and seeing that all seemed in order, so did I.'

De Louvois pounded an angry fist against the mantelpiece. 'The cup! Of course. No wonder several people drank the same chicory water with no ill effects. It was the goblet they had tainted, which we did not think to examine.'

The requisite autopsy on Henrietta had been extremely thorough, performed by the king's surgeon and attended by physicians chosen by the suspicious Lord Montague. The doctors decided that Madame had died of cholera morbus and of a consumptive constitution weakened by childhood convulsions and rickets and the adult venereal disease which had also killed six of her eight infants. But the whispers of poison still abounded.

'Gomberon, why did you not report to us such horrific plotting?'

'I was afraid to be implicated, Your Majesty. I am but

a lowly servant. It would have been my word against those of highborn gentlemen, and they are also Monsieur's dear friends.'

Louis stared at him. 'A word from you could have saved her life.'

Gomberon had the grace to redden and hang his head.

Louis was pale. His lips moved stiffly. 'I gave you my word that you should have your freedom, and I will keep it. But you will forget everything you have told me. You will never again mention any knowledge of plot or poison or anything else about this ugly affair, or I will have your tongue ripped out and broiled for you to eat. I hope you have marked me well. Now, get out of my sight.'

Under the king's towering disgust, some of the valet's aplomb quit him. He bowed, stepped back, and darted a swift, apprehensive glance at the two other men in the room. De Courcillon stepped over and flung open the door, and the valet, his head still ducked, hustled his bulk through the portal.

Seeing the door secured again, Louis rose and walked to the window. He stood there, running a finger over his slim, divided moustache, looking out with unseeing eyes at the lovely fountain and orange trees of the Garden of Diane.

'Will I ask Monsieur de Courcillon to arrest the gentlemen in question?' de Louvois asked, his cold gaze unblinking.

'And give credence to the public notion that poor Henrietta was indeed poisoned? And, as they are so anxious to believe, perhaps by my brother's orders? No, de Louvois, I think we are forced to leave the vipers unmolested in order to keep any hint of murder in the shadow world of rumor, where our calm attitude will work to squelch it.' The ruler turned from the window, dark circles underlining his eyes, mouth set. 'But I shall have the murderous scoundrels in to see me. And I shall inform them that if Monsieur's second wife, whoever she might be, suffers as much as a hangnail to harm her, they will find themselves not just talking to the rats at

Pignerol for the rest of their vile lives but drawn and quartered.'

'Yes, sire.'

'And do you agree with my point, Marquis?'

'Most well taken, sire. Indeed.'

'Then, what is more, you will effect the official return of the Chevalier de Lorraine to France, and in good odor. That should help to bury Lord Montague's rampant suspicions of a long-distance plot.'

'At once, sire.'

Louis turned his regard to the captain of his élite corps of swordsmen. 'De Courcillon, smoke out d'Effiat and Beuvron, and quietly bring them to me this evening before supper. Use my valet's small staircase to avoid attention. I shall await their attendance on me here in this room.'

Nicolas saluted, right hand on heart. 'By your orders, sire.'

Louis seemed to deflate, the silver-embroidered satin coat too heavy for his shoulders. 'You may withdraw, messieurs. I need solitude to digest the loathsome reverberations of this whole situation and those involved in it. It is true, you see, the old saying, "Not even a king can pick his own relatives."' He turned once again to the window.

Bowing to his back, the two men replaced their plumed hats and exited. Once among the courtiers in the anteroom, Nicolas and de Louvois, never enamored of each other and now suddenly rivals for the affection of the provocative Comtesse de Lowry, found themselves striking off in the same direction. Silently, they walked the same path through the huge, ornate guardroom, de Courcillon broader of shoulder, de Louvois somewhat longer of leg. The gentlemen lounging there on king's duty, seeing them both stony-faced and frowning, let them pass with only nods for greeting.

At last, de Louvois said, 'Take as few men as possible to bring in those vermin. Discreet men. De Brissac, in fact, may be all you need. I doubt if they will give you any trouble, since we can no longer prove anything.'

Nicolas threw a sideways glance at the scar-jawed

minister. 'I had intended simply to go myself, since I agree with your assessment. But I will take de Brissac.'

In the frescoed anteroom, they halted just as a page in the Duchesse de Montpensier's green and white livery slipped up to Nicolas. 'Monsieur de Courcillon, the Comtesse de Lowry wishes to inform you that my mistress and her suite have arrived and are now installed on the first floor of the palace overlooking the court of the Hercules Fountain, should you have a moment to greet Her Highness.'

De Louvois's eyes flickered and grew hooded over his slight smile.

'Tell Madame de Lowry that I will send her a note later requesting a visit,' Nicolas mumbled, having no intention of making de Louvois privy to his arrangements with Julie. The young man bowed and spun on his heel. The two gentlemen walked on, Nicolas intending to slip away as soon as they reached the stair.

'Did you believe the valet's tale?' de Louvois drawled.

'Most of it. It matched what we had already surmised.'

'What did you not credit?'

'That the knave himself had so little to do with it. He has a mild-faced appearance and a direct manner, but I think the man is a conniver. I wouldn't trust him from this pillar to that.'

'Exactly. We are again in accord. I shall arrange to have the man removed.'

De Louvois halted, and since they were in conversation, Nicolas had to stop, too. De Louvois contemplated him with eyes so dark one could not see the pupils, but the meaning behind the sudden ferret smile that stretched the thin mouth was all too evident. 'I would not doubt that Gomberon's account of this interview with the king is already on its way to inform Lorraine, who, I fear, will not believe that His Majesty would so easily let him off. But Lorraine's presence is necessary to create the illusion of Madame's suspicionless death. The English are so incensed about the rumors that King Charles had to send a detachment of guards to protect our ambassador at Whitehall. Therefore'—he smiled mirthlessly—'I must assign you to fetching Lorraine here immediately, for you have the tact and ability to convince him that his skin is safe. You will leave for Milan tomorrow, monsieur.'

Under the falls of lace at his wrists, Nicolas's hands clenched into fists. It was no more necessary to chase after the Chevalier de Lorraine than to chase the moon when it set; the man would return without question, overjoyed to be allowed home with free access to his royal lover. All the journey would do was remove Nicolas from Fontainebleau for two weeks so that de Louvois would have a clear field with Julie. But as long as he was on his formal tour of duty, de Louvois was Nicolas's superior.

'I could send de Brissac as easily, rather than go myself. The king——'

'Not acceptable, since de Brissac would know little of the situation and would not be able to act to soothe Lorraine. Last fall, the king insisted that you take that special prisoner to Pignerol because the situation called for discretion. This is the same. A delicate matter, de Courcillon, fit only for a chief officer of the Garde-du-Corps. De Brissac can act in your place as temporary captain here.' Now the sardonic smile had gained a definite mocking twist.

Nicolas gazed at him stonily. Only the king could supersede de Louvois's orders, and Louis had never been known to do that. The monarch might even think the minister's point well taken. The game went to de Louvois this time; Nicolas had no choice but to obey. He thought he was succeeding in keeping an unaffected attitude, but he felt a muscle in his jaw jump, and his nostrils flared in spite of himself.

'Very well, Monsieur le Ministre. At your command. If you will send me official authorization, I will depart tomorrow.'

De Louvois nodded with false affability. 'Of course. *A votre service*, monsieur.'

Any spectator to their *de rigueur* bows as they parted might have sworn an iron rod had been rammed up each back.

* * *

Julie dismissed the page and read and reread the short note in her hand, her back turned to the ladies at the far side of the chamber. They were taking turns reading to Mademoiselle the latest news in the Paris *Gazette*, while Dant and the maids went to and fro across the patterned rug unpacking trunks and boxes. Because they had not come to Fontainebleau the easy way from Paris, along the Seine by roomy barge, but had made the long and dusty trip south by coach followed by a caravan of guards, retainers, cooks, maids—almost the entire household, along with numerous wagons piled high with baggage and Mademoiselle's favorite furniture, without which she could not last the summer—they were all wilted and tired. Julie and Madame de Plessis-Rabat, especially, for having to endure the Duchesse's cries and clutches each time they forded the smallest brook.

But now energy tingled along Julie's nerves to flush away fatigue, released by the note she held. It was from Nicolas, telling her she must meet him that very night, after Mademoiselle had retired. And he had set as meeting place not the garden or a corner of an empty salon when all were at *appartements*, but his own chamber, where he had invited her to take supper with him, carefully asking her to bring her servant if she wished. Her heart had begun a slow pounding, which she was sure was loud enough to be heard across the room.

To be closeted alone with a gentleman in his quarters, going there masked or not, was to be compromised; some snoop would see it, and sooner or later her identity would be guessed and the gossips delighted. Did she care about that? Had she enough gumption to go to him alone for the first time since she had slept in his arms in a coach in Flanders, alone in the place of comfort he had deemed worth waiting for on that cold, cramped night? If he wanted her, would she let him make love to her, become his mistress—as she had done a thousand times in her reveries, in her waking dreams, in her sleep in her too big, too empty bed?

She felt herself blushing at the erotic images that invaded her mind, and she dropped her hand in her lap, trying to compose herself and think more steadily.

Nicolas wrote that his valet would await her just outside Mademoiselle's apartment, after the *coucher*. Primly, she told herself not to be flustered. She had until then to decide whether to go or not. But she laughed silently at such subterfuge: you'll go, *ma fille*. To use Nicolas's own phrase, wild lions couldn't keep her away from him.

Mademoiselle ate her dinner of lamb, partridge, and carrots, followed by a honey pudding, from a tray on her rug-covered table, preferring to read from the rapturous and flowery Quinault, her favorite playwright, to conversation that afternoon. The servants set up another table by the window, and Julie, Diane de Greu, and mesdames d'Epernon and Puysieux took their dinner there. It was a gay little party in spite of their lingering fatigue. At least Julie thought it was gay. Her mind seemed to be floating around in her head without an anchor. She hoped her eyes were not drifting loose in the same witless manner, and she kept forcing her attention back to the chatter. If she was this distracted now, hours before seeing him, how would she hold up by eleven o'clock or midnight? She stole a glance at her little timepiece. Half before three o'clock. Seven hours to go. A glance told her Mademoiselle was engrossed in her reading. That was good. Without a nap, the royal lady would retire early.

Outside, beyond their table littered with plates and goblets and crumbs, a soft summer rain was whispering down from a dun sky. A mild breeze brought in the smell of wet grass and rambler roses and of the warm, moist marble pavement. They all ate too much and drank too much and sat cracking nuts, at ease, happy to be settled from the trip. Soon after, leaving the table to lounge upon settees, their eyelids drooped, their muscles relaxed, and they all dozed, even Mademoiselle in her big chair, head lolling to one side, leather-bound book fallen to the floor. Julie, somnolent too, quieted her heart finally and allowed herself to nap, relinquishing the time to daydream about Nicolas only because she was anxious to be fresh and clear-eyed that night.

They all woke toward five, bleary-eyed, cramped,

feeling a little sheepish, amazed that the servants had cleared the tables without waking them. Mademoiselle sent Dant running for cool drinks, to fetch up her other maids and order the lackeys to bring in her bath. Refreshed from her nap, the king's cousin announced that she was going to make a special toilette that night for her first appearance at court in a month, if one did not count the few sad hours at Saint-Cloud. When the maids arrived, she genially released her ladies to their own quarters to refresh themselves and change attire.

The chamber assigned to Julie, on the floor above Mademoiselle's, was cramped, for she shared it with Diane de Greu and their two maids, but she was used to going about her business as if the others weren't there. Blanchette filled Julie a tub from buckets delivered to the door by the palace servants, and the tepid water, sprinkled with dried flower petals, revived her. She swabbed her face energetically with a wash cloth until it glowed, and she splashed happily about. Blanchette washed her hair with the finest of Marseilles soap, and she sat in her silk dressing gown just inside the window to let the warm breeze dry it while Blanchette stirred up the charcoal in a brazier on the cold hearth to heat the curling irons.

She went to study her gowns, worrying because she had to look perfect and unfortunately nothing in her whole wardrobe was perfect enough for the evening to come. Frustrated, she searched once more through the neatly hung or folded piles of wide-skirted, narrow-bodiced gowns, all in fine fabrics and iced with Venetian lace. She settled on one at last, a shimmering purple silk that complimented her eyes. Pink rosebuds caught up the looped silk braid defining the low neckline, and there was an underskirt of pleated pink satin and short, puffed sleeves, which would leave most of her rounded arms bare if she removed her long silk gloves.

She leaned over to settle her breasts high within the corset. She pasted a tiny heart-shaped patch on the soft curve of her bosom above the bodice edge. Blanchette dressed her jet hair fashionably in back in a high Psyche knot, at the side in long curls, and over her forehead in wispy tendrils. Since her skin was poreless and her lips naturally tinted, she needed few cosmetics, merely a touch of pink color on the cheeks, a dot patch at the corner of her eye, and a dab of pomade to add shine to her winged eyebrows. With her best pearls to adorn the smooth column of her neck, pearl drops in her ears, her favorite essence of white hyacinth dabbed on the nape of her neck and on her bare shoulders, she was ready. She picked up her fan and waited for de Greu, who was very animated tonight because a new beau was awaiting her.

How was it possible for a night to drag like a year and yet seem no longer than a minute?

Julie tried to immerse herself in chatter and in watching the new gambling game called Hoya which, so the gossip went, had already ensnared Athénais de Montespan to the tune of hundreds of thousands of livres every evening and at which the king's mistress was even now animatedly engaged. She drifted from one salon to another while Mademoiselle held court with Cardinal Rohan and diverse other luminaries; she even peeked into the billiards room, where the gentlemen disported themselves. But Nicolas was nowhere to be seen—and although this disappointed her in one way, it made her glad in another. She did not want to see him until later. It occurred to her briefly that the Marquis de Louvois, too, was absent—not that she cared—and, in fact, even the king did not make an appearance at the *appartements*.

She rejoined Mademoiselle, whose group intermittently included the Comte de Lauzun, at which points the Duchesse's color went quite high and her eyes became brighter.

Suppose the Duchesse, whose *coucher* she was obligated to attend, didn't go to bed before one or two in the morning? Julie fretted, eyeing her animated mistress. The woman looked ready to stay until dawn. Wine! That was it. Wine would make her sleepy, especially the heavy, sweet southern wine she enjoyed.

Mademoiselle was having too good a time being in the thick of things to notice that her solicitous lady-of-honor was always presenting a fresh cup of wine at her elbow.

But the Duchesse was too busy talking to drink much; she merely held the goblet and sipped once in a while. Finally, ignorant of Julie's silent fidgeting, Mademoiselle abruptly stood up anyway as the hour grew late, announced that she was retiring, and bid all an expansive good night. Grateful, Julie accompanied her, collecting de Greu and de Plessis-Rabat on the way. The ladies-in-waiting followed as their mistress made her proud exit between the bowing, glittering courtiers, who even in their great numbers did not begin to crowd the long François I gallery and adjoining high-ceilinged salons of Fontainebleau.

Later, Julie could not remember much about helping the maids and ladies attending Mademoiselle's *coucher* remove the royal lady from her clothes, fripperies, and plumes. She seemed to be talking, walking, smiling in her sleep, looking surreptitiously at her little clock, which was in her pocket, every few minutes. Mademoiselle yawned heavily, and at last she was abed, having insisted that she was much too exhausted to have her hair combed out or her heavy rouge washed off. The twittering ladies bowed and went out the door. Julie said good night, acknowledged Dant's curtsy with a nod, and then she, too, was beyond the bedchamber portal.

De Greu was waiting for her. 'I think I will return to *appartements*. Not that I have any silver left to play with. Just to watch.'

'Wait, maybe I will. . .' With a trembling hand on de Greu's arm, Julie had no idea why she was detaining the girl. Perhaps she was afraid to leave the antechamber and find there was no one waiting for her beyond it. She was cold, she felt faint, the lemon ice she had lapped up earlier must have disagreed with her, frozen her liver——

'What, Julie? Are you all right?' Little de Greu peered at her with owlish concern.

'Oh. Why, of course I am. It's not anything, I'm just still tired. I'm going to my bed. You enjoy yourself, *chérie*,' Julie fluttered.

She watched de Greu head for the door leading to the long gallery, the heels of the young woman's shoes clicking on the parquet floor. Then she drew from her pocket a small purple mask and donned it. The candles in the room flickered in the night breeze from the open windows and scattered yellow light as she walked slowly toward the opposite door. A thought struck her, and she colored. Surely he had not sent Skandahet-se to fetch her? The whole court knew to whom that savage belonged.

But in the next room, a quiet chamber, an ordinary man in a dark coat and breeches and simple white fall at the throat left off his staring at the richly painted ceiling and advanced toward her. 'Madame? Forgive my impertinence. Do you seek a certain Monsieur de C.?'

Through the phlegm blocking her throat, she whispered, 'Yes.'

'Suivez-moi, s'il vous plait.'

The strange thing was that as soon as she saw the servant awaiting her as promised, her mood instantly changed. Her lips curled upward in an anticipatory smile, her eyes took on sparkle behind the silk concealer, her heart began to beat again with excitement as she followed the valet's thin, straight back. And she realized that all night she had simply been afraid the man wouldn't be there, that she would wait in vain for Nicolas to remember her, and that she would then die of rejection right there on the spot.

It was a rendezvous she desired with every fiber of her being.

Silence. Mademoiselle's ears strained to hear if anyone remained outside her door, and then, with a conspirator's cry of glee, she pushed back the sheet and swung her long legs out of bed. Dant hurried up with a satin dressing robe and helped her mistress pat her hair back into place and puff a bit of powder onto her nose. Then the maid went to the small door on the wall with the bed, which led to a back stair, knocked softly on it, and was answered by a corresponding knock. Dant pulled it open. Outside, fussy with lace and shining in silver and white brocade with jeweled buckles on his shoes, stood the Comte de Lauzun, stoically enduring his long wait.

He brushed by the maid and went immediately to

Mademoiselle, kissing her hand. 'Your most gracious Highness,' he murmured, agreeable for once.

'Oh, Antonin, I am sorry for the delay. My ladies are too solicitous of me,' the Duchesse simpered.

'I was aware of no delay, Your Highness. My thoughts were so busy with you and the prospect of your coming marriage with Monsieur.'

'Oh no, but you are misinformed,' she gasped, almost withdrawing her hand from his clasp. 'That is not in the least decided yet, my dear Comte, not at all. The king merely informed me there was a possibility—a situation vacant, as he put it, and asked if I wanted it. I evaded answering directly, of course, but when I indicated I could never be happy with Monsieur and did not wish to marry him, the king said he would think on it. I told him the truth, you see, in spite of that little lecture you gave me on duty and how you were looking forward to addressing me as Madame.'

She pouted, accusation in her tone.

He heard it, and his mouth turned down. 'I am a loyal subject of the king, Mademoiselle, and whatever it is I might personally wish has no standing against the desires of my monarch. What other advice to you would you have me say?'

'The truth, Antonin, what is in your heart.' She moved closer to him and would not let him relinquish her hand. 'I wish to hear it.'

'Highness, it is summer, and yet here I stand numb with cold. You are making fun of me. I am a commoner and a soldier. I know of battlefields and politics, not of women. Even though the king often takes me into his confidence, I still have no rank but that of an ordinary courtier.' He looked up into her eyes, and although his tone was forthright, she thought she read pain in his face. He said more softly, with some embarrassment, 'I do not wish to allow your female frivolities to make me ridiculous.'

'But I swear to you, I was never more serious or more determined, my dearest Comte.'

She drew him with her toward a settee, with a quick glare at Dant, who bustled to leave, mouth pressed in a prim line. She thought her mistress was abasing herself to meet this man secretly—and in her dressing robe.

Anne-Marie-Louise de Montpensier felt sure of herself now, for the man who perched himself next to her, as she insisted, looked at her with the eyes of a stricken dog, all his bluster and bravado and strutting dissolved by the fear of losing the object of his desire to a state-arranged marriage. Now she could tell him what they must do, because there was no more time to hesitate. She moistened her lips to begin and saw his eyes rove to her bosom, that still attractive and rounded expanse of soft flesh, and a little *frisson* of joy climbed her spine. Her Antonin was the most intelligent of men, but underneath that stiffly formal shell lay a passion she'd heard many pining ladies had also perceived but which was only ready to be uncovered by her, she was sure. He would see the rightness in what she was going to say; he would cease to resist his human feelings. He would agree that a tenderness like theirs, between two grown and responsible adults, should no longer be denied.

She leaned forward to declare what he had never allowed her even to hint at before, that she was exasperated with his modesty and subtleties and that he was the man she wished to marry; and she thought she saw, at last, in the red-rimmed blue eyes, hope flood in. Ah, Antonin, she whispered in her head, for all your masterly control of our situation these many months, it will still be love of me that rules you. Ah, my charming obstinate little man, *je t'adore*.

The valet opened the door for Julie to enter, then quietly closed it behind her.

Nicolas was standing inside, behind him a table finely appointed with plate, goblets, and silver candelabra. At least, that was her impression, for all she really saw clearly was him, a vital presence comprised of masculine assurance and strength and blue eyes alight with welcome. He was wearing a silvery blue brocade coat, which emphasized his narrow waist and ended at the knee to barely show his matching baggy breeches. White silk stockings outlined his muscled calves. The dress sword at his waist was slung from a gold-fringed baldric slanted across his chest. His luxuriant cinnamon locks fell to his broad shoulders.

She removed her mask as he strode up to her and bent his head to kiss her fingers. She wanted to run her hand over the loose-waved hair that slanted forward about his face. 'Madame la Comtesse,' he murmured against her skin.

Perhaps he felt her hand tremble. He straightened up and folded her hand against his chest, moving in closer to her. 'It was almost beyond my wildest hopes that you would come, Julie,' he told her softly. He held her hand caged in both of his, like a captured bird.

'Liar,' she answered in a tone just as soft. 'You knew I would. And by myself. From the very beginning, when you stole my carriage, you knew.'

'No, not knew. Hoped, prayed, desired with all my heart.'

Julie watched his lips move and wished she didn't have to answer with coy gush. What she wanted, single-mindedly, overwhelmingly, immediately, was for him to wrap her in his arms and kiss her. Mortified with her own bold urges, she attempted to take some control of the situation. Extricating her hand, with a smile, she slipped past him and glanced around the simple chamber that had been assigned him. There were some impressive gilt-framed paintings hung on the walls, which she thought were Italian masters, and these had to be his, a quiet indication of both his wealth and taste. Several small rugs of peculiar design were strewn about, but before the hearth was spread a spectacular rug of white shaggy fur—the Arctic polar bear, he told her later. His bed, up against one wall, was long and narrow, quite utilitarian, but it had a blue velvet canopy and a spread embroidered with the d'Aubièrre arms.

Julie stood by the table set with gleaming silver forks and plates and asked, oh so brightly, 'But will you not offer me something to drink, Monsieur le Marquis, for my throat is dry. And perhaps some food? I am famished.'

He belied his grin with a solemn manner. 'Of course,

madame. I have an excellent hippocras, from a receipt of Monsieur le Prince de Condé himself. And if you glance under that cover, you will find a salver of cold roast fowl and other succulent morsels my own cook prepared with much loving care, since his head was forfeit if you were not pleased.' He came up close to her and slipped his arm behind her to take up one of the full goblets from the table. With a little bow of his head, he presented it to her and then picked up one for himself.

She wished he wouldn't stand so close, and yet she wanted him to stay right there. What did they exchange remarks about so gaily as they sipped the heady wine? Inane subjects, the weather, the success of the day's hunt, which had bagged a boar and a sow for tomorrow's banquet, the state of Mademoiselle's health—quite fine, in fact! His eyes never left her face, and finally, breathless, she ran out of aimless chatter and stopped for a moment. It was then she realized he wasn't smiling. His gaze was consuming her.

His regard dropped from her mouth to the swell of her full ivory breasts, where the heart-shaped black patch rose and fell above the sheen of her purple silk gown, to her tiny waist, and then moved up again, roving over her features, her hair, and at last coming to rest on her eyes.

She did not look away but stared back at him, although her smile faltered. Now her lower lip trembled. Surely she could not allow this thing to happen, she thought frantically. She was plunging into waters too turbulent for her to navigate——

'You're not l-listening.'

'I haven't heard a word you said,' he confessed. 'But if you will tell me how God made you so exquisite, my lady, I will treasure every syllable that falls from your lips.'

Gently, his eyes still on hers, he took the cup from her hand and set it down. Her fingers opened without her knowing it. She thought she swayed toward him. And in a moment, she was in his embrace, his mouth was on hers, and she was happy at last. He kissed her long, hard, and deep, and she answered, winding her arms about his neck and pressing against him, letting him drink from the reservoir of passion that had survived hidden within her until he had stirred up its depths.

He hugged her against him. He kissed her chin and nose and eyes. Then he swept her up lightly into his arms and whispered against her fragrant cheek, 'Tell me, love, are you still famished?'

Out of her uncontrollable need for him, the *'Oui'* that she breathed, her eyes heavy-lidded, left him no doubt about how to assuage her. He started for the bed but then stopped, changed his mind, and carried his burden instead to the fluffy white fur rug, setting her down on it. Kneeling beside her, he pulled from his neck the snowy fall of lace cravat and shrugged off his baldric, impatiently sending the sword and belt skittering across the floor. Nimbly and quickly, he undid the numerous buttons of his coat and flung it aside.

It seemed too much effort to close her parted lips. Julie's attention was focused on his passionate eyes, his responsive mouth. She was hardly aware that her hand fumbled behind her with the buttons closing her bodice. He unbuttoned his full-sleeved shirt down to the tight band of his breeches, and when he leaned toward her, she could see a mat of sandy hair curling at the base of his tendoned neck where the pulse beat strongly.

Stilll kneeling, he expertly pulled the pins from the Grecian knot so that her hair slithered down her back. He took her shoulders in his hands, drew her against him, and tasted her lips deeply. And then, without preamble, he did a stunning thing that made her senses reel: he quickly, tenderly scooped one breast out from the confines of her bodice and bent his head to lick at the nipple, back and forth, with a hot, expert tongue. A short, sharp cry escaped her, but her desire hurtled along as inexorably as his. She flung her head back and abandoned her body to him. She only knew she might faint from the tremors his encircling lips, his mouth, his breath on her skin were sending through her system. He ran his hot tongue all around her breast, up her chest, then fastened his lips in the hollow where the pulse throbbed unmercifully in her throat. Uncaring, wanton, lost in her need, she tried to turn her back, begging,

'Take it off for me. Please. Quickly,' and pulling at her gown. He obeyed, reaching around behind her, so near that she closed her eyes, and by feel rapidly unbuttoning her bodice, unhooking her skirt, drawing the gown down to her knees as she knelt. He untied the strings of her two petticoats. Then, tenderly laying her down, he pulled off everything at once. For a second, his burning eyes took in the formidable lacing of her corset; in a fluid motion, he stood up and went to the table, returning with a hilted knife. Unflinching, she watched the sharp edge of the knife descend toward her heaving bosom, heard his breath ragged, impatient, and then he guided the blade in a swift and delicate slice right through the laces. Released from tension, the corset fell away. She lay on the shaggy fur, nude except for the ribbon-tied drawers and white silk stockings. He hoarsely asked her, devouring her with his eyes, 'Quick enough for you, madame?'

She held out her arms, and he came into them, curving her soft body into his, kissing her deeply as she kissed him, one of his hands slipping under the waistband of her drawers to grip the firm smoothness of her *derrière*. The possessive hand on her flesh heated her; so did the feel of his naked chest, his demanding mouth. Frantically, she pulled the shirt free from his breeches and then slid her hand under it and up his muscled back to the mass of his shoulders. She had no defense against what was driving her, and she didn't care. The world had narrowed down to this one minute, to being in the arms of this one man. She pulled her mouth from his and pressed it warm and demanding on the corded side of his neck and heard him groan. From every extremity, flames raced along nerves to collect in her groin and belly and sear her with her need. There was only him and her ungovernable wish to take something from him and give him something back. She flung a leg over his; he pressed her so closely against him that she was able to glory in his aroused hardness. She moved against him insistently.

Then he drew back, and he was glowering at her, at her swelled lips, her slitted eyes, her tumbled black hair. With a soft curse, he ripped the front of her drawers down. He fumbled at his own breeches, and then he loomed on top of her, his weight on his elbows, kneeing her legs apart, rhythmically probing, probing her——

She panted, trembling with anticipation, digging her fingernails into the flesh at the side of his ribs as she tilted her pelvis and came to meet him. She gasped. She moaned aloud with pleasure as they locked together as one, and as one they rode the wild horse, spiraling round and round on an upward course, reaching, straining for the top in a frantic crescendo, clutching each other, and then the wild leap into space—first her, the convulsions of her body soaring away with her; then he followed, a surging, long release and a low, hoarse cry as if from pain.

He collapsed on top of her, his chest slick with sweat, but the momentary suffocation of his weight meant nothing to her; she was far out of reach. He rolled aside, pulled off his shirt, and flung it away, then subsided beside her inert form on the fur rug, nuzzling his nose into her damp neck. They rested that way, their breathing slowing, the storm of their motions subsiding to a rumbling on the horizon, the chamber coming into focus again around them.

Finally, heaving up on one elbow, he placed his hand on her belly to rouse her. She opened her eyes, gazed at the intoxicated homage in his, and thought he was the greatest miracle God had ever put on earth. With a languid hand, she brushed away the damp hair from his brow, tucking a wavy lock behind his ear. He let her do what she wanted, the lines soft about his mouth. Then he caught her hand roughly and kissed her palm.

'You raped me, woman, damn it,' he growled. 'It is totally against my principles to make love that fast. You have used me ill.'

'Would you wish to call out the guards, *mon pauvre petit* monsieur?'

'Yes. You are dangerous to my equilibrium.' He rubbed his hand softly over her belly.

'Nicolas?'

'*Oui, cher coeur?*'

'This—this is the first time I have ever done that.'

'The first—well, you are a most experienced *virgo intacta*, my love. And your late husband must have been moribund when you married him.'

'Shhh.' She smiled. 'Do not disparage the dead. No, I meant it is the first time I have ever. . .enjoyed love in just that manner. Reaching the. . .the pinnacle together. Both at the same time.'

He understood her now. The blue eyes held a tender, proud light. 'And did it please you?' he murmured, commencing to stroke the side of her neck. 'Because that depth of response has much meaning.'

'Oh yes,' she whispered. 'Tremendously. I am—stunned.'

He kissed her lips softly. 'You do me much honor, *mon coeur*. In every way.'

And then it took hold, what he had said before in jest, except that it was true. She practically *had* raped him. She couldn't believe how frenzied she had been for him to take her, how forward, how unbridled. With no more modesty than a *grisette* off the streets. She remembered her clutching hands, her insistent mouth, and with a groan she turned her hot face away from him, burying it in the rug. But, as if he read her mind, he would not let her hide from him and gently forced her face back again.

'Julie? What bothers you?'

She kept her eyelids lowered as she lay there, half turned from him. In a tiny voice, she answered, 'I am ashamed. I simply threw myself into your arms. I blush for my brazenness, my immorality——' Her voice trailed off. She covered her bosom as best she could with an arm.

The bold cinnamon brows drew together. 'Sweetheart, I will not allow you to say that. Never feel so, Julie, never. You must promise me that anything we do together to give each other pleasure, anything at all, will make you happy, not ashamed. For you to want me, without pretense, is a gift so precious that you shine in my eyes like a goddess. If you cover your body from me who worships it, *doux coeur*'—and, ignoring her resistance, he made her take her arm from her breasts—'you are hiding the sun from me.'

Weak before the feeling deepening his voice, Julie looked up at him and then dropped her gaze, hardly able to stand the tenderness and reverence in his regard. At least she thought that was what she read there.

She felt his breath on her; she felt his hand glide slowly, warmly over her skin, her thighs, her belly, and up between her breasts to the flawlessly smooth plateau of her chest. Her nipples tingled, stirred her. She felt the hand withdraw and opened her eyes to the sight of him quickly peeling off the rest of his clothes. Then he flopped over onto his belly, his face hovering over her.

'Did you miss me?' he grinned, referring to the second he took disrobing.

'Yes, yes, yes. . .' She sighed and caressed the smooth bulge of his shoulder. 'It is as if your hand on me tells my body to live, to feel.'

'Ah! My hand. And what about my mouth?' Deliberately, teasingly, eyes on hers, he slipped down, then lowered his head and pressed his lips to her navel, his soft moustache brushing her skin. Delicately, he inserted his tongue, circling it around the shallow depression, plunging it in. Delicious shivers took her as his hands slipped under to cup and stroke her buttocks.

Her breath caught in the back of her throat. Her toes curled convulsively. She was starving all over again, only this time it was evident that he was in control of her. 'Kiss me. Up here. Please,' she begged.

'With pleasure,' he murmured. But he made his way slowly and sensuously up to her mouth by planting his lips all over her quivering belly, her sensitive breasts, her arched throat, and by the time they fastened over her eager mouth, one wetted finger massaging her hard and erect nipple, she was straining up against him. He pulled away what remained of her drawers, and she wriggled to help him.

Now they experienced what there had been little time for before, the delicious, voluptuous feel of willing form against form, hers soft and yielding, his hard, tempered, excited. He took his mouth from hers. 'Your body is so beautiful,' he whispered hoarsely in her ear. 'I am drunk with the joy of you. I cannot get you close enough to me.'

Inflamed, she hugged him passionately. 'Never let me go, Nicolas, never,' she whispered back.

'Never, my love.' He hugged her to him. His hand stroked the silkiness of her back and buttocks. Their kisses grew long and deep. It was a communication that needed no words.

Finally, his hips moved against hers with sensuous suggestion so that she trembled all over in answer. He looked down at her with eyes dark with desire and murmured, 'I love you, Julie.'

She heard him, her heart heard him, and it almost leaped from the body he was so expertly caressing into ecstasy. But she didn't answer. She pushed away the treacherous words and, arching toward him fiercely, begged, 'Kiss me—there. There. Oh. . .Oh. . .' And again they scaled the unbridled heights together toward the ultimate, most intimate giving there could be between two humans.

Later, sated, they lay in each other's arms for a while, damp and content, with heavy limbs, and never had Julie experienced such perfect peace.

Eventually, Nicolas got up and went to fetch the two goblets of wine, and because, as he walked away, he couldn't observe her lingering voluptuousness, she let her eyes boldly drink in the robust male beauty of his broad-shouldered, slim-waisted torso; his hard, small buttocks, where the skin was lighter and smoother than the rest of him; his strong, straight thighs covered with light curly hair. He returned, handed her a goblet, and, dropping down beside her, watched her gulp the cool hippocras. He leaned toward her, passed his thumb over her wine-wet short upper lip, and licked the sweet moisture from his finger. Solemnly, he said, 'I love you. From the minute I saw you enter Mademoiselle's study in that bright yellow gown, like a blithe sun sprite, I have loved you.'

Even though they weren't touching, she could sense the heat of his body, she could smell him. Their flesh still seemed as one flesh. But she put insistent fingers over his mouth. 'Don't say that. It isn't necessary to say such things.'

The light blue eyes regarded her with some surprise. '*Ma chère*, you are probably the only woman in the world who doesn't want to hear those words.'

'Oh?' she responded, and she gave him a sideways glance. In spite of her sudden feeling that she was standing on the edge of a chasm and might fall headlong, she asked, 'Have all the ladies you have favored been delighted when you made that vow? The Princesse Margarethe, for instance?'

He pulled back from her. '*Nom de Dieu*, madame. You are a cool one. I tell you I love you, I adore you, and you jealously accuse me of making such a momentous declaration to all the ladies. I hope you know better than that. I hope you are just being coy.'

'I beg your pardon, Nicolas. It wasn't my intent to insult you. You needn't make such a long face. It's just that—must we profess a deep love in order to enjoy each other?'

She had never thought to see the undauntable Nicolas d'Aubièrre, Marquis de Courcillon, shocked to his core, but now she did, and she quailed under his disbelieving stare. She had gone too far, been too bold in her flight from becoming entangled in the net of love again. Now he really would think her wanton.

The light in his eyes lost its softness. He said slowly, 'I had hoped, Julie, that you would feel the same way. Just now I could have sworn you did. Well, so be it. That I love you is a fact. If you do not return my affection, that doesn't change it. I am thirty-one years old, *mon amour*, almost at middle age. I have obviously not spent all these virile years chaste. And yet there has been no woman I have wanted as much as I do you——'

Wanted *to marry*? Her heart proffered in silence the words struggling to emerge from her welter of ambiguous feelings. She saw disappointment tighten the muscles of his bearded face. To marry, Nicolas——?

'. . .Wanted to marry.' He echoed her heart aloud, and she thought she would faint with joy and with fear. How could she explain to him that she both adored and distrusted him? He neither looked like the Earl of Lowry nor sounded like him, and Richard, in all their short months as married lovers, had never known how to draw from her such deep and exquisite physical response. And yet Nicolas's open personality, his easy grace with women, and his involvements with them to the point where at his age he was yet a bachelor contrived to panic her. The emotional pain of Cuckfield, not even a year behind, still lay heavy on her. She could not allow herself to love a man such as Nicolas, for her only profits from having loved the elegant, cruel Richard were the hard lessons she had learned about certain men. Learned, by heaven!

He was waiting for her to say something. She put her hand on his swelling biceps. 'Nicolas,' she pleaded, drowning in her own confusion. 'I could not marry you.'

His mouth was now a straight line. 'Because there is someone else? François Michel de Louvois, for instance?' His voice was barbed.

'No, no, not at all. I beg you to understand that if I have given myself to you, my heart is entangled nowhere else. In my life there has only been my late husband—and now this moment, with you. If you do not believe me, then everything that was beautiful in what we have done will turn to ashes. I care much for you. I desire you, wanton woman that I am. But'—she desperately flung out the words more for herself than for him—'I cannot love you.'

His stare went from angry to bewildered to noncommittal; she could see his forceful will driving the hurt from his eyes, replacing it with his more customary insouciance. He shrugged. 'Very well, madame, if that is how you feel. I cannot force you to love me——'

Suddenly, he pulled her roughly up to her knees, and she found herself again enveloped in his warmth, crushed in a fervid embrace. In spite of the turmoil within her, her body seemed to melt into his again. Without volition, without even hesitation, she raised her head and offered up her mouth to him, responding to his deep, searching, open-mouthed kiss not with her brain or even with her fenced-about heart but out of the very essence of her being, the pulsing core from which her life sprang.

He finally released her mouth and said hoarsely into her hair, 'I hear very clearly what you said, *mon cher coeur*, but I hope you don't mind if I simply do not believe you. I do not discourage so easily.'

Reluctantly but firmly, he put her aside then and stood, scooping up her petticoats and dangling them before her. She rose too, flushed and a bit flustered, and snatched them to cover her nakedness. She turned her back to don them, as well as to hide her smile at the sight of his physical response to their last embrace. She picked up her ruined corset and drawers. 'I suppose we might consign these to the trash heap,' she said with a rueful laugh.

'What use could you have anyway for such stupid instruments of torture? God made you naturally beautiful.' He made his point with his hands in an appreciative, affectionate caress of her high, full breasts. He quickly kissed each rosy nipple.

Pleased, still she slid away, trying to regain her poise. She shrugged her shimmering purple gown over her head and turned her back to him. 'Will you help me button up my bodice, monsieur?'

He nuzzled the nape of her neck but complied. 'I would rather help you unbutton it,' he muttered, fumbling with the loops. At last, she was presentable, if missing some undergarments. She stooped and felt in the fur rug for the pins from her hair and then went to his ornate framed mirror to repin the Psyche knot. In his breeches and shirt, filling a plate for her at the table, Nicolas watched her, admiring the slim curve of her silk-covered back, her rounded arms, the midnight gleam of her hair in the candles' soft light.

Filled with well-being and suddenly ravenous, Julie sat in the chair he offered and literally attacked her food, and since he was starved, too, they both enjoyed the sumptuous meal in silence at first. She was licking the grease of the last cold mutton chop from her fingers when he said, 'I must leave tomorrow with Skandahet-se on a confidential mission for de Louvois.'

'Leave?' Her tone echoed her dismay, the chop bone remaining in midair. 'But we have only just arrived here.'

He gently pushed the bone toward her mouth again. 'Only for a few weeks or so, *minette*, and then when I return, I shall be finished with my tour of duty for the year, and we will have plenty of time for picnics and promenades and rides beyond the town, *à cheval*——'

But she pouted, 'I am disappointed.'

'So am I, and especially I do not like to leave such a fragrant blossom among the hungry bees. But a soldier receives his orders and must obey. If you want to know the truth of it, I have no doubt de Louvois concocted this wild goose chase just to make his access to you easier. I came very close to throttling him.'

It was on the tip of her tongue to tell him of the mauling she had suffered in de Louvois's carriage, but her instinct held her back from giving him more to hold against his superior. Instead, she wiped her fingers on the napkin, got up, and came around the table. She pushed aside his crossed leg and plumped herself in his lap. 'Will you be jealous?' she demanded softly, wriggling about a little. She popped a sweet biscuit into her mouth.

'Will you be faithful?' he chuckled, pinning her to sit still.

She swallowed her cake. A sincere frown appeared between her eyes. 'Although he does not interest me, Monsieur de Louvois is a very attractive man. But there is—something—about him that frightens me. A facet of his manner that draws me and repels me at the same time.'

'He has that effect on many people. It is a cleverly cultivated characteristic. But just keep a cool head around him and remember that I love you. And that I will dismember with a few especially painful strokes any gallant who touches you, king's minister or not.' He surveyed her possessively for a moment, taking in the glow on her cheeks, the clarity of happiness in her violet eyes, the languorous curve of her lips. 'You have the look, madame, of a woman who has just been thoroughly made love to,' he observed with satisfaction.

Julie blushed. She scrambled up from his lap and put her hand out to forestall him as he reached for her. 'No,

Nicolas. I must leave. It must be close to three or four in the morning. Any later, and all the servants will be stirring.'

He grabbed her hand and kissed it, but because he cared not to compromise her, he did not insist that she stay longer. At the door beyond which the valet sat waiting, probably nodding, she donned her little mask again. Nicolas stood looking down at her intently, as if memorizing her face, and she had all she could do not to step close to him again, run her hands up his loose shirt, and smooth her palms over his brawny chest. She saw the Adam's apple bob below the trim cinnamon beard. The little squint lines about his light blue eyes crinkled.

'Will you miss me, Julie?' Incredibly, there was a wistfulness in his voice.

In answer, she threw her arms around his neck and clung tightly to him. 'Oh, Nicolas!'

He buried his nose in her fragrant hair. 'Miss me, *doux coeur*. And when I return and there is more time, I have some things to tell you, certain circumstances that have to do with you, certain things about me I want you to know.' And when she drew back and looked at him questioningly, he shook his head and chuckled. 'If anything, at least curiosity will keep my memory green in your mind.'

Reluctantly, they parted then. But for the next few weeks, she relearned all over again the lonely ache of terribly wanting someone who was absent—even though this someone was coming back.

CHAPTER
~ 13 ~

Because the dauphin fell ill, the court returned to Paris early that year, fortunate that the end of the summer offered unusually decent weather for that humid city. Actually, most of the court was glad to get back to the greater elbow room of the city or to their own comfortable hôtels, no one more so than Anne-Marie-Louise d'Orleans, Duchesse de Montpensier, who swept into the Luxembourg palace joyously planning her wedding and with drawings already in hand for the lavishly appointed apartments to be designed for her husband-to-be, Monsieur de Lauzun. So much had happened at such a pace, it was no wonder the lady rode so high on her cloud that she did not hear the ominous rumbles of outrage below her.

De Lauzun, having first consulted the pregnant Athénais de Montespan before they left Fontainebleau regarding the king's outlook and having solicited that lady's aid in the marriage matter, had also enlisted several friends, among them the Ducs de Crequé and de Montausier, and they had made formal request on his behalf for the hand of La Grande Mademoiselle.

And, wonder upon wonders, responding finally to his cousin's impassioned petitions as well as to this impressive delegation, the bemused king had given his consent for the two lovers to marry.

De Montausier, who literally ran with the wonderful news through flotillas of servants scurrying about the rooms of Fontainebleau packing and preparing their masters to depart, could not seem to penetrate Mademoiselle's delirious joy with his added most serious warning not to lose a moment but to tie the knot quickly, even that very night. And Madame de Sévigné, quickly informed of the stunning turn of events, arrived to echo the advice, begging her friend not to tempt God and the king but to seize the moment as it was given.

Julie definitely agreed with them. Something about the way Athénais had so suddenly become solicitous of the couple she'd always reviled and ridiculed jarred her. Athénais never did things just for friendship. But, behaving like intoxicated adolescents at last given their head, the transported pair refused to listen.

'I have no intention of seeming hysterical to be married, making it look as though my life has been spent in a panic and I was grasping at my last chance,' Mademoiselle declared pompously. 'And my dear Monsieur de Lauzun wishes the sacrament to be taken openly, with all forms observed and in the chapel of the Tuileries, with all the country's nobility in finest regalia observing,' she trilled. 'We intend to dazzle *le tout* Paris.'

De Lauzun, once pushed over the balance line, became drunk with his own success. He felt secure, with the king and the Marquise de Montespan firmly on his side against the deeply shocked princes of the blood and the angry ministers Colbert and de Louvois. He said calmly to his friend the Duc de Richelieu, who the next day offered his house at Conflans for immediate nuptials, 'To marry in haste would make me seem too greedy to grasp my good fortune. And in any case, my dear monsieur, we must wait to reach Paris for Her Highness's lawyers to draw up the settlement papers.' He smiled his stingy, pursed-mouthed smile and lowered his voice. 'The title of duc will come to me, along with the duchy of Montpensier, and she is also settling on me the principality of Dombes. Not too generous, eh? But I think I can induce my beloved to throw in the county of Eu as well, which represents the first peerage, and then I shall be well served.' He offered his friend his beautiful snuff box, a new affectation, and then peered up at him with one eye half squinted. 'Still, I have to admit that when I shall soon be master of the Luxembourg, I need all my self-control to keep my head from ballooning.' He gave a harsh cackle.

The Luxembourg was crowded all day long with nobles and commoners coming to congratulate La Grande Mademoiselle, to fawn over her and curry favor, or simply to ogle the haughty royal lady who had refused half the kings and princes of Europe and was now blithely giving her hand to an ordinary gentleman of an obscure house—a commoner, to be exact. The ecstatic Duchesse took all this flurry of attention to be a sign of how right her action had been in declaring her choice of marriage partner; her ears remained closed to the less obvious truth, the deep distress of the social hierarchy upon which the country's order was based. For she, of all people, had seriously failed in her duty as a daughter of France by totally ignoring caste lines. And, more shocking, the king had not opposed it.

No one could understand such an unwise breach of protocol. It was an age when lovers separated by station could easily complete their happiness privately while maintaining correct marriages and public decorum; the bastards resulting from these liaisons were accepted as inevitable and often named heirs in the absence of legitimate inheritors. Seeking answers to this strange situation which had the nobility, the Parlement, and the higher bourgeoisie outraged kept the whole city whispering. Even the *canaille* were in a state of consternation. A tempest was about to break.

Madame de Sévigné, her aging but still pretty face worried, drew Julie into an alcove off the queen's oratory one morning. 'Can't you do anything with her? She cannot be so besotted as to think the king will stand against the tremendous pressures they are bringing to bear on him. I see it all about me. The queen weeps constantly, Condé and Conti implore, Monsieur wants her locked up in an asylum, the Maréchal de Villeroy throws himself on his knees in tears before his old pupil. If Anne-Marie-Louise wants the Comte de Lauzun, she must marry him now and damn the banns and contracts and the Tuileries chapel. What makes her so blind, I ask you, madame?'

'Love,' Julie answered bleakly. 'She acts only on Monsieur de Lauzun's advice, and he gives total reliance to the king's word and to the fact the king recently caused the announcement of Mademoiselle's marriage to be sent to all his ambassadors.'

The Marquise's hand plucked nervously at her draped moiré skirt. 'As, of course, he would. Louis will not easily admit an error in judgment. But Her Highness has no idea of the forces arraying themself against her. When the news first came out at Fontainebleau, I wrote my cousin Madame de Coulange in Lyons a letter so excited and so thrilled I could carcely contain my pen from jumping off the page. But now—they have let two weeks go by, much too much time for the kettle to boil, and boil over.'

'It really isn't her fault, madame. She wished at first to marry quietly at the Marquise de Montglat's Cheverny or at Eu, but the Comte said these chateaux were too far away. Still, if it will ease you, I think Her Highness is truly becoming aware of the hostility. This morning , in fact, after her *lever*, she spoke to Monsieur de Crequé about the use of his chateau in Charenton for the nuptials.'

The Marquise de Sévigné, often exasperated with her royal friend but always loyal, gave a little gasp. 'Oh, madame, indeed this is better news. Charenton is close to Paris, and the marriage could be held there quietly and with dispatch. Do what you can to push her quickly toward such a decision. Truly, I fear for them otherwise.'

The next day, Julie stole an hour in the late afternoon to take a calming stroll in the Luxembourg gardens, using a painted paper parasol to shade her face, enjoying deep breaths of the fragrance of summer's last blooms. The crickets had already begun their song, and on one variety of small tree the leaves were turning yellow. The pebbled paths began to hurt her feet through the thin soles of her shoes—a reason many gardens were more admired than used—and so she sat on the rim of the great round reflecting pool, sighing her lovelorn sighs and smoothing once more the letter from Nicolas in her pocket, which she had read and reread for days. It was written from Milan, where his return was delayed because the Chevalier de Lorraine was being treated for a fever, but the man was recovering, and they would soon be on their way home. And he wrote other things, too, things that made her blush and catch her breath. She stared in the placid aquamarine water and saw his handsome, bearded face with its quirked smile. She imagined the sun-glinted ripples were the merry sparkle in his blue eyes when he was pleased, and she thought lovingly about the tight line of his jaw when he was not.

She had only to count how many times a day she thought of him and how she could make a quiver run through her by remembering the touch of his hand on her breast; and how she could watch a ballet performance in the company of de Louvois and other gentlemen and be totally unaware of what was happening on the stage because the music conjured waking dreams of their lovemaking; she had only to feel her heart skip its beat at the sound of his name on someone's lips in order to know the depth of her infatuation with him. It made her deliriously happy even while it upset her; it made her skin glow and her eyes shine, as her admirers unwittingly proclaimed. But the very need she had for Nicolas de Courcillon strengthenend her fear of his hold on her emotions.

Becoming aware of a crunch on the gravel behind her, she swiveled her head around, and her smile grew wide and welcoming. She held out her hand to Mercure de Vosges, who limped up and took it in his cool fingers, the shy warmth in his fine dark eyes signaling his pleasure at seeing her. He wore a coat of yellow embroidered linen with pale green turned-back cuffs and a froth of icy-white cravat. There was a white plume pinning back the brim of his hat. The uncharacteristic lighthearted effect of this costume removed years from his pale features. The Comte de Vosges was not handsome or irresistibly magnetic like de Courcillon, Julie thought. And he limped. But there was an attractiveness to his gentle bearing. A woman could do worse than welcome the friendship of so sincere a gentleman.

'How are you faring, dear madame?' he asked her, hobbling to join her on the pool's rim.

'Just barely, *mon ami*,' she joked. 'But well enough, I suppose, if it weren't for all the commotion.' She glanced at him, not wishing to bore him with complaints, but he seemed willing to let her go on. 'I mean—oh, it's not the painters and upholsterers and drapers and trailors I mind so much—in fact, I would be so happy with the bustle of such a joyous occasion, except that it's—it's not reallly real, I fear. It's all going to crash in, isn't it?'

The slim shoulders lifted in a mild shrug. 'The mood about the city isn't gay,' Mercure admitted.

'A wedding should be joyful. Instead, I have this terrible feeling of doom soon to come, like that Greek in the tales, what was his name? With the sword always hanging over his head?'

'Damocles,' Mercure smiled. 'And yes, the king seems not at all inclined to change his mind about the marriage.'

Now she shrugged, a graceful gesture that drew her companion's worshiping eyes to contemplate the snowy roundness of her shoulders. 'I suppose we could all be fighting with shadows. And yet, even Mademoiselle has gotten edgy now.'

Julie had lately taken to confiding in the Comte de Vosges, for she needed someone uninvolved to talk to, and he was so reserved, so discreet. She had no doubt she could trust his silence. And it flattered her that his interest in the whole affair of Mademoiselle's projected marriage was more centered on her, in sympathy for her position of foil to Mademoiselle's bumptious moods.

'Her Highness is truly devastated that the Prince de Condé, her ally, her cohort when they were young together and fighting the War of the Fronde, has come out so vehemently against her. I thought for a moment she would faint when she heard of his bitter opposition. It rather surprised me, since they are not very friendly beyond the courtesies. The news that it is *he* leading the princes of the blood in their hostility to what they deem a deep insult has extinguished some of the dazzlement in her eyes.' Julie sighed.

'And Monsieur de Lauzun?'

'He grows truly furious when she wonders if they shouldn't drop all their plans and marry immediately. He glares at her with that stern eye of his and declares that he trusts his king, he trusts Athénais de Montespan, and the only one he doesn't trust is her, Mademoiselle. He wouldn't even stay to sup with her last night and called her indelicate for even suggesting such an impropriety—dining with her alone, that is.'

'He is not very nice to her under the circumstances, is he?' Mercure murmured. 'But I suppose the Comte is under a great strain. It is difficult enough choosing to marry and presenting one's suit, but to do so in such a gale of resentment must wear on the nerves.'

'Well, today he apologized to her for his sharpness, not that she ever minds it,' Julie added gloomily. 'But I so wish they would quietly do what the king allowed them already weeks ago and not fly in the face of all the ill winds just for pride's sake.'

De Vosges took up her hand from where it lay on her lap. His fingers felt a bit clammy, trembly. 'Come, madame, there is little you can do for them. You must not lose your smile,' he cajoled somewhat clumsily.

Julie immediately brightened. He was right. Her anxious mood was not going to help anything. Determined to be fetching, she twirled the parasol as it rested along the lovelock on her shoulder and called up her dimple. 'Indeed, you are right, monsieur. But you know how I admire her. I sometimes forget that her problems aren't mine.'

He looked at her with his soft-as-velvet black eyes. 'Do you. . .' he began, blushed, and started over. 'Do you ever think yourself of remarrying, madame?'

She glanced sideways at him from the corner of her eye, always the flirt. 'Why, of course, monsieur,' she said archly. 'I am still young, and every woman wants a fond husband and beautiful children. And I would be pleased to have my own hearth again.' She was dandling him, she knew, not with what she said, which was the truth, but with what she didn't say: that she had little interest in marriage declarations at present, not with her heart so inflamed with Nicolas de Courcillon. But she saw no harm in encouraging him anyhow, in what, after all, might be a three-year courtship. Mercure was so timid and patient. He'd never done anything braver than gingerly hold her hand. Nor might he ever find the courage for anything more, she admitted to herself.

He shifted his gaze so that he was looking just a tad past her; he barely perched on the pool's stone coping, poised as if to run. 'If—if a gentleman wished to present his suit for you, to whom would he do it? That is, you have no immediate elder of the family, or brother. Or even a guardian, as you once told me.'

Julie was stopped for a moment. 'Why, I suppose I hadn't even considered. In fact, my uncle de Montespan is exiled so far to the south he is scarcely reachable. And there is no one else. It looks as if the gentleman who sought me would simply have to speak to me, does it not?' She looked down modestly, not wanting to chuckle and discomfit him.

He realized how long he had been holding her hand and, embarrassed, let it go. 'You are in an enviable position for a woman, *chère madame*, for you may follow your own inclinations in so important a matter. But who is there to tell you what is really of benefit to you? That steadiness and loyalty and a kind heart are often more worthy in a man than a fine figure and flamboyant ways?' His pale forehead showed a sheen of perspiration. 'Who is there to advise you that the heart that holds you in greatest esteem might not be one that can dance the *gaillard* prettily or fetch you a pear from the highest tree?'

'But don't you believe, monsieur, that an adult woman who has already been married might already know such things for herself?' she asked softly. 'And, in fact, she does.'

'You d-do?' he stammered. There was a pause while he gathered his courage, during which the tinkle of laughter and chatter from a group of strollers coming down the gravel path came to Julie's ears. And she saw, from a different direction, a page hurrying toward them. 'Julie, I. . .oh, I do hope, madame, you will honor me with the pleasure of using your baptismal name and that such an intimacy does not offend you, for I should like to believe we have built a close enough friendship. Th-that is, I carry you in the highest regard and hope that you also have some. . .some. . .ah——'

She took pity on him and touched his arm. 'Of course, Mercure. It would please me for you to call me Julie.'

His earnest smile widened, stretching the little black moustache above it. Quickly, he blurted out, 'My mother, she has heard me speak about you and has professed a desire to meet you. She is old and does not get about much or go to court. But if you would be willing to honor our house with a visit. . .'

The page reached them, puffing, and bowed. 'Your pardon, Madame de Lowry, but Her Highness requests your presence in her apartment immediately. Without fail.' The plump youth, new to his post, wiped his forehead with his green and white sleeve, his eyes popping out with excitement.

'Good heavens! What has happened?' She quickly got up.

'I am ordered to conduct you to her. Immediately,' the page repeated.

'Monsieur, *je suis désolée*. . .' Julie swung around to apologize for having to rush off, although she was secretly relieved that Mercure had not yet made his invitation fully, for she would have had to accept, and she didn't think she wanted to be scrutinized by the dowager yet.

De Vosges stood up unsteadily. 'Never mind, dear Comtesse. I certainly understand. But perhaps you will ride with me this week as consolation?' he ventured and, at her smile and nod, added eagerly, 'I will take the liberty of sending my footman around to inquire what day and time would please you.' Sincerity and timid passion tinged his voice. 'Of course, any time you choose would be my pleasure, dear Comtesse. Julie.'

He kissed her hand, and Julie curtsied briefly, leaving him with hope lighting his eyes.

Julie found a distraught Mademoiselle, attended in her sumptuous bedchamber by her newest friend, Madame de Nogent, de Lauzun's sister, and Mademoiselle de Greu. The face Mademoiselle turned to her held terror. 'Ah, God save us, you were not far, madame. Oh, I am undone! My marriage! My marriage is broken, I am sure of it. The king has sent for me. He has commanded my presence within the very half-hour. What else could such urgency mean?'

The other women looked at each other, foreboding in their glances.

De Greu murmured to Julie, 'The carriage has already been ordered. It is waiting.'

'You will come along with me, the three of you,' Mademoiselle choked, wringing her handkerchief. '*Le bon Seigneur* only knows what is to happen. Oh, *Sainte Vierge*, I tremble. . .' she whispered as her servant prepared her to leave. They followed her out, the glum Dant slipping Julie a vial of spirits of ammonia to keep in her pocket, just in case.

The tense ride across the bridge to the Tuileries palace, where the king was currently making his quarters, was broken only by Mademoiselle's painful muttering under her breath, 'I told Monsieur de Lauzun. . .I said so. . .he is too naïve. . .' Julie arched her brow at Diane de Greu for more information. De Greu shrugged. She knew nothing more than Mademoiselle; they had been chatting together when the king's minion arrived. Madame de Nogent, a simple woman, sat looking straight ahead, her startled, thin eyebrows like chevrons over her pale, anxious face. Julie's apprehension began to deepen into depression.

To make matters worse, at the Tuileries, they were stopped on their way toward the king's apartments by a gentleman of the royal suite and directed to go to the king's private study via a back stair and through his dressing room, a secretive and, in this case, ominous way to enter into the royal presence. At the dressing-room door, the women were met by the Duc de Rochefort, the current captain of the Garde-du-Corps. Mademoiselle was ushered in, the three women with her allowed to wait on the small landing. De Rochefort, being a considerate man, sent a servant with folding stools for them.

Julie bit at the skin around her thumbnail. She was praying that the Sun King would not, could not, be so ruthless as to crush the two middle-aged lovers in his godlike, absolute fist.

Louis had not altered his wretched expression in the ten minutes since he had announced to his white, hand-wringing cousin, 'My dear, I am forced to inform you that I cannot permit this marriage,' and he had had to endure the piercing shriek that issued from her throat. She staggered and dropped her big body into an armchair, then mewled, 'Ah, sire, sire, what are you saying?'

He had come to the agonized woman and taken her cold hands, sincerely moved with pity. 'Try to calm yourself, Mademoiselle. But the fact is that my ministers are fearful of the appearance that I am sacrificing my relative—you—to benefit my favorite, de Lauzun. They swear this is injuring me with my own people and is doing the same in foreign courts. What is more, I am informed by a certain source that de Lauzun declares he does not truly love you—that it was you who inveigled him into this betrothal.'

He did not like to cause his supercilious and silly cousin such pain, nor was he happy to abrogate his word. But more so, he couldn't understand why he had even given it, in what state of mind he had casually allowed such a corruption of tradition. Madame de Montespan had come to him several times in the week with concern written in the furrows of her brow. She had related what someone had heard de Lauzun swear and then described the mocking, angry tales making the rounds among the populace. The shafts and barbs against the king coming to her ears had caused her to reverse completely her original murmuring, as their heads lay on the pillow, that from his great height of majesty it cost little to grant his spinster cousin the wish of her heart. Athénais, in fact, reinforcing his new decision, had just left him, her heavy satin skirts just clearing the closing dressing-room door as the Duchesse de Montpensier entered by another. And the rest of his nobility—distraught with him, bitter...

Mademoiselle pressed her clasped hands to her heart.

'Not love me? Oh, sire, that is a base lie formulated by an enemy. The man adores me, and anyone can see it who looks beneath his always proper deference to my rank.'

Morosely, Louis continued, 'Nevertheless, cousin, such reports are spreading everywhere and are compromising me in my royal person and tarnishing the crown of France. My duty as a monarch is supreme. This is my will. You may not marry the Comte de Lauzun.'

Grief contorted Mademoiselle's features. She jumped up, and, forgetting everything but that this absolute ruler, her own blood relative, was again sacrificing her life to his own position and needs, she raised her fists and pounded on his chest with heedless fury, tears flooding down her distorted face. Louis of France let her strike his august person, comprehending that she had much reason to revile him, pitying her, bearing the weight of her anger as payment for his guilt in having made his original decision in haste. She stopped beating at him and slid down to the carpet, hugging her face against his knees. 'Ah, sire, I implore you. You cannot withdraw your word, the word of a king. I beg you to kill me, kill me rather than forbid my marriage to the only man in whom I find any repose and salvation. I will forgive you my death rather than bear separation from all that I love in the world. Oh, Your Majesty, Your Majesty. . .' She sobbed into his hose, beating her grief against a rock.

Gently, he disengaged himself. Looking down at her bent head of thick, silver-threaded curls and her heaving bosom, he felt tears well up in his own eyes, not so much for her but for the buried memories her plight unearthed in him. He was assailed by memories of Marie Mancini, the first overwhelming love of his youth, who had been forced from him by his mother and Cardinal Mazarin. Marie had been a dimpled and dancing-eyed girl whom he had worshiped and whom he had been seeking in vain ever since—in his marriage, in his mistresses, in his passing affairs. The remembered agony of a rent heart struck at him in spite of the intervening years, and the tears that wet his cheeks were to soothe his own scars, for they still could ache.

Thus, extremely moved, the Jupiter king of France himself knelt beside his sobbing cousin, embraced her ample figure in his arms, and, leaning his cheek against hers, wept with her. The man inside the monarch was desolate that life exacted such terrible sacrifices of those who dwelt in the demanding air of Mount Olympus. To ease her, he called her by the endearing names of their childhood, stroked her hair, did everything he could to stop her tears except rescind his decision to deny the marriage.

They remained this way in misery together for many minutes. Finally, with a last pat, he kissed her hot forehead, rose, lifted her up, and pressed her into a chair. His cousin raised puffy, reddened, and dull eyes to his. 'Ah, sire,' she whispered. 'Never before have I loved anyone, and now I have chosen one of the truest gentlemen in your kingdom. I beg you to let me live with Monsieur de Lauzun. I beg you to consider, my king.' She raised trembling, ring-bedecked hands to him in supplication. 'Consider that no one can have any true ill or joy of my marriage but myself, and I will suffer what rocks are cast at me, in poise and without complaint.'

It was a mistake to say. It recalled to Louis his purpose, to rescue the dignity of the royal family, and gave him an opening to recover his bearing. His expression turned stony; his long dark hair and the diamond sunburst pin on his satin coat vibrated with his sudden indignation. 'You will excuse me, Mademoiselle, but I must strongly contradict you. The fact is that the honor and stature of the ruler of France, the dignity of his court, and the esteem of every crowned head of Europe are involved with your affair. *You* have forgotten that you were born a daughter of France, but I, Mademoiselle, I remember it, and I shall without a doubt shield your rank and my royal name from dishonor.'

Scarcely hearing him in her extremity, she flung herself at his feet again. 'Oh, sire, hear me. De Lauzun is no ordinary man. He is great, good, heroic. Oh, I implore you, do not make my life a desert. I cannot—I will not—give him up.' The tears rolled again, and she blubbered. She grabbed for his hands with her cold, desperate ones.

Becoming impatient, he raised her up from the floor and put her once more in the chair, where she hid her face in her sodden handkerchief. 'Anne-Marie-Louise, why in the name of heaven did you give me that time to change my mind?' he demanded, his dark gaze full of sharp reproach. 'Why did you not act while I was still blinded by the stars of passion in your eyes?'

She shook her head into the handkerchief and cried, 'Alas, when did you ever break your word, my king? How could I know it would begin with me and Monsieur de Lauzun?'

A hot stain rose on Louis's face. She had touched a sore issue, one that embarrassed him. His long, jutting nose pointed down at her. 'Not even a monarch is his own master, Mademoiselle, in affairs which concern the honor of his country. Sacrifices must be made,' he snapped.

Removing the lace square from her eyes, she squinted at him through swollen lids. 'To whom are you sacrificing me, then, my cousin? Could it be Condé? I saved his very life once. I. . .stood with him in every danger. Why does he wish me so ill? Is it to remove me from a gentleman who vexes him because the man recognizes no master but you?'

Louis was uncomfortable with her accurate thrusts, but he tried not to show it. 'Anne-Marie-Louise, I ask you to obey me in this, and you can command me in every other way. Be assured your obedience in this matter will make you doubly dear to me.' He plumped himself down in his armchair. He was unable to suppress a nervous yawn.

Mademoiselle wrung her hands still. 'I beg you to have pity on me. Have mercy. Do not give heed to others only to destroy me.'

'It has grown late, Mademoiselle, and we have nothing more to say. I shall not change my mind.'

'Those to whom you sacrifice me will jeer at you for allowing them to influence you!' she flung at him in desperation.

Ignoring her insulting tone, he got up, took her firmly by the elbow, and led her to the door. Trying once more to placate her, he said, 'Let me deliver you to your ladies, cousin. Give yourself some rest, and then come to me tomorrow. Come and tell me you forgive me, and we shall begin anew to love each other.' He kissed her on both cheeks. 'And now, *bon soir*.' And so saying, he thrust her through the door.

Louis shut the door behind her and puffed out his lips in relief. At last, the painful affair of his cousin's marriage was almost done with. He went to his table, which was supported by brass cherubs, and rang the bell for his captain. There was one more difficult interview to get through tonight, and then he could go to bed without the month's nightmares of accusing faces telling him he had been soft-headed. The affair of Montpensier and de Lauzun was about to be finished, and de Condé and Conti, de Louvois, Colbert, de Montespan, the ministers, and his ravening subjects could all go to the devil. He was tired. He wet his handkerchief with the tip of his tongue and wearily rubbed at the tear stains on his peach-colored coat, with the resigned wish that all the expectant mob of courtiers awaiting his *coucher* in his bedroom would disappear so that in a little while he could lay down his burdened head without ceremony and sleep.

Her worried companions gasped as Mademoiselle stumbled out of the king's dressing room, hair disarranged, eyes and nose scarlet, face crumpled and stained with tear tracks. There was no need to ask what had happened. They rushed to her, practically supporting her on either side. By using the back stair and hastening through the kitchens, one of them going around to the main entry to fetch the carriage, they managed to hustle the limp, uncaring royal lady almost unnoticed into her coach. Through it all, she remained wordless, only an occasional muffled and broken moan issuing from deep inside her. Her swollen eyes were half shut.

But once in the vehicle carrying her back to the Luxembourg, the dam broke, and, throwing back her head, with an unearthly screech, she yelled, 'No, no, no, I will kill him, that heartless monster! I will kill myself! I will smash the palace, the whole dirty world!' And before any of her unprepared friends could stop her, she snatched the cold and empty charcoal warmer from under the seat and began smashing at the window next to her with crazy strength. Madame de Nogent squealed. Julie grunted. They tried to catch her flailing arm, but the woman had the power of her fury behind her. The window shattered with a dreadful sound, and she started on the next one, crashing the heavy wood object against it and screaming imprecations. The driver's hatch popped open to alarmed queries, but Julie yelled at the man to keep going, to reach the Luxembourg palace as fast as possible, and to restrain the footmen in their seats.

The coach rocketed forward. De Nogent and de Greu cowered in corners, squeaking and shielding their faces with their fingers. Julie tried again to stay Mademoiselle's insane destruction, but the woman was in the grip of apoplectic hysteria and with wild eyes shook her off like a fly to continue her pounding attack upon all the windows and doors, uncaring of flying glass. A splinter of glass nicked the Duchesse's cheek, and blood started to flow. Julie looked down to quickly jerk out a shard of glass, which had shallowly penetrated her own sleeve, and dodged the flailing virago as best she could. Taking in the shocking state of the coach as it swung into the court and hearing the uncontrolled screams of his mistress, the quick-witted butler sent footmen running to quickly dismiss the people loitering in the salons or in the Duchesse's chamber, their curiosity unhidden about why she had left so precipitiously. Mademoiselle flew out of the coach, treading on the assisting footman's toes, and ran into the Salle du Gardes, weeping and gesticulating. Some of the more snoopy visitors lingered long enough to see the disheveled woman shake her fist at invisible enemies, a tragic and frenzied figure hurling curses to heaven. The tearful de Greu and others of Mademoiselle's ladies who hurried up tried to shield her by surrounding her. Julie ran ahead to make sure the bedchamber was empty of strangers, and then she stood back against the door as Mademoiselle barged past her and flung herself on the bed, writhing, almost howling, with a fury welling up from decades of frustration.

Although the other women and some trusted retainers were pale with shock at such behavior, Julie tried to appear confident. Her heart was thudding with the violence of Mademoiselle's reaction, but Julie knew all about such hysteria. She remembered flying to pieces and crying herself into exhausted unconsciousness when it finally sank in that Richard was going to keep her incarcerated at Cuckfield for the rest of her life if he wished and that she had absolutely no recourse against him, against his sadistic cruelty. 'Get the tincture of camomile drops,' she ordered Dant, who appeared about to do so anyway, 'and cold cloths for her eyes and forehead and to swab away the blood from that scratch. And send someone immediately for the doctor. Tell him it is delirium.'

But the rigidity was leaving Mademoiselle's limbs; her cries were fading into gulping sobs. Hardly in the same world with them, she allowed her ladies to undress her limp body and tuck her under her perfumed sheet. The cold cloths, the ammonia bottle held briefly to her nose, and the nerve-soothing camomile in water that she uncaringly swallowed, helped. By the time the doctor made her drink the powders he had mixed in some strong wine, she was recovering. At last, she turned a long, more composed, but ravaged face toward Julie, who had just changed the compress on her head. Her lips struggled with a forced smile. 'Do not look so distressed, madame,' she whispered. She patted Julie's hand. 'I have not died. Physically, at least.'

'You must rest, Your Highness.'

'He has refused to permit my marriage to Monsieur de Lauzun.'

Julie could only regard her silently, deep sympathy in her eyes.

'If I do not marry Monsier de Lauzun, my life is over. It is that basic. There is nothing, nothing else.'

'You will feel stronger in the morning. The doctor has given you a draught. . .'

'Pah, the doctor's draught! It does not affect my system much. I can defeat it whenever I wish. He should know that by now, the dolt.'

A footman knocked and whispered though the narrow opening of the door to Madame de Plessis-Rabat. She approached the bed. 'Messieurs de Montausier, Crequé, and Guitry are here, Mademoiselle. And Monsieur de Lauzun.'

Spots of color stood out like fire against the Duchesse's pallor. Her swollen eyes gained some life and opened wider. 'Allow them in, madame. And then you may all retire, and I thank you for your kind ministrations.' She caught Julie's hand and muttered without moving her lips, 'No need to make them jealous. Go, and then come back in a while. Now perhaps we'll find there are many ways to skin a cat.'

For all her staunch attempts not to come unstrung, this last defiant remark didn't help Julie to relax over the situation. She left with the others but went right to her chamber, claiming fatigue. There Blanchette helped her refresh her face, arms, and back with a damp rosewater cloth and then don a fresh gown. She sat down for a moment and nibbled at some biscuits dipped in a glass of strong wine which Blanchette had poured out. So much had happened that her head was buzzing. The world had again turned topsy-turvy in a few hours. She closed her eyes to rest them, relishing the quiet and peace of her room compared to the astonishing storm that had just blown itself out. A vision of Nicolas rose against her closed eyelids. He was smiling his quirked smile at her, pleasure in his light eyes as he listened to her, and she ached for him to be near so she could relate the day's shocks and alarms and draw strength from his comforting. And, in fact, it should be very soon that he would leap up the Luxembourg staircase and open his arms to reclaim her. She had found that all the whirl and swirl at court, the flattering attentions of several gentlemen, the gilded salons and crowded *appartements* had become boring, hollow. All interest had fled since there was not the chance of even a glimpse of him.

No, she really had no time to allow herself to conjure

up the daydreams that daily sustained her, the anticipation of their private reunion, the sensuous intertwining of her own limbs with his, the hot meld of lips and bodies and pounding hearts. . .

Pinching her arm to erase such unbridled, lascivious visions, Julie jumped to her feet and brushed the crumbs from her lap. She had promised Mademoiselle to return, and it was time.

CHAPTER
~ 14 ~

'Oh, Antonin! Oh, what I have suffered!' Mademoiselle cried out as her little beau rushed forward through the *ruelle* gate to take her hand. 'I must look near death's door. Oh, whatever shall we do, *mon cher*, whatever shall we do?'

Gone was the rampaging termagant of an hour before; in her place lay the tearful dependent woman looking to her gallant hero to make things right.

The dour lines about de Lauzun's mouth chiseled themselves deeper. Astonishingly, there was a hint of accusation in his tone, as if he blamed the prostrate Duchesse for all their troubles. 'I have just come from a private interview with the king. I admit it was a terrible struggle to greet his broken words with the constancy and submission required of a loyal subject. Yet I think I projected admirable restraint.'

Tears glistened in her eyes. 'But, monsieur, I cannot understand. Don't you care that our lives have been forfeit? You should have raged, cried, made every objection...'

'And so I did, but not at my ruler. At Madame la Marquise de Montespan, who sat there so coolly and unmoved in the background, the treacherous bitch, of whom I could reveal enough scandal to make Louis dismiss her. It was she whom I reviled and called a filthy whore for using her power and personal purposes to turn my master against me. It wasn't until His Majesty raised his gold-headed stick and, crimson in the face, made as if to strike me that I realized the insults I had hurled at her in my momentary lapse of reason, and I fell on my knees begging him for his forgiveness.'

The glances his friends threw at each other held shocked disbelief, for they had not heard this story before, but the royal lady's eyes widened in admiration.

'Oh, Antonin,' Mademoiselle quavered. 'And did he give it?'

De Lauzun combed satisfied fingers through the waves of his wig. 'Yes, of course. Very angrily but, notwithstanding, yes, for he has always valued my genius. And what is more, in compensation for my shattered heart, he presented me with five hundred thousand livres and the government of Berri! An extremely handsome elevation, *n'est-ce pas*?' He sat down on the edge of his ex-fiancée's bed and fussed with his lace cravat as his worried friends conversed in low tones outside the *ruelle*. Then de Lauzun looked up to fix his hand-wringing lady with his usual stern, disapproving look. '*Vraiment*, you should be pleased with his generosity to me, Anne-Marie-Louise.'

'Why should I be content with what the king gives you, monsieur, when *I* can give you so much more? Antonin, I want him to give you *me*,' she wailed. 'Nothing else will ever stop my tears. I love you. You are my life,' she cried, casting all modesty to the wind, grasping his arm, pleading with her red-rimmed, almond-shaped eyes.

The stubborn acceptance overlying de Lauzun's crabbed features dissolved for a moment. 'I had vowed, Mademoiselle, never to tell you I loved you until we were wed,' he said bitterly. 'But'—and he drew his handkerchief and then softly dabbed at the tears leaking from her eyes, the most intimate gesture this correct man had ever allowed himself to make toward the august spinster, at least with observers present—'but the king has not forbidden us to see each other, and *écoutes, ma chère* Duchesse, he even repented enough to suggest I continue to be your adviser and best friend. He then swore upon his dead mother that he would never withdraw this permission for our friendship.'

Mademoiselle's damp eyes lit with hope. 'Did he say that? Oh, Antonin, my gallant knight. Do you see what that means? Do you see he is saying we do not have to give up our love? We just must not marry.'

De Lauzun's mouth turned down, his pursed lips compressed. 'Your Highness speaks ignobly, from despair. Never, Your Highness, would I allow you to compromise yourself. Never could I treat you with such dishonor. You know me by now. I respect my king, I respect myself, and most especially I respect you. Stolen kisses are an insult to both of us, and I will not abrogate my principles.'

'But you cannot mean. . .'

'I mean exactly what you hear,' he stated.

She stared at him, and a thousand confounded thoughts jostled through her head. He would not stay with her as a lover. He felt it would debase her to know her without sacrament. He would leave her to sigh out her life a dried-up spinster. Reckless beyond reason, she jerked her high-minded lover closer to her by both of his brocade-covered arms and shoved her flushed face close to his to whisper dramatically, 'But they need not be stolen kisses, Antonin. Only secret ones. We could marry in secret, my dearest love, with only a few trusted witnesses to our happiness, and in this way our love would be sanctified and the king's good graces retained nevertheless. Everything of legality is already prepared—the contracts, the settlement—and you must say yes, Antonin, for it is our only salvation,' she begged, practically shaking him.

His first reaction was to recoil. 'Go directly against the king's commands? Do you know what you are saying, woman?' he demanded harshly.

'Yes, for this would not be the first time I have defied him. And does the courage of a woman pale before that of the girl she was?'

Her heart rising and her eyes coming alive, Mademoiselle's thoughts tumbled from her beset brain. 'The king would never know, nor would the gossips; they might whisper that we were lovers, but whom do they not lance with their *poignards*? Only we would know the truth. All protocol would be satisfied, and in fact, we shall walk about rending our breasts for a while to allay suspicion. But think, monsieur. What we so fervently wish for we will have. Not nuptials at the Tuileries, not celebrations, but each other!' She finished triumphantly and drew in her breath.

She was dazzled to see his tight mouth slowly relax into a contemplative smile. 'Ah! And at the same time have beaten our enemies at their evil games!' He nodded. Then the smile faded, and he said most seriously, 'But what if our transports of delight should cause you to conceive, my dearest person?'

'Then we shall call the child illegitimate, but God would know better. And on our deaths, the truth would come out, and this lovely child would inherit all.' She was blushing violently.

'All——' de Lauzun echoed.

'This time, we must move most quickly, Antonin, while the court believes me in seclusion nursing my wild grief. Let me think how a moment. But dismiss your gentlemen, monsieur, for we shall need only the most trustworthy of them tomorrow.'

For once, a bemused de Lauzun took her orders and did what she said. A moment after the gentlemen left, there was a scratching at the dressing-room door, and Dant admitted Julie. 'Ah, Madame de Lowry, come here and attend us at once,' Mademoiselle called out in a voice so firm and clear that her lady-of-honor's step faltered in surprise. 'Dant, serve us some of that cherry wine on the table. Now we will confer. . .'

Excitement rose in Julie as Mademoiselle, in a half-whisper, unfolded the plan that had sprung into her head full-blown, out of crisis. 'There is, just outside of Paris and near the gentle fields where we often used to picnic in my youth, the little town of Choisy-le-Duc. Located there is an inn and also a small religious community, built with my money and administered by an ordained and pious Franciscan who is beholden to me and whom I trust beyond doubt. There we will marry, *mon cher* Comte, and even stay the night, and no one the wiser. Then we shall part and appear in our separate places, and innocence reigns and all will appear as expected. *Voilà!*'

'But we must have witnesses,' de Lauzun interjected.

'Your dear friends Madame Sévigné and the Princesse Palatine, Your Highness?' Julie suggested.

Mademoiselle shrugged in annoyance. 'La Sévigné is ill abed these few days, and La Gonzaga has gone to the Rhineland to visit her sister. But you will do, madame, and Antonin, your loyal friend de Montausier, perhaps. And then one or two of the good brothers.' Mademoiselle's tendency toward command was functioning normally again. She cocked her head regretfully. 'Ah, I wish my godson de Courcillon were here.'

'So do I,' Julie muttered.

'Tomorrow night, then, at ten o'clock. I will gather my forces, monsieur, and you will gather yours, and we shall meet in two coaches just behind the Saint-Sulpice church.' In her element now and forgetting to defer to de Lauzun, she ordered, 'Julie, you must go and pave the way—but in a hired coach, so as to awake no suspicions—and I shall give you a letter to Monsieur l'Abbé Prevertin de Cristus explaining all. And you, dear monsieur, must comport yourself as if your hidden heart is broken but you are bearing up bravely in your usual manner.'

De Lauzun stared at her, but with slumped shoulders. For once he was allowing Mademoiselle to pull and prod him, too distracted by his own tumbling thoughts to take over the leadership from her. 'That will be no problem,' he said glumly.

Mademoiselle pouted. 'You do not sound overjoyed, monsieur.' Her tone had become kittenish again. She had forgotten that her face was washed of the cosmetics and powder that ordinarily camouflaged her mottled skin. She appeared plain and heavy-featured, but she arched her neck, and her hand plucked at his sleeve coquettishly. 'Perhaps you do not love me enough to find the courage for such a risky business?'

He straightened his back, returning to his bravado. 'You cannot believe that. I am just thinking, planning.'

She brightened. 'Ah, good. How very like you, *cher* monsieur. But now you must retire. I shall arrange all, and we must both play our parts with more skill than Monsieur Molière in his finest role. We will meet again tomorrow night behind Saint-Sulpice. Without fail.' Her smile bathed him with her overflowing love.

De Lauzun nodded, still frowning and bemused. He kissed her hand and for a moment held it to his elegantly attired breast. '*Au revoir*, dear Highness, queen of my heart. Until tomorrow.'

'Oh, Antonin, I am so very happy. *A demain*, then, and dream of me sweetly tonight.'

Julie stood back as they parted, the soft smile on her face mirroring her pleasure that the two star-crossed lovers were to be united. They had gone through so much, been denied so much, dared so much. Each was so stiff-necked and proper that even the king's tacit permission that they might have an affair did not help them. But even Julie felt a pang of envy in her heart for that limitless dimension of love that demanded vows of commitment before God, even if in a short and secret ceremony.

Tossing his riding gloves to a servant and yodeling a bawdy song in an exuberant baritone, Nicolas bounded up the stairs of the Hôtel de Courcillon. He was free of his mission, free of his duty to the crown for another nine months, free of the evil, amusing, simpering, and Adonislike murderer of the house of Lorraine, who had rolled great blue eyes at him through the whole trip and blown him sardonic kisses when his two officers weren't looking. Skandahet-se followed him up the stairs, grinning at his master's pleasure to be back in Paris again.

Nicolas called out to the butler, 'A bath, Maître Cousteau, my man, clean clothes, a fine scent, new boots, my barber with his scissors and razors—whatever else will make me presentable to the most beautiful lady in all Paris!' He flipped his dusty hat to the smiling valet as two servants scurried about opening the drapes and filling the water pitcher.

Skandahet-se knelt to help him pull off his streaked and cracked boots, the Indian's great strength making short work of the gritty job. 'We had a coach,' Nicolas explained to him, 'but Lorraine chose to ride in it, and therefore I did not. My good horse was better company. I let him try his wiles and little pouts on Giles La Roussie, poor fellow.' He gave a roar of laughter. 'One doesn't trifle with that *petite fille*, though; he's a wily swordsman, like a scorpion with a sting. Puyghilm de

Cresson trained him, more's the pity. Fencing masters ought to pick their pupils with more discrimination. . .' He sighed and slid down on his spine in the chair, legs planted apart, happy to be home. De Louvois was away from Paris for a few days, which required him only to leave a written report with the secretary that the Chevalier de Lorraine was safely ensconced in his Paris quarters. Mission completed.

He said to Skandahet-se in Huron, 'And what news have you for me, Skandahet-se, son of the great Tipaguma of the land of the big waters beyond the peaks? I charge you to say what has transpired that might amuse me.'

The reddish-skinned man folded his brawny arms on his chest, which bulged his coat sleeves to the straining point and shook his many skinny braids. 'Some things have happened, misyoo, but none of it will you like,' he responded, in badly accented but passable French. 'There is much to wonder at.'

Nicolas had seen enough grave Indian faces to know when they were really solemn or when there were grins hidden behind the stony expressions. Skandahet-se was serious. 'Ah, the devil shove it in his ear, can a man have no peace? Very well, spit it out, and it better be facts and not the half-chewed gossip you get from your kitchen maids.' Skandahet-se's bulk and scandalous manners might offend ladies, but the grubby female scullions found him seductive and intriguing, their only connection with the exotic world beyond pots and pans. He often spent his free time lingering about the big, hot royal kitchens where worked a tall black woman who particularly appealed to him. He patted her jutting behind (with sometimes a little of the same to others) and snatched food tidbits. But few people, including his women, knew that he could understand and speak French.

Skandahet-se grumbled in the back of his throat. 'Plenty facts, monsieur, what everyone knows for truth.' The valet reentered, guiding servants pulling a sled with buckets of hot water for filling the metal tub. 'The great Duchesse lady, your relative, got the permission from the royal king to marry the tiny man she like to live with, by name of, I think, Misyoo de Lauzun. And much wedding plans were made and special papers made in order to call this special king's man a duc. And over the whole court everyone babble, babble, babble, much surprised, much angry. . .'

'What!' The blood had drained from Nicolas's bronzed face. He jumped up and began to take off his garments, throwing them left and right. 'Devil take it, how could that happen? The king would never. . .I can't believe. . .I have to stop her, that foolish woman. Cousteau, get me washed and combed and out of here before a quarter-hour has passed, or I'll hang you up for bear food. And you'd better be telling the actual state of affairs, warrior of the rainbow tribe, for I intend to lock myself with my godmother and lecture her until she finds her senses again. The blasted silly woman! Just to have that conniving, posturing cockerel to her bed, she is signing away her fortune, her position, her whole life, in goddamn fact!'

He stepped into the hot tub and howled, and the servants leaped to douse the steam with buckets of cold water. Cursing, muttering, Nicolas splashed about unmercifully. His valet, done up in a large apron, made a valiant effort to soak his back. 'I will not allow it, I will not——' the Marquis de Courcillon raved, slipping down the tub's high back to douse his soaped hair and coming up blowing and snorting.

Skandahet-se, having observed in silence and with a certain interest his master's violent reaction to what was already old news compared to that of yesterday, and having quelled the valet into silence with a narrow-eyed, intimidating glance, grunted, unmoved. Then he continued as if he hadn't let minutes go by. 'But royal king has changed his mind yesterday, and there is no more wedding. Wedding treaties are torn in two. My wench in king's scullery says your Duchesse and her ladies came running through kitchen, the Duchesse was wild-eyed like crazy animal and tearing out her hair.'

Caught midway out of the tub, Nicolas stood there dripping. 'You miserable savage! Why did you not say that first? *Queue de diable*, I ought to strangle you with your own braids.'

'Could not say first what happen second,' the Indian replied reasonably. A ghost of a smile touched his lips. The valet came up with a towel. 'You want me to order up horses?' The plural was Skandahet-se's request to be taken along to the Luxembourg. He was bored.

His anger fading, now that he had learned that the emergency had been avoided, Nicolas relaxed and allowed the valet to rub him down with heavy white toweling so that his skin glowed. 'No, order the coach. I want no Paris dust to spoil my pristine appearance. I am going to hear the details of this horrendous episode from two sets of female lips, and I want their scrutiny to fall on me approvingly, *hein*?'

Especially that of the Comtesse de Lowry.

As he stood thinking of her and waiting fresh drawers and shirt to pass from a servant to his valet, Nicolas felt his breath come faster, at the prospect of seeing his winsome Julie. He would take her gorgeous face, with its limpid flower eyes, so tenderly between his hands, and the parted lips would offer honey and spices for him to taste, and the satin-skinned breasts would swell to his touch, inviting his caress. Fantasizing, with a smile on his face, he could hear the tiny moans of joy he would draw from her with his hands, his body. He could smell the perfume of her soft, satiny white flesh. . .He glanced down at himself, his member erect as a soldier, and an eyebrow lifted with cynical amusement. He hurriedly drew up his britches, casting a sidelong look to see whether his valet was smirking, although a quick glance at Skandahet-se told him nothing. The Huron never had much expression, anyhow, except one of diabolical glee when he had frightened somebody. Calm yourself, de Courcillon, he jibed at himself, you needn't daydream now. The lady you dreamed of as you tossed in those lumpy Italian beds is close at hand, and you can soon fill your lovesick and infatuated eyes with her.

The emblazoned carriage, rolling quickly over the Paris cobbles to carry him in his silk coat and Skandahet-se in his incongruous tilted hat to the Luxembourg, somehow contrived with its bumpy rhythm to carry his mind back to another ride with Skandahet-se. But that time, long ago, he had been dressed in a deerhide jerkin, and they rode on horseback through a dappled forest, along a lake path thick with pine needles. They had ridden fast and with excitement toward the Huron encampment, for Skandahet-se's sister had just been delivered of twin daughters. Nicolas's daughters. He didn't know what he had expected to see when the tightly wrapped babies were shown to him, Skandahet-se's handsome reddish-tan skin and his distinctive, strong features perhaps, along with his own light eyes and hair. But the infants seemed, to his young and European eyes, just two moon-faced, homely Indian babies, still flushed and angry from the struggle to be born, and their d'Aubièrre blood did not show itself one bit.

Had he been in love with Shanat-a, perhaps the tiny girls might have moved him more—or had they been at least male children. But looking back now, in the light of his ensorcelled feelings for Julie, he knew his affection for Shanat-a had been more gratitude for her devoted nursing of him when he had almost died of snakebite, and pleasure in her shy adoration of him. It was the loneliness of a young man trying to set up a trading outpost in the wilderness that had led him to keep her in his wigwam after she first crawled uninvited under his blanket. Her skin was soft but lightly pitted, and her black hair smelled of bear grease. But he had put his arms around her frailness and taken what she offered in the spirit in which she gave it, a mutual liking. Or so he thought, for Indian women were not held to chastity until they became pregnant and subsequently married.

But Shanat-a wept great silent tears when, after six months, her high-spirited, strong white brave, now bronzed and bearded and almost as silent and efficient a hunter and trapper as any Indian, departed his hide-walled wigwam for his white man's cabin over the ridge, leaving her pregnant and heartbroken. For she had refused to understand that their relationship was to last for only a short while.

Skandahet-se, hefting great bundles of otter skins delivered by his fleet of sixty Huron canoes to the counter of the post's enlarged trading room, reported to Nicolas in his passable French, 'She thinks you find her too ugly, that you look for prettier wife. I tell her I find her a good husband as soon as papoose is born, but she cry all the time. I tell her same as before, that you chief's son from far away, someday go home, maybe never come back. I tell her look what pots, what blankets and skins and food and wampum, what knives and needles and beads you have provided for her wigwam. I tell her I will find her new brave to warm her backside. She cry more. One day, after babies born, she see white, golden-hair lady French trapper carry in canoe, and she stop crying. She feed babies, she give them to grandmother, she sit and stare on ground.'

Nicolas stirred uneasily at his memories. He had done what he could from a distance, everything he could think of, full of pity for the gentle but stubborn little savage who had fallen in love with him, but refusing to see her and make it worse, especially since, by then, he had trained Croixverte to handle the post and had himself moved into Trois Rivières to expand their operation. His successes in putting together a trade fleet more dependable than that of the government company exhilarated him, and his head was filled with bright plans. And then came the news that his brother and nephew had died; he was the inheritor of the estates and entitlements of the marquisate of Courcillon, as his father and brother had been before him. Skandahet-se, an unusually curious red man, living with him in the bustling frontier town, asked to go to France with him, and such was the huge fellow's stoicism that Nicolas believed he would withstand the cultural shock with his usual imperturbability.

But three days after Skandahet-se arrived at the Huron encampment where he had gone to make his *adieux* and bring Nicolas's presents to his sister, the devastated Shanat-a took her life, leaping into the river with one of her year-old babies and drowning them both, a vast humiliation to her family. Skandahet-se told his employer and friend nothing of it until they were already gazing out on the foam-topped waves speeding them on to a new existence. This nephew of the tribe's chief had never blamed the bearded white man, who had come only to trade and to learn their ways, for the weak, womanish behavior of his sister. He himself had children and two squaws, one in camp and one in the small settlement of Saint Vars on the Saint Lawrence River, and he missed neither. There were squaws everywhere.

But Nicolas arrived in Cherbourg a somewhat older and more heart-burdened man than the new marquis who had embarked in Tadousac, New France's port on the Atlantic.

There was nothing at all similar between the thin, dusky-skinned Shanat-a and the beautiful and graceful Julie de Lowry. The one, as a callow young man, he had given a patronizing, selfish affection; the other he loved with the scarred heart of a worldly man. And yet, of the many women he had known, only these two brought up images of one when he thought of the other. The rest were only passing shadows, leaving no marks behind them.

This time, Nicolas's entrance into the Luxembourg's private apartments was strongly opposed, in spite of Skandahet-se's dark glower. 'Monsieur, I insist. Her Highness is highly indisposed and has given absolute orders that she will receive no one,' the butler stated. He and five footmen barred the way down the corridor of salons toward Mademoiselle's private rooms. 'Absolutely no one, Monsieur le Marquis. I beg of you to respect her wishes.'

Nicolas scowled at him. 'I somehow have the feeling, my friend, that no one does not include me. But perhaps her lady-of-honor, Madame de Lowry, is available? At least, may I see her? I would take it very badly should you deny me that much,' he threatened. Behind him, Skandahet-se folded his big arms and stared.

The butler hesitated. He certainly did not want a ruckus with his mistress's favorite gentleman, and he knew how often Monsieur de Courcillon was privately admitted to her presence. 'Please wait here, monsieur. I shall inquire for the Comtesse.' He stalked off stiffly, leaving his underlings on guard. Nicolas and his companion seated themselves on red velvet upholstered stools under the jaundiced eyes of Mademoiselle's gold-framed ancestors, to enjoy the evening breeze from an open window, in company with a few other petitioners and vendors hoping Her Highness might relent and see them. Scarcely five minutes passed. The gilded portals flew open as the butler returned with Julie behind him, her full taffeta skirts billowing, her violet eyes wide and shining, her cheeks pink.

Nicolas jumped up and grasped the hand she held out to him, and he cursed all his daydreams for never once capturing the vivid reality of this radiant, round-armed, midnight-haired woman. 'Oh, monsieur, I am so glad you are here,' she breathed as he fervently kissed her delicate hand and squeezed her fingers. She withdrew her hand, coloring. 'Come with me,' she whispered, 'away from the others.' Nodding to the butler, she turned and went through the line of guards toward the doors leading to Mademoiselle's chambers. Leaving Skandahet-se to wait, he followed, enjoying the view of her erect back and tiny waist hugged by the slithery green silk, and especially the natural, graceful sway to her walk.

The next room, a small drawing room displaying an elegant collection of porcelain on its mantels, was empty. Nicolas closed the doors behind them and Julie turned to him. Even in the half-light her beautiful eyes were eager as she scanned his face. He walked up to her and drew her to him, the delicate hyacinth perfume wafting like a spring morning around him, the feel of her supple body quickening his heartbeat. He crushed her against him and heard her delighted squeal of protest, and as he laughed and molded her to him with possessive hands, six trying and lonely weeks fled away. Her warmth, the unique female scent of her, renewed his happiness that this woman was his. Of all women anywhere, everywhere, she was the one God had made for him. Except for one minor point—that she didn't understand that. Had she a relative, an aunt, anyone, he would have brought all his considerable assets to bear in demand for her hand, and, by God, she would have to marry him, girlish reluctance or not. But there was only her to consult, and she had pointedly ignored his proposal even as they lay twined together on his bearskin rug.

The woman he held imprisoned, so obviously joyful to see him, lifted her slightly parted coral lips to his. Nicolas captured them in a kiss that for one little minute was a normal gesture of greeting but turned swiftly into intimate recognition, their mouths opening to each other, their tongues finding each other, their breaths mingling, bodies pressed together in the need to blend into each other. There was mutual passion in the kiss, and sweetness and desperate need. There was surrender in every trembling inch of her body.

Helpless as a youth in the throes of his first encounter with love, he said passionately when they finally attempted to breathe again, 'I love you,' words he had never uttered to anyone, except for his first fumbling encounter with his tutor's daughter sixteen years before. How easy, how right it was to say them to this woman who looked at him with eyes that bespoke her soul, her vulnerability, her wounds, her loving heart.

Her lips curved in a soft smile, and the dimple appeared, but she gave him no answer back. Instead, she shook her head and breathlessly pushed away from him, saying in a shaky voice, 'Later, *mon coeur*. Later we can better greet each other, and you will tell me of every hour and every minute of your journey. Oh, Nicolas, how I've missed you! But come with me now, monsieur, come. Mademoiselle waits to see you, and God has surely sent you at the right moment. So much has happened. Perhaps you have already heard?'

'About the betrothal and its demise? I heard an outline of it, to my utter disbelief. And now I see my godmother has secluded herself to grieve. How does she fare?'

'Fine, fine, truly. Come, see for yourself, but hurry. The hours are passing swiftly——'

Too enthralled with her to be puzzled, Nicolas smiled

down, his eyes devouring her, 'Very well, then, lead on, *ma chère* madame.'

He had, in fact, expected to see the Duchesse listlessly weeping into her handkerchief. But 'fine' was an accurate description of the imposing figure who stood impatiently in the middle of her chamber while her kneeling maid took some last stitches in the hem of her white silk gown she wore. Her face was as pallid as the several white rosebuds adorning her elaborate coiffure, but her blue eyes blazed with nervous excitement. At the sight of her beloved godson, she threw up her hands and rushed toward him, causing Dant to prick herself with the needle.

'Nicolas, Nicolas, how wonderful! Now you shall be a third witness, and how happy it makes me to know you will be present at the most joyous event of my entire life!' she gurgled.

Bowing first to kiss her hand, he then turned up to her a quizzical expression. He said in his pleasant voice, 'I have been hearing some incredible tales since my return to Paris today, Your Highness. Did you in truth ask the king for permission to marry the Comte de Lauzun, or have I been fooled?'

'No, you have not been fooled, monsieur, for so I did. And permission was granted, I swear to you. Left to his own decisions, my cousin has compassion for me in his heart and a sense of proportion. But in the end, what prevailed were the evil voices at his elbow—oh, I cannot bear to think of the cruelty of it.' Pain crossed her face for a moment, and she shuddered dramatically.

'What evil voices?'

Mademoiselle sailed back to the kneeling Dant to get her torn hem finished, and Nicolas followed her. She fluttered her fan to cool her face and said in a voice trembling with outrage, 'Do I have to make a picture for you, monsieur? De Louvois and Colbert, of course, in league for once. And that daughter of Satan, de Montespan, who at first gave my Antonin every promise of her cooperation and then, when our hearts were overflowing with happiness, unveiled the face of her venom and destroyed us.'

For clarity and fairness Julie prompted her, 'But there were also the princes of the blood and entire council. . .'

'No doubt,' Nicolas drawled, casting a jaundiced eye over his godmother. 'And it goes well without saying, most of the court and half of Paris as well.'

'Ah yes, the wretches. But the worst blow for me was Condé, that ungrateful dog!' Mademoiselle cried, twitching her finished hem from Dant's hands and stalking to a mirror to arrange the white velvet-and-pearl edging looping the bodice that half exposed her bosom. 'His was the most damaging voice of all, and he yammered day and night into the king's ear. *Bien sûr*, no one around the throne cared a bent sol for me, as they never have in all my life. It is always the state, the state, the state!'

'You used to be punctilious about the dignity of the state,' Nicolas reminded her.

'And so I still am, when honor has anything to do with anything. But I am not in line for the succession. What does it matter whom I choose to marry as long as he is a recognized gentleman? And Monsieur de Lauzun is surely recognized, would you not agree? He is favoured beyond most by his king.'

'That much is true,' Nicolas muttered, deciding not to remind her of the also-favored-beyond-most princes and dukes she had once snubbed as not good enough for her. But instead he probed, 'And so the betrothal was broken?'

'The king went back on his word. Can you believe such a thing? He broke all precedent and bonds of trust and thrust a knife deep in my heart, his closest adult blood relative besides his brother,' Mademoiselle declaimed, her hurt deepening her voice, 'and so he withdrew his permission.'

Nicolas studied her in puzzlement a second, then glanced at Julie, but she was looking at Mademoiselle and smiling, seemingly transfixed by the story. He transferred his frowning gaze to his godmother again. 'You will pardon me, Highness, but I don't quite follow what is happening here. You are supposed to be prostrate with grief, secluded, allowing no one to comfort you. You have suffered by your own account a terrible emotional blow—and yet, miraculously, here you stand, well and able, and in remarkably good spirits.' He looked from one women to another for an answer and saw them exchange glances. Suspicion gripped him. Sternly planting his legs apart, hands on his hips, an incipient storm hardened his features as he faced the two foolish females unsupervised by cool head or anything more than misguided emotion. 'And I see you are garbed in a very white and virginal dress, too. Just what is taking place here?' he demanded, the unconscious snap of command in his voice making them both shrink into themselves.

Blinking rapidly, Mademoiselle turned to face him, but she seemed not to be able to open her mouth, just as if she were some young and guilty maiden whose father had challenged her. Julie, however, slid protectively in front of her and answered with an upward tilt of her chin and forced confidence. 'She is wearing white because she is to marry Monsieur de Lauzun tonight in spite of everything, for they are in love and they wish to be one. But in the greatest secrecy, outside of the city at——'

With a harsh gesture, Nicolas cut off the flow of her words. 'Don't even say it, madame, I don't want to know!' he responded angrily.

Mademoiselle found her voice and walked toward him, her hands out in appeal. 'But, Nicolas, I want you to come with us, to be witness to my joining hearts with Monsieur de Lauzun. You are like my own blood to me, closer than my half-sisters. . .'

He grasped her hands. 'And with the deepest regard I talk to you now, Mademoiselle, I appeal to you, you must not do this thing. It will place you in the greatest jeopardy. You are going against the king's direct order. No one will raise a finger for you. . .'

'But no one will know! The priest is a man of solid honor, and only de Montausier, Julie, and now you will have any factual knowledge of the marriage. Monsieur de Lauzun and I in public will observe every decorum. And in private, as well. We are expected, you see, to profane our love by maintaining a quiet affair, sneaking about behind doors. But if we are forced to observe the letter of this immorality, at least we will abjure the spirit.'

The righteous ring of her tone added fervor to Nicolas's plea. 'But think, Mademoiselle! Nothing remains secret in this court. Surely you know that. The news will be out by tomorrow.'

'I don't see how that can happen. Antonin's good friend de Montausier would be putting his own neck in the noose, and Julie and you are beyond questioning. When I begin to receive again, I shall go on weeping and gnashing my teeth for a while, and soon no one will be interested even to start a rumor. We are going well masked and with only one trusted driver. Our secret will be safe.'

Nicolas's wide shoulders bunched under their elegant covering. 'Your Highness, I beg you, give up this dangerous idea. You are a royal princess, the king's only full cousin. Your obstinacy could cost you too dear. You will pay too high a price for humiliating the monarch of France. No secret is ever inviolate where there are those whose greatest benefit would be to know.'

His very brusqueness seemed to stiffen her backbone. 'I hear what you say, monsieur, and I know you care for my welfare. But you do not care for my heart, the heart and soul of a woman too long deprived of love, of the sweet bonds of matrimony, of children, and I will not spend one minute more, not one, in the toils of a lonely spinsterhood, to die alone and without issue. Not for the king, not for the state, not for the cruel Condés and Longuevilles and Contis. I do not care a sol for my life if I cannot be wed to the Comte de Lauzun—who will soon become the Duc de Lauzun by my gift, if only on paper.'

Nicolas's face flushed. His jaw clenched, and it seemed as if every hair in his closely clipped beard stood rigid. Totally forgetting himself, he grabbed her arms and shook her. 'I will not allow you do to this to yourself. I cannot be responsible for such a selfish, stupid action right in the face of an army of virulent enemies——'

Mademoiselle jerked her arms from him and shoved his chest to make him stand back. Her voice trembled, but her tone was full of wrath. 'How dare you, de Courcillon! How dare you speak to me in such a manner!' Red mottled her cheeks. 'You allow me nothing, monsieur, for I am not in your thrall. Let me remind you. I am a grown woman, and I shall do what needs to be done.'

They stared at each other, both shocked at the division that had opened between them. Mademoiselle blinked again, and her manner softened. Eyes pleading, she groped behind her and sat down heavily on the velvet chair. 'I know you mean only for my best, Nicolas. I know you. But trust me. In this instance, you cannot feel what I do. I would deeply wish you to be a witness to the ceremony.'

He stepped back. His hands were clenched into fists. He said through stiff lips, 'And I deeply beg pardon of you, Your Highness. I have no right, of course, to give you more than heartfelt advice. I beg you to forgive my churlish action and presumptuous words. But I regret I cannot connive with you in this sorry affair. I have no way to stop you. Therefore, it is best that I hear no more about it.'

Mademoiselle had gone pale again, the white dress making her skin look gray. She heaved a half-irritated, half-sad sigh. 'Very well, monsieur. You shall have your wish. You may forget all that has been said. And you may retire now. I have had quite enough.'

He kept his attention on her a moment more, his light blue eyes filled with distress. And then his gaze went to Julie, and the look she returned him flashed with anger.

He bowed. 'May I have your permission to speak privately a moment to Madame de Lowry?' he asked. 'And then I will depart.'

'Of course, if she so wishes it.' Then Mademoiselle told Julie, 'I will have Dant arrange my scarf and cape now. Don't be long, comtesse, my German clock says it is almost time.'

Nicolas went toward the anteroom and opened the door.

'I will not be long, Your Highness,' Julie promised, and with head high, she slipped past him. Motioning from the low-lit, empty chamber the lone footman only half finished with touching his flaming taper to all the sconces and candelabra, Nicolas closed the door softly.

She rounded on him, her eyes deep purple. 'I don't understand you! You are so dear to her, she adores and respects you, and yet you treat her so cruelly. To refuse to share the most momentous occasion in her life——!'

'And I don't understand you, madame, a supposedly grown and experienced woman who would lend herself so readily to a furtive marriage doomed to failure and an action the king could easily call treason. Have you lost your senses?'

'No, not lost them, consulted them—those senses of intuition and feeling and pity, which is more than I can say for you, in your anxiety not to become involved in an intrigue.'

'Becoming involved is not at all the question. There is much more to my objection than just her disobedience to the throne. Yet she is so touchy, I don't dare use truth to bolster my arguments. I want to tear away the veils from her eyes once and for all.'

'And what truth might that be?'

They were standing facing each other, arms at their sides, fists clenched, fire spitting back and forth between them. Now he turned his back to walk away a few paces, then spun about on his heel. 'What *is* there about that little man that so many women cannot see the scoundrel behind the strutting *poseur*, the bumpkin's greed beneath the stance of upright, proper, elegant gentleman? De Lauzun not only plays the clown often, he is a clown.'

His mouth became a straight line. 'Did you know that one of the reasons Athénaïs de Montespan may have agreed to take his side is that he was probably attempting to blackmail her? The little worm once insinuated himself *under her couch*—do you hear—so that he could eavesdrop on a damning conversation between the marquise and Minister de Louvois about how best to manipulate Louis into giving the post of Commander of Artillery to de Louvois's candidate rather than to de Lauzun.'

'And how do you know that?'

'De Louvois is not the only one to have some eyes and ears in the Louvre,' he retorted sarcastically. 'The men under my charge have ears, too, *n'est-ce pas*? There are sharp eyes and ears and tongues everywhere, and that is why I have no hope for this supposedly secret marriage.'

'I won't believe such insulting nonsense as you just told me. Half the rumors at court are false. Monsieur de Lauzun may overreach at times, sometimes he has been too rasping in his behavior, but he loves her very much, and she loves him.' Julie jutted out her chin. 'Don't you believe that people who love each other and are free should be able to marry? Don't you believe in the affection, the deep loyalty that can blossom in marriage? Or in the real pleasure of the bonds created by being responsible for each other's happiness and best welfare?' she demanded.

He was so beside himself to get her to listen to some reason that he disregarded what he thought were merely obvious rhetorical questions, deserving of no answer. 'Julie, it is her gold he loves, her lands, her houses, her titles, her royal blood. Should the little Gascony upstart manage to give her a child, his get would have royal blood! And *that* is what he loves.'

'Y-you only presume this. You do not know it,' she flung back. But she was devastated, for his very lack of response to the questions that had flooded out from her own heart *was* an answer.

'Everyone knows it but Mademoiselle.'

'They die with jealousy of him, those whom the king does not favor so highly. And those as well who wish to inherit from her. They would say anything to discredit him.'

He strode to her and grasped her shoulders, the remaining control on his rare but sometimes towering temper fast shredding. He thrust his face at hers, his eyes narrow with anger. 'Do *I*, madame? Answer me! Do I die with jealousy of him?'

'N-no.'

'Ah, but you are not sure.'

'Y-yes, yes, I am sure.'

'Then why will you not see the truth in what I say and help me to discourage her from this folly while there is still time?'

'B-because,' she said deliberately, biting off her words. 'Because she l-loves him. Very deeply. And that is what you don't understand.' Her black curls quivered as she accused him. Her brows almost met across her forehead. Her eyes spat purple sparks at him as her own temper erupted. 'She *wants* him. She would give him everything of hers if he asked it. And does he want from her any more than those many royal suitors and princelings who were to receive her as a gift from the king? Or some who even in the end rejected her? The point is, Monsieur de Courcillon, that for the first time she is wildly in love with a man who wants her, and the true depth of that word *love* you most obviously do not comprehend.'

He let her go then, but his expression said he would have loved instead to fling her across the room. 'My godmother is unreachable. But she can use Dant as a witness. I don't want *you* to involve yourself in this incredible and dangerous defiance of the king,' he grated as they stood glaring at each other.

'And why? Because I might help her gain what she wants?'

'No. Because she is a royal princess, and you are not. You are putting your head in a noose she is concocting, but it might strangle only you and anyone connected with you.'

'Oh! Are you afraid, monsieur, that your friendship with me, a woman who acts on her convictions, might compromise your safety? How loyal, indeed. So much for the bond of friendship, I see. Or any other bond beyond that.' Shocked and hurt, she allowed cold sarcasm to drip from her lips.

'It takes a true ninny not to see that friendship can also include strong objection to stupid behavior. And how dare you impugn my loyalty, de Lowry!'

'Would you rather I impugned your courage?' Julie flung at him. She was reckless now of consequences. Images were flashing through her brain—Richard carelessly shoving her away from him, Richard caring nothing for her pleading. . .'It takes a true coward to walk away from a woman who is begging for help.'

His eyes narrowed in his effort to control himself. A cord stood out on his neck. 'You are fortunate you are a woman. A man would forfeit his life to me for that insult. You are very quick, madame, to assign me the personality of a poltroon when I have done nothing in the past to deserve such a low opinion from you. Courage may also mean using one's intelligence. A man is allowed to refuse to take part in an action he believes is the height of insanity when it appears he cannot stop it. A woman, too. Perhaps it is you who haven't the courage yourself to oppose her, if it means losing your position. And so much for the bond of friendship when it comes to clinging to one's social rung.' He was mimicking her phraseology.

She glowered at him. 'You do not understand, monsieur. Neither you nor I have any business telling Mademoiselle what to do. The difference is that I am faithful enough to support her in her decision. You have no right to sneer at me for that.'

'*Le diable!* It is you who does not understand,' he roared. 'I am not sneering at you. I care about you, you addle-headed, silly-witted, stubborn and foolish wench, you—oof!' She had landed a stinging blow to his face with her palm, all the strength of her angry contempt behind it.

'You have n-nothing to say about what I do, either, Monsieur de Courcillon. You are not my m-master. And I do not need so insulting a person to care for me, especially one who reviles me and sh-shouts at me and treats me with such great disrespect.'

Her chin tilted up and with burning cheeks, she ordered vehemently, 'Stand aside, please. I have no more time or inclination to hear your nasty descriptions of me.' Her fingers ached from the slap; her heart ached with disappointment in him.

A muscle twitched in the clench-jawed, taut face. The blue eyes, full of disgust, burned down at her over the marks of her fingers on his cheek. She thought for a moment that he was going to hit her back. His lips twisted then. 'I apologize for raising my voice, Madame de Lowry. It was ungentlemanly of me. And I shall immediately relieve you both of my presence and of the friendship for which you have so little use. But you will understand if I cannot wish you more than "God watch over you" in your folly. Your servant, madame.'

He did not even kiss her hand, just turned on his heel and strode away, boot heels thwacking the parquet with a hard and angry sound.

Bosom heaving, Julie watched him yank open the door to the next room and disappear through it. Underneath her wrath, she was appalled. She had not meant for things to get so out of hand, to strike him, to imply that she no longer desired his friendship—the euphemism they had both used for the intimacy of naked bodies and deep passion. In fact, she was stunned. Not until her last desperation had she raised her voice so to Richard or challenged him or done anything but meekly obey him. Yet with Nicolas, she had somehow come to this point of defiance so soon. Her whole personality had changed. But was that so much better?

She stood trembling, tears pricking behind her eyes, hardly daring to face the fact that she had probably lost him. Yet lost what? Another Richard? Selfish, unfeeling, unrelated to anything but his own shallow beliefs and pleasures?

She remembered the time then. She whirled and reopened the Duchesse's door, groping for the chain of her little clock, fighting back the vexed tears. *Mon dieu*, it must be half after nine already.

Standing close to the door, her head swathed in a white lace scarf, Mademoiselle scrutinized her as she came in, the woman's stiff posture and concerned eyes giving away how much she had heard. Silently, she watched Julie drop a quick curtsy and go to retrieve her cape she had draped over a bench. Mademoiselle said huskily, 'He loves you. He is speaking to you for your own good. Perhaps you should listen.'

Touched by the concern from a woman who seldom thought about anyone else, Julie answered with a casualness she was very far from feeling. She was determined not to shadow her mistress's wedding night. 'Oh, give it no credence, Your Highness. We have quarrelled like this before,' she lied. 'He always comes back seeking forgiveness. Men are just blind in the ways of the heart. And they have so little tact.' She consulted her watch. 'It is time for us to go now. The coach will be waiting at the side entrance.'

They both attached full vizards and pulled up the hoods of their capes. Dant fussed about with Mademoiselle's skirt, which had only a short train, for ease in maneuvring.

'Well, we do not need him as witness, anyhow, since we had originally not counted on him,' Mademoiselle said with a false airiness as they walked through the salons, deserted except for some servants. 'Still, I would have hardly in my wildest dreams believed that I would have to say my wedding vows with a tiny suite of one.' She threw Julie an ironic glance but then smiled. Her tone took on a softer sound. 'A most devoted and important one, however, my dear. *Ciel*, how nervous I am. See, my hand shakes. Where is my courage?'

Dant hurried forward to catch up with them. 'But where does Your Highness go to say the vows?' she ventured to ask. 'To a church nearby?'

'To—no, never mind, good Mistress Dant. The less known, the less chance of a slip. Madame returns tonight, and I tomorrow, just at dawn, by the same gate. It is in your charge to see that no one realizes I am absent. Go back now and pray for me, my faithful Dant.' In the hand with which she waved Dant back, Mademoiselle clutched a small white Bible.

Dant did not hide her disappointment at not being allowed to see her mistress of twenty-five years taken in marriage. Her pleated upper lip pulled under her teeth, her shoulders rounded dejectedly. 'Yes, Mademoiselle.' She dutifully curtsied, faded eyes full of reproach, and fell back. In fact, Mademoiselle had earlier declared Dant's presence within the bedchamber essential to forestall any chance visitors. Dant thought the possibility of visitors was slim, given that it would soon be the middle of the night.

The maid watched the two masked ladies glide away through the long, dim chambers toward a back stair, the rustle of their skirts becoming only a mysterious whisper as they grew small in the distance. She sucked in one cheek as she always did when she was thinking.

Jean-Pierre Anselm d'Aubièrre rolled about on his bed in pain, his lank hair plastered to his forehead, his stomach knotting, gripping, knotting again. His heartbeat was rapid, his breathing shallow, and nameless dread squeezed his throat into a dry, convulsive tunnel. He gulped incessantly. His shirt was drenched.

He had no illusions about what was wrong. But help was on the way if the boy he had sent to La Voisin's connections in Paris used his legs fast enough. He groaned as the threatening vision of his depleted purse assailed his clenched eyes. Gold would always buy him help, but he had little left and little to expect. The rents from the abbey lands were laughable. And a youngest son inherited nothing but derision. A muscle spasm in his leg caused him to moan and groan out loud. He rubbed the calf frantically, then drew his knees up to his chin and rocked. Where was that damnable toad of a boy?

A scratch, a peremptory knock, and the door banged open. His brother stood there hulking in the square of light from the candelabrum held aloft by the butler behind him. Jean-Pierre's ringing ears suffered Nicolas's sarcastic, 'What ho, brother mine! Dissipating your youth as usual?' The man made his inexorable advance on the bed, motioning a servant to light the sconces around the room.

Jean-Pierre hid his face and aching eyes from the light. 'I see you are at home,' he groaned.

'And I am told you are ill again. Let me look at you.'
'What for? So you can read me a lecture, *ma mère*?'
'So I can determine what should be done for you.'
Jean-Pierre heard the soft knock of a metal scabbard against the carved bedpost, and then his arm was flung unceremoniously off his face. A sharp knotting in his gut

at that moment turned his vehement protest into a moan and a convulsive grab at his belly.

'*Morbleu*, you look execrable! Your eyes are filmed, and you are green at the gills. This is the end of it, Monsieur l'Abbé. I am summoning leeches to you, and I will hear no protests.'

'No, no, please, brother. I will soon be fine. No doctors, I beg you. It is only something I ate. . .'

'Or drank. . .'

'A bad fish, ingested at a small fête for the Cardinal de Retz. It will soon leave me as it always does, this bad digestion, as always, you will see.'

But he began to shiver. His valet, who had entered the room, rushed to pull up a blanket about him. Struggling to control his trembling, Jean-Pierre sneaked a direct look at his brother and looked again, for there was a dispirited sag to the usually assured face, and the degree of his brother's anger with him seemed excessive, as if it were stretched over another and greater irritant he had suffered.

'Does he vomit? Has he fever?' Nicolas demanded of the valet, who shook his head.

'But he has scarce eaten since yesterday, Monsieur le Marquis.'

'Shut up, you *crapaud*.' Jean-Pierre struggled to sit more erect on the pillows. 'I've sent someone to the herbalist for medicine,' he croaked. 'It always works, dissolves the bad bile. Go away so I can sleep. In the morning, you can relate to me your Italian odyssey. Always wanted to go to Firenze——'

Some of the ire left Nicolas's expression, draining away into the bleakness behind his eyes. Nicolas rubbed impatiently at his beard. 'I was in Milan. And if you are not better in the morning, I shall have you tied down so the doctor can attend to you.'

'I'll be better, one hundred écus on it,' the young Abbé swore. Then he clamped his lips on a torsion of pain. When he recovered, he said, 'Ah, dear brother, talking about money, I have been desperately low in my coffer, and when I went around to your watchdogs on rue Passy, they refused me another franc without authorization from you.' A tremor rattled Jean-Pierre's teeth, and for a passing second he started. He stared in terror as great tongues of fire burst out crackling from the large crucifix on the wall behind Nicolas, while the nailed figure on it writhed its hips in a halo of red light and issued a plume of black mist from its mouth.

Nicolas whirled around, saw nothing to stare at, and turned back, puzzled and concerned again. 'What's wrong with you, Jean-Pierre?'

The vision was gone. Christ hung most quietly from his silver and jasper cross fixed to the wall. 'N-nothing,' he stuttered, 'just air in the belly.' He managed to break wind to prove it. He felt too weak, too full of that gnawing, baseless fear to talk, but his financial need was urgent. 'It is necessary I have money,' he demanded, with no shame for his profligacy.

Nicolas slapped at his thigh with his gloves. He walked to a table, swooped up the wine the valet had poured out for him, and slugged it down, putting his glass out for more. 'Hardly news, my little brother,' he responded at last. 'Money flows through your fingers like water. Women, gambling debts, more horseflesh than you could ride in a year, lavish dinners for your friends. But none of them as murderous as the ocean of drink you are drowning yourself in. Look at you! In your excesses, you are sick as a dog, and you will die like one someday. Do you truly expect me to go on contributing to your death? No, Monsieur l'Abbé, not anymore.'

Nicolas was warming to his subject, taking out the whole evening's distress on his miserable brother. 'You were purchased a place of honor by our father. You are the leader of a respected religious community and as such are allotted a generous part of the house's income. But you are an administrator who does not administrate except through underlings. You are never there. You are shaming the family of d'Aubièrre, and a scandal will surely brew up if you continue so irresponsibly.'

Hands planted on his hips, Nicolas's eyes glowered with indignation. 'No. Not a penny more. Recover your health, and then retire to spend some months carrying out your duties, directing your chapter. Six months away from the temptations of the court, and you will have accumulated enough to pay for the following six months.'

Jean-Pierre choked over his answer. He threw back his head, bit his lip, and groaned with pain. The worried valet offered him a goblet of water, and he took it to wet his cottony throat. Then he flung the metal goblet at his tormenting brother, but Nicolas nimbly dodged it, and it thumped dully against a rug-draped table. 'I should not have to ask you for money,' Jean-Pierre screeched. 'It was my father's gold, his estates, his rents.'

'And then it was Eugene's, and now it is mine. Not yours, Jean-Pierre Anselm. And I am not ashamed to remind you that, by my own wits and labor, I have augmented what was a modest fortune into a large one. None of which you have any right to unless I die. I have been more than generous with you, and I shall continue to be, for in spite of what you think, I am concerned with you. You are my brother and only blood relative. I care enough for you to tell you that only if you take yourself away from court and your expensive mistresses and the cards and the spirits that consume you, only if you recover by your diligent attention to your responsibilities some of the respect due to the name of your forebears, will I ever give you one miserable sol again!'

By this time, Nicolas was barking. Even the suffering Jean-Pierre could read in the flared nostrils and wrathful eyes his autocratic determination to end the underwriting of his brother's dissipation. Jean-Pierre stiffened with hate; the stupid, selfish, arrogant dog, he railed to himself, squeezing his eyes shut to eliminate the picture of his nauseatingly righteous, rich, and domineering brother. He drew a sharp breath, but then he couldn't stifle an outcry at the stab of pain in his cracked and dried nasal passages. It was the seer's yellow-fumed inhalant that did that, the pungent cloud of smoke that grabbed a man by the ears and kissed his mouth and hurled him feather-light down a giddy, light-swirling tunnel trailing laughter that danced lovely sprites about his head and teased away every thought, to fill him with joy like a fat, bounding balloon. . .

A footman was admitted, shoving before him a ragged boy. 'I got your medicine, monsieur,' the boy called out, and Jean-Pierre heard him. The valet swabbed the sweat from his brow, but Jean-Pierre knocked away the cloth. 'Quickly, Le Brun,' he croaked. 'Mix three of those powders he has with no more than half a cup of wine, stir it well, and let me drink it. Damn you, man, hurry.' The valet scurried, pendulous mouth half open, and did what he was bid. Jean-Pierre struggled up, gulped down the potion, and fell back on his pillows.

Nicolas stood rooted amid this activity. He had seen men sick before, but shivers and staring at unseen apparitions were usually caused by high fever. Yet the valet reported that his brother's head was cool. The same symptoms, however, could be caused by compulsive imbibing of the harsh distilled spirit sold by apothecaries. And this was a product not easily obtainable in the village where the Petits Augustins were located.

He came close to the bed and looked down at the waxen face and the limp, dark hair pasted to Jean-Pierre's brow and cheek and sweaty neck. He noticed something else, too. The man's hands were covered with dry and grayish sloughing patches. The boyish charm that usually fueled his brother's smile and personality had disappeared; the thin, drawn, pasty-faced man of twenty-two in the bed seemed aged by twenty years, and sour lines were etched between his nose and mouth.

Nicolas was smitten by guilt. His brother was sick, even if it was by his own doing, and yet here he was raving at him, pouring on his head the spleen left over from his bitter quarrel with the ignorant woman who had almost dazzled him into believing she was more than a porcelain-faced doll. He already had one damn fool, Jean-Pierre, bent on destroying himself. He did not need another.

However, Nicolas hated doctors, for it was obvious to him that they caused more pain and death than they ever prevented, and so he would force himself to allow his younger brother one more day to recover on his own. Chastened by the man's bad color and shallow breathing, Nicolas put his hand gently on the thin shoulder. 'Jean-Pierre, open your eyes. I shall make you a proposition. It is worth listening to.'

The grayish lids opened slowly, but the eyes behind them had gained some clarity. In fact, Jean-Pierre's limbs had stopped their convulsive writhing and were more relaxed. The medicine, whatever concoction it was, seemed a prodigiously quick remedy for the ills of wanton dissolution. But the brown eyes that stared at Nicolas were filled with rancor.

'Jean-Pierre, on the premise that a few days in bed will find you fit, I will give you what money you need now to pay your debts and obligations. And in some months' time, I will again be willing to add a reasonable supplement to your income. But both of these offers are predicated on your leaving Paris for Ancy-le Franc almost immediately, to take up your duties with the Petits Augustins, at least through the winter. I won't make any bones that I wish to remove you from some of the temptations that have overwhelmed you, but I think a time of quiet and contemplation and prayer among the good brothers, and some simple fare, and you might pass this tempestuous passage between youth and maturity without crippling yourself along the way. Don't bother to accuse me of coercion, for that is just what it is. I am forcing you, and you have no choice. Otherwise, I will give you nothing, and you may dodge your creditors and live how you can.'

Jean-Pierre was swiftly coming back to himself. 'And how do you know I will be a good boy in Ancy, *ma mère?*' he mocked bitterly.

'Your face and your health will tell me.'

The brown eyes took on a shrewd light. 'And if I agree to being treated as a chattel, will you give me enough money to extricate myself from my obligations? It will not be cheap. My luck has been bad, and my *amours* are greedy.'

'You will have whatever you need. But I expect you to be gone by the end of the week. In fact, in a month or two, as soon as I look into my business affairs and consult with the stewards of my other estates, I have decided to leave court for the winter months and spend time at La Toque, hunting in the brisk air. So we shall meet again after this winter, both of us fresh and new and bouncing as a maiden's tits.'

Jean-Pierre relaxed now on his pillows, his color much better. He stretched his mouth into a weak version of his toothy smile, surprisingly agreeable. 'Whatever you say, *mon frère*. There's not much choice you give me. Moreover, it pains me to admit you are probably right. I need a rest.'

Nicolas punched him lightly on the arm, thinking to himself what a wonderful persuader money was. At least, with Jean-Pierre. With some others, nothing would help. They would march with dreamy eyes directly into the dragon's mouth, sustained by unreasoning sentiment, oblivious of truth. '*Très bien*. Then we are settled. Sleep well. I will look in on you in the morning.' He saluted and turned away.

'I am sure you will,' Jean-Pierre murmured softly to his retreating back. The valet, straightening the bedclothes, looked up from under his brows and saw the eyes of Monsieur l'Abbé, fixed on his brother, glisten with spite. As soon as the door closed, the sick man demanded, 'Where is that boy from the herbalist, Le Brun?'

'Without, monsieur, awaiting payment.'

'Good. Bring him in. You see how well the curative dose works? I want to give him a much larger order. A precaution. Just in case my digestion rebels so far away among the good friars.'

CHAPTER
~ 15 ~

Mademoiselle finally left her bed of woe; one did not go more than eight days without paying tribute to the king. But she went about drooping and sighing, bravely attending various social functions but often fainting and having to be carried out, to the seeming mortification of Monsieur de Lauzun. He could not abide shows of emotion and did his best, in her presence and out of it, to treat the whole situation, with his usual tart aloofness, as water under the bridge.

The several times in the next weeks that Nicolas found himself briefly in his godmother's vicinity, they both performed the proper courtesies, no muscle moving in either face to indicate anything more than her depression and his ordinary male wish not to linger too close to such moaning. But it didn't escape his glance that she had extraordinary high color and bright eyes for a woman who was broken-hearted. And in spite of her convincing spasms of grief—and why not convincing, since the fact remained that she had been forbidden to take de Lauzun as a husband—the probable reason he suspected for her inner radiance made him grind his teeth. And so did de Lauzun irritate him, whose great disappointment had not one whit affected his fawning around the king or confident strut as the new governor of Berri.

Madame de Lowry, on the other hand, was less perky than usual, although when they did accidentally encounter each other, her color and her chin came up, and she sailed right past his unsmiling scrutiny with disregard. But in the restless and sleepless weeks that followed, his own equilibrium began to restore itself. His anger began to dissipate, overridden by a greater affliction, jealousy rampant. Reason told him that what Julie and the Duchesse may have perpetrated was done. What use was it to miss her, to care nothing for the smiling faces looking up at his with flirtatious smiles and seductive glances when the eyes in the back of his head told him she was behind him on the other end of the salon gaily enjoying a hand of cards in a foursome with the Comte de Vosges, who followed her everywhere lately like a devoted lapdog.

But his first tentative attempt at reconciliation was illtimed, for Minister de Louvois came up to her side with the fan she had just dropped. Nicolas's greeting came off more sardonically than he had intended, and Julie's nostrils flared as she stared right through him. The Marquis de Louvois nodded, but his scorn was barely concealed, and he quickly steered his lady away through the strolling buyers patronizing the overpriced shops in the Palais Royal's arcade.

Several things had worked to distance Nicolas from the irked pride of a lion who had roared in vain. Jean-Pierre's fast recovery from his illness and docile departure from Paris helped. The on-time sailing from Cherbourg of his three leased merchant ships, to return before the onset of winter laden with Croixverte's fresh shipments of dressed furs and skins as well as various other paid cargoes, helped. So did his intendant Beraite's efficient performance in getting the captains and crews in hand, the ships laden with trade goods, and the whole enterprise sent off some days earlier than scheduled—added insurance for an early return. Vigorous, long sessions of practice with the sword every morning helped, too, toning his muscles, putting spring and balance back into his legs, and making him sweat profusely, which he hoped would wash away the itch in his blood and the flashes of regret that he had handled Madame de Lowry much too roughly. *Tiens*, he grumbled to himself, she couldn't help it if she had no perception of things. Women were simply not good at reason, witless little souls that they were.

'*Et voilà! Touché!* That stroke would have cut you in half, de Courcillon, had this edge not been blunted,' gloated Apollon de Vivonne, pleased as punch, for as able as he was with the sword, he seldom got the chance to beat his flashy friend.

Nicolas grinned good-naturedly and walked to the edge of the mirrored practice room in the Palais Royal to swab the sweat off his face with a cloth Skandahet-se held out to him, rather than with the falls of fine lace edging his full sleeves. His linen shirt was stuck to his chest. His diaphragm above the tight waistband of his knee breeches moved in and out with his panting. The lanky de Vivonne followed him, accepting a towel from his own valet. 'You are getting soft, *mon ami*,' he teased, and gave Nicolas a backhanded slap across the muscled belly, which still, unfortunately, showed an extra pound or two from the starchy Italian cuisine.

'Not for long.' Nicolas grimaced, retying the ribbon that held his flowing hair to the back of his neck. 'Another week of keeping you from hacking me to pieces, and the extra lard hasn't a chance.' There was a shout, and they both turned to view the two remaining duelists who were still on the floor, one of whom had just dodged the blunted tip of his opponent's twisted-grip rapier by a hair.

'Monsieur le Duc isn't bad for so foppish a youth. I thought he had injured his knee in Flanders,' observed Nicolas.

De Vivonne sucked on a tooth. 'He did. It goes in and out of its socket. Today it seems it is in.'

They stood and watched the elegant dueling style of the Duc de Rohan, who was actually a prince, since he was the head of a French family claiming descent from a ruling house. Nicolas finally threw back the towel to Skandahet-se. 'Let's join them,' he suggested to de Vivonne. 'You draw off de Grignant. I've not had a chance to try de Rohan's arm, but I've heard that last year he studied under Alferi at the Fencing Academy in Padua. Not bad training.' But before they could move on it, the gentleman in question delivered a clever parry and recover and, with a bruising blow of his fencing sword, rendered his opponent's sword arm theoretically useless. The loser, a stoutish but agile member of the Vendôme clan, flung his sword down in exasperation.

'*Merde!* I all but had you, de Rohan.'

'Not once did you get near me, monsieur,' the Duc

drawled superciliously. He came to the chamber's side to dab his baby-skinned, fine-boned hatchet face and long neck with the towel his valet provided. 'And "all but" has seen many a man spitted and dead, *n'est-ce pas*?' He pressed a finger to the side of his chiseled nostril and noisily blew his nose on the floor, then did the same with the opposite side.

Nicolas came up to him and said smoothly, 'I hope you're not going to quit, *cher* monsieur. We were just going in after both of you.'

'Were you, now?' The hazel eyes flicked lazily over them. A smile played about the patrician lips. 'Well, I have already crossed swords with Monsieur de Vivonne, and he gives a good fight. But you, Monsieur de Courcillon, would be a challenge. We have somehow missed each other at practice here, but I know your reputation. Unfortunately, although you truly tempt me, I shall have to make my excuses.'

'That is disappointing, Monsieur le Duc. As you said, we seem never to have found the opportunity to oppose each other. Can you not spare another quarter of an hour?' In Nicolas's opinion, de Rohan fenced with a precision that augured a certain rigidity of thought; an unusual move would catch him unable to switch gears in time. Nicolas was eager to take him on. A good and hostile challenge could draw all the depressive toxins from his system.

De Rohan fanned himself with the crested face cloth and raised an eyebrow. 'But it is not the time, monsieur, it is the energy. I happen to be in the pageant for the queen's birthday tonight, and though I have few lines to say, I must admit I have the devil of a time remembering verse. So I must retire to my study—to study. Since you were not in Paris earlier, when the parts were assigned, I presume you will be a spectator to the play?'

But Nicolas didn't feel like being put off. 'Is your role so taxing, then, that I cannot persuade you? With a handsome bet, perhaps?'

De Rohan flipped his head to get the damp hair off his forehead. 'Not taxing but important. I play a villain on horseback, the King of the Night, who with his minions steals from the absent Glory of the Sun—which is His Majesty, of course—the three Dryads of Earthly Grace, and that's really the substance of it since the rest is the Sun's quest through strange and savage kingdoms to find the all-powerful Goddess of Beauty—Madame de Montespan, of course—who will restore harmony to Terra. A silly story and even sillier verse, certainly not on the order of Racine, but the costumes and settings will be superb. My own is almost as spectacular as the king's.' He hesitated, considering, smoothing down the hairline brown moustache. 'Still, a handsome bet is a handsome bet.'

De Vivonne said casually, but not innocently, to Nicolas, 'Monsieur le Duc has had the fantastic good fortune of rehearsing his role for weeks with the three seductive beauties who play the Dryads—the blond and pert Duchesse de Cantroux, the titian-crowned Eloise de Floque, and the raven-haired beauty the Comtesse de Lowry, whom he swoops into his arms and carries away on his saddle as she quite dramatically proclaims her lines predicting his downfall at the Sun's hands. I just happened on one of the rehearsals last week. It was—fascinating.' His lips twitched.

'Yes, except for the verse, it has been a delightful experience, to say the least,' de Rohan drawled. 'And, between us, a fine excuse to lay hands on some of the most luscious ladies in all France and hear them giggle about it, women who would publicly blanch at a lascivious stare.' He chuckled at the memory.

'Lay hands on them, eh?' Nicolas attempted to keep his polite smile from turning deadly. He felt the bunching of his shoulder muscles under his shirt and was aware that a wicked shine had come into his eyes. 'Twenty thousand livres, Monsieur le Duc, for a strike to the death and to pit my own former master, Guyon of Nantes, against that of Padua.'

An acquisitive gleam lit the hazel regard. 'Twenty thousand! That is a great deal of money, monsieur.'

'But worth it, monsieur, to show you the difference between your dancing master and a true genius of fencing technique. We shall have done with it in five minutes, and then you may be off to your study. I was taught to dispatch my victims swiftly.'

Stung, de Rohan abruptly yanked his rapier from the scabbard held by his valet and jerked his head toward the center of the gleaming practice floor. 'Come on, then, de Courcillon. I have five minutes to take care of a braggart. You shall soon see what I was taught. Perhaps messieurs de Vivonne and de Grignant would watch closely, as attestors?'

Following his antagonized prey to the center of the floor, Nicolas looked over his shoulder and threw some casual sentences in Huron at Skandahet-se, who responded with a grunt.

'What did you say to that aborigine?' de Rohan asked as they took their stance, intrigued by the strange sound of the language.

'Merely told him to get ready to collect your order on your banker this afternoon,' Nicolas said, and he was pleased to see the jut of the sharp jaw. 'He speaks little French.'

From the Vicomte de Vivonne's point of view, the accident that took place ten minutes later was just that, an accident; the Duc de Rohan had slipped on the mucus from his own nose, even though the other attestor said he thought de Courcillon's miserable savage had deliberately curved his foot out to wipe it away too late and that it was no accident that he had hooked the howling Duc's bad leg out from under him. 'After all,' de Vivonne offered reasonably as the Duc lay writhing on his back, 'as stupid as the redskin is, he would have had to be blind not to see that his master was in total control of the contest at that point and needed no such help from him, wouldn't you say? You saw de Courcillon's furious drive. He had de Rohan dancing back from that flurry of strokes like a cat on the coals, and in the very minute he came up under the Duc's frantic high lunge—a move which would have taken the Duc through the throat— why, then, at that very moment, would the faithful servant have spoiled the victory? It makes no sense, Monsieur de Grignant.' De Vivonne dabbed at his nose and stuck his handkerchief back into the breast of his velvet coat with a self-satisfied air, ignoring the other's scowl.

Nicolas, meanwhile, knelt by the groaning, suffering de Rohan and deplored the incomprehensible stupidity of his servant. 'He will certainly be whipped for such witless action, most properly punished, I assure you, Monsieur le Duc, for causing me such mortification and you such pain. It is sometimes hard to predict how an Indian might think. I could swear he was only trying to save you from slipping and misjudged your distance, but, nevertheless, I will see he pays well for it.'

The Duc struggled up, leaning on his elbows, one leg turned inward at a peculiar angle, sweat beading his high brow. '*I* will see he pays well for it. Send him to my steward for punishment,' he gasped. 'And you cannot tell me I did not feel him yank my leg sideways—as perhaps you told him to do,' he accused, grimacing. 'Ah, *sacre Dieu,* this damn knee——'

Nicolas's head came up sharply. 'I shall ignore that unworthy remark, monsieur, as coming from a man beset by great pain. My Indian acted on his own, but without malice. Nevertheless, I shall most certainly forfeit the twenty thousand livres for his clumsiness, and you shall have it by suppertime.'

'Oh?' The Duc squinted at him. One could see his feathers lie down again as he reasoned that surely de Courcillon wouldn't order his man to cause an accident and then relinquish the prize. 'That is only fair, of course, monsieur.'

'Of course,' Nicolas agreed.

But then de Rohan smote his forehead, and the one arm remaining to support him quivered. 'Ah, *mon Dieu,* the play tonight! I will never be able to walk, much less ride. The scene will be in ruins and the king furious— oof, *Dieu me sauve,* this blasted thing hurts! Where is that miserable valet? Does he think to find a stretcher in Flanders? Two chairs and some strong footmen would do.'

For a moment, Nicolas had the grace to feel shame, viewing the spasms of pain lancing across the pale aristocratic face, but twenty thousand livres would make up for his nasty deed, considering he had actually won the match. Skandahet-se's timing had been superb. 'Monsieur, I beg you to allow me to try to take your place tonight, as added penance. We are almost of a size, and if you would spare me a few minutes after the surgeon makes you comfortable, you could instruct me in the role. I would not play it as successfully as you, no doubt, but at least the theatrics would not be disrupted. It is the least I can do,' he offered, hoping the downturned corners of his mouth indicated that he did not relish the idea of displaying himself before the whole court.

The miserable de Rohan stared at him. 'The costume would fit, I suppose,' he conceded, groaning. 'And you must use your own horse. But how will you learn the verses?'

With a deprecating shrug, Nicolas said, 'One of the few things my tutors didn't slam my knuckles for as a child was my quick memory. I demand, monsieur, that you allow me to redeem my servant's deplorable misjudgment.'

The door to the big fencing room opened to admit de Rohan's valet, followed by servants carrying a full-length settee with which to transport the Duc to his quarters in the nearby Louvre, where a surgeon would settle the joint back in place and bind it. 'Very well. Come to my apartment in two hours,' de Rohan muttered, gritting his teeth as the men lifted him onto the makeshift stretcher. 'I've neither the mind nor the time to find another substitute now, the devil with it. And bring the twenty thousand with you, de Courcillon,' he demanded as he was carried carefully away, his valet and de Grignant accompanying him.

Skandahet-se came from where he had stood hangdog and penitent behind the fallen Duc. He helped Nicolas don his coat, but when their eyes met, the Indian's facial muscles stretched into one of his rare grins. Nicolas regarded him fondly from beneath knitted brows and murmured, 'We shall have to do something about you, you miserable savage.'

'I hope that fabricating this encounter with your lady

will be worth twenty thousand livres, *cher ami*, for you'll make a fool of yourself out there if you don't know the part,' de Vivonne drawled as they sauntered from the room. 'The sound of the audience's laughter will do much to cure de Rohan's knee.'

'I've made a fool of myself before,' growled Nicolas, 'and for nothing so important as patching together what was a charming friendship. It seems the lady and I both lost our tempers, but I'll bet another twenty thousand she's as willing as I am to forget it, once I can get near her.'

'This beauty seems to have tripped you up, for once,' his old friend observed with an amused glance.

'Trussed me up like a boar on a pole, you mean,' Nicolas declared, slapping his hat back on his head. He shrugged his acquiescence to that fact. 'I don't know what it is that makes her so different in my eyes. Maybe that she's so vulnerable yet thinks she's so strong. But I'd like to go back to sleeping at night, damn it!'

Julie closed her eyes tightly for a moment, hoping to capture her elusive first lines by seeing them written large on her eyelids. When she opened them to peer from the wings, she was shaken to see that the Glory of the Sun, in his gilded and garlanded chariot, was about to make his departure from the stage to shine his bounty on the 'halcyon lands beyond the vast, bottomless sea.' Louis was almost blinding in billowing robes of glistening red-gold silk fabric encrusted with big, flashing paste diamonds and rubies. A shimmering cloth-of-gold cloak was swirled over one shoulder, and a huge sunburst headdress of shining gold rays surrounded his dark curls, which were glinting with sprinkled gold dust. At the crack of his jeweled whip, his arched-necked and gilded horses, reins dripping gold and silver tassels and rosettes, quickly drew his divine figure off the stage and behind a sky-blue partition lavishly painted with clouds, birds, and garlands and supported by gilded columns.

There were soft, heelless slippers secured to Julie's feet with pink ribbon. Her close-fitting Grecian robe was of clinging pink silk with satin ribbons that trailed down behind like a train. Her shining hair was loose down her back, with a wreath of pink and white flowers over her brow; her arms were bare to suggest girlish innocence.

She knew she looked charming, but she felt in a panic; her voice was stuck in her throat, and she couldn't remember one word of her verses, not one! But fate gave her no time to bolt. Madame de Floque, playing Napaea, nymph of glens, grabbed her by the hand, and in a moment their flower-bedecked float girt with real shrubs and grass moved smoothly forward, carrying the three Graces out onto the outdoor stage set up on the Tuileries vast terrace. Finger-snapping applause washed over the three pretty women as, with arms intertwined and pastel-shaded robes rippling against their figures, they made a striking tableau for a moment, heads held high, staring into infinite distance with their semigoddess eyes.

Aided by sprites, the Dryads descended the steps of their platform, and the play went on. Julie dredged up her first word through sheer terror of the rustling many-headed monster called an audience, which she could see beyond the footlight candles. The rest of her lines flooded back to her, and the fright of her acting debut receded in the excitement of the moment. The scene was short but pivotal. She was lucky to have been cast as one of the Graces; it gave her prestige and a chance to show off her acting ability and, luckily, required little memorizing. She would not have been able to manage a larger role in her present benumbed state of mind, where nothing could hold her attention for long and she wept a river of tears every night in her dreams, if not in fact. It all went smoothly enough, however. She and her companions praised the Glory of the Sun and his benevolent rule over all earthly gardens, swooping and gliding about the stage as they had been rehearsed, attended by voile-draped children strewing flower petals in their paths.

A gauze curtain descended slowly over the backdrop, depicting a sunlit garden. Concealed strings pulled closed metal covers that hid the light of strategic candles outlining the stage, and the stage took on the look of twilight. Julie, who had the most important role, gave the cue word then, enunciating it clearly and loudly, for de Rohan had been known to daydream and come in late. But the high wooden partition rattled a bit, and, right on time, out from behind it burst the King of the Night on a rearing black stallion whose shining hide was draped with strings of scintillating crystals. The man was stunning in a bespangled midnight-blue satin tunic and tights all of one piece and smoothed over shoulders, belly, and strong thighs. His entire face was hidden behind a rigid and full silver mask, and on his arrogant head was a headdress of a crescent moon under a fall of shimmering stars. Six minions, all in black and with small silver masks, ran beside him and encircled the women.

'Hold, O beauteous creatures of the dawn, hold in your flight, for you have crossed the line between day and night and, not seeking your own beds in time, are now forfeit to rest in mine!' The ruler of the dark menaced them.

Julie's mouth dropped in astonishment, for the voice did not belong to the Duc de Rohan; it was deeper and stronger and very familiar. She gulped and backed away from the pawing horse, frantically buying a few seconds to find her line. 'S-sisters, fear not, and keep your place, for surely even night will give us grace to light our candle, and in doing so push back the shadows, the dark cloaks behind which. . .' Mechanically, she went on, entering into a brief exchange with the shimmering king. Her stage sisters flicked tense eyes to hers as they, too, realized that the dark rider on his towering horse was not de Rohan. But the man under the silver mask answered impeccably, and they relaxed, stepping forward to make their speeches.

It was Nicolas, of course. Julie knew very well the timber of the voice, the broad-shouldered build, the mockery in the tone. What he had done with the poor Duc she couldn't tell, yet he certainly knew the verses. But he hadn't rehearsed, and he would make a shambles of the action. How dare he ruin the scene just to goad her, the *cochon!* As the others declaimed, she felt her hot cheeks flush deeper than her stage makeup.

The short exchange of dialogue, with vile threat of rapine on one side and maidenly pleadings on the other, might have gone decently enough if the brute hadn't thrown in lines he made up: 'Ah, Limoniad, gentle nymph of meadows, one peep into your limpid violet eyes, one glance at the lush divinity of form you display to tantalize men into your perfumed reach. . .' He raved on and on and then, blessedly, it was time to exit, the minions of night affixing silver collars and chains to the drooping swan necks of Julie's fellow actresses. The King of the Night was only to look on regally, and so he did, but then he held up his hand, and, to her indignation, Julie heard him continue to rewrite the play.

'Take them hence, good henchmen, and into my gloomy, thunderous keep cast them and throw away the key. Get thee gone, I charge you now, and leave this one for me.' A deep laugh issued from the mask's rigid silver mouth. Obviously having been reinstructed in their roles, the men snatched up the lissome Dryads and quickly bore them away as they wept and called to the Glory of the Sun to be saved. Julie stood transfixed and embarrassed upon the stage, heart pounding to hear the unsuspecting audience quiet with suspense behind her, and she couldn't think what to do.

The black stallion, guided by its rider, took some steps toward her. She gasped, looked wildly about, and dodged to one side. The rider turned the horse and followed, a stream of evil chuckles coming from the silver mouth. She dodged again, feeling like an animal at bay. The fire that lanced from her eyes toward the rider was not feigned as he expertly and swiftly positioned the horse again and again to keep her from the two exits off the stage. The pig. He was making her look ridiculous. She could hear her own breathing in the expectant silence. She hated him. She faced him with defiance and hurled her own improvised lines at him. 'You shall not touch me, monarch of shadows and hooting owls, for I am beloved of the flaming Sun.'

'And I shall touch you, glorious maiden, for away from me you cannot run,' he responded in execrable rhyme, and trotted the horse toward her again.

The float was up against the backdrop. She could scramble under its wheels, but how humiliating to be thus holed. In her desperation, praying to faint and shut out all the eyes upon her, (and, beyond the rider, a startled pair belonging to the king) she made an error and ran up the steps of the float—an advantageous height for the hunter. He immediately reined the horse past and swooped her off her perch, an iron arm hauling her into the saddle as she kicked and beat at him but was nevertheless carted away into the wings like a sack, past the surprised actors and stage hands who quickly parted to make way, and carried in a canter down the ramp of the terrace. She heard the burst of applause from the audience behind her, some confused shouts from her cohorts, and the heavy sound of her captor's breath behind the silver mask. They cantered down a long double lane of shrubs into the privacy of a hedge-screened grotto, and there he pulled the horse up.

Julie twisted her head around, skewering him with a glare. 'Now that you have frightened the wits out of me with your horse's hooves and made an exit worthy of Monsieur Molière, you may let go of me,' she ordered, matching her hauteur to her vexation.

For answer, he merely swung a leg over and got down, and then, when she refused to come into the arms he held up, he proceeded to haul her down, ignoring her stiff noncooperation. He ducked back from the blows she swung at him, caught at her, and, with one hand locked around her wrist, used the other to fumble off his mask. A laughing, bearded face emerged in the bright moonlight.

'I thought my ending to the scene was much more dramatic than the stupidity the author wrote,' he exulted. 'The audience was enthralled. Didn't you hear the ovation?'

'No, but you will surely hear from the king about the temerity of changing the work he commissioned translated from the Greek. And for what purpose this farce, may I ask?' she bit off.

'Because, *ma chère*, to watch you from the audience

would have been too far away, and you avoid me otherwise.' Provocatively, he studied her mouth, then leaned toward her and rumbled softly, 'You devastate me in your simple little robe and fragrant wreath, dear Dryad. In fact, I am quite ready to believe you wield the power of an unearthly being. At least, over me.' He put his hand up to brush back the long, loose tendrils of hair the night breeze stirred about her face. She stepped back.

'Stop.'

He shook his head. 'Ah, Julie, we had merely a difference of opinion. What has been done is done. As to Mademoiselle, she carries grudges for a while. I must wait before I try to salve the hurt I caused her. But you and I—could we not at least fly the flag of truce?'

'Never. I shall never forget the ugly names you called me.'

'I have a bad temper.'

'You have a *vile* temper.'

'Won't you forgive?' He rubbed his cheek above the trim beard. 'I seem to remember you were not so calm yourself.'

'That was in defense. Let me tell you, monsieur, I can forgive you, yes. I was raised to be humble in the face of apology. But I cannot forget. Temper frightens me. I flee from it.'

He contemplated her rigid, hostile expression. His mouth drew into a sarcastic quirk. 'I suppose you prefer to that the cold blood of a de Louvois. You must *like* steel emotions and almost limitless power.'

Deliberately ignoring the never-again-repeated scene in the minister's carriage, she responded, 'The difference is that Monsieur de Louvois doesn't insult me. He is very aware of acting a gentleman.'

'He is very aware of you, you mean, and he is insidious. He will bide his time and entice you stealthily. Which might have been my method, too, had you not deliberately lured me on.'

She drew in her breath in a gasp. 'What! Lured you on? Oh, villain, that is not true. Your ego is insufferable, monsieur.'

He dropped his eyes to her indignant mouth and soft, full underlip; his gaze followed the slim line of her throat to the velvety ride of bosom, and for the first time he realized she wore no chemise under the thin and clinging fabric of the Grecian garment that fell in graceful drape to her ankles. Her nipples showed erect under the supple cloth, raised either by rubbing against the fabric or by her reaction to him. Or, quite possibly, by the very mention of her persistent gallant, the Marquis de Louvois, he thought with chagrin. The green dragon of jealousy that clawed in his heart prompted him. 'That is an immodest costume, madame. You do yourself a discredit to be so bold.'

She looked down and colored and made a helpless gesture with her hand. 'It was designed for the Dryads by Madame de La Rochefoucauld herself, from a Grecian urn her husband owns, and it was approved all around.'

'It is a suggestive disgrace, madame,' he said, unjustly incensed. 'I would allow no female relative of mine to go around so brazenly garbed. For whose benefit do you show yourself so, eh? To attract Monsieur de Louvois? Or perhaps that pasty-faced knight de Vosges?' He dropped the mask on the grass and grabbed her up into his arms. 'Do they hold you like this?' he demanded furiously. He was driven on by images of the woman he loved being fondled and kissed by the saturnine de Louvois, her silky flesh yielding to the touch of those long, insidious fingers. 'Do they embrace you, hug you, make love to you——?' He rained kisses on her imprisoned neck and shoulders, on the tip of her ear, and forced her chin around so he could clamp down on her lips. He pressed his mouth cruelly against hers and forced open her unwilling lips. He knew he was hurting her in his unyielding grip, but she was hurting him. Who knew what she might have been enticed into doing with de Louvois, what blandishments might have influenced her gullible heart to forget him, to give her love elsewhere?

He tasted salt on her lips, lips that no longer resisted his but were cold and still as marble. She was crying. Then he realized he was insane. She was neither foolish nor promiscuous. He was driven crazy with jealousy because he wanted her, and he was acting irrationally, abominably. He knew what it was—bedevilment, because he had lost control of the situation. He was deeply in love with her.

He released her mouth and, holding her more gently, wiped away the tears on her cheeks with his thumb. 'Ah, Julie, I am sorry,' he said in an anguished whisper.

She said nothing, merely stood looking small and white. There was deep fright in the look she gave him.

'I have never before been jealous of a woman. I don't know how to cope with it. I am unstrung because you have taken over my heart. I want you, but you are angry with me. And so I buck like a wild horse and act crudely.' He pressed up her chin with one finger. 'Forgive me, *mon coeur*, I must be touched to stupidity by the moon. Say you will forgive me.'

She looked back at him silently. Moonbeams caught in the raven mass of her hair glinted blue. Her eyes were huge, dark, unfathomable pools. The gay dimple that had always enchanted him had fled.

Julie felt paralyzed. Was it Richard standing there, as he had those few times he had visited her, lower lip curled around a cruel smile while he prodded her to tell him why she begged so hard to return to court? he sneered. Hadn't he saved her, by removing her to Cuckfield, from the virulent plague that had carried off even a dozen of the king's very intimates? What made her so restless, so anxious to be away from her goodwife existence at the manor? Was she missing the homage of the gallants who were always dancing about her at court? Was she missing a lover, perhaps? Had she entertained a lover in London when her husband was absent?

No, no. She had shaken her head, horrified. She had tried to deny it, but he would not let her. He went on and on, telling her what she was missing of her secret lover's performance, relishing the prurient details in his mouth as if he were chewing on candy, detaining her with a relentless grip on her arm so she must listen to the workings of his vile imagination and be hurt, wounded. But for what? For what?

And to what avail her protests, her hysterical tears, over his accusations? Richard decided what he wanted to believe, and from then on, that was the truth.

'Julie, say something. Please. Call me monster, lout, anything, but at least speak to me,' Nicolas pleaded. But she remained mute, like a wooden doll. He dropped his arms, freeing her. 'Did the passion we found together mean so little to you, then, that you can just pass it by? Won't you take my hand and let us start afresh? It was only because I love you——'

'If we go back now, we will not ruin the king's last scene by our absence,' she said tonelessly.

'Julie——'

She put his hand away from her. 'We must go back on the horse. We will not arrive in time otherwise.'

He studied her face. 'Maybe I am mistaken. Maybe your heart sings an air discordant with mine. Perhaps you have no heart.'

'That is very likely, monsieur. I have had much instruction in the art of pitilessness.' Her features were frozen; only her lips moved.

He snorted softly, deriding himself. 'It is no more than I deserve. So many women. And now fate deals me this card in revenge. A wax doll, soft and melting when the fire is applied, hard and unfeeling otherwise. You never said you loved me. You've been very scrupulous about that. Then why do I feel as deceived as an ex-virgin crying after her departing amour?' He waited an instant and then spoke out. 'Say something. Damn it, I don't allow women to toy with me!'

If he expected an answer, he got none. A muscle in his jaw moved. His eyes narrowed. 'Very well, madame,' he said. 'As you wish. I'll not bother you again.'

Staring up into his angry face, Julie felt drained, buffeted by his emotions and her own. His gaze remained on her for a moment, and her heart tortured her to make peace with him, but she could not ignore her fright of his jealousy, her fear of his tumultuous personality. She remembered his merry light blue eyes upon her, she remembered his tenderness in Flanders as she had shivered against him in the coach, and the words he had breathed in her ear on the bearskin rug were graven on her heart. But the man frowning down at her was too easily capable of outburst against her. She was hers alone to give; she wasn't going to injure her life a second time.

And yet, and yet—As Nicolas helped her up on the horse, she told herself something, her eyes on his bent head, her hand wanting to stroke the waves of his silky-coarse cinnamon hair, which was not yet obscured by the starry headdress he had retrieved. And yet Richard had never been jealous of her, not for one minute, not from the beginning, no matter how he declared his love. He had never cared enough even to worry that another man might desire her. It was his sadism that had created nonexistent lovers for her.

She had seen the jealousy darken de Courcillon's face as he imagined her with de Louvois, imagined losing her to another, even dared to wonder if she had strewn her favors about, the contemptible *cochon*. Surely that said something.

But she wasn't sure what.

Nicolas adjusted the silver mask over his stony face. Sitting stiff and erect as they trotted back to the terrace, Julie resisted the temptation to sigh and lean back against the broad, hard chest. It would be so easy to give in and let later take care of itself. But God had not rescued her from Richard de Lowry's cruelty for nothing.

They reached the wings in time for the last scene, in which the King of the Night is vanquished by rays of fire from the Sun's glorious fingers and the three Dryads are returned by the Goddess of Beauty to the Gardens of Earth. They both moved through their parts woodenly, with mercifully few lines to repeat, and Nicolas made a creditable slinking, slumping exit, leading his horse into exile, darkness forever conquered. At the end, Julie remained embedded in the excited and milling cast and crowd of well-wishers that surrounded the actors, gaily smiling and giggling, and carefully not looking in his direction.

* * *

A month later, the king gave a sumptuous banquet for the new papal legate, at which just he and the august cleric dined *tête-à-tête*, although many courtiers attended and watched as eighty different dishes were served to the two men, not counting thirty-eight for dessert. The spectators were titillated by the rumor that just that morning, Colbert had thundered in a report to the king that such a useless meal, costing a thousand crowns, gave him an incredible pain when so many of the people went hungry. Mademoiselle and the Comte de Lauzun were among the onlookers, and the *Gazette de Paris* reported that the Comte took snuff from a gold box that had on the lid a diamond-ringed ruby the size of a thumb.

The following evening, perhaps incidental to the gossipy report, the Comte de Lauzun was arrested and taken to the Bastille. No reason was given for his detainment; only the king's *lettre de cachet* was needed.

Nicolas was informed about it almost as it happened, interrupted at his supper by a friend, the Seigneur d'Elbrouse, who had recently been appointed a lieutenant in the Gardes. D'Elbrouse also imparted the news that it was probable that de Lauzun would be transported down to Pignerol by another captain, Monsieur d'Artagnan, very shortly.

Nicolas scratched at his beard, cursing softly, then went to his writing table, where he dashed off a letter telling Mademoiselle of the arrest, pledging to get her what information he could, and begging her to keep a cool head and do nothing precipitous. He drummed his fingers on the table, picked up the quill pen again, and wrote another note—this time to Madame de Lowry, consisting of three short words—and he enclosed within its confines a white rose clipped from his garden, which he drew from a vase on his table. Summoning the fastest page in his house to speed the messages on their way to the Luxembourg, he poured two glasses of wine, gulped his down, and accompanied d'Elbrouse back to the Louvre.

Mademoiselle shrieked upon receiving the note and ripped it into little shreds. She immediately sent a maid to summon Julie and tore at her graying curls in frustration while tears of terror slid down her cheeks. Totally ignoring Nicolas's cautions, she ordered out her carriage and prepared to dash to the Louvre to snatch her Antonin from the king's wrath, which could only have been occasioned by one thing. Pacing her chamber as Dant hurried from the *garderobe* with a wrap, she declared in a voice tense with fear that she would swear, she would crawl on her knees to her cousin, that there had been no marriage, that whatever he had heard was baseless, unproven, untrue. She moaned and clutched at her heart. 'Where are my ladies?' she demanded of Julie.

'In the Grand Salle, playing at cards with visitors and entertaining the Bishop of Vaillon, who has requested an audience with you this evening, some charity of his, I think,' Julie answered.

'Good, leave them there. We will go around the other way and. . .'

There was a low scratch on the door, and Dant went to open it. 'An envoy from the king, Your Highness.' The butler hardly had time to announce this before Monsieur de La Merveille, the current captain of the Garde-du-Corps, came around him. Mademoiselle paled and stepped back.

The Duc de La Merveille was punctiliously polite. His bow as he swept off his plumed hat was extravagantly low. But the message he carried to her, on the king's heavy parchment with the royal seal, was black, and no courtesy helped it. The Duchesse de Montpensier was hereby exiled from the presence of the king and from his court for an indefinite period of time to any of her farther properties that she wished, accompanied by whomever she wished. Furthermore, she was strictly enjoined by His Majesty from entering his royal presence or his houses without his express permission and informed that her exile was to begin immediately, with a grace period of two days to prepare.

'But why?' she cried out. 'Why, monsieur, has he arrested the Comte de Lauzun and banished me from his sight? Why? What have we done?'

'I am sorry, Your Highness. I simply do not know.'

'It cannot be. I will go to His Majesty. I will tell him he is deluded. I will go on my knees as a simple woman,' she begged, her voice breaking. 'I cannot believe this.'

De La Merveille had the respect to look quite unhappy, although he had been for years one of de Lauzun's most bitter detractors and in his heart he thought this woman a fool. 'I am desolate, Mademoiselle, but I am instructed to inform you that His Majesty wishes his orders complied with to the letter and that if there is any deviation at all from his commands, he will be forced to believe that his measures against Monsieur de Lauzun have not been stringent enough and that further action could be warranted. I beg you to heed this serious warning.'

The threat against de Lauzun was enough. Mademoiselle's large body sagged, and she fell into a chair. Julie hurried to the stricken woman to chafe her limp wrist, and Dant scurried for the ammonia vial. But Mademoiselle raised her head and croaked, '*Très bien, monsieur*, I hear what you say. But may I at least address a letter to my cousin to beg his leniency? In the last resort, is that, at least, allowed me?' She wanted to ask in the letter if she could at least see de Lauzun, but she feared that to do so might bring more punishment on his head. She closed her eyes in pain. 'Dant, where are you? Bring pen and paper and a writing board; if I move, I shall break into pieces. Madame de Lowry, call my butler and steward, gather my attending ladies, set wheels in motion. My fate has been decided. My heart is dead.'

Julie still had in her pocket her unopened letter. She was hollow inside, her eyes big with shock. The whole world seemed to be collapsing on her. The king of France had turned his awesome wrath on this household, de Lauzun was jailed, Mademoiselle la Duchesse de Montpensier, princess and daughter of France, exiled to the country perhaps for years. And what was to become of her? She had just arrived at court hardly a year before. Mechanically, she moved to do her mistress's bidding. Life had lost much of its pleasure since her bitter falling out with Nicolas over Mademoiselle's plan to marry secretly, and since his insulting, jealous remarks to her. It was losing more of its savor still, filled with her pity for the oppressed and distraught Duchesse. Wretchedly, she drew Nicolas's letter from her pocket. She did not plan to open it. For her own sake, she was going to send it back. She must take care of herself.

No one slept. Madame de Plessis-Rabat sniffled into her handkerchief. Mademoiselle de Greu went about with tears in her eyes. Visitors were chased out. Hundreds of candles burned all night in the salons and chambers as platoons of tired servants packed trunks and boxes and furniture and then carried them to the drays lined up in the courtyard. Sleepy-eyed drivers using two teams hitched and unhitched them to bring in the big wagons from the private livery sheds where they were stored, a great bang on the door and loud 'By Her Highness's orders!' having driven the owner of the sheds from bed and persuaded him to cooperate.

The steward walked about with lists of maids, cooks, equerries, scullions, hostlers, and footmen in hand, assigning who would go with Mademoiselle into exile and who was not necessary. No one was forced to go, of course. They had the option to refuse and quit the job, and some did, although a skeleton staff was left at the Luxembourg to keep it ready for the owner's return. Mademoiselle's attending ladies also had the choice of going with her or not, since some were married and some had commitments. Nor would those who remained be dismissed. But if they resigned to seek another situation—since some exiles were forever—Mademoiselle generously offered them back half the money each had paid for her prestigious position.

Finally, in the hour or two before dawn, everyone laid down his or her head to get a little rest before starting up the packing again in the morning. Julie felt so overwrought and wide awake, she thought she would never sleep. But she did, in spite of the tears that leaked from her eyes when she laid her head on her pillow. And somewhere between sleeping and waking, she found she had decided what she would do.

'I would be pleased to go with you, Your Highness, if but for the winter, to see you settled in.'

'You are too young to bury yourself in the country. You may stay here, in the Luxembourg, until I return. Mesdames d'Epernon and de Puysieux have already decided to come to Eu.'

'But neither has a legible handwriting.'

'I cannot understand you, madame. A bird whispered in my ear that the Comte de Vosges, a man of wealth and refinement, has made an offer for your hand. Were I your guardian, that is a match I would surely approve.'

'I have not made any decision yet. If the Comte de Vosges holds me in the esteem he professes, he will surely not change his mind in six months.'

'Consider. You will surely miss all the gallants who collect about you.'

'Not much.'

'And, ah, Nicolas? Can you not forgive him as I have? *Malheureusement*, the man was right in his judgment of how harshly my cousin's wrath would fall upon poor Monsieur de Lauzun and me. He is not the finest diplomat, de Courcillon, but he has a true heart, in spite of it.'

'I. . .the situation is not so simple, Highness. There are certain complexities involved.'

'Indeed. They must be very vexing to have stolen your good humor and given you so somber an expression when you think no one observes you.'

'It is the strain of keeping the equilibrium between Monsieur de Louvois and myself.'

'Really.'

'He is a man who takes what he desires or else will not give up seeking it. Yet, especially now, I don't wish to offend him. I feel in as delicate a position as a juggler on a high wire.'

'*Tiens*. You need a husband to defend you, madame, a man of honor like my dear Antonin—oh my——'

'Look here, Mademoiselle, take my handkerchief. It is dry.'

'Is there no end to these tears, no end to my grief? Oh, I cannot believe what has happened, I simply cannot. Ah, Julie, my dear, I must go meekly into exile to protect my dear love from the anger of the most powerful ruler in all the world. But your life is here.'

'Whatever informant the king believed would probably have also reported my complicity in your affairs. In fact, I am surprised that nothing has been said to me. But perhaps a season's absence would be discreet.'

'It will be lonely.'

'I am used to that. The sea air will clear my head, help me think out my future. And I will work along with you and ride every day. Please allow me to come, Your Highness.'

'*Ciel*, what can I say to such devotion? You are welcome, my dear.'

'Thank you, Mademoiselle. Blanchette is already at my packing.'

'One more word, madame. Monsieur de Courcillon sends notice he will say his *adieux* to me tonight. He will probably be unhappy to hear you are leaving court, too, except that he indicates he is soon to make a trip to his estate at La Toque in Brittany for several months.'

'I. . .sincerely beg to be excused if I am in the room when the gentleman arrives.'

'La Toque is not terribly far from Eu.'

'That holds no interest for me.'

'How stubborn you are. Surely it was not that silly riding off on the night of the queen's birthday that has turned you against de Courcillon?'

'No, not really.'

'Well, I would not want to pry——'

A footman entering with a communication on heavy cream paper interrupted the conversation, to Julie's relief. Mademoiselle took it and broke the seal. She read for a moment, her puffy face drawing into itself as her eyes traveled over the words, her lips compressing until they were white. She stood up, crumpled the letter with angry strength, stalked to the cold hearth, applied the paper to a lit candle on the mantel, and tossed the burning missive onto the stone with a curse. Julie waited for her to remark on the letter, but she clamped her jaw and remained silent. She walked to the window sunk in her thoughts and stood staring out as the wind whipped the limbs of the boxed orange trees in the park.

It would have been rude to invade her privacy, and Julie forbore, even though the red and yellow ribbon under the seal signified that the letter was from Athénais de Montespan.

The Duchesse de Montpensier, her three ladies, and a great household left Paris for the exile of Eu the next morning. Her caravan was long and most imposing, transporting everything from great trunks of clothes to extra coaches to carpets to paintings and commodes to Dant's fancy pigeons roped atop a baggage cart, a farewell gift from the servant's sister-in-law. The train clogged up the narrow streets of Paris. Even in high disgrace and with leaden heart, Mademoiselle let no onlooker forget she was a princess of the royal family, and the richest woman in Europe.

CHAPTER
~ 16 ~

Mademoiselle's favorite dwelling, the Norman Chateau des Comtes d'Eu, looking over the Atlantic just north of Dieppe, had years ago supplanted in her esteem her former place of exile, the Burgundian chateau of Saint-Fargeau. Hearing Mademoiselle's tales of the site's long history, of the illustrious Artois, the Cleves, and the Guises, Julie had halfway expected a hulking pile brooding over the land. It lifted her heart to see instead an airy, rectangular palace of dressed stone and brick with high peaked roofs, numerous windows, and flag-stoned plaza. The large house sat on a low rise to one side of the town of Eu, a community made prosperous by a glass factory and fabric, lace, and brass makers.

The present chateau was built on the site of a fortress where William the Conqueror married Mathilde of Flanders in the year one thousand and fifty, but it was not venerable. Begun a century before by Henri de Guise and finished just ten years ago by Mademoiselle to her own taste, the house had an openness, a windswept grandeur, that helped to ease the depressed state in which its owner, her three ladies, and her large staff arrived.

In fact, the combination of gracious domicile and salubrious sea air roused the Duchesse from her wan stupor, and as soon as the trunks were unpacked, she set about continuing with her interior decoration of the many apartments, thus causing more prosperity for the carpenters, painters, gilders, and furniture makers who visited the house daily. Her hundreds of fine paintings, when they arrived in their crates from Paris, were immediately distributed among the salons and bedchambers. Her precious porcelains were displayed on mantels and tables, each hearth of the wing they were using enlivened by tapestried fire screens to shield the occupants from the crackling fires her servants were ordered to keep high and cheerful.

Mademoiselle courageously forswore any more tears, and her demeanor had recovered some of its dignity. But it touched Julie to see how she lavished rich furniture and rugs on the empty apartment above hers, a small suite of rooms connected to hers by a hidden staircase— a suite perfect for Monsieur de Lauzun to occupy when he was released and free to visit—along with other members of the court, of course. Mademoiselle existed by the belief that the king would not continue to hold a man whom he had previously given such favor on charges unstated and unproven. It was a matter of a year or two, at most.

The bustle of craftsmen and tradesmen and servants busy furbishing and polishing the chateau gave the ladies a false sense of purpose, for in reality there really was little reason for the fuss. Except for Mesdames de Sévigné and de Nogent and the Princesse Palatine, who sent word that they hoped to visit in the spring, no guests were expected. But it was a way to keep busy, as was, for Julie and Mademoiselle, at least, continued work on Mademoiselle's memoirs, which the lady had again taken up with a vengeance. The Duchesse undertook as well the civic activity of transforming a hospital she had once endowed into an orphanage for girls, a project requiring much consultation with local authorities and the Sisters of Charity, who would run the home and teach the girls lacemaking. There were warm feelings between the people of the town and the Duchesse de Montpensier who rented them their lands.

The evenings were quiet. They sat to *ombré* or other games while violinists hired from Abbéville played Mademoiselle's favorite music. Or Julie played the clavier for them or they read aloud or they went to bed early. Mademoiselle wrote letter after letter to de Lauzun in the Bastille, sending them off by fast rider even though her Paris confessor, the Archbishop of Luynes, had advised her in a letter that the man was being held incommunicado. She kept her letters carefully circumspect in case of censorship, but there was never an answer. Mystified by the king's need to keep de Lauzun deaf and mute, she wrote to Nicolas and to her friends, begging them for news; they had none. And then, at the beginning of November, came a letter from Nicolas. De Lauzun had been transported to the dreaded Pignerol, a fate reserved for the most damned of political criminals.

Mademoiselle ate nothing for two days. Her skin was pasty, her eyes red-rimmed. Yet she did not let go of the idea that in a while, a matter of two years, perhaps, the Jupiter king would surely relent and free his sinless prisoner.

When Julie's presence was not required by the Duchesse, she read or wrote letters of her own or shopped in the town. She rested by the old fountain outside the huge and beautiful Gothic collegiate church and watched the children at play, surrounded by the bright laughter of their innocence and envying them. They did not wake like she did in the middle of the night to the imagined sound of a special voice, the imagined warmth and delight of certain strong arms about her, the imagined impression of his kisses on her yearning body, yearning because her physical need for him was like a drug she could not cast from her system. Watching the children frolic and remembering her own childhood, she felt old. She felt empty.

And so she went galloping almost every golden fall afternoon, wearing a plumed hat and a brown and silver hunting coat and breeches fashionably modeled after those worn by gentlemen and thus allowing her to ride astride. She had a sleek chestnut gelding, a gift from Mercure de Vosges, who knew how well she could ride and who begged her to accept the animal to ease his distress that she was leaving the court until spring. She called the young horse Caprice, because he danced on the end of his tether and always wanted to run no matter in what direction, sometimes even following after a darting bird. She rode him far and fast, past Eu to the beach at Tréport and for leagues along the hard-packed sand. Or in the opposite direction, along the valley of the Bresle River toward Gamaches, into the gentle folds of the Norman countryside, past orchards dense with apples, fields of cabbages, slopes tenanted by fat cows and tansy and purple gentian, past the dense forests of Eu. Ultimately, she delivered the horse back to the groom lathered and blowing, and herself to Blanchette pink-faced and tired. But the exercise did not seem to pick up her appetite or keep her eyes from opening before dawn.

Sometimes, on a particularly dull night, she had to pinch herself to make sure she wasn't at Cuckfield still, dreaming all that had happened, even though she knew the circumstances were entirely different and she was hardly a prisoner. Sometimes she snorted mirthlessly under her breath as she contemplated Mademoiselle and herself, just two women struggling with sore hearts.

After the night of the queen's birthday, Nicolas had made no further attempt to breach her barriers and, in fact, had gone jauntily back to entertaining the ladies, including the Princesse de Margarethe, who one cool evening had displayed a glossy sable shoulder wrap that could easily have come from him. Nor did he even write her one word of goodbye on their hasty departure from Paris. Not that she would have responded to it.

There was only one answer to the consuming pain while she waited to get over him, for time to erase the memory of his gaze resting on her like a light blue flame, his ribald chuckle, his easy, quirked smile. Only one response to the aching in her body that forced her shameful fingers down to the throbbing place where his had been, although it never made her feel the same. That answer was to marry, and one day early in December, as the household made subdued preparations for Candlemas and Julie lingered in the pale sunshine of the chateau's park taking deep breaths of cold, salt-fresh air in her lungs to dispel the heaviness that dragged at her heart, that answer came clear as a bell rung in her ear, a truth she must embrace.

She had received several letters from Mercure, two from the Seigneur de Crequé, who had turned out to be more sincere than she had thought, and indeed a pleasant note from the Marquis de Louvois urging her to return to a court from which she had removed three-quarters of the beauty and all of the sparkle. De Crequé could be discounted. He was handsome but shallow and spoke of little besides the entertainments of the night before, his horses, and his three gorgeous, concave-bellied white hounds from Russia, one of which he had presented to the king. De Louvois was already married, although his wife insisted on raising her children by herself in the country. That left de Vosges, if her object was marriage upon her return to court, and fortunately he had already declared for her. Even more fortunately, the Dowager Comtesse, his mother, had received her kindly and seemed as gentle a person as her son.

Julie tiptoed about in the recesses of her mind. What did she really think of Mercure? That he was lame had no bearing. She saw him as a fine man, not a knight-errant needed to rescue her from dragons. As for his looks, she had gotten used to his pale complexion, and he had expressive eyes. He carried his frame slightly stooped, and he had a hesitant manner, but he was serious and conservative, contemplative, quiet. And he was wealthy, scion of an old and distinguished name, like hers. This was a man to trust, to give one comfort in one's middle years, and to grow old with. And that was her answer to the turmoil the dashing Nicolas de Courcillon could produce in a woman's life, the tatters such a one could make of a woman's heart and then walk away laughing, back to the Princesse Margarethe. The fact that it was *she* who had run from Nicolas did not stop her further flight.

When she told Mademoiselle of her decision, the lady contemplated her sadly. 'Years ago, I would have nodded smugly at your sage choice, knowing nothing then of love or of passion or of caring. But it is important that I ask you now, since you are your own mistress to select whom you wish: do you love de Vosges?'

Julie chewed on the side of her lip, then raised her head to meet the piercing gaze straight on. 'Love has been little necessary to marriage all through the centuries. I am confident a friendly rapport can also bring happiness, especially if the man is as gentle and devoted as Mercure de Vosges.'

'Well, you are no child. You must know your own mind.' The regal head cocked as Mademoiselle showed more curiosity about Julie's past than she'd done before. 'Tell me, were you in love with your late husband?'

'No—I mean, yes, I worshiped him. Yet I was but sixteen, and it—it did not last long.'

'Do you mean you suddenly found him distasteful?' The question was delivered in a surprised tone, the groping of a woman still a novice in the convulsive relationships between the sexes, a woman who had little idea that the fine sentiment of love can twist into hate.

'No, Your Highness, it was the Earl who suddenly found *me* distasteful,' Julie answered, bitterness in her voice. 'He was a man of sophistication, of earthy tastes and a low tolerance for domesticity. He was also a gambler and a cheat and a cruel master who locked me away where I could neither witness nor object to his excesses,' she went on. 'And when the love he professed for me evaporated and he was done with me, he humiliated and mistreated me. So much for love as a value for marriage.'

'*Mon Dieu*, I had no idea. And so you have no trust for love, madame. Do you think perhaps it was the man who failed you and not the state of emotion?'

Julie dropped her eyes and studied the herringbone pattern of the newly installed parquet floor. 'It could be possible. But there are many men like the Earl of Lowry.'

'I see. And if one were hurt enough, it would be hard to distinguish a sincere man from a veritable cad,' said Mademoiselle, staring at Julie thoughtfully. 'How much easier the system of marriage arranged at puberty so a young woman does not have to bother herself with choosing.' Then she drew in her chin and looked up at Julie. 'Well, fortunately, my Monsieur de Lauzun is a man of undeceptive reliability. He does not shower one with endearments, so much is true, but what he does say is firmly meant.' She heaved a large sigh. The blue eyes began to water, the fleshy lips to droop. 'Ah, Antonin, Antonin——'

Julie said quickly, 'Will you ride with me today, Your Highness? The sun warms the air, and it looks to be most bracing outdoors.' Mademoiselle did join her sometimes, riding sidesaddle, bringing sedateness to the outing.

The Duchesse's shoulders slumped. She laid down her pen and peered across the small, warm study toward the window, which framed an unusually blue sky for Normandy in winter. 'Yes, I believe I will,' she agreed unenthusiastically. 'But not too long. The sisters from that pitiful old ruin they call an orphans' shelter are bringing me some financial records today.'

And so the winter slowly passed, mostly gray and chill and drizzly, noisy only with bluejays chasing from the feeders the titmice and house finches. Inspired by Mademoiselle, Julie tried her hand at writing poetry. She felt better now that she had resolved to accept Mercure, less taut, less frightened by her misstep of allowing de Courcillon into her heart. Yet in her perky and rambling letters to Mercure, she made no mention of her decision. She thought it would make a happy surprise for him, a gift, so to speak, when she returned to Paris.

This time, Mademoiselle crumpled the cream-colored paper and hurled it across the room. 'Never, never, never,' she cried. 'I will see her in hell first, the dreadful witch!' And she collapsed onto a settee, a trembling hand covering her face.

Gray-haired Madame de Puysieux looked on in alarm, tufts of white cloth protruding from her aching ears where the doctor had poured in warm oil to ease the pain. The lady-in-waiting's fluttery hands were encased in fingerless gloves against the chill of the high-ceilinged salon where she had been working a large tapestry along with two Sisters of Charity and the wife of the local seigneur when the missive from Paris arrived. She had hurried to bring it to the Duchesse in her study, never dreaming it would cause such fury.

'Go, go, *chère* madame, back to your industry. We have promised that work to the collegiate church by

Eastertide.' Mademoiselle waved the curtsying woman out, not removing her other hand from her eyes.

Julie bent to pick up the crushed letter and walked with it to the hearth, where she posed it over the tongues of yellow fire that jumped and crackled and kept the little room snug from the March winds. 'Shall I burn this, Your Highness?' she asked dryly, somewhat miffed that she hadn't been taken into her employer's confidence regarding these mysterious communications that drove the woman so wild. It was the third one with Athénais's seal, and all had produced this violent reaction.

'Consign it to the flames indeed, and that she-dragon along with it!' the Duchesse cried from behind her hand. But she said no more than that. She went about the next few days distracted and irritable, a state of mind that might have caused the grievous accident that occurred, since she was not ordinarily a stumbler.

It was one false step on the wide stair, Julie was told. Mademoiselle's heel had caught in the short train of her heavy velvet gown. It sent her tumbling head over heels in a welter of skirts and underskirts the short distance to the bottom, where her ladies and several footmen rushed to her. Her visitor, the bishop of the diocese, quickly knelt at her side, thanking God to hear her dazed moan, for at least she was alive. But they were all appalled to hear her scream out, 'My leg, my leg,' as the servants tried to move her. Realizing that the leg must be broken, the purple-cassocked religious directed the footmen to maneuver a large cloak under the fainting woman as a quivering Dant passed the ammonia vial under her nose. Thus, they were able to lift and carry her, weeping in shock, up the stairs to her bed. Julie, rushing in from an errand in the town, found her thus, somewhat relieved of pain by an opiate draught administered by her own physician and weakly awaiting the arrival of a surgeon.

In spite of the surgeon's assurances—as his practiced hands ran down the leg from which one of the women had drawn the green silk stocking—that the break in the bone was simple and not a more serious complex fracture, the bone-setting was harrowing. Julie held one hand, d'Epernon the other, and two strong footmen held the suffering woman down at shoulder and hips. Julie saw de Puysieux's strained face and knew she must look the same as Mademoiselle cried out, wept, and squashed her hand in a convulsive grip as the surgeon manipulated the lower leg bone into place. He then applied the stout splints he had brought and bound them tightly, and an ashen, shaken Mademoiselle rested exhausted against the pillow, her eyelids gray-purple. Dant fussed about her.

Julie hurried after the departing surgeon, who was talking with the doctor. 'Monsieur, how long will Her Highness be laid up?'

The surgeon peered at her from small, bright eyes. 'Six weeks, perhaps more. The bones knit slowly in an older person. She must be kept absolutely immobile for the first month, but I shall come every few days to observe her progress.'

Mademoiselle's physician puffed himself up. 'I shall see to alleviating her discomfort, Comtesse. Her Highness will have little pain,' he declared, taking the conversation away from the surgeon, whose profession was considered by physicians to be much inferior to their own. And this despite popular opinion that, even with their bloody saws and tools, the surgeons at least *tried* to cause less pain than the doctors. 'But she will be a terror to keep motionless. If she is not listless and pining—for which I give her certain excellent nostrums, since she will not be bled—then she is agitated and restless.'

'*Tiens,* but she cannot dance the *Branle* on one leg.' The surgeon shrugged, cheerfully dismissing the problem of Mademoiselle's temperament.

Julie turned away, sighing. Why did this have to happen now? She had begun to make definite plans to return to Paris, was every day looking more forward to it and every day becoming more tired of the life at Eu. And now her royal mistress lay helpless, unable to move from her bed.

Mademoiselle's eyes opened blearily as she approached the bed. 'Julie, my dear, you shall have to be my eyes and my ears while I endure God's punishment for my transgressions,' she croaked, reaching for Julie's hand.

Julie gave it, but hunched further into her soft wool shawl. No amount of logs on the fire heated the big bedchamber, and the chill of early spring seeped through her. Dully, she answered, 'Yes, Your Highness.' If the beset woman noticed her gloomy expression, she gave no indication of it.

'The construction at the new orphanage site must be inspected at short intervals. And you must bring me reports of how the masons are progressing in the far wing of this house. Consulting with that pompous architect de Meergin is no substitute for seeing the work firsthand.'

'Yes, Mademoiselle.'

'*Bon*. You are a great comfort to me, madame. I am thinking that when I write my weekly letter to Monsieur de Lauzun, I will say nothing of this accident. It will only upset him to think I could be stupid enough not to watch where I was going. Now I will sleep,' she announced to the ladies hovering about her, and she settled herself, eyelids drooping. 'Shoo, shoo, all of you. Ah, *Dieu*, how fortunate that I am staunch and used to adversity, or this latest indignity would surely destroy me.'

'Yes, Your Highness,' Julie intoned. She reserved her resigned groan for later, when she had reached the privacy of her luxurious little chamber, made even more pleasant by the glowing hues of some of Mademoiselle's sixteenth-century canvases mounted on the walls. Walking her fingers morosely along the brocade cloth on her table, she finally sat at the writing board to finish her letter to the soon-to-be-married Diane de Greu. She enjoyed de Greu's letters because they gave her all the gossip, such as who was pursuing whom. And which of the king's gentlemen had been absent from court most of the winter. . .

The four riders crested a hill together and saw beneath them at the end of the gentle slope the crossroad leading southwest toward Paris. They'd had a good gallop. Apollon de Vivonne leaned his lanky body over to pat the neck of his lathered horse and then pushed back his plumed hat, wiping his forehead with the cuff of his gauntlet. 'Well, there it is, *mon ami*. Are you sure you won't ride back to Paris with us? My son still has not assuaged his appetite for your tales of the mysterious forest and painted natives of New France. And you would not miss the nuptials of the decade this June, would you? Louis has promised Monsieur an even more spectacular celebration than marked his wedding to poor Henrietta.'

Nicolas's eyes automatically traced the road, but to the northeast, toward the greening hills and beautiful valleys of Normandy. The men started down the hill, keeping the horses at a walk so that the following vehicles, carrying de Vivonne's wife and two children, their servants, some men-at-arms, and baggage carts, could catch up. De Courcillon and de Vivonne, who had brought his family north for a visit, rode first, followed by Skandahet-se and the overseer of the many hectares of orchards and fields in cultivation on these ancient lands of the d'Aubièrre family.

'I'll be there,' Nicolas assured him. 'I've had enough of rustication.'

'Hmmm. And with *her*?'

'With her. Without a doubt.'

'I don't understand how you can be so sure that she is not totally committed to marrying de Vosges. The man is quite suitable, after all. Perhaps she is set on it.'

'She is not set on anything. She is pig-headed. I would wager I have understood the message of Mademoiselle's letters correctly, from what I could decipher of her hand. She writes them herself, when Julie is absent.'

'God knows I wish you good fortune, you know that. It is time, *mon ami,* that you settled down to the connubial hearth. It has its various points. And you need some sons.'

Nicolas smiled, squinting his eyes against the sun. He drew off his velvet glove to wiggle the fingers of his cramped rein hand. 'If you want to know the truth, it was watching you, Apollon, that really decided me—you and your delightful lady, who for the few weeks I have had the pleasure of your company did not leave off secret smiles and stealing glances at each other like a pair of mooning newlyweds. Madame de Vivonne has my old snorting satyr of a friend wrapped about her finger.'

'My little wife is a good woman,' de Vivonne allowed modestly, with a chuckle. 'More than good. She makes me happy, as you have noticed. I do not know why she pleases me so much, why I am charmed by her face and her character and her giddy laugh; she is not so different from other women, not even as beautiful as some, and it was my father who first chose her. But I presume I love her, if what I have said defines the word, and that, I suppose, makes all the difference.' He straightened up his lanky form in the saddle. '*Tiens*, you are making me sound idiotic, like a calf-eyed boy.'

'And that is how I felt as I watched with envy the two of you all these weeks—idiotic to suppose I could find the same contentment with *her*. And yet I think so, for no glorious bouquets of seductive females, no Margarethes or Contis or du Vals can take my miserable mind off her. If I do not take her to wife, I think I will spend the rest of my life looking for someone like her, making do with a demi-love here or there, always imperfect for my taste. Not a very happy outlook,' Nicolas growled.

'But you can't just ride up and steal her away like a loaf of wheaten bread,' de Vivonne said. 'How can you win her if she won't even talk to you?'

Nicolas grinned and cast a scoffing glance at him. 'You're getting old, de Vivonne. What has happened to your imagination? Trust me, I'll find a way.'

They heard the thunder of de Vivonne's matched coach horses coming up behind them amid the chink and rattle of brass and leather harness and a whooping boy riding postilion. With a strong clasp of hands, the two men bid each other farewell. Nicolas rode back to stop at the coach window to say another goodbye to the vivacious Celine de Vivonne and her young son and daughter, and then watched the whole entourage disappear beyond a curve in the dusty dirt road, past a stand of tall, thin cypress and early-budding wild shrubs, which were just waiting for the chill to break in order to burst into bloom.

The three men wheeled their horses about and started back to the village on the estate where Nicolas meant to visit a laborer who had been badly injured by a collapsing cider press.

What he hadn't elaborated to de Vivonne, since it had seemed too long a story—perhaps too personal to go into during the convivial hours they had stretched their feet to the fire—was that Mademoiselle had mentioned, among other tidbits about her lady-of-honor, some facts about Julie's marriage, that he hadn't known before. This information—as his doting godmother-playing-Eros intended—gave him a workable clue to the lady's sudden and stubborn denial of interest in him.

CHAPTER
~ **17** ~

The two gentlemen from Paris arrived unannounced one evening. Panting for news of de Lauzun, or at least the possible lifting of her own punishment, Mademoiselle admitted them immediately into her presence. They no sooner had doffed their hats and made their bows when the spokesman announced in smooth tones that they came as emissaries for the Marquise de Montespan. Mademoiselle went rigid. She immediately dismissed her ladies, including Julie.

The ladies went no farther than the anteroom, glancing at each other in whetted curiosity. They went about their bead embroidery in a busy manner, but their ears were cocked toward the firmly closed door of Mademoiselle's bedchamber, where she was ensconced in a chair, her splinted leg propped on a padded hassock.

At first, there was only palpable silence, a heavy sort of silence that made Julie think everyone was holding her breath. And then it was broken by a crash, loud and startling, and another, louder, slamming against the closed door, along with the sound of shattering glass. In a crescendo of fury, Mademoiselle's voice pierced the thick wood, bulging a wild counterpoint against the mollifying voices of the men. The ladies sat transfixed, needles paralyzed. Their eyes darted to Julie, aghast; perhaps Mademoiselle was being murdered and a phalanx of footmen was necessary to invade the room and save her!

But before Julie could do more than rise from her stool, the door flew open, and the two gentlemen, with hunched shoulders, jostled each other desperately to emerge. Another object flung from the table at Mademoiselle's elbow shattered on the floor at their heels. 'No, no, no, no!' the Duchesse screeched at their departing backs. 'Never! That is my answer, now and always. And you can tell the Marquise I will not be distressed with this again, you hear? Now leave my house, you jackals!'

Startled looks crossed between the ladies. They had seen Mademoiselle moon lovestruck, act foolish, laugh, sigh, weep hysterically, bristle, swell with snobbery. But when it came to indignation, she seldom went further than a stiff and piercing glare.

A footman came to meet the discomfited gentlemen, who settled their clothes, clapped on their wide hats, and, without a glance at the staring women, stalked out behind the liveried servant.

Julie spared them one glance and then rushed into the room, followed by the others. Nimbly stepping over the shards of glass littering the floor and a gold and enamel carafe lying in a puddle of spilled hippocras, she stepped quickly to Mademoiselle's side, concern in her eyes. Breathlessly, she asked, 'What has happened, Your Highness?'

The royal lady sat erect and rigid, indignation flaming her cheeks and burning in her eyes. But she did not answer.

'Dant, fetch some wine. Quickly,' Madame d'Epernon wisely ordered. She used her painted fan to bring more air to her mistress, who seemed paralyzed, staring inward, intent upon a progression of thoughts only she could fathom. The Duchesse took the wine mechanically and drank it down. And then she seemed to subside in her seat, as if the air had been let out of her.

Passing a hand over her face, she whispered, 'I am very fatigued. Call the doctor. I will take a draught, and then I want to sleep.'

Two burly servants helped her to hop over to her bed, splinted leg crooked up, a maneuver she had only begun to manage now that the first month of her confinement had passed. Relieved of her clothes and jewelry, her thick graying hair lightly brushed and covered by a nightcap, she leaned back with a sigh, and within ten minutes of taking the medicinal drink, she fell into a snoring sleep. But without a word to explain the upsetting incident.

The other ladies twittered at Julie for information, but she shrugged helplessly. She knew as little about it as they did.

The sky beyond her window, where Blanchette had forgotten to pull the drapes, was still black with night when Dant, backed by a nervous Blanchette, pushed back the bed curtain, shook Julie by the shoulder to awaken her, and said that Mademoiselle was demanding her presence. Frowning against the flicker of the candles in the small candelabrum Dant held, and blinking back the beginning of a headache, Julie uttered a tiny groan, but she obediently slipped from the bed and stuck her arms in the dressing robe Blanchette held up for her. She followed Dant, also in a robe and with gray hair tumbling from her nightcap, hurrying the brief distance to Mademoiselle's apartments to enter the darkened bedchamber with apprehension nibbling at her. She was always frightened of some dread occurrence when abruptly awakened in the middle of the night, stemming perhaps from when her mother had died in the early hours when she was a child. The last time such a thing had happened, she had loaded a pistol and fired—

Mademoiselle sat up in her bed, a ghostly figure in a pool of light, her white lace cap askew. But even in the poor illumination from the two candles on her bedside table, one could see that her features were composed, in fact, set in wide-awake determination. 'Julie. Come here, *mon enfant*,' she said huskily. 'Stand by me. I wish to talk to you.' She patted the edge of the high bed. Her splinted leg made a long mound under the bedclothes.

'You are not ill, Mademoiselle?' asked Julie anxiously.

'No. Indeed, I am fine. At last. For I know now what I must do in order to save my Antonin. Dant, light a few more candles. I abhor the dead of night. I am sorry to break your rest, madame, but I shall have no peace in my soul until I have removed myself from that. . .that strumpet's clutches. There is much I have to tell you.' She paused to stare at Julie for a moment, the lines between her mouth and nose chiseled deeply. 'Do you sometimes wonder why I trust you, madame? Uniquely, it is your eyes. They are so vividly amethyst they ought to be opaque. Instead, they hold so luminous a clarity, one can see your very soul shine through. My life has been made and broken by people, people high and low, a myriad of them. I am a great judger of souls by this time. And yours, in spite of what misfortunes life has already dealt you, is as pure as spring rain, madame. And loyal.' Mademoiselle lowered her head, her eyes drilling into Julie. 'Even so, do you swear by *le bon Dieu* and all the saints and apostles and on the memory of your father and mother that you will never, ever breach my confidence in what I am about to tell you?'

Julie looked at her tautly. She was flattered by Mademoiselle's opinion of her, even if she knew she was not quite so perfect as the Duchesse believed. She had a prickly feeling that the woman was going to involve her in something she would surely be better off avoiding. Nevertheless, she murmured, 'Of course. I do swear so, Your Highness.'

The Duchesse relaxed her jaw. '*Très bien*. Now, if you have been wondering about the letters I burn and the two blackguards I drove from my chamber this evening, you need wonder no more. They were all from Athénais de Montespan, the presumptuous concubine, and she demands to make a bargain with me. She indicates that she will do what she can to persuade the king to free Monsieur de Lauzun from Pignerol if I will cede to her little son, the Duc de Maine, my counties of Eu and Dombes, with all their large incomes, as well as the barony of Bois-le-Vicomte, near Meaux, so that the bastard, who has been only poorly endowed by the king, will have a princely portion. It is the usual disgusting case of the mouse droppings wishing to mix with the pepper.' Mademoiselle glared, the ire not meant for Julie. 'Otherwise, as she has made the thinly veiled threat through her emissaries, she has no choice but to support the king's animosity against my Antonin. And my response to all of her petitions is *no!*' The double chins quivered with outrage. 'How dare she think to blackmail me!'

Julie was silent, appalled at Athénais's mean exploitation of Mademoiselle's tragedy. Suddenly, it occurred to her that de Montespan might have maneuvered the whole situation, hoping to force Mademoiselle into a secret marriage and thus deliver the king's cousin into her greedy toils. No, no. She dismissed the idea as too complicated. It just couldn't be possible.

'It is my wealth,' Mademoiselle continued. Her hand plucked restlessly at her woolen blanket. 'It is the inheritance of my birth and estate which has already devoured most of my life by causing the king, my closest relative, to ignore my lonely spinsterhood. He was never diligent about proposing me to foreign princes, who are the only ones lofty enough to merit my hand and dowry. And those he did propose were so unsuitable or disgusting or otherwise repellent that he knew I would not meekly consent, nor did he insist. I have finally realized what his game is. He wishes to keep my money here in France, perhaps even for himself and his heirs, for he was not ever serious about uniting me, even with his brother—it would aggrandize once more the Orleans branch of the Bourbons. My money is crushing me to death, because I have no child to claim it.'

Julie was shocked. 'But surely Your Highness does not believe that—that——'

'That the king is blackmailing me, too? No, madame, I do not believe such a thing. I think he does not know what that snake in his bed is doing. But she is safe enough. He will not hear anything against her. He turns purple with anger should anyone complain of her imperious excesses.' Mademoiselle cleared her throat. She swallowed. '*Vois-tu*, if I had an heir, a French-born son or daughter, none of this calamity would have happened. A direct descendant would legally inherit my wealth, and the king's fears about poor Monsieur de Lauzun laying hands on a Bourbon legacy would not be.'

Feeling sorry for the middle-aged woman who, in spite of her station and enormous fortune, was so alone, Julie murmured, 'Perhaps we should search for some other, more realistic solution to Madame de Montespan's demands?'

One imperious eyebrow rose. 'No, madame, there is no other solution, none I have ever found since my seventeenth birthday, when I began to struggle to be recognized as a woman of worth, apart from my riches. In the beginning, I was mistreated by my weak and wavering father, Gaston, and after my sire's death. I was left languishing by my Jupiter-cousin, who could not decide on a husband for me. But, you see, I shall have the last laugh on them. For I *do* have an heir, a prince of the realm, born twenty-two years ago of my body and the Prince de Condé's seed.' Triumpantly, she let this shell burst into the silence and then, in the face of Julie's open-mouthed speechlessness, continued. 'And now I intend to find him, this young man, and show him to the world as my legal heir, and he will buy for me surcease from manipulation and blackmail and from the suspicion that if I die first, Monsieur de Lauzun, who is seven years younger, could inherit my fortune.'

As if exhausted by this incredible revelation, she fell back on her pillows and squeezed her eyes shut against Julie's stare. 'Ah, *ma chère* Julie, *comme je suis malheureuse!*' The shallow heaving of her bosom told of her difficulty in disinterring this decades-old secret, her one shameful indiscretion. 'Dant will tell you that what I say is true. It was the very end of the war against Mazarin and Queen Anne, Louis's mother, who some say was the Cardinal's secret wife. You have heard of the civil war people called the Fronde? We were being driven from our stronghold in Paris. The Prince de Condé, my comrade-in-arms and leader of the nobility's rebellion against Mazarin's yoke, was preparing to bolt for Spain, where he would regroup our tattered forces to continue the fight. We were very young, he was infinitely handsome—just as he is now, if one looks beneath the bloat of drink—and we were anguished. Our armies were decimated, but what was worse, a tragic number of our dearest friends, the very cream of the aristocracy and the companions of our gay childhood, were dead—gentlemen and, tragically, some of the ladies, too, struck down fighting in the streets, blown apart by Louis's cannon on the roads to Paris, or swept away by the years of fighting in the provinces. We were alone in our riven headquarters, we turned to each other in farewell, we wept in each other's arms, and then, even though he had chosen to marry another, we forgot everything. It was very romantic and moving. And very temporary—just that once. We did not love each other. I did not know the real meaning of the word then.' She opened sloe eyes, haunted by memories. 'As I think about it now, though, how similar he was to Monsieur de Lauzun, you see. So able, so commanding, the very master of the world——'

The room was cold. Dant came up silently and put a woolen scarf about Mademoiselle's shoulders. 'And so much for romance,' Mademoiselle finished, the resilient timber having crept back into her voice. 'When we finally surrendered, my cousin Louis was surprisingly lenient to me in view of the fact that once I accidentally fired the Bastille cannon in his direction and almost blew him up. But I went into the exile he imposed with relief—no, scuttled into it would be the word for it, for I was pregnant and mortified and frantic to take my shame into hiding at Saint-Fargeau.' Involuntarily, she looked down at herself as if once more seeing that huge and heavy belly she had so loathed, along with the squalling child that was born from it. 'And so the infant was born in utmost secrecy. The Prince de Condé has no idea. No one knew except Dant here, who paid off the midwife and then took the child away—and two others whom I needed as witnesses to the bastard's lineage. Just in case.'

She shook her head, and the lace ruching of her cap trembled above her eyes. 'I wanted no part of that screaming, unfortunate bastard. I was a royal princess, young and full of hope for a powerful match with a brilliant ruler, and such scandal would ruin me. I felt nothing but fury toward the baby. And yet the blood that ran in that little being's body was royal purple, and it united the two major branches of the Bourbons. Some vague reservation compelled me to write out a document, with witnesses, and Dant cut a good nick in the tiny ear for identification. And then she bound his wound and took him away. And I never thought of him again. Until now.'

Julie put a hand on the bed to steady herself. Both the hour and the revelations were making her knees weak. Mademoiselle noticed her little stagger and called to her servant. 'Dant, bring a seat for madame. Sit down, Julie, you must not be faint, even though I am plunging you into a maelstrom. But I have never found you stinting in my service, and I am forced to tell you these things because I must enlist your aid now. There is little I can do for myself since I have an entire tree attached to my poor leg.'

Julie sat down, more heavily than usual. She had to give her mistress an answer. 'I am at your disposal, Your Highness,' she said, but slowly, for her brain signaled she was surely known to the king as Mademoiselle's close confidante, and knowing all these explosive secrets was dangerous for a woman with little family protection.

'I must produce this child—er, man, now—and use him to remove the pressure from me and Monsieur de Lauzun before that she-devil does us more damage. You must find him for me. There is no one else I can ask.'

'B-but, M-mademoiselle, is it wise to unearth this person at all? Your reputation——'

Mademoiselle forestalled her, snorting. 'My reputation? I am forty-four years old and probably beyond bearing a healthy child. At this point, I will scarcely be proposed to by a head of state; even a doddering old man demands a young girl to warm his bones and fill his house with offspring. All I have of my hopes and dreams is my money and my Antonin, and no one, not even the king of France, shall take either away from me!' Her jaw jutted, her eyes burned. She was as ferocious as a bear defending a cub.

'What name did you give the child?'

Mademoiselle twisted her mouth and looked down. 'I didn't. I told you. All I wanted was for it to be taken out of my life. The family with whom it was placed named it—him. Dant knows who they were.' She looked over for help to her longtime servitor, who hovered discreetly at the edge of the bed.

'The child was taken north to the village of Bonneval, a long distance from Saint-Fargeau. I knew a baker there,' Dant offered in an unsteady voice. 'They had been married many years and had no children. They took the infant and asked no questions. They named him Edouard. Edouard Courbier.'

Mademoiselle said, 'All you have to do is travel to Bonneval and seek out the baker's family and then in all haste bring the young man to see me, and I shall reveal to him who he is. I will give you more money than you need and a letter with my seal, in case he proves obstinate. Peasants are always persuaded with money and official-looking documents they cannot read.' Now she smiled into Julie's serious face. 'Come, madame, I have not asked you to murder somebody, merely to bring back to me a son.'

'Mademoiselle, I feel constrained to say that I am not sure the idea is a wise one.'

'No? You and Dant, too. Both doubters. But *I* am convinced it is my only salvation, and I am not ashamed, at last, of this bastard. He has, after all, the blood of royalty, a brilliant pedigree on both sides. He will be happy as my legal heir. And all will go better. I am sure of it. The royal family is dangerously small. The king will welcome another member, just as he has rejoiced in his own bastards.'

Still Julie hesitated. It was not the long trip. She would be happy to be doing something and traveling. And she could accomplish the mission and still be in Paris in plenty of time for Monsieur's marriage to the German princess who was niece to the Princesse Palatine. It was her uncertainty of the outcome for Mademoiselle of unveiling a bastard heir that made her stumble over accepting.

Mademoiselle leaned forward. 'Julie, come here. Give me your hand. I have told you this history because I trust you and because I need you to do this thing for me. I have just one bit more to tell you. One of the witnesses to the birth of this child was the Bishop de Liagre, my trusted confessor. And the other was the Vicomte de Croixverte, your father, a respected man of total discretion and a friend whose lands at that time adjoined the estate of Saint-Fargeau.'

'My father!' Julie exclaimed.

'I...you cannot imagine how my heart aches for the suffering of Monsieur de Lauzun, shut up and held in silence in that cold, distant fortress, with only a valet to attend him. You cannot imagine how I weep to think of it. My heart is cracked and dying, even if it may not show. In fact, on account of feeling too much, I end up by feeling numb. But think, madame. You can bring the key to unlock his prison door and to end my exile. I beg you to help us. Go to Bonneval, do anything necessary to find Edouard Courbier—he may be a baker, he may be a farmer in the area—and bring him back to his rightful place.'

Unable to withstand the tears that glistened in the blue eyes and the cracking of the stentorian voice, which had sunk to a hollow whisper, Julie straightened her shoulders. 'When do you wish me to go?' she asked briskly.

'Immediately. Tomorrow or the next day. *Merci à Dieu,* the weather is good, so your coach will not become mired. I have already consulted my equerry's maps. If you go by way of Gournay and Vernon, you will skirt delay at Rouen. Just hurry, madame, hurry.'

Mademoiselle's complete confidence in her scheme was catching, the more so because Julie was bemused by her father's involvement in the secret. In fact, the mission began to appear just the adventure her bored spirit craved. Julie gave the Duchesse her dimpled smile. 'If Your Highness will allow me to get some sleep, I promise to be ready to depart after the one o'clock dinner tomorrow. Is that quick enough?'

'Yes, of course. You have a good heart, Comtesse. I will not forget it.' Mademoiselle nodded gravely at her, then subsided again on her pillows with a sigh. 'Now go back to your interrupted dreams, madame.' Her almond-shaped eyes closed on a sly smile. 'Perhaps they will surprise you and come true.'

At dawn, a small window in the chateau's roof, high and sloped like the brow of its owner, opened, and a hand launched into the air a gray and white pigeon, which tentatively flapped its way into the rosy-streaked sky. Then it banked right and shot away east, a feathered messenger aimed at Paris.

Anne-Marie-Louise d'Orleans believed she knew intimately all her own faults. When she was young, there had been a fad for writing self-portraits painfully honest down to the last pimple, and she had written—in excellent prose, of course—of her tendency toward overbearing behavior, her selfishness, her inability to sympathize with lesser mortals. But no failing irked her more than her precipitous nature, which caused her to rush into action without enough calm consideration. Not that she regretted her desperate decision to unveil Edouard Courbier and recognize him, even if it meant the loss of her status as a maiden lady. That cost her little at this late stage. But in the several days since Julie's coach had pulled away from the chateau with the capable Poilettier cracking the whip over four big, spirited horses, she had grown more and more guilty about sending the young woman off so far by herself, without even footmen, just to maximize the privacy of her quest. The roads were infested with highwaymen, and innkeepers were often unscrupulous. Travel was risky unless one was well escorted. Mademoiselle chewed on her knuckle. She might have selfishly and stupidly sent her lady-of-honor into real danger. Robbers thought nothing of murder to accomplish their looting. Yet the task had to be done, and who else could she have sent?

Therefore, it was with cordiality and great relief that she received the unexpected visit of her godson de Courcillon, and then, after sharing news back and forth, with scarcely a blush, she made him party to the mission on which she had sent Julie. She waited for him to get over the shock of her youthful indiscretion, reconfirmed that the circumstances were true, and then drove on.

'I know you oppose Monsieur de Lauzun, Nicolas, but you surely can see that once the question of inheritance is settled, even the king will have to give the man his freedom—for what will there be to fear from him? His friendship with a lonely woman? Even that serpent de Montespan will have to unwind her greedy coils. All that distresses me now is that I should have sent some men with Madame de Lowry. But I was afraid of too many eyes and ears. You know the swift nature of gossip, even from here.'

She bit her lip and pulled in her chin defensively. 'I wish, monsieur, you would not stare at me with such reproach in your eyes.'

In fact, his light blue eyes held incredulity. 'First, Your Highness, you decide to skewer your reputation and prepare for all France the juiciest bit of gossip of the century in order to free a man from prison who, believe me, will be neither grateful to you nor charmed to know about your heir. And then to top it all, you send an unescorted female on a long journey to find this lost person. If you were not a lady most dear to me, I could only think the sea air has rusted away your good sense.'

Out of necessity, the Duchesse ignored this bit of effrontery. 'But *le bon Dieu* has sent you, dear Nicolas, just at the right time to correct the error of a distraught woman. I was wrong to send her alone, with only her maid and the coachman. You *will* ride after her, will you not? I would be most grateful if you could relieve my mind of this stupid mistake.'

But Nicolas persisted. 'I seem to remember you holding forth that no person of quality would abandon her honor and that honor was so beautiful a thing you could not comprehend how a person could despise it. And yet here you are contriving to throw your honor to the wind.'

'You are cruel, for you do not answer my request.'

He tossed back his head and gulped the last of the fermented apple cider in his cup. He stood up, and a cynical smile quirked the corner of his firm mouth. 'But of course I will go after her. You know that very well.'

'But you will not impede her from what she has to do?' Mademoiselle clasped her hands in entreaty. 'Nicolas, I implore you to help me.'

The woman looked so pitiful to him just then. Loss had hollowed out her long face and was reflected in her miserable eyes. A crutch of polished wood leaned against the side of her armchair, and the broken leg under her embroidered skirts was still stiffly extended on a hassock. He had not the heart to deny her the solution she thought was the key to all her problems. He wondered if anyone had written her the news of the cache of love letters de Louvois's agents had recently found among de Lauzun's personal effects—torrid missives to and from at least twenty women in the past ten years. He decided not to mention it. His empathy to the condition of love had matured. One sometimes could not control or answer reasonably for the runaway heart.

Nicolas slipped down to one knee by the side of the chair. 'Trust me, Your Highness. I will do nothing to hurt you. My only wish is for you to be happy. And for Julie to be safe. I will leave immediately.'

Mademoiselle put a fond hand on his solid, brocade-covered shoulder. Then she lifted it to pat the side of his face, where the close-clipped cinnamon beard hugged the strong jaw. 'You have always been my good and loyal friend, Nicolas. I am thankful.' He kissed the knuckles of her hand, but she was glancing toward the window. 'Still, it will be dark soon. You might as well leave at dawn. Julie has taken the Gournay road to avoid Rouen, but my equerry warned that it was not an easy road. She won't have gotten too far. You can easily catch up, you and that barbarous servant of yours, on your swift horses. But perhaps tonight you will regale me and my ladies with what news and gossip you have had from court?' She added wistfully, 'Eu is my favorite home besides the Luxembourg, but we are lonely here for the excitement of Paris and my cousin's court.'

Nicolas rose and smiled down at her. 'I will do my utmost to entertain you, Your Highness.'

She was right, of course. There was no use setting off in the dark, and Julie would have halted, too, wherever she had reached. But impatience ate at him, and concern. He hoped the impetuous woman he craved had taken that pistol with her. Sighing, he resigned himself to being the gallant and amusing cynosure of Mademoiselle's tiny salon that night. But his head and his heart were on the road somewhere between Eu and Bonneval.

CHAPTER
~ 18 ~

There was something about the man's face that disturbed her; it was a square face under a thatch of long straw-colored hair, a heavily freckled face with a snub nose and thin lips that contrived to hide his teeth when he smirked at her. In spite of his good clothing and the rapier at his side, he did not impress her as a gentleman. She had seen him twice already, once two days ago, frankly staring at her as she ascended into her coach in the morning to leave the inn at Magny. Another time, she had just a glimpse of him, a face in the crowd at the market in Houdin, where she had stopped to purchase some candied fruit to make the trip more pleasant. And now, here he turned up again, seated in the corner of the inn's taproom, which she passed while looking for the landlord to order supper sent up for her and her maid. Even while speaking to the innkeep, she could see from the corner of her eye the man's speculative stare, and she drew herself up as if to form a shell against it. It shouldn't be surprising that he turned up in the same places as she did. Inns, after all, were not plentiful in these parts, and travelers tended to time their progress to reach a haven every night. But there was something insolent about his expression that irritated her and made her notice him. His two companions, one nondescript, with a yellow feather in his soft-brimmed hat, the other large, with a belly to match, seldom glanced in her direction.

Julie leaned into the horn comb Blanchette was using to untangle her hair and enjoyed the mild, rhythmic scratching on her scalp. The trip so far, *merci à Dieu*, had been uneventful but surely more interesting than just biding at Eu. It had been foolish of her to leave without an escort. She had realized that the very first night when dusk caught them still on the road. But turning back held no appeal. She used what caution she could, covering her fine clothes with a lightweight and ordinary traveling cloak, sending Poilettier or Blanchette to hire the chamber, and retiring to it as inconspicuously as possible. The big coach, plain black trimmed with red, upholstered in ordinary leather, was also innocent of Mademoiselle's diamond-shaped fleur-de-lis crest, and Poilettier had prudently exchanged his green and white livery for plain jerkin and breeches. This time, she was careful always to bolt the door of her chamber, and her late husband's pistol was close to her hand at night, and during the day in the coach as well.

As for the freckled man, she had no reason at all to fear him or suspect him of anything more than the crude attention any unescorted woman might receive. But she felt better to think that in two days more they would reach Bonneval and the end of their journey east, and she would no longer have to turn and find those small, hard eyes upon her.

Looking down from the steep incline, Nicolas saw the vehicle on the road below him, a black and red coach joggling at a moderate clip down the curves of the slope. He was certain it was Julie. By taking to the roads before dawn and pushing the pace, he had shortened the gap between them until the innkeep at Houdin, soothed by some francs in his palm, told him a lady answering Julie's description had departed his premises not two hours before in a black and red coach and a team of four.

He lost the coach from his sight for a moment as it entered the shadow of a rocky overhang, but then it emerged, rattling around the curve and down into the straight lower road. He grinned at Skandahet-se and jerked his thumb up. He was just about to spur up his horse when his eye caught horsemen, three of them, galloping around the bend below and proceeding in the same direction as the coach. What stayed him was their curious action on the lightly traveled road. For the coach had suddenly pulled up to a halt at a clump of bushes, and the driver climbed down to relieve himself behind them—and so did the three riders pull up short and halt, as if deliberately maintaining their position an unnoticeable distance behind the coach. They remained discreetly staring down at the vehicle from the last of the series of angles descending the steep hill, the wind ruffling the plumes on their hats and billowing their short capes. In a few minutes, the coach started up again, and so did they, keeping a steady, remote distance behind it.

Nicolas's frown deepened. He had intended to ride up and surprise Julie now that he'd caught up at last, but it appeared that the three rascals trailing her were thinking to try the same thing. But for different reasons. 'Do you note those riders below?' he asked Skandahet-se, who grunted. 'I think we will stay far enough behind them that they don't suspect we are hunting the hunters. Whatever mischief they may have in mind, we will be happy to accommodate them, the whoresons.'

Skandahet-se grinned and loosened the long dagger stuck in his belt. Nicolas drew his flintlocks, loaded them with ball and powder, and thrust them back into his silk sash. Then, digging in their spurs, they spurted after the coach, following along for several uneventful hours into the threatening clouds gathering in the evening sky. They reached Maintenon, where there were two small hostels Mademoiselle's equerry had noted on the hand-drawn map he'd made for Nicolas. Riding into the narrow single street of the village, Nicolas saw the top of the black and red coach over the low wall surrounding one of the inns. There was no sign of the unknown riders, but Nicolas felt correct in suspecting them. People innocent of evil would not have kept so artificial a distance between them and the coach. He had no doubt they were highwaymen, but he was puzzled about why they had made no move to catch up with the coach and go about their robbery.

Skandahet-se was disgruntled to be left with the horses at the other inn, but the great Indian was too noticeable. Nicolas walked back the short distance across the square to the hostel Julie had chosen. Since he had no wish to frighten her, his first order was to see what the scoundrels were up to. He knocked some of the dust from his brass-buttoned coat and lace cravat and went in the open door.

There were six or eight plank tables. Travelers and villagers sat at them, wolfing down their early suppers off wrinkled, none-too-clean cloths. The airless interior was too warm, and their faces glistened like the grease on the meat they consumed. The odors of food and spilled wine and ale and a scattering of rancid straw on the floor mingled with the fainter whiff of leather and unwashed bodies. Nicolas didn't expect to see Julie; she would have gone immediately to the chamber let her, so he sat on the end bench of one table and ordered wine and some round rolls and cheese. From under his hat brim, his eyes traveled over the faces about the room. It took only a moment to spot the yellow feather in the hat of the smallest of the trio, and there they were, deep in conversation on the high-backed wooden benches of a corner niche. One face took his attention immediately—the freckled, stolid features of a petty nobleman whom he knew mostly by sight, a greedy climber and a henchman of de Louvois, a man named—he scowled and searched his memory—de Troisac. The idea that the group following Julie were highwaymen winked from his mind, replaced by surprise and then confoundment. What reason would de Troisac have to follow the Comtesse de Lowry, who had not been at court all winter? And how would the men have found her in the first place, unless they had been in Eu, which was highly unlikely. It was possible they were just innocently traveling the same road, but a glance at de Troisac's sly face and a prickling under his skin told him that probably wasn't so.

Slumping against the back of the wooden bench, Nicolas turned so that the large brim of his tilted felt hat hid most of his profile from the group in the corner. He broke the roll and ate the pieces thoughtfully. What would they want with Julie, after all? Yet they had acted most suspiciously, keeping a careful distance behind the coach, stopping when it did—hardly normal behavior. It was a peculiar situation. It bore watching. Surreptitiously. He drained the thin, acid wine and strolled out the door again. In the yard, he flipped a coin to a young hostler in wooden sabots and nodded towards the big coach from which the horses had been unhitched.

'See that conveyance there, boy? The coachman is having his supper inside. Find him and tell him a gentleman wishes to speak with him and will make it worth his while.' He looked about for a less conspicuous place than the middle of the dirty, packed-earth inn yard. 'I'll wait there, to the side of the shed, in back of that old beech.'

The boy bobbed his head with a grin and trotted into the rambling stone and timber hostel. Nicolas waited behind a vine-draped, gnarled tree, his thumbs hooked into his sash, watching the twilight sky darken further with the swift sailing of swollen rain clouds. Presently, he heard a shuffle of boots on the gritty ground, and Poilettier stood before him.

'Monsieur de Courcillon!'

'*Oui, mon homme.* Finally I have caught up with you. It was careless of Her Highness to send Madame de Lowry on a substantial journey with only you and her maid in attendance. Since Mademoiselle had her reasons for allowing the footmen and mounted guards she supports in abundance to rest on their arses instead of protecting her lady-of-honor, I volunteered to come after you, along with my Indian companion.'

Poilettier's jowls sagged with relief. 'And a good thing, Monsieur le Marquis, a good thing. These here roads are infested with assassins. 'Twas only as we left I realized we would not have any escort. Too late to complain. I would not let madame know how many times on a lonely stretch I have held me breath and prayed at the sight of horsemen approaching.'

'It is not the horsemen approaching but the three riders following you who are the problem, Poilettier.'

'Following! I ain't noticed 'em.'

'They're experienced. They keep back a very discreet distance.'

'Brigands, monsieur?' Poilettier asked, his expression worried but his tone steady. Nicolas was glad to note that he was a man who didn't rattle easily.

'I doubt it, for I recognize one of them, a man I have

seen at court. But obviously they are up to no good. I wanted to warn you that they are at your back, although I want you to do nothing about it. Act normally, pretend they are not there. Have you a weapon?'

Poilettier puffed up his ample chest. '*Mais oui,* monsieur,' he announced proudly and swept back his leather vest. Two pistols protruded from his belt, one at each hip.

Nicolas cocked a raised eyebrow at him. 'Do you know how to use those things?'

'*Mais oui*, monsieur. My brother carried a matchlock gun in the service of the Duc de Longueville. He taught me. And these were given to me by Her Highness's steward.'

'Good. It will be your business to keep a sharp eye out for whatever other rascals might be lying in wait.'

'Will you ride with the Comtesse, monsieur?'

'Listen carefully, coachman. Do not tell madame as yet that you have seen me. I am going to keep the three riders in sight as I have been doing—secretly, from behind them—for I hope to learn their game before they play it. I do not wish madame to have unnecessary anxiety or to get herself mixed up in anything. Just continue as you have been, and say nothing. When we reach Bonneval, I will contact you again, unless there is a reason to do so beforehand. Is that clear?'

'*Oui, oui,* monsieur. As you say. My lips are sealed.' He gave Nicolas a sheepish grin. 'But pistols and all, I was not a happy man. The old heart is much lighter to know you and that great pagan are coverin' my flank.'

Nicolas drew some coins from the purse on his belt. 'Buy yourself some cider, coachman. It is well fermented this time of year. But stay sober. Put your pallet close to madame's door, and keep watch over her. I don't think these men wish to confront her; they seem content just to follow, as if to determine where she goes. But vigilance seems wise. If you need me, I am lodging on the other side of the church, at the sign of the pheasant. Tomorrow, Skandahet-se and I will form a rear guard. Just keep your pace moderate.'

'*Bien sûr,* monsieur. I am a moderate man.'

* * *

Cloaked against a slow patter of rain that blurred the gray morning, Nicolas and the big Huron sat their horses quietly, lined against the wall of an alley to the side of Julie's inn, damp hats dipped over their eyes. From this point, they were able to observe everything but were indistinguishable themselves, screened by a lively traffic of wagons, slogging peasants, peddlers seeking a sheltered spot, and dampened townspeople called to early mass by the pealing church bell. Finally, they saw the four horses drawing the coach trot out from the hostelry's gate. Then the black and red vehicle itself appeared, and Nicolas caught a tantalizing glimpse of the profile of the woman he could not dislodge from his mind as the equipage rumbled across the bustling square to regain the road to Bonneval. He and his companion did not move. They waited. Nicolas's mount snorted softly and pawed the ground. A heavy hay wagon drawn by the huge, feather-fetlocked working horses of the area creaked by their alley. And then, almost to the instant that Nicolas reckoned they would appear, the three riders trotted out of the gates and off in the same direction as the coach, hats pulled low against the softly falling rain. Skandahet-se grunted. Nicolas smiled grimly.

They lingered some minutes more and then rode out to cross the cobbled square, tracking the trackers. It was, in fact, infinitely easier than following the spoor of a prime winter-pelted rogue wolf who might lope in any direction and who could hear a twig snap a hectare away. This trio suspected nothing, and there was only one road to Bonneval, albeit a bad one of deep ruts, rocky rubble, and indistinct borders. To keep back far enough to blend in with the local users of the road was no great issue, as long as they had a glimpse now and then of their quarry. The morning's journey was uneventful.

'They want to know where she is going, not to stop her,' Nicolas confirmed to his stoic companion, whose braids glistened with silver drops. 'But why? Were they sent by de Louvois? And how can they know the goal of a mission only my godmother and she and I have knowledge of? Shall I believe that Monsieur de Louvois carries his amorous interest so far as to be jealous of madame's movements, not that I will allow it to avail him anything? Passing strange, indeed.'

The road was flat and looped widely along a stretch of planted fields and open meadows so that beyond the three riders he could see, small in the distance, the coach-and-four disappearing into low-hanging mist. He thought of Julie, of that glimpse of pert profile, and how close he was to that distracting dimple, the soft, sweet lips. He ought to knock together the heads of the men who followed her, jump into her carriage, grab her in his arms, and stop her protests with his mouth. For the two hundredth time, he touched the memories of the night they had spent together, gently, as if they were too delicate for inspection, although the muscles in his belly contracted as he remembered the smoothness of that satin body avidly twined with his, the tiny waist his hands could span, the full breasts, the round arms around his neck——

Skandahet-se broke into his erotic daydreaming with a grunt. 'Road marker, misyoo.'

They were close to Bonneval. Which meant close to finding out what de Troisac was up to.

It was easy to locate the baker in Bonneval; Poilettier just followed his nose. Stepping gingerly from the coach onto the wet, muddy cobbles before the little store, Julie sniffed appreciatively at the mouth-watering odor of fresh breads baking and also displayed in a basket posed in the shop's leaded-glass window. She looked up as a check, but there was no name above, only a wooden sign of two crossed loaves. Squaring her shoulders and priming her smile, she opened the plank door, which squeaked on its iron hinges, and went in.

The rosy-cheeked woman in apron and white kerchief turned from the heat of her brick oven to lean chapped and floury hands on a table grooved with wear. *'Oui, madame, je peux vous aider?'*

Julie threw back the heavy, damp hood from her knotted, ribbon-bound hair. Her spirits were good in spite of the weather and the tiring trip, for here, finally, was the goal of her mission. Her curiosity about what this lost prince of the blood and child of the houses of Orleans and Condé would look like, her anticipation of his mystification over the summons she would issue in behalf of the royal La Grande Mademoiselle, were soon to be satisfied.

'Courbier? Madame Courbier?'

The woman's brows rose to the rim of her pleated kerchief. '*Nom du ciel,* madame, that poor woman has been in her grave these two years, God give her peace. I can serve you with what goods you wish. If you are just passing through, you may not know how excellent are our white loaves, light as air, and our poppy seed turnovers have just been taken from the fire, madame——'

'No, you don't understand. I am actually looking for one Edouard Courbier, and I am in hopes you will be able to tell me where to find him. Or perhaps the baker himself, Maître Courbier?'

Curiosity kindled the gray eyes. 'And who wants him?'

'A friend. A powerful friend who has need of him.'

The eyebrows rose again. 'A powerful friend? Courbier?' The woman wiped her hands slowly on her apron, obviously considering whether she should say anything at all. But curiosity got the best of her as she studied the simply dressed but without a doubt wellborn woman before her. 'I am sorry, madame, but you are too late. Both Maître Courbier and his wife are dead. My husband bought this business from the town council, which seized it when no one claimed it. I do not know of an Edouard. Perhaps he was their only son, who went away years ago, I have heard. We were not at all acquainted with the Courbiers. We are from Voublery, the other side of the river. I fear I cannot help you.'

Some of the wind spilled from Julie's sails. '*Mon Dieu!* I am confounded by what you are saying. But who might know where the son Courbier went? Surely there was someone in the village who was his friend?'

The bakewife shrugged. 'As I said, madame, he departed a few years before we removed here. Perhaps the mayor can help you. Or Monsieur le Curé.'

'Yes, the mayor,' Julie repeated, set back. She had never imagined that the young man would have left Bonneval, where he was raised. Ordinary people did not travel about like the aristocracy. She grasped at the woman's suggestion. 'That's a good idea. I shall inquire of the mayor.'

The round chin lifted to indicate a particular direction beyond the shop. 'Go up the stepped street. His house is there, the tallest one before the fountain and the washing trough. His name is Petitjean.' The woman shuffled out from behind the table, wooden sabots on her feet. Grudging respect grew in her eyes as she peered through the window at the big coach that crowded the narrow street and took note of Blanchette in her white cap with long tails waiting outside the door. 'I regret, madame, you may have come a long way for little.' She reached under a towel covering a tray on the table and drew out a still-warm little cake redolent of almonds and honey, which she pressed into her visitor's gloved hand. 'For good luck, madame.' She smiled, bobbed her head, and waved away the coin Julie tried to pay her with. But she accepted it for several more cakes that Julie purchased for Blanchette and Poilettier.

The ensuing visit to the mayor proved just as fruitless. A rotund individual, not so good-natured as the baker's wife, Monsieur le Maire said sourly that Courbier's boy, a dreamer and a layabout, had gone off four or five years before, and no more had been heard from him, even by his grieving parents. 'Not worth his keep, not worth it,' the wheezing mayor grouched. 'There's no respect these days from children. But the old ones accepted his caprices with fond smiles, and how does he pay them back? By leaving one day, forever, with scarce a word. I said good riddance then,' he huffed. 'And I say good day to you now, madame. I must attend to my cow in back, who will drop her calf momentarily. I regret I cannot help you.' He bowed her out stiffly.

The Curé, a little man with watery eyes, pulled tight the rope around his black cassock, waggled his tonsured head, and answered sadly that, no, he had no idea where the boy went, but the lad was always running away from the time he was little, and the baker several times had fetched him back by the ear. It was too bad. When the boy was eleven or twelve, he had already learned to make excellent raisin buns, but he grew restless again. Adopted, the boy was, child of the baker's cousin. The blood will always tell. The father must have been a wanderer. No true child would leave his parents like that. He peered with his tearing eyes at Julie. 'You say there is some money to come to him? Hmm. Well, my daughter, go out to the square and rest on the bench there. I shall go fetch a sinner I know who may have an idea of Courbier's whereabouts. He will come to you there, since he will not come to the church.'

Julie walked back to the fountain, on her way impulsively stopping several villagers to query them. She got only curious stares and shakes of the head for her trouble. Dispirited, she sat down on a long bench fashioned of saplings to think what to do next, for she was certainly not ready to give up. Peeking through the omnipresent cloud cover, the sun sent down some weak, tentative rays to warm her head; it felt good after the constant rain. She looked at her toes. Her shoes were a mess. She sighed, slumping, but immediately twitched up again at the sound of a rusty voice at her elbow.

'Whatcher want 'im for? Edouard Courbier?'

She turned to stare into shrewd, rheumy old eyes in a wrinkled and worn face spotted with age. The ancient had settled himself on an opposite edge of the bench, a knife and a whittling stick in his gnarled hands. There was a guarded expression on his features. He hawked, spat, and repeated his question. 'Eh, my lady?'

'Why, I. . .I have good news for him. A relative has lately died and left him an inheritance. Only he must appear himself before the judge to receive it. And now I cannot find him.'

'Eh? An inheritance? Never heerd tell the baker had a rich relative. Never heerd that. And where might this poor rich corpse have died?'

'In, ah, Normandy. But I am sworn to discuss the circumstances only with Edouard Courbier, and alas, no one here knows where he has gone.' She lanced a sideways glance at him. 'Would you, perhaps?' It was a forlorn hope. The old man gumming his toothless jaws did not look like the source of much information.

But the old fellow, wielding his small knife so that the sharp, curved blade bit deep into the half-carved piece of wood he held, said conversationally as he gouged out slivers, 'Me name's Balouse. Henri Balouse. I knowed the youngster well. He was a different 'un, he was, a good boy, but as hungry as a starvin' rat to hear me tales of the wide world. I was a seafarer all me life, sailed from one end of t'earth to the other. Come home here fifteen years ago to die in the town where me mam give me birth, an ole barnacle washed up on the beach, and I'm still here. But the boy, 'e kept me company, them shiny blue eyes o' his all lit wi' dreams o' the painted black men o' Africky what eats human flesh and the Chinese heathen and the cruel Turk in his war galley, deadly swift. Aye, I knows where he be. If he ain't on a ship.' The faded eyes, under surprisingly dark eyebrows, bored into hers. 'But how do I know you don't mean 'im harm? Who are yuh, anyway?'

Julie got her rising excitement under control. 'My name is Julie Croixverte. And as you can see, I am but a woman, and I have no one with me but my coachman and a servant. It is my mission just to deliver a message to the *bonhomme* Courbier. How could I harm him?'

'Be it a goodly amount the fellow has come into?'

'Yes, a goodly amount.'

The old sailor put his carving, the emerging shape of a dolphin, down beside him. He rubbed a dirty palm on the ragged canvas breeches that covered his shanks and then pulled at his nose. 'Enough ter make it worth me time ter tell yuh where to find 'im?'

Julie was annoyed with herself for forgetting the power of a few coins with the poor. She reached under her cloak to slip her fingers into the money pouch in her pocket and came up with a silver écu. 'Does this amount suit you?'

The gray stubble on his chin quivered, the faded eyes gleamed. 'Aye, madame, it'll buy me a new blanket to warm me old backside now this bag o' bones don't please no good woman no more.' The dirty blue-veined hand reached out for the generous offering and closed over it tightly. From under the neckline of his greasy tunic, Balouse pulled a little pouch on a leather cord and slipped the écu into it, patting the bag with satisfaction. 'See, madame, that 'ere boy weren't no one to bake tarts when 'e could be rovin' the seas. It were maybe five years ago, 'e ran away and none did he tell 'is heart to but me. He went to Honfleur, up on the Norman coast, there to apprentice to any channel vessel would have 'im so's he could learn. He was big and strong fer his age. 'Tis me guess that's where you'll find 'im if you inquire at the quais. And that's me story. I know no more.' The oldster cackled again and patted his windfall. He made a wheezy joke. 'And if you can't find the lucky one, I'll take what's comin' to 'im. 'E was a decent lad, that 'un.'

She stood up, smiling. 'I thank you, seaman Balouse. And I am sure Edouard Courbier will be grateful to you. I will go on my way at once.'

Balouse squinted up at her. 'I don't guess you'd ever seed him? Well, 'e is ordinary-lookin' enough, but you'll know 'im by 'is left ear. Someone went and sliced a piece o' his ear when he was a babe. And you can tell 'im that his mam died—only she weren't 'is real mam. He were a cousin's babe.'

Julie thanked the old sailor again, and then hurried past the knots of women slapping their laundry at the stone trough below the fountain, heading back down to the lower street, where the coach and her companions waited. She was smiling, exhilarated to have found a trail to the man she sought. It was still early. They could turn right around and go northwest again, back to Normandy. They could probably reach Honfleur in four or five days if the weather got better and the roads dried out.

But even as she wished this, the drizzle started up again, forcing her to pull up her hood as she descended the worn and ancient steps. It had been such a chilly and wet spring, and the roads were becoming soggy. The glow she had experienced not to have lost her quarry quickly faded into the gloominess that sat within her lately, lying in wait to devour any stray smile or laugh. She could not remember ever being so moody—one minute up, the next minute crushed. Keeping her skirts raised off the wet and gritty cobbles, she forcibly elevated her chin as well. The sooner she found Courbier and brought him back to Eu, the sooner she could return to Paris, give her hand to the Comte de Vosges, and get on with her own life.

The old sailor, who, were the truth to be told, had never taken ship farther east than Italy, watched her go, cackled, patted his chest again where reposed a shiny silver coin he had hardly hoped to see, and went back to his skilled carving.

Happily, the town of Bonneval was small. If the local inn did not reveal a black and red coach, neither did the trio of hunters or Nicolas have to search far to find it. In order to stay unnoticed, Nicolas decided to circle the perimeter of the town, leaving Skandahet-se with the horses, and he had come up on foot in a few minutes from the other direction to observe the coach halted at the baking shop. Then he watched the coach move on again, deeper into the morning-busy community, and saw the three followers emerge from a nearby street to trail it. He retrieved his companion, and they threaded their way in the same direction, drawing back just in time as they came across the coach, stopped at the base of a street of wide steps between old houses. De Troisac could not be seen, but there was no doubt he was somewhere about; a little way beyond the coach, one of de Troisac's men leaned unobtrusively against a wall, holding the reins of the horses and enjoying a short flirt with two laughing wenches.

There was nowhere the Comtesse de Lowry could have gone but up the steps. Leaving Skandahet-se to keep an eye on the coach, Nicolas hunched into his cloak and went up the street, which led to the communal spring and small town square. At the top, he slipped into the deep recess of an old doorway to wait until he could spot either his lady or her hunter. In a few minutes, he saw Julie emerge from a house just behind the fountain, bowed out by its resident, and then, skirting the villagers filling their water pitchers or slapping their wash at the trough, she headed for the church just opposite, into which she disappeared. He waited, twitching impatiently. Soon she appeared again, asked a question of several passersby, and then went to sit down on a bench, a discouraged slump to her shoulders. It didn't take a necromancer to divine that she hadn't found the man she'd come for.

A graybeard sat down with her and commenced to talk with her. They talked a bit, and money changed hands. The conversation was soon finished. Julie got up, nodded her head several times, then turned and hurried back to the steps leading to the lower street. In his doorway, Nicolas had to control an impulse to dart out and draw her back into the shelter with him, except that de Troisac must be watching her from somewhere and he didn't wish to tip his hand yet. So he drew back farther into the shadow and watched motionless as she swept past him, almost close enough to touch, her cloak billowing about her heels. A trailing aroma of hyacinth reached him, and he felt his heart speed up at the glimpse of her, smiling, her gaze bright under the dark, winged brows.

He realized—he was struck by it, in fact—that his memory had failed him over and over, never actually reproducing the true vitality of her beauty, the delicate purity of her profile shown now to advantage by the simple Psyche-knotted coiffure. But it was not just her outward charms that drew him—it was her personality, her impulsive eagerness to embrace life, her staunchness to a cause, her silver laugh. A stab of resentment twisted in him that her spirit seemed so carefree while his was so enchained. Was she smiling because of that limp de Vosges, or because she had not given one thought through the winter to the man she had made love with and then dismissed as a sacrifice to her unreasonable fears? But reason fortunately cut off his building irritation. It made more sense to think she was merely pleased at that moment because the old man had pointed her toward her quarry.

A gaggle of children skipped past the doorway, shouting and laughing, running from the rain that had started up again. Nicolas glanced around the edge of the embrasure and saw de Troisac and the other man, having come out from wherever they had lurked, heading toward the old man, who looked up and then ducked his unkempt gray head to his carving again. De Troisac addressed him, but the old man shook his head without taking his eyes from his work. Slipping his hand into his coat, de Troisac withdrew a purse from which he extracted some silver. The old man's eyes widened. The coins changed hands. There was a short conversation; the ancient shrugged and shook his head. Leaning casually against the doorframe, Nicolas tried to interpret the tableau at the far end of the small square, annoyed with the ordinary life of the town that passed before him and hid them temporarily from view. He thought he detected a puzzled expression on de Troisac's face. Then a cart loaded with kindling lumbered from another street into the square and halted right in front of them as the besmocked boy who had been riding the faggots jumped off and hauled down a bundle.

'Peste!' Nicolas hissed between his teeth, slapping his hand against the stone of the doorway. He set his jaw and waited. But when the cart drew away, the old man was gone, and de Troisac stood in the drizzle talking to his underling, frowning, intense, evidently impressing something on the man. The man nodded, and the two turned to regain their horses, hunching against the chill and wet. Nicolas shrank back and flattened again into the shadow, but, hardly suspecting observation, they passed his doorway without a glance.

When he finally emerged and hurried down the steps, the coach was gone, and de Troisac and his men were gone. Skandahet-se strode over the cobbles to him, leading the horses, followed at a respectful distance by some round-eyed urchins and awestruck loungers who had never seen so strange a being. Skandahet-se greeted him. 'I talk to the coachman when he go to make water. He says madame orders him to take her as swiftly as possible to Honfleur. He says he will go by way of

Nogent, Verneuil, and Bernay. Bad roads, he says. He knows these places.'

'Honfleur! But that is all the way back on the Atlantic!'

Skandahet-se shrugged. He had no idea where the town was.

'And the other three?'

'Only two went after madame. And one galloped off this way, opposite direction.'

'Back to Paris,' Nicolas muttered. He shook his head and swung onto his horse, squinting off into the rain in the direction taken by the coach and the hunters. A long roll of thunder rumbled out of the low clouds; lighting cracked in the distance. A few stragglers scurried by them bent under bundles on their back, and a horseman trotted past. 'I've had enough of this cat-and-mouse skulking,' he grumbled. 'It's time to find out why de Troisac is trailing her and who has put him up to it.'

Skandahet-se grunted. His lips stretched into a wolfish grin. 'Then we slit throat?'

'That depends on what their business is. Probably, we'll just tickle them a bit. Detain them long enough for them to lose the scent. It is my fervent wish that madame quickly accomplishes her goal and then returns to Paris. I am tired of this damnable rain,' he growled. He opened the flap of a saddle bag, drew out a parchment map of the north of France, hand drawn for him during the campaign in Flanders in 1668, and studied it. 'Ah, here. If we take the faster road, through Saint-Paul, we will reach Verneuil before them. A little ambush on the road, and we can truss up our chickens before they can squawk. *Allons-y!*'

And they spurted off after the objects of their pursuit.

The coach wheels ground through the muck with a sucking sound, but Julie risked getting her face spattered by mud by letting down the window to look back along the road stretching behind them. And for the fourth time that day, she noticed in the distance the same two riders. Frowning, she sat back in her seat again. It was that freckled man, she was sure. She had caught a glimpse of him again just as she left Bonneval, and it bothered her enough so that she kept glancing back from the coach whenever they reached a curveless stretch. The two mounted men could be seen, always at the same distance, even when she asked Poilettier to vary their speed. She took her pistol from its felt bag and put it on her lap, to Blanchette's askance but silent look.

She had no idea what the freckled man wanted of her, but she had no wish to be robbed or perhaps to lead him to Edouard Courbier, if that was his aim. So that meant having a plan. She mulled over an idea that seemed most likely to divest her of the unpleasant company and decided to go ahead with it; the trouble was worth being free of the sinister surveillance. At their next halt, she would confer with Poilettier and Blanchette.

'But, madame, I am not happy to leave you. It don't seem wise to do,' Poilettier objected.

'In fact, I will be safer in a farm wagon than in the big coach, which is conspicuous in these parts. And by leading those men away from me, you will be doing a necessary service. Even if they catch up to you, all you need answer is that you know nothing, you only followed my orders. See, Poilettier, they could not just be common thieves. They've had opportunities to accost us, but they have merely been following us since Magny. And you have your pistols.'

'*Oui*, right here.' Poilettier patted his weapons.

'What is that man's name again, your good friend in Trouville, so I can remember it?'

'Le Carré, Augustin, madame, the harnessmaker on the Touques River quai.'

'Good. Go there finally, as if you were visiting your friend, and let them puzzle out how you could have lost your way so badly. By the time they see they've been duped, I will have done my business, hired a conveyance, and turned back to Eu, where I have no further fear of them.'

'But supposin' there is no one willing to oblige us in Verneuil?'

'You worry too much, coachman. There is always

silver to induce the reticent. And if not, we can try again in the next village. But I must make an effort to elude these men.'

Poilettier tried again. 'Her Highness made me responsible for you. I should go with you.'

'If they don't see you on that box, Poilettier, they will smell a rat. Blanchette is a witness to the fact that I refused to allow you to come with me. It will be all right, I am certain. I will transform myself into a little country woman, and who would wish to bother me?'

'The churl who will be drivin' you, for one. You are carrying much money in your purse, madame.'

Julie laughed at his fears. 'What, a maid just dismissed from service, to have any money? Besides, I have my pistol, too. Just find me a fellow who looks honest, at least.'

Poilettier waggled his eyebrows as he saw her determined chin. Finally, he shrugged. He was inclined to agree with her reasoning, and he couldn't stop her. Besides, de Courcillon was behind them and would surely stay with her once the coachman slipped him the change in plan. '*Très bien,* madame. I will do my best for you.'

The coachman clumped out of the chamber, and Julie turned her attention to Blanchette, who stood with head hunched into her shoulder like a turtle, obedient to the new arrangements but dubious.

In the common room below, Poilettier cast only a furtive glance at the two seated hard by the rude steps to the upper floor. They were still there; they were always there. He passed through the antechamber and looked about the inn yard. He marched over to the two other small lodgings the town offered. He stood irresolutely in the square, rocking on the balls of his feet, hands in his tunic pockets. De Courcillon was nowhere. For the first time since the Marquis had secretly joined them, he could not spot him or his big Indian. Scratching his head, he waited a long hour more, eyes darting back and forth between the streets giving onto the square as various horsemen clopped in and past him. Nothing. He whistled tunelessly between his teeth, pressed an elbow against the pistols under his tunic, and lifted his shoulders. *Eh bien, c'est la vie.* He had done his best. He departed then to help Madame de Lowry put her little scheme together.

CHAPTER
~ 19 ~

After a few snapped orders to the astonished Poilettier, Nicolas quickly waved the coach on to hold around the bend, out of sight. He was careful to pull up his kerchief mask before the occupants in the coach's dim interior could identify him. It had begun to rain again, the slippery muck slowing up what few vehicles were abroad and making his job easier, not that he expected any trouble in capturing the two he was after.

Screened in a tangle of brush and vines, he let a peasant lad with hair like a haystack ride past on a swaybacked horse. Some minutes more, and then there they were, just cantering around the curve, de Troisac a few hoofbeats in the lead. Nicolas drew back into the brush in a semicrouch and made ready with his rope, which lay hidden in the muddy ruts of the road and was attached to a tree opposite him. Timing his move as much by the sound of the hooves as by eye, he suddenly hauled strongly on the rope, and it jumped up taut before the surprised riders, the horses whinnying, rearing, and rolling wild eyes at the barrier, the unsuspecting horsemen pitching off into the muck. Almost immediately, they scrambled up, groping for their weapons, but they were already facing a masked brigand with two pistols aimed steadily at their hearts.

'March!' Nicolas commanded in a muffled roar, jerking his head toward the thick forest. 'In there. Quick.' He herded them in among the dripping trees, where in a few paces they were unobservable from the road.

An angry de Troisac, hands in the air, turned his head over his shoulder. 'See here, *mon homme*. If it's money you want, take it and be quick about it. We are on special business and must not delay. Take what you wish, but let us go,' he demanded.

'Shut up!' Nicolas barked. 'Keep moving. And keep your eyes in front of you, or you'll never leave these woods.'

After shuffling through the wet leaves and greening underbrush fifty more paces, Nicolas quietly hung back, allowing Skandahet-se to rise up silently behind the two prisoners, a pistol reversed in his hand. Two swift, light taps behind the ears, and both men pitched forward, knocked out.

'You have an elegant touch, dogstar warrior,' Nicolas grinned, shoving his pistols back into his belt. Quickly, they securely tied the hands of both men behind their backs and then carefully blindfolded them, for there was no way to disguise Skandahet-se, and Nicolas wanted them to believe they'd been taken by two of the murderous highwaymen infesting the roads. A gag was also shoved into each mouth. Then Skandahet-se went back to collect the men's horses.

As soon as they stirred, groaning, Nicolas jabbed them in the ribs until they lurched blindly up to their feet and then made them form a stumbling procession farther into the woods until they reached the shelter of bent saplings, canvas, and leaves that he and Skandahet-se had hastily thrown up and stocked. Nicolas had determined that he would get his information more quickly from de Troisac's companion, whose mouth, he noted, was not set in so grim and stubborn a line. Looping enough rope around de Louvois's agent to keep him solidly attached to a tree, he then grabbed the other man by the arm and hauled him out of earshot of de Troisac. Roughly, he flung the man sprawling on his back, then followed him down, kneeling and holding him prone with a hand on his chest. He pressed a stiletto against the man's neck hard enough to draw blood. The man screamed in fear and tried to roll away from the wicked point.

'Tickles, *non?*' Nicolas grunted. 'So. What is your name, my friend, and tell me quickly. Don't let me get impatient.' He pricked the stiletto's sharp point into a new place on the neck.

'Bartois,' the man gasped, 'André Bartois. I don't

have much money, I swear. But I have a gold ring. Look, look at my finger. You can take the ring. Just don't kill me——'

'That all depends on you, Bartois. It's not the ring I want. Yet. First, I want you to warble a little. Answer my questions. If you lie, I'll know it. If you do, or if you're too slow, you'll know it. My knife shaves closer than a razor.' The point jabbed in again. A thin ribbon of red was already seeping down the man's taut neck into his cravat.

'Yes, yes. I don't know what you want,' Bartois gurgled desperately.

'Why are you following that big red and black coach?' The knife pricked again. 'Quick. No lies.'

The man's Adam's apple bobbed. 'We were ordered to.'

'So? And by whom?'

'By M-monsieur de Louvois. The king's own minister.'

'Oho! I think I have caught myself two big fish here. And what is so interesting about that coach? Speak up!'

'Yes, yes! There is a lady in it, the Comtesse de Lowry. We are to report where she goes.'

'Don't stop now, *mon ami*. And why does Monsieur de Louvois watch this lady's actions? Eh?' There was silence for a moment. Bartois began to twitch. Nicolas growled in his ear, 'Cooperate, *mon ami*, or I will dispatch you and start on your friend, who may value his life a little more. It makes no difference to me whose throat I cut.' He placed the cold steel blade against the convulsive Adam's apple. '*Dépêches-toi. . .*'

'No, wait, don't kill me. I am but a very little fish,' Bartois cried. 'It is her father. De Louvois thinks she will lead us to her father. She has been watched since the day she came to France. He thinks she knows where her father has hidden himself.'

Nicolas sat back on his heels in astonishment. De Morlé? De Louvois was searching for the Vicomte de Morlé, who was supposed to be dead for six years? *Nom d'un chien!* But why? He glared at the blindfolded Bartois and doubted that this fish knew that answer, or de Troisac either, for that matter.

'What does he want her father for?'

'I...don't know. I swear to you, I don't know,' the man agonized as the blade pricked his neck again. 'He didn't even tell de Troisac, who is the leader here. Why would he tell me?'

'There were three of you. What happened to the other one?'

Now it was Bartois's turn to be surprised. His body stopped quivering as he considered that this murderous varlet must have been observing them at least since Bonneval. Another prick got his tongue moving again. 'Uh...uh...he was sent back to Paris to report to Monsieur de Louvois. The lady seemed to be looking for someone else—a...a baker called Courbier.'

'Does that mean anything to you?'

'No. We don't recognize the name. But perhaps Monsieur de Louvois will and give us further instruction.'

'Do you know where the Comtesse is going?'

'To Honfleur. But if the old dodderer gave her a location for Courbier, he did not give it to us.'

'And what were you to do in the long run, in case the lady led you to her father?'

'Detain her. Both of them. For questioning. I don't know about what.'

Nicolas got to his feet. Disconnected thoughts ran like mice around his brain, all going back to de Morlé's furtive appearance in Canada, his request to be immediately attached to one of Nicolas's remotest outposts, his stubbornly unexplained statement that everyone in France believed he was dead. And now Julie, innocent of what machinations had occurred, was being drawn into her father's intrigues. He'd have to talk to her and tell her about de Morlé. Perhaps she even held a piece of the puzzle and did not know it.

He got up, aimed the toe of his boot at the man's rib, and kicked, but not too hard, just enough to intimidate him. The fellow was merely a lackey. 'And what were you to do if this Comtesse merely met a lover and not her father?'

'Nothing. Just follow her back to Eu or wherever she

went.' The man curled his body up, his shoulders hunched, dreading the next blow.

'Get up. Move!'

Bartois wriggled to his knees, cringing, then rocked up unsteadily to his feet. Nicolas seized him by the back of his collar and marched him forward, half lifting him off the ground. When they reached the lean-to, he shoved Bartois into Skandahet-se's waiting arms. 'Gag him again,' he ordered, and then he went on in a deliberately loud voice, designed to reach the ears of both captives. 'I told you it was worthwhile to trail the batch of them. This one's spilled a very interesting tale. There's ransom here someplace if I figure it out, but meanwhile there's a little dove of a lady traveling by herself in that coach, a jewel or two on her fingers, perhaps. I'll get our companions and ride after it. You stay here with these rubbish until I come to get you.'

De Troisac, whom Skandahet-se had allowed to sit against the tree but tied with a rope around his neck, struggled with blind strength to his knees and wrenched at the ties that bound his elbows, making muffled, furious noises. Skandahet-se stepped over to him and silently jammed the muzzle of his flintlock pistol against the man's ear. The noises stopped. De Troisac stiffened and bowed his head. But he was shaking with anger.

Drawing his companion aside, Nicolas whispered, 'I was right. It is for de Louvois that they ride. But something is very strange here. It is not madame's present mission they are interested in but information about de Morlé, her father. Keep them here three days, then let them go without their horses. By the time they grope their way out of the forest, we will have spirited away the man she is seeking and be on our way back to Eu. Make your way to Honfleur. I shall seek you at the largest inn or leave a message for you if we must leave before you arrive.'

Skandahet-se grunted, arms folded. The handle of a hunting knife peeped out of the brass-buttoned coat, whose fabric strained over his chest.

'You should have enough food, and the stream is nearby. Keep these two dry under the canvas. I don't want them to die of croup—yet.'

Another grunt. And a grin. Skandahet-se would keep himself busy by trapping rabbits and squirrels, perhaps shooting a deer. He wouldn't mind that at all. Nicolas clapped him on the arm.

So that the blindfolded and gagged prisoners would not guess for a while that one of their captors had left, he tried not to snap twigs as he slipped over to where the horses were tethered. He freed his own to take him back to the waiting coach and to his lady, who must by this time be in a towering dither over whatever excuse Poilettier gave her for halting so long.

'What are you pulling off, Poilettier?' Nicolas bellowed. 'That scabby woman in there in the back is not Madame de Lowry. What have you done with her? Get down off that box, villain, and your answer better please me, or you're a dead man.' The horse dancing under him did not waver a fraction the pistol aimed at the coachman's grizzled head.

As hastily as he could move his hulking frame, Poilettier clambered from his perch and snatched off his hat. 'No, no, monsieur, you don't understand. 'Twas not me did anything to her. 'Twas by her own orders, monsieur. She finally discovered those louts that was followin' us, and she decided to trick them.'

'Trick them? Explain.'

Poilettier looked into the bore of the pistol and swallowed; he had regretted letting the woman go off by herself the minute he'd pulled away from the inn, and the man who held the pistol was fixing him with eyes like pale blue ice. 'She insisted on changin' clothes with her maid, Blanchette, back there in the coach, the woman'll tell you so. And then she made me hire a wagon and driver to take her away another route and a poor woman to wear Blanchette's cloak and travel with us, so's they'd think there was two. I was to take the fork at Breteuil and lead those monkeys a merry chase, round and about, to give her time to reach Honfleur and find that man she's looking for. 'Tis the truth, monsieur. Would I be standin' here waiting for you if I'd done her harm?'

'By all the saints and apostles, Poilettier, you let her go on alone? With some stranger to drive her?' The baleful stare had turned into pale fire, but the gun was lowered. 'Where is your sense, man?'

'I couldn't stop her, monsieur. I am only a servant. I do what I'm told.'

Nicolas shook his head. 'Which road did she take, then? Quickly!'

'The path from Verneuil to L'Aigle. The wagon was old and the road was bad, the fellow warned. He had a Percheron, though, could pull that wagon at a good speed till it fell apart. Maybe if you ride in that direction 'cross these fields and don't hit no woods you can catch up to her.'

'I'd better catch up to her, coachman, or I'll feed your stupid liver to the seagulls. Where were you to rejoin her?'

'Yer in my own territory now, monsieur. I was born in Saint-Malo and know Normandy well, too. My brother lives in Trouville, south of Honfleur, on the river quai. I was to wait at his house.'

'Well, go there. And if she manages to get to you before I reach her, get her back to Eu as fast as you can. If she gives you any trouble, just throw her in the coach and lock the door, on my authority. Say I will explain.'

Poilettier looked up from under his bushy eyebrows. '*Oui, oui*, monsieur.'

'Then pay off that pimply woman and find her a ride home. There is no one following you anymore.'

A smile spread over Poilettier's features as he fingered his hat. '*Mais oui,* sir. Just as you say. I wasn't much happy with all this hugger-mugger business——'

'Get on your way, then, man, and so will I. That woman puts more trouble into my life than a wolverine trapped in a torn net bag,' he muttered. He wheeled his horse. 'That way, you say? And are you certain?' he demanded.

'Absolutely, monsieur. She could not make very good time on such a back way, and I think not much distance separates the roads yet from here. If you ride across the fields diagonal—so'—he chopped the air with the edge of his hand in the direction he meant—'you will surely come upon her.'

'Pray that I do. Farewell, Poilettier.' Nicolas dug in his spurs, and the horse jumped.

'*Au revoir,* monsieur.' Hands on hips, the coachman, with the heads of the two women poking out from the coach behind him, watched de Courcillon's horse arrow off, leap a ditch, and stretch its legs in a gallop toward the gray horizon. Scratching his head, he wondered what this captain of the king's bodyguard had done to stop in their tracks the rascals who had been following the coach. Beaten them? Tortured them? Left them with that terrifying savage to be strangled? All three, maybe.

A raindrop hit Nicolas on the nose, and another plopped on his cheek in quick succession. Damnation, more rain, he cursed to himself, squinting up at the rapidly darkening sky. If she was ahead of him, that would only drive her on faster to reach L'Aigle for the night. Reining in his horse to an easy lope, he guided the animal around the craters in a humped, straggly path through a patchwork of fields and stone walls. He'd made good time across the open meadows, but she could be either ahead or behind him on the path. He bet on ahead, since a Percheron could run for hours without losing his wind. But if he didn't spot a likely wagon in a quarter-hour, he would just wait to see if she caught up.

He pulled his hat lower against the splattering of raindrops and then noticed ahead of him a copse of elm trees standing on a knoll. He smiled at his luck: the only appreciable rise he'd seen in this flat country ought to give him a good look at the way ahead, past the low walls in the way. He spurred up the horse and topped the small hill, just in time to see, about half a league ahead, an uncovered wagon bumping in haste along the rutted path, the cloaked figure clinging behind the driver drawing up the hood of a cloak over dark hair. As he watched, the driver flung a whip over the great horse, and the wagon lurched around a curve at higher speed.

'That's them,' he muttered into his beard. 'Hardly five minutes between us. Stretch your legs, Al-Minyah, and close up the gap.' Again, he touched the glistening dark flanks with his spurs, and the sturdy Arabian obeyed, miraculously flying over the holes, stones, and tree roots. But as he drew close, he saw Julie spot him, too far away to recognize him, and jerk upright. Coming down a slope, he caught the wagon driver using his whip again, and the unwieldy vehicle spurted ahead to where the road veered and disappeared behind a screen of trees. Pushing his mount, Nicolas reached the bend and saw that the path now ran along the edge of the high banks of a turbulent river, and the wagon ahead was jolting crazily along, the wheels threatening to fly off in different directions.

As if God had suddenly turned a spigot, the rain began a steady downpour, drenching him, his mount, and the narrow path, whose edges, soaked by days of rain, crumbled under the flying hooves of both horses. Cursing at the weather that kept her from hearing his shouts as he drew within earshot and at Julie's understandable fright at a rider bearing down this abandoned road at full tilt, Nicolas was just about to haul up and stop chasing her when the Percheron thundered around a narrow curve. The wagon's back wheel slid over the edge of the crumbling bank, and, in a nightmare of motion that seemed to him slow as a stately dance, the heavy wagon tilted and slid backward. Nicolas heard the terrified screams of both the woman and the struggling horse as the wagon toppled. The humans were pitched out and fell into the dark, rushing river below.

Heart stuck in his throat, Nicolas galloped up, leaped off his horse, took one look down, in a sweat unbuckled the belt that held his pistols, and flung off his coat. Racing a short way forward on the bank below which Julie was struggling in the river to keep her hold on a wagon plank, he scrambled down to a jutting ledge of earth and jumped off in a shallow dive. He came up from the cold shock, gasping into the rain, and bobbed with the swift current for an instant before starting a strong, steady stroke toward her.

I'm drowning, dear God, I'm drowning, Julie's mind

shrieked as she fought to hold on to the plank and keep her head above the swirling water. She tried to recall how she had come to be immersed in that dark water, and then the horrid memory of that crazy jolt came back. The whole world had tilted over sickeningly, and she had gone flying out into space. Then eternity had grabbed at her in an eerie, silent moment and she had plummeted downward. She must have smacked the water, gone under, and come up—she was in too much shock to remember. But she did remember what happened then, the terrible image of the broken remains of the wagon with the crazy-eyed, battling horse attached to it sweeping by her while she grabbed frantically for the small purchase she now had. The roar in her ears kept her from knowing anything else except that she was fighting for her life. She clung with one hand while with the other she struggled to loosen the strings of her sodden cloak, which was dragging her down and away from her hold. With uncanny strength, she ripped at the knotted strings strangling her and burst them apart, and the clutching fabric whipped away from her, at the same time pulling her locked fingers further loose from the slippery plank. Her fingers were growing numb; her legs were numb, too. The rain beat at her face; the river swirled and swelled around her and crashed over her head and into her mouth, stopping her breathing with relentless red, purple, and black finality till she bobbed up and rackingly coughed it all out again. Stop it, stop it, she wept silently, powerless to scream or beat back the inevitable fate that demanded her life, battling to keep her hold a minute more, incredulous that this catastrophe was hers all alone, that no one would ever know——

Something bumped her hard in the back, and, gasping, she bobbed about to fend it off with her free arm. Then she shrieked her terror aloud, for the bundle of rags that swirled and circled away from her had a head in it, a head caved in at the back, limp hair trailing behind like streaming seaweed—the reckless country youth whose wagon she had hired. Stark horror tore loose her fingers, and, clawing, she went under, water rushing into her nose and mouth, the roaring of the current cutting off into a ringing in the void of death, and the pain of not breathing was crushing her chest. Sudden noise again as the maddened river pushed her up into the rain and rolled her around, coughing, choking, no time to get a breath, a torment of wet above her, beneath her. I am drowning, she screamed out silently. I can't swim, she cried in her horror-stricken soul as the river tossed her. The water and the cruel, weeping sky and the heedless, rocky banks whirled before her frantic eyes. So cold and wet and lonely a death—no, no——

She went under again. But she felt something grab her hair and yank her up, and something else jabbed under her arms to support her upper body. She was being towed, tugged, little by little against the current. She coughed up water, gasping, gagging, and dragged back her consciousness. It was an arm clamped around her, a human arm, and beside her, a dark head with features hidden by plastered hair strained forward across the insistent current as a man labored to pull them both to the riverbank.

It burst upon her like the white light of heaven, like a clanging together of the hereafter's cymbals, that she was being rescued from death. Someone had seen her. But a delirious panic swept through her that maybe he would not be strong enough, that he would let her go, lose her, let her die. And coughing and choking, she seized the arm about her and grappled with violent strength to work her way up the shoulder, trying to anchor herself more firmly to him, clinging harder as he tried to push her away, grabbing at his neck, his head, anything, hysterically attempting to climb on him, holding him tightly so that he could not, would not, leave her to drown. The man had stopped swimming and struggled with her as the rain beat down on them and the flood swept them along. She wanted to scream out, No, don't let us die, man, but instead, spitting out water, she grabbed his hair and, because the current was tugging them apart, tried again to climb on him. Beleaguered, he fought her. He raised an arm out of the water in protest——

And life boomed in her head like a gong, whirled around sickeningly, then went black.

Hurting. Everything hurt her. Her chest and her back. And her jaw. She moved her jaw a little, and one side twinged cruelly.

She moved a little. There was something heavy over her. It smelled strange. Something crackled under her. She was warm. She heard the snapping of a fire, smelled it. But this wasn't her own soft bed. Where was she? Alarmed, feeling spent and sore, she opened her eyes. And the room spun. She opened her mouth as if to cry out, then she remembered the river, the inexorable, suffocating water beating her down. Had she drowned? She didn't feel dead. She couldn't be dead, because she could see above her a stained, thatched roof and below that a plank-shuttered window in a fieldstone wall.

She heard a soft sound, like someone poking up a fire. She turned her head, and sure enough it was a fire, a lively conflagration on a rude hearth, the leaping flames wrapping an orange glow around the man who tended it, his back toward her.

Naked. Her widened eyes told her he was naked. Close to the fire, a pole was extended from a plank table to a bench, and on it clothes hung drying in the considerable heat. In fact, she was roasting. She pulled an arm from under the heavy, curly sheepskin that was weighing on her but then lifted the cover a bit to stare at herself. She was naked, too.

Her eyes flew again to the broad, smooth back of the man hunkered down by the fire, and memory returned of a strong arm fighting to hold her against the drag of the current. This must be the man who had saved her life. She stared at him as he concentrated on his task, settling with a green stick one log back on the other. Her gaze followed the reddish hair that spilled to the muscled shoulders—hair the color of Nicolas de Courcillon's, who was so far away, who probably cared nothing for her anymore. She might have died in that river without knowing one more tender-mocking glance from those light blue eyes. The disturbing sight of that hair and the powerful nude male form brought back some feeling into her lassitude, strangely not joy for having been delivered from an untimely exit from the world, but the familiar ache of regret for a man she couldn't forget.

Keeping a bashful silence, she watched the man feel his linen underdrawers, which were hanging on the pole along with his breeches and shirt and her gown and underthings. Deciding they were dry, he stood up and drew them on over his tight haunches, and her eyes followed the play of muscles in his thighs. Seeing that he was covered, she dared to raise her sore body on one elbow, the whimper she heard in her ear being her own. Her throat was arid, but it was time she thanked this Norman, whose house this must be, for her life.

The fellow heard her and turned, straightening up. Her startled eyes stared at a close-clipped, bearded face. She put out a protesting hand as if to stop a ghost from overwhelming her and opened her mouth, but nothing came out but a weak squeak. She was seeing things. The man looked exactly like Nicolas, exactly. Her mouth remained open even though her breath had stopped, and she felt that her eyes were as wide as saucers. The man came over to her pallet of heaped straw covered with a soft skin and dropped to his knees on the sod floor. He took her hand between his, and light blue eyes twinkled at her.

'If you had been cruel enough to drown yourself, madame, and doomed me to a life devoted only to your memory, I would have never forgiven you,' he teased, but there was relief in his voice.

'I don't believe this,' she whispered, incredulous. 'Is it you, Nicolas?' She was aching to believe he was real but afraid to credit her eyes and ears. 'How could you possibly, possibly have found me? *Mon Dieu*, not only found me but suddenly to appear in that river just as I was about to be swept away and drowned? Am I dreaming?'

'I didn't just appear, my dear. I deliberately jumped in after you. And the Lord knows you gave me a difficult enough time.' He chuckled. He reached out and fingered her jaw on the left side. 'Does that hurt? I think I tapped you a little too hard, but you were doing your best to drown the both of us.'

'But is it a miracle? I still don't understand,' she breathed, her mouth still open with shock. Gently, he closed it for her.

'No, madame, no miracle, just hard work on my part to keep you in sight, you foolish woman, running all over France by yourself. The Duchesse told me where you had gone and why, and I have been fairly close behind you since Houdin.'

The tone was gruff, but the light in his eyes dissolved her disbelief in his presence. She put out a tentative hand and touched his bare chest. It was real; it pulsed with life under her fingers. And now that she believed it, the acceptance of his being there fountained through her like that new fermented wine bubbling up in a goblet. She was overwhelmed by the magnitude of her debt to him. With a soft cry, she sat up and flung her arms about him, unconcerned that the musty sheepskin slipped down to her waist. 'Oh, Nicolas. Oh, thank you for being here,' she cried into his neck. 'Oh, Nicolas, I am so glad to see you!'

In a minute he took her arms down and held her out to look into her eyes. 'I wish that were true,' he said.

She colored a bit. 'Well, of course it is true. You saved my life.'

'Just gratitude isn't good enough,' he said huskily.

But she had realized she was bare above the waist, and her blush grew deeper as she pulled away from his grasp and wriggled down under the sheepskin again to cover herself. '*Piu*, this great thing smells.' She laughed shakily, still incredulous to think that he had been following her all these days and then turned up in time to drag her from death's door.

'Don't hurt its feelings, madame. It had a great deal to do with your current state of health. When I carried you in here, you were dripping and shuddering with cold and only half-conscious. That old sheepskin, in fact this hovel, belongs to the shepherd who saved both of us, appearing as he did out of the rain just as I staggered from the river with you. He was searching for a lost lamb. Now he's left his dog with his flock and gone to the village to get us some food.'

'*Ciel!* It has just occurred to me that I lost everything in that miserable accident—my handcase, my money, all at the bottom of the river.'

'Not the money, anyway.' He grinned and rocked up to his feet to walk to the table, where he picked up a purse. 'This was still in the pocket of your gown, and no wonder you couldn't stay afloat. We're lucky to have it, though, for every franc I had was in the purse on the sword belt I threw off, or in my saddlebag. We will never see those again in this land of empty-bellied peasants. But your money will be enough to get us to Honfleur and then back to Eu. That is, if you will permit my company?'

Honfleur. More memories returned. She watched him pour hot water from a steaming earthen pot into a wooden cup of the shepherd's coarse wine. He stalked over to press it into her hand.

She said, 'I would be grateful for your company, monsieur, even though you don't think gratitude counts.' She dimpled at him, noticing how the light of the fire gleamed golden on the hairs on his chest. Modestly, she held the sheepskin against her bosom so she could gulp down the warm potion. But as she sat up, she winced.

'What ails you?'

'I seem to ache all over. My poor jaw, of course. But especially here.' She indicated her breastbone. 'And my back.'

With a wry expression, he said, 'My fault again, I'm afraid, but the soreness will leave you soon. I had to pound some water out of you, and the rock I draped you over wasn't exactly soft. Still, it worked. You gave up half the river and coughed yourself back to life. Would you like me to rub the sore places? No, I didn't think so——' He went to feel the clothes still on the pole, which she saw was the shepherd's long crook. Blanchette's simple gray gown hung limply next to her own petticoats, and chemise. Blanchette's white cap now rested on the gravel of the riverbed. Nicolas tested his brown breeches. 'Not all the way dry yet,' he muttered, 'but they'd do for supper.' And he drew them on.

The wine flowed cozily through her veins and put some strength in her limbs. 'Could I. . .' She felt a bit bashful, realizing that it was he who had undressed her. 'Could I put on my clothes and come out from under this hide?'

'*Bien sûr*, if you now feel warm enough, but your gown is still damp.' He picked her cotton petticoats, chemise, and underdrawers from the pole. 'But these are nice and warmed through, and decent enough for our supper, whatever that may be. Here, catch.' He tossed them over to her. She reached to retrieve them, and the sheepskin slipped down again, exposing her for a second before she was buried in a welter of underclothes.

She giggled. The wine had already reached her head via her empty stomach. What was more, the lonely ache of her soul was gone, washed away not in the flooding river but in the pleasure of his presence, which as always, seemed to fill the room. He was shrugging on his soft shirt, full-sleeved, lace at the wrists, but he wore no stockings, and the effect, with his bare feet and knotted calves, was funny. She giggled again.

He looked around from shoving his boots closer to the fire. 'What, *ma chère*, is so funny?'

'I don't ordinarily dine with gentlemen in such a costume, bare legs sticking out.'

He growled, 'I certainly hope not. Get dressed, then, while I tend to the fire, and consider yourself blessed that it was May and not December, or the cold alone would have done you in. I seem to hear no rain beating on our roof. Maybe the Lord has taken pity on us and quelled this evil deluge we've been suffering for weeks.' He turned his back to let her dress.

She crawled gingerly from the pallet and drew on her knee-length underdrawers, slipped the low-cut sleeveless chemise over her head, donned one drawstring petticoat and reserved the other, which she arranged over her bare shoulders and arms like a shawl. She looked down at her feet, wiggled her toes, and then glanced around the low-ceilinged room. 'But I haven't any shoes,' she said, dismayed. 'I lost them in the river.'

He turned back to her, and his gaze took her in with amused approval. 'That's true. We'll have to think how to remedy that so we can get to the nearest village tomorrow. We've only our feet to get us there.'

With both hands, she pushed back the mass of still damp hair that tumbled about her face and then held out one gleaming black strand. 'And whatever shall I do for a comb? I must look a fright.'

'I shall be charitable and ignore your frightful state until we come to a town where we can purchase what we need. And I seldom dine with ladies without stockings, either.' He chuckled. He walked over to her and let his hand span her waist. 'You look delicious. Pale, perhaps, but who wouldn't be in the circumstances—almost drowned, punched in the jaw, and subsequently pounded black and blue?' Gently, he turned her face into the light to inspect her jaw. 'Not as bad as I thought. Only a small area is turning purple. Matches your eyes,' he consoled her, one eyebrow quirked up. She made a pout and then smiled back as he studied her bruise.

'Julie, I'm sorry I had to hit you. There was nothing else to make you relax.'

'I forgive you. And I am mortified that I panicked so. I remember I thought you might give me up and leave me to drown.'

'Leave you?' he murmured. 'I will never willingly leave you.'

She stared into the suddenly serious pale blue intensity of his eyes. She ached to caress his face, the soft beard, the hard cheekbones, and yet she could not. She felt paralyzed between the pleasure of what he'd just said and her inability to believe it. Her struggle with herself turned her expression blank and tied her tongue. He waited for a moment for some reaction from her. His smile hardened. His Adam's apple dipped in the strong column of his neck.

Just then, the door squeaked back on its hinges, and a skinny youth in a tunic of tanned leather entered. It was the shepherd, carrying a basket, accompanied by a draft of cool, clean night air that made Julie realize, as she pulled the petticoat more modestly around her shoulders, how hot Nicolas had made the hut. The fellow glanced at her shyly and then said to Nicolas as he put the basket on the table, 'Here's some o' yer coin back, monsieur. There ain't much extra victuals in the village. But my sister, she spared you some.' He scratched his head. 'Say, I found yer fine horse, monsieur, ambling on the road where you said he might be. Good thing it was raining, no one else abroad to find him. But I looked all about and didn't see neither yer coat nor yer pistols. Could be some'un went by and didn't think to look in the woods fer the horse. I've put the mount in the shelter with my flock and with hay that I bought him. Rode him back, I did, if monsieur doesn't mind. 'Twas my first time in a real saddle,' he said proudly.

'I could hardly mind, shepherd,' Nicolas was beaming. 'I never thought you'd find that horse.'

Pleased, the fellow ducked his head. 'I'll go see to me flock now,' he mumbled, and, with another glance at Julie, he was gone.

Nicolas began to unpack the basket and saw that the fellow had told the truth. The repast was not Lucullan: a half-loaf of bread, four cooked eggs, a small piece of local cheese, a wooden bowl of turnips and parsnips cooked in pork fat, and a small bottle of the region's hard wine. But it was enough to get them through to the next morning, with a bit saved for breakfast. He arranged the part of the bench not supporting the drying pole, then drew Julie to the table.

'Come, madame. First fill your belly, and then we will talk and plan for the morrow.'

'I'm not very hungry,' Julie demurred. And then she gobbled up in an instant the shelled egg and piece of bread he handed her.

When they'd finished everything except for a bit of bread and wine reserved for the morning, he put the bench back closer to the fire for her, and she sat there to please him, although her cheeks were beginning to feel toasted. He leaned casually against a wall, arms folded, studying her. It occurred to her that maybe that's why her cheeks were hot. '*Dis-moi*, Nicolas, were you aware that there were some men following me? That's why I sent Poilettier off with the coach, to trick them. Except I have no idea what they wanted. Surely they could not know about Mademoiselle's son? And who would have sent them, and how——?' She lifted a puzzled face to him.

'That was the information I wanted, and the reason I stayed behind you. In fact, Skandahet-se and I caught them just before Verneuil and squeezed some facts out of them, some of which still don't make much sense. They had no idea you were looking for Courbier, not until they got to Bonneval and talked to the same old man you did. And then they sent one of their number galloping back to Paris for further instructions.'

'Instructions from whom?'

'The Marquis de Louvois, one of them confessed. Your good friend,' he said pointedly, unable to resist the acid dig.

'De Louvois?' Julie's brow wrinkled. 'But I am so confused. Why would he want me watched? And where did those men come from? From Eu?'

'No, I can only believe from Paris and that they intercepted you on your route. Which can only mean they received a message from Eu.'

'But who——? I don't understand.' She shook her head helplessly, her hair, dry now, floating around her head like a midnight cloud. 'If they were not after me in the interests of finding Courbier—which was *my* purpose, after all—then why?'

He pushed off from the wall and came to sit with her, crossing his legs to rest one elbow on his knee and leaning his bearded chin on one fist. 'Julie, what do you know about your father's death?'

She blinked and gave him a startled look. 'Why, my father died when the ship bringing him across the Channel from England foundered and sank. It took a month for me to hear of it, by letter from the new ambassador in London. I even received a letter of condolence soon after, written by a secretary and signed by the king.' She searched his face for more meaning.

'It seems, *ma chère*, that de Louvois, at least, does not believe your father is dead, for these men were following you in the belief that you would lead them to him. Can you think of a reason why de Louvois would be so anxious to lay hands on your father? Was de Morlé in disgrace with the king, perhaps? Had he misused his office? A vast gambling debt?'

Julie shook her head again. 'I don't know. But then, I was far removed from him and knew little of his business. I was always under the impression that the king held him in very high esteem.'

The cinnamon brows were drawn together in annoyance. 'I am certainly going to have the full story from de Morlé at this point,' he muttered. 'A stern message by the next ship should bring us back some enlightenment.' He saw Julie peering at him, bewildered and anxious. He uncrossed his legs and took her hand. 'See, madame, I have some very special news for you.' His tone was gentle. 'Your father is not dead. He did not perish in the wreck, but got to shore, hid his identity, and took passage to New France on a trading ship. The Vicomte is, in fact, my partner in my trading enterprises and has amassed a new fortune. It was he—through me—who purchased La Vallette from you.'

Julie thought her breath had left her. She couldn't quite encompass what he was saying. 'Y-your partner?' she echoed. It penetrated slowly, what he had told her, that her father, her reserved, stiff-necked gambler of a father, was alive and well and prosperous and, more than that, with attachments to Nicolas de Courcillon, of all people. 'But why didn't he let me know that he lived, at least?' she cried. 'I am his daughter.'

'He wanted no one to know; he only trusted me because he had no choice and because he was afraid for his life. I took him to a remote trading outpost north of Quebec City, and there he remains, only no one would recognize him now for the former aristocrat Henri de Morlé. Don't think too harshly of him, Julie. I want to tell you, he suffered greatly in his heart for having decimated your dowry by his gambling. At this very moment, I have with my banker, under my name, his accumulated funds that are yours by his wish. I had given my word to keep his secret, and so I've been racking my brains to think of some way to present these monies to you. At last, now I can.'

Julie was speechless. She waited for the old anger and resentment toward her father to surface again, but somewhere in the course of her eighteen months in France, such vexations had evaporated. Now all she felt was thankfulness that the Vicomte de Morlé yet lived and she was not totally alone in the world. She even experienced a sudden wish to be with him.

Nicolas rose and retrieved her cup. He poured them both a small amount of wine. 'Drink it,' he ordered.

'Nicolas, did he never tell you why he is afraid to show his face? Couldn't that money you have, after all, be used to pay off his debts?'

'I don't think gambling debts have much to do with it. I like your father, Julie. He is both keen and honest, once kept away from the card tables. In fact, it was his considerable money which in 1662 allowed me to start trading for furs. I knew him when I was still with the king's troops in Montreal, so that when he came to ask me for asylum, it was as a partner. He did not say what brought him to abrogate his life in Europe, and I did not press him. In the bosom of that vast black wilderness stretching from horizon to horizon, whatever transpires here in France seems remote, unimportant. But now—because it is involving you—I am determined to find out what he ran away from.'

Julie concentrated, sipping absently at her wine. The petticoat had slipped off one of her shoulders unnoticed. 'But what shall we do? And what has become of those men who followed me? One was very freckled. I noticed him everywhere.'

'That is a greedy character named de Troisac, one of de Louvois's familiars. Skandahet-se is holding him and the other trussed up in the woods for several days, which should give us enough time to reach Honfleur, extract Courbier, and be on our way back to Eu. That they have had Courbier thrown in their path is not important. They could not know who he is.'

But Julie suddenly thought of something. 'Nicolas! My father was at Saint-Fargeau when Mademoiselle was delivered! She told me that he and the Bishop de Liagre were the only two witnesses.'

Nicolas blinked. There was a connection somewhere, a thread in all of this, but he could not quite pull it out. 'I still believe we are dealing with coincidence and they do not know who Courbier is,' he said slowly. 'And digging about in Honfleur will avail them nothing in respect to your father,' he concluded and shrugged.

He saw her strained face and drew her up from the bench by her shoulders to try to reassure her. 'Julie, don't be afraid. There is nothing to fear. The Marquis de Louvois wants your father for some reason, not you, and if he were certain you knew his whereabouts, he would already have squeezed it from you. When his minions inform him that it was only some personal business for Mademoiselle that took you from Eu and back again, he will retract his claws.' He curved an eyebrow. 'But at least now you know what his interest in you was.'

She caught the hint of smugness in his voice and bridled. 'I suppose you think that Monsieur de Louvois has not any other interest in me except my father? Well, monsieur, you are wrong, very wrong. In fact, I could tell you of a time when. . .when. . .'

'Yes?' A dangerous light had come into his eyes.

Good sense for once overrode her ego. 'When he has been most attentive to me, at many of the court functions,' she finished lamely. She gently disengaged herself from his grip and pulled the petticoat back up on her shoulders. 'Well, what is to be done now?' she asked, and suddenly felt droopy.

He gave her a sideways glance and went to poke up the fire. 'Now we are going to get some rest. You are more exhausted than you realize. And tomorrow, since we have fortunately regained my horse, we can ride in style to L'Aigle to buy you some shoes and a comb.'

'And then? Won't we need another horse?'

He brushed off his hands and stifled a yawn, then leaned back against the table. 'I've thought of something better—certainly easier on your posterior than riding mounted all the way to Honfleur. L'Aigle is on the Risle River, and the shepherd tells me there are barges traveling from there down to the sea at Tancarville, close to Honfleur. We'll be less conspicuous traveling by barge, in the unlikely event that de Troisac and his friend collect themselves to search for you again. How does such transport strike you?'

Julie gave him a dimpled smile. 'I'd be delighted to be drawn peacefully along a nice, smooth river. That ride in the farm wagon wasn't so easy on my anatomy, either.' She was excited by the thought of several days in the close confines of a river barge with him, of several days with him anywhere. She peeked at his face. His expression was very calm, as if the sensuous thoughts that were flitting through her mind, romantic thoughts, thoughts of an inevitable and fervent closeness between them, did not at all occur to him. Maybe—the idea turned her heart chill—maybe she had been too cruel, too supercilious with him when he tried to apologize during the play at the Tuileries, and now he no longer wanted her? Yet he was here, wasn't he?

'I. . .I was under the impression, monsieur, that you have been angry with me,' she finally ventured timidly. 'We have not been in touch all these months.'

He gave her a polite smile, but he did not move from his easy position against the table. 'Does madame forget the letter I sent her in Paris which was returned to me with the seal unbroken, enclosed white rose and all? And my tendered apologies beforehand and afterhand, all unheeded. I submit it is you who is angry with me.'

'Not anymore,' she confessed, looking down. 'How could I be so ungracious to a man whom surely God must have sent to prevent me from drowning? And who has offered to help me accomplish Her Highness's charge?'

He unfolded himself and came to stand before her, and there was something closed about his expression. 'And whom you don't trust for a sol's worth,' he stated.

She felt flustered. 'I can't think where you get that notion. I've actually had nothing to trust you about.'

'That is a matter of opinion, I would say. Unless your memory is very short.'

He was pressing her, she sensed, and he was coming close to touching something that made her uncomfortable. They stared at each other, the little space between them almost shimmering with unspoken words, with suppressed desires. Why is he just standing there? she thought. Why doesn't he hug me, kiss me? I was right. He no longer wants to. My fear of him, my flouncing about angry so that I could be safe from him, has pushed him away. What is he thinking? What is behind that mildly mocking expression with which he views the world—and views me now, here? Why doesn't he reach out for me? I want him to take me in his arms, and I just won't think anymore, not on the dreamlike journey this has become. An idea occurred to her that distressed her further. He is only here as a favor to Mademoiselle, to keep her lady-of-honor from harm. He would do that for her. He is contrite about his treatment of Mademoiselle when she wanted to marry de Lauzun.

'Nicolas,' she started, not knowing what she was going to say, only knowing he was hurting her. Irrationally, against her stubborn decision to forget him, she did not want their story to end. She wished he wouldn't look at her so coolly, as if they had never lain pressed against each other, as if he had not drawn from her body, her brain, and her heart every response she knew how to give, as if he had never said to her, 'I love you' or asked for her hand. Unless it had meant much more to her than to him. She searched his eyes. 'Nicolas——'

It was then that he moved, but only to rub a knuckle against her cheek, as if soothing a child. 'We've talked enough for tonight, Comtesse,' he said softly. 'Go back to your sheepskin and get some sleep. I'll let the fire die down some. I think you're past any chills now.'

No, she wasn't. She suffered an invisible chill through her body remembering his lusty inability to withstand her charms at other times—the way he would stare at her mouth, the flare of his nostrils when she came close to him. She swallowed her disappointment. He was tired, that was it. She told herself that to discredit the sting of her tears.

At that moment, the door was kicked open, and a great mound of straw staggered in, under which appeared the shepherd's skinny legs. Julie went and lay down on the shepherd's pallet. She pulled up the sheepskin and watched them heap up two beds on the sod floor, the soggy youth's before the fire, Nicolas's in the corner away from the heat, which she now realized he had suffered for her sake. Through her lashes, she saw him remove his breeches and rumpled shirt. She had never forgotten how beautiful his body was, the muscular grace of it, the heat of it. The memory of his hard flesh under her hands had often risen unbidden as she lay on her bed at Eu and had made her heart tremble.

He must still have a remnant of that passion he had shown her, he must. And they would have a few days on the river all to themselves. She would laugh, she would flirt, she would make him remember how he had wanted her. And that twice he had said, 'I love you.'

Life was so short. It would be stupid to deny herself what she could have of this man. Life would probably prove long enough when she was the wife of the sedate Mercure de Vosges.

CHAPTER
~ 20 ~

May burst open at last, the very day Julie found herself happily crossing the short gangplank of the *Berceuse*, followed by Nicolas, who led his Al-Minyah onto the flat, crowded deck of the shallow-draft barge. A blaze of sun was set, jewellike, in a miraculously brilliant blue sky unblemished by a single cloud. Warm, soft breezes brought the exquisite fragrance of apple blossoms from the orchards, by some peculiarity of the lovely day mingling compatibly with the pungency of tarred timber and fresh whitewash from the barges moored to the riverbank. Of the two of these vessels that could take passengers, Nicolas had chosen the smaller, which was also cleaner, and there were pots of pink azaleas set out on the roof of its cabin. The good-sized cabin, built to indulge the owner's young wife, was partially raised above the deck. It contained a window, a bed with a down mattress, a table and two chairs, a broad chest with an oil lamp, and enough room to move around. It was also swept and neat, and the barge master's wife proudly showed them a set of laundered linen sheets she had to offer—her treasured wedding sheets, used only on special occasions. It was the owners' own quarters, but for the generous passage fare offered, they were happy to sleep on straw-stuffed cotton mats under a canvas on deck.

'And so will I,' Nicolas murmured offhandedly to Julie when they had completed negotiations and stood on deck to watch the lines cast off.

Julie glanced at him sideways. She said nothing, just continued to smile into the enchanting spring morning, but her toes wriggled impatiently in her new red leather shoes. She had half expected such a move on his part. But, luckily, she had caught him watching her as she tried on the pleated white cap at a stall that morning, setting it on her tumble of black hair and tying it under her chin, turning her head this way and that in the vendor's bit of mirror, the ringlets at her temples stirring in the mild breeze. In the mirror, she saw her own eyes clear and bright with pleasure, her cheeks pink. Her face glowed in spite of the ordeal not twenty-four hours past, and she knew it was his presence that filled her with such effervescence. And behind her, she could see his eyes shining, too, admiring her, although when she turned full toward him to elicit his comment, his smile became merely one of polite approval. Hope gave her courage then. Underneath his wounded pride, she might still find the enamored man she knew last summer. He was just obstinately waiting for her to make the first move.

The barge master's boy clucked at the two large, sturdy horses hitched one behind the other on the towpath. 'Hui! Hui!' And with the animals straining at their traces and the master heaving on a pole at the stern while his wife took the tiller, the *Berceuse* glided away from the quai and joined with the flow of the gentle current on its downstream journey to Tancarville.

The barge master's amiable plump wife lashed up the tiller and then came and bobbed them a curtsy, at the same time using a self-conscious hand to mask a wide, gap-toothed smile. 'Madame, monsieur, you will be more comfortable under that bit of awning on the cabin roof. It is pleasant to sit there and view the countryside,' she offered. But Julie was anxious to wash her face and comb her hair properly and don the new garments they'd bought from the town tailor to replace Blanchette's torn gown: a simple, square-necked gown but of a very becoming blue stuff, along with a gaily flowered challis shawl. They'd also found a new coat for Nicolas, of a light tan wool, with bone buttons. The gown was a little too loose, the coat a little too tight, both yanked right off the forms in the tailor's little shop window where they had served to advertise his trade.

Once she got herself feeling less bedraggled, Julie reasoned, she would be more adept at bringing a lecherous gleam into her cavalier's eyes again. She asked the wife, Maîtresse Pontaguze, to bring a basin and a cloth, and with a gay wave to Nicolas, she hurried purposefully to the cabin, where their few things and his saddlebag had been deposited.

Yet later, in spite of her endearing country cap and wide smile and the fit of the blue gown over her full bosom and the charm of the balmy day, outside of taking her hand to guide her up the short ladder to the cabin roof where a folding seat awaited her, Nicolas did not touch her. He was pleasant, witty, and relaxed, but whereas her hand tingled from the grip of his as he helped her up, he seemed not to notice the contact at all. Nevertheless, they passed a delightful, lighthearted morning on the *Berceuse*, and when Maîtresse Pontaguze brought them a dinner of stewed lamb and tiny onions and beans, with a good Loire wine to wash it down, Julie announced that not even the queen enjoyed such delicious picnics on her royal barge. There were chuckles from the good woman and the barge's grizzled mate. Neither one had ever even seen the queen and didn't think the plainly dressed little bourgeoise complimenting them had, either. Julie and Nicolas proved starved; they cleaned their bowls with gusto and accepted second helpings.

The sunny afternoon slipped by in languid ease, the barge taking them leisurely past scenes of country beauty—half-timbered farmhouses, orchards of gnarled-trunked old trees buried in blossom drifts like pink and white snow, meadows carpeted in young spring green, grazed by particolor cows and their newborn calves, thickets along the river brilliant with the deep pink of rhododendrons, peasants plowing in the fields. At the thatched-roof settlements, people walking on the towpath called out greetings to the barge master, familiar with him and the owners of the two barges behind them. In their wooden sabots, the villagers ran along with the vessel, holding up by the feet flapping, scrawny chickens, vegetables, net bags of eggs, hoping to barter the food for flasks of wine—the cargo—stoppered by cloths soaked in olive oil, which Maîtresse Pontaguze had prepared for good-natured, if truncated, bargaining.

Between the villages, they glided in a lush quiet, defined by the rippling of the water, the barge's creaks, the soft plod of the horses' hooves, and the call of cuckoo birds. Silence had fallen between Julie and Nicolas, too, and they sat in a contented, companionable reverie watching the vine-draped tree trunks on the reedy riverbanks go by. From the forward section came the pleasant humming of Maîtresse Pontaguze as she mended her husband's vest. Julie had many questions she wanted to ask Nicolas about her father. But, much more, she wanted to push away reality for a few days and envelop herself in the sweet, graceful dream of this unlooked-for idyll. Her father had once abandoned her to the Earl of Lowry and then totally disappeared from her world. He could wait a few days more for her attention.

Nicolas had arranged their low stools so that they could lean against the elevation of the cabin wall. He lounged side by side with her, slid down on his spine, booted legs straight out before him and braced against the roof edging. His new floppy-brimmed soft hat was tilted over his eyes, which were closed, but Julie didn't believe he was sleeping. There was the curve of a contented smile under his smooth moustache. On an impulse, she snuggled her hand through his folded arms and up to where she could nestle it under his. The smile deepened slightly, and his warm hand squeezed hers a second and then relaxed. And that was all. He continued dozing or thinking or whatever he was doing. Feeling a little foolish, she waited a few minutes until Pontaguze clomped by, then withdrew her hand—with no opposition—and asked the barge master to help her down. She had some business with the earthenware pot kept under the bed, but more than that, she wanted to regroup her thoughts.

Wandering about the cabin later, pinching off a tallow drip from one of the candles, touching his saddlebag, rubbing a finger along the decorative iron edging protecting the corners of the chest, Julie realized that she wasn't very learned in the deliberate provoking of a man's interest. Men had always been interested in her without much effort on her part. A bit of perfume here, a heart-shaped patch there, *et voilà,* she was enticing. But, she thought in frustration, she had neither perfume nor patch, satin gown nor plume fan to help her cause, not even a bit of kohl for her eyes. None of her warm and dimpled smiles or seductive glances all afternoon had made one dent in his reserve. Not that her actions had been feigned—very little, in fact. It had been a glorious spring day, she was alive, she was with Nicolas, and her laughter and cheerful chatter were genuine indications of her delight. But something else needed to be added to bring him around, and she wasn't sure what.

Maîtresse Pontaguze brought her husband a sweet peeled onion, which she had obtained at the last village, and with relish he bit into it as if it were an apple, winking at her fondly. He worked the steering pole with one sinewy arm as he chewed.

'I am beginning to think these two are innocent cousins after all. The monsieur has taken a bag of hay from the horses and slung it atop the cabin roof with that cotton blanket you gave him, and that is where he intends to sleep,' the bargeman remarked between crunches. 'Too bad. They make a fine-looking couple.'

His wife wiped her hands free of the onion smell on her apron and cocked a good-natured eyebrow. 'Well, cousins they may be—though there's no resemblance I can see—but not innocent, *mon chou.*' She chuckled. 'Ah, no. If you can see how she flirts with him, over her shoulder, so'—she raised a shoulder and looked back archly—'and her pretty mouth always parted, so, as if to catch a fly. And he pretending not to see it but studying her profile from under his hat as if she were a priceless painting hung on the archbishop's wall.' She let loose a peal of laughter, which made her husband grin.

'You think they're really going to see a relative wed in Honfleur?'

She leaned her ample behind against a wine cask and threw him a provocative look. 'They're going to see somebody wed, *bien sûr,* but mayhap each other,' she declared. 'Although, if they've run away—and they have the look of it—they don't so much as hold hands.'

Finishing his onion in one last huge bite, the barge master wiped his hand on his baggy breeches and then reached out and gave his young wife's big breast a squeeze. 'Or hold anything else, neither, eh, *mon ange?*'

Laughing, she knocked his hand away. 'Well, he bought her a packet of new clothes. Must have cost his life savings.'

Pontaguze scratched at the graying bristles of his erupting beard. 'I dunno. They have the feel of quality to me, not any small town's petty bourgeoisie. That's good horseflesh he brought on board. But I guess he could have won it at gaming. Or stole it.'

'Well, they're a nice pair, anyhow. He handed me enough francs to do my best with the victuals—which means we eat good as well, eh, Maître?' With a laugh and a saucy flounce, she poked him in the ribs, sidestepped his lunge and outstretched hand, and took herself forward, rolling her lips.

When it grew too dark for the mules to see the path, the barge was hauled against the high banks and anchored for the night with a lantern hung from a pole on its stern. Maîtresse Pontaguze served her passengers supper on the table in the cabin, a hearty repast of an omelette made with cheese, an eel stew, and a freshly baked round loaf of wheat bread, all miraculously turned out on the small brazier on deck. Wine she drew off from one of the Loire barrels on deck, which were covered by canvas to insulate them from the sun's heat. And one of her last jugs of strong cider cooled in the river at the end of a cord.

Julie found Nicolas most charming to her, relaxed and talkative, recounting, at her prompting, the daring military exploit in Flanders that had brought him to the attention of the king. She listened with growing admiration, her elbow propped on the table, chin in hand, and while she paid attention to his words, she was also absorbing him—his amused eyes, which deepened to aquamarine at remembered adventures; his expressive, square-tipped fingers gesturing, describing. He was handsome, this bearded, strong-willed man. He projected both grace and strength and a prickly independence, and for the first time, she felt inadequate before his splendor. De Courcillon was just as Athénais had once described him—dashing, whether in court silks or his present commoner's coat of tan serge, a man at the height of his powers. How could she hope to keep his attention forever, to believe him when he murmured, 'I love you'? Here he was, closeted with her and by no means unhappy, and she was already jealous of all the other women he might look at.

Stupid, you are simply being stupid, she clucked at herself, crushing up all the deflating thoughts in her mind and ejecting them. Her chin lifted minutely as her ego asserted itself, for she was not ordinary, either. Her name was as good as his, her spirit as strong. She almost interrupted his animated tale to tell him that.

After supper, they wandered outside to take some air on the cabin roof, she pulling her shawl closer about her, he taking off his coat to let the cool air flow over him. She wanted to sit on the folding stool, but he gestured toward the hay sack that would be his bed. 'It's more comfortable here, and you can lean against this raised section,' he suggested. When she acquiesced, he helped her to sit and then folded himself beside her—but not too close. She wished he wouldn't be so proper. The old Nicolas would have just plumped her down and then leaned forward to steal a kiss as well.

But it was a beautiful night, a full moon drifting in a cloudless black-velvet sky full of tiny diamond chips, the tops of the dark trees touched with silver, shining ripples spreading out on the river. Upstream, the yellow pinpricks that were the lanterns of another barge twinkled. Astern, their animals, fed and watered and sheltered under canvas, moved restlessly. A night warbler sang his pure song from the shadowy brush along the bank; a bullfrog added his bass croak. Forward, where Pontaguze and his mate mended the torn mesh of several eel traps by the dancing light of a large oil lamp, the plump barge wife began to hum and then to sing in a soft, clear voice:

Te souviens-tu, Marie, de notre enfance aux champs?
Te souviens-tu, m'amie, nous dansions les bontemps...

For a long while, they listened, charmed, lulled by the sweet, melancholy country airs the woman sang and by the water lapping below, gently rocking the vessel. They found themselves sitting closer together, somehow, their arms brushing, and Julie could feel Nicolas's heat through the cloth of his shirt. She was so aware of him next to her, her nerve ends tingled. And yet he remained merely contentedly gazing up at the shadow-pocked luminous mass that was the moon. She sighed to herself, thinking of how many moons she had stared at alone, yearning for him, and yet here he was, sitting as innocent of passion as a chaste monk.

'It is so beautiful, isn't it?' she ventured in a murmur more like a sigh.

'It is magical,' he agreed quietly. 'Almost unreal. I have spent so many nights under the sky, in the woods of New France, in the Flemish sortie camps, I find it hard to believe that I am really here, indolent on this peaceful Norman river, surveying the lunar orb from the comfort of this great hay mattress——' He broke off for a brief chuckle.

'And with me?' She prompted the most important part in a small voice.

He returned to face her. His shirt glimmered purple-white in the swath of silvered light; his eyes were in shadow. He did not touch her, but she could almost feel his fingers trailing along her cheek. She brushed back the silky strands of hair the breeze blew across her lips.

He remained still, saying nothing, but an errant sparkle came out of the shadow, and starlight caught in his eyes. 'I think we should retire now,' he said finally. 'It has been a long day, and you should have some rest.'

'But I'm not sleepy yet,' she said coquettishly.

'You will be once you lay your head on the pillow. May I escort you to your portal, madame?'

She was confused but willing to oblige him. It was obviously privacy he wanted, a closed door behind them before he would reach for her. Shyness was not one of the Marquis de Courcillon's ordinary traits. It must be her vulnerable position in the exposed world of the barge that had muted his brashness, although this was the man who had carried her laughing and protesting away from the blindman's game at Saint-Germain and swept her offstage on his horse during the Tuileries theatrical. Her heart caught when she remembered those intoxicated times and the night they had spent together, and she was glad the darkness hid her heated cheeks.

She gave him her hand, and he helped her down from the roof. They both nodded to bid good night to Pontaguze, whose wife, mate, and boy had already retired to their own beds. In a few steps, they were at the low door to the cabin, and he threw it open for her. Smiling, she went by him and down the few steps, confident he would follow, but when she turned around, thinking she would just step into his arms, invited or not, and ease her terrible need for his touch, she saw by the lantern that he was still outside, his outstretched arm propped against the cabin roof.

'Aren't you going to say good night?' he asked mildly.

She was confused again. 'Don't—don't you want to come in?'

'I think that would be unwise. I have a tendency to take from you what isn't mine to have. My conscience seems to have developed knots in my old age.'

'N-Nicolas, I simply don't understand your actions. You once said you loved me——'

'And so I do, madame, but you don't love me. And I don't relish the precarious position of unrequited lover. You might forget me tomorrow, and I don't like to be hurt. Someone did that once when I was very young, a flighty woman who adored to count her lovers in multiples of ten, and it has since made me wary.'

'But that is. . .but you're being incredible. I do care for you; *mon Dieu*, shouldn't you know that? Do you think I. . .I consort with any man who smiles at me? Nicolas, you are making me very angry.'

'Something I do not wish to do, *ma chère*, I have only the highest thoughts of you. I told you; I love you. But the quicker I get over being enthralled by the soon-to-be-betrothed of the Comte de Vosges, the better for my health.'

Julie's shawl had slipped off one shoulder. 'Oho, so that is the problem. Mademoiselle has been talking to you.'

'And wouldn't you have mentioned it?'

'Yes, of course, when I had. . .I m-mean, I haven't quite made up my mind, you see——'

'Ah! A flighty woman.' He shook his head, turning down the corners of his mouth mournfully. 'Just as I thought.'

She stamped her foot, wishing he were under it. 'But that isn't true.' Becoming exasperated, she put her hands on her hips. 'See here, monsieur. I am no more going to stand here and talk to you for all the people on this barge to hear——' She caught herself and continued more reasonably, 'Won't you at least step in for a moment? Please?'

He rubbed his beard, considering, and this distressed her further, to see how strong his will was when hers was so weak and she wanted him so much. 'No, Julie,' he said finally. An unadorned refusal without any graceful apologies.

She asked, 'But then why did you come such a long way after me? And risk your life plunging into that rushing river? How can I understand you?'

'It's not hard. Since I love you but do not wish to be your lover, I must then be your friend for a while, until I see you safely bestowed into other keeping.'

'My friend?' she wailed.

He reached for the door. 'Go to bed now, madame. Thing will look brighter to you in the morning. We have a long way to travel yet and your mission still to accomplish. If we cherish each other in friendship, the road will be smoother.' He smiled, teeth gleaming in the half-shadows. With one hand on the latch, he swept off his floppy hat and made an elegant bow, then pulled the door shut firmly.

Tears of hurt came to her eyes, and she did not brush them away. Shoulders slumped, she whispered,

'Friends?' After they had made love together that night at Fontainebleau with a wildness and a passion she had never dared imagine, with a depth of intimacy she had never dreamed existed?

Friends?

And then she whirled, grabbed up a pewter cup, and flung it at the closed door, swallowing the screech that would have accompanied it. 'I'll show you friends, you *gros cochon!*' she choked.

Te souviens-tu, Marie? Te souviens-tu?
Le temps que je regrette c'est le temps qui n'est plus.

Outside, leaning against the cabin wall, arms akimbo and one booted leg crossed over the other, Nicolas heard the loud clunk against the door and favored the night with his quirked smile. Good. Now, if she'd do some thinking before she closed her pretty eyes, perhaps she would compare her stubborn fears that were wrecking them with those he had just pretended to have about her and come up with the proper answer: one welcomes the gift of love the present offers. The future branches into too many unknowable paths to be considered. He hoped she thought fast—if his little lesson was to work. He didn't intend for this enchanted voyage, so removed out of time and place, to end with their being friends.

Meanwhile, he could use some sleep himself. It was better than seeing again in his mind those violet eyes clouding over with unhappiness as he did his best to act the cooled-off swain. That was one of the things he loved about her: she could not keep her feelings from her face, her mobile, delicate, obstinate little face.

The next day proved even more exquisite a spring jewel, with the sun sparkling on the water, the air warm and perfumed, as if nature were making bountiful apology for the weeks of mouse-colored skies and chill drizzle it had inflicted upon its creatures.

In the morning, several other passengers came aboard to ride to La Lague, where a large fair was being held, including a white-haired country priest in a stiff-brimmed round hat, a simple, friendly man who was pleased to be invited to share Julie and Nicolas's breakfast and who sat without fuss cross-legged on the cabin roof.

'Ah, *mes chers enfants,*' the cleric beamed, waving about the wedge of bread and cheese he'd chosen. '*Le bon Dieu* sends us such days as this now and then, to make us ache for Paradise. Do you travel far, then, in this chariot of the angels, might I be so bold?'

'All the way to Tancarville, *mon père*, and thence to Honfleur. Another two days,' Nicolas told him.

'Ah. I perceive from your manner of speech that you are not from these parts. Has no one told you of the veneration and celebration of our local Saint Exuberin in La Lague? We shall miss the great procession, unfortunately, where one can see the saint's actual finger, preserved in holy water, carried on the shoulders of strong men. And the whole town marches with branches of apple blossoms, treading on flower petals strewn the whole length of the way. The celebration is renowned for leagues around, and a great glory to one of God's holiest men. You must attend it.' He winked slyly at Julie and tapped a finger on his reddish nose. 'I dare say this fair young woman would be excited to see our beautiful representation of the life and martyrdom of Saint Exuberin. It is played every year by a troupe of actors from Rouen, good Normans all, and so talented the tears flow down your cheeks and you would fain rush upon the stage to stay the executioner's cruel hand!'

The plump barge wife, passing by with buckets to be emptied astern, called up cheerfully, '*Oui*, Father Paulinus, 'tis true what you say, but say also about the fire-eaters and the balancers on a rope, the dancing bears, the fearful man with two heads, and the Liron! A real, live Liron from Africky, so the crier read from the notice in the town square last time we went through, a frightful beast with giant teeth who would just as soon eat you up as look at you.' She giggled and then added, 'We stop at La Lague for the night, anyway.'

Julie's eyes had begun to shine. She turned to her companion. 'A lion! I've never seen one. Even the king's zoo does not have one, for the beast they had died. Oh, Nicolas, can we go to the fair? Please?' She laid an urging hand on his bare arm. They were far from the protocol of the court, and his sleeves were rolled up to greet the warm day.

He looked at her wide-eyed, eager smile, and his reserve melted. Was this guileless girl the widow of sad experience and mature outlook who was determined to protect herself from loving too much? Or even the cool accomplice to the Duchesse de Montpensier's ill-considered demands? Julie was breathtaking in her beauty. Her raven hair was tied casually loose and waved down her back. Her porcelain complexion, already pinkened by the sun, was now more wisely protected by Maîtresse Pontaguze's crownless straw brim with ribbons tied under the chin. Her sweet lips were parted in excitement, displaying the glisten of white teeth. He expected this breathless milkmaid any moment to clap her hands and bounce in her seat, and he would deny her nothing just to keep that artless excitement in her flowerlike eyes.

He knew he was staring at her. He would never forget how lovely she looked at that moment. It wasn't necessary for the barge wife, who was just as eager as Julie to see the 'Liron', to repeat coaxingly, 'We do stop there for the night, monsieur.'

'Well,' he responded expansively, 'if that is the case, I suppose we will go to the festivities.' His hat brim was pulled down to shade his eyes against the early sun, which slanted under the bit of awning. He smiled from under it at Julie. 'Does that please you, *ma jolie cousine?*'

'Oh, yes, it does,' she trilled, and she did clap her hands, entirely lost in the pleasure of the moment, and he wondered if she had ever been allowed to attend a fair during her years in Sussex. 'And will you buy me a honey apple? I had one once. I adore candied honey apples.'

He would buy her the world if only she knew, if only she would continue to look at him so ingenuously, as if he were God, as if her world began and ended with his merest word. He sighed, for ordinarily that was not

Julie. But word be damned, if only she would continue to look at him. With a spirit suddenly as weightless as the pale butterfly that came to flutter airily above her head, he smiled at her. 'You may have two honey apples, *minette*. I do not cringe from women who have left their teeth behind in such sweet traps.'

Grinning, he ducked away from her make-believe blow, catching her hand. And smiling and laughing they remained all day as the *Berceuse* slipped between narrow banks covered with tiny, starlike wildflowers and glided under the trailing withes of chartreuse weeping willows, with an occasional cow peering placidly at them through a break in flowering hawthorn hedges. Idly fingering the smooth edges of the ribbon securing her straw brim, Julie regaled him with pleasant tales of her childhood, including her mother's stories of La Vallette, the estate she had thought lost to her but which, could she credit her ears, now belonged to her father. She also related, laughing over them, funny anecdotes of her schooling at the convent and her youthful friendship with Athénais de Montespan.

This last made him remark wryly, 'I hope you will take it kindly, madame, if I make mild mention that at present the Marquise de Montespan would betray her own children to keep the king's favor. Her friendship is to be taken with grains of caution.'

Wondering what commotion he would make if he knew about Athénais's connection with La Voisin and the dread Black Mass, or his brother's horrid apostasy, and determined never to tell him, she wrinkled her brow. 'Athénais has always been more ambitious than loyal, Nicolas. You may be sure I know it, and I haven't forgotten how she tried to use me. But I don't think she would deliberately do me great hurt. There has also always been a sort of truce between us. And anyway'—the thought tickled her to a giggle——'I was not thinking this week of wresting the king away from La Montespan.'

He studied her for a moment with his discerning eyes. 'I couldn't prove it, Julie, but considering the demands Mademoiselle has received from the Marquise, I wouldn't be surprised if the woman had manipulated the entire affair with de Lauzun——' He held up his hand quickly to forestall her objection. 'Peace, peace. Not with de Lauzun's knowledge, of course. But how else to put La Grande Mademoiselle in a position of desperate need for Athénais de Montespan's intervention with the king? It was one reason she needed to know exactly what was happening at the Luxembourg almost as it happened.'

He could be right, of course. It made a terrible sense. 'And what do you think she will do when Her Highness produces an heir and removes her riches from Athénais's grasp?'

He shrugged. 'Get her adherents to try to disprove it, of course.'

The barge went under a squat stone bridge hardly an arm's length above their heads, and they waved to two children watching the laden craft go by, drawn by the patient, plodding horses. The littlest girl threw down a field poppy, which Julie laughingly caught and stuck into the bosom of her gown. Unwilling to break their languid mood, she changed the heavy subject, asking him then about New France, and he was not averse to following her lead. She wondered how did he come there, how did he become a trader, and he told her all about his service with the Carignan-Salière regiments and how he had noticed that trappers working for independent agents had more experience in eluding hostile Indians than those employed by the government.

'And they made a damned lot of money, too, for their agents, a very tempting opportunity to an impecunious young officer. That is where your father came in. He saw me as I watched how many cargo ships arrived and left, and he learned about my bribes to study the ships' manifests in order to know how many bundles of skins went out on each tide. He offered to advance me the capital to being a trading business when my tour of duty was up, and six years ago he joined me there, as I've told you. It worked out very well. It freed me, of course, to come back to France to see to my estates. And to take my place at court.'

She peeked around her straw brim. 'And were there many ladies of quality in New France for you to consider?'

'Saints and martyrs, no. There were then only perhaps twenty-five hundred Europeans in all of New France, in Montreal, Quebec City, and Beaupré, with families of any fortune sending their daughters back to France to be educated and married. The king, in fact, had been sending shiploads of women and ordering all bachelors to marry within fifteen days.' He grinned at her. 'King's officers excepted, God be thanked.'

He told her of how he had met Skandahet-se and of his stay in the Huron camp and of the ambush by hostile Senecas that put an arrow through his chest and almost ended his life. A swift, comprehending look passed over her features. He knew she was remembering the night they had spent together on the bear rug and the jagged white scar she'd fingered under his collarbone. As they traveled sedately northwest across Normandy, he spoke to her of everything that had touched his life, except for Shanat-a, an episode he was not proud of, best left for another time.

Once, forgetting himself, he absently rubbed the back of her hand as it lay daintily beside her on the hay sack. Her glance at him was startled, hopeful. He turned the intimate gesture into a mere friendly pat and quickly drew her attention to a little church set in a slope of ribboned fields, covered to its conical Norman tower in freshly green ivy that lifted and wavered in the light breeze.

Stretching their legs on the towpath as the sun lengthened its downward glide, they played a game popular with the court in which one party gave the initial of a name—either courtier, statesman, or famous artist—and the other must guess the person. He stumped her on General Horace de Menil and the legendary Roland, ancient hero of the Spaniards' battle against the Moors, for both of which she merrily accused him of making up names, and she got great pleasure out of his ignorance of England's John Milton, for which he accused her of the same. Pontaguze rested the horses downstream a bit and waited for them to catch up. And then, at dusk, just after they had taken a little evening collation of bread and jelly and cider, they reached the lively, lantern-hung La Lague and maneuvered for space to tie up alongside the busy quai. A glow from the nearby torchlit church plaza lit up the sky behind the precipitous tile roofs of fifteenth-century houses that hulked over alleylike streets leading from the riverside docks. And the joyful noises of a country hurdy-gurdy and bagpipes wound their droning about the clear night.

They all went together, the two couples, the priest, the mate, and the boy, everyone already in buoyant spirits primed by Pontaguze's gift of a glass of fermented hard cider. The barge wife had donned her best outfit, taken from a chest in the hold with the liquid cargo: a vividly embroidered wide sash, which joined a full white bodice fluttering with ribbons to a brilliant blue calf-length skirt. Below this, she sported red stockings and silver-buckled black shoes. Her mop of curls tumbled from a gossamer pleated white cap. The ruddy-faced barge master had adorned his person with a short purple blouse of shiny cotton sporting a jaunty sprig of white azalea his wife had pinned to it. There was a little bunch of azalea in the breast of Nicolas's tan coat, too, and a long speckled feather had been added to the floppy hat under which his light blue eyes twinkled. He was failing to maintain much reserve in the face of his resilient mood and his lady's animation.

The priest soon found a gaggle of round-bellied fellow clerics whom he knew, and the mate and the boy peeled away to follow after some maidens who giggled by in their bright skirts and charming caps.

Perhaps it was the result of her sober winter, but Julie found herself as uncontrollably excited as a child. She almost skipped as she pulled Nicolas here and there through the crowded lanes of stalls and food stands from which mouth-watering smells of onions and butter and sizzling meat emanated. She had donned her gauzy Norman cap, and Maîtresse Pontaguze had generously lent her a family heirloom, an apron of beautiful lace to wear over her blue gown, and a lilac ribbon for her neck. And she had clipped from somewhere a bit of fragrant hyacinth for her passenger to tuck into the modest square neckline of her gown, because Julie had mentioned that it was her favorite scent. The women of the town in their holiday finery wore gold crosses and amber beads, and instead of sabots, the men strutted in polished leather shoes that pinched and prodded, but they smiled anyway. Delighted children darted everywhere, some still clutching the bright nosegays they had carried in the afternoon's solemn religious procession. All around the surprisingly large square situated before the church, residents in the facing buildings had hung out flapping sheets and white cloths painted with *fleur-de-lis* emblems, with the arms of the guilds or scenes of the lives of various saints colorful with writhing dragons and rampant beasts, as well as foreign banners confiscated by war veterans as souvenirs.

The boisterous barge mistress grabbed Nicolas by the hand and pulled him and Julie into a ring of dancers circling to a country tune played by foot-tapping musicians on bagpipes, drum, and concertina, and the surrounding onlookers clapped enthusiastically in cadence. Giggling, joining hands, and matching her steps to the others', Julie threw back her head and abandoned herself to the jolly dance, circling with a hop and skip first right, then left, and then, like the others, Nicolas picked her up and whirled her around so vigorously she thought she was going to fly off into the night, except that he had strong hold of her. She laughed and hugged him, and then they were drawn back into the circle again, stamping out the rhythm.

> *Et sur la mousse l'on se trémousse*
> *L'on s'entrepousse comme des fous!*

They danced with townsmen and peasants and the local gentry, on and on until the music wound up in a wild flurry and they fell into each other's arms, laughing and exhausted, and then hunted up a refreshment stall to down wooden mugs of cool, delicious hard cider.

They watched the tame bear lumber about and box with its trainer, they exclaimed at the scraggly-maned lion pacing in its cage, staring with empty yellow eyes. They gaped at jugglers and wrestlers and acrobats and a daredevil on a wire strung over the stalls from one end of the square to another. They gorged on *fougasse,* a flat, crispy festival bread and smoked sausage, fried eggs and peas, crackling strips of roasted pig skin, and washed it all down with more cups of bubbling cider. Julie devoured her candied apple for dessert and licked her sticky fingers with relish. Being silly, she held one finger up for Nicolas to lick, and when he did, little shudders of pleasure went through her and made her catch her lower lip with her teeth. They wandered among the vendors, and he bought her a tiny carved patch box of ivory, and she insisted on buying him a ring for his little finger, made of polished olivewood.

The hour grew late, strong cider and sweet wine had turned some of the revelers rambunctious, and there were rowdy youths who ran through the crowds in big papier-mâché heads wielding soft, rolled-cloth batons to strike people with. The Pontaguzes found them, and, along with other departing fairgoers in a gay mood, all four strolled back to the barge, arm in arm along the cobbled street, flushed and mellow with drink and the entertaining evening.

'Hop-la, good woman, you are so sozzled you can hardly keep your feet,' the barge master bellowed in mock disapproval as his plump, giggling wife stumbled.

'*Gros cochon*, you pushed me!' she cried back.

'*Faut t'embracer, tu sais,*' he announced, and picked her off her feet in a bear hug to plant a big, smacking kiss on her mouth. Setting her down, he hauled her along with them. 'Come, you've kept me from my sleep long enough and spent all my francs, Jezebel,' he croaked, and then he began to yodel in a cider-soaked basso:

> *Ma femme boit comme une éponge*
> *Et moi comme un trou d'été.*
> *Qui fait que jamais elle ne songe*
> *À notre nécessité...*

Laughing at the bawdy ditty, Julie and Nicolas settled on a less suggestive song that they warbled together, she giggling when he made up words because he couldn't remember the true ones, but it wasn't until they reached the barge, the crew not yet returned, that she realized his arm was about her waist and he was keeping her steady. In fact, he followed close behind with both hands on her shoulders when she maneuvered the short gangplank.

His coat was unbuttoned, his hat pushed back rakishly on his head. Gaining the deck, she untied the strings of her cap and pulled it off, shaking out her curls, but then a great hiccup shook her. She collapsed in giggles against him. Life was so funny.

'You are shamelessly drunk, madame,' he rumbled through his grin, looking down at the top of her head. 'I wouldn't trust you to walk two paces on your own.'

A grand idea bloomed in her somewhat befuddled head. *That* was how to seduce him. Be helpless. Another loud hiccup made her bounce in his arms. '*Pouffe!* I am—*hiccup*—fine,' she announced.

'Monsieur, madame, a special toast to this night and to good St. Exuberin!' With his beaming wife carrying a lantern behind him, Pontaguze stumped up, in his fist a small leather wine bottle which had a long, bobbing wood spout. 'This is a wine from Tours, gone old and so delectable and sweet, it is like sugar from the lips of a virgin. You must drink it from the spout, like this, and good fortune will follow you.' He threw back his head, raised the bottle high, and ejected a pale stream of wine directly down his gullet.

'I don't think——' Nicolas began, but Julie interrupted, clapping her hands.

'Oh yes, I want to do that,' she said.

'Julie, you have had enough.'

She flounced her shoulder and looked up from under her lashes at him. 'Monsieur, you are truly being impolite. This is a special gift from our host. You just—*hiccup*—don't think I can do it.'

'I know you can't. Not without drowning yourself.'

'Well, neither can you.' She hiccuped.

Loosened by the merry evening, Nicolas merely raised

an eyebrow for answer, put her aside, and reached for the bottle. He tilted back his head and, with a neat, well-aimed squirt, poured himself a mouthful of wine. And then another. Wiping his mouth on his sleeve, he handed the bottle back to Pontaguze. Pontaguze passed the bottle to his wife, who expertly aimed several swallows into her mouth, and then, with a whoop and a frisky, naughty glance at Nicolas, she passed the bottle to Julie.

Julie grasped it in both hands, planted her feet firmly on the gently bobbing deck, threw Nicolas a tipsy smirk, and raised the bottle. The grinning Pontaguzes began to clap in rhythm. She really wasn't sure she could do it properly. The nozzle was so long and floppy, she had to hold the bottle almost at arm's length. But so what if she failed? *Tant pis.* The world was a pleasant place where anything was possible. She opened her mouth, aimed right at it, and squeezed—and hiccuped—and the stream of wine jetted off the point of her chin and down into the cleft of her bosom, and it took her befuddled reflexes a second to realize what was happening. She shrieked and dropped the bottle, thoroughly wet down her front, and stood staring down at herself in disbelief.

Maîtresse Pontaguze burst out laughing, and her husband guffawed behind his hand. Nicolas's shoulders shook.

'Oh, *nom du ciel!*' Julie squeaked, trying to flap her wet bodice. 'Oh, *mon Dieu*, what a disgraceful performance. My eye is not all it might be,' she tittered.

Nicolas pulled a red kerchief from his pocket, caught her by the arm, and began to swab off her chest, wiping her up like a child as she stood there with a silly grin on her face. 'Your eye is about the same as with a pistol,' he chuckled.

'It is good luck, madame, simply that you have tried it,' Pontaguze averred, and his wife echoed, '*Mais oui*, good luck.'

Julie shifted her gaze to the barge mistress, and suddenly the cabin behind and the whole of the barge began to wheel around. Her eyes grew wide. 'Whoops.' She swayed and reached out to clutch at Nicolas.

He scooped her off her feet to carry her. 'Bid you good night, kind hosts, with thanks for the excellent wine. This lady has had too much reveling. I'll see she finds her bed safely.' He nodded pleasantly to them, but there was a tone to his voice that separated them now that the evening was over, that made the owners of the barge *Berceuse* duck their heads respectfully as they said good night. Pontaguze hurried to open the cabin door for Nicolas and his burden, who was now humming happily between hiccups.

'I will clean madame's dress for her in the morning, monsieur,' the barge mistress called out. 'She may have to stay abed until it dries.'

But when her husband came back to her, she put her arms about his thick waist and said huskily, 'I don't think he will mind that, eh, *mon grand liron*? I think the fine cousins will not arrive in Honfleur as they left L'Aigle, *hein*? He'll keep her feet warm tonight.'

Pontaguze steered her forward toward their own pallet under the canvas. 'Get away with you, woman. My own feet need warming. And we start off right at dawn tomorow, no excuses.' Nuzzling her ear, he also gave her behind a hearty pinch.

Nicolas dropped her on the bed as if she were a sack of beans and dusted off his hands. 'You're drunk, madame,' he noted.

'Oh no, you're mistaken,' she giggled, struggling to sit up. There was a big wet stain down the front of her dress. She ogled it and then collapsed backward. 'Oooh, this barge is funny. It goes up and down, up and down. . .'

Hands on his hips, he viewed her with fond tolerance. 'You're a mess,' he chuckled.

'A mess, a mess,' she crooned, and she let her head hang off the bed, throat exposed, one arm and her dark mass of hair drooping to the floor. Her eyes closed. 'I think I'll go to sleep.'

'Well, you can't go to sleep like that, sopping wet and smelling like a wine vat. Julie, wake up. You can't. . .'

'A mess, a mess,' she tittered, bouncing her hips.

'Nicolas, let's sing. *"Sur le pont d'Avignon——"* she piped, and upside-down she saw him shake his head. She saw him divest himself of his coat, his boots, and the simple cravat he had purchased for his neck. He went over to let down the woven curtain that blocked the small window.

'L'on y dans-e, l'on y dans-e. . .'

'Come, madame, sit up. In the absence of your maid, I'll help you to remove your gown.' He leaned on the bed on one knee and hauled her up by her arms. She collapsed limply, her hair flowing forward to hide her face.

'I don't need any help,' she protested, and hiccuped.

She felt him unbuttoning the bodice of her gown and untying the strings that drew the skirt together and the ties of the lace apron, vaguely aware that she had no corset over her flimsy chemise. Wrinkling her nose at the wine smell that rose from her damp skin, she chuckled. 'Phew! That scent has stayed in the perfumer's vats too long.'

He pulled her close to him to hold her while he tugged the bodice sleeves from her arms, and she kept her eyes closed to treasure the feel of his arms about her. Then he laid her down and deftly swept off the whole gown and her one petticoat. *'Tiens,'* she heard him mutter. 'I'm getting plenty of practice peeling wet clothes off of you, *chérie.*' She heard him step away from the bed and peeked. He was pouring water into the basin and wringing out the cotton kerchief in it. But when he came back onto the bed again with the obvious aim of swabbing the wine smell and sticky residue from her chest, she grabbed his hand with the wet cloth in it and patted it on her hot face. 'For some reason, I'm very warm,' she hiccuped.

Kneeling on the bed beside her, he shoved a pillow under her head and then ran the cloth over her neck and upper chest. He tugged with one finger at the neckline of her chemise. 'This is soaked, too,' he growled, but when she focused her eyes on him, she saw him gazing hypnotized at her breasts, outlined by the thin wet cotton partially plastered against them. Her heartbeat quickened, her heart lifted. 'Well, take it off, then,' she whispered wickedly. 'It won't be the first time, and there's no more will you see with me naked.'

He flushed, like a boy caught peeping through a keyhole. His eyes darkened, sought hers. Suddenly, a delicious surge caught her in its thrall, an interior contraction of overwhelming desire and obsession, and with sinuous grace she twisted up to her knees and flung her arms about his neck. She cried out the first thing that came clearly to her jumbled mind. 'Oh, Nicolas, Nicolas, oh, I love you!' Tears came to her eyes as she hugged him convulsively, because it was the truth and she would die if she had really lost his love. 'Oh, *mon coeur,* I mean it.'

His arms went around her. She heard him draw in a deep breath, almost a sigh. Then he said gruffly against her temple, '*Eh bien.* That's better. Yet how do I *know* you mean it?'

Pulling back to stare into his smiling but intense gaze, she complained, 'But you are being mean. Of course I mean it.'

He wrapped her in his expansive embrace again and rubbed his cheek against hers. 'Then I apologize. Because I know you and love you, I know you would not say—or do—what you don't mean. And because I love you, I trust you.'

With relief, she heard him say again, 'I love you,' and it finally dawned on her that all of his cool behavior had been linked to making this one point, that without unquestioning trust, there could be no love. And she felt ashamed of her suspicious spirit.

He let her go, ignoring her abashed expression, and put a finger on the tip of her nose. 'Julie, take off that wet chemise before you get a chill.'

His tone was matter-of-fact, but he wasn't that calm; she could see in his gaze that he was barely containing his mounting desire. It returned to her a feeling of some control. She sat back on her heels on the bed and licked her lower lip sensuously. She lifted her arms straight up. 'You take it off,' she whispered.

He stared at her for a moment. There was a vein

throbbing in his brow. He reached out and slowly drew the garment over her head and then flung it away. He groped for the damp red cloth, laid it flat over her breasts, and gently washed away the wine down to the base of her ribs. He jumped up to fumble among her discarded garments, then brought over the petticoat to wipe her dry. And in his hand was the drooping tip of hyacinth which he rubbed over her shoulders and bosom. She watched him with desire-slitted eyes. Then, without touching her otherwise, he bent his head and delicately kissed the tips of both breasts and ran his tongue up the marble valley between them, ignoring how her body quivered. He pressed her down full-length on the bed again, then slid up and kissed her mouth passionately. Moving his lips against the corner of hers, he whispered, 'I don't want you to budge. Not a muscle. I'm going to take you very slowly tonight. Because if this is a dream, I want to make it last a long time.'

She sighed, a long, wavering surrender. She sought his lips again, feeling their smooth texture and firm softness, the only soft part in that brawny body. 'Make it last forever, my love,' she breathed against his lips, and she experienced anticipation so voluptuous that it made her heart skip and turned her limbs to melted butter.

This was where she belonged, in the circle of his arms, in the protection of his body. She lay still while he slipped off her long underdrawers and rolled her black stockings down upon their garters and off her feet. Then he swiftly shrugged off his own garments. She closed her eyes and tried to make her breath come more slowly as she felt him settle his naked body against hers and begin to stroke back the dark curls from her brow. She could drink in his warmth now, she could smell his skin, that wonderful, dry musky scent, a compound of maleness and male power, that rushed from entrancing her nose to quickening the pit of her stomach. He drew her to him and pressed her against him, and she moaned to feel the silky-rough length of his body against hers. But she followed his orders and remained passive. With difficulty.

'Open your eyes,' he demanded, and so she did. 'Your

flower eyes,' he murmured, peering into them and then kissing her lightly on each lid. 'They have haunted me from the day I met you. They made a hermit out of me this winter, because if you were not in court, I had no wish to be there, either. They enslaved me. A willing slave.' He smiled. And meanwhile, one hand caressed her back, her slim waist, the curves of her hip and buttock, and ran along the silky smoothness of her firm, round thigh.

'Don't move,' he ordered again. Slipping down her trembling body, he began with her foot, kissing it, the sole, the toes, the dainty arch. She could feel the soft tickle of his beard. And then he moved his lips up her leg, cradling it with his hands, her knee, her outer thigh. Her breathing came harsher, her back arched slightly in spite of her determination to stay quiet, but then he skipped over the place that burned and circled her navel with his tongue. He pressed his mouth in short, hot kisses against her soft belly and then continued to move up, and she could feel against her the hard proof of his desire. Her fingers clenched convulsively. She wanted to touch him, to feel him, and even in its fuzzy state, her mind staggered with shock because she wanted to kiss him—there.

His warm breath made her breasts swell and feel heavy, he squeezed her breasts gently and kissed them, and then his hot mouth coming over her nipple sent her senses reeling. She flung back her head with a desperate gasp and a cry; and with a lover's sixth sense, he immediately snaked his hand down to press flat against the throbbing dampness between her legs. Her body arched up, and she exploded. She thought she was coming apart, she heard herself squeal, and then she thought no more against the profound, rapturous undulations that shook her and shook her. And then he was holding her tight until her tremors subsided. She drew in a sobbing breath; tears leaked unheeded from her eyes. He held her for a while, kissing her temples and forehead, until her body totally relaxed.

He raised himself up on one elbow to peer down at her.

'What happened?' she asked in a half-quaver, half-laugh.

Vastly pleased, he shook his head and teased her. 'You couldn't wait again, *ma petite chatte*. I thought I told you not to move.'

'Oh, that was mean. Don't you ever make me do that again. I want to make love to you, too.'

'Do you, *mon coeur? Eh bien*, start now, then,' he invited her.

She blinked at him, for the moment at a loss how to begin. He grabbed her hand and wrapped it around his warm, hard member, erect as a soldier. 'You could start here,' he said in an encouraging murmur.

The shock of touching him ran up her arm; her pulse began to beat raggedly again, and a reservoir she thought was totally empty commenced filling once more.

Nicolas watched her wakening, elated all over again to suspect that the woman he craved, for all her widowhood and natural passion, had never been loved erotically. She was his to please and to teach and to delight in. He clenched his jaw against the movement and joyous grasp of her slim fingers and with an effort of will removed her eager hand from him before his control evaporated. Catching her in an ardent embrace, he kissed her long and hard, opening her willing mouth to plumb its depths and taste her sublime sweetness, caressing her satiny back from her neck down to the cleft at the end of her spine, holding back his clamoring need by dedicating all his attention to rekindling hers.

He smiled down into her eyes, where purple flames leaped and slowly, with his hands and his mouth, he worked upon her body like a master at a harpsichord. And she made it easy, moving and responding in just the way he elicited, and it seemed to him, to his delighted astonishment, that their bodies began to vibrate in unison.

She groaned, pulled his head to her bosom, her hips moving against him. 'Please,' she whispered, 'please. . .'

He took her then, plunged into her with every sensitized fiber of his being and thrust again and again, and then, feeling her body quake against him and his own control plummeting toward oblivion, he pressed his finger below on a private spot. She yelped, her body arched like a bow, and he followed her, telling her with his profound physical response of the desire and deep love he felt for her.

Afterward, he held her close until their panting subsided, and then his arms relaxed and they both drifted off somewhere.

She felt totally at peace. Happy. Sad. She twisted to lie on her stomach and looked over at him. He lay just as they had fallen apart, one arm across his eyes, cinnamon hair damply tangled, the little flicker from the oil lamp illuminating dimly the planes of his face, the regular rise and fall of his broad, golden-haired chest. She thought he was asleep from the sound of his breathing. She smiled, then realized that at some point he had pulled the bedclothes up around her. She found the edge of the sheet and flapped it over him, too, then snuggled against him, nuzzling into his shoulder. He turned on his side, unwaking, but an arm slipped over her and a solid leg hooked over her own. She was more than contented to let herself slide into the dark billows of sleep that way. She was enchanted.

They made love again the next morning. They woke about the same time, cozy in each other's warmth. He gave her a conspiratorial smile and moved to face her on the pillow, his lips just touching hers in voluptuous suggestion. With languid hands, they caressed each other, stroked each other. It was a quiet demonstration of love, but it soon built into heated ardor and carried them away again to their own private heights of elation.

Then she washed from the basin while he swam in the river, and she noticed from the window the Pontaguzes admiring his steady, strong stroke. They wolfed down a breakfast of bread and preserves, hard-boiled eggs, and onion soup, and since her gown was not dry yet, they simply retired back to bed again to wait. To talk. And soon to find fit amusement.

In the afternoon they lolled, sated, contented, under the canvas on the cabin roof, watching the countryside slip by, the others on board discreetly leaving them to themselves. Maîtresse Pontaguze cooked a fine dish of stewed partridge and cabbage for supper, and afterward they sat up late, the two of them and their hosts using Pontaguze's battered deck of cards for several lively rounds of *Bezac*.

Finally, the Pontaguzes retired, but Julie and Nicolas were loath to go down. He put his arm around her, and she leaned her head against his shoulder. Tomorrow, in midmorning, they would arrive at Tancarville, and the trip would be over. The real world, their mission, their problems and needs and doubts, would intrude again. It was so like a dream, Julie thought, so impossible to have happened, unimaginable to the woman who had left Eu barely two weeks ago. She rubbed her cheek against the soft fabric of his shirt, feeling safe and secure in his embrace. He loved her, she couldn't doubt that; at least, right now he did. They might have conceived a child on this barge in their lust for each other. That did not frighten her, at least right now; bearing his baby would give her joy. She would not think farther than that. She would not allow the goblins of distrust into this encapsulated happiness. She snuggled against him with a happy sigh.

Nicolas looked down at her delicate profile and tilted nose and wondered what she was thinking. She was moody, his raven-haired beauty, sometimes prone to extremes. He had no doubt that she loved him—her whole soul lived in her eyes when she gave herself. But even so, he still sensed, apart from the lushness of her physical response, a stubborn kernel of reserve. It would probably annoy him later, this deep-seated wariness. He was an open man, and what he felt and how he felt stood out in plain relief. But that was for later. This magic time had no room for criticism. He did not remember ever in his life being so content.

Louis XIV walked from his gilded chapel feeling better for his morning prayers and ready for the day's ministerial conferences and public petitions, the piles of decrees and documents on his desk to be read and signed, and the new Portuguese envoy greeted before duty might release him to more amusing pursuits. He was not a very religious man, but there was a satisfaction in prayer, in putting the desires of his heart into words, that soothed him. He attended mass every morning.

Surrounded for a moment by his bowing, smiling courtiers, the ladies and gentlemen spilling like summer blossoms down the broad marble stair which led from the ornate balcony overlooking the chapel, he caught the eye of the Marquis de Louvois, and they walked ahead in solitary conversation down the echoing gallery of huge allegorical paintings, continuing the talk they had begun before mass.

'So, she is searching for a fellow named Courbier in Honfleur?' Louis eyed de Louvois sidewise. 'Have you any idea why this quest? Who is the fellow?'

'I don't know, sire. The name is unknown to me. But my men are following behind her and will report all that she does.'

'*Au diable* with merely what she does. I want to know everything that transpires—what she thinks, whom she sees, what conversation takes place, why she is after this particular man.'

'It might be easier for me to elicit this information if I had some idea to what purpose,' de Louvois said blandly. 'Sire.'

The king of France chuckled, but his tone was pointed. 'My dear Marquis, there is only one pair of eyes in this realm whose blinks you cannot count—mine—and it plays havoc with your self-esteem. But such is my will, monsieur. My interest in Madame de Lowry, while not personal, is a personal matter and, as I have indicated before, will remain so. Allow me this discretion, if you please.'

De Louvois's nostrils pinched in, but he inclined his head in obedience. 'I beg your pardon, Your Majesty. Yet a keeper of the national security might be expected to have some curiosity, sire.' Wisely, he then backed away from the touchy subject. 'My man de Troisac is both dogged and effective. I can reach him by messenger pigeon through my agent in Le Havre. I am certain he will gain us the information you desire.'

Louis scratched his chin, contemplating his canny Minister of War thoughtfully. 'No, not him, monsieur. You. It is my desire that you take a few days from your staff and your heavy duties and conduct this investigation personally. Have de Troisac continue to hold her until you arrive, disable her coach, something surreptitious. If you can learn what she is doing without her being the wiser about your motive, that would be best. Should you need to face her, I have no doubt you can pass the meeting off as one of a more social nature.' His knowing glance as he brushed an invisible piece of lint from his silver-embroidered brocade coat was sly. He was long aware of de Louvois's attraction to his cousin de Montpensier's beautiful lady-of-honor.

The Minister of War's smile was as controlled as his smooth tone. *'A votre ordre, mon roi.'*

They talked of another matter briefly, and then Louis turned to the groups of people trailing behind them to beckon forward his brother and the Duchesse d'Angoulême, with whom he wished to discuss last-minute additions to the plans of their forthcoming wedding. De Louvois dropped back, chatted briefly with several members in the peacock tail of courtiers fanning out behind the king, then, joined by his deputy, Gévaudon, turned on his heel to return to his bureau and make plans for an immediate departure.

Now he allowed himself the sarcastic smile he had hidden previously. Louis would like to think that the few state and personal affairs he did not share with his adept chief of the country's military and domestic security were safely secret. Not so. François Michel Le Tellier knew much more about the person Courbier than Louis imagined, although not all. Years before, he had traced a trail backward toward its beginning, but it had finally evaporated into nothingness, leaving him still with the bafflement of who, at last, was this ordinary citizen whom the Jupiter-king had singled out. The lack of the full story rankled him, along with another situation—the king's disbelief that the old Vicomte de Morlé was dead and his subrosa search for him.

But what yesterday were territories obscured by opaque clouds now suddenly seemed destined to appear clearly. The crossover of de Morlé's daughter into the puzzle of Courbier was not just coincidence. There was a link here that, when finally understood, would give him the solution to both mysteries. He had a gut suspicion that knowing the answers to either circumstance might not prove to be of much use to him in the long run, but it was not in his nature to leave a door unopened if he stood before it.

He stretched his wiry body and fingered the grim sword scar along his jaw. Actually, he welcomed a reprieve from work days crammed with meetings and plans and charts and requisitions for another military campaign to bedevil the Spanish in Flanders. And he had no objections to spending an evening with the desirable Comtesse de Lowry. She might be so grateful to be rescued from the singularly unpleasant de Troisac that the evening could prove quite rewarding.

He would prepare an immediate message for de Troisac in care of Blum, the Le Havre agent, a good man. And another to Blum himself, to watch all possible routes of entry into Honfleur; Madame de Lowry might have slipped away from de Troisac. At the least, bringing Blum in would give de Troisac more support should any complications arise.

CHAPTER
~ 21 ~

Nicolas stooped and came down the four steps into the cabin, bringing with him the fresh, sweet air of a May morning. His face lit with a smile.

Julie stood, in her knee-length chemise and black stockings, arranging her hair at a bit of mirror, her bare arms raised to the twisted knot at the back of her head. Glancing at him, she teased, 'And what are you smirking at?'

'You, Aphrodite. Such lovely arms, white as alabaster. So lately wrapping their smooth roundness about my neck——' In two steps, he caught her up, soft and yielding in the flimsy chemise, giving her so enthusiastic a hug that her coil of black hair, still unpinned, slinked down her back and unraveled.

Laughing, she pushed at him. 'Stop it, barbarian. Look what you've done. Be serious. I need to converse with you.'

He wouldn't let her go but growled in the back of his throat and nuzzled the tender spot where the side of her neck joined her shoulder with a make-believe bite. 'But I *am* serious. Unfortunately, you have left me but the wreck of a man, and therefore serious will do me no physical good.'

'But truly, Nicolas, what do we do now?'

Seeing that she would not be put off, he sighed and swiped up an apple that remained from their breakfast. '*Eh bien,* my love. Neither cart nor spare mount is available in this little hamlet, and since we have only one horse, we are going to do two things. I will go into Honfleur, and you will stay here.'

She had expected him to say that, but she made a face anyway as she began to pin up her hair again. 'But I don't want to stay here,' she complained. 'I want to find Courbier.'

He said patiently, 'Listen, sweetheart, Skandahet-se was only to hold those two rascals a short while. If by some chance they managed to get to Honfleur, they will be looking to play out de Louvois's game with you, *not* me. You will be safe here on the quai, which is more than I can say for Honfleur.'

'I could wear a mask,' she insisted hopefully.

'*Tiens*, if we can locate Courbier, so can they. This is not Paris, after all. If they are watching him to find you, any masked woman approaching him would be suspect.'

'We could go at night. I could wear a hood.'

'Now you are being silly, madame. If you were Courbier, would you open your door at night to hooded strangers?'

'But, Nicolas. . .'

He tossed the half-eaten apple onto one of their wooden plates and reached to take her hands. 'I know, *minette*. You've come all this way, and you deserve to be the one who finds Mademoiselle's heir for her. But there are too many peculiarities going on for me to allow you to be exposed to any more of it. And, most important, we have only one horse,' he noted again, to placate her.

Grudgingly, she nodded her head in assent, not the danger but the practical matter of transport stopping her protests.

'Pontaguze says he unloads his cargo here for the exporter to transship to his vessel bound for England, and he does not expect to turn about until tomorrow noon, which gives us plenty of time. I will also fetch Poilettier here with the coach.'

Unresisting, she continued to dress, stepping into her petticoat and tying it about her waist, then doing the same with the blue gown.

He pursed his mouth and studied her. 'Hmm. You are too quiet. That makes me nervous.'

'It's just that you are right.' She shrugged. 'It would look peculiar for us to ride up sharing one horse and tell the poor man we are from Her Highness and he must come with us. Not that I am not badly disappointed. I'd really like to go with you.'

'Oh, *mignonne*,' he crooned, stepping forward to hug

her again and rock her. 'I know. But be patient. You will soon get to meet this fellow.' He gave her a final squeeze and a kiss on the cheek and then strode over to the chest to buckle on the low-slung belt and sword he had purchased in L'Aigle.

She missed him already. 'How long do you think you will be?'

'Hard to tell. Assuming I can find him, however long it takes me to persuade him to come with us.'

'That might not be so easy without the letter Her Highness furnished me that had her seal. The one that was lost in the river with everything else. . .'

'Don't worry. We have enough money with us and the promise of more to ensure that he will come. People who mean you harm don't usually pay you for it.'

He already had one foot on the step, but she ran and caught at his brown coat. 'Nicolas——'

'Yes, love.'

She held his eyes for a moment, cherishing their warmth. But the world was already intruding upon them, and a vague finger of fear scratched at the door of her happiness. 'Nothing. I love you.'

He brushed his fingers along the petal-soft skin of her cheek. 'I love you, too. It won't take me long to slip that fellow away without fuss. And when we return to Eu, we'll talk. There are things we must talk about.'

She followed him out on deck and watched him swing a leg over the horse he had saddled previously. And then, with a jaunty wave to her, he rode away, loosely erect on his Arabian, which was snorting and delighted to stretch its legs again. The horse pranced with arched neck, carrying its master between the stalls of the fish vendors along the length of the quai. She watched Nicolas negotiating the hamlet's single dirt street, until he rounded the corner near a dilapidated building and disappeared from view.

Pontaguze and his deck hand had that morning poled the barge under a block and tackle, which now creaked noisily, hoisting flat beds of wine barrels from the barge to the timber-shored packed earth of the quai. Feeling useless and lazy, Julie enjoyed a luxurious yawn.

A horseman studying the activity on the barge picked his way slowly down the quai. She gave him a casual glance and paid no more attention. He was an ordinary man on an ordinary horse, perhaps looking for a relative or friend. A girl passing with a tray of pastries took Julie's attention, but out of the corner of her eye, she was aware of the man's scrutiny as he rode by. And then the scent of the delicious, buttery, and fresh-baked *oubliés* compelled her to call out to the vendor, and shortly she was the owner of two fragrant little cakes, which she blithely demolished.

She decided to get some exercise by walking around. Perhaps she would help Maîtresse Pontaguze make her purchases for noon dinner, and so she proceeded across the short gangplank with the aplomb of a seasoned mariner.

Entrepreneurs had lined up their shallow-bedded, two-wheeled carts, shielded from the bright sun by canvas over hoops, to display neat rows of glistening, silvery, pop-eyed ocean fish—sole, skate, mackerel, whiting, mussels, oysters. Smiling, humming to herself, Julie wandered along amid the fishmongers, admiring the shining scales and the oysters' bumpy, tight-closed shells, the eye relieved of fish here and there by the verdant counterpoint of baskets of dandelion greens, leeks, and mushrooms. She found the barge mistress haggling over a black blood pudding offered by an old woman whose nose met her chin. Maîtresse Pontaguze was glad to have Julie's company, and the pleasant morning passed in poking and prodding and purchasing of various food stores and some new mending needles. At one point, a man jostled by her rudely but stuck out a hand to steady her, looking directly into her face as he excused himself with a careless shrug. She thought it was the same person who had gone by on a horse earlier.

The afternoon passed, too, but more slowly, making her aware of how useless she was at that moment to her own mission, sitting on a barge in Tancarville when she should have been in Honfleur. Various thoughts intruded, dispelling her lassitude of the morning. She felt foolish for missing Nicolas so much, just in a few hours' separation. She hugged her arms around her and considered that somehow she must be unique to have attracted the love of this special man. When she thought of him, pictured his bearded face, heard his mellow voice, she felt she was floating somewhere above the earth. And yet some tiny part of her brain tugged at her, seemed to be crouching, bewildered.

He wanted her for his wife, he had said that before, and that he loved her. And she wanted him desperately; her being craved toward joining her life to his. Yes, just as it had years before to another dashing, unpredictable, ultimately unattainable creature—Richard, Earl of Lowry. Her heart was not at all to be trusted with her life.

It seemed one of the longest days of her life, in spite of the fact that Julie had begged the barge mistress to allow her to stitch some of the pattern on the embroidered mitts the woman was making. At last, from across a broad marsh and behind a bank of clouds that marked where the rollers of the distant ocean hit the beach, the sun's final rays became diffused to fingers of gold. Julie went in and lit her two lamps and candles, preferring to eat her supper of grilled fish and blood pudding by herself in the cabin. Later, staring at the darkened square of the window, a little snuffle escaped her, worry that Nicolas had been gone too long. She tried to calm herself by considering some of the obstacles that might have confronted him. Honfleur was a small but very busy port, and there were many ships putting in and out, or the trail may have led to someone who was then at sea——

Nothing stirred on the barge. Julie cocked her head and listened to the mild lapping of the river at the vessel's flanks. The simple cabin, which had seemed so wondrous the past enchanted days, now seemed too empty. But she could see him everywhere. In fact, she now spotted his extra shirt lying half under the bed, obviously waiting for a laundress. It put a wry smile on her face. Men were not neat without their valets to attend them. Richard, too, in the short time she'd been invited into his bedroom, had shed his things just where he stood and, even in the absence of any servant, left them there. She rose to pick up the shirt, flipping the curtain down across the open window as she went. She was just about to stoop to get it, for she wanted to hug it to her, to smell it, to hold him, when the door burst open with a huge bang, and she stood transfixed, mouth open in surprise, so startled that for a moment she merely gaped at the dark patch at the top of the steps. And then it was filled with the thigh-high boots and broad-shouldered shape of a man, and she almost cried out, 'Nicolas!' But the face that appeared under the cocked-brim beaver was square and flat. And heavily freckled. De Troisac!

She pressed clasped hands against her chest as he swaggered down the few steps into the room and stopped to contemplate her with an unpleasant smirk. She demanded hoarsely, 'What is the meaning of this intrusion? Who are you? What do you want?' She fought to control her voice.

'Good evening, Mademoiselle Croixverte, as you have been calling yourself, Comtesse. But between us, we do not need little subterfuges.'

She wouldn't answer him, merely lifted her chin angrily.

'De Troisac here, Martin de Troisac. I am most happy to greet you, madame.' He came a step closer, impudent enough to expect her to give him her hand. She kept her elbows rigidly against her body. He shrugged, looked around, and then glanced up toward the door, where a silhouette had appeared. He made a signal, and the door was pulled shut. She heard footsteps, receding toward the stern of the barge.

With a sweeping gesture of sarcastic courtesy, de Troisac indicated the two chairs at the table. 'Shall we sit down, Madame la Comtesse? There are some little matters I must discuss with you. No reason why we cannot conduct our conversation in comfort.'

Julie took a deep breath to scream for help, but there was uncommon quiet from without, and de Troisac's unconcerned stance told her the crew was probably being held at pistol point. She clamped her lips and prepared to defy him, but then it occurred to her that perhaps she could learn as much from him as he was after from her. Surreptitiously, she moved her foot, trying to push the rest of Nicolas's shirt under the bed, covering the movement with a haughty nod. She then advanced with silent dignity to seat herself where he indicated.

'That is very intelligent of you, madame,' he murmured. He pulled the other chair forward and put his foot up on it so that he leaned casually on his whitestockinged knee as he stood facing her, looking down slightly, a crude show of arrogance.

She noticed he had scratches on his face such as might be made by a cat or thick bramble bushes. There was a gleam in his small eyes, but she couldn't tell whether it meant cunning or intellect. A belt about his waist held both sword and pistol, and in his hand was a riding crop with a long leather tip. Finally, she said, 'You have been following me for days, monsieur, and I demand to know why.'

'Very simple. I wanted to know—that is, my employer wanted to know—where you were going. We've been very patient up to now, merely coming along behind you, but this may not be the end of your trip, and our patience has disappeared.'

'Your employer? And who is it who sends minions to trail me and burst down my door? Obviously no friend of mine. Name him!'

'You are not in any position to question me, *ma belle*. Now, I am a very courteous gentleman and I wish to treat you with all respect, seeing you are so far from home and completely alone on this vessel, with the owners occupied and unable to help you. That was an irritating trick you pulled on me at Verneuil, and I'm not proud to have been stupid enough to fall for it. But one stupidity is all I allow myself, madame.' The gleam in his eyes deepened. 'Where is your coachman? What are you doing on a barge, and why are you here near Honfleur? To what purpose was this trip that took you so far from Eu?' He fired the questions at her rapidly.

She set her jaw and did not answer, glaring at him.

When she didn't respond, he reached out and jabbed her shoulder with the crop, not hard but in warning. 'It is my advice that you talk to me, madame. I like to hear the sound of your voice. And I have a bad temper when I'm thwarted. Now, what is your business with one Edouard Courbier, eh? I'm sure you will be polite and tell me.'

She didn't miss the menace under his tone. She lied through stiff lips. 'He is a good baker. *My* employer wanted some of his special raisin buns. I came to get them.' Not that she expected him to believe it, but she had no intention of delivering the truth.

De Troisac stared at her over a tight smile. 'I told you, I have already been stupid once, and it caused me much trouble. My patience has been worn through. What are you after Courbier for?' He chucked up her chin with a flip of the crop. 'Do not anger me, madame. I am not a violent man, but my companions are.'

Companions? Were there more men with him than the one he'd trailed her with? She'd been confident that Nicolas, returning finally, would somehow deal with the unsuspecting de Troisac and his man. Now, considering de Troisac might have too many confederates with him to be overcome, tendrils of trepidation began to wrap around her heart.

'You are obnoxious and insolent, monsieur. I am sure this employer of yours would not condone mistreating a lady.'

'I grant you that. But it is my way to persuade you to answer my questions. Once I gain him what he wants, he might not be particular about my methods.'

'My business is none of yours.' She braved it out. 'And I warn you, I have influence. I presume you consider yourself a gentleman. The king himself shall hear of your ruffian behavior, and His Majesty is not fond of crudeness toward women.'

'Aha, but would you care for the king to raise his own questions about this journey, eh, madame? Now, please cooperate with me, *ma belle*, and I shall soon rid you of my presence. I would not like having to ask for help from the big-bellied rider you saw accompanying me—no gentleman at all, but a true bully, lately a jailer on one of the king's Mediterranean prison galleys.'

Julie drew her brow together and glared. 'Do you think to threaten me, you villain? It will do you no good. I am not afraid of you. Now, get out!' She rose up quickly and made a rush past him, but with a show of his yellow teeth, he aimed a vicious backhanded blow at her with the crop, catching her on the side of the neck with the leather tip. She gasped; shock and a stinging pain enveloped her, and she sat back down in the chair. Her hand flew to the burning spot and came away crimsoned with blood. Tears sprang to her eyes. Obviously, de Troisac's orders did not prohibit him from harming her in order to get what he wanted.

His eyes gleamed maliciously. He held up the crop in front of her frightened eyes and snarled, 'I am doing what I can to curb my temper, woman, but I have no time for games. My employer demands a good job from me, and I will not disappoint him. I didn't want to mark your milky neck. I would not like to scar up your pretty face, either. Unless you force me to. Eh?' The crop shivered in his hand as if he were holding it back from doing its sadistic will.

She shrank back, knowing he meant it. 'I-I cannot t-tell you what I don't know,' she whispered.

'Who is Courbier?'

'Just as I said, a baker who once lived in Bonneval and is now possibly in Honfleur.'

'And why do you want him? Is he who you originally set out to find?'

'No. I m-mean yes. Her Highness the Duchesse de Montpensier ordered me to find him. That is why I went to Bonneval.'

'Why does she want this nondescript baker so much?'

'I t-told you, I don't know. She said nothing to me except she wished me to find him.'

'And then. . .'

'To bring him to her.'

'Why?'

She rolled huge, nervous eyes at him. 'I told you, I d-don't know.'

'Oh, most certainly you do, dear madame. Now, why?' he barked, and he brandished the crop warningly. 'Do not make me loose your tongue.'

With an agile twist that surprised him, she jumped up again, eluding the crop and knocking it up with desperate strength to dash past him toward the table, where lay the knife she'd used to cut her loaf of bread. But he whirled about and came instantly after her, tripping her so that she fell across the table with arm outstretched. The knife was pushed to the floor on the far side. He pulled her up by the hair and dragged her away. He yanked her against him, jerking her arm up behind her back so viciously she screamed in pain.

'A feisty one, aren't you, black hair?' he panted in her ear, emphasizing his words with painful jerks on her arm. 'Thinking to stick old de Troisac, eh, madame? *Quelle méchante.*'

He was putting so much deliberate pressure on her arm, she feared her shoulder joint would soon part. With a panting sob, she pleaded, 'You are breaking my arm! Please——'

'No, you please me, so old de Troisac can keep his post. I'll break more than your arm if I don't hear from you something I wouldn't already know.' His breath on her cheek made her skin crawl. The cut on her neck throbbed painfully, and she felt blood running down, snaking into the hollow of her throat. He yanked on her arm once more, and she shrieked again in pain and terror. A tiny bit more, and something would rend apart. She shivered.

His gravelly voice turned oily again. 'And your father, de Morlé, madame, where is your father? And don't tell me he is dead. If we believed that, I wouldn't be here. But tell me something, bitch, very quickly, or we will have to explain how you accidentally injured your arm—and your face, eh?'

There was a splash outside the curtained window and a shuffle of footsteps. De Troisac froze, listening. But there was little fear in his voice as he muttered, 'What was that?' She could only answer with a moan under his fierce grip, and she drooped against the other arm which clamped her waist.

There was a loud kick, and for the second time the door burst open, which made de Troisac whirl around. He was forced to release the pressure on her arm, but now the other arm almost cut her in two as he cocked a pistol unwaveringly at the scowling man who moved down the four steps like a stalking leopard, bloody sword in hand.

The command came, curt and deadly. 'Let her go, de Troisac.'

Julie felt the rumble of a mirthless chuckle vibrate the chest she was pinned against.

'*Tiens!* What have we here? A fancy *soirée* at court? It is the Marquis de Courcillon, upon my word, the king's captain. A surprise for me, eh? Aha, madame. I see there could be many reasons for your journey here. But it seems to me a far trip for a mere assignation.' The pistol jutted warningly at Nicolas's further glide forward. De Troisac did not intimidate easily. He nodded at the stained rapier. 'I see one of my men has made the mistake of annoying you.'

'He made the mistake of not following orders as docilely as your other two henchmen. I suggest you be more careful. Let her go.'

'You listen to me, de Courcillon. Move one step closer, and I'll blow off your head—or hers, it doesn't matter which. You are interfering in official business.'

Nicolas's eyes narrowed. 'Which official?'

'What matters is that you are obstructing the wishes of an authority higher than yours, which wants this woman questioned. Don't antagonize my employer. He is a dangerous man.'

'So am I, my friend.' Nicolas moved a step closer. De Troisac backed up. 'I am usually not inclined to kill a man, but if you don't turn the lady loose, your employer will never know what happened to you. You are in no position to bargain.'

With de Troisac's harsh breathing in her ear, Julie lifted her head. Nicolas's eyes flicked to her neck and held there. His nostrils were white and flared. 'You are bleeding, madame,' he observed in an ominously quiet tone.

'He used the c-crop,' she whimpered against de Troisac's convulsive grip, her gaze going automatically to where the goad lay on the floor. 'Nicolas. Be careful. He'll shoot——'

But the frigid blue eyes shifted their gaze momentarily just over de Troisac's shoulder, and a split second later Julie heard a whistling sound, a thud, and a cursing cry of pain as de Troisac's grip fell away from her. The pistol thumped to the floor, there was a loud report which made Julie scream and put her hands to her ears, and a hole appeared before her panicked eyes, not in Nicolas but in the wall to one side of him. Nicolas kicked the smoking weapon skittering under the table as Julie's erstwhile captor struggled to pull out the dagger that was lodged in the flesh of his upper arm. Blood coursing down his sleeve dripped and laced about his fingers.

'Julie. Come behind me,' Nicolas snapped.

Stumbling, she complied and then, facing about, saw Skandahet-se grinning in at the window, his plumed hat askew, satisfaction written all over his face. Without taking his eye off de Troisac, who finally jerked the knife out, Nicolas reached into the breast of his coat and shoved the red kerchief into her hand. 'Take this, love. Press it against the cut hard. 'Twill stop the bleeding.'

With his right hand, de Troisac snicked his sword from its scabbard. Sweat glistened on his forehead, the freckles standing out on his coarse face. 'Come then, monsieur. Even with only one arm, I am ready for you,' he croaked.

Nicolas flushed and raised the tip of his sword. 'I'll say this for you, lout—you're brave if stupid. But I have no intention of spitting a wounded man. That's too easy to be interesting. I'm just going to cut you up a little bit, eh, de Troisac? The sort of thing you like to do. *En garde!*' He called the challenge.

Julie pressed back out of range as the two swords clashed together, Nicolas attacking, a grim smile on his face, de Troisac desperately defending himself from the flashing rapier darting over and around his guard. There was little room to move for either one, but even had de Troisac's left arm not been hanging by his side, it would have been just as quick a defeat as it proved now. He was a decent swordsman but no match for the relentless shower of strokes that drove him back and pinned him against the table. In hardly a minute, the weapon went sailing out of his hand, and he was defeated. Before he could recover, two controlled lightning slashes of de Courcillon's rapier point on either side of his face laid his cheeks deeply open to the bone.

Gasping, de Troisac staggered back, mouth in a grimace of pain and shock, sword hand raised to his face, which was streaming blood.

'A good lesson to be learned,' Nicolas grated coldly. 'Never use a crop on a lady.'

He turned to Julie and winked, but his mouth was a mean line. She quailed inside. Was this unbending avenger the same man who treated her with such tenderness? She recognized a streak of steel in Nicolas, a flash point of temper beyond which the softness in his nature did not extend.

He scooped up de Troisac's sword with a flip of his own and, spying the lace cuff of his shirt peeping from beneath the bed, scooped it up and flung it to the bleeding man as a sop. He nodded to Skandahet-se, who had slipped quietly through the window, where now appeared the awed faces of Pontaguze, his mate, and his wife. And a grinning Poilettier, who had kept his trusty pistol on the two remaining henchmen outside. He grunted to the Indian, 'Take this vermin out and put him on his horse, along with the other two. Maybe he'll bleed to death before he finds help.'

Expressionlessly, the big Huron stepped forward, grabbed the pale-as-death, blood-covered, buckling de Troisac by the collar of his coat and the seat of his breeches, and hustled him up the stairs.

'My advice to you, de Troisac, is to get as far from here as you can,' Nicolas hurled after him. 'The next time I see you, I'll finish the job.' He flung the two weapons, one crimson-stained, on the table, muttering to himself. Then he turned to Julie, who was still pressed, speechless and huge-eyed, against the wall, holding the bunched kerchief tightly to her neck. 'Let me see that,' he said in a softer tone. He stepped over and took down her hand to examine the cut, which ran diagonally almost to the large tendon of her neck. His frown reappeared. He shook his head and bellowed to the window, 'Maîtresse Pontaguze, have you something clean for a bandage? Bring it here at once; madame has sustained a wound.' He took the kerchief from her hand, put his arm around her, led her to the bed, and sat her down.

There was a pitcher of water on the table. Nicolas rebunched the kerchief to an unbloodied spot and poured water on it. Then, tilting Julie's head, he gently swabbed away the blood from the cut. The pressure she'd been putting on it had almost closed the edges of the long, straight wound. She winced, and he stopped for a moment to peer into her eyes. 'Are you faint, sweetheart? No? Good. It's shallow, only a bit more than a scratch.'

'I'm fine,' she murmured weakly, enjoying his ministration.

He kissed her on the forehead, then pressed the cloth against the wound, which was still oozing blood. When she whimpered, he growled, 'I should have killed that filth; he could have laid open a blood vessel for you. But somehow, I can't believe de Louvois gave him permission to mishandle you; that would not be the minister's method in such a case.'

Maneuvering her bulk gracefully through the door, Maîtresse Pontaguze approached, carrying a small jar of ointment and a sleeveless soft white bodice, her summer spare. She clucked in sympathy at the sight of Julie's slashed neck and blood-speckled gown and proceeded to tear strips from the bodice.

'You will be well compensated for this, maîtresse. I appreciate the sacrifice.' Nicolas smiled at her as he sat beside Julie.

'Think nothing of it, monsieur. It was a pleasure to my heart when you jumped upon the back of that scoundrel who had knocked my poor husband on the head.

Pontaguze has a great lump right there, and his ears are ringing. But who were those men?' Just as she asked this, Skandahet-se stooped and came down the stairs silently. She looked askance at the impassive Indian. 'And this one!' It was plain she was somewhat in awe of Nicolas now—her passenger was an experienced swordsman, certainly of higher quality than she'd supposed, and probably so was the lady. Run away from her husband, most likely. The titillating thought ran through the woman's mind in spite of the distracting circumstances.

'This man is my companion. He is a Huron Indian from the Americas. As for the others, it makes no difference, you'll not see them further.'

'Nicolas, but did you find Courbier?' Julie broke in, no longer able to contain herself.

'Shhh. Let me bandage you up first. Hold still.' He applied ointment with one finger, folded a soft strip into a pad, and then, while the barge mistress held it firmly in place, secured it by winding the other tight about the slim neck and making a knot against the pad.

With half a choke, half a chuckle, Julie complained, 'You are strangling me.'

'Not quite, *mon amour*. I can still hear your voice.' He took her face in one hand and brought her mouth to his, kissing her lips with as much pleasure as Julie had in eating her honey apple. He was not eager to let her go, but a soft clearing of the barge mistress's throat reminded him that they had spectators. He broke off and with a regretful sigh asked Maîtresse Pontaguze to find them what late supper she could—he'd had little to eat all day—and especially to bring some of the good, sweet Muscat to revive madame.

The woman bobbed him a curtsy. With a quick glance at Nicolas, Skandahet-se followed her up the stairs, only Nicolas noticing his fingers twitching at the tempting sight of the barge mistress's plump rear. He strode to the window, where the mate, the boy, and some of the curious from neighboring barges hunkered staring, and closed the window firmly and dropped the curtain over it. He walked back to where Julie sat slumping, propped two pillows against the wall that served as a headboard, and, taking her by the arm, got her to lean back, then bent and lifted her legs onto the bed. 'Now. Tell me what happened, madame.'

'Not much more than what you saw. He was trying to get me to tell him who Courbier is and where my father is, just as you believed.' Her face lit for a moment as she proudly considered her fortitude. 'But I told him nothing, Nicolas, not a word. Nothing that he didn't already know, even when he was hurting me.' She rubbed her shoulder ruefully. 'I had just realized he was truly going to break my arm when you arrived. You can't imagine how frightened I was. But I'm so anxious to know. Did you find Courbier?'

'I don't doubt you were frightened. This party has become too rough for you, my love, and I have a notion it's far from over. I'm sending you back to Eu, where my godmother has guards galore to handle any sort of invasion. Tomorrow, before dawn, in fact, we shall both be gone from here.'

She sat upright quickly, indignant. 'Back to Eu? I will not! I beg you to remember, Monsieur de Courcillon, that the task of finding Edouard Courbier was given to me, not you, and I intend to accomplish it. You have no authority to send me home.'

He stood over her with drawn brows, a fist on a hip. 'My authority is that I love you and I don't want you hurt.' Seeing her adamant expression and prepared for it, he said bluntly, 'Do you want to go to England?'

She blinked and gawked at him; he thought for the millionth time how astonishingly beautiful were her eyes, even unrivaled by any hint of pink in her cheeks.

'England! Are you jesting? Nicolas, I will kill you. . .'

He shook his head, trying to keep his expression solemn. He was telling her the truth—it just needed a little embroidering. 'No, not a joke, unfortunately. Our quarry is the peripatetic sort. I inquired all over the docks, of ship captains, sailors, general hangabouts, but nobody knew him, and I had half trod my boots through, leading Al-Minyah by the reins. I was just about ready to tromp through the town and inquire of all the bakers when I saw just before me a chandler's establishment. It occurred to my hunger-weakened brain—for I had not taken much breakfast, what with the distractions in this cabin—that an inexperienced lad might not so easily find employment as a mariner, even on a river barge. So I entered, demanded the proprietor, and lo, my surmise had been correct. He remembered Courbier. He had given him work as a rope coiler and then, some months later, as a general clerk of stores. But the fellow had an unquenchable hankering for the sea and finally managed to wangle a berth on an old cargo vessel plying the Channel. The chandler could go no farther in his story than a few months past that, when Courbier once or twice visited him and then came no more.'

He hooked a foot in the stretcher of one of the armless chairs and, pulling it close, sat on it backward, then took off his floppy hat and skimmed it to the bed. 'But the chandler directed me to a small dock almost beyond the walls of Honfleur, where our luck held. The creaky old ship happened to be in its berth, and its captain remembered Courbier well, in fact made no bones about his disgust with the youth, who, it seems, got so deathly seasick every voyage that he finally left the ship.' Carefully, he watched her expression change at the very mention of the word *seasick;* he had not forgotten her vivid tale of her own crossing of the choppy Channel. 'Courbier had encountered a maiden in England whose father owned a small bake shop in Bournemouth. According to the captain of the tub, he took up his old trade and soon married the girl.'

'Across the English Channel? *Mon Dieu!* I hardly expected that,' she said faintly.

He dropped his head for a moment to hide the twitch of his lips, hoping there was suitable sincerity in his eyes when he looked up. He shrugged. 'Well, that is where we shall have to go after him. Or perhaps we will find he has taken up wandering again, since the captain had a strong feeling Courbier might have decided to set up his own little establishment on a large island in the North Sea, an island they'd once put into that had real need of a good French baker,' he lied smoothly. 'If so, it would only be a sea trip of a week for us—unless the cross winds stir up those rough North Sea storms, which can rage and blow for days on end. Even in spring.'

'Storms?' Her smile was so tentative, it didn't even generate her dimple.

'Yes,' he continued, feeling mean but doing it for her own good. 'Violent storms are the norm for that body of water. They blow all the time. But we've started this business, we might as well finish it. I wish there were a better ship available than the only one departing tomorrow with the tide, but the quicker we fetch Courbier to Eu, the better. Speed is essential.'

Unconsciously, her fingers were twisting the fabric of her blue skirt. 'Uh, what is the matter with the ship?'

'Oh, nothing serious, *minette*. She is seaworthy enough but a little down at the heels and small. That just means she'll ride the swells like a cork, bobbing up and down a lot but able to scoot out from under the big waves and otherwise just head up one side and down the other. Up and down, and sometimes around if the storm is as fierce as usual,' he added innocently. 'We might get very wet, but we'll be safe enough. I think.'

A scratch at the door, and the barge mistress entered laden with a tray. Nicolas rose to make room on the table for the steaming bowls of lamb and lentil soup and black bread. The woman laid out spoons and coarse napkins, picked up Julie's gown to try to wash the blood from it, and, with a smile, disappeared. Nicolas poured amber wine from an earthen pitcher. 'Come to the table, love, and eat.' He held out an inviting hand.

Julie swung her legs off the bed and joined him, but the memories he had stirred in her of seasickness were too vivid; the heavy smell of the soup caused creepers of nausea to climb her throat. She pictured herself gagging and gasping and retching the way she once had, all stringy-haired and suffering, unable even to smile at him, and shuddered at how ugly a picture she would make. He fell to heartily, tearing a big piece of bread to dip into the broth. Slowly, she spooned up a few minute mouthfuls.

There was silence for a few minutes, broken only by the clink of his pewter spoon against the pottery bowl. 'Um. . .Nicolas?'

'Yes, love?'

'I've been thinking you might be right. Perhaps I should go back to Eu, if only to reassure Mademoiselle. She must be very anxious about what has happened to us. And you probably can travel much faster without me.'

He stopped his spoon halfway to his mouth and looked up at her from under his brows. 'I can't do anything much better without you, but I think you're being wise. I shall have to elude whoever else might be allied with de Troisac and get onto that ship undetected, much harder for two than one, and those Channel cross-chop waters make for unpleasant sailing.' He went on with his eating.

She thought she caught a smile, a fleeting expression immediately hidden behind a piece of black bread, but she decided she was wrong. At last, having satisfied his empty belly, he sat back and regarded her. 'You haven't eaten much.'

'In fact, I have already had my supper. I'm just keeping you company. But it just occurs to me. Wherever did you find your Huron and my coachman?'

'Skandahet-se was at one of the inns on Honfleur's wharfs. I sent him to Trouville to collect Poilettier while I did my searching. When from a distance down this quai I saw no lanterns lit and hung on the barge, something in my gut told me there was trouble. So we left the coach and horses in the alley behind the wharf buildings and crept up quietly behind barrels and bales of cotton and whatever else could cover us. The two men outside had herded everyone under the deck canvas, out of sight of the other barge people. And since they expected no trouble, taking the rascals was easy. Although I had to run one through, unfortunately.' He got up to take her hand and help her up. 'In any case, *douce coeur*, we'll have to leave before dawn; we've only a few hours to get some rest.'

Nicolas's plan was for her to make the trip back to Eu as fast as possible, with Skandahet-se riding alongside the coach as escort. He himself intended to enter Honfleur and board the Channel ship before daylight, for since the old man had not told de Troisac of Courbier's yearning toward the sea, he might this way elude any chance surveillance.

He finished his supper and went outside to talk with the Indian and Poilettier and settle with the Pontaguzes. When he came back, they extinguished one of the oil lamps and lay down on the bed, only partially undressed, to rest for the few hours before Skandahet-se would wake them. He gathered her in his arms, careful not to disturb her wound, and thus they lay tranquilly for a while, spoon fashion, until he felt a wetness on his hand, which rested alongside her cheek.

'Why do you cry, love?' he whispered, stroking her hair back from her temple.

Gulping, she whispered in a teary voice, 'It was too short, this interlude together. Too short. We always seem to be separated.'

He hugged her closer. 'Only for a while now. You need some sleep tonight, or I might find you other things to do. But at Eu we will not be pressed, and we will talk seriously of the future.'

'But I'm afraid for your safety. This simple mission has turned out to be a dangerous puzzle. Who knows what will happen? It doesn't seem possible that de Troisac will give up.'

'Once I am on the ship and bound for England, they will never find me. I paid the chandler well to keep his mouth shut on the truth of Courbier and fed him a tale of evil relatives following after me looking to take inherited money from the man. And once I have Courbier and spirit him to Eu by a roundabout way, our mission is done.'

'But the Marquis de Louvois?'

'De Louvois is in Paris. Even if they send news by pigeon, it will take time for him to replace his agent or find another strategy for his aims.' He chuckled softly. 'He thought you'd be alone. A little chicken easy to pluck.'

'But there must be someone at the chateau who informed him I was leaving on a journey and by what road. In fact, just by your mention of pigeons, I am reminded of something.'

'Of what?'

'That Mademoiselle's personal maid, Dant, was given pigeons by a relative as a farewell gift.'

There was a silence. The river slapped softly beneath them. She wondered if he had fallen asleep when he finally said, 'That could explain many things. If I could just edge the puzzle pieces closer. It is as if one key bit of knowledge is missing.'

'Oh, I cannot bear the thought that it could be Dant who is spying on Mademoiselle,' Julie groaned. 'She has been so loyally at her side so many years.'

'Perhaps not as loyally as you think. You must promise me you will do nothing to show any suspicion of the woman until I arrive with Courbier. Just see that Mademoiselle keeps her guards on alert, no one allowed entry except those she utterly trusts and any royal messengers. Promise, now, that you will do as I say.'

He made her turn around so she was facing the glint of his eyes. He kissed her on the nose. 'Promise, madame. On your word before God.'

'I promise. Truly. I will tell Mademoiselle in private only that the trail led you on to England and that I was too fatigued to go farther.'

'Good. Now close those magnificent eyes and sleep,' he ordered.

But in a few minutes, she mused sleepily, 'Nicolas, doesn't it seem strange that a child of two royal houses of France, Bourbon and Condé, is naught but a village baker, leading his simple life and working hard to earn his living? And now he is about to be named heir to one of the greatest fortunes in all Europe? I wonder what he is like, this lost prince. Perhaps this news will overwhelm him. It might stop his heart. Eh? Nicolas?'

But her lover's breathing had become deep and even. He had relaxed onto his back. In the weak light of the one lamp burning, she could see the sandy lashes against his cheeks, a faint smile just barely curving the corners of the strong mouth under the moustache. She leaned closer toward him and touched her lips briefly to his, feather light, breathing him in, and then subsided. She sighed. She wasn't sure what would come of it all. Except for the fact that she was deeply in love with him, she just wasn't sure of anything.

Nicolas lounged on the lumpy slat bed nailed to the floor of the ship's cabin, one leg crossed over the other, and watched his foot bouncing up and down as he mulled over the sequence of events. It had not been difficult to slip onboard the square-rigger *St George and St Jude*, with his horse in the purple dark before dawn. He had startled the watch, who finally called the mate with whom he'd made arrangements for passage the day before. Now, comfortable without his coat and sword belt, he was whiling away the hours until the tide turned and they stood far enough out from shore for him to emerge on deck for some air. He sniffed and wrinkled his nose; the narrow sleeping quarters smelled of previous occupants' unwashed clothes and bodies, and there were mouse droppings in the corners. It was nowhere near as clean as Pontaguze's commodious cabin. But it was the first ship leaving, and speed was more important than comfort.

He hadn't mentioned to Julie one of the most worrisome aspects of what was going on, that both the chandler and the captain of the old ship Courbier had sailed on mentioned that there had been others making queries about the fellow some years before. They had no idea who the others were, nor remembered their names—ordinary men, they said. But, as the grizzled owner of the leaky tub chuckled, taking the three écus offered him for his cooperation, 'Seems to be a good business knowing something about Courbier. He was a pretty ordinary lad, not bad in 'is way. Got a chopped-up ear. What's the fellow done, anyway? Them others wouldn't tell me neither.'

The cabin, belowdeck, had no ports, but Nicolas had an onion-shaped timepiece in his saddlebag and saw by it that it was another hour at least before he could come up into the fresh air. He sighed and amused himself by listening to the slams and bangs of the last of the cargo being loaded, the heavy footsteps marching above his head, the shouts and curses of the crew lashing down crates, the creaks and squeals of tackle. As the preparations for sailing died down, he contemplated lying down on the thin mattress and grabbing a nap. Then there was a loud rap on the door. Yawning, growling out a question, he heard the mate's voice in answer to him. He swung his legs off the bunk and went and drew the bolt.

Three men burst in, one immediately slipping around behind him, as it happened between him and his sword, toward which he recoiled reflexively. They were professional guardsmen, jack-booted, in mustard-yellow coats and plumed hats and bristling with swords and pistols. The leader, of large stature and tiny moustache, held two flintlocks aimed at his heart. 'Monsieur le Marquis de Courcillon?'

'What of it?'

'You will be kind enough to accompany us. Peacefully, monsieur. I have more men outside than you could escape from.'

'By whose orders do you coerce me with firearms? You are in lawless disregard of my personal rights.'

'By the warrant of His Majesty's Minister of War, Monsieur de Louvois, who wishes to speak with you. You have no choice, monsieur. I intend to accomplish my orders no matter what humor you receive them in. Please comply.'

Nicolas stared at the cocked guns, cast a sideways glance at the alert men on either side of him, and cursed himself for having underestimated de Louvois's determination. Sullenly, he shrugged. 'Very well, but allow me to don my coat.'

The officer nodded. 'Of course. Leclerc?' He motioned to one of his men, who got the coat and held it for Nicolas to shrug into, then gathered up the sword and saddlebag. 'We will take these things along, monsieur, in case you do not come back this way. And if you will permit——?' The remaining guard held a strip of leather. 'Just a precaution.'

With a black look, Nicolas held out his wrists, which the guard bound tightly. Actually, he had considered a quick dive off the narrow strip of deck, where only one could walk at a time, and an underwater escape into the dark forest of pier pilings. Yet it would gain him nothing in the long run.

'Now, monsieur, I shall have to ask you where is the lady with whom you travel.'

'The lady is not with me. She has returned to—her home.'

The officer motioned with his head, and the man behind him disappeared. They waited in silence, the officer putting up one of his pistols. Then the guard reappeared. 'They say he never boarded with a lady, sir.'

The officer frowned. Then he shrugged. '*Eh bien. Alors*, that is not our problem. Get monsieur's horse saddled. Quickly.'

Four more men in dark gold uniforms lined their way to the gangplank, holding back with drawn swords the curious crew members, who peered behind them. Nicolas was hustled onto the quai, helped onto his horse, and urged along in the midst of an impressive escort. They rode around the perimeter of the square port crowded with ships and then cantered away from it, to the edge of the town. There they proceeded under the squat Norman gateway of an inn, a low-gabled, timbered old building with a thatched and mossy roof and cages of chattering squirrels set beside the heavy main door. There were a variety of local vehicles lying about on the old, cracked tiles of the court, but standing apart from them, badly mud-spattered, as if driven hard, was a large and elegant coach with an impressive coat-of-arms on its door.

Nicolas was escorted through an outside passage to a small entrance and then up a curving stone stair. This let into a chamber of large proportions filled with heavy Henri IV furniture and two antique iron chandeliers suspended from the beamed ceiling. The Marquis de Louvois, finely attired but hatless, sat in an armchair before the cold hearth reading a book. He put down his volume as Nicolas and his guard entered, unfolded his lean length, and stood.

The officer saluted. 'The Marquis de Courcillon, monsieur.'

'You did well, Massigny. But you are too finicky. I bid you unbind my guest immediately. He is, after all, a gentleman and an officer of His Majesty's household.'

Nicolas chaffed his wrists where the leather straps had bitten in. 'What is this all about, de Louvois?' he growled. 'I don't enjoy being arrested like a common criminal. I hope you have a worthy explanation.'

'Arrested?' The supercilious black eyebrows rose. 'There is no question of arrest, *mon cher* monsieur. But I needed an immediate conference with you, and seeing you were about to depart our shores, this was the best way to ensure it. I most sincerely apologize to you for my method. Please, will you sit?' He indicated an armchair opposite his.

Nicolas was not deluded; de Louvois's tight, sardonic smile showed no sign of regret. The minister was used to getting what he wanted, one of his virtues of value to the crown. He muttered stiffly, 'I will stand.'

'As you wish.' De Louvois eyed him. 'You are not in your usual sartorial form, Marquis. You must have done some hard traveling. All the way from Eu, perhaps? And through Bonneval?'

'Why ask me what you already know? Come to your point.'

'But where is the charming Madame de Lowry? I understand from my badly wounded agent, de Troisac, that the lady was with you last night. Really, de Courcillon, need you have cut the man up so badly? He has lost much blood and is in a high fever. He was only seeking information.'

'Madame de Lowry is on her way back to Eu. With a bloody crop wound on her neck, delivered by your overeager agent.'

Nicolas judged that the annoyance that darkened the suave face was genuine. 'Crop wound? The dog! He struck her? I shall see to the man for that—if he lives. But *revenons aux nos moutons*, monsieur. The Comtesse is hastening back to Eu, I would imagine, and just as well, since my need to know about her father is almost moot.'

'Julie de Lowry knows nothing of the Vicomte de

Morlé. She lived far removed from him in England, and following that, he died. The man has been dead for years.'

De Louvois measured him with brooding eyes. He ran his tongue over his lips, drew them in, and then pursed them as he contemplated the heavy-shouldered man before him, standing with stubbornly folded arms. 'De Courcillon, I will come directly to the point. You are seeking a man named Courbier. I know you think to find him in England, and that is why, after questioning de Troisac upon my arrival late last night and then having him sewn up, I ordered my men to inquire if there was a ship leaving today for Bournemouth. I must thank you for not embarking at Le Havre and making my task more difficult.'

'Sheer, rampant stupidity,' Nicolas muttered, shaking his head.

'Or merely one too many delightful nights in the company of an adorable beauty,' de Louvois responded with an oily smile. He held up his hand as Nicolas, flushing angrily, made a motion to clap a hand on a sword that was not there. 'Peace, peace. As you can see, the window is barred and my men are outside the door. I did not mean disrespect to the lady. I merely meant to exonerate you somewhat from your own conclusion. Besides, I have something you will find more valuable than defending your lady's honor. We are men among men, after all. If you have won the damsel, I have won the game.'

'What game?'

But de Louvois had seen Nicolas's glance toward the rapier suspended from his own embroidered baldric and moved cautiously away from him to lean back on his hands against a rug-covered table of heroic proportions. 'Why don't you tell me who Edouard Courbier really is, just to confirm my suspicions?' At Nicolas's stubborn silence, he continued. 'Very well, monsieur. I will sweeten the pot to where resistance out of misplaced loyalty buys you nothing. You tell me *why* you are after Courbier. I will tell you *where* he is. And he is not in England.'

Nicolas blinked. 'But he is alive, then?' He could sense the puzzle pieces were coming together.

'He is alive, and he is well. But you will never find him without telling me what I wish to know: his true identity. Do that, and I will exchange with you the full story of Courbier. Neither of us can have success, you see, without the other.'

There was not much choice. The trail had run out, and de Louvois could be believed that Courbier was not further traceable. But the factor that decided Nicolas to embrace the bargain was that Mademoiselle was determined to reveal Courbier's lineage anyway. 'Do I have your word that you will give me full access to him?'

'For my part, you may have any access to him you can devise. I have no personal involvement with Courbier, monsieur. But in my position, I *will* know everything that transpires in France. Just that simply. It is an instance of my thoroughness. And my personality, probably.'

In Nicolas's estimation, de Louvois did nothing for simple reasons. But he nodded toward the chair. 'I think I will accept your offer to sit, Marquis.'

'By all means. Let us be comfortable. May I offer you some wine? The landlord has a surprisingly good cellar.'

The minister's smile was all blandness and courtesy now, without its usual sharp edge. Such mildness in a crafty man who had never been enamored of him made Nicolas uneasy, but he could only go forward. He accepted the goblet of wine and sat back in the chair, appearing relaxed even if he wasn't. Since de Louvois seemed to be waiting for him to fill the silence, he drew a breath and began. 'Are you aware that Madame de Lowry and I have been trying to find Courbier, not on behalf of her father or any such wild surmise, but at the request of the Duchesse de Montpensier?'

De Louvois's stiff lips stretched farther in a suave smile. 'Not as a fact, of course. Merely a strong suspicion.'

'But it is a fact. And the reason for it is——' He hesitated. De Louvois remained motionless, but in the sheen of illumination from the window, Nicolas had the overwhelming illusion of a jackal crouched in the brush, expectantly licking his chops. 'The reason is that Courbier is her natural son, and she wishes to recognize him.'

De Louvois's head jerked up. 'Indeed! How much light is beginning to become shed on dark places. And who was the father of this repudiated child some, ah, twenty and something years ago, as the man looks to be?'

Nicolas felt sweat spring out underneath his moustache in spite of reason's telling him that reticence would avail nothing. 'I give you the information, de Louvois, because it is something Her Highness will herself make public as soon as Courbier is located. The father was a prince of the blood whom she was constantly thrown together with during the Fronde, a man she supported and admired, a married man, unfortunately.'

The minister's dark eyes gleamed. Leaning forward, he gripped the carved-wood arms of his chair. 'Are you, in fact, telling me, monsieur, that it was the illustrious Grand Condé who fathered Courbier? Is there proof of this?'

'Yes. To both questions.'

De Louvois jumped up to commence a jerky, victorious stride about the room, hands clasped behind his back. 'Of course. Now it makes sense. The wily fox!' he muttered. 'He prepares well, for any contingency.' He stopped to stare out the window but did not register, just outside, the glory of an old apple tree in full bloom shedding its pale petals and delicious scent over the inn yard.

Nicolas stirred. Bot curiosity and disquiet were overwhelming him. 'That is my part of the bargain. Now take care of yours, monsieur,' he demanded.

De Louvois turned, and the assumed blandness was gone. His expression held its usual sardonic veneer. He flicked at his lace cravat to shake a mote of dust from it. He said expansively, 'Of course, monsieur. But first let me refill your glass.' He brought the ewer and poured the ruby-red liquid. 'As I noted before, Marquis, Courbier is no longer in England. In fact, he is in France and has been for the past six years. And the reason this information will do you no good, de Courcillon, is that, ironically enough, he is the prisoner whom, with his special jailer, you escorted from the Bastille to Pignerol almost two years ago. Do you remember? The man called only Prisoner X?'

Nicolas stared at the king's most important official, who, with head lifted back, returned his gaze from under dropped lids. He felt the pulse beating in his temples. 'But——' He cleared his throat. 'That man was wearing a mask of rigid black leather clamped about his head, which covered all of his face but his eyes and mouth. You say *that* poor wretch is Courbier? God protect us! But why? And if *you* did not know who he was when he was imprisoned, then who did?'

'The king did. Ah, but he is sometimes quite wily, our majestic ruler. It is not often like him to think so far ahead. I am going to gell you a little tale, de Courcillon, because you are in this up to your neck, and you might as well drown in it, my friend.'

Nicolas stood up, tipped up his glass, and then strode to the table to pour his own refill and recover his composure. When he turned to face de Louvois, he saw sly satisfaction in the man's expression. De Louvois flicked calmly at his cravat again.

'I knew nothing of Courbier until, six years ago, His Majesty asked me to arrange to personally escort to the Bastille a prisoner arriving from England by ship at the tiny port of Etretat. The youth who came off the vessel was shackled, manacled, and grotesquely locked into a face mask. He was accompanied by a private jailer. Nor did it avail anything to talk to him, for his shock was profound, and he said little. But once in a while, he would mutter or weep, or a muffled and terrified shriek would issue from that heavy device that hid his features. It became clear that he was nothing but a little person who had no idea why he had been arrested, much less held on a royal *lettre de cachet*, taken from his bed in the middle of the night, hustled onto a ship, and so bizarrely hooded. Beyond orders to mentally break the wretch into submission but to keep him physically well and well cared for, the king would say nothing of his reason for imprisoning this Courbier. In fact, I am certain it amused him to hold this secret from me. Such an arrangement did not suit me, of course, nor did it add any luster to my position.'

De Louvois picked daintily at a tooth with one long fingernail. He looked thoughtful. 'Beginning with the ship the masked individual arrived on, I had my agents trace him back to Bournemouth, where they heard Courbier's wife's story of three armed French gentlemen who had kidnapped her husband. I will shorten the story by saying merely that I was able to trace Courbier all the way back to Bonneval. And then nothing. Courbier remained an everyman who normally should have lived and died in obscurity.'

'Why was de Morlé involved?' Nicolas asked.

'As I piece it together now, he may have been the one who originally located Courbier in England for Louis. Perhaps he had some way to identify him.'

Nicolas shook his head, saddened. 'I suppose I can confirm that. De Morlé was present at the baby's birth and signed an attestment to the birth.'

'Ah, indeed! There it is,' De Louvois crowed. 'So Louis recalled him from England then, and I think de Morlé began to suspect that the king might wish to rid himself of the only other person who knew the true identity of this wretched man in the mask. Conveniently, on his ill-fated voyage across, de Morlé drowned. Or he let it be thought that he drowned. His Majesty never quite believed it, and again, without furnishing me a reason, demanded vigilance from my agents for any clue to his existence. When the delectable Madame de Lowry surfaced, it seemed logical to take note of her comings and goings. An agent sent me notice that she was leaving Eu for Bonneval. Since I had not been aware of the connection between de Morlé and Courbier, you can imagine my excitement, which ran even higher when de Troisac sent word that madame was seeking not her father but, in fact, a baker named Courbier in Bonneval.'

Now de Louvois reseated himself. He propped his

elbow on the high arm of the antique chair and rested his chin on his fists, dark eyes looking inward, almost talking to himself. 'At that point, I was first able to propose to myself a motive for all this activity, because now, in Julie de Lowry's shadow, I caught a tiny hint of La Grande Mademoiselle, Her august Highness's involvement. And I am amazed at how accurate my hypotheses were.' He shifted and tented his fingers. 'The moment the king learned of the existence of this lost heir to his cousin's fortune, he decided to seize the man and use him as a control—to keep him hidden in case of a de Lauzun, you see, or in case Mademoiselle decided to bring the heir forward herself in an effort to preserve her estates intact. Which I presume is her reason for acting now? Louis wished to keep the man alive in case Mademoiselle made a foreign alliance. She would not likely have any issue of it now; thus, a living heir of this lineage would bring her money back to France when she died. We must assume that the king has documents proving this heir's bloodlines.'

Nicolas nodded. 'Mademoiselle has the original attestment, but there were copies.'

'Yet why the torturous mask? It is unlikely that Mademoiselle or her few witnesses could identify a grown man from a newborn infant.'

'Partially, they could. They had clipped off some of his ear.'

De Louvois raised an eyebrow. 'Ah. Just so. And the Duchesse has such strong features, he might thoroughly resemble her. The poor wretch tried twice to escape his cell in the Bastille, once even carving a message on the back of his tin plate and tossing it from the window. Unfortunately, it was found by an illiterate prison laundress, who brought it to the warden. That is why he was ordered removed to the remote Pignerol.'

'The question is, who informed the king of Courbier's existence?'

De Louvois shrugged. 'I do not think it was de Morlé. It was in all probability the same person who also offered herself into my employ. The Duchesse's longtime personal servant, Louise Dant.' At Nicolas's pained look, he smiled cynically. 'Come, come. Money will buy anyone. But further than that, I know her background. She has a brother who was arrested in 1664 for the murder of a watchman yet who is treated in jail with some leniency—favor which she must have bought by offering the king the full tale of Mademoiselle's illegitimate brat and who the witnesses were. Yet, although she was also keeping me informed of developments at the Luxembourg on other matters, including finding de Morlé through his daughter, she kept the king's silence on Courbier.'

As if the revelations themselves were not upsetting enough, the very fact that they all rolled so easily off de Louvois's tongue now brought Nicolas's sense of unease into sharp focus. He rose so forcefully that the chair almost fell backward, and he stood over de Louvois, his mouth a grim line. 'Why are you telling me so much, Marquis? I have never known you to part with any information except for a purpose. It would have sufficed just to relate that Courbier was dead. Whether I believed you or not, I had little chance of ever discovering that he was the Prisoner X in the mask, unreachable in Pignerol. Why are you being so confidential?'

De Louvois reached over and scooped a handful of shelled walnuts from a bowl on a table beside him. He began to nibble on them. 'Your perspicacity comes too late, monsieur. My purpose has already been achieved. Just by knowing the identity of the man in the mask, you have already compromised your freedom. Perhaps it escaped you that de Morlé could have feigned drowning because he feared he knew too much? And that our monarch does not care to share this secret of this hidden pawn in his back pocket with anyone? If not with me, whom he has entrusted with state secrets of vastly greater import, then certainly not with you. Sit down, Monsieur de Courcillon,' he commanded suddenly, and when Nicolas, stone-faced, complied, he smiled.

Nicolas had a sick feeling that this time fate was going to collect her dues for all favors previously dispensed to him. One cannot win all the battles, he primed himself, just keep your head.

'I am constrained, of course, to inform the king of your involvement in all this. The rest becomes a matter of indispensability. His Majesty will be much wroth that I have come to share his little secret with him, for Mademoiselle aside, you can imagine the scandal and the outcries of the Condés and their partisans the Contis if the identity of the rumored man in the mask is leaked out. But I am too valuable to the king, too embroiled in his government, and he will be forced to trust my discretion. But you? Understand, monsieur, I am aware of the fact that he admires you and considers you among the most capable of his nobility. But you are dispensable nevertheless, and he will not stand for your partnership in his shameful detention of an innocent party in whose veins runs the best blood of France. Regrettable, but a fact. Therefore, I have some advice for you.'

Nicolas held up a warning hand. 'You but speculate, monsieur. I have not deliberately sought entrance into this situation. The king will certainly consider that.'

'It will have no bearing, I assure you.' De Louvois sighed. 'I will be direct. The king will wish to ensure your silence. I do not need to describe to you, de Courcillon, the several unpleasant ways he might accomplish this, although I believe he will be inclined to show you some clemency. The least painful punishment would be exile, a very distant exile, to New France, perhaps, where you already have ties. I will try to convince him of the justice of this.'

Nicolas rubbed at his bearded chin. He glared. 'A favor from you, monsieur, carries too many poison spines.'

'Very well, I admit I don't like you, I never have. But helping you aids me, too. Death or imprisonment would make you a martyr, a hero worshiped by a lady in whom I have a most special interest. But a man exiled to the wilderness? That would produce a much more sour impression.' He swung his crossed leg up and down, pleased with himself.

Nicolas marveled bitterly at how easily fate had set up this little trap in de Louvois's favour. There was not even a step he could berate himself for as stupid unless he went back and cursed his simple trip to Eu in the first place, a ridiculous reaction. He rose from his chair. 'I would not be so naïve as to discredit your power to bring about this exile, monsieur.' Stalking to the window, he frowned out, battling with the rage that threatened to break through the veneer of his icy composure. He turned to see satisfaction relaxing the lines of de Louvois's face, and he read there a certain scorn as well that came close to goading him into revealing his helpless fury. 'Let me tell you, de Louvois, if your reference was to the Comtesse de Lowry, she has no interest in you. And I intend to make her my wife. I will not be able to resist the will of the king should he banish me from his court, but you are very mistaken to think such a situation would avail you any notice from the lady.'

De Louvois uncrossed his legs and got up. 'Ah, yes, I know the rosy promises a lovers' idyll on a springtime river might seem to hold, but you do not know women very well, Marquis, in spite of your reputation with the beguiling creatures. The Comtesse has not been long out of enforced lonely years in the country. She is young and vivacious, and her own mistress. She has related to me herself, several times, her joy in being with the court, and this past winter's duty in Eu could only have sharpened her appetite. Very frankly, I believe that once she knows you must leave France, she will not come with you. I am almost certain of it.'

'I would like to knock that certainty down your throat!' Nicolas glowered.

Able to afford amiability, de Louvois made a friendly shrug. 'Without a weapon, monsieur? And fists are for peasants. I beg you to remember that exile is only the least of what the king's irritation might require as balm. Keep me on your side.'

'The game is not up yet, de Louvois.'

'You err. It is very nearly played out, de Courcillon.' The minister drew a tiny snuff box of polished horn from the lining pocket of his rose silk coat and withdrew a pinch. 'Since Julie de Lowry could know nothing of this dénouement, you will, for her own safety's sake, not tell her. Nor Her Highness, either. It would only give

Mademoiselle another reason to break her heart against Louis's will and in her—forgive me—silly arrogance might push him into causing a fatal accident for Monsieur de Lauzun. I doubt he will ever let de Lauzun go, and it is possible Courbier, too, will spend his life hidden in a dungeon in Pignerol. Ironic that the two of them are both there. Do you see? It would be a shame to burden the august lady with more useless grief.'

Eyes narrowed, Nicolas nodded. 'For once we agree. I will tell them both the man is dead. You have my word on it. I would not risk either one of them.'

De Louvois relaxed. 'Accepted. Well, I have at least saved you a tiresome Channel voyage.'

'By dint of substituting an ocean voyage for me?' Nicolas sneered. 'We shall see.'

But the minister merely nodded. 'I know my employer. I have taken the liberty of engaging a chamber in this pleasant inn for you, Monsieur de Courcillon. You might wish to refresh yourself before journeying on to Eu, as I presume you will. As for me, I shall return this day to Paris, where my problems clamor for me. And where, as she has written to me, Madame de Lowry will return for the nuptials of Monsieur. When I report to him, in the circumstances, His Majesty will demand your attendance upon him. Yet for the two ladies to believe your tale and forget Courbier, you will need to allow some time to pass, the time it would take to sail to England and back, assuming good weather, and thence to Eu to report to them. Shall I assure His Majesty that you will attend him within the fortnight, three weeks at most?'

Nicolas's nod was curt. He did not trust himself to speak.

'*Adieu*, then, monsieur. I think we understand each other.'

Nicolas made a sketchy bow and turned his back on de Louvois's corresponding courtesy. De Louvois followed and ordered one of his footmen to show Monsieur le Marquis to his chamber.

Arriving there, where his sword and saddlebag awaited on the bed, he slammed the door behind him.

Grabbing up a large painted tankard holding a bouquet of fresh flowers, Nicolas drew back his arm and hurled it with all his might and inchoate rage at the stucco wall. As he stood staring at the spreading puddle of water and scattered jonquils and lilac branches, he found he could not even spit out a curse to rail at being so thoroughly in de Louvois's clutches. The connivance of sheer coincidence here was so enormous, and so unescapable now, by himself or even the king, that there were no bellowings loud enough to mitigate its impact.

He had never before, in his active life, experienced so humiliating a checkmate.

Nicolas rode back to La Toque, sent his staff and caretakers there into a bustle, and soon slept in one of his own beds. The enforced wait was difficult. Anger and inaction gnawed at him and caused him to slam himself around the old but pleasant chateau, to hunt the area's foxes and hares with a vengeance, to spend too much time and money taking his seat as seigneur and betting heavily on the bloody dog fights held in the village.

But when at last he and two accompanying servants rode off and reached the busy, rutted coast road running north past Le Havre and Dieppe, he cantered more calmly along with the ebb and flow of travelers and commerce. He had come to some sort of accommodation with the turn of events, should Louis choose to exile him. Looking into his deepest heart, Nicolas knew that such a decree was far from anathema to him. The real truth was that the aimless, fussy life of the loyal courtier had begun to bore him.

It was, in essence, a continuous search for amusement and for esthetic occupation for the mind, the most luxurious and lavish sloth ever encouraged upon a noble class by a shrewd ruler grasping for uncontested control of the state. By certain background and by dint of his commercial involvement, Nicolas had an eye clear enough to escape the pervasive lure of insipid court routine—the *levers* and the *couchers,* the *appartements* and ceremonial attendances that made up the hours of most aristocrats—except when the gentlemen eased the vacuousness of their days with wars designed as sops to their energies.

If he and Julie were forced to retreat to New France, they would be writing on a clean, fresh slate where pushing back the wilderness demanded energy and involvement from all the citizens, no matter what their station. There was a possible empire of trade and wealth to be built there. What was caring whether one had the privilege of standing for hours watching the king eat to that? Yes, he had enjoyed the victories of war and the prestige of the king's favour and the captaining of his bodyguard. But he had always suspected that for a man who had spent years on the rugged New World frontier, it would all seem too precious eventually.

Nicolas found himself close to smiling as the leagues melted away from under Al-Minyah. It was as if a heavy boot was lifting from his neck, from his damaged self-esteem. By all the saints and martyrs, let de Louvois plead his exile, in vain hopes of separating him from Julie. The crafty minister was outsmarting himself. It would not cause him too much unhappiness to lead his raven-haired darling by the hand onto the awesome shores of the virgin land across the ocean. Greeting New France once more, with a beautiful bride on his arm, seeing the wide-skied land through her eyes as well as his own vision, grown more mature, more appreciative, became ever more exciting as he thought of it. Its sudden aspect as a barless prison, his first reaction, totally receded from his mind.

He pushed back his hat, a fine beaver with the wide brim folded back over a bright crimson plume, and enjoyed the sun on his already bronzed face. The two attendants riding with him had to kick up their horses to match his sudden spurt of speed.

CHAPTER
~ 22 ~

It was Anne-Marie-Louise d'Orleans's conceit that adversity had finally made steel of her heart. She had not wept much in months. But now, in spite of Nicolas's regretful tone, his words struck like a lance through all her defenses, to where hope had dwelt fiercely in its resilient cocoon. Her knees went to jelly, and she would have staggered had he not grasped her arms.

'Dead! Ah, *Dieu me sauve!* That cannot be. But I need him!' she wailed. 'I have no other bulwark against the avariciousness of my enemies. I have no other way to release my dearest, tormented Monsieur de Lauzun. Courbier is yet young. He cannot be dead.' In her grief, she pushed Nicolas from her, walked stiffly a few paces away, and turned on the two who confronted her. She stared at her godson's strained face and her lady-of-honor's tightly clasped hands. Well may they look miserable, but it was she whose last card was played, whose last hope was gone. It crossed her mind that for propriety's sake she should feel sorrow; after all, she was the mother of the man called Courbier, or had been, eons ago. But the harsh truth was that she felt nothing but futile anger for the unknown and long forgotten fruit of her body. How dare he die when a daughter of France wished him to live!

'Is it true, then?' she whispered to Nicolas, her lower lip trembling with disappointment.

'I fear so, Your Highness. Of the measles. I saw his grave in the small Catholic churchyard at Bournemouth. And so, of course, the priest confirmed.'

'And the wife?'

'Died giving birth to a stillborn. There was no other issue.'

'No issue,' Mademoiselle said in a hollow echo. 'Well, Nicolas, I am sorry that you suffered such a hard voyage for nothing. I have already thanked Madame de Lowry for her considerable effort on my behalf. Now I thank you.'

Nicolas felt sullied, wretched, as mortified as a bear with its paw caught in a jug. Yet, as hard as it was to tell the simple yet convincing story, it was easier to bear the disappointment etching deep grooves along his godmother's features than the horror and perhaps militance the truth would have created in her—that her own flesh and blood was the pitiful prisoner in the mask, half forgotten now, once the object of so much speculation. His glance touched on Julie, standing just beside him, lovely in spite of her distress, in a pale peach silk gown, her thick hair in a simple knot. But sorrow for Mademoiselle clouded her gaze.

Too much sorrow, he thought with a harder judgment. He wondered if Julie was going to have trouble disentangling her life from the lady she served so loyally.

Mademoiselle said sadly, 'It will finally come to giving that scandalous bitch what she seeks. I cannot abandon my Antonin, for that is love, you see, sacrificing for each other. I will give her the counties she covets for her offspring and pray her humbly to intercede with my cousin for the Comte de Lauzun's release.' She raised her eyes to plead for Nicolas's understanding of her heart. 'What other way is left for me? I have attempted everything else. Louis turns a deaf ear to my weeping. All my letters to Monsieur de Lauzun have been returned, undelivered, still sealed. He is being cruelly kept from all news of me and obviously not allowed to write to me. Perhaps he thinks I care nothing for him now, that my heart is so fickle I would further wound his imprisoned soul with indifference. Oh, I cannot bear it. I must grasp at the only slim hope that is offered.'

For one miserable moment, all three stood staring at each other, and then Nicolas came to Mademoiselle's side and took her elbow. 'Please, Your Highness, will you sit. It must pain your leg to stand so long.'

She gently put his hand aside. 'No, monsieur, it is not my leg that is tired but my heart, beating for almost half a century under the duress and loneliness of everyone else's designs for me. Tired. Tired. I will return to my chamber and rest before attending vespers at the Collegiate. You will come to vespers too, Nicolas.' Then she shook her now fast-graying head at Julie. 'No, stay. Madame de Puysieux is near, and she will attend me. Since monsieur insists on riding back to Paris tomorrow, perhaps you have things you wish to say to each other. It is of great importance to convey the feelings of the heart. Alas, how I know. . .' She lifted her head and, with a wisp of a smile, walked slowly from the salon, assisting her stiff-legged gait with an ebon walking stick, which had been resting against a chair. The train of her gown made a sad murmur.

Nicolas hastened around to open the door for her with a respectful bow, then noiselessly shut it behind her.

They met in the middle of the room in joyful embrace, and Julie could not believe it was really Nicolas, the reality, not one of her yearning daydreams, who was hugging her, kissing her lips, her forehead, her cheeks, the tip of her nose. On his arrival, he had only kissed her hand, taken a swift peek at the healed cut on her neck, and quickly and briefly explained why he was alone before Mademoiselle, having seen his little party ride up from her window, sailed with urgency into the salon. Now the grip of his hands on her shoulders was hard and real, the dancing lights blue eyes gazed into hers, he was murmuring the wondrous words of how he had missed her, how drear the days were without her, how empty the nights.

The nights. Desperately, she clutched at all her resolutions before they melted like so much snow before his heat, resolutions she had struggled with while surrounded by the spring glory of petal showers from the chateau's flowering shrubs and the boxed cherry and almond trees in the gardens. There had been plenty of time to think on the rattling journey home and during the suspenseful weeks of enduring a nervous, depressed, querulous Mademoiselle. Among the several letters she found awaiting her there had been another soft plea from Mercure de Vosges for an answer to his suit, as well as an elegant expression of hope from the Marquis de Louvois that he would have the pleasure of greeting her in Paris shortly. But neither had to do with her resolve.

She was not going to become Nicolas's mistress, in spite of her love for him. From the beginning, there had been little choice for either of them, short of removing themselves to two different countries. The magnetic, irresistible attraction between them had inevitably led to the bedchamber. But until she could master, could understand, her conflicting feelings and why she shrank from marriage with him, she could at least master the frailty of her body. They had drunk too much from the cup already. The deliriousness he caused in her had caused her good sense to run away.

His arm across her shoulders, Nicolas led her to a window seat, then sat down beside her. He still wore the fawn coat he had bought in L'Aigle, although there was finer attire awaiting him in the baggage he'd left here before riding in chase of her. The coat brought back so vividly to her those enchanted few days on the Risle, even though his hat was not the floppy-brimmed countryman's gear he had worn on the river. She remembered the afternoons under the awning on the barge, the drunken night at the fair, the slap of the river against the craft's sturdy sides, the cocoon of their cabin, invaded only by the scent of apple blossoms. She remembered the soft-rough feel of his naked skin, her hands caressing him from strong shoulders to smooth, taut buttocks, the erotic responses he drew from her, this broad-chested, blue-eyed cavalier gazing at her so possessively now. But there was a painful constriction in her chest, strong enough to make her clamp a stubborn lock on her runaway thoughts. She veered the conversation toward a safer subject.

'Nicolas, guess what? One night I had a dream, but perhaps it was more of a memory. It was something that has been tickling at my head all this time. Do you remember that coach you exchanged with me when I first arrived in France? You were taking a prisoner to Pignerol?'

'Could I ever forget it? It almost cost me my life.'

'Nicolas, that prisoner had scratched something into the veneer of the coach, behind one of the curtains. It was a name, and I think I remember it said "E. Courbier"!' She waited for his surprised reaction, searching his face. But after a second's absorption of what she said and a momentary stiffness of his features, he merely shrugged and shook his head.

'I regret, *mon amour*, that you did not read it right. That prisoner's name was Emile Courtrier, a dangerous assassin.'

'Oh.' She felt deflated. She thought she'd found an important clue.

'What is more important right now is whether you will come back to Paris with me in the morning, sweetheart.'

'Ah, Nicolas, you are so unfair.' She smiled at him. 'I could hardly get ready so soon, and my gown for Monsieur's marriage, which Mademoiselle's seamstresses are working on, is not finished.'

He grinned back. 'Shall I guess that it will strike chagrin into the hearts of the other ladies and make me the envy of every male in Paris?'

'I hope so, for that is the whole purpose. But I have some news. There is a possibility that at the last moment, the king will invite Her Highness to come to Paris for the wedding, just for that one day. But even should that come to pass, I am so anxious to leave here that I will start off well before her—with an escort this time, I promise. But I had hoped you might stay a while so we could leave together. What is your hurry?' She saw the smile leave his face and a more serious look replace it.

'Julie, before I returned here, I made a short detour to my chateau at La Toque and found there a letter from Beraite, my Paris intendant. It seems that grave problems have arisen across the sea in New France.'

Concerned, she asked, 'Is it my father?'

'No, he is well. These are problems of supply, rival shippers springing up and luring away my trappers, such things.' He took a deep breath. 'What it means is that there is every chance I may shortly be required to return to New France. Perhaps for a very long time. It would mean giving up my appointment to the Garde-du-Corps. I have even thought I might settle some of the family properties on my brother to see that they are properly looked after, for with the big estate at Courcillon and the tracts of fine riverbank land I already own in New France, it would hardly cheat my heir out of his due inheritance. It is a situation to be considered.'

'Oh, Nicolas, New France? The wilderness? You can't mean it?' She was shocked. She recoiled from the hope in his eyes.

He could hardly miss the dismay in her voice, but he hurried on. 'I want you to marry me, my darling. No, let me say it differently. It isn't an order, it's a plea. I am asking you for your hand in marriage. I adore you. I want you for my wife, the mother of my children. I put at your feet all that I have and will ever have, and perhaps now, as well. I will offer the excitement of a life in the New World.'

She said unbelievingly, 'Amidst the savages?' and she thought his answering chuckle too hearty.

'*Vois-tu, mon amour,* it is not at all what you are thinking. We would be among the leading aristocrats in a colony of more than five thousand Europeans now in several prosperous settlements, hustling and full of vigor. Granted, the class of elegants and *haut bourgeois* is small, but there are parties and balls, and you would shine like the sun. Perhaps you might even start a literary salon or a theater. I will build you one in a garden grotto like that at Versailles. We can import actors, musicians, dancers, whomever you wish. . .' He stopped, no longer able to ignore that her head was turned away. 'What is the matter, Julie?'

'Nothing. I. . .'

Gently, he forced her chin around so she had to meet his penetrating gaze. 'Do you love me?'

'Oh, yes, yes. You know I do.'

'But what? The next step is simple. You will honor me with your hand in marriage. Although we cannot ask his blessing in advance, I am sure your father would approve. And Mademoiselle will surely witness the contract. We can marry in Paris, or at my estate at Courcillon, or even here, to include my godmother. However you wish it, my love.' But he had to shake her by the hand to elicit more from her than just her unhappy stare.

Julie took a deep breath. It was going too fast, running away with her. 'Nicolas, I can't speak to you of marriage yet,' she cried. 'I need more time. I need to consider. . .'

'More time? You've had months. You've had weeks. We are in love with each other. We are free to marry and consecrate this love. What is the issue?'

She hung her head. 'You don't understand.'

'No, I don't, and I'm afraid neither do you. Is it the prospect of making a life in New France that stops you? Is it?'

'N-no,' she stammered, and yet that was not true. She was appalled at the very idea of removing once more far from the civilization and sophistication of the glittering court of *Le Roi-Soleil*. It would not be the very temporary exile of the Norman countryside at Eu but a long-term residence, almost a banishment, thousands of leagues across the sea in a vast territory of forests where Europeans huddled in fortresses for their lives. It was terrible. It was unjust. It was ungracious of him to ask it of her. It was without any consideration at all of her deepest feelings. She would not incarcerate herself again.

He was trying to read her face. 'I had hoped—Julie, I don't know how to soothe this baseless fear you have of me. If my love and my offer of marriage are not enough, I do not know what would be. I realize the prospect of living in New France is not, at first, appealing. But if a woman says she loves a man, she should wish to marry him and be where he is, even if it be in farthest Russia.' His mouth tightened. 'I cannot think you gave yourself to me so lightly.'

She recoiled and reddened. Even though she knew that her reluctance was jabbing once more at his ego and that he was angrily striking back, how dare he cast aspersions on her morality? 'You have no right, monsieur, to wound me with such insult. Lightly? Do you truly believe that? Lightly?'

Gripping her by her bare shoulders, he desperately studied her eyes, as if he could drill through them into her head and uncover the mysterious why of her actions. 'Then why won't you marry me? Tell me what is wrong, and I will fix it!'

Fix it? Erase in himself the very essence of the dashing, romantic male she had fallen in love with—both times?

'Nicolas, please. I did not say yea or nay. I ask you for more time to think about it. It is an irreversible step,' she whispered miserably.

A muscle jumped in his jaw. He stood up with finality. 'But you *will* say yea or nay, and before I depart tomorrow. I am thirty-one years of age. I have been looking too long a time for the right woman to share my life, and in that I've been irresponsible. Now that I have found her, I have no more time for frivolity. You know what is in your heart. No more days or weeks or months will subtract or add to that. I ask you to give me your decision tomorrow, Julie. Not later. Now I will go to change my attire before we leave to hear the mass.'

She peered into his hardened expression. 'Don't be angry with me, Nicolas. I beg you,' she whispered.

Stiffly, he bent to kiss her hand. 'Not angry, madame, never. My feelings for you run too deeply. Just disappointed. You need give me only one little word tomorrow morning. I want to ride from here with rejoicing in my heart.'

She watched him stride away noiselessly over the thick carpet, his back rigid. Why did he always seem to be going away from her? Why was her heart pounding in such a panic? Hadn't she already faced the decision of what was best for her to do?

They said very little to each other that evening, in the company of the somber Duchesse, her ladies, and a few invited guests chosen from among the town's richest merchants. Julie played the clavier for them, but she was not at her best form. Then they listened to Mademoiselle's violinists and a specialist on the hautbois. Julie felt Nicolas's brooding eyes on her often, but every time she glanced at him, he looked away. Once, as they passed from the salon to another chamber and brought up the rear of the company, he grabbed her hand and squeezed it, as if willing a message to flow from his fingers into hers. But there was irony in the tight smile he gave her, in his guarded eyes, and he said nothing. They sat later to cards, four to a table, and Nicolas seemed to enjoy amusing the ladies who were his partners. He was a man always attractive to the ladies, Julie thought jealously, putting more warmth in her own smile for the eager gentleman opposite her.

She soon excused herself from the game to return to her chamber, claiming a very bad headache. The men stood politely as she rose, and Nicolas made a move to escort her.

She held up her hand to stop him. 'No, please, monsieur, do not disturb yourself or inconvenience your partners. I shall be fine,' she refused firmly and, with Mademoiselle's penetrating gaze upon her, fled from the room before Nicolas could protest.

When she arrived in the privacy of her chamber, she let the tears leak out finally and sat simply staring into space. She thought maybe he might come to see how she fared, but he did not, and the laughter of the ladies he had pleased and flattered rang as an echo in her ears. In a while, Blanchette undressed her, and she crawled into bed to still the tumult within her. In the broken stretches of sleep that finally overtook her, she dreamed of weird places, a series of cold stone caves in which she hid from a wild boar with Richard's face that was snuffling and snorting to get at her, to hurt her, and she tried to scream for Nicolas, but there was a cut on her throat preventing her——

She woke in the gray of a rainy morning and felt a million years old.

He made his *adieux* first to Mademoiselle, who stood before the main portals of the chateau with a pallid smile of noble suffering on her face, the damp breeze blowing wisps of graying hair from the wired curls of her coiffure. There was a light shawl about her shoulders. 'You must not worry about me, *mon cher* Nicolas. I have survived this far and will continue to,' she said. 'I only ask that you remember me as I shall you, and write to me when it is convenient. I do miss you.'

'And you must promise that you will care for yourself well. The ocean air is often chill and damp.'

'Ah, but I love it here, were it not so lonely, so far from Paris. . .Yet I don't think we will meet again for a while, eh, monsieur? Why do my bones tell me that?'

He tried to use his roguish smile to lift her up. 'We shall surely meet sooner than you think, especially if the king will allow you to the wedding. And if I sail to New France, it might be possible that I pass through here on the way to my port.'

'God travel with you, Nicolas, my dear.'

He kissed her hand. She took his bearded face in her big palms and brushed both cheeks with her lips.

Julie stood clutching a wrap about her shoulders and saw his unsmiling regard turn to her. She had not appeared that morning until just before it was time for him to leave, and then she had quietly joined them, answering his probing look with downcast mien. He stood staring at her now, but she, feeling lifeless as a wooden doll, could only lower her eyelids. No word passed between them. Then he said softly, 'I bid you *adieu,* madame.'

Sensing the strain, Mademoiselle said anxiously, 'Surely not *adieu* but *au revoir?* The Comtesse will depart for Paris soon herself.'

Without taking his harsh gaze from the mute Julie, Nicolas murmured, 'No, Your Highness, I believe it is *adieu.*' Julie raised her head, but he seemed not to notice the glint of tears in her purple eyes. He inclined his plumed hat slightly into her meaningful silence, turned, and ran lightly down the wide stair to where his mounted servants, footmen, and Skandahet-se waited, along with the baggage carts.

She thought her heart would crack in two. She could

not wipe from her mind the image of his last stare. There was disappointment, anger, wounded pride in it, but most of all there was cold finality. She would not have to fear the future, his possible infidelities or his unearned wrath, or the unknown, precarious existence of New France. He would not come seeking her again.

Her own *adieux* to Mademoiselle a fortnight later were just as sad. No word had yet come from the king about allowing Mademoiselle to witness her cousin's wedding, but there was still time. Even so, Julie did not think she would return soon to Eu, and Mademoiselle knew it, in fact was dejectedly resigned to it. Julie had had offers for her hand, after all. She deserved a life.

'It is none of my affair, of course,' remarked Mademoiselle, 'but you seem to have rejected my godson's suit. Anyone can tell you he offers an establishment quite as grand as the Comte de Vosges and, better still, without a prying mother to whom you would have to bend and scrape.'

'The Dowager Comtesse is a very nice lady. She seems quite amiable.'

'Bah! You're not in love with that wispy de Vosges. I do not understand how you could turn away a man of such parts as De Courcillon. Every woman at court, married or not, has tried to snag his interest.'

'I wouldn't doubt it.'

Mademoiselle waited for her ordinarily open lady-of-honor to say more, but there was nothing but silence. Finally, the sharp blue eyes that were boring into Julie drifted sideways. Mademoiselle shrugged. 'So be it. I suppose I am the last one fit to instruct you on affairs of the heart, since I have been the last one to discover the power and the anomalies of love. I can only pray you find what is in your best interest.' Spots of red burned in her cheeks. 'I will miss you about me, madame.'

Julie fell on her knees and pressed the Duchesse's large but well-shaped hand to her cheek. 'And oh, so shall I miss you, Your Highness. I will write and tell you all the news, every week. I shall always be in your debt for all your kindnesses.'

'Nonsense. I am not a kind woman,' Mademoiselle declared. 'I am quite selfish.' But then she put her hand on Julie's bowed head and stroked back the raven hair, an unusual tender gesture.

CHAPTER
~ 23 ~

'You do not look at all well to my eyes, Monsieur de Courcillon.'

'It is merely fatigue, sire. According to Monsieur de Louvois's instructions, I traveled as swiftly as possible to return to Paris,' Nicolas responded, thinking of the four days he had had to wait anyway for the summons to private audience, like waiting for the headsman's ax to fall.

'I will take for granted, monsieur, that you are aware of my irritation with your accidental discovery of the identity of Prisoner X. In fact, de Courcillon, I am vastly angered.'

Displeased, frowning, the ruler sat in judgment on his majestic velvet-cushioned throne in a formal audience chamber empty of all courtiers, not a usual circumstance. The Swiss guards at the portals were too removed to hear what was being said. Nicolas fell to one knee and bowed his head. He did feel quite ill, but by force he kept his voice true. 'I am your most loyal subject, Your Majesty, I beg your consideration of that. I swear that I have long forgotten whatever it was about such prisoner that I might have stumbled upon. As, I am sure, has Monsieur de Louvois from his end.'

Louis rubbed a thumb across his lower lip impatiently. 'My minister exceeded himself in his unbridled passion to know, I will give you that. But one person privy to my business is bad enough. Two is too many. Monsieur de Louvois is a valuable instrument to me, a gentleman whom I cannot lightly dismiss for the indiscretion of excess curiosity. But you, my dear Marquis, make me nervous. You are too much an intimate of my poor, misguided cousin at Eu.'

'Sire, at this moment she weeps for a dead heir. I would never risk her life—or that of the accidentally involved Madame de Lowry—by breaking the silence I swore to Monsieur de Louvois. And that I now vow to you.'

'I believe you, monsieur. You may rise now. You must understand that this is not a punitive action on my part. You know I have favored you much in these past years, and for good reason. You are a capable officer. But with the knowledge you have, I will not be comfortable seeing your face about me, monsieur, not for a long while. I could imprison you, I could do away with you, I could banish you to your farthest estate in France. But it makes more sense to me to remove you from the political machinations of this court through a military commission. Killing two pigeons with one stone, as it were.'

Louis chuckled dryly at his own deftness. He patted down the hair of the luxurious waved wig he wore more often now that his head was balding. But as he viewed the cinnamon-bearded cavalier standing before him, his brows drew together over his shrewd eyes. 'What ails you, monsieur? You are swaying. I fear you are not well.'

Nicolas felt as if there were no blood in his face. His heart was thudding heavily in his chest, and there seemed to be a cord knotted tightly about his throat. By sheer will, he stiffened his stance and kept his voice even. 'Just a small indisposition, sire. It will be gone by tomorrow.'

Louis eyed him sternly. 'Very well. For, although I am removing you from my court, monsieur, it is for an urgent purpose as well, an end in itself that will shield both of us from gossip. I am outraged with the English attitude toward the Americas. They seem to believe the entire continent is rightfully theirs. If they would only be satisfied with being traders and let us conquer the land, an arrangement could be easily worked out: we will take one quarter of the world's commerce and leave them and others the rest, providing they honor our territories. But between English incursions and Indian atrocities, there is turmoil in our Canadian colonies.

'I am sending over, along with laden supply ships and

more colonists, four of my crack companies, a fresh infusion of twelve hundred men and officers who have fought all over Europe from Italy to the Lowlands, and who will swell the New France garrison and citizens' militia. Because you already have good experience in the rigors of the New World, I am appointing you commander of these units, monsieur, going in advance of the Duc de Frontenac, whom I intend to name Governor of all New France. I trust you to be an efficient military arm of France in the colonies, Monsieur le Marquis. That is, if your commercial interests will allow?' The tone was dry, mildly sarcastic, even amused as he looked into the somber-shadowed, intent eyes of his soon-to-be-ex-captain of the Garde-du-Corps.

'I am your most obedient servant, sire. This commission honors me. I would allow nothing to interfere with my duty to you and to France.' A wisp of shrewdness filtered through Nicolas's dulled brain, and he added, 'Of this you have an excellent guarantee, Your Majesty. I someday hope to be released from forced absence from your side.'

'Someday, perhaps. But at this moment, troops are needed urgently overseas. It will take more than another fortnight to equip them and load the other ships that sail in the convoy. I shall have your commission drawn up and your orders. You will be under direct command of the Maréchal de Grammont, but you will inscribe your reports in duplicate, and one will come directly to me. It is my desire that my subjects and properties in New France be secured from savages and Englishmen alike. Do not disappoint me, monsieur. And now you may retire. God go with you.'

Hat under his arm, Nicolas bowed and retreated, stepping backward. He had not expected the splendid command he had just been awarded. It poured a measure of oil on the injustice of his exile and the turmoil in his life. If only he were feeling physically better. Perhaps he should accept bleeding——

'Monsieur le Marquis!'

He looked back to see a troubled expression dipping the end of Le *Roi-Soleil's* long nose. *'Oui, mon roi?'*

The royal fingers drummed on the gilded arm of the throne. 'If you are too busy preparing your departure to attend my court, I will understand,' the king suggested pointedly. He paused and then went on. 'I wish to repeat, I deeply regret, monsieur. I will miss having your strength and intelligence about my throne. But from time to time, certain court intrigues might provide you with too much temptation to disclosure. I have no doubt of your oath of silence. But greater wisdom is to remove you from the eye of the storm. You understand.' Louis being the most absolute monarch yet seen in the Western world, the last was neither question nor apology. It was a command.

'Yes, Your Majesty.' Nicolas made a slight incline of his head.

'You may go, monsieur. *Le bon Seigneur* keep you and guide you.'

'*A votre ordre, mon roi.*'

Julie arrived at the Palais de Luxembourg past seven on a drizzly June evening. She went straight to her chamber and in short order stopped Blanchette from unpacking her things, realizing that continuing to live in the silent palace, with most of its myriad salons and chambers darkened and furniture draped in cloths, was a mistake. Without its owner and her vast entourage, her visitors, petitioners, guests, sycophants, literary salons, and soirées, the rooms echoed eerily to the footsteps of the small staff and deepened her feeling of depression. She should have accepted either Athénais de Montespan's invitation to use the Hôtel de Montespan or the eager one from Diane de Greu, now wife of the Duc de Lesdiguières. In the morning, she would send a note around to her former colleague accepting with pleasure. It would be good to see again the pleasant young woman with whom she had shared much laughter and certain confidences. She would have to endure the night at the Luxembourg, but she would use the time to pull herself together, to put on her Paris face.

How different her entry into Paris was this time, she thought bleakly. When she first arrived from England, she could not contain her joy at the sight of the city. She had been thrilled to her toes then, and how long ago that seemed. Not that it didn't please her to set eyes once more on the crowded, noisy city, the Louvre and Tuileries palaces, every window blazing light, the deep clang of Notre Dame's bells, the construction scaffolding about the dome of Les Invalides, the bustle of vendors closing up shop on the glistening, dirty quais. But she couldn't escape the dejection that had been her constant companion from the moment she had decided for Mercure over Nicolas. She hoped a sound sleep in a good bed, for once, would help. But deep down, she knew it wouldn't.

She glanced at the crystal vase full of dozens of pink roses tied with silver bows which had greeted her when she entered her chamber, a gift from Mercure. He was awaiting her messenger telling of her actual arrival and would most likely come back with the man. But she thought she would wait until morning before announcing herself. She sighed. She didn't expect him to wait much longer for a definite answer to his suit, and her situation this very night was indicative of what her answer must be. She did not want to spend any more of her life at Eu as part of Mademoiselle's train, but unless she bought a place in another royal establishment, she had no residence of her own, in Paris or elsewhere. She supposed, from what Nicolas had said, that she had enough money with his banker to buy herself a house, but such a thing caused lewd gossip if a woman had no family or children to live with her.

Nicolas. Ensconced in his Marais mansion across the Seine, perhaps readying himself for an evening of gaming or the theater with the Princesse Margarethe or whichever other vapid *belle* now took his fancy. Julie knew how quickly he recovered. She squeezed her eyes shut to blot out the vision of his face as she had last seen it and called down a more impersonal thought: she must write and tell him to transfer what monies he held for her to her own banker's coffers. It would not compromise her father in his need to appear deceased. Let the world think her fortune came from the wealthy de Vosges;

lovers could be very generous.

Blanchette helped her out of her travel-dusted clothes and into a cool ribbon-striped dressing robe in which to eat her solitary supper. She had directed the footman to light all the candles in the sconces about the room, for it made her feel better. She was going to accept Mercure, of course. A woman needed an establishment of her own, a husband, children, a place in society. But she would have to wean Mercure from his shy and tentative ways and his dislike of crowded court functions. In her mind's eye, she plotted herself mistress of brilliant gatherings in his imposing hôtel, its century-old stodginess lifted by the luster of new chandeliers, pale-painted and gilded paneling, and the strains of dance music, and what remained of her own gloom brightened by pearls the size of quail eggs resting on her bosom. As for the man himself, retiring, embarrassed about his deformity—well, he was sweet. He would be generous, too. And perhaps he might be a bearable lover. With dedication, she could be a good wife to him.

Julie was nodding over a new novel by Madame de La Fayette that de Vosges had sent, when Blanchette entered to install in her armoire a freshly ironed gown for the morrow. There was a footman following behind her. 'A letter arrived for you yesterday, madame, and a packet,' the maid announced, her perpetual expression of timid surprise always in place. 'They only just remembered it.'

Julie reached for them as the footman came across the parquet to her. She smiled to herself. How confident Mercure was becoming. Letters, gifts, roses. The heavy ivory paper carried no crested stamp in the wax that sealed it, still, as soon as she had the letter unfolded, she had no doubt about the distinctive handwriting. Her smile faded fast as her eyes scanned the paper. It said, 'I do not forget that I owe you a debt of friendship, and now I shall repay it. A gentleman of the king's guards and very dear friend of yours, whose brother we once encountered under very strange circumstances, lies very ill and will soon be dead of poison administered by said greedy, half-mad brother. It is a drug that little by little stills the heart. Go to this man immediately and make use of the antidote, which I send you here—a strong infusion of foxglove, powdered bloodwort, and various other potent substances, which must be taken undiluted, half a cup every two hours. It is all that will save his life. Speed is essential. I pray for your success and beg you not to mention my name in any connection.' There was no signature.

Julie was aware that she made a strange noise, a cry perhaps, that turned both servants' heads sharply toward her. She tore the parchment wrapping from the packet and found a dark flask wrapped in a scarf. Her heart squeezed in fright as an unbidden vision of Monsieur's late wife, Henrietta, rose before her, the woman writhing and screaming, dying in agony. Dying...

'Blanchette, help me into that gown and bring me some shoes, quickly. You, footman, go immediately to order my coach and driver. I wish them ready for me at the main portal in ten minutes, and tell the driver if he brings me to the Hôtel de Courcillon in the Marais in less than that, he shall have a bonus.'

In feverish haste, she dressed, not stopping to reknot and recurl her hair but tying a chiffon hood over the black tresses that spilled over her shoulder. Clutching the precious flask wrapped again in the scarf, she climbed into the coach, Blanchette beside her, and they were whirled away into the Paris night. Accompanying her agitation was anger: the letter and packet had been sent by Athénais yesterday and not produced by the dolt of an interim butler until precious hours had passed tonight. *'Entendez-moi, cher Seigneur,'* she prayed under her breath. 'I beg you, let him be alive. If he is dead, it is I who have murdered him by not warning him of his brother's evil ways. And if he is dead, I shall die too!' she wailed inwardly, uncaring of the contradictions in her soul. She was squeezing Blanchette's hand convulsively as some comfort to her fear. 'Dear God, help us!' Her lips framed the silent plea.

A footman admitted her through the outer door of the Marais mansion, but two others moved to bar her way at the foot of the stairs as the liveried butler descended toward her. 'I must see Monsieur le Marquis. I am the Comtesse de Lowry. Please announce me at once.'

The man insolently looked her up and down, making her aware that she must appear somewhat disheveled. 'The Marquis is indisposed, madame. He will see no one.'

'He will see me, I am sure. I demand that you announce me or let me pass.'

'I have my orders from Monsieur l'Abbé d'Aubièrre, madame. I shall have to inquire of him.'

'No, don't...Very well, then, but quickly. I am in most urgent haste.'

The butler sighed and shook his head, knowing the mission was useless, but he turned and went up the stairs again. She wrung her hands and paced under the imperturbable stares of the footmen and Blanchette's round-eyed gape. Finally, the butler returned, his manner, as he slowly came down again, regal as a duc's. 'I regret, madame, but Monsieur l'Abbé says that the Marquis is not to be disturbed, nor he, either, for that matter. You will have to depart,' he insisted into her upturned face.

'I will *not* leave, you imbecile. This is Monsieur de Courcillon's house, and he would want me admitted, ill or not,' she replied in a fury, and she tried to force her way past the lackeys' shoulders which were drawn together to block her passage.

'There is no use to this, madame,' the butler huffed, coming around the footmen and grabbing her arm. 'My master was quite clear. No visitors. I will escort you out.'

'You will let me go, you oaf!' Julie cried. She twisted around to free her arm and stamped the high heel of her satin shoe into his instep so that the man yelped in pain. She glanced up desperately toward the balustrade around the first floor landing and called out as loudly as she could, 'Skandahet-se! Skandahet-se!' She struggled with the angry butler and one of the footmen, who had grabbed her elbows and were shoving her toward the door, warding off Blanchette's indignant slaps at them at the same time. The fracas should have wakened the entire household.

'Let go!' bellowed a deep voice, and it froze the servants in place. The big Indian loomed at the top of the stairs, arms akimbo.

'Skandahet-se, allow me up. I know monsieur is ill. I have something that will help him,' Julie cried. 'Help. For monsieur,' she repeated clearly, trying to make the untutored savage understand. 'Please!'

The taciturn Huron stared at her for a moment. Then he glowered down at the butler. 'Let go!'

'Listen, you heathen barbarian, my orders are to let no one further than this foyer—arghh!' The man's voice stuck in his throat as the Indian, seeming to fly down the stairs, grabbed him by the front of the coat and almost picked him off the floor. The butler's eyes popped, for there was a knife point threatening his belly.

'Let go!'

'G-Guillaume, release the lady's arm, for God's sake,' the man gurgled hastily, and he was dropped back on his heels again.

Skandahet-se shoved the knife back into the belt about his tight, button-popping coat. He nodded gravely to Julie. 'Come.'

Straightening her hood and the shoulder of her gown, which had been pulled askew, and throwing an acid glance at the butler, she followed the Indian up the stairs and through two small but finely appointed salons before stopping at a pair of portals heavily carved in the style of the last century. The Indian frowned at the footman guarding the door and threw open one of the doors, stepping back to let her enter. He motioned Blanchette to wait outside.

The room was in semidarkness, but she could easily see the large bed that dominated the far end. She started to hurry toward it, but at Skandahet-se's grunt, she looked around to her right and realized that Nicolas was sitting slumped in a high-backed chair, clad in a white shirt and breeches, his head fallen forward so that his hair hid his face. The table next to him held a lit two-branched candelabrum, a half-full wine decanter with a sticky goblet, a napkin, and a scatter of papers. She approached, her heels making a *tic-tac* on the floor, but he gave no sign of hearing. Her heart contracted with terror at his stillness until she stood by him and saw the faint, quick rise and fall of his chest and heard his labored breathing. 'Nicolas?' she whispered. 'Nicolas?'

There was no answer.

She put her hand under his chin and lifted his unresisting head and was shaken by what she saw—great dark circles under his closed eyes, as if he had been struck, sunken cheeks covered with stubble, a tinge of blue on his lips. His eyes opened, a glimmer of pale blue rimmed with red, a bleary look, vacant, uncomprehending, centered on her but unfocused. *'Le bon Dieu nous aide!'* she whispered, appalled. She brushed aside the tangled hair on his brow and laid her palm on it and then on his cheek. Clammy cold. Too cold.

'Have there been doctors?' she asked Skandahet-se. 'Doctor?'

'The doctor has come twice, madame, but misyoo gave hard orders he not be bled. The doctor does not know what is his ailment. It is very strange, he says, and needs study. He left medicine, but it does no good.'

'Is he in pain?'

'No, madame, nor air in the belly or vomit. He just becomes weak, much weak like a baby, till he cannot swallow food or speak much and fights to breathe.'

'But why is he not abed when he is so desperately ill that he does not even recognize me?'

The Indian shook his head. 'Misyoo would not allow. This morning he says he rather die sitting up, and makes his valet dress him and he drinks wine. Makes me swear not to put him back in bed. But past few hours he does not talk. I go to misyoo his brother and ask him to call doctor again, bleed him maybe, but the brother laughs. He is sick himself.'

Julie had held the packet containing the antidote in an iron grip under her arm. Now she feverishly opened the bundle and drew out the flask. 'Here I have medicine which may work if we are not too late. You must help me to get it down him,' she told Skandahet-se. She glanced at the goblet, which showed the dregs of wine, scowled and gave it to the Indian to wash well with soap. He went into a connecting dressing room, and she heard him pouring water into a basin. When he brought back the clean goblet, she unstoppered the flask, measured out what she thought was the correct amount of the oily yellow fluid, and, with the Indian holding his master's shaggy head steady, tipped the antidote Athénais had obtained little by little into the slack mouth, rejoicing that Nicolas seemed to make some effort to help her with his lips.

Julie put down the empty goblet and beckoned to the Indian. 'Come, carry him to the bed. I absolve you from whatever silly promise he forced you to make.' Obviously relieved to have someone directing, Skandahet-se immediately complied, lifting Nicolas by the arms, insinuating a big shoulder under him, and heaving him up to be borne like a sack of stones across the room. Julie piled up pillows to help him breathe and pulled aside the bedclothes.

As soon as Nicolas was installed, she sent Skandahet-se to order more blankets and a brick heated in the oven and wrapped in flannel. It was all she knew to do. She had felt his hands, his stockinged feet. They were cold, those same hands whose warmth had sent *frissons* of pleasure along her skin as they caressed her; they were icy cold. She pushed aside the unbuttoned neckband of his shirt and pressed her finger to the side of his neck as she had seen doctors do. There was a pulse, but as she compared it to hers, it was frighteningly slow. She hung over the pale, still face and whimpered, 'Oh, Nicolas. Oh, my love, don't die. Oh, I beg you, don't die.' She pressed a hand against her mouth as she thought again of her culpability in this tragedy, her stupidity in letting him live with a dangerous satanist just because she was embarrassed by her knowledge of it.

There was a scratch on the door, and a servant handed in woolen blankets, which Julie and the Indian wrapped closely about the comatose Nicolas. The brick, when it arrived, they would put against his feet, under the covers. His garments they would leave on him, for added warmth. They stood looking down at him, knowing nothing more to do. Julie was torn. She should surely get a doctor to him. And yet each doctor was jealous of his own prescriptions and might not allow her to administer the medicine she had. It was all that might work, Athénais had written. She looked at the little timepiece she had hung about her neck, a last-minute thought before she had rushed from the Luxembourg. Less than two hours from now, she could give him another draught of the antidote——

The Indian cleared his throat. 'That medicine you bring will cure misyoo? Make him better?'

She looked up at the hawkish nose, the reddish skin, the stolid features. The eyes, a dense black that emitted no light, were staring fixedly at the man in the bed. But the corners of the stern, wide mouth drooped, as if the hard lines from nose to mouth could no longer hold them up. It was as much sorrow and distress as the Indian could show, she supposed.

'I don't know, Skandahet-se. I am told by someone who is wise in these matters that it is the only thing that may save him,' she muttered. 'We can only pray and wait.' Then she jerked her head abruptly and gave him a startled look. 'But——! You speak French! It just occurred to me.'

A shadow smile passed over the somber face. 'Misyoo teach me to speak his words when we were still in my land.'

'But you keep it secret? No one is sure you can even understand French.'

He shrugged, a little uncomfortable under the surprise in her eyes. 'Not waste words when there is nothing to say, madame.'

Her smile was faint, too. It was all she could manage with the dragging, heavy breathing of Nicolas in her ear.

'Then tell me what happened. How did monsieur fall ill?'

The big man shook his head. 'Since we returned from Eu, misyoo is very unhappy. He fight with Misyoo l'Abbé, who is always sick and with no gold in his pocket. My misyoo drinks much, spirits that burn and special wine his brother brings from his monks' house. He sits and drinks, but not getting drunk. Once he goes to meet with the king, and then he tells me we are going back to New France, which makes my heart happy. Not see my wives and my children in a very long time. But every day he look sicker and sicker. Two days ago, in spite that he yells no, his brother call doctor, but it does not help. My misyoo stands by the window to breathe better. He drink more wine to make his blood more rich, he write on his papers, but yesterday he was too weak to stand. He will not send for his friend de Vivonne. He thinks he will soon get well, does not wish king to know he is ill.' He glanced at the man wrapped in blankets, looked at his own big hands, and grunted. 'In my tribe, we would have powerful man of medicine to call out the bad spirits that are eating his liver. We dance, we chant, we chase them out. But here in this foreign land, my prayers have no power.'

Julie walked to the table, picked up the decanter of red wine, and sniffed it. It smelled like a young, fruity wine from a Burgundy vineyard. 'Is this what he has been drinking?'

'Yes. Very special good. Every day Misyoo l'Abbé bring him more. Make him feel better, Misyoo l'Abbé says.'

'Mon Dieu, mon Dieu.' Julie shuddered. Holding the decanter gingerly by the neck, as if it were a live snake, Julie crossed the room with it and flung it with all her strength into the cold fireplace, the crash of the glass and splash of deep red liquid underlining the frightened anger within her; there was hardly a doubt in her mind that Nicolas was being murdered by his possessed brother. She thought then of Nicolas's older brother, the one who had died suddenly of unknown causes along with his little son, and Nicolas's sister-in-law, unhinged, incarcerated. How long ago was it that the jealous Jean-Pierre Anselm d'Aubièrre had begun his slide into evil and the depravity of satanism?

She turned from the shattered vessel to the unblinking Indian. 'Skandahet-se, listen carefully. That wine was poisoned. Perhaps his food, too. It is even possible the things he wears closest to his skin, his linen, his shirt, are poisoned. Let him drink nothing, understand, nothing but water from the common barrel, and eat nothing but food from the servants' pot, both of which only you shall carry to him. You will bring one of your own shirts, and we will put it on him; and yourself wash and dry some of his own and some linen. I have heard talk that even fiber of clothing and the paper of letters can be made poisonous.'

'Is it misyoo's brother who does this?' The corners of the hard-set mouth pulled down farther.

'I cannot answer that. Just follow my instructions.'

The few candles lit were guttering when Julie awoke with a start, blinking into the shadowed room, her back aching from having dozed off in the rigid chair. Was it time to give Nicolas more of the antidote to the poison he'd ingested? They had given him three more doses through the night. Was it time? She groped on her chest for the little clock and then noticed Skandahet-se in a listening attitude by the door. 'What is it?' she called to him in a low voice.

'Misyoo's brother. I think he comes.'

A moment later, the door was flung open, the Indian stepping back to become half-hidden behind it. Jean-Pierre Anselm stumbled in, his worn-looking valet following, only to be ordered to remain outside. Jean-Pierre hooked the door with his foot to close it, not remarking the Indian who stood in the shadows. The Abbé's thin body was encased in a black floor-length soutane, badly crumpled, carelessly unbuttoned at the neck. He was unshaven. Julie rose, shocked at his appearance for the second time in that house, for she had only seen Nicolas's brother—with the exception of that one terrible night at La Voisin's—in the fine garb of a courtier, a relentlessly smiling man with a certain boyish charm. This person before her, whose eyes burned in his crumpled face, was almost unrecognizable.

'You are not wanted here, madame. I order you to leave.'

She stubbornly lifted her chin. 'Monsieur de Courcillon is very ill. I have come to take care of him.'

''Twill do you no good. He is dying. Any fool can see

that. He'll be dead by the morrow. You can't help him. My dear, dashing, officious brother is doomed.' And there it was, to her horror, that curious little falter in his speech, which she had heard issuing from the bizarre demon mask at La Voisin's.

She heard him give a ghastly laugh. But she took a step forward, unafraid of him. 'And from the looks of it, so are you, Monsieur l'Abbé. You, too, are ill.'

'Me? I am fine. I do not need your solicitude, madame. All it takes is enough gold coins, and my boy can run to fetch my medicine, which is exactly what he is doing now. The poor Marquis, my brother, has much money, as you may have noticed, funds which will come to me, of course. Then I shall be better able to take care of my health.' His voice surged high; his giggle was half hysterical. But then his rumpled eyebrows clashed together, and his tone dropped to a threatening whisper. 'Get out, madame! I order you out of my house. I shall send in my servants to remove you by force.'

'It is not your house, monsieur, and you will not l-lay a finger on me. I know you for what you are, you servant of the devil, and I know what you have done here. You p-pray to a forgiving God that your brother lives, for I am not the only one who knows you are a murderer! Furthermore, you will allow me f-free access to this house should I require it, or I will lay before the king himself enough information on your apostasy as to earn you a swift p-place with the headsman, regardless of God's will for Nicolas. I swear it, Jean-Pierre Anselm d'Aubièrre. I will destroy you if this man dies!' Her voice broke, and there were tears of fury in her eyes. Stunned, he glared at her.

Julie could not bear to look at him. She turned and ran to the bed, to peer down in fresh grief at the unconscious, desperately ill man who had been her vigorous lover, her hearty friend, who might now never return to the remote New France settlements that drew him back. Tears streaked her cheeks.

And then she realized that Nicolas had moved; in fact, he had pulled one arm from the blankets and flung it across his forehead. Staring at him, she saw that his chest rose and fell more regularly and his breathing was much less harsh. She felt it was warm. His forehead, too, was of normal temperature, the clamminess gone. The pulse beat she located in his neck gave a quicker tempo. She bent, a moan of relief escaping her lips, and laid her wet cheek against his relaxed hand. Then she heard shuffling footsteps behind her. She straightened up and turned, spreading her arms as if to protect Nicolas with her body.

With narrowed, venomous eyes, Jean-Pierre croaked, 'How does he do?'

'I warn you. I meant all that I said. If the Marquis dies, I shall expose you and your dreadful cult to the world. If he lives, I shall tell only him your part in it, as I should have done before, and I will let him deal with you. But you will not enter this room again until your brother is totally well and in control.'

'You want his wealth, too, is that it, harlot? How do you dare upset my plans, my needs, my life!'

'I will see you burn, you vicious monster!'

The trembling hands Jean-Pierre raised to strike her were like claws, his face so twisted with anger it seemed his burning eyes looked out from a mask more grotesque than the one he had worn in his office of priest of the Black Mass. Julie shrank back, but she was not afraid, for Skandahet-se had come up noiselessly behind the shaking man. The Abbé loomed over her for a second, and then, suddenly, the clawed hands clutched at his own face and he burst into racking sobs. He sank to the floor on his knees, hunching over as if in pain and making a wrenching noise. Julie stared in horror. She'd hardly expected her threats to produce such a violent breakdown.

'You don't understand. No one understands,' came Jean-Pierre's broken, hoarse voice. 'There is that within me which has devoured my soul. I am caught in its meshes like a struggling fish in a net. Even now it grips me with furious, demanding fingers, a demon of agonizing power. I must feed it, I must. . .' Racked with sobs, retching and moaning, he sprawled disabled on the floor at Julie's feet. 'You don't understand. If Nicolas lives, I will die. He hates me! He wants me to die. . .' he wailed.

She twitched her skirt away, revolted. 'He is mad,' she muttered to Skandahet-se.

'It is as he says. A spirit of evil visits him, and only the medicine he takes drives it away. Footman tells me that yesterday he collect all the silver in the house, plate, spoons, everything, and take it away. Before you come, he sends his boy for the medicine, and soon now he will recover.' He eyed the groveling man. 'In forest near my home, a root grows, and in winter sometimes the hungry fox gnaws on it. It helps him live, but it drive him mad. He runs in circle, tries to climb trees. Yet fox still gnaws on root. His spirit crave root. Misyoo l'Abbé is like fox. Spirit sick. Better that I kill him. He is evil.'

'No! You will do no harm to him. Call his servants to take him to his apartment. It is not up to us to punish him.'

The sun had come up by the time Julie administered to Nicolas what was probably the next to last dose of the antidote. He still slept, perhaps the result of the medicine, but his breathing and temperature were normal, and a touch of color had chased some of the deathly pallor from his face. She lowered his head back to the pillow and gently smoothed the soft hair off his brow and from the sides of his face. She stared at him hopelessly for a moment.

'I believe he will be all right now,' she told Skandahet-se. 'We have done all we can. I will leave now. Do send a messenger immediately to fetch Monsieur de Vivonne here to help the Marquis recover, but make no mention of the scene we have just endured. When the sun is almost halfway toward noon, give him the rest of the medicine, and if he wakes, make him stay in the bed if you have to tie him there. Let no one near him but yourself and his valet, if you think the fellow trustworthy. And see that monsieur's food and drink are taken from the common sources.'

The Indian nodded. 'Misyoo l'Abbé will demand entrance.'

'Perhaps now he will not. But should his own illness cause him to forget what I threatened him with, remind him that the Comtesse de Lowry's notary holds a sealed letter wherein are stated all his vile secrets.' It was a safeguard she intended to write as soon as she reached her own quarters. Sadly, she brushed her fingers over Nicolas's face. The features were sharp and tight over the bones, sapped as he was by the deadly, heart-stopping poison. Yet they still showed the same resolute set that defined him.

'This afternoon, I will have delivered to you a letter for the Marquis to read when he is able, which will explain to him everything that has happened. You will also tell him that it was you who administered the antidote, which arrived here by messenger from me. Do not, under any circumstances, tell him that I was here with him. Do you understand?' She peered at the Huron's dispassionate face, and the officious manner that had held her together all night crumbled a bit. 'Please?' she asked him.

He nodded again.

'When—when is it monsieur's intention to leave for New France?' Her throat tightened over the question.

'We leave Paris on twenty-sixth of June. Then sail with army regiments from the port of Cherbourg at moonrise the last day of June.'

'Ten days.' She stared down at Nicolas again, but sweet memories of his quirky smile, his tender eyes, were squeezed by visions of embattled towns huddled behind wooden forts in the black depths of the North American forest—as she envisioned New France—more isolated and more lonely than Cuckfield had ever been. There was no doubt that life for her was here, not there. Tears burned in her eyes again. Her heart ached desperately. Oh, my love, my love, how will I ever forget you?

She whirled around to Skandahet-se. 'I shall be residing at the Hôtel Lesdiguières in the rue Montmorency. Send me some word by tonight about how the Marquis fares.'

Drawing a small mask from the purse dangling at her waist, Julie donned it and then tied on her hood. Fighting bone-deep fatigue, she went out to collect

Blanchette, who had slept on a settee in the anteroom. She was anxious to flee the mansion where her love had almost left this life, his fine Paris premises that soon would see him no more, perhaps for many a year.

CHAPTER
~ 24 ~

A Son Altesse La Duchesse de Montpensier
Mademoiselle:

There is so much I have to relate to you. Therefore, as I promised, I shall set it all down in this letter, except I necessarily must be brief, or I shall not come to the end before more is to be inscribed. However the case, I pray that your health is continuing good and that the bad-weather ache in your leg has eased as the weeks have flown.

My first news is unfortunately most sad, and I shall repeat it first so that what follows later may cheer you—although you may have heard of this calamity by earlier courier. Nicolas de Courcillon's younger brother, Monsieur l'Abbé d'Aubiérre, is dead, having passed on in his sleep one week ago, some say from a gross overdraught of a certain medicine he was in the habit of taking to calm his nerves. This great tragedy has affected all of us, for the gentleman was but twenty-three. Needless to say, Monsieur le Marquis was desolate at the demise of his only remaining brother—so I am told. And all the more so for having at that time not quite recovered himself from a debilitating illness, which I am happy to say has quitted him entirely—so I hear. In fact, at the funeral mass yesterday, which I attended in the company of Monsieur de Vosges, I could see for myself that, *merci à Dieu*, in spite of sorrow and the marks of grief writ upon his face, the Marquis, your godson, seems to have recovered his strength and his élan, which fact I hope will ease your mind.

I could speak only a few words with him at this melancholy ceremony, merely to offer my most deep condolences, and as Monsieur de Vosges and I slipped away directly the funeral was over, I know little else of him. Except that the king has given him command of four regiments of soldiers being sent to New France a few days from now. He is understandably busy putting in order his affairs and is hardly seen at court. Perhaps he will write to you himself with more details. . .

With a sigh, Julie laid down her pen and flexed a cramped finger. She happened to gaze at the quill and then looked away. It had been dyed a light blue, and it reminded her of the color of Nicolas de Courcillon's eyes. Eyes that had looked down at her—and at de Vosges—with guarded greeting, eyes bracketed with more etched lines than had been there before. If she could only have recalled the letter she had written to him about Jean-Pierre, she would have; but out of worry for Nicolas's safety, she had sent it the very day she had been at the Hôtel de Courcillon, without knowing that the tormented Abbé had been found dead that afternoon, empty powder papers crumpled on the floor. If only she had stayed her hand another day, Nicolas could have buried his brother without the grievous knowledge of how diabolical the man had been, how full of hate, how inclined to murder. If only, if only—She squirmed in her seat, uncomfortable in her own skin. If only she had never been exposed to her bitter, instructive existence with the Earl of Lowry, would she now be writing the next sentence?

. . .a much happier event to take place, for I have decided to betroth myself to the Comte de Vosges, an exemplary man and one of whom I am fond. The banns will be published on Sunday next, and we have talked of being wed in September. . .

Again she laid the quill down to stare out the window of the small but very pleasant chamber the new Madame de Lesdiguières had assigned her, although she could see nothing but the windows on the farther side of the house's square court. After a few days, she had received from Nicolas a few lines penned in his big, blocky handwriting, to wit: there seemed no words beholden enough to thank her for sending the potion that had saved his life; the facts that she had related to him about Jean-Pierre were horrifying enough to contemplate but not so much as the man's sordid death; yet it must have been a forgiving God who had intervened at the last to remove his brother's soul from the additional pain of earthly punishment for his heinous sins, etcetera, etcetera, and once again a graceful *remerciement* for her extraordinary service to him. It was only because she knew how Nicolas had loved his brother that she detected the pain behind his calm words.

She read the letter three times, looking for something else, she knew not what. But it was no more than a dignified expression of gratitude, reserved and correct. Somewhere inside her, she had expected he might express anger that even for one night she had been foolish enough to involve herself with sorcerers, in spite of the fact that it had kept him from dying, for that would have been Nicolas's way when he had cared about her. But he coolly accepted her tale and made no comment regarding her. He hadn't even come to see her himself. He had sent Skandahet-se with the letter.

She sighed again and dipped the pen in the tiny inkpot. Well, what did she expect? He had had his fill of her indecision, her inability to trust him. In fact, Athénais, whom she had gone to the Louvre to see to thank for her warning and help, had casually cautioned her. 'Don't expect great gratitude from your Marquis, Ton-Ton. Men are so peculiar—lovers, husbands, all of them. They are not happy if we know something they don't whether it saves their lives or not. They sense it as a sort of power over them. A man like Nicolas de Courcillon, for instance, will chafe at the thought that you could know a mysterious apothecary who divined just the right medicine to make up to cure him.'

Julie rubbed her forehead. She'd done even worse in respect to Nicolas's ego than Athénais had imagined, for Nicolas now understood that she had known about Jean-Pierre's diabolical connections for a long time and had never told him. For him, that was surely the last straw.

...Madame de Montespan is more stunning than ever now that she has given the king another daughter. Her star is still most high and firm in the heavens, and her influence with His Majesty is secure. She expressed to me her regret that you did not avail yourself of her friendship in the matter of Monsieur de Lauzun but vowed she would never cease to offer it to you, knowing, of course, that her determination to have her way would get back to you. Having produced another child for him, she is even more disturbed by the king's financial neglect of her children, even though his frequent visits to them, a tattered secret, pleases her. I would not doubt Your Highness will receive yet another overture on her part to trade her influence for a duchy...

...and even Monsieur de Louvois, who continues his attentions to me, in vain, he shall soon discover, professes not to know why His Majesty holds Monsieur de Lauzun incommunicado at Pignerol. He said to me, obliquely, that perhaps if the king allows you to Paris for the wedding, you might petition His Majesty again in person. As for the certain disagreeable man I told you of whose curiosity gained him great pain in Honfleur, neither Monsieur de Louvois nor I speak of him or of what might have been behind his quest. It is as Nicolas said. They could only have discovered the same sad and unarguable end of the trail as he did. Better to let the thing lie...

Her mouth twitched into a mirthless smile. Her skin was so pale that the straight, deep pink scar on the side of her neck was easily noticed. In fact, de Louvois had remarked on it with deepest sympathy. A runaway horse and the whipping of a thorny thicket was her excuse. Then he had remarked, in a form of obtuse consolation, that she could be certain so cruel a thicket had been amply punished. By God, presumably.

...I have hired an additional maid-cum-seamstress, a more mature woman than Blanchette,

therefore much more experienced with the needle. . .
. . . Diane de Lesdiguières has been so gracious to me. She insists I am to be her guest until my wedding. I am more than comfortable here, in this household with her courteous husband, adorable stepchildren, and her little dogs. . .

Yes? she mentally chided herself. Then why don't you allow Blanchette and Aurore to unpack most of your trunks? You can pack them all back up when it is time to move to the Hôtel de Vosges. You need only supervise your servants. You are even too lazy for that.

. . .is giving a *soirée* on the evening of 25 June at the Hôtel de Lambert for Monsieur and the advance envoys from the Palatinate. *Le tout Paris* will be there, and oh, how I wish so were you, Your Highness. Surely a part of France's special glory will be missing by your absence. But I am sure that between Madame de Sévigné and myself and the accounts I will cut from the Paris *Gazette*, you shall be so well informed of what transpired that you will most certainly feel you were present. . .
. . .and again with a prayer for your health and happiness, I sign myself
Julie de Lowry
Hôtel de Lesdiguières, 23 June, 1672

Once more, she put down the pen and again sighed. The twenty-third of June already. Just seven more days to the glitter of Monsieur's gala wedding. The hard-used streets along the route from the Tuileries to Notre Dame were already being divested of any construction sites and major eyesores, and on the day of the wedding, they would miraculously turn into fragrant, flower-strewn paths to Parnassus. Mercure vowed that in her honor he would order the grandeur of six red-plumed horses to his coach that day, to distinguish them both in the gala procession. Mercure was so quietly happy. . .

And in three days, Nicolas de Courcillon would quit Paris and then France. She pressed her lips tightly against the disagreeable thought that he might not even come to say goodbye to her.

Nor, in the days that followed, did he.

The Duchesse de Lesdiguières, née de Greu, had always thought the Comtesse de Lowry was one of the court's great beauties, albeit less conceited than most. But seeing her attired and standing in the center of her chamber ready for the gala soirée was an exciting experience, made the more so for de Lowry's long absence from the court. Entering the room, the new duchesse gave a pleased gasp, and as her guest's maids stepped back, flushed with pride and excitement, she glided forward, her hands clasped passionately. 'Ah, Julie, how utterly enchanting you look! Let me get a good view of you.' Her pink-cheeked friend laughed but stood still, and Diane circled about her with exclamations of admiration.

It was both the woman and the gown that gladdened her eye. The hairdresser who had once attended Mademoiselle had visited that afternoon, and the result was the artless-looking coiffure de Montespan had just introduced, a whole head of silky, shining, blue-black ringlets, some of which tumbled prettily onto the pristine forehead, with pearls on tiny bow knots shimmering here and there amidst the curls. The dark mass made a perfect frame for the delicacy of a faultless complexion, great lash-fringed violet eyes, and tilted nose; and the eyes were finally lit with some pleasure as Diane exclaimed over her.

Julie's gown, which brought out the drama of her violet eyes, was of a marvelous shot silk that shimmered from indigo to lavender to purple as she moved. Her wide skirt over side panniers was held open below the tiny, pointed waist by silver roses fastened with amethyst bars, and it sported a three-foot silk train bordered with silver roses. Her pleated underskirt was of embroidered silver gauze, and silver ribbons puffed her lace-trimmed sleeves. The very low-cut neckline displayed smooth, white shoulders and her full bosom, which in turn was the tender showcase for a sparkling square-cut sapphire, pendant from pearls about her neck, a gift from the Comte de Vosges. Her graceful arms were encased to the elbow in perfumed white kid gloves. Long eardrops sparkled in her ears, and she held a fan of a single splendid curled white ostrich plume.

Diane came back around to face her friend, secure in the fact that her own finery, sheer black gauze over white satin, and with diamond-fastened ostrich tips in her blonde hair, had brought her pleased husband quickly to his feet when she had entered his chamber. 'But wherever did you get that incredible chameleon silk?' she asked, awed.

'Isn't it wonderful? It was a saint's-day gift from Mademoiselle, and she told me it had been presented to her years ago by a visiting prince from the Indies. We had so little to do at Eu, we made all sorts of trips into Dieppe to purchase fabrics and had gowns and petticoats and *robes de chambre* sewn and fitted. I have a finer wardrobe than before I left Paris.' Julie declared this with a gay little flip of her shoulders to signify that she was a woman with no care in the world. But Diane knew better. They had talked and talked, for Julie had confided in her. Now she was sorry to see the momentary shine in the splendid eyes dull again. And the smile that decorated the coral lips stiffened and seemed affixed with glue.

Diane wondered what she could do. As a more bashful type, she had always admired Julie's poise and easy grace, but she hadn't realized that the woman was so stubborn. In fact, she thought her wrong to disdain the Marquis de Courcillon merely on suspicion of future infidelity. It seemed so childish, so injust. Almost all husbands were unfaithful at one time or other. But, although it seemed to hurt, Julie was adamant. Well, the temptation of de Courcillon would soon be removed from her.

Diane slipped her arm around her friend's waist. 'The Comte de Vosges is a lucky man, *ma chère amie*, for tonight he will be the envy of every man present. Come,' she urged. 'My dear husband awaits us. You remember the ditty, "Let us away to the ball, away, away."' Diane warbled cheerily and batted her eyelashes. And together, laughing, fans aflutter, they rustled through the salon to the foyer, where the satin-coated Duc de Lesdiguières stood, ready to offer an arm to each lady.

The line of coaches waiting to drop their passengers moved forward slowly into the court of the Hôtel de Lambert, and people relieved their impatience by sticking their plume-adorned or elaborately hatted heads out of the windows to see who was alighting at the steps. It suited Julie to do this, too. She thought the somewhat cooler air outside the coach would help her dull headache. It was thus she saw Nicolas emerge from a calèche and go up the stairs to the portals alone, no Princesse Margarethe, no Vicomtesse d'Angerville, or any other *belle* on his arm. He held his head high, and his step was in his usual confident manner, but his gray brocade coat and white-plumed hat made a muted costume, and over his baldric he wore a wide lavender band of mourning.

Julie pulled back her head and for an instant closed her eyes against pain. She hadn't been sure he would attend this function, since his regiments were to leave at dawn the next morning, so Skandahet-se had mentioned in delivering the letter. But she supposed it was an easy way to bid the most people goodbye. She wanted desperately to avoid him. If, in spite of what they had shared, he could not find the courtesy at least to make his *adieux* to her in private, she had no wish to instruct the whole court on what it was like to bid farewell to a lover.

The crowd was so great, there seemed a good chance they might not meet. Four hundred preening aristocrats were jammed into the blazing ballroom of the great hôtel, and between the body heat and the heavy aromas of perfumes, brilliantine, and the white jasmine hanging from baskets everywhere, one could hardly breathe. Still, in spite of her discomfort, when they appeared at the head of the steps leading down into the long, ornate salon, and the majordomo knocked his staff against the floor and announced Monsieur le Duc de Lesdiguières,

Madame la Duchesse de Lesdiguières, and Madame la Comtesse de Lowry, the buzz and murmur that ran around the room gave Julie a lift of pleasure. Many pairs of eyes stared at her with open admiration or, just as good, with scarcely veiled envy.

She greeted this one and that and soon collected a little flotilla of the usual eager gallants, but when Mercure finally found her, she was willing to leave their endless, witless flatteries. Mercure smiled down at her anxiously, his pale face showing splotches of red, occasioned, she thought, both by her splendor and by his discomfort with parties and crowds. They made their way to a smaller salon, which was less crowded and where they could sit to keep Mercure off his bad leg and still hear the elegant music of the orchestra. Since the king and queen had not arrived, there was no dancing yet.

The evening went by in a blur for Julie, unable as she was to generate her normal enthusiasm for this affair. Mercure began to irritate her with his repeated apologies for not being able to stand long enough to enjoy watching the dancing, and each time she was invited by one of her admirers to essay a *branle* or *pavane* and accepted, she returned to his sad smile feeling guilty. People stopped to chat with them, however, and they did hasten over to the doorway to see the arrival of the king. Louis, resplendent in white silk and crimson taffeta, led in the small, stout Marie-Thérèse. Behind them glided, with a long silken train, the scintillating Madame de Montespan, all flashing eyes and expanses of creamy skin and jewels, easily overshadowing the subdued La Vallière. At one time, Julie might have maneuvered to stand along the path opened for the monarch's arrival, for she had always liked to be seen by the approving royal eye; it stroked her ego. Tonight she did not care much one way or the other.

It grew warm amid the ebb and flow of chatting couples and groups who passed their settee. Julie pulled her hands from her kid gloves and tucked the mitts under at the wrist. Mercure volunteered to go fetch her an ice from the collation table, which bore great pyramids of them, and she gratefully accepted. With measuring eyes, she watched him limp away leaning on a slim rosewood stick with an ivory knob, and she thought for the hundredth time that his countenance was certainly pleasant enough, his build slim—what a pity his lameness had driven him so within himself.

Beyond the people standing before her, she saw a group of her giddy friends enjoying one of Monsieur's waspish stories, and she decided to join them. But on rising abruptly, a pendant jet on her bracelet caught in one of the ribbon knots holding back her skirt and was pulled off, dropping. She bent to feel about on the velvet seat of the settee and even ran her fingers between the seat and the back, and then, having had no luck, began to scan the floor just below.

A voice behind her said, 'Is this what you are looking for?'

Her heart turned over. She whirled about as if someone had slapped her on the rear. Nicolas stood there, straight and stiff, proffering on his open palm the tear-shaped jet with its twisted hook, gleaming balefully. He was not smiling. He looked at her with eyes empty of familiarity. His hat, with a white plume holding cocked the gray velvet brim, was pushed back on his head. It would ordinarily have given him a jaunty air, but his somberness now turned his features to granite.

She picked the little jet from his palm, murmuring distractedly, 'Thank you. It was careless of me.'

He shrugged. 'An accident.'

The moment's silence seemed to stretch for an hour. Finally, she got out, 'I thought you were not even going to say goodbye to me.'

He said stiffly, 'It is my impression that we have already said our goodbyes.'

His matter-of-factness chilled her.

Then, seeing her visible hurt, he bent a bit, his tone warming up slightly. With a faint smile, he said, 'May I at least tell you that you are especially gorgeous tonight, madame? If I were a poet, I might say that Venus would blush in your company.'

'You are too kind, monsieur.' She gave him the

formula response, for she was too flustered to be original.

'But I once knew a lady who will always outshine you. She wore a plain gown of blue stuff and a stiff, lacy cap, and she was modest and loving. She was more than beautiful. She was a dream. I imagined her.'

There was accusation under the cool, even tone, but it was better than empty words. Disconcerted, she didn't know what to say. She glanced around, hoping Mercure was on his way back but knowing it was too soon.

Nicolas saved her by finding another subject, returning again to neutral formality. He stated in a lowered voice, 'I thought you might have a word or two you would wish me to deliver to your father.'

Father? The word burst like a firecracker in Julie's head. In all the turmoil of the past weeks, she'd almost forgotten that she still had a father on the earth. Horrified and embarrassed by her self-absorption, she sought refuge in a lie. 'Yes, of course, but there is so much to say. It takes time. I have been composing a letter, which I will dispatch after the wedding. In care of you, if you will permit.'

'Of course. I shall be headquartered in Quebec City.'

'Meanwhile, please say to him that I am overjoyed to know he still lives and is well, and that a letter follows. Would it be dangerous to him if he wrote back a few words to me?'

'I could include a brief letter in one of mine to my intendant at the warehouse, Jean Beraite, a trustworthy fellow to whom I have given a fifth share in my fur business. In any case, I will convey to the Vicomte your verbal message.'

'I thank you, monsieur.'

Julie was well aware that courtesy alone would require her to inform this former lover that she was soon to marry the Comte de Vosges, rather than have him hear it from her father. Yet she could not struggle out the sounds from her throat. Her eyes ran desperately over his set face, a very compelling face, even devoid of its quirked smile and amicably tipped eyebrow, even in its deliberate stoniness. How would she ever get this cavalier out of her heart? She thanked God that he was leaving France, leaving her to her own life. Oh, Mercure, where are you? Why don't you come back? Had she seen in a mirror how stricken her expression was, the feeling of plummeting inside her would have turned to sheer panic. Yet she couldn't move to walk away from him.

He took her hand. So familiar a grip, so warm the strong fingers. An invisible tremor ran through her, both at his touch and because she remembered the frightening iciness of his hands and feet a fortnight before. More thanks to God went up in her mind that he was alive and hale. And bidding her *adieu* forever? Oh, merciful God——

'I will take leave of you now, Comtesse. I wish you every happiness. Sincerely. I will never forget the joys of our short friendship.' Over the faint irony in his voice, his regard was steady, cool. He bent his head and kissed the back of her hand. And then, propelled by an impulse he could not master, he turned her hand over, pressed his lips to her palm, and then closed her fingers tightly over the impression, as if for her to save it. '*Adieu, Julie*,' he said gruffly, and left her.

Clutching her fist to her breast, she watched him recede from her, saw him deftly avoid colliding with strolling couples until a knot of well-wishers swallowed him up, one gentleman pounding him on the back in conviviality. She was peripherally aware that people had been glancing at them with open curiosity, the gossip mills ever needing fodder, but she didn't care. Her palm burned, and her heart shriveled. A touch of nausea rose in her throat.

Mercure returned, along with a page bearing two delicate porcelain cups of strawberry sherbet on a tray, an apologetic smile on his face for his slowness. She was able to smile back at him, but not even spooning the cold, sweet ice into her mouth could put out the searing misery of her soul. Now that it was too late, much too late, vulgar reality had finally pounced and sent her reeling with its crystal-clear message: she would never be happy without him.

* * *

'Poilettier, can't you make this heap go faster?' Julie shouted up to the beleaguered coachman, who already had the four horses keeping a jingle-and-crack pace that would totally wind them if he did not pull back soon. 'Faster, *mon homme,* faster!'

The coachman complained to the hired guard sitting hunched on the box beside him, 'That lady can keep you jumping, I tell you. Always in a hurry. Look at that one, for instance.' He jerked his jaw at the advance rider galloping about one hundred paces ahead of them, employed to see that the road was clear and watch for pitfalls. 'Postilion boy not good enough for her this time. Never needed a forward man before. Never traveled almost all night, every night, before. *Eh bien*, look back, friend. Is the other vehicle keeping up our pace?'

Clinging to the thin iron rail about his seat and with one hand holding his wide-brimmed hat on, the man twisted his thick neck around to squint past the other guard jouncing on their rear jumpseat. He goggled at the less fancy but four-horse conveyance swaying and bumping along a hundred paces behind. 'Yes, stickin' with us,' he reported.

'*Bon*. He is a good driver, that Michel Brunet. But not as good as I am, I can tell you. That is why the Comtesse takes me with her to New France.'

Respect dawned in the guard's dust-reddened eyes. '*Tiens,* you would go there? Across the sea?'

'Well, and why not? I ain't got no family t' speak of— she found me out in that a long time ago. And she ain't thinking to get them dainty shoes of hers mucked walking about like a peddler's wife. That fellow there, out ahead, he'll take this vehicle back to the Luxembourg along with the baggage coach; they belong to the Duchesse de Montpensier, eh? But me and the two maids, we go with de Lowry. A new place. Start a new life.' A smile creased across Poilettier's creases.

The guard's grin showed broken teeth. 'Ain't you afraid the savages will roast you alive in yer skin? I heard that the redmen are murdering them fools and their families that leave good French sausage and wine to freeze their bazoos in the northern woods. The savages stick them full of poison arrers and hack off the tops of their heads *glymphh!* like a melon, and leave what remains for the maggots to feast on.' The guard declared this gleefully, licking his lips. 'You going to chance leaving your bloody scalp on a hatchet blade, eh?'

'Ahh, only an imbecile thinks every man, woman, or child lives in a hut in the woods there. They got real towns with big forts and troops of soldiers. The ships we're chasin' after are carrying heavy cannon and four regiments of soldiers along with lots more settlers. That oughter take care o' the barbarians. I ain't afraid.'

Undaunted, the guard went on. 'My uncle, he's a warder in the Bastille. They ain't got any women in New France. My uncle says the king is emptying the jails of gals to give those poor devils of colonists something to lay with so's they don't sin with each other. Lots of them fellows younger than you, coachman. What you going to do of a cold night?'

Poilettier winked. 'My lady hired herself a new maid—young, strong, not bad in the face. Calls herself Aurore. Fancy name fer a hired woman, eh?' He pulled back evenly on the reins to slow the horses, calling out to them soothingly, and stuck up an arm for the following driver to see.

'What would she want with an old man like you?' The guard grinned at him.

'I managed to save a few livres in my life. She might see a well-fixed, lusty old man better than a lice-scratching trapper with hair all over his face.' Poilettier grinned back.

'Poilettier!' The Comtesse de Lowry shouted up again. 'Why are we slowing down?'

'Because we don't want to kill the animals, madame. The poor beasts can only run full out so long. Dead horses won't bring us nowhere, madame,' he called back. 'Don't worry, 'tis me on the box. Poilettier will get us to Cherbourg in time.' He growled to the guard, 'Women! The maids tell me everything. First she dances the Marquis a dandy tune, then she sends him away, then she breaks a few hearts in Paris so's she can chase after him now, and God only knows how we will catch those ships. For if we don't, she could change her mind again and not go, and I've got me mouth set for a bit of adventuring. But I ain't going to be stupid and break these horses till we see the Cherbourg church spire on the horizon. We could even be lucky and be able to change teams in Bayeux. I know a stabler there——'

Julie chewed on the ragged thumbnail that was already below the sore flesh. For the twentieth time, she leaned to see her timepiece under the dim glow of the little lantern affixed above the seat. Almost ten o'clock. They had barely an hour to reach Cherbourg. The suspense kept her from feeling the fatigue of the dash she was making, but butterflies were plunging around in her stomach. Nervously, she stroked the silky little brown dog clipped like a lion sleeping in her lap. It had been a gift from poor Mercure, the only one she hadn't returned to him.

What if Nicolas simply would not have her? What if he refused to allow her on the ship, even though she came with a baggage coach carrying most of her possessions in and atop it, as well as Aurore, Blanchette, and an extra guard? Well, she thought, indignation rising to cover her fear, he was not the captain of the ship. She would say she was going to visit her father, and if there was any cabin available, she was going to squeeze on board. A partial letter to her father, in fact, was in the purse that hung from a silk cord about her waist. She had begun to write it three days ago, putting in everything that had occurred in her life since Richard's death. But when the last page and a half talked about nothing but her father's partner, stubborn, overbearing, beloved of women, and who had proposed marriage to her, she suddenly stopped writing. She stood, carefully folded the letter, calmly rang for Blanchette, sent a page running to her notary and banker, and prayed with all her might that regiments with foot soldiers could not travel as fast as a full-teamed coach with an expert driver.

A knock on the trap roused her. 'Eh, madame, there are lights,' Poilettier yelled down. 'If we are on the right road and have not lost our way, it is Cherbourg ahead. I shall make a lantern signal to the baggage coach.' In a moment, she heard him blow a horn signal to alert the forward rider, too.

We had better be on the right road, Julie grumbled belligerently to herself to cover the chill prickles creeping like ants along her spine. Oh, *Sainte Vierge*, how would he receive her, what would he say? What could she do to make him love her again? Could he fall out of love so fast? Well, she hadn't. How could he? Yet she had been so despicable, so miserably childish, so dreadful to him. How could he care for her anymore? That kiss in her palm at the Hôtel de Lambert? It was nothing. He was a gallant, after all. That was probably his way to take leave of any woman——

Suddenly, the coach shot ahead, throwing her against the seat, but she didn't mind. Poilettier knew this port city and the fastest way through it to the docks. He was a good man, her coachman.

To the noisy tune of barking dogs, which woke up the warm little creature on her lap, they whirled into Cherbourg and rattled past households already asleep, empty squares, lantern-marked inns, and noisy public houses with raucous customers spilling out. Loiterers dodged the dashing vehicles with sailor's curses. The main wharf, lumpy with tarpaulined cargo, showed yellow pools of light from lanterns hung from almost a dozen looming, square bows and from a forest of masts and ropes. A shouted inquiry from Poilettier to a watchman elicited that the ships for New France were out along an arm of the quai, all loaded, boarded and ready to sail upon the tide soon to turn.

They clopped out on the indicated jetty. 'The Comtesse de Lowry to see the Marquis de Courcillon,' Poilettier boomed down at the sentinels guarding the secluded dockage where the ships were lined broadside to the quai. 'It is urgent, so let us through, *mon homme*.' One of the men held up his lantern to the coach window and, seeing merely a lady, half her face muffled in a chiffon scarf, deemed her undangerous. Both coaches were passed. 'The ship at the very end,' the sentry called. 'But you haven't got much time if you're goin' to board.'

The broad jetty was illuminated by lanterns strung across it. It was littered with hay, smashed crates, sprung barrels, all the accidents of loading departing vessels crowded with men and beasts. The poor were picking about among the trash. More lights hung from the riggings of the sturdy vessels preparing to depart upon the ocean's broad bosom; dark forms moved about beyond the ships' rails, snatches of song floated on the soft night, sailors shouted to each other. A huge moon lay low on the horizon, like an actor waiting to make an entrance.

The coach hauled up with a flourish at the far end of the jetty. There was only one figure at the end of the quai, standing above the water, watching the silver orb beginning its rise, hands clasped behind his back. But Julie knew the set of those shoulders, the gold-red glint of the hair resting on the brocade coat. At the sound of the halting coaches, the figure clapped on its hat and turned about. But grudgingly.

'Nicolas!' Julie called from her window as Poilettier descended quickly to let her out. 'Nicolas!' Her heart was beating wildly. She saw him stop, arrested in midstep. Poilettier took the dog from her and tucked it under one arm, with the other setting the stair and helping her down. Nervously, she smoothed her skirt, then screwed up her courage and faced him with lifted chin as he stared at her. He came forward slowly, but the surprise on his face was turning into something like disappointment.

'I thought you were one of my under-lieutenants, the Duc de Trémouille's son. He missed us at Caen, and I hate to sail without him. He's a good officer.'

He could not have deflated her more if he'd pricked her with his rapier. Frightened beyond words at such an unemotional reception, she looked at him over the few paces that separated them and drew the letter from her purse. She showed it to him. 'I was writing this l-letter to my f-father, but then I decided to deliver it in p-person.'

He glanced behind her at the heaving horses and the

outrider with his torch and lanterns hanging at each side of his saddle. 'Such a decision evidently cost you a few nights on the road. Would not a courier have done as well?'

'N-no, you don't understand. I mean truly in p-person. I wish to s-sail with this ship, along with my servants. I shall p-pay whatever passage asked.'

At last she got a reaction. His brows knit like a storm cloud. 'You mean to sail with us to New France? Do I take your meaning correctly, Comtesse?'

'Y-yes, that is my intention.'

He put his hands on his hips. He was irritated. 'Boarding this ship is not like taking a sloop ride to Forges for the waters. We set out on a long, difficult journey, and if we hit a blow, your life might be in peril. You cannot change your mind in the middle of the ocean, madame, and summon a shallop to take you to shore. And you will not find soirées the size of Madame de Lambert's in New France, nor too many gallants of the proper station to lead about by their noses.'

'I am not interested in g-gallants. I am going to New France to live with my father, and th-that is my r-right. And neither will I change m-my mind in midocean.'

'Your father lives in the forest in a log outpost, madame, where the long arm of the king cannot reach him. You would hate it there. I suggest you turn about and return to Paris.'

'You are hard-hearted, m-monsieur. He is m-my only relative.' She looked at him beseechingly, for she was suffering under his cold gaze. 'I don't w-want to return to P-Paris.'

'Why are you stuttering? Stop it.'

She felt her lip tremble. 'Because you hate me,' she wobbled.

He shook his head as if at an uncomprehending child. 'I do not hate you. I merely have no use for perfidious, fickle women.'

'And I am neither of those, you will see, Nicolas. I was just so frightened. Love had done me so badly before.'

'And what contrived to calm you at this last second?'

She swallowed. 'I realized that, no matter what, I did

not want to be where you were not, not in Paris or France or anywhere. I want to be with you. If you sail to New France without me, I will die!'

His eyes traveled over her face. 'You might even die on this tub of a ship,' he said coldly. 'The bottom of the Atlantic is littered with sunken vessels.'

'You think I am such a coward that the thought of foundering will deter me, or of Indians or outposts or what not? Well, since you don't understand, I suppose I can't blame you. But the only threat that shakes me is that you will leave me here. I knew all along I was going with you. I never even unpacked my trunks in Paris.' She held out her hand in entreaty. 'Nicolas, please. I love you.'

She did not see the angry frown relax, but in his eyes, it seemed to her, a tiny, surprised gleam began to melt the ice. A bell sounded several times on board the ship. He turned from her to look up at the mate hand-signaling him from the railing. He turned back to her and made a brief bow. 'I appreciate your sentiment, madame, but there is no room for you on the ship. All the cabins are filled. I am sorry. I must board now, for we are sailing. *Adieu*, madame.'

He turned on his heel and walked from her, back stiff and unyielding. 'I could stay with you, in your quarters, Nicolas.' She ran after him desperately, uncaring that she humbled herself. 'I would take no space at all. I would make no noise and eat very little, hardly a nubbin, I promise. . .' Anguished, she tugged at his sleeve to detain him, then held her breath as he stopped and faced her. Was she imagining a ghost of a smile twitching the corners of his mouth? Were there wisps of amusement warming the light blue eyes?

Nicolas looked at her, her sweet lips half parted in her painful anxiety, her violet eyes full of pleading, and knew that in spite of all reason and his injured ego, the damnable woman was, as usual, making his pulse beat harder. He remembered the lurch of his sore heart as he turned to see the miracle of her descending the coach steps. He narrowed his eyes at her, as if he could see her more clearly that way and see, of course, that she was just another woman, not worth burdening his life with. All he saw was a beguiling and beautiful female whom, by some kink in his personality, he wanted very much. The words she said had sent his heart soaring, like a ferocious falcon released from the cage. He had already resigned himself to a life without the muddled woman, yet what sense did it make to leave her here on the Cherbourg quai, and his heart with her? He gathered his courage and told her, 'No matter how little bread you cost me, Comtesse, I could not allow you to share my quarters—and my bed, for there is only one, and the floor is too hard for a six-week voyage—unless we were wed. I must watch my reputation, after all,' he stated primly, without the hint of a chuckle. 'I am beginning a new regime. In fact, there is a priest on board whom I can scare up directly we sail. What say you, madame? Will you put your life in my hands? Quickly!'

Choked by gratitude, by love, she could scarcely watch the fierce light that had come into his eyes. Tears came into her own. 'I would be most honored to marry you, monsieur,' she whispered. 'I love you.'

Suddenly, she felt herself gathered up and crushed against him, accepted again into that circle where there was the only safety in the world. He kissed her temple and whispered against it, 'It will be no good if you continue to saddle me with another man's failures. I am the man I am, and no one else. Just as you are unique. And I love you. That should suffice.'

'Oh, Nicolas, it does, it does,' she said passionately. She raised her head to him. 'I have been a fool. I allowed a dreadful human being to reach beyond the grave to hold me prisoner, just as he did in life. But that is finished. I finally swept all his poison out of my system at last, because I was losing you and that could not happen. I want you. I love you.' Wonder arose in her. She thought his eyes looked suspiciously moist.

But he stood her away from him. He put his hands behind his back again and stepped sideways to look at the sea, not at her. He stated brusquely, 'There is no doubt, madame, that you are of good breeding and a beautiful woman. But who says I am looking for beauty?

No, indeed, I am looking for a woman of modest temperament and deportment, a quiet hostess for my home. I shall demand obedience of a wife. I shall expect her to be submissive to my will. In fact, she must, without questioning, do all that I tell her and acquiesce to all that I do.' His glance at her, from the corner of his eye, slid quickly away again.

Julie's brow wrinkled. 'She must?' she quavered.

'Yes. Do you agree to that?'

Her mouth went dry. She swallowed. She opened her mouth to speak, but nothing came out. Helplessly, she gaped at him.

But he had turned to her, and he was laughing. He grabbed her up and whirled her around and chuckled in her ear. 'Never mind, never mind. Now I believe you. You couldn't tell me what was not true just because you thought I wanted to hear it. Oh, *mignonne*, I love you.'

Her own laugh, the first real one in weeks, brought back her spirit. 'Oh, but you know me very well, *mon coucou*,' she giggled happily, the dimple showing.

'Indeed, I am very thorough. I know everything about you, how you laugh, how you cry, how you fight with me, how you make love. . .' he exulted, and swung her around again.

It made her dizzy. She saw the side of the ship, rising like a wall behind him, bobbing up and down as the tide changed. 'And how I look when I am seasick?' she groaned to herself, trying to quell the faint nausea that already began to grip her. A bride, after all, should be radiant, not nauseated.

He signaled to his seamen to board the people accompanying her and the baggage. She preceded him up the swaying gangplank, dainty head held high, and her courage as well. If Nicolas de Courcillon did not realize right now, by her coming on this miserable voyage, how much she adored him, he shortly would.

Bravely, she gave a jaunty shrug. *Tant pis*. One could not always be gorgeous.

AUTHOR'S NOTE

Released from banishment, La Grande Mademoiselle finally signed over various sovereignties in favor of the Marquise de Montespan's son; but Antonin de Lauzun was not released from Pignerol for ten years. His subsequent behavior toward the Duchesse was often ungrateful and graceless. He neglected her, ridiculed her, and flaunted his many infidelities in her face. Their mounting arguments and fistfights were the talk of the court. Finally, in 1684, she threw him out of the Luxembourg forever, and when she died, she left the major part of her vast fortunes to Monsieur, Philippe d'Orleans.

There was never any actual proof exhibited that Mademoiselle and de Lauzun had really married.

Athénais de Montespan's gaudy reign as Louis XIV's mistress spanned fifteen years. She was deposed, in part, by Louis's discovery of her degrading participation in the Black Mass and his suspicions that his terrible headaches derived from foul concoctions she put in his food. Her successor, whom Louis secretly married in 1683, was Madame de Maintenon, a middle-aged and militant social reformer who had once been governess to the Marquise's children. Two of the de Montespan daughters married princes of the blood.

The mysterious masked prisoner, fictionalized by Voltaire and Dumas as wearing an iron mask and being a royal personage, was reported by the modern historian Arthur S. Barnes to be a man of obscure station who, the scholar concludes, most probably did not know why he was locked up or treated with certain deference. Some stories have him a valet of an important French Huguenot conspirator, abducted from London because of certain of his employer's 'secrets' that Louis XIV and de Louvois thought he knew. Long after such secrets had lost their value, the prisoner remained in the toils of French red tape and a system of secrecy that seldom released its victim.

So many legends, wild or plausible, circulated about the dramatically shrouded prisoner through the centuries that connecting him with Mademoiselle seems one of the more realistic theories. The masked captive, never truly identified, died suddenly in 1703.

As for the fictitious, newly wed Marquise de Courcillon, formerly Julie de Lowry—being extremely happy as well as extremely vain, she simply refused to become seasick on her honeymoon journey.